KT-214-673

Ian Irvine was born in Bathurst, New South Wales, Australia, in 1950, and educated at Chevalier College and the University of Sydney, where he took a PhD in marine sciences in 1981. He has worked in a variety of jobs, including sweeping up in a cement factory, as a research assistant in microbiology and as an environmental project manager.

In the early 1980s Ian led several disastrous expeditions to Sumatra, which gave him many ideas for his books. He has spent too much of his life diving on filthy harbour bottoms investigating pollution.

Ian Irvine set up his own consulting firm in 1986, carrying out environmental studies for clients in Australia and overseas. He has worked in many countries in the Asia-Pacific region. An expert in marine pollution, he has developed some of Australia's national environmental guidelines.

Ian is married and lives in the mountains of northern New South Wales.

Ian Irvine can be contacted at ianirvine@ozemail.com.au

By Ian Irvine

THE VIEW FROM THE MIRROR QUARTET

A Shadow on the Glass
The Tower on the Rift
Dark is the Moon
The Way Between the Worlds

THE TOWER ON THE RIFT

VOLUME TWO OF
THE VIEW FROM THE MIRROR QUARTET

IAN IRVINE

An *Orbit* Book

First published by Penguin Books Australia Ltd, 1998
First published in Great Britain by Orbit 2000

Copyright © Ian Irvine, 1998

Maps copyright © Ian Irvine, 1998

The moral right of the author has been asserted.

All characters and events in this publication are
fictitious and any resemblance to real persons,
living or dead, is purely coincidental.

All rights reserved.
No part of this publication may be reproduced,
stored in a retrieval system, or transmitted, in any
form or by any means, without the prior
permission in writing of the publisher, nor be
otherwise circulated in any form of binding or
cover other than that in which it is published and
without a similar condition including this condition
being imposed on the subsequent purchaser.

A CIP catalogue record for this book
is available from the British Library.

ISBN 1 84149 005 9

Printed and bound in Great Britain by
Mackays of Chatham PLC, Chatham, Kent

Orbit
A Division of
Little, Brown and Company (UK)
Brettenham House
Lancaster Place
London WC2E 7EN

'The irony of history is inexorable.'

BARBARA TUCHMAN, *THE MARCH OF FOLLY*

CONTENTS

PART THREE

PART OF THE SOUTHERN HEMISPHERE OF SANTHENAR

LEGEND

Mountains
Hills
Desert
Salt Lake
Marsh, Swamp
Conifer Forest
Broadleaf Forest
Tropical Forest
Grassland
Reef

NYS
Banthey
FARANDA
Flude
TARANTA
Huccadory
CRANDOR
Bel Torance
Taranta
DRY SEA
Katazza
Strinklet
Jepperand
Tar Gaarn &
Havissard
Roros
Ashmode
CARENDOR
Guffeons
KALAR
Gosport
STASSOR
Maksmord

20°
30°

Maps by the author

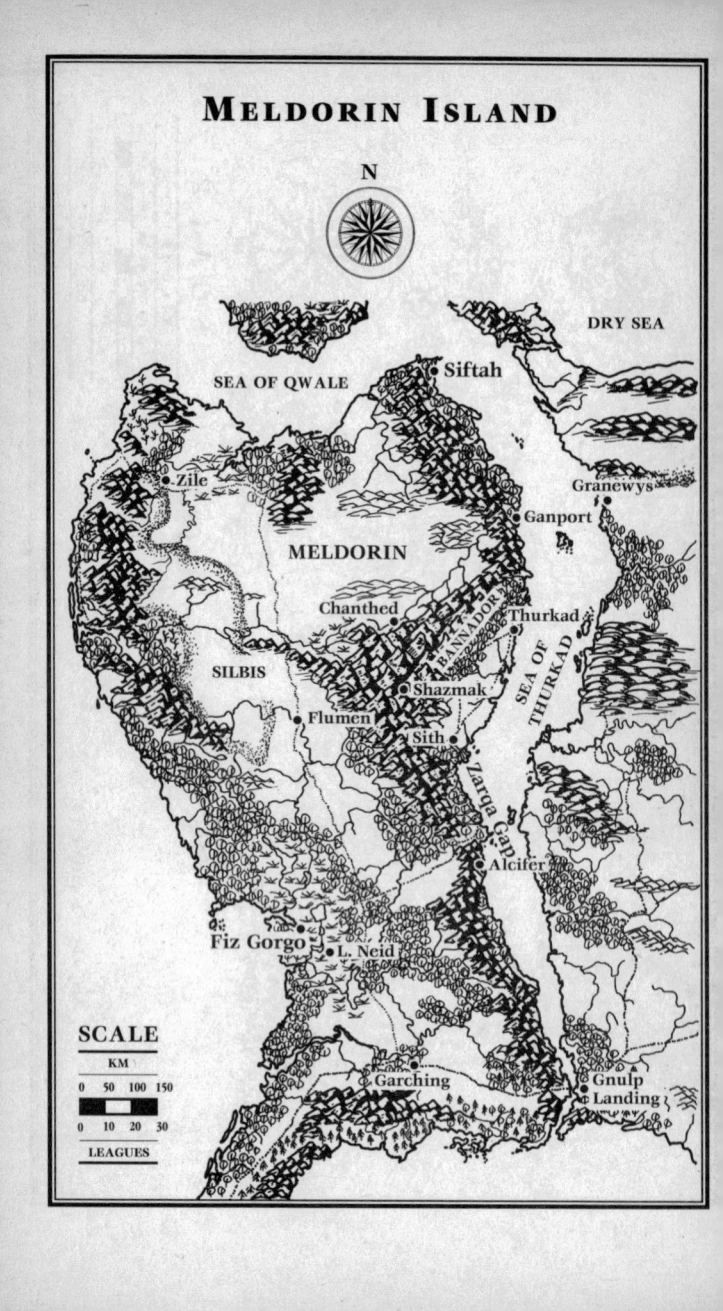

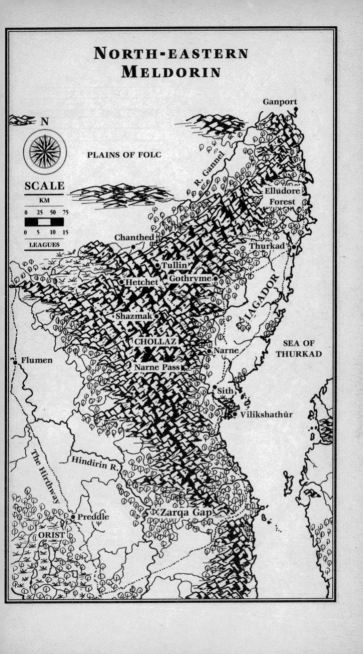

NORTH-EASTERN MELDORIN

N

PLAINS OF FOLC

SCALE

KM
0 25 50 75

0 5 10 15
LEAGUES

Ganport

R. Gannel

Elludore
Forest

Chanthed

Thurkad

Tullin

Hetchet

Gothryme

Shazmak

IAGADOR

CHOLLAZ

Narne

SEA OF
THURKAD

Flumen

Narne Pass

Sith

Vilikshathûr

Hindirin R.

The Hirthway

Preddle

Zarqa Gap

ORIST

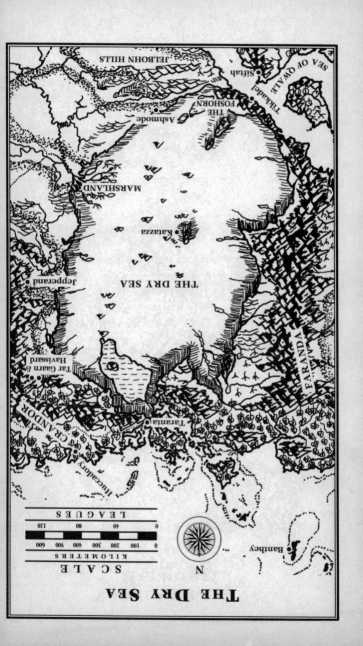

SYNOPSIS OF

THE VIEW FROM THE MIRROR

The View from the Mirror is a tale of the Three Worlds, *Aachan, Tallallame* and *Santhenar*, and of the four human species that inhabit them: *Aachim, Charon, Faellem* and old human. The setting is Santhenar, a world where wizardry – the *Secret Art* – is difficult, and doesn't always work, and every using comes at a price – *aftersickness*.

Long ago a whole race was betrayed and cast into the void between the worlds, a Darwinian place where life is more desperate, more brutal, more fleeting than anywhere. In the void none but the fittest survive, and only by remaking themselves constantly. A million of that race died in the first few weeks.

The terrible centuries ground on. The exiles were transformed into a new human species, but still they could not survive the void. Reduced to a handful, they hung over the abyss of extinction. Then one day a chance came, an opening to another world – Aachan!

They gave themselves a new name, Charon, after a frigid moonlet at the furthest extremity of the void. Escaping it, they took barren Aachan from the Aachim, reducing them to servitude. The Hundred, as the remaining Charon became known, dared allow nothing to stand before the survival of their species.

Despite their efforts, they did not flourish on Aachan.

One of the Hundred, *Rulke*, commissioned the golden flute, an instrument that could open the Way between the Worlds. Before it could be used, *Shuthdar*, the old human who made it, stole the flute and fled with it to Santhenar. Unfortunately Shuthdar blundered. He opened all the paths between the worlds, and the four species scrambled to get the flute for themselves. Rather than be taken Shuthdar destroyed it, bringing down the Forbidding that sealed Santhenar off completely. Now the fate of the Three Worlds is bound up with those marooned on Santhenar. They have never ceased to search for a way home, but no way has ever been found.

Volume 1
A SHADOW ON THE GLASS

Llian, a brilliant young chronicler at the College of the Histories, presents a new version of an ancient Great Tale, the *Tale of the Forbidding*, at his graduation *telling*, to unprecedented acclaim. But *Wistan*, the master of the College, realises that Llian has uncovered a deadly mystery – evidence that a crippled girl was murdered at the time the golden flute was destroyed. The crime must have occurred to conceal a greater one, and even now such knowledge could be deadly, both for him and for the College.

Llian is also *Zain*, an outcast race despised for collaborating with the Charon in olden times. Wistan persecutes Llian to make him retract the tale, but Llian secretly keeps on with his research. He knows that it could be the key to a brilliant story – the first new Great Tale for hundreds of years – and if he were the one to write it, he would stand shoulder to shoulder with the greatest chroniclers of all time.

Karan, a young woman who is a *sensitive*, was at the graduation telling when Llian told his famous tale. She loves the Histories and is captivated by the tale and the teller. Karan returns to Gothryme, her drought-stricken and impoverished home, but soon afterwards *Maigraith* appears. Karan owes an obligation to Maigraith, the powerful but troubled lieutenant of *Faelamor*, and Maigraith insists that she repay it by helping to steal an ancient relic for her liege. Faelamor is the age-old leader of the Faellem, exiled on Santhenar by the Forbidding. Desperate to take her people back to her own world, she believes that the relic may hold the key.

Yggur the sorcerer now holds the relic in Fiz Gorgo. Karan and Maigraith steal into his fortress, but Karan is shocked to learn that the relic is the *Mirror of Aachan*, stolen from the Aachim a thousand years ago. Being part-Aachim herself, she knows that the Aachim have never stopped searching for it. Either she must betray her father's people or refuse her debt to Maigraith – dishonour either way. And Karan has a dangerous heritage: part Aachim, part old human, she is a *blending*. Blendings, though prone to madness, can have unusual talents, as she has. They are also at risk: sometimes hunted to enslave the talent, as often to destroy it.

Maigraith, captivated by something she sees on the Mirror, is surprised by Yggur. Finally she is overcome but Karan flees with the Mirror into the flooded labyrinth below the fortress, pursued by Yggur's dreadful *Whelm* guards. Karan is clever and resourceful, and eventually escapes, but is hunted for weeks through swamp and forest and mountains. The Whelm, who are also sensitive, are able to track her through her nightmares. In a twist of fate, Karan saves the life of one of the Whelm, *Idlis the healer*. She heads towards Chanthed, a place of haunting memories for her because of Llian and his wonderful tale. Pursued by the Whelm and their dogs, she thinks of Llian as a saviour and reaches out to him in her dreams.

Mendark, a mancer who is Yggur's bitter enemy, hears that the Mirror has been stolen and sends out his lieutenants to find it. Learning from *Tallia* that Karan is heading for Chanthed he asks Wistan to find her. Wistan, who would do anything to get rid of Llian, orders him to find Karan and take her to Mendark's city, Thurkad.

Llian is terrified to be cast out of his secure world, yet knows that if he does this task well, Mendark's name will open any door, and he will surely solve the murder and make his Great Tale. He travels into the mountains in a romantic dream.

At the tiny village of Tullin he dreams that Karan is calling for help and wakes to find two Whelm at his throat, trying to trace her *sending*. Llian is rescued by *Shand*, an old man who works at the inn but is more than he seems. After asking Shand for help but being refused, Llian heads out into the snow to find Karan. Eventually he does, after many perils, but crashes into her hiding place and knocks himself out at her feet.

At first Karan feels that Llian is a dream come true, but the great teller is revealed to be callow and awkward. Worse, he does not take her seriously, and when he tries to get her to go to Thurkad with him Karan grows angry. Sith is her destination, and to pay her debt she must give the Mirror to none but Faelamor. That night the Whelm find her again and, full of mixed feelings about Llian, she flees with him into the high mountains.

After a number of narrow escapes they lose their pursuers, but Llian gets mountain sickness and they begin to run out of food. Karan has no choice but to head for Shazmak, a secret city of the Aachim, where she grew up. She is afraid to go there with the Mirror, and more afraid to take Llian to a place forbidden to outsiders.

Eventually she talks the Aachim, among them her cousin and friend *Rael*, into allowing Llian in, but soon learns that *Tensor* is on his way to Shazmak. The leader of the Aachim is so dominating that Karan knows she can never keep the Mirror secret. Karan agonises over whether to break her vow and give it to the Aachim, but realises that the Mirror would be too great a temptation. They are proud but not wise, and their history is littered with disastrously pursued follies. Rulke the Charon was the architect of all their misfortunes, and though he has been imprisoned in the Nightland for a thousand years, Tensor has never ceased to search for a way to exact revenge on him.

As it happens, Tensor has already heard about the Mirror from Mendark. Tensor sends a message to Shazmak, to *Emmant*, a cunning blending with a thwarted lust for Karan. While Llian searches Shazmak for evidence that will help him with his quest, Emmant shows him a book of Aachim Histories, but he has put an enchantment on the book and Llian reveals that Karan knows about the Mirror.

Tensor returns and Karan is brought to trial, for the Mirror cannot be found. It is impossible to lie to the *Syndics*, but Karan, in a desperate expedient, plants a false dream in Llian's mind, and through a *link* with him, reads it back to the Syndics at her trial. Because Llian believes it to be truth, it *is* truth, and despite Tensor's protests she is freed. However, Emmant is spurned by the Aachim for his dishonourable act, and this drives him into madness.

That night, with Rael's aid, Karan and Llian escape from Shazmak, hotly pursued by the Aachim. Stealing a boat, they flee down a wild river. Rael and several of the Aachim are drowned in the chase, and Karan is devastated. Despite the trial they were her friends.

In Yggur's stronghold, Maigraith is tormented by the Whelm, who have an instinctive hatred of her. Later, under Yggur's relentless interrogation, she gives away Karan's destination, the city of Sith.

Yggur is desperate to get the Mirror back, which he needs for his coming campaign. However, as the weeks pass a bond grows between them, Maigraith finding in the tormented Yggur the complement to her own troubled self. She also sees that, though the Whelm serve Yggur faithfully, they despise him, especially for the relationship with her which to them is a fatal weakness. But the Whelm are born to serve, and they lost their true master so long ago that they have forgotten him.

Now readying his armies for war, Yggur is torn between his growing regard for Maigraith and his need for the Mirror. One night the Whelm come for Maigraith when he is away, and under their torment she betrays the truth about Karan's origins. The Whelm are exultant – now they know how to attack her.

The same night Faelamor appears, using her mastery of illusion to get into the fortress. Overcoming the Whelm, she snatches Maigraith away. However, Faelamor is furious when she learns that Karan has escaped with the Mirror. Faelamor hates Karan because she is a sensitive and a threat to her plans, and threatens to kill her if they ever meet again. Inwardly Faelamor despairs because the Mirror, that she has sought for so long, has eluded her again. Once before she almost had it, but *Yalkara* the Charon, her greatest enemy, defeated her. Yalkara used the Mirror to find a warp in the Forbidding, the only person ever to escape from Santhenar. Now Faelamor's own world, Tallallame, cries out for aid and she is desperate to return. What Yalkara could do, Faelamor *must* do, and she has corrupted herself trying to. She has been hunting for the Mirror, one vital part of her age-old plan, ever since.

Faelamor and Maigraith set off towards Sith. Maigraith is reminded that whatever she does, Faelamor is never satisfied. She falls back under Faelamor's domination.

Yggur returns to find Maigraith gone. He feels her loss keenly but he can delay his plans no longer. His armies march on the east.

Karan and Llian flee through mountains and caverns, hotly pursued by Tensor and his Aachim, and down into the forests of Bannador, Karan's own country. At a forest camp she has a terrible nightmare and wakes to find that the Whelm have tracked her down again. This time she is helpless for they know she is a blending and how to control her. Desperate, Karan seeks out with her mind and finds Maigraith not far away. But the link is captured by a terrifying presence, who uses it to speak directly to the Whelm, reminding them that they are really *Ghâshâd*, ancient enemies of the Aachim. Karan sends Llian away but is captured herself, though the Whelm are unable to find the Mirror.

Maigraith feels Karan's link but by the time she gets to the camp Karan is gone, and the Mirror too. Faelamor is furious. Maigraith rebels, abandoning her. Faelamor is captured by Tensor and sent to Shazmak, where to her horror she learns about Karan's Aachim heritage. Faelamor already suspects that Karan has Faellem ancestry as well. If so, she is *triune*: one with the blood of three worlds. A terrifying prospect – no one can tell what unpredictable talents a triune might have. Faelamor decides that the risk to her plans is too great – Karan must die. She sends mad Emmant to hunt Karan down. Through him the Ghâshâd find a way inside Shazmak and butcher the Aachim there, but Faelamor escapes.

Llian recovers the Mirror from Karan's hiding place, eventually finds her and tries to smoke the Whelm out of the house where they hold her prisoner. The building catches fire; Karan and Llian are lucky to escape. Llian hires a boat and *Pender*, a magnificent boatman who has fallen on hard times, takes them down the river to Sith. On the way, Karan and Llian find that they can deny their feelings for each other no longer.

Reaching Sith, they discover that Yggur's armies have taken all the lands to the south and are massing on the other side of the river. The city cannot stand against him. Nor is Faelamor there to take the Mirror. Karan collapses, unable to drive herself any further. She is wracked by nightmares about the Whelm, who since she was captured seem to have grown more powerful. As the invasion begins she is betrayed, but escapes with Pender, a perilous journey where Karan is so tormented that she casts herself into the sea. Llian and Pender drag her out again. Now there is nowhere to go but to Mendark. Karan is afraid of him too.

They reach Thurkad not far ahead of the war. Llian goes to the citadel, not realising that Mendark has been overthrown by *Thyllan*. A street urchin, *Lilis*, guides Llian to Mendark's refuge. Mendark and Tallia offer to take Karan in, but angered by Mendark's imperious manner, she refuses him.

Not long after, Maigraith comes to Thurkad. Karan is overjoyed and tries to give her the Mirror, but Maigraith asks her to keep it one more day. Before she returns, Emmant appears in disguise and attacks Karan in a murderous fury. She stabs him dead but is driven into madness; then Thyllan captures Karan and the Mirror.

As all the powers gather in Thurkad, Mendark realises that the only way to recover the Mirror is to call a Great Conclave, which even Thyllan must obey. During the Conclave they all put their case, and Karan tells her story. As the Conclave ends, a messenger bursts in with news that the army is defeated and Yggur is at the gates of the city. Faelamor shatters Tensor by revealing that the Whelm are actually his ancient enemies, the Ghâshâd, one-time servants of Rulke, who have taken Shazmak and slaughtered the Aachim there. She lies, blaming Karan for this treachery.

Karan is sentenced to death, while the Mirror is given to Thyllan to use in the defence of Thurkad. Seizing the moment, Faelamor calls forth Maigraith, whom Tensor has never seen before, and Tensor knows by her eyes that she is descended from the hated Charon.

Tensor breaks and uses a forbidden *potency*, or mind-blasting spell, that lays the whole Conclave low. Only Llian the Zain is unaffected. Thinking Karan dead, in grief and fury he attacks Tensor but is easily captured. Tensor sees a use for someone who is immune to the potency. He flees with Llian and the Mirror.

PART ONE

PART ONE

1

THE WAIF

T he Great Hall was dark. The glow from the burning city did not penetrate the velvet drapes. The shouts, the screams, the clash of weapons up the hill – all just a murmur from far away. In the room there was no conscious being, no intelligent life. The broken door banged in the wind, the hinges bawled, striking a dreadful lament, crying to the dead to rise. The members of the Conclave lay silent.

Hours passed. In the darkness one man dreamed. Dreamed that he lay cast down and senseless while the army of his mortal enemy poured through the gates of Thurkad. *Get up!* he screamed. *Only you can save your city.* But he could not wake.

The tramp of marching feet echoed in his dreams – they were hunting him! He gave a wrenching groan that tore through the fog in his brain and woke, bolt upright in the dark. His heart was racing. Where was he? Hardly knowing his own name, aware of little more than a growing terror, he felt around him. The things he touched were blank pieces. He could not put a name to the least of them.

A horn blasted, not far away. Panicking, the man clawed himself to all-fours, sagging across the room like a rubber-kneed crab, tripping over bodies, cracking his head against a table leg. Something smashed under his weight, the shards stabbing into the palm of his hand. He picked out pieces of curved glass, feeling the blood run down his arm. Smelling spilled oil on the floor, he felt around for the lantern but his numb fingers snapped the flint a dozen times before it lit. He lurched in swaying arcs back and forth along the rows of benches, then fell down in front of a tall woman who lay on the floor like a fallen statue. Yellow light bathed long limbs, dark hair, skin as rich and smooth as glazed chocolate. Her eyes were open and her lips wet, but the woman made no sound, gave no sign that she saw anything.

With shaking hands he brought the lamp down to her eyes. It registered nothing. The light showed him clearly – a slim man of average height and uncertain age, with blue eyes and thin, wild hair. His sallow skin was sunk into deep creases; his scanty beard was lank.

The man's face was wracked. 'Tallia!' he sang out, a wail of pain. 'For pity's sake, wake!' He rocked on his haunches, overcome by the magnitude of the disaster, shuddered and bent over her again. Putting his bloody hands around her head, front and back, he tried to force open the blocked channels of her brain, straining so hard that his breath came out as a series of little groans.

In his head the tramping grew so loud that it blocked out all thought. He closed his eyes but the images shone out brighter than before, row after row of soldiers. The mind that directed them – his enemy – was as cold and unstoppable as a machine.

'Tallia,' he screamed. 'Help! Yggur's coming for me.'

Tallia's pupils, which had imperceptibly contracted to points of darkness, expanded in a rush and she knew him. 'Mendark!' she whispered.

Mendark threw his arms around her. Tears starred his eyelashes. They struggled to their feet, swaying together, then Tallia's eyes rolled and the room tilted in slow-motion confusion. He clung to her until she was steady again.

'What happened?' she asked. 'I don't remember anything.'

Mendark held the lantern high. It showed the hall in chaos: tables and benches overturned, lamps smashed, papers and people scattered like hay.

'Tensor violated the Conclave,' he said, grim-faced.

'Conclave?' Tallia rubbed her forehead as if she could stir her brain back to life.

'I called a Great Conclave,' he replied, 'to recover the Mirror from Thyllan the usurper, and to free Karan.'

'I can't remember,' said Tallia, shaking her head.

'Yggur's not far away. I can *sense* the hate in him.'

Tallia did not ask him about that. Mendark was a sensitive. He *knew*. She squatted down, rocking back and forth on her heels.

'Tensor struck down the Conclave with a mind-blasting potency,' Mendark went on. 'A terrible spell.'

'Tensor betrayed us?' she whispered.

'Yes, and fled with the Mirror. What's he going to do with it? I'm afraid, Tallia.'

'It's starting to come back!' Tallia slumped on the chair. 'Oh, my head is bursting!'

'And mine, but we must get going.'

Mendark handed her a jug, a tall, wasp-waisted vessel of dark-blue porcelain. Tallia drank from it greedily, spilling water down her chin and her shirt. She wiped her face with the back of her hand, nodded, which made her wince, and said, 'What do we do now?'

'I can't think. The Council is in tatters.'

The Council was an alliance of wizards and scholars, of which Mendark had been Magister until his recent overthrow. He ticked the members off on his fingers. 'Tensor's gone, Nelissa is dead. Thyllan is my enemy and will never be otherwise. Old Nadiril is far away in Zile; he hasn't come to a meet in years. Wistan is likewise out of reach in Chanthed. That only leaves me, Hennia the Zain and Orstand between us and ruin. Where's Orstand?'

Tallia looked around. 'I can't see her.'

'Find her and Hennia. Protect them at all costs! I've got to get to the citadel. If Yggur learns that they lie here helpless . . . Ahh!' he wailed. 'There's no time!'

Mendark looked as bad as she felt. They were both wracked by aftersickness, the by-product of using wizardry, the Secret Art, or being too close when someone else did.

Outside, where all had been silent, they now heard shouting and screaming. Mendark wobbled his way to the door. The street lamps still burned. The street was wet, though it was not raining now. People streamed past, clutching pathetic treasures.

'What news?' cried Mendark, but his voice went unheeded. He picked up a spear that lay on the road and stepped into the path of the refugees, blocking their way. 'I am Mendark!' he thundered, though it took most of his strength. '*What news?*'

'The enemy has come through the northern gate,' said a bearded man, grey hair plastered to his head. He cradled a whimpering baby in the crook of one arm. Little blue toes stuck out of its sodden blanket, curling and uncurling. 'It's said that Thyllan is dead. Who leads us now?'

'*I lead!*' Mendark cried. 'I am Mendark. Magister once more! Go, tell everyone that the real Magister is back. We will defend the walls of the Old City and strike outwards until the whole of Thurkad is free again.'

The crowd, which was growing every minute, stared at him in silence. He raised the spear above his head. 'Go, you fools!' he roared. 'I am your only chance.'

As they scattered he heard a few thin cries of 'Mendark! Mendark has returned!' though whether they went in hope or in fear of him Mendark could not tell.

'Poor fools,' he said under his breath. 'What chance is there for Thurkad now?' He lumbered back up the steps.

'Tallia,' he shouted, and she came running, awkwardly, as if her knees had frozen solid.

'There are . . .' she began.

'No time!' he snapped. 'You must do as best you can. I will rally our armies, what's left of them. Bring the Council to the citadel, and anyone else who can help us. I'll try to send aid, but don't wait for it.'

'But Mendark . . .'

'Whatever it is, you must deal with it.' He stood there for a moment, his face haggard, then ran out. His unsteady footsteps echoed on the stones.

'But most of the people here can't even walk,' Tallia said softly. 'Important people, vital for our defence. How am I to deal with them, alone?' Thurkad was the greatest and oldest city of Meldorin. If it had fallen so quickly, where could they hope to find refuge?

She went to the door and looked out, but now the street was empty, silent. Misty rain began to drift down. What could she do? Hesitating in the doorway, Tallia noticed a movement in the alley across the street. Someone had put their head around the corner and quickly pulled it back again. The little thin face was curiously familiar.

It was the street urchin who had guided Llian to Mendark's villa several weeks ago. Llian had so charmed her that she had refused a silver tar in payment, a fortune for any street child. What was her name?

'Lilis,' Tallia called softly. 'Lilis, come forth.'

The head peeked around again. It belonged to a hungry-looking girl who seemed about ten, a long-faced waif with platinum hair. Her ratty clothes were spattered with mud up to the waist.

'Come here, Lilis, I need you.'

Lilis emerged onto the street, looked this way and that and slunk across to Tallia. In the light from the doorway she looked even shabbier than before.

'What does you want?' she squeaked, looking tremulous.

'Come inside.'

'Into the Great Hall?' The squeak became a horrified whisper. 'Could be whipped for that.'

'Nonsense. The old Magister is back and I am his chief lieutenant.' Tallia took Lilis's thin wrist and led her inside. 'Look,' she pointed. Many of the richest and most powerful people of Thurkad: justices, legislators and wealthy merchants were strewn about like carcasses in an abattoir. 'We've got to get them to the citadel.'

Not far away a tall man twitched and shuddered. He was mean-faced, with a misshapen cudgel of a nose and a swollen gash across one cheek. His pale, almost colourless eyes stared unseeingly ahead. It was Thyllan, who had ended Mendark's tenure as Magister not long before the Conclave.

Lilis's eyes bulged. '*The Magister!*' she said.

'No more! The usurper is overthrown. Mendark is back – the real Magister. Help me.'

Tallia hurried around the room, checking for signs of life. The guards had recovered and fled, save one who lay in a puddle of blood on the far side. He was dead – had fallen on his sword and bled to death, by the look of it.

As she turned away to the next, Lilis caught sight of a small bare foot protruding from under the guard's billowing cape. She lifted the cloth to reveal a small woman with a pale face surrounded by a wild froth of fiery red hair.

'It's Karan,' said Tallia, 'Llian's friend.'

Various emotions crossed Lilis's face: concern, envy. 'Is she dead?'

Tallia bent down swiftly. 'No, but without help she could die.'

Karan's face was set in an expression so sad that it made tears spring to Tallia's eyes. If only I had helped her, she thought, none of this need have come about. She rolled Karan over. Her shirt was bloody from breast to hip. Tallia tore the shirt open, expecting to see a mortal wound, but there was none. It was the guard's blood.

Tallia looked around. 'That's strange,' she said, furrowing her brow.

'What?'

There had been many people at the Conclave but a lot were gone, including several faces that she was looking for: Faelamor, Maigraith, Llian. 'Where's Llian? He would never have left Karan.'

'Llian's gone,' said Lilis. 'The big man took him.'

'Big man?' Tallia asked, checking Karan's vital signs. The pulse was erratic, her skin clammy, and her eyes flickered back and forth under her eyelids. Tallia lifted one. The eyes were deep green; the pupils hardly reacted to the light. She was probably not in immediate danger though, if kept warm and dry. Tallia tore the cape off the guard, wrapped Karan in it, round and round, and then put her out of the way against the wall. Nothing more could be done for her at the moment. She turned to the next casualty.

Beneath a window was a mound of fallen drapes, half-covering a huge jelly of a woman swathed in the scarlet and purple gown of the High Court. The dignity of the office was marred by a red mouth sagging open and dentures hanging out. Her face was as round as the moon, with eyes that looked tiny in their pouches of fat. Yellow-grey hair was cut straight across at the level of her ears.

'Who is *she*?' Lilis piped up.

'Justice Orstand,' said Tallia, greatly relieved. With Orstand on their side there was always hope. She was the most powerful intellect on the Council, a friend that Mendark relied on greatly. 'Water, quickly!'

Lilis scurried away to return with a blue jug, which she promptly poured on the judge's face. Orstand shuddered and tried to get up, but wobbled on her legs. Tallia hurriedly thrust a chair under her.

Orstand looked around the room. 'Is Nelissa – ?'

'Dead!' Tallia said harshly. She explained their situation.

'Oh!' said Orstand. 'But Mendark's right – the Old City is our only refuge.' Its walls were high and strong and the citadel inside it stronger yet. Though surely not enough to resist Yggur.

'Can you walk, Orstand?'

Orstand gave a smile of sorts. 'See to the others, my friend. When they're ready to go, I will be too.'

Embracing the old woman, Tallia went on with her work. There were other dead, quite a few, mostly the old and the frail. Too late for them, but several people were on their feet already after Lilis's rough ministering with the water jug and a wet cloth.

Tallia remembered something Lilis had said earlier. 'What did you say about Llian?' she asked, but before the child could answer there was shouting, screaming and sounds of battle nearby. Dread shivered down Tallia's backbone. They would be trapped!

'Lilis,' she cried. The waif's eyes showed the fear they both felt. 'Go and see what is happening. See how close the enemy is.'

The girl hesitated, staring at her with those huge eyes. Tallia, thinking that she wanted payment, fumbled for the purse that hung at her waist. Lilis struck her hand aside; then, realising that she had hit the chief lieutenant of the Magister and might be slain on the spot, leapt away saying, 'I go, I go!'

'Lilis!' Tallia called. She came back warily. 'Be careful.' Tallia embraced the grubby little urchin. Lilis looked astounded, then a tiny smile broke across her face. 'You *will* come back?' said Tallia. Normally so capable, she now felt overwhelmed.

'I come back,' Lilis said, her eyes shining, then she was gone.

Tallia hurried across to Orstand, who was bent over another of the bodies, trying to bring it back to consciousness. She looked about to collapse again; every breath rattled in her massive chest.

'I can't decide who to take and who to leave,' agonised Tallia. 'Is a judge more important than a doctor? A wealthy merchant more valuable than a young woman?'

'You can't choose that way,' said Orstand, looking up. The flesh sagged off her face like overly wet dough. 'The group must come before the individual. Anyone who can't walk, or falls down and can't get up again, must be left behind. And that includes me.'

'I could never leave *you* behind,' said Tallia, staring at the old woman.

Orstand wheezed with laughter. 'I'd like to see you carry me!'

Tallia smiled at the thought. Soon seven people were more or less ready to walk. They included Thyllan, his hair sticking out in all directions as though electrified, and Hennia the Zain, the other member of the Council, an old, saggy woman whose eyes had gone blank. A badly bitten tongue hung out the corner of her mouth. There were also two members of the Assembly, the puppet government of Thurkad, long dominated by the Governor on one hand and the Magister on the other. The other two were strangers, though they both looked important.

They were in much the state that she had been in before Mendark woke her, but she did not know how to do the same for them. Several more were in worse condition, flopped over chairs and benches like dolls stuffed with grass. If they could be roused she might be able to get some of them to safety too. And there were quite a few like Karan, who might live or die, but would have to be carried. Worthy people all.

Save for Orstand, her seven could have been senile. Thyllan was wandering aimlessly around the room, but most of the others just stared at the wall, mumbling to themselves. Hennia kept saying, 'I don't want to go. Mendark is finished!' Tallia was almost in despair by the time Lilis came running back.

'Soldiers coming!' she cried. 'Must go now!' Grabbing Tallia's hand, Lilis tried to pull her toward the door.

Tallia resisted. 'We've got to take them with us. Give me a hand.'

Between the three of them they got the able-bodied into a shambling line at the door, but it took all of Lilis's efforts to keep them there while Tallia tried to rouse the other group. Outside, the shouting and noises of battle grew louder.

'Must go *now*!' Lilis screamed.

Tallia looked back at Karan, torn between her feelings and her responsibilities. It was not just that she liked Karan. She was a sensitive too, a priceless talent, especially in time of war. Anyone left behind was probably condemned to death, but not everybody could be saved. She ran back to Karan and took her hand, then laid it down again, unable to choose.

'Go on, Lilis. I'll catch you.'

Karan moaned, flinging her head from side to side. Suddenly coming to a decision, Tallia bent down to pick her up, then one of the comatose sat up, a short, rather stout man called Prathitt, a wealthy merchant and legislator. A fussily trimmed spade beard drew attention from his rapidly receding hairline. He staggered towards the door, waving his arms and shouting gibberish.

Tallia caught him just outside and slapped her hand over his mouth and nose, cutting off the racket. A small knot of people ran past, shrieking and moaning, then a signal horn called from up the street. Another answered it from around the back of the Great Hall. She looked about frantically, to see Lilis shepherding her crew into a mean alley. Orstand, at the rear, moved with the tottering, wide-legged gait of a toddler.

'Hurry!' Lilis screamed.

Tallia agonised in the doorway. There were about a dozen people left and she knew most of them. Some would die without help. Maybe all of them, if the enemy found them. Her patient began to thrash about again. If she carried Karan, this fellow would give them away. Then someone attacked the back door of the hall, the hammer blows echoing inside. Too late! Pulling the door closed, she hauled Prathitt across the road.

The rain was falling more heavily now. Within the alley it was almost as black as tar and slippery underfoot. Another clot of people ran down the street. Behind them Tallia heard the rhythmic tread of a squad of marching soldiers. She moved up the alley, slipping and skidding on what felt like decaying leaves. There was an odour of rotten cabbage, and the further up she went, worse filth.

'Lilis,' she whispered hoarsely.

There was no answer. Tallia heard the sound of falling water and the next second walked right under a torrent discharging from the roof. She wiped her eyes and stared uselessly into the darkness. The mouth of the alley was a lighted rectangle, partly obscured by mist. The tramping grew louder.

Prathitt, roused by the soaking, shouted an obscenity and flung up his arms. One fist caught her a painful blow on the cheek. Tallia struggled with him, making more noise than she liked. He was very strong, and when she eventually got her hand over his mouth, he bit her so hard that he drew blood. Cursing, she struck him on the side of the head, knocking him down.

Someone yelled behind her. Yggur's soldiers were moving back and forth in the road. One approached the alley, holding up a blazing torch. Her patient began to stir. Tallia put her foot on his back, pushing him down into the mud. The torch went away, though the soldiers could still be seen in the street lights. The rest of the squad must be checking the Great Hall, she supposed, feeling her failure very strongly. Where had Lilis gone with her lot? Probably abandoned them as soon as the soldiers appeared. Who could blame her? There was no one to look out for her but herself.

Tallia heaved Prathitt to his feet, hauling him backwards up the alley, when without warning he put his muddy hands on her face and shoved. She overbalanced and fell backwards against a water barrel, hitting her head. For a moment she stared into a whirlpool, like being back in her earlier trance,

13

then her head cleared and she sat up, trying to clean the muck out of her eyes. Reeling footsteps disappeared up the lane.

The light appeared again, and the silhouette of a soldier. Tallia bowed her head, praying that he would not come up. After a long interval the light faded. She crept back to the mouth and saw a squad of soldiers standing guard up the street. No chance of going back for Karan now. Nursing her bruises, Tallia headed up the alley to find her sick.

Two hours later, in pouring rain, she reached the gates of the Old City, having been hopelessly lost in the back streets. Not only had she failed to find Prathitt but she had not come across Lilis or any of her seven either. She felt like an utter fool and was tempted to go back to the Great Hall, but Mendark's guards summoned her to the audience chamber.

The large room was crowded with splendidly garbed officers and aides, while twenty clerks sat at a row of desks along one wall, writing orders furiously and passing their strips of paper to the messengers who ran in and out. Mendark stood before a large canvas map of the city, arguing with an officer gorgeously attired in the Magister's colours, scarlet and blue. That put Tallia in an even worse mood.

It was Berenet the dandy, Mendark's other chief lieutenant, his magnificent mustachioes freshly waxed and coiled. His garments were silk and velvet; he wore a ruff of purple lace at his throat that helped to conceal a sunken chest. Tallia wondered where he had been lately. What with her own travels, and his, she hadn't seen him for half a year. She nodded curtly. Grinning, Berenet inspected her from head to toe.

Mendark looked haggard, though she noticed that he'd had time to bathe and change his clothes. 'What happened to you?' he asked more brusquely than usual. 'Don't drip mud all over the carpet. Oh, what does it matter?' as Tallia stepped to one side.

'I lost them,' she said, feeling like a schoolgirl caught out in some childish negligence. Berenet smirked.

'What are you talking about?' Mendark asked, his brows knitting together. He was furiously angry about something.

'The survivors of the Conclave. I got some of them out but I lost them in the alleys.'

'They've been here for an hour!' said Mendark. 'Some street brat brought seven of them to the gate, all looped together like a camel train.'

'Lilis brought them?' Tallia was amazed. 'How is Orstand?'

'Not too good.' He waved a hand.

Tallia saw the big woman sagging at a table on the other side of the room. 'And Hennia the Zain?'

Mendark lowered his voice. 'I think her nerve has broken. We may have to replace her on the council, after this. What else have you to tell me?'

'I had to leave the rest – I was lucky to get away myself. I lost Prathitt. He hit me and ran away in the dark.'

'Not one of your greatest successes,' said Mendark sourly. 'Thank heavens for Berenet. He has come back with vital intelligence about Yggur.' An aide tugged at his sleeve. 'Just a minute!' he snapped.

'I left Karan behind,' said Tallia. 'The soldiers came before I could get her out . . .'

Mendark swore. 'A sensitive like her would have been useful.'

Tallia took that as another criticism. Sensitives could be invaluable, to sense out danger and to advise what an enemy might do. Some could even relay messages by means of a mind-to-mind link. Karan had that rare talent. But they were a terror to control and often an emotional liability.

'I suppose she'll be dead in the morning,' Tallia said unhappily. Everything she'd done today had been a failure.

'We might all be! Why did you send Thyllan back?'

So that's what the problem was! 'How could I leave him behind? He's on the Council.'

15

'How could you miss the chance to rid me of my enemy?' Mendark raged. 'No one could have blamed you. Now everyone knows he's here and I don't dare allow any harm to come to him.'

'Do we obey the rule of law or not?'

'In this case your judgment is faulty. Berenet would not have been so scrupulous.'

'I'm sure of that!' she said acidly.

'Aah! Get something to eat; I need you to look at the situation on the north side.' The aide attacked his sleeve again. Mendark turned away to the new problem.

Tallia remained where she was. 'I'd like to go back to the hall with a squad and get the rest of them.'

'Impossible,' Mendark barked over his shoulder. 'I need you here. Anyway, Yggur holds that part of the city now. Forget them!'

Tallia knew that he was right, but it still hurt. She turned away, then swung back. 'What happened to Lilis? I didn't even pay her.'

'The brat? The guards gave her a couple of grints before they chased her away. Now stop pestering me!'

Again the smirk from her rival, Berenet. Tallia gritted her teeth and ignored him, though it took all her self-control. She stopped by Orstand's table for a moment to enquire about her health.

'I don't think I've felt worse in my entire life,' said Orstand, though she found time to ask about everyone by name, and was dismayed at Lilis's shabby treatment.

Snatching food and drink from a tray, Tallia hurried out to spend hours more reviewing the reports that streamed in, doing the rounds of the walls and relaying orders in the desperate defences of the night.

In the early morning of that bitterest of all days for Thurkad – the first time that an enemy had come within the gates in more than a thousand years – Tallia learned that

Yggur's First Army had been beaten back from the quarter where the Conclave had been held. Several small victories gave hope of larger ones to come, so instead of snatching a few hours' sleep, she took a small detail down to the Great Hall to find Karan and the other wounded if she could, and bring them to safety.

She picked her way through streets strewn with valuables discarded in flight and not yet taken by the looters – here a red cloth bundle, burst open to scatter silver cutlery in the gutter; there a carved wooden donkey with one ear broken off; a jacket embroidered with silk and garnets; a rolled tapestry that could have come from a bawdy house. Further on there were bodies and the marks of war – blood and broken weapons; men and beasts, women and even children dead of terrible wounds or sometimes no wound at all. And everywhere she saw the smoking shells of houses, once homes. Nearer to the Great Hall there were no signs of war; perhaps it had swept around that place.

By the time she arrived it was late morning. Tallia regretted bitterly her failures of the night, Karan especially. It felt like a personal betrayal. As she approached the hall there was smoke and the smell of burning wood. Closer, the odour of burning flesh, too. Black smoke groped for the sky. Tallia ran up to the pyre.

'Nothing else to do, lar,' said a tall, lean man with a little round pot of a belly that looked so incongruous it might have been pasted there. His grey hair was shaved to stubble. He wore the leather apron of a butcher and there was blood on the front of it. 'If we leave them there'll be plague.'

There were a lot of bodies on the pile and as she stood there staring, two men came up, carrying another between them, and heaved the corpse up onto the fire as if they were loading sacks of coal onto a wagon. The flames were too hot for her to get close enough to recognise any of the faces, and she did not care to watch the burning or to smell the stench. She went into the hall. It had not yet been ransacked; indeed the chaos inside was as they had left it the previous night, save that the dead were gone, and the dying.

There was a huge bloodstain on the floor where the dead guard had lain, and drag marks away from it. Over against the wall, where she had left Karan wrapped in the bloody cloak, she found a tiny smear of blood. Near the far wall was Nelissa's stick, broken in two. Tallia ran outside, back to the pyre, calling out to the butcher with the grey hair.

'What of the dead in the hall? Are they burnt?'

The man thought for a moment, scratching the end of his nose with a bloody fingernail. Tallia found the mannerism particularly offensive.

'There were five, perhaps six, that we took from there,' he said, frowning. 'I can't remember now; so many dead! We did that place hours ago. I remember the old one – we knew her, of course, even if she hadn't been in robes. Nelissa the Sour! Who will mourn *her*, I wonder?'

'Was there a young woman with red hair?'

'Can't remember, lar. There were several women, that I know, and one very striking, but after a while you don't look too closely at them, except to be sure that they're dead. No matter how beautiful they are, once they're gone, their dreams are finished. No use having your own over them.' It seemed he needed to talk about his experiences. 'Remarkable the gap between life and death – at first you can hardly tell it, but as the day wears –'

Tallia was not interested in his philosophy. 'Are you sure you haven't burnt her? She was little, about so tall; red hair, pale skin, blood all over her shirt, but not her own. You would have noticed her hair, a fiery red. She was still alive last night.'

'Then you should have taken her last night,' he said, scratching his nose again. 'That was a bitter night to be dying alone. The women we burned from there had no blood on them, as far as I remember, nor the men either, save one. One woman was tall and dark, not unlike you. I don't remember the other. But we didn't burn any live ones. There were only two breathing this morning, both men, and we sent them away to be nursed. That's all I know.'

The others must have recovered or been taken prisoner in the night, thought Tallia. If only I had carried her with me. But I didn't, and now it's too late.

2

THE UNDERBELLY
OF THURKAD

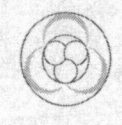

W hen by perilous ways Tallia returned to the citadel
she found that the defence was already failing. Yggur's
forces now surrounded the city's armies on all sides but the
east, forcing them back towards their last bastion, the walled
Old City, which was not even a tenth part of Thurkad. She
ran to the audience chamber but Mendark was not there,
and after a long search, for not even his officers seemed to
know where he was, she found him on one of the wall
towers, directing the defence of the southern wall.

'It's hopeless,' he said wearily. Grimy with soot and
spattered with blood and mud, he was quite as exhausted as
she was. Berenet stood beside him, as beautifully groomed
as ever. Weeping, Mendark swept his arm around the smoky
horizon. 'Look at the destruction. The Gallery is on fire from
end to end; all that remains of the Old Stockade is ash. Four
thousand years of history gone! The longer we fight the more
will die, and defeat is inevitable. But how can I surrender
Thurkad? I love my city with all my heart.'

'Where's the Governor of the Assembly?'

A messenger hurried up with the latest despatches.
Mendark tore open the seal.

'That treacherous cow!' Berenet spat. 'She's fled with her
barges loaded to the waterline.'

'The whole Assembly is in disarray,' Mendark added. 'They couldn't govern a playground! There's only me!' He bent his head to the papers.

'Then your duty is clear,' said Tallia. 'You must defend Thurkad and do what you can for the people, whilever there is hope.'

'That I will do, though a higher duty becomes pressing: to uphold the purpose of the Council. Never was that needed more, with Tensor amok with the Mirror.' He stared down into the city, where Yggur's flag, black crucible on a white circle, was hoisted over a hundred buildings. It looked more like a raised fist; the townspeople called Yggur's soldiers the blackfists.

'I have a plan you may be interested in,' Berenet said, polishing his silver buttons.

He looked smart and efficient. Tallia was uncomfortably aware that she was still covered in mud.

'It'd need to be a good one,' Mendark grunted, not looking up from his despatches.

'It is,' said Berenet smugly. 'Look!'

He unrolled a map of the city on the paving stones, tracing the irregular line of the walls with a manicured fingernail. 'According to the latest intelligence, Yggur now holds five of the eight hills of Thurkad – the whole of the southern and western districts and most of the north. Now he presses towards us in the east.' Berenet marked the areas that Mendark's forces still held – the eastern hills area and, at its centre, the walled Old City. 'But he is vulnerable!'

'How so?' Mendark muttered.

Berenet flipped hair out of his eyes and spread a series of gold coins – a display of wealth that Tallia found vaguely offensive – across the map.

'He has his First Army, headed by Drossim, the most capable of his generals, here holding the centre of the city. The Fourth is stationed in the south, here, controlling the western and southern gates. Morale is not so good in the

Fourth Army. Yggur has overstretched himself – his other three armies are sorely pressed to hold the lands he's conquered and cannot come to his aid.'

'Mmm!' Mendark said indifferently.

'He's brilliant in the field, no doubt of it, but he's never fought for a city this big before. Look!' cried Berenet, moving his golden markers. 'The Fourth Army is barracked all through here.' He marked an area of tenements and labyrinthine alleys. 'And the First Army sleeps here, also in the labyrinth.'

'Get on with it!' said Mendark, still writing furiously.

'See how narrow the roads are, here and here and here. If there was an emergency in the night, the streets full of people, he'd never move his troops through.'

Mendark looked up. 'Go on.'

'Half a million people live in the slums. Another fifty thousand in the wharf city. Suppose we were to fire the labyrinth here and here and here.' His finger traced a line from the northern gate down to the wharf city. 'Everyone would panic, and the streets would be blocked. That whole area is built with timber – walls and floor and roof. His troops would never get out.'

'It would burn all the way to the western wall, even in this weather,' Tallia exclaimed.

'All the way,' Berenet exulted. 'No stopping it! And there'd be so many people in the streets he'd never move his army. The only way out would be through the western gate, so if we brought a battalion of archers around outside in the night and moved your other forces here and here and here,' more gold glided across the map, 'we could finish him in a stroke. His superior numbers would be a weakness rather than a strength.'

'He *could* go into the wharf city,' said Mendark, standing up and beginning to pace back and forth.

'This battalion would stop him if he got that far,' said Berenet, caressing a gold piece. 'Besides, the Hlune are vicious fighters when they're defending their own.'

22

'It might succeed,' said Mendark, tapping the map with a pencil. 'Though I don't like it overmuch.'

'It's desperate!' Tallia retorted. 'If the wind shifted, it would burn us out instead of him.'

'No worse than what we presently face,' said Berenet. 'Utter defeat!'

Tallia could scarcely believe what she was hearing. 'Burn the labyrinth and thousands will die. Tens of thousands!'

'It's worth the sacrifice,' said Berenet. 'If you lose the war, which is almost certain, many of them will die anyway.'

'I can't believe you're seriously considering this, Mendark,' said Tallia urgently. 'It's a shocking betrayal of trust.'

'She's right, Berenet,' said Mendark, shaking his head.

'How can I serve a fool who doesn't want to win?' cried Berenet.

Mendark went very still. 'If you no longer wish to, you know where you can go.'

Berenet clenched his fists until they shook. 'Damn you!' he whispered. 'You question *my* loyalty?'

'Not your loyalty, only your judgment.'

'I offer you the chance of victory, and you choose certain defeat.'

'Enough,' said Mendark, shaking. 'I cannot do it to my city.'

Berenet picked up his gold, rolled the map and, without saying another word, walked away.

'You made the right choice,' said Tallia.

Mendark's pencil snapped. He looked up at Tallia and his eyes were like windows into a torture chamber.

'*Did I?* I've just given up my city and my people, and maybe more will suffer than if I *had* burned Yggur out. And for what?'

He stalked along the wall in full view of the enemy, not noticing as an arow tore through his cloak. Tallia ran after him, urging him to shelter.

Hunched down in an alcove, she broached another issue.

'The Mirror is, perhaps, more important than the fate of Thurkad. And it was Tensor's in the first place.'

Mendark buried his head in his hands. 'Yes, but what is he going to do with it?' Arrows whizzed close overhead, but he ignored them. 'We even spoke of Tensor's quest once or twice, while we were still friends and held to a common purpose. But the ruin of Shazmak has driven him to despair. What more can he lose? He has no honour in his own eyes anymore.'

'All the more dangerous for that,' she said.

'Where can he go?' he went on after a pause. 'My spies have learned nothing. How can we find him in this chaos? There's only myself between him and ruin.'

Tallia put her arm across his shoulder. 'Since *you* are the Council now, and Thurkad is finished, better we go after him.'

'We must. But he was my friend for a long, long time. The bonds still tug at me, Tallia.'

Tallia had a sudden thought. 'Llian was gone too.'

'What?' Mendark roused slowly from his reverie. '*What?*'

'When we recovered last night, Llian was already gone.'

'And there is no trace of him?'

'Nothing –'

'Llian would not have abandoned Karan.' Mendark paced the wall, looking very agitated. 'This is very bad! Did Tensor take him? I must know.'

'Why would he want a chronicler?'

'I haven't got the faintest idea.'

A rock flung from a catapult smashed into the battlement, peppering them with chips of stone. They ducked down hastily. Mendark put his hand to his cheek, where a curving gash began to ebb blood. Tallia fished out a rag but he pushed it away. 'It's nothing! What were you going to say?'

'Remember the night Llian arrived? The guide who brought him to us was Lilis, the street brat that you cast out ungraciously.'

'There are thousands like her in Thurkad. What of it?'

24

'Llian offered her a silver tar in payment but she refused it. She said he had paid enough already. What street brat would refuse a tar?'

'He has charm enough,' said Mendark grudgingly, but intrigued for all that.

'Later that night I saw her in the street outside. And last night she was hanging around just after you left the hall. She said that the "big man" took Llian.'

'*The big man!* Tensor? You think she followed them? You'd better track her down. Orstand knows everyone; she'll find you someone who knows the streets. Dear Orstand! Where would I be without her? Without her, the Council is a hollow shell.'

'There is also Hennia the Zain,' said Tallia carefully.

'The Zain measure their loyalty as sparingly as a moneylender his coin,' Mendark spat. 'Speaking of which, better go to the treasury – it could cost a pocketful of gold.' And, suddenly remembering something else, he said, 'Oh, Tallia!'

She was already walking away. 'Yes?' she asked absently, thinking about the new quest.

'I came across some things of Karan's this morning while I was going through the rubbish that Thyllan left in my office. A diary, a knife, some trinkets.'

Tallia came back, raising a deliberate eyebrow. Surely he wasn't feeling remorse?

'Well, do you want them?' he asked roughly.

'I've got enough to carry. She's gone. What does it matter?' Then, suspicious, 'Why do you care?'

'Llian might want them.'

'You mean he might do what you want in exchange for them,' said Tallia. 'Don't you ever do anything out of altruism? Oh, never mind, where are they?'

He told her, then she put it out of her mind and went to find Lilis. She was given the name of an old soldier named Blustard, a reprobate and drunkard who lived in one of the squalid lean-tos that festered against the western bulwalk of the Old City. Eventually she tracked him down on the wall, for such was the necessity that even he was doing his duty. After speaking to his officer, Tallia took Blustard aside.

He was one of those people who knew everyone and everything, and he recognised her at once. He was drunk, of course, but for him that was normal. If he knew anything about Lilis she would get it out of him.

Blustard had once been a handsome man, tall and slim with a ripe red mouth and high cheekbones, a noble forehead and a mane of black hair billowing down over his collar. But now the forehead and the hair, rusty grey, were all that was left of him. His hands and fingers were twisted and scaly, his nose a swollen, bulbous, red-veined horror, and his flaking lips were grey. His breath stank, his teeth were rotten and his arm trembled even when he rested it on the table. He was afraid of her, as well he might be. Even more afraid than of the enemy outside.

She questioned him but soon realised that he could, or would, tell her nothing. He was too afraid, not drunk enough.

'Come,' she said at last. 'This is no place to talk. Let's step down to The Barrel,' naming a soldier's inn nearby.

Blustard was only too happy. They found the inn to be almost deserted, with only a few old men, too ancient to serve on the walls, drinking in a corner. The barmaid, a plump old woman with the hairstyle of a girl, a froth of golden ringlets, was rinsing mugs in a bucket. She stood up as the door chimed.

'Get out and do your duty, you craven sot!' she screeched as Blustard stepped into the room.

He stopped just inside the door so that Tallia had to push past him. After a word in the barmaid's tiny ear, she banged a large jug of black beer and two mugs on the counter and moved away smartly, triple chins jiggling, wig slightly askew. Blustard scooped up the jug and the two mugs and set off before she fumbled a copper out of her bag. She turned just in time to see him catch his toe in the rug, crashing to the floor so hard that the windows rattled in their frames. He slowly climbed to his feet. One of the mugs was chipped but he had not allowed a splash from the jug.

'Not a drop spilled! Look at that!' He grinned his black-toothed grin at her, wiping a dribble of blood from his nose across the back of his hand. 'You can rely on old Blessie, eh!'

Tallia was astounded. The sot was actually proud of himself! 'Very good,' she said curtly. 'No, this table,' pointing to one in the darkest corner of the room.

Blustard sat down with a thump, filled both their glasses to the brim and with great cheer raised his. She clinked mugs with the best grace she could muster and took a sip. The beer was strong but sour, as if the barrel had not been cleaned properly. Blustard drained his mug in a single swallow, belched and poured another. His ghastly nose still dripped blood into grey stubble. Tallia looked into his eyes.

'The street child, Lilis,' she reminded him. 'You know her?'

He mumbled. 'What?' she said.

'I can't remember!' He was looking down at the table. He would draw it out, to get whatever he could out of her.

He raised the mug toward his lips. Her hand shot out and caught his wrist. Despite his appearance, he was very strong, Tallia discovered. But she was a master of the Secret Art and of unarmed combat, too, and few in Thurkad could match her will to will, or wrist to wrist for that matter. She couldn't let this street bully defeat her. Though he terrorised the poor and the weak, she knew that he was rotten at the core, a coward when faced with someone stronger.

Blustard forced back, and for an instant she thought he was going to overpower her. She imagined little Lilis in his hands, and that gave her the strength she needed. She twisted hard; after a short struggle the mug fell from his fingers. Beer flooded his lap. She twisted his wrist harder.

'I'll break it. Don't mess around. Lilis?'

The drenching of his trousers did not bother him. He was used to that one way or the other, but he looked down mournfully at the wasted beer. She twisted further, the wrist bones creaked then his resistance was gone. 'Yes, I know her.'

'Where does she live?'

'Live! They don't live anywhere, those kids. They sleep in a barrel one day, up a drain the next.' Blustard looked toward the jug. 'I need my drink,' he whined.

'It's my drink,' she said, applying more pressure, wondering if she would have to break his wrist to get what she needed, 'and you don't get any more till you tell me.'

'Easy to find her if there was no war. But everyone is hiding now.'

'You must know who to ask.'

'They disappear all the time. Taken! *Sold*.' Blustard spat on the floor.

Sold! I thought I knew Thurkad. 'Find out!' she said curtly.

'When you ask, they vanish.'

That was entirely understandable, but she knew he could find Lilis if he wanted to. For all his drunkenness, Blustard was a powerful man in the alleys. How could she motivate him? What promise would he not break, once he was away from her?

Tallia tightened her grip on his wrist, looking coldly into his bloody eyes. 'Tell me exactly what I must do to find her,' she said, emphasising each word. 'Who I talk to, what I say to them. Then you are going into the dungeon cells with nothing but water until I return. If I don't come back, or I come back without her, Mendark will forget that you are there. You know what a vengeful man he can be.'

Blustard did. He stared back at her, seeing her utter resolve. His eyes strayed to the jug.

'After you tell me,' said Tallia softly.

Again he hesitated, lusting for the drink, looking down at his clamped wrist, anywhere but into her eyes. He wiped his nose with the back of his other hand, smearing blood halfway across his cheek, and then it suddenly burst out of him.

'I can't find her!' he moaned. 'There is only one person that can, in the war. S'Courcy!'

Tallia shivered despite herself. S'Courcy was a diseased spider at the centre of the web of wickedness and corruption that made up the underworld of Thurkad. No one ever saw him, but everyone knew that he was there. This was more than she had planned on. But when you served Mendark you did whatever it took. He did not accept excuses, nor would Tallia think of offering them.

'Tell me how to get an audience with S'Courcy,' she said. 'And how to get out again safely, or you will die a sad and sober man in the bottommost level of Mendark's dungeon.'

Blustard would do anything to avoid that. She listened, noted, clarified, and when she was satisfied, let go his wrist and poured him a mug. He drained it in a swallow then she stood up, caught his wrist again and led him to the door. On the threshold she whistled, a sound that made him clutch his ears. Up the street two of Mendark's personal guard looked up. One of them she knew, a very reliable fellow, fiercely loyal.

'Torgsted!' she yelled.

Torgsted was short, curly-haired, with a smile to roast chest-nuts and a line that could charm the most jaded barmaid. He was exercising those talents in animated conversation with a very pretty girl a full head taller than himself, but he broke off and ran up, saluting Tallia.

'Take this man to the lowest cells and put him under guard there. He is to have no drink but water till I return. And hold him tight on the way.'

Torgsted saluted her again, the two stepped forward and, gripping Blustard tightly, led him away whining and sniffling to the citadel.

There was no getting out of the Old City secretly until dark, so Tallia went about her other affairs until the late afternoon, snatched a meagre sleep, little more than an hour, exchanged her finery for street drab, oiled cloak and hood, and, not willing to risk any of the secret ways, lowered herself over the wall with a rope into the unlit alleys. From there, consulting only the map she had memorised, she worked her way into the squalid labyrinth of unpaved lanes and passages, tall rotting tenements and tiny market squares where more than half the people of Thurkad existed. It was a place which only a mighty army could command, so Yggur's troops wisely kept to the wider streets, the more lighted ways. Though they controlled who went in and out they did not interfere with what went on within. Not yet.

Tallia went where Blustard had told her to go and spoke to a man there, saying precisely what she had been told to say. She gave the correct tribute, a tar. The man led her through the streets to another place, she gave the woman there another tar, the woman looked at Tallia through glazed eyes, nodded, flicked a glance at the man and led her again through the lanes. He goes the direct way, thought Tallia, to tell S'Courcy I am coming.

This process passed through several more stages. Finally they went inside a stone building, up six flights of steps, down a hall and into a large room which was undecorated, though partitioned by screens into a number of smaller spaces. The walls were water-stained; there were no windows and the air was smoky and stale. Round a partition she was led, into a larger space where there were rugs on the floor, and in the centre stood a large square bed with gilded posts and a canopy of painted silk. It was also stained and had a tear in the middle. In the bed lay the man she had come to see.

He was very fat, with pallid skin but remarkably thin arms and legs and a small head. His sharp lips were pursed. Had he twice the number of limbs he would have greatly resembled a spider, she thought. No, not fat at all, his body was bloated by disease. His shiny eyes fixed on her.

'Tallia bel Soon! Right hand of Mendark. Welcome. Show yourself. I am S'Courcy.'

His voice was soft, sibilant, but might easily have become venomous if he was thwarted. He waved a stick-like hand and a servant took her cloak and hood. Tossing back a river of black hair, she stepped toward him and put out her hand. He screwed up his lips. She stopped at once.

'I do not touch,' he said. 'Ah, but you are indeed even more beautiful than it is said.' She inclined her head. 'And most expert in combat without weapons, I hear. Please do not be insulted, but stay well back.' S'Courcy's voice went hoarse and he broke into a fit of coughing that went on and on. Finally he gasped it to a close. 'This is the end of the Magisters in Thurkad, I think? We must all reach new accommodations.'

'The situation is fraught,' Tallia replied.

'But you did not come here to talk about the war. How can I possibly help the Magister? You want someone found, I believe?'

'A street urchin. Her name is Lilis. She guides, from the eastern waterfront.'

S'Courcy gestured to an aide. 'Find out about this child,' he said, and the aide bowed and ran out.

'And why do you want her?'

'We think she saw something last night.'

'Saw something?' His eyes closed momentarily and he looked down at his hands.

Tallia knew what he was thinking. Maybe this was something that Yggur would pay for. Maybe he would pay more than Mendark. Maybe at a time such as this it would be better to do the conqueror a favour. The situation looked hopeless for Mendark. But then, he *had* been Magister for an age and he was wily beyond belief. And it was said that Yggur was a law-maker, a regulator, an upright man. Perhaps he would not do business.

The aide came back in, bowed and stood waiting. S'Courcy looked up.

'The child who came out of the citadel yesterday, before dawn,' said the aide.

'Ah! The one who led the Council to safety after the Conclave. The price has gone up.'

'Where is she? And what is the price?'

'The price. That is something to negotiate. Ah!' He examined her with glittering eyes.

He wonders how desperate we are. He knows we have little time. The price will be outrageous.

'My price is one hundred gold tells.'

More outrageous than she had imagined – a colossal fortune. But her face showed not a twitch. 'A *hundred*! With that I could pay a hundred spies for a year. She was not the only one with her eyes open last night.'

'Ah, true. But a hundred spies cannot tell you what you need to know today.'

'Ten tells,' snapped Tallia, 'and I want her now. Where is she?'

'Not far. We have been instructing her in her responsibilities. Perhaps we can make a compromise. Fifty tells.'

Tallia's eyes narrowed. His words gave her a cold feeling inside. 'Twenty tells, as long as she is in good health. Otherwise she is no use to me.'

'There will be a small wait. Take this chair; let me offer you refreshment.' He waved at an orderly but Tallia shook her head.

'I will stand, thank you.' She moved back slightly, turning so that no one could come behind her. Two guards lounged in the doorway, apparently at ease, but their eyes never left her.

'As you will.' Aides came in and out. S'Courcy busied himself with his ledgers, broken with frequent coughing fits that left him white-faced and hoarse. Finally the first aide returned, speaking briefly with the spider.

'They bring her,' said S'Courcy. 'She is . . . a little damaged. Perhaps I can compromise. Twenty-five tells.' He drew back his lips in a travesty of a smile. 'Shall we agree on it now?'

'I will see her first,' said Tallia coldly, already wondering what her options were and whether she would get out of here alive.

Another aide appeared, carrying a bundle of bloody rags from which thin legs and arms hung limply. He flung the bundle down in front of Tallia. She went to her knees, smoothing the hair away from the pinched face, though not forgetting the guards behind her. It was Lilis, and she had been savagely beaten some time ago, for she was covered in purple bruises and newer swellings that were yet to discolour. There were fresh welts on her legs. One eye was black. She was unconscious.

Tallia stood up and her face was cold as stone. '*Instructing her in her responsibilities?*'

'All coin earned on the street comes here,' S'Courcy said with a sickening smile. 'For her deeds she must have been rewarded handsomely, yet she yielded none of it. So we taught her her duties, as we would any who so failed.'

'She was never paid, only a few coppers by the guards before they drove her off. And she is but a child.'

'*Never paid?* Is that the quality of the Council who protect us? Even on the streets we pay our debts. But what is one child, anyway, out of the teeming thousands in this city? Her life-price is only half a tar.'

Tallia wanted to smash him through the wall, and could have, in spite of the guards. But where was the profit in that?

'And that is what I should pay you,' she said. 'But I, too, pay my debts. Because she *is* damaged, and has been beaten since I came here, I will pay only my initial offer.'

Pulling a handful of coin from her pocket, Tallia counted ten tells and threw them on the end of the bed. Then she tore her cloak out of the hands of the waiting servant, wrapped Lilis in it and heaved her over one shoulder. Her eyes met those of S'Courcy. 'Let me give you this warning. Mendark is down, but still powerful, and he never forgets an injury. Ensure that we get back to the citadel, or one day when you least expect it he will burn the labyrinth to brick dust and ashes.'

She whirled and stalked out of the room. Mendark doesn't even know where I've gone, she realised on the way down the stairs, fearing a knife aimed at her back, or a stone dropped from above. But by the time she reached the bottom one of the aides was beside her, leading her. On the streets pragmatism was all. S'Courcy had ten tells for nothing; why make an enemy unnecessarily? And he *was* very vulnerable.

Still, it was not until she was back at the side gate and calling out the password that she could relax. The gate opened a crack, a lantern was directed onto her face, up and down the street, and she slipped wearily within.

Shortly she strode up the stairs of the citadel and found Mendark once again in the audience chamber, as frantically busy as before. The atmosphere was not as gloomy as it had been earlier; evidently Yggur had suffered a setback. That explained why she'd had such an easy passage back.

'Beaten!' she said savagely to Mendark's inquiring glance, 'because she did not hand over the *reward* for saving the Council.' Mendark's eyes slid away from hers. 'I will take her to my room. You can question her later, *if she lives*.' She strode away, sweeping people aside with one arm and calling for a nurse.

Upstairs, Tallia and the nurse cut off Lilis's rags, bathed her thin little body, washed her hair and cleaned and bandaged her wounds. They found her left shoulder to be dislocated, and some ribs cracked. Basia the nurse, the most wrinkled old woman in the world, though still nimble, soon put those injuries right. Finally they slid Lilis into a nightshirt and rolled her into Tallia's bed. She was breathing shallowly and her skin was cold.

'What do you think, Basia?' asked Tallia, her heart going out to the waif. 'Will she live?'

The nurse, who had come from her rocking-chair and her

hearth to aid the war, said, 'Oh, I think so, if she survives the night. The injuries would soon mend if she were well, but she is frail – listen to her chest rattle. That's the hazard of life on the streets. I've some herbs that will help her, though.'

'Tell me what you need and I will run for it,' said Tallia, unclenching her fist and kneading the taut sinews.

'I have to make the medicines first,' said Basia. 'I'll go. Why are you so worried?'

'She's just a child!' Tallia did not understand what Basia was getting at.

'I can see that. I care for her, as I do for all my patients. But you are one of the powerful, with great responsibilities. Why do *you* care so much?'

'Perhaps I'm trying to make up for past negligence,' murmured Tallia. 'Go for your medicines. I'll watch her.'

Tallia pulled up a chair and sat by the bed. She felt so tired. Time passed, an hour. She took Lilis's hand, felt her feet. The urchin was cold, too cold. Tallia threw off her own clothes and slipped into the bed, taking Lilis in her arms and enfolding her with the warmth of her body, comforting her and even drawing a little comfort from her, and finally slept better than she had in more than a week.

When Basia returned in the early morning, Lilis was sleeping peacefully in Tallia's arms, her face serene. Basia looked down at them with a smile, then touched Tallia on the shoulder. She woke instantly. 'It's morning,' said Basia. 'Already the child is better.'

Tallia was out of bed in a flash, water splashed in the adjacent room, then she was back, dressing hurriedly. She sat down beside the bed to pull on her boots, and at the creak of the chair Lilis opened her eyes. The most beautiful golden smile that Tallia had ever seen spread across her thin face.

'I dreamed about you,' Lilis said in a scratchy voice. 'You held me in your arms and made all the hurts go away. It was so warm, so wonderful that I was afraid to wake up. Where am I?'

'You are in the citadel, child,' said the wrinkled old dame. 'Tallia went into the labyrinth and took you from that evil spider and brought you here. You owe your life to her.'

'I did,' said Tallia, 'but you helped me too, Lilis, and were beaten cruelly for your trouble. Let us not talk of owing.'

Lilis stared at Tallia for ages. 'T-Tallia,' she said finally. 'Where do you come from?'

Tallia smiled. 'Why do you ask?'

'You look different, and you talk different to everyone else in Thurkad. And you are nicer.'

Laughing, Tallia kissed her on the nose. 'I am from Crandor, halfway across the world. When I was your age, old Mendark found out that I could do . . . things. He sent me to a special school, then brought me to Thurkad to work off my debt.'

'Do you have a mother and a father?'

'I do, in Crandor, but I don't see them much these days.'

Lilis sighed heavily and lay back down. 'Now,' said Tallia, 'I want you to rest and grow strong, and after that the Magister himself will ask you some questions.'

Tallia went up to Mendark's offices and collected the little bundle of Karan's gear. There wasn't much. A small knife with a plain soapstone handle, the blade a good, rather dark steel with worn patterns chased into it. The trinket, as Mendark had called it, was a globe the size and shape of a plum, made of some polished mineral, grey in colour, with silver leaves at the big end. It was a curious ornament, rather too big to be worn on a chain.

Examining it more closely, Tallia saw that there was no provision for that, for there was no way of attaching it. Then she noticed something quite remarkable: in the dark room her fingers left glowing marks on the surface, faint patches that slowly faded. *It must be a lightglass!* Tallia knew of such things, but only as ancient artefacts that had long since failed.

Mendark had one, quite different to this, though five hundred years had passed since it last gave out any light. A wonder he hadn't realised what it was. Where had Karan got such a thing?

The other item was a small book of many pages, carefully wrapped. A beautiful, costly volume with the soft feel of rice paper. The handwriting was tiny. There were occasional dates scattered through it, the earliest more than six years ago. It was a diary or journal, though the intervals between entries were irregular, sometimes weeks apart. The last was dated two weeks ago, just after she'd reached Thurkad.

Tallia did not care to read Karan's private thoughts. There was an inscription inside the cover but she did not know the language. It ended with a single word – Rael. A gift; a precious book; a valuable record. Karan's family would certainly want it. Karan came from Gothryme, a poor place in mountainous Bannador, Tallia recalled. Llian would want to see it too, if he ever returned. Wrapping the items carefully, she went down to carry out her next task.

From each of the seven that Lilis had rescued Tallia extracted (in one case extorted) the proper ransom for their lives. Converting that to gold, she put it away for Lilis. The child would need it to live on, if they survived, though the way the war was going that was looking less likely every day.

3

AFTERSICKNESS

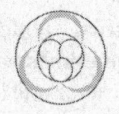

Faelamor tried to sit up but found that she could not; her arms had no more strength than string. Tensor's potency had drained her cruelly. Nonetheless she had to find Maigraith. Faelamor had never been physically strong, but now just dragging herself up the stairs to the balcony exhausted her. She lay on the floor for an hour before summoning the strength to raise her head again. As she did, a lantern flared and she heard voices.

Maigraith had not stirred. One arm hung through the balcony, her glasses still clutched in her hand. Faelamor eased the arm back lest someone see it and remember her. However, in the confusion and haste downstairs, and the shouting and clangour outside, no one did. Someone banged on the back door, then all was silent.

A lamp still guttered below. She crawled back down the stairs, finding quite a few people still alive, though none stirred when she touched them. So tired. She lay down for a moment, then snatched herself out of sleep. Among the wavering shadows of the lamplight she saw a bundle against the wall. It turned out to be Karan, wrapped in a cloak, her eyes racing under their lids. Not long ago, Faelamor had uncovered a secret that even Karan did not know: that she was a blending of three different human species, a triune.

Triunes were incredibly rare, mostly mad, but could have remarkable talents. What might this one be capable of? Deadly, treacherous creature! Faelamor thought. She put her hand to Karan's throat but lacked the strength to squeeze.

Suddenly Karan groaned, a horrible endlessly drawn-out wailing cry of terror, cut off by a shuddering inward gasp, and flung her head from side to side. The hairs stood up on the back of Faelamor's neck. She found herself backing away involuntarily, filled with such a bleeding horror that she could not find the courage to approach again. She was as weak as if she had no bones. Ahhh, I will die here, and the hopes of the Faellem with me, she thought despairingly.

The Faellem were one of the three off-world peoples marooned on Santhenar by the Forbidding, but unlike Aachim and Charon they had never made a new life here. They were so bound up with their own world, beloved Tallallame, that any other planet could be no more than a dimensionless shadow. Here they lived, and sometimes died, but they made no home. They could not. They knew themselves to be the greatest and noblest of the four human species, and nothing but Tallallame would do for them.

The broken front door creaked open. An officer and a pair of Yggur's soldiers put their heads in cautiously. Faelamor tried to fashion a concealing illusion, but found that her powers of the mind were quite gone. She lay on the floor like a corpse on a slab. The soldiers held their weapons out while the officer inspected the room, then made some notes on a sheet.

'No danger here,' he said in a clipped accent. 'But something is not right. We will come back when the quarter is secure.' They went out, someone shouted outside and the street was silent again.

Must get help! Faelamor thought. She crawled out onto the wet steps. There was no one in sight. The air was smoky; flames were visible beyond the rooftops. Shortly there came running footsteps. Two men appeared, a tall, very fat one whose flabby belly and thighs jiggled as he ran, and another with stumpy legs and a chest as big as a barrel.

'Help!' she cried, lying helpless in the rain.

They did not break stride. 'Help yourself,' said the tall man, breasts as big as a woman's dancing beneath his water-sodden shirt. Stumpy said nothing; he did not even look at her.

Faelamor willed their feet out from under them but nothing happened, their wooden-soled sandals clapped on the cobbles and they were gone.

I *am* the Faellem! she told herself. I *do* have the will.

Soon another man appeared, limping badly. 'Help!' she cried again.

'I am useless,' he said dismally.

'You *will* aid me,' she gasped, trying to force strength out of a vacuum.

The man stopped. He was a short fellow, young and slender, with a bloody rag wrapped around his right foot. Half of his ear was missing too, leaving a raw hole, and his torn coat was daubed with blood.

'I have gold,' she whispered. Oh, to be so helpless that she must beg a *gah*, as the Faellem derisively termed the old human species.

'Gold!' he choked. 'Can I eat it? Will it bring back my father? Will it help my mother now?'

'You live!' she said. 'Gold will repair your injuries, buy food, pay for a room.'

'I have all that,' he said indifferently, staring through her. His hair was a coarse black mat, his face broad, the cheekbones high and prominent. There was just a trace of fuzz on his chin. Not quite a man – an appealing youth, save for the vacant eyes.

Faelamor found a new approach. 'I am older than your mother,' she said, and felt it. Lying in the rain with her hand reaching up to him, she felt like an aged crone.

The grey eyes focussed. 'So you are,' he replied respectfully, and that struck her even harder. 'I will take you to my mother's house.' Reaching down, he lifted her to a sitting position.

'My friend needs help more than I do,' she said, holding herself upright with her arms. 'She is inside, at the top of the stairs on the balcony.'

'Is she older than my mother?'

'She is, though she does not look it. Bring her glasses too. Go quickly, please.'

He limped inside, leaving blood on the stone with each step. The rain washed it away.

'Is this your friend?' asked the youth, lurching through the door with Maigraith over his shoulder. He slipped and fell heavily. Maigraith's head flopped back. Raindrops spotted her cheek, smooth as marble. Her eyelids flickered but she did not rouse.

'It is.' Faelamor felt a little stronger now, though she was growing very cold.

'She doesn't look as old as my mother,' the youth said dolefully, staring at Maigraith.

'She *is* old, boy. Now do as I tell you. Take her to your mother's house, then come back for me.' She spoke as a woman to a child.

'*All right!*' he said, as a child to a nagging parent. He eased himself out from under Maigraith, lifted her awkwardly, shrugged her into a more comfortable position and hobbled off. Faelamor watched him out of sight.

'What have I done?' she said aloud. 'The boy has lost his wits and I am no better.'

The rain intensified. The sound of marching came down the street. More soldiers! Faelamor felt strong enough to stand, though as soon as she did so found that her knees would not support her. She flopped her way back into the hall and crawled behind the door. There she lay in a daze, taking no account of time, until she was aroused by a plaintive voice outside.

'Old mother? Where have you gone, old mother?'

'Inside!' she gasped.

The youth, a shadow against the dark, felt around until his hand touched her shoulder.

'Is it you, old mother?'

'It is. Take me to your mother's house, boy, and be quick.'

He lifted her easily and carried her back out into the drenching rain. It was quite a distance, and his gait grew more uneven with every step. Faelamor lost track of time. Once he skidded, fell and dropped her hard on her bottom, but even that did not shock her out of the creeping lethargy.

'Sorry, old mother. Very sorry.' It was the last she knew.

Maigraith's eyes fluttered open. She was exhausted and dull-brained as if she had slept for a week. Her cheek felt tender too, a big lump from some fall that she could not remember. She focussed on a plaster ceiling decoration, painted in many colours and touched with gilt. She lay in a huge cedar bed in cream linen sheets, though they were damp and her clothes were too. The room was a long, high-ceilinged rectangle, with curtains of blue velvet and a blazing fire at the further end. Beside the bed was a table with bread, fruit and a painted flask of yellow wine.

Maigraith slowly came to her senses, bewildered by the gaps in her memory. Fate conspired to play cruel jokes on her, flinging her from one terror to another, snatching her friends away as soon as she found them, never allowing her to know what was happening and never permitting her any control over her existence. Each time she felt she understood the world it would turn topsy-turvy again.

She reached for a piece of bread. Her head throbbed and she groaned. The moving hand seemed not part of her. An answering groan came from the armchair by the fire.

'Faelamor!' Maigraith cried. 'Was it you brought me here?'

'In a fashion.' The voice sounded even more lethargic than Maigraith felt. 'How are you?'

Maigraith sat up. 'I ache in every part, and my head is all fluffy inside. If this is aftersickness it is the worst I've ever felt. I can't even remember . . .'

'We have much the same troubles then.'

Maigraith looked across at her liege. Faelamor had led the Faellem to Santhenar in the hunt for the golden flute, long ago. The Faellem were smaller than old humans, with translucent skin that showed pink flesh beneath, and the blue nets of veins. Normally they concealed their differences by cosmetics or illusion, but now Maigraith could see Faelamor's blood flowing under the skin. Even Maigraith, who had served her for many years, had never seen her looking so Faellem. The greatest illusionist on Santhenar, Faelamor's voice could be anything she wanted it to be. Now it was just a choked little whisper.

Her colourless hair normally had an almost luminous glow about it, swirling about her like a restless cloud of static electricity, but today it lay on the chair back like sodden noodles.

Maigraith was distinctly different. She was of average height but willow slender, with perfectly straight chestnut hair that hung down to her shoulder-blades, and skin as smooth and amber as honey. She would have been beautiful except that she always looked melancholy, and but for her eyes, which were an unnerving colour between indigo and carmine, depending on how the light caught them. Lately she concealed the colour with tinted glasses.

Maigraith wondered, as she was wont to do, about the differences between her and the Faellem. She knew she was different; she looked old human save for her eyes. But where she came from, who she really was, were unknowns. It was the greatest torment of her life, but she could not find out. Her parents were dead, a secret so shameful and shocking that Faelamor refused to talk about it.

Now Faelamor was speaking again. 'Tensor has taken the Mirror. Do you recall that?'

'I remember that you called my name at the Conclave. I went to the balcony, and after that my mind is empty.'

'Thurkad is taken!' said Faelamor. 'Yggur's troops are everywhere. We are in great peril. Especially me, especially like *this*.' She meant her inability to disguise herself.

'What about Karan?' Maigraith asked. Karan was the only person who had ever treated her as a friend. Would that she had done the same. Maigraith had dragged Karan into this business in the first place, and she could never stop feeling guilty about it.

'Dead by now, I would say,' said Faelamor coldly.

Maigraith did not even cry out, just stared sightlessly up, knowing that she was to blame. The hollows of her eyes flooded with tears, filled eventually to overflowing and washed down her cheeks. Not wanting Faelamor to see her in her misery, she turned over and pulled the sheet across her face. The pillow grew wet.

After a while the emptiness in her belly forced her up again and she took a little bread moistened with wine. Faelamor had not moved. 'Where are we now?' Maigraith asked.

'A young fellow has taken us into his home, but he is a very strange one.'

'Where is he?'

'I don't know. I woke up in the next room, yesterday. Everything was as you see it now – the fire, the food – and I heard him coming and going, but I did not have the strength to get up. The Conclave drained me to the dregs. I slept the day and the night away.'

'What are you going to do now?'

'I cannot think. We are trapped. My powers are gone.'

The Faellem, in whose civilisation machines of any sort were frowned upon, and use of magical devices utterly forbidden, had developed their powers of the mind, of deception, confusion and concealment, to a high art. To lose those powers was worse than going blind.

'You can't do anything at all?'

'Nothing. I have failed my people. I want to die.'

This was a new experience for Maigraith. Faelamor was normally so dominant, her every action so carefully planned. Now Maigraith felt the bonds breaking, one by one. Interesting possibilities arose, and the most interesting of all was Yggur. He had held her prisoner in Fiz Gorgo last autumn, but after weeks of talking, a kind of friendship had developed between them, as each recognised the pain that the other was in. Subsequently his frightening servants, the Whelm, had taken Maigraith and tortured her. Had they done so at Yggur's orders or on their own behalf? Maigraith still agonised about that. She could not believe that he would do such a thing to her, after what had grown between them. But then, he *had* been desperate to get the Mirror back.

Not long before the Conclave, Maigraith had gone to Yggur's encampment to meet him, to lay this demon to rest one way or the other, but he had not been there. Now the very mention of his name set off a great yearning in her. She was afraid of Yggur, but she longed for him too. She said nothing about that to Faelamor, of course.

Just then the young man limped in. The stained and tattered clothes of the other night were gone. He was dressed in fine cloth of sombre brown. The bloody remnant of ear was cleaned up and bandaged, the black thatch oiled flat to his skull in the formal Thurkad way, and knee-high black boots were polished to a brilliant shine. His eyes were fever-bright but he spoke very courteously.

'Good morning, old mother; young mother.' He bowed to them in turn. 'Did you sleep well? When you are ready, come down the hall, where I have prepared a hot bath for you. After that, I have laid your breakfast out. Usually our honoured guests are invited to the jade terrace, but it is cold and wet there today. However, you will find the old parlour very comfortable.'

Maigraith and Faelamor looked at one another, wondering if there was some jest. He became an anxious boy again.

'I hope everything is to your liking. My mother . . . Hospitality was a sacred duty to her. She would be sorrowful if I fell below her standards.'

'Thank you,' they said together.

'We will come directly,' Faelamor went on. 'We are very tired.'

'I could carry you to the bath . . .'

'Not necessary,' said Maigraith. He bowed once more and disappeared.

'This is not right,' said Faelamor. 'I am uneasy. Yet I do not sense violence in him.'

'Then let us humour him and be on our way. A bath is something I had not even dreamed about.'

The bathroom, a weary walk away at the end of a long hall, was grander than anything Maigraith could have dreamed: a vast room walled and floored in black calcite, with a square tub the size of a cart, half-filled with steaming water.

'Wealthy folk indeed,' said Maigraith as she scrubbed herself with soap perfumed with rose petals. 'But even so he must have laboured half the morning to prepare this.'

Soon they were sitting in the parlour, clean and refreshed, eating a magnificent breakfast. Maigraith normally cared little what she ate, but she had a passion for hot chocolate and a huge jug of it was put before her.

When they had done, and even the jug was drained, the youth came back. 'You are satisfied?' he asked. He seemed to be under some strain.

'Thank you. We could not have asked for better hospitality.'

'Then please to come with me.'

They followed him silently down another hall and into a room of similar quality to Maigraith's, with a bed equally grand, though larger. A fire glowed near the door; there was a barrel beside it.

'Come in,' he said, his voice cracking. 'Please pay your respects to my mother.'

Maigraith stepped inside and almost fell down. Even Faelamor felt the stab in her breast.

A woman of middle age, small and slender, was laid out on the bed in a gown of rose-coloured silk. There were embroidered slippers on her tiny feet, and her black hair was brushed until it gleamed, braided many times and the braids spread fanwise on the pillow. The wound in her side had been carefully bandaged, though the bulge was visible through the silk. Folded one in each arm were the bodies of her sons, twins about the age of nine, and they were as carefully dressed as their mother, even the wounds, the black hair oiled, the eyes closed.

'Come, pay your respects, old mother, young mother. Give her thanks for her protection and hospitality.'

Maigraith was struck dumb. Going forward, she touched the woman on her hand, which held a single night-black, trumpet-shaped moonflower, and thanked her. Faelamor was moved despite the hardness of her heart and her lack of empathy for any species except her own, and she also thanked the dead woman and laid her hands upon her brow.

'She would be proud,' said the youth, tears quivering on his lashes. 'How beautiful she was, my mother.'

'How did they die?'

'My father went to the war seven days ago. I promised him that I would look after my mother and my brothers. He went bravely, and he was killed in the first hour of battle.'

They stared at the burden on the bed.

'I promised. Look how I kept that promise!' he wailed, tearing at his ruined ear until the blood flowed. 'Beloved father, I failed us all. The soldiers came and my mother and brothers were slain. I'm sorry, father. I'm sorry, mother. I'm so sorry, Tasie and Ben.'

He turned to Maigraith and Faelamor. He was quite calm. The tears were gone. Maigraith had never seen such dignity in one so young.

'Go now,' he said simply.

They turned away at a loss, thinking to leave him to his grief, but scarcely had they reached Maigraith's room when a high-pitched cry pierced through the whole house. The silence was devoured by a roar and a crackle.

Maigraith ran stiff-legged back to the room but could not get inside. The barrel lay on its side in the middle of the carpet, a burning brand smoking beside it. The room reeked of burning oil and the whole of the bed was enveloped in yellow flame, flames licking to the ceiling, dripping onto the floor, and highest where the youth lay across the bodies of mother and sons, enfolding and protecting them with his arms.

Maigraith turned away. Faelamor took a step through the door but the heat forced her back. She bowed her head. 'I never knew his name,' she said.

They took refuge in a rotting shed among the shrubbery at the far end of the garden while the mansion burned until there was nothing left but the stone of the walls. No one came to watch the fire or to see if help was needed, except a pair of soldiers, and they soon went away again. Neither Faelamor nor Maigraith could bear to stay but they had nowhere to go, and Faelamor, lacking the strength to defend herself against even the most miserable ruffian on the street, dared not try to find a better place.

They spent the rest of the day in the shed, huddling as best they could among the spiders, out of the rain and the wind and the drips, for the walls were just timber slabs put vertical with a gap between each, and the roof mere cracked and rotting shingles. The shed was small, four paces by three, with an earthen floor that was a bog. One end was full of stacked firewood, while the other held broken furniture and the oddments that accumulate in the lifetime of a house: a small table with a cracked top, pieces of a rosewood bed that spiced the moist air of the shed, a cupboard filled with chipped pots and plates and cups with their handles broken, a child's wooden horse with the inscription 'Dearest Ben' underneath.

The next day they went out onto the street, clinging together like two old women in the constant rain, for, as the youth had said, they could not eat their gold. Maigraith had conjured an illusion of sorts to disguise Faelamor and herself, but it was a miserable effort that even an apprentice scryer would have seen through.

They did not get far. Their part of the city had been fought over for days but had finally been taken by Yggur. His soldiers were on every street corner.

'Name?' demanded the lanky guard a bare two blocks away. His eyes, as blue as sapphires, watered constantly from the wind, crusting his cheeks with ice.

'Telliuliolellillallamammamor,' said Faelamor, which was not true but might have been, for that was the way names went in the part of the world where her people now lived. She had to write it down for him.

'From where?' He rubbed crackling strands of ice off his cheek.

'Mirrilladell,' which was true. The Faellem dwelt in that vast land of lakes and bogs south of the Great Mountains, months' journey east across the Sea of Thurkad.

The guard shivered, stamping his feet in a futile attempt to warm himself. 'Where is your pass?'

'Was not needed when I came to Thurkad, weeks ago.'

'Where do you live now?'

Faelamor gave another street, another place.

'And your business today?'

'To find something to eat,' she said tersely.

Finally, after more questioning, the guard consulting a list, scrutinising her carefully and making notes on a slate, he waved her on. Faelamor waited, sick and sick at heart, while Maigraith went through the same interrogation. She passed through as well.

Two blocks away they did it again, and again later, but

not for money could they find any place to take them in or any food to buy. The market stalls and shops were all closed and shuttered, as were the inns and the private homes, and there was never an answer to their knocking. Neither could they leave that quarter, for no one was allowed in or out.

'I can't do this,' Faelamor gasped. 'I am weaker than ever. We'll have to go back.'

It was late afternoon by the time they got home. Faelamor was staggering, Maigraith supporting her. They splashed past the charred rubble to their shed.

'Look,' said Maigraith, pointing. In the winter-ravaged remnant of a vegetable garden, pillaged of everything edible, a few turnips had been exposed by the rain.

'I loathe turnip,' Faelamor replied, and while Maigraith gathered three or four of them, Faelamor sat down on a lump of wood out of the rain and cried. Her failure seemed absolute, her loss of powers permanent, their discovery inevitable. For one who had for the whole of her very long life been a leader, this inability to control her destiny was a devastating blow.

It grew dark. The rain came down heavier than ever. Maigraith washed the turnips clean under the torrent from the roof. They were long gone to seed, wrinkled and wormy. She handed the larger one to Faelamor.

'Enjoy your dinner,' Maigraith said with a rare smile.

The turnips were fibrous and pungent, almost as hot as a radish. Maigraith gnawed hers thoughtfully. She was beginning to recover. For most of her life she had felt the powerlessness that Faelamor suffered now. She was not happy, but neither was she in despair.

Faelamor took nothing but water and wasted away visibly. Maigraith endured the shed for another day, eating the turnips and a few other roots dug from the garden, but she knew that each day Yggur's control of the city grew tighter. The opportunity to escape was already gone. Hunger was weakening her. In another day she wouldn't have the strength to help herself.

In the morning Faelamor lay curled up in her cloak in the only dry corner and would not get up. She looked very frail and refused the offered turnip, though she sipped a little water when the battered cup was held to her lips.

Maigraith had come to a decision. She had one chance left in the world, if she had the courage. And even if it failed, it must be better than this.

'This is impossible,' she said. 'I am going out. Will you come too?'

Faelamor flopped a transparent hand at her. 'Do what you will. Nothing matters.'

4

A RECONCILIATION OF SORTS

Maigraith placed food and water by Faelamor's hand, then covered her with a tatty rag of carpet. Putting on her glasses, which made her eyes a washed-out blue, she went out. She did not go far, just to the nearest guard post. 'I am Maigraith,' she said simply. 'You will find me on your list. I would be taken to Yggur himself.'

Well-trained as he was, the guard seemed shocked at her approach. He looked her up and down, consulted the list and sent a messenger at once, a small, timid, black-haired woman called Dolodha. Maigraith remembered her from the time of her captivity in Fiz Gorgo. Within minutes Dolodha returned with an officer, two guards and a Whelm that Maigraith also knew, for he was the one she had struck down at her very first interrogation in Fiz Gorgo last autumn. His name was Japhit. He was gaunt even for a Whelm, with long grey hair and a face that was all planes and angles, a mirror to the inside.

These people, Yggur's terror-guard, were an angular race, often so thin that they seemed to be no more than grey skin over club-like, knotted bones. Unless they swore to a master and a purpose they were incomplete. But having sworn, as the Whelm had to Yggur, they would do anything to ensure that their master's goals were met. Recently, however, many of Yggur's Whelm had repudiated their oath to Yggur, reverting to their ancient name, Ghâshâd, and swarming into Shazmak. In ancient times the Ghâshâd had served the Charon prince, Rulke.

The officer checked the list, inspected Maigraith carefully and took Japhit aside. 'Yes, it is her,' he said. The guards stepped forward to take her.

She raised her hand. 'Put your shackles away,' she warned. 'I go of my own will. This Whelm has felt my sting.'

They hesitated; the officer looked to the Whelm once more. 'Allow her,' Japhit rasped, with a shiver that he could not suppress.

Maigraith relaxed a little. Her bluff had not been called. Even when fit she seldom used her powers, mindful of the warning Faelamor had driven into her over a lifetime: 'The Secret Art must be used sparingly: the more it's used the blunter it gets.' Maigraith always felt self-conscious when using it, and her timing was always wrong. In spite of her strength it was always too little too soon, or too much too late.

It took several hours, questionings at progressively larger posts, more messages and changes of guards, before she found herself outside Yggur's headquarters, an ancient, grim bastion of grey stone that looked down on the walled Old City and the Magister's citadel inside it. It was nearly dark. They ushered her inside. A different Whelm made the mistake of gripping her arm. Maigraith raised her fist. The first Whelm flicked his fingers at the second, who let go. They tramped on.

Now they stood outside the big double doors. Her skin tingled; her heart was pounding so hard that she was sure *he* would hear it knocking. The call came. They brought her up a long room to a table set on a dais of one step. The table was stacked with papers, maps and charts. Yggur sat behind it.

He stood up, seeming even taller than she remembered,

and limped around the table. His raven hair was longer than before. The frosty grey eyes were set in sockets dark as bruises. He looked stern and commanding, a relentless machine. Maigraith grew afraid. Thousands had died during his march through Iagador; thousands more in the assault on Thurkad. She had given herself into his hands and he would treat her with no more mercy than any other prisoner.

What was she doing here anyway? How could she have built a castle of dreams on the few tiny kindnesses he had shown her when she was his captive in Fiz Gorgo? At that time each had seemed to find in the other the complement to their own crippled selves. Yggur was obsessed by fear of Rulke, who had driven him mad before being imprisoned in the Nightland. Maigraith was a creature of Faelamor's will, but trapped by her own desperate longing to know her identity. Surely his kindness had been just a ploy. How could he care for someone as unlikeable as her?

'Why did you come?' he asked. His mellow voice was rigidly controlled.

'Because I wanted to.'

'Then why not before? Why only now, when I was within hours of having you?'

She wanted to ask how he really felt about her. Getting the words out was like trying to leap a chasm. She stalled at the edge; the words froze in her mouth.

'*Me?*' she said with feigned scorn. 'I think *not*! I tried to see you even before the war began. I went right into your camp, disguised as a . . . camp follower.' Maigraith was a modest, reserved woman, brought up that way by the prudish Faelamor. Even the euphemism was embarrassing for her. 'That was hard: your camp was well-guarded, well-warded too. But when I reached your tent you were not there, and the Whelm were eyeing me. I went away again.'

She stopped abruptly, reminded of the consequences of that trip. Karan had begged Maigraith to relieve her of the Mirror, but Maigraith had not dared to take it into Yggur's camp. She had broken her promise, had not been there when mad, depraved Emmant attacked Karan. And all this has come of it, Maigraith thought.

'That's a long time ago,' said Yggur.

'Since the Conclave I would not go against Faelamor.'

'And now?'

'She is sunk in a sickness of the heart.'

Dolodha came running in to whisper in Yggur's ear. He looked up at Maigraith, searching her eyes. 'We'll soon know,' Yggur said coolly. 'Bring her in!'

Maigraith could not conceal her shock. 'How did you find her?'

'My dear!' he replied with a thin-lipped smile. 'Knowledge is my business.'

Shortly Faelamor was carried in on a litter. She raised her head with an effort and her eyes flicked past him to Maigraith. 'You have betrayed me,' Faelamor said bitterly. 'I will never forgive you!'

Maigraith had expected such a reaction but it hurt her nonetheless. 'You are alive. That is the best I could do for you.'

'Yggur and I are rivals for the Mirror,' Faelamor said, looking absolutely deathly. 'We always will be. And you have put me in his power. *How long before you share his bed as well?*'

'I only did what was inevitable,' Maigraith replied stonily, so mortified that she did not dare look at Yggur.

Faelamor laid her head down and the litter was taken away by two Whelm. Maigraith began to follow her but Yggur growled, 'Stay! We are not finished, you and I. Your liege will be taken care of and not harmed, whilever you please me.'

Maigraith could not help wondering what lay behind his carefully chosen words. What did he want of her? It did not bear contemplating. Her dreams were now laughable.

'Faelamor claimed that Karan was dead,' Maigraith said,

desperate to get onto safer territory. 'But I cannot believe that. Do you know anything about her?'

'I have also been looking for Karan,' he said with an ominous smile. 'Chaike!'

Chaike was a thin, nervous man who, whenever attention was on him, went into a fit of rapid blinking that twisted up his forehead and made his eyebrows dance.

'What do you know about Karan Fyrn?' Yggur demanded.

Chaike blinked nervously.

'The sensitive!' roared Yggur. 'Where are your wits, man?'

'I spoke with those pr-prisoners who survived the Conclave,' stuttered Chaike, his eyebrows oscillating furiously. 'One of them remembered seeing her alive. I also questioned the men who burned the dead the next morning. Someone else asked after her that day; but they had not burned her body.'

'Who asked?'

'It was T-T-Tallia bel Soon.'

'Mendark would want Karan,' said Yggur, dismissing Chaike. 'As do I. I remember her well – a remarkably clever young woman. Not even my Whelm could catch her.' He spoke admiringly. 'I can use her. Sensitives don't last long, alas! I've burned out half a dozen this week. Then again, perhaps she did die, and her friends buried her.'

Maigraith turned away, chilled by his words. But Karan had only one friend in Thurkad, she thought, and he is missing too. No, I will not give her up.

'If she were dead I think I would know it,' said Maigraith, 'because of the link that was once between our minds. I must find out what happened to her, dead or living. If anyone can find her it is you. What do you know about her friend, Llian of Chanthed?'

'For a prisoner, you question me very boldly,' he said, but answered nonetheless. 'The teller? Rumour says that he was taken by the Aachim. We are pursuing them at this very moment. When we catch them I will have him brought here. But as for Karan . . .' Yggur considered the means. 'If her fate can be learned I will learn it. Who can I send though?'

'Not a Whelm!'

'No, they failed last time. It requires a particular kind of person. Sitala? No, she has gone to Bannador. Pran took an arrow in the eye. If he lives he will probably never see again. Ah, Zareth the Hlune! He is reliable and tenacious. After we take the citadel I will give him an unlimited warrant.'

Maigraith had done everything she could. What was going to happen now? She looked up and met Yggur's eyes. They were hard as chips of agate. Impossible to raise the question that was in her heart. Then he took a quick gasping breath, as if he was troubled too. Perhaps he wasn't as hard as he pretended to be. Maybe she bothered him as much as he did her. Get on with it, she told herself. If you don't, you'll regret it forever.

'Yggur,' she began, but just then a pair of messengers ran in without knocking. Their faces were alight with eagerness.

'Be so good as to go over there,' said Yggur, pointing to a chair and table on the far side of the room.

Maigraith did so. She sat at the table, wondering what was going on, for she could hear no more than a murmur. The messengers spoke in an excited rush of words, and at the end Yggur let out a whoop and pounded one fist into the other palm. Good news about the war, Maigraith presumed.

A long discussion ensued. At the end of it she saw broad grins on their faces. The messengers hugged one another, bowed low and ran out. Truly his people love him, she thought. He is not as black as he is made out to be. Perhaps I have made the right choice after all.

Yggur did not call her back, so she sat at her table watching him at his work, taking the reports of scouts and spies and generals, conferring with his advisers, then issuing a string of orders.

Maigraith was hungry; thirsty too, for no refreshment had been offered her. Indeed, in the excitement, Yggur seemed to have forgotten all about her. Then, hours later, he looked up and, catching her eye, abruptly waved her across. She went slowly, feeling her status as a prisoner.

'Leave us,' he said to the guards, the Whelm, the clerks and messengers, and silently they filed out, closing the door behind.

'What am I going to do about you?' he asked softly. A muscle spasmed in his cheek. 'Tell me the truth – why did you come?'

'You treated me kindly in Fiz Gorgo,' she replied. 'I felt that you . . . cared for me, a little.'

'I did, *then*!'

Why don't you help me? she thought in anguish. Must I bare myself to your humiliation? 'And I care – cared for you, *then*. There is one thing I *must* know –' she hesitated, afraid. 'Why did you send the Whelm to torture me, that last night in Fiz Gorgo? That was not a deed of the Yggur I knew.'

'I warned you – I must have the Mirror!' Yggur stared down at her from his great height, intimidating her. 'Nothing has changed!'

'I did not think you would do that to me.'

He stooped down to her level. 'And I never did. I can be very harsh when I must, but not against *you*.' He spoke the word with soft emphasis, and his eyes were glossy. Yggur's eyes followed the curves of mouth and chin and breast and hip with heart-quickening terror. Woman, so mysterious that she might as well have been another species. How she could hurt him, if she had a mind to.

'I had to go away,' he went on. 'The Whelm acted in defiance while I was not there. They tortured you cruelly!'

'They hurt me,' she said, though without emphasis.

'When I returned, you were gone.' He paced back and forth, limping badly. 'Faelamor had taken you away. I tried to forget you after that, but every night and every morning you were back in my mind.'

'So it was for me,' said Maigraith, 'though I could do

nothing about it. But the chains of duty that bound me are fractured now. *I am lost between one world and another.*'

'Ahhh! This talk chases its own tail,' he cried. He drew away from her and he looked uncertain, even afraid. The side of his face began to go rigid, the speech became halting, as it had been on their first encounter. He paced across the wide room, his limp growing worse and worse. At the table he turned abruptly, almost fell and had to prop himself up. His face twisted, he tried to take another step but his leg had locked like a log of wood. 'I cannot . . . endure it,' he said thickly.

Maigraith felt his pain now, and it was worse than her own. She pitied him. She began to walk towards him, looking down at the floor, unable to bear the pressure of his staring eyes. Keeping her gaze fixed on his feet she paced the distance between them. Finally she stopped, just two steps from him, still looking down.

'Maigraith,' he said hoarsely. 'Look at me.' She looked up. 'Will you . . .'

She felt just as anxious. What did he really want? She could never know; the feelings of other people were blank to her. 'I will stay,' she said, '. . . if that is what you want.'

She put out her hand, and after a hesitation he took it in his own.

5

THE FALL OF THE OLD CITY

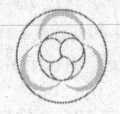

Mendark had taken heart from Tallia's earlier advice and rallied what was left of the city's forces. Even the people who had turned against him before the Conclave were glad to see him now. During the night there had been further small victories, parts of the city taken back, and there was even talk of driving Yggur out of Thurkad. Mendark knew that this was just a temporary reprieve, perhaps meant to give them false security, but he kept his thoughts from all but Tallia.

'Is it hopeless, Mendark?' They were climbing the stairs to her room to talk to Lilis.

'Utterly! Yggur is just waiting until everything is ready. He doesn't want to waste good soldiers, good lives. We've days at most. Fortunately I've already secured the secrets of the Council, those we were unwise enough to commit to print, and my meagre war chest.'

Tallia knew that he dissembled. Long before his overthrow Mendark had begun moving the Council's secrets and its wealth, to say nothing of his own, out of Thurkad in the custody of those lieutenants that he trusted, and on solitary missions by himself. Did he forget that she had participated in several of those trips? Any war chest that he now had to dispose could only be a fraction of his wealth.

Lilis was sitting up in Tallia's bed, chattering non-stop to Basia, though she went quiet as soon as Mendark entered the room. It was impossible that the Magister would even deign to notice a street child.

But Mendark could, if the humour chose him, make himself seem small and humble, so as not to intimidate. Taking the chair vacated by Basia, he hunched down with his head resting on his hands, looking like a kindly old gentleman. Lilis was disarmed.

'I'm glad that you are better,' he said in his kindliest old-gentleman tones. 'I'm afraid your beating was partly my fault. I should have taken you in the first time. But the war, you see. I have so many things to think about that I can't do them all.'

He touched her cheek below the black eye. She flinched.

'It wasn't so bad,' she said. 'That is yesterday. On the streets we only think today.'

'That is the trouble with being Magister,' said Mendark confidentially. 'I have to count the yesterdays, the todays and, most of all, the tomorrows. And that is where I need your help.'

'My help!'

'Yes. I must know what you saw at the Great Hall, before Tallia met you.'

'I saw lots of people coming and going, all day. Important people: councillors, judges, rich merchants.'

'No, just before you saw Tallia.'

'Nothing then. I had just come back.'

'But Lilis, what did you see before you *went*?'

'A soldier ran in, a messenger. It was raining. Then there was shouting inside. Then it went quiet. Then I heard a tremendous noise and a bright light. Then it went *very* quiet.'

'What happened after that? That is what I must know.'

'A great big man came out; his beard was black. There was blood on his face. And he had my friend Llian, my other friend,' she said, looking sideways at Tallia, 'by the arm, and dragged him down the steps. I was so afraid.'

'Ahh,' said Mendark. 'Just as I thought. And then? Did you follow them?'

'I tried to. At the bottom of the steps Llian fell down but the blackbeard picked him up and took him away. They went up Bellmaker's Street, north then west. On the way the man saw me. After that they went too quickly for me.'

'Where did you lose them? What streets?'

Lilis named a street, and another that crossed it.

'Yes,' said Mendark. 'Tensor once had a villa down that way. You have been a great help. A great help,' he repeated, taking Lilis's hand. 'You are a clever child.'

He got up, gesturing to Tallia. They walked to the door together. 'Though not enough,' he said. 'They'll be long gone by now and you are stuck with her.' He looked old and mean-spirited.

'Sometimes you shame me!' she replied. He grunted and she changed the subject. 'What do you want me to do?'

'Take charge of our escape. Make sure all is ready by the morning.'

'It's in hand,' said Tallia.

'And the boat?'

That was his greatest anxiety, she knew. 'It's there now. What about the Assembly?'

Mendark spat out the window. 'That pathetic lot! We'll have to give them the opportunity to get away, I suppose. At least the people will know that I cared to do *my* duty – unlike our miserable Governor.'

'And Thyllan?' she asked tentatively, recalling his previous temper.

'Don't remind me of your stupidity!' He sighed heavily. 'Even Thyllan must be taken, though it is against my inclinations. Keep watch on him. He will be my greatest trouble.'

Almost immediately they suffered a series of stunning reversals. Tallia was in the war room with Mendark when a messenger came clattering in, a tiny woman dressed in black tunic and ludicrously big boots that almost came off with every step.

The messenger reeled up the room. 'Dabys reporting, Magister,' she gasped out, trying to salute but unable to lift her arm. 'We've lost the East Hills quarter!' She fell on her face.

Tallia ran down and lifted her under the arms. Dabys moaned, for there was a savage gash in her armpit, so rudely dressed that the bandage was falling off. Tallia shouted for a nurse. 'What happened?' she asked.

'They knew our battle plan,' Dabys said through clenched teeth. 'Surely they did, for they were waiting for us and prepared for everything we did.'

Mendark looked shaken. 'I expected to lose the Hills district,' he said, 'but not so quickly.' He bent over Dabys. 'How badly are we defeated?'

'The whole army is lost,' she said. 'I am the only one to get away.' She slumped down, breathing noisily through her nose.

It was not long before the next blow fell. A dozen soldiers appeared at the door, battered and bloody. They were all that was left of the army that had held the south-east sector, and they too had a tale of unexpected defeat, of an enemy who seemed to know every detail of their battle plan.

An unpleasant suspicion began to take shape in Tallia's mind. How many people knew such details? Only the left-over rump of the Council – Mendark, Orstand and Hennia the Zain – and herself and Berenet. Not even Mendark's commanders in the field knew each other's orders.

Tallia had always disliked Berenet for his strutting, boastful ways, his ostentatious display of wealth and his arrogance, but she had never found cause to question his loyalty before. But who else could it be? Only Orstand or Hennia. That either would betray them was ridiculous.

She remembered Berenet's face after Mendark rejected

his earlier plan. Such rage she had seen in his eyes! It had to be him. She said nothing, having no evidence, but went about more watchfully than ever.

By the end of the day they had lost everything outside the Old City. They held that fragment through the night, for the walls were strong, though it seemed that Yggur was playing with them, just testing their defences or their resolve. He would send out a foray against first one wall, then another, and while each was beaten off easily, it kept everyone on alert night and day.

The following evening Tallia had just lain down on her bed, hoping to snatch a few hours' sleep, when an explosion of fire lit up the night like a harsh blue-white sun. She sprinted back to the wall, hearing the sound of sword clashing on sword. As she raced up the steep stairs another spark soared into the sky, and another, and each burst with brilliant light like the first to drift slowly down.

Reaching the top of the parapet she saw that there was a melee down at the corner watch-house, four defenders against two of Yggur's soldiers, but even so they were being beaten back. All along the wall, guards stared up like wooden soldiers at the descending flares. Tallia looked over. Scaling ladders rattled against the wall in their dozens, and the enemy were swarming up them. There must be a thousand below this section of the wall, to face less than a hundred above. They were hopelessly outnumbered. Where was Mendark? Where was Berenet, for that matter? He had come down earlier to take charge of this area, but there was no sight of him.

A flight of arrows whispered over her shoulder. Tallia ducked, snatched a round stone from a stockpile and flung it at the shadows on the ladder below her. Not stopping to see what happened, she sprinted along the wall, sword in hand, rallying the guard as best she could. They were already defeated – she could see it in the way they stared at the uncanny flares, in the listless way they fought and fell.

A spike-helmed head appeared further along the wall. She

slashed as she ran, but he merely ducked and bobbed back up again as soon as she went by. Tallia shouted orders, getting a detail armed with stones above each ladder. The falling missiles relieved the pressure somewhat. At the watch-house three of the guard had fallen to the two intruders. That's our lot, Tallia thought. In five minutes we'll all be dead. What will happen to little Lilis then?

She leapt into the air, crashing into the back of one of the enemy. His head cracked against the wall and he lay still. At the same time the remaining guard skewered the second intruder in the thigh and he collapsed, blood pouring from his leg.

'Where's Mendark?' she screamed over the din of exploding flares, clashing weapons, and the wails of the wounded.

The guard pointed down the wall with bloody sword. His chest was heaving, his teeth bared like the skull of a racehorse. 'Tower!' he gasped.

Tallia climbed into a watch-post, trying to see through the confusion of battle. Just inside the eastern wall was an ancient watch-tower, smoke-stained and grimy, one of the oldest buildings in Thurkad. It was taller than the topmost dome of the citadel, with a view over most of the city, and Mendark occasionally used it as a refuge or a place for contemplation. An aerial bridge connected it to the wall of the Old City. As she watched, half a dozen enemy came over the wall and sprinted for the bridge.

More flares soared into the sky. One failed to ignite, falling as a glowing spark that went out as it struck the parapet. To Tallia's dismay she saw Mendark's white face in the doorway of the tower. He seemed to be trying to work some defence with his hands, but whatever it was, his attackers must have been protected against it. He ducked back inside.

'Mendark, go down!' she shouted, though he could not have heard. Then she saw that the enemy were already inside the wall, swarming around the base of the tower and setting up defensive formations there, while others attacked the lower door. They were Yggur's finest, and they fought with a deadly purpose. They *knew* he was there, Tallia realised. We are betrayed! And Berenet was not at his post.

Tallia climbed down, leaning against the ladder for a moment with her eyes closed, trying to think what to do. Ahead, the way to the bridge was being defended desperately, but the defenders were falling under the weight of numbers. Mendark was in desperate danger. They all were, for if he fell the city must, and none of them would ever get out. Worse, Mendark held Council secrets that would make Yggur impossibly powerful.

'What's the matter?' someone cried, shaking her arm. It was curly-haired Torgsted, the guard who had taken Blustard away. He was one of Mendark's most loyal soldiers.

'Torgsted!' she gasped. 'Mendark's trapped in the tower.'

'Then you'd better work one of your tricks, lar, otherwise we're all dead.'

'I'll need help!'

'Osseion was beyond the guard post a while ago.'

Tallia felt a little encouraged. Osseion was the captain of Mendark's personal guard, a huge, dark man, a tireless fighter, always reliable. 'Get him here – if he's still alive!'

Torgsted ran off. Tallia agonised about what to do. She had no little skill at the Secret Art, though it did not extend to blasting people with her fingertips or conjuring sprites out of the ether. Her frantic gaze centred on the aerial bridge. There was no one on it yet – the defence was occurring on the wall beyond. She concentrated hard, building an illusion in her mind, of the bridge tearing away and crashing down against the watch-tower.

That wasn't difficult. She'd had long training in such things. What would be hard, though, would be to send the illusion to all the attackers and defenders alike. If she failed to convince a single one, the illusion would fail.

Little Torgsted came running back. Osseion pounded behind him, one shoulder wrapped in a blood-stained bandage.

'Get rid of those ladders, Osseion!' she snapped.

Tallia released the illusion. Nothing happened. Strange things were going on in her mind – the image of the bridge stretched like rubber then broke into pieces. She could not get it back. Yggur must be using the Secret Art too. Of course he would be.

'I can't do it,' she gasped, clinging to the wall. It felt as if one of the flares had gone off inside her head.

Torgsted appeared out of the smoke and dark with the fallen flare in his hand, a swollen cylinder about the length of his forearm, swathed in red and gold fabric. A stub of unburnt fuse hung out one end. As he walked he was binding cord around it, end to end. Tallia watched in bemusement.

He finished his work. 'Light it,' he said, holding the flare back over his head.

'It'll burn your arm off,' she said, afraid.

Osseion had rallied the stone-dropping teams, temporarily cutting off the flow of enemy up the ladders, but at the bridge the last of the defenders fell. Yggur's soldiers began to swarm towards it.

'Do it!' said Torgsted.

Snatching a lantern off its pole, she slid up the glass and touched the flame to the fuse. It caught and Torgsted instantly flung the flare towards the enemy. 'Look away!' he yelled, dropping flat.

The flare soared, bounced on the parapet, before skidding along the stones into the group at the end of the bridge. Tallia peeked through her fingers. The fuse winked out. Then the flare burst with a light so bright that it turned the soldiers into black stick-figures flying through the air. The explosion made her ears ring.

'Come on!' Torgsted shouted, dragging her by the arm. Tallia still felt strange in the head. For the moment she was glad to be told what to do.

All the soldiers were down, though several were crawling around, blinded by the flash. Part of the flare was still revolving on the path, emitting brilliant light and white smoke. Mendark leaned listlessly against the door of the watch-tower, not trying to defend himself. What was the matter with him?

When she got closer she saw a long bloody gash on the side of his head. His hair and neck were wet with blood. Tallia tore the coat off a fallen soldier, threw it over her shoulders and snatched up another. It was singed black, but at least Yggur's colours showed. Several enemy were on their feet now, staggering towards them. 'Hold them!' Tallia cried, and ran out onto the bridge.

Mendark did not even recognise her when she took his hand. There was blood on the leg of his trousers too.

'Mendark!' she screamed, right in his face. His pupils hardly reacted. More soldiers were coming over the wall. It was hopeless.

Tallia wrapped Mendark in the cloak. He was dazed, one arm listlessly clawing at the cloth. She strained to lift him over her shoulder. Her head, still throbbing from the explosion, shrieked at the effort. Staggering across the bridge, she looked around for the best way out.

Osseion and Torgsted stood back to back, fighting like dervishes. Suddenly Osseion slipped on the bloody stone and landed hard on his knee, awkwardly trying to protect himself with his upraised sword. He was attacked wildly, the sword smashed out of his hand. The big man scrabbled forward, going bare-handed at his opponent. Tallia held her breath – Osseion was doomed. But somehow he ducked under the flailing sword and caught his opponent's leg. The man reversed the sword, raising it to stab down. Desperately Osseion tried to stave off the blade with his bare hands.

Torgsted, who had despatched his opponent, hurled himself at the other soldier. The man turned to defend himself, but Osseion lifted him by the legs and he toppled backwards over the side.

Tallia stood on the bridge, looking down. The battle was

far from over. The yard below was full of Yggur's troops, fighting in dozens of little melees. Torgsted was staggering, Osseion not much better.

'Come on!' she roared, stripping the cloaks off two more of the enemy.

Tallia's voice rang through a sudden quiet. The two donned the cloaks, Osseion threw Mendark over his shoulder and ran for the stairs. The enemy were swarming over the far end of the wall. She could not bear to see lives lost in something that was utterly hopeless. 'I'll sound the surrender,' Tallia yelled, snatching up a trumpet from a dead signaller.

She blew three rising notes and three descending, the day's code for what up to now had been unthinkable, then they dashed down the steps. The yard was already thick with Yggur's troops. Ahead was the citadel gate.

The cloaks concealed them just enough to get to the gate a few steps ahead of a mob. Torgsted must have found a second wind for he propped, his sword working like a weaver's shuttle. They leapt through, he followed, the gates slammed shut and the bars banged home. Safety, until Yggur attacked again. Defeat was inevitable. In twenty minutes of bloodshed and terror the defences of the Old City had been overwhelmed.

And Tallia could not help feeling that they had been betrayed – that the enemy had known exactly where to find Mendark. She knew just who to blame for the betrayal.

6

BETRAYAL

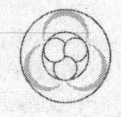

'**M**endark, you've got to listen!' Tallia yelled. 'There's a traitor among us.'

He was still suffering from concussion, while the citadel panicked around him. Yggur's siege engines were methodically reducing the walls to rubble.

Mendark turned his head away. Tallia shook him. 'Look! Yggur knew the battle plans of both armies. And he knew you were alone in the tower. Don't tell me it's a coincidence. Only five people knew all that. You, me, Orstand, Hennia *and Berenet*.'

'No!' he said. 'It can't be Berenet.'

'Look at the evidence.'

'No!'

'Then who? *Me*? Orstand –'

There was another terrific crash outside. The walls of the citadel shook. They could not last another day.

Berenet came in, limping. His clothes were torn to shreds and he was daubed with blood, but he did not seem to be carrying any injuries.

'Where the hell have you been?' Tallia said savagely, sure that he was putting on an act. 'Mendark was almost taken. You were supposed to be supervising the south wall.'

He ignored her. 'I've been on the east wall, Magister,' he

said to Mendark, panting hard. 'Had to take command; all your officers are dead.'

'Yes, yes?' cried Mendark. 'How did you fare?'

'We fought hard but it was hopeless. No one else got away. I'm sorry!'

'How convenient,' Tallia said under her breath.

'Go on then,' Mendark waved tiredly. 'Get ready. We go within the hour.'

Berenet nodded curtly, gathered his rags about him and swept out. Mendark groaned, demoralised by his near capture and the implications behind it, that he could not face up to. 'It hurts, to abandon my city like this. You can never know how it hurts.'

Tallia understood what he was going through. Mendark had been Magister for a thousand years, and dwelt in Thurkad all that time. She gave him a minute, then began again. 'We must escape, so we can fight for the city.'

'Give me a little longer. I have some tasks to do before we go.'

'What tasks?'

'Things that are the Magister's responsibility!' he snapped. 'Make sure that Orstand and Hennia are ready – the Council has to escape no matter what. Now get out!'

Tallia busied herself with her own frantic arrangements. She saw Mendark a few times, limping around with a cane, looking like death. Around midnight they met again in the library.

'We've got to go *now*!' she urged. 'The guards are beginning to believe Thyllan's lies: that the downfall of Thurkad is your fault. You must put him down.'

'He *should* be put down,' Mendark said bitterly, 'but I cannot be the one to do it. I'll take him and the others as far as the wharf. There they can make their own arrangements. The boat is ready?'

'It's waiting. But –' Tallia clenched her fists. She hesitated. 'I don't know what to do about Lilis.'

71

'Lilis?'

'The street child. You can't have forgotten her, surely?'

Mendark pressed his hand to the bandage around his head. Blood stained the cloth above his ear. He inspected a bloody fingertip. 'My head aches shockingly!' he said. 'What were you saying? Oh, *her!* Leave her, she'll be all right!'

'Lilis comes with me.'

Mendark screwed up his eyes against the pain. 'Are you mad?'

Tallia's dark face flushed. 'I can't leave her here. It was you who taught me the price of loyalty.'

'I have a city of a million people to safeguard. Likely she'd be safer here than with us.'

'Perhaps, but it makes no difference.'

'Well, bring the little scrag, but keep her out of my way,' Mendark said irritably. 'Let's go while we still can.'

Tallia made allowances. Mendark was not as hard-hearted as he pretended. At least, she hoped he wasn't.

'I'll give the order to surrender at dawn,' said Mendark. 'That'll give us a few hours. Meet me by the escape way.'

Tallia ran, soon to return, followed by Thyllan, his scarred face thunderous, all traces of the madness gone. There were chains on his wrists and ankles. Mendark signed for the ankle chains to be released. Thyllan was flanked by six of the citadel guard. After them waddled the other refugees: merchants, lawyers, legislators. Men and women, fat and thin, but all mourning the loss of everything they owned.

Hennia the Zain walked by herself as always. She was a saggy, jowly, large-breasted woman of advanced years, full of resentment at the world, and at Mendark for being trapped with him. Her feet were so tiny that they might have been bound as a child. Berenet, who had changed into his finest, followed, aping her small shuffling step. Mendark kept giving him dark looks but said nothing.

'Are you coming or not?' Mendark yelled at Hennia, who

had squatted down over her pack, taking things out and putting them back again.

'What a mess you've got us in,' Hennia grimaced.

'I might have done better with a bit of support.'

'I gave you as much support as anybody,' she said.

'I know!' he said coldly. Hennia twisted words to suit herself.

Osseion, the captain of Mendark's guard, was tall, broad as a tree, black as coal. One of many scars lifted a corner of his mouth to show large square white teeth. Ugly, fearsome Osseion, gentle as a kitten.

Lilis, close behind Tallia, was a scrawny, well-scrubbed, big-eyed, silent shadow. She had recovered rapidly, though her eye was still yellow and black, and the dislocated shoulder was supported in a sling. She wore new trousers of good woven cloth, a coat slightly too large for her, and the first pair of boots she had ever owned, judging by the clumsy way she walked. Lilis kept looking down at her boots as if what had happened was not possible. Her platinum hair shone in the lantern light. The little canvas pack on her back contained undreamed-of possessions – two more sets of clothes, underwear, socks, soap, a brush and even a knife!

Hennia turned the corner and stumbled over Lilis in the gloom. 'Look where you're going, you little wretch!' she said, swatting at Lilis's head.

Lilis evaded the blow with practised ease and moved back under Tallia's wing.

Another huge missile shook the walls. The glass pieces of a chandelier clashed together. Torgsted came racing in, skidding on the tiles. 'They're inside!' he shouted.

Mendark reeled, dropping his pack. His face went the colour of dough. 'They can't be! Orstand, can they have broken our protections and we not know it?' He swayed as if he was going to faint.

Orstand sniffed the air like a bloodhound, and looked like one, too, with her sagging dewlaps. 'They must have if they're inside, though I can't imagine how. Where are they, Torgsted?'

'The advance guard came up through the cellars. They must've tunnelled in.'

'Ah, I can feel it now,' said Orstand. 'Mendark, are you all right?' Catching him as he fell, she lowered him to the floor. 'Osseion, seal all the corridors and stairs into this part of the citadel. Make a stand at the top of the stair outside. Tallia, water!'

Tallia dabbed Mendark's brow with a wet rag and shortly he began to revive. 'My head,' he said.

'Maybe the escape way is compromised now,' said Tallia, helping him up.

'Impossible!' snapped Mendark. 'Only the Council and I know about it.'

'No one else?'

'And Berenet,' he said reluctantly. 'Take charge, Orstand,' not realising that she already had. 'Tallia, come with me.' He limped the other way.

'If they've been underground, making tunnels,' said Tallia, 'their scryers might have traced ours.'

'Not this one! It's protected! Not all the scryers in Iagador could trace it.'

'The citadel is protected too, but they got in.'

He stared at her. Sweat was pouring out of his forehead. 'Better check it, I suppose.' He pressed a stud on the wall next to a bookshelf. 'Hold this in!'

Tallia put her finger on it. Mendark went behind another bookshelf. She heard his fingernails scratching on the timber, then a sound like steel marbles rolling over each other. The panels of the wall moved apart to reveal a locked door made of metal. He unlocked that and went through into a dark passage.

'Close the door behind you. There must be no light at all!' He put his ear to an identical metal door in front of him.

Tallia closed the door. It became perfectly dark. 'I can't hear anything,' he whispered. 'Get your knife out and be ready with the lantern.'

The lock clicked; the door was eased open. Tallia sensed Mendark moving forward. His hand felt around in the dark, caught her arm and felt his way up to her ear.

'Careful,' he said, his breath tickling her ear. 'There's a steep stair in front of us.' He edged forward to peer down into the dark.

'It's safe,' he whispered. 'I can't *sense* anything. Let's get going.'

As Tallia turned to go back there came the faintest rattle a long way down, like a pebble knocked down a set of steps. Mendark ground his teeth and prodded Tallia painfully with the staff. They went back through the doors, locking and barring them carefully. In the library, Mendark cursed fluently. 'How could Yggur have found it?' He smote his fist against the wall. 'How?'

Treachery, Tallia thought. 'Can't we take them on?'

'Yggur knows me too well. He'll have hundreds down there. We're trapped.'

Tallia felt her own panic rising. 'You don't have another way out?'

'Not from here. It's right across the other side of the citadel, at the top of the eastern stair. I don't see how we can get there, now.'

Yggur had just taken Maigraith's hand when there came a persistent rapping at the outer door. 'I'm sorry,' he said irritably. 'The war is at a critical stage.'

'Can Mendark still win it?'

Yggur's smile was close to a sneer. 'Win! He's holed up in the citadel with only a few hundred soldiers left. As soon as the news comes from my delving team, we go in.'

Yggur opened the door. A swarm of messengers were waiting outside. Yggur listened to each then snapped a series of orders. Maigraith sat silently, watching and listening, remembering his military efficiency.

The message came not long before midnight. 'All is ready,' said the messenger.

Yggur smiled, showing clenched teeth. 'Come, Maigraith. I want you to witness this.'

'Where are we going?'

'To take my enemy.'

Maigraith stood behind the front line, waiting with Yggur for the final attack on the walls. She was weak from hunger, having had nothing but turnip for days. The mail coat was incredibly heavy. She wanted to go to bed. There was plenty of time to dwell on her own failings.

Faelamor had required her to steal the Mirror in the first place, but she had lacked the courage to do it by herself and had forced Karan to go with her to use her sensitive talents. That had been Maigraith's first failure. Had she done her job properly Faelamor would have had the Mirror months ago, and none of the other disasters need have happened. But Maigraith had looked at the Mirror and been captivated, as though it was the door to a whole new life for her. That was how Yggur had caught her.

There was a clamour ahead of them. The assault was beginning. 'How I've waited for this day!' Yggur said, grinding his teeth.

Shortly a tall, dark-haired man came running in. He was lean with big feet and hands, and he wore his chin-whiskers plaited, the plait ending in six small braids.

'Zareth reporting, sir!' he said briskly, giving a four-fingered salute.

Yggur raised an eyebrow.

'We're ready. The citadel wall is breached in three places!'

'And every possible way out is watched?'

'Those that we have been able to identify,' said Zareth. 'Each is monitored by a pair of illusionists, and the scryers are sensing out hidden escape ways. Wherever he goes, we will find him.'

'I hope so,' Yggur replied grimly.

Maigraith knew, because Yggur had told her the story in Fiz Gorgo, why Mendark was Yggur's enemy. Yggur held Mendark responsible for the failure of the Proscribed Experiments long ago, the Council's scheme to trap Rulke the Charon. Though the Experiments had failed disastrously, eventually Rulke had been hurled into a specially made prison, the Nightland, a place separate from the reality of the world. But before that, Rulke had possessed Yggur, taken control of his mind and left him crippled and mad. Even now, centuries after he had recovered, Yggur still suffered the memory of Rulke, like the sting of a giant scorpion.

'Go!' Yggur said. The guards surged forward. 'This place should be called rat city,' he muttered to Maigraith, who had to run to keep up with his long-legged stride. 'There are a thousand grubholes under the Old City – I've spent more time tracing them these last four days than I have fighting the war. And still my enemies escape me. But not this one!'

They raced through the main gate of the citadel, across a courtyard swarming with Yggur's troops.

'Where is he, Zareth?' he said to the officer running beside him.

'The south-western corner, high up,' Zareth replied, 'as far as our scryers can tell. It is . . . not an exact art.'

'I know that!' Yggur snapped. He stopped in the middle of the courtyard to confer with his officers.

A messenger came running out the front door of the citadel, the same young woman who had been at the guard post when Maigraith surrendered. She wore a dark cowl and drab robes, and her thin face had a pinched, underfed look.

'What is it, Dolodha?' cried Yggur. 'Mendark is taken?'

Dolodha skidded to a stop, almost tripping over her long robes. She bowed to Yggur, edging away from the Whelm on his right, a bony woman whose name was Vartila. She had also been at Fiz Gorgo. Maigraith was afraid of her.

'We broke into his workroom but he was gone. Not long, though.'

Vartila gave a menacing growl. Dolodha skipped sideways out of the way.

'I don't believe he's yet escaped,' said Yggur. 'Run, do the rounds of every squad and report to me.'

Dolodha looked uneasy, but ran back inside. Shortly Yggur and Maigraith followed. Other messengers reported as they pounded down the main corridor of the citadel. They passed a pair of Whelm, who were beating captured soldiers with their knotty staves.

'Enough!' cried Yggur. They clattered up flights of broad steps. Maigraith had a stitch in her side. 'I can't go on,' she gasped, but Yggur did not hear.

'The library,' sang out a different messenger, running up. 'This way!'

They turned right at the top of the stairs, down another corridor and burst into a large space panelled in rare timbers and filled with tall bookcases. It was a beautiful room, built in the shape of a short-armed cross. In the centre was a long table, bare of paper or ornament. The ceiling rose up in a twelve-sided steeple panelled in pale wood. The room was full of the scent of books and fragrant wood.

There were soldiers everywhere, milling about, trampling mud and blood into an exquisite carpet of knotted silk. Three illusionists, robed in black or white, huddled in a corner, broken by the strain. A sensitive, a pretty, violet-eyed girl about fifteen, wept beside them. 'I want to go home.' She had been snatched from her family a few days ago and was quite bewildered. 'Please let me go,' she wailed.

'*Where is he?*' Yggur cried furiously.

No one spoke. No one knew. Maigraith felt pity for the girl. All was not perfect in Yggur's empire after all. Everything had run clock-like for months, but now something had gone wrong and he could not work out what it was.

Finally Zareth came running back, his chin-plaits whipping

from side to side. 'He was here, in this room,' he said. 'He can't have got far.'

'Drag my chief scryer up here,' Yggur shouted.

Zareth stuck his head out the door and bellowed. A little round ball of a man puffed in, carrying a green leather bag in one hand.

'Damn you!' Yggur roared. 'Find him or you're finished!' With a scrape of steel, one of the Whelm drew a curved blade. The sound made Maigraith shiver.

The scryer fumbled a circular blank of glass out of the bag, almost dropping it. It was concave on the upper side, like the mirror of a telescope. He set it on the library table on a brass stand, warmed a flask on a candle, unstoppered it, then poured a quantity of quicksilver into the hollow. From another flask he dribbled spirit onto the quicksilver, touching it with the candle. A pale blue flame spread across the surface, burned for a minute, then went out. Immediately the scryer threw a cloth over his head and began to sway and mumble.

He looked up at Yggur, puzzled. 'It's strange. It's as though he's here, and yet not here. His aura is very faint.'

'Of course it's faint,' Yggur snapped. 'He's using a charm of concealment, but it's not strong enough to hide him from me. Quickly, man, or you'll suffer *their* fate!'

The scryer darted a glance to the corner where the illusionists and the sensitive crouched, and bent to his glass again. After a long silence he spoke. 'He's close by; not a dozen steps from us! That way!'

'At last!' Yggur exulted. 'Take the place apart.'

'Isn't there a secret stair up to the top floor from here?' cried Tallia.

'Yes,' Mendark said, 'but his scryers will track me and he'll be waiting when we get there.'

'I've an idea,' said Orstand. 'What if we were to make a simulacrum of you and hide it here. That would confuse them. They won't know where to look.'

'He can't be more than a few minutes away. He'd break it the instant he got here.'

'But in a few minutes, with luck, we can get to the other escape way.'

'How would you do it?'

'Principle of similarity,' Orstand replied. 'Whatever happened to the portrait of you that used to hang in the library?'

'It's in the storeroom next to the privy,' scowled Mendark, 'where I don't have to look at it.'

Tallia ran and brought it back. It was a miniature done in sombre brown, an unflattering portrait that imbued Mendark with a look of greasy, rat-like cunning. And depending on the light, he could be looking in one direction or the other.

'I see what you mean,' she said, smiling. 'Two-faced.'

'But ideal for our purpose,' said Orstand.

Together they worked a charm on the portrait to give it the faintest life-aura of Mendark, then put it between two locked doors. Immediately they hurried to the secret way. It was a steel ladder that ran up inside a wall right to the top floor, a terrifying climb for many.

Tallia was grimly amused to see the differing ways that they took the climb. The refugees were ill-at-ease, more used to their counting stools and their couches. Flabby Malkin, who had been elected leader of the Assembly after the flight of the Governor, was splendid in his furs but he had to be coaxed up each step. Hennia looked more angry than terrified. Still scowling, Thyllan followed, but more quickly than any, in spite of his hampering chains. He reached the top, shouting down at the others to hurry, as if he was in charge. As if he soon would be again.

Berenet came next, with almost exaggerated confidence, but his was the confidence of one seeking to impress in everything he did. Mendark watched him with narrowed eyes and never turned his back. Then the citadel guard, some assured, some uncertain, but they were elite and well-trained, and whatever they felt it did not show on their faces. Osseion followed, an expert climber, with Lilis scuttling up after, hindered by her sling. Finally came Tallia, moving slowly under her heavy pack, the lantern held out to one side, the black hair concealing her face.

She stepped lightly off the last rung. Mendark's gaze lingered on her flushed face in the golden lamplight. When all had passed through he heaved on a lever and a counterweighted slab swung down with a squeal, sealing the shaft behind them. They emerged next to a stairwell. Now they had to get right across the top floor of the citadel, the length of a city block.

'Quick, Tallia, scout out the best way.'

She ran and was back again in a minute. 'The passage along the southern side!'

A crash came echoing up the stairs, hammers being used on the secret door below. They took off, knowing that a minute could mean the difference between escape and capture. In the first cross-passage they ran right into a pair of Yggur's soldiers. There was a short, sharp melee, but Berenet's sword, wielded expertly, accounted for both of them. They broke through, slipping on the bloodstained floor as they hared off down the hall.

Halfway down, Hennia swayed on her tiny feet. 'I've had enough!' she gasped, sitting down where she was.

'You must,' cried Mendark, taking her arm. 'The Council –'

She snatched her arm away. 'The Council is damned,' Hennia said limply, 'and it's all due to you, Mendark.' She got up and plodded back the other way.

'Useless Zain!' Mendark cursed, then kept on. He soon caught Orstand, who was lurching down the corridor, every part of her great body in wobbling motion. Her face was scarlet, but though she was working hard she was going slower and slower.

'Come on, old friend,' Mendark said, taking her arm gently. 'Hennia has abandoned us. We need you desperately.'

'I won't let you down,' she replied, trying to smile. 'But this mistreated old body might. My chest is burning.'

Osseion ran back and gave Orstand his shoulder. With Mendark supporting her on the other side they staggered down to the end of the corridor. Someone roared behind them. A fireball whizzed over their heads, bursting into coloured sparks that skidded down the wall. 'It's Yggur!' Mendark groaned.

They crashed through a swinging door, crushing a guard on the other side. Finally the staircase was in sight. They milled about there while Mendark fumbled with concealed buttons on a massive stone column that des-cended through nine floors of the citadel. Again there was a roar behind them and more fireballs splattered on the end wall, setting a priceless tapestry alight. Flames dripped off the tasselled fringe. Now they could hear running feet behind them, and others coming up the stairs. Lilis cried out.

Tallia looked around frantically. The guard took up their defensive positions, though there was no hope of defending against so many. 'Where's Hennia?' she cried.

'Gave up!' Berenet spat.

'I have it!' Mendark shouted. He wrenched open doors in what had appeared solid stone. Inside were folding gates of wrought-iron. He flung them apart, revealing a dark metal cage with a big wheel at the back. 'In!' he screeched. Then, at their hesitation, 'Or stay behind!'

They squeezed in. The cage swayed dangerously, tilting down on one side. 'Come on!' he shouted at the guard. They fought their way in. Huge Osseion sprang in last of all, his weight sending the cage rocking wildly, and forced his way through them to the wheel.

Just then a dozen soldiers hurtled up the stairs. Twice that number appeared round the corner from the passage they had just run down, Yggur at their head. Mendark slammed the iron gates closed. 'Spin the wheel, Osseion,' he cried, almost choking on his fear.

The wheel creaked into motion. The cage did not move. Mendark and Yggur stared at each other, then Yggur smiled and slowly raised his hand. 'Come out,' he said, 'or I will grill you alive.'

Mendark stared him down. Out of the corner of his mouth he whispered, 'The other way, Osseion, you bloody fool. Knock the brake right off.'

The wheel clacked but still they did not move. Yggur's face hardened. 'Is there no one that you value, Mendark? The child perhaps, or faithful Tallia? I'll make a lesson of them that you will never forget.'

Tallia pushed Lilis behind her; Orstand gathered the child in her arms. 'That won't do any good, Tallia,' said Yggur. 'From here I can burn the lot of you. Come out!'

Still nothing happened. Yggur ever so slowly raised his hand. Mendark sighed. 'All right,' he said, reaching for the gate. As he did so, something snapped behind Tallia and the cage fell so abruptly that she tasted her dinner. They plunged headlong down a black shaft.

'Not so fast!' Mendark roared.

'Brake's broken!' Osseion shouted back, forcing his boot against the whirring wheel.

The sole began to smoke; they slowed a little. The ropes screeched, the cage swaying from side to side in its tunnel. Through the wrought-iron roof they saw a fireball high above, dripping glowing sparks down at them. 'If he burns through the rope, we're finished,' Mendark muttered.

'How far to go?' shouted Osseion.

'A few floors,' Mendark replied. 'Slow it right down.'

Fire licked against the sole of Osseion's boot. They slowed slightly, then fireballs rained down all around them and the cage fell free, accelerating. It ground against the stone wall with a shower of sparks, bounced off and struck the other wall. Lilis, who had pulled back her fingers only moments before, gave a frightened yelp. Tallia took her under her wing.

'Slow it!' Mendark screamed.

'I can't! Rope's gone.'

There was a bang high above them and a shower of metallic sparks. Something clanged on the roof of the cage. In the weird light from Osseion's boot Tallia caught sight of Mendark's face. It was absolutely stark. 'We're going to hit the –'

They struck hard, hurling everyone off their feet. A roaring corona of water burst up the walls of the tunnel and poured in through the sides of the cage. Osseion's boot went out, plunging them into darkness, then the water went over their heads.

'Light!' Tallia shouted, fighting her way upright. Standing up, the water was only breast deep. She felt around among the press of bodies. 'Lilis, where are you? Light, dammit!'

A dim light came from the end of Mendark's staff, barely enough to see. She reached down, hauling up whoever she touched by the first handhold – hair, shirt, nostrils in one case. 'Lilis!'

Her questing fingers caught a tiny wrist. She dragged Lilis out from under someone, clinging to her as if she were her own daughter. 'Mendark!' Tallia said urgently. He was hanging off the metal gate, looking dazed. 'Mendark, I don't know where to go from here.' She smacked his face. 'Quick! How do we get out?'

He staggered, righting himself. 'There's a door that leads out of the shaft,' he said, wrenching the gates open. 'Here, somewhere. Orstand, where are you?'

Tallia felt around again. Fat old Orstand was floating face-down, quite dead. Her heart had given out. 'Mendark . . .' Tallia began, then fireballs began to fall around them, fizzing in the water. Someone screamed; the group stampeded out through the gates, and she could not find Mendark in the dark and the crowd.

In that chaos it took ages to find the door, and longer still after the fireballs stopped, to force it open against the weight of water. Tallia could see the shadows of soldiers coming down the shaft on ropes. She and Osseion dragged the last sodden, battered and dazed people out of the cage, now almost fully submerged, and through the door just as the first soldier dropped onto the roof. Orstand's body was left behind, along with the corpse of a lawyer whose name Tallia could not remember. Osseion slammed the door closed then Mendark pulled a lever that dropped a slab of stone behind it, blocking the tunnel.

Mendark looked over his party, counting under his breath, then frowned. 'Where's Orstand?'

'She's dead,' Tallia said softly. 'Her heart couldn't take any more. I'm sorry.'

Mendark put his head in his hands and wept. They watched awkwardly.

'We must go,' said Tallia after a long interval.

'I know, I know. But of all people to lose, why her? How are we going to manage without her? She had the best mind on the Council. She was my oldest friend.'

No one answered. They proceeded along to an open shaft. Brass rungs went down, five to a span. The light did not show the bottom. Mendark went first, gingerly, for he was heavily encumbered and his injuries still troubled him. When he reached the bottom, about twenty spans below, he set the lantern to one side and moved hastily out of the way, as if afraid that someone might fall on him.

'What about the gold?' asked Tallia.

'It's hidden further down. I had a feeling we might be leaving in a hurry. A trek to get to it from here, though.'

They pursued a wandering way through a rat's nest of tunnels, terrified that they would run into Yggur's guards. But they did not, and eventually found the gold where Mendark had hidden it. The guards lifted the chests. Stony-faced, Mendark led the way down the tunnel.

'This tunnel comes out in the sewer, I believe, though it hasn't been used during my term,' he said over his shoulder.

'I'm not sure of the tide. If it's high we may have a wait. We'd better hope that it takes Yggur a while to break through and trace us.'

'The tide is falling,' said Tallia. 'We'll be gone before he gets here.'

They went along at a steady pace for more than an hour, zig-zagging through many cross-tunnels, before Mendark splashed into water that was deep and foul-smelling.

'We must be near the old shore,' he said, working his way around the edge of the pool, and shortly they reached the exit, a thick round iron door with a double row of bolts circling the rim, but rusted through in the middle. They heaved at the door but the hinges were immoveable. Osseion smashed the centre out with a hammer. They climbed through.

Outside they found themselves in a huge tunnel, one of the main sewers of Thurkad. Down it a current was running swiftly, the tide being at full ebb. They moved cautiously along the edge, over sloping slippery stone, then Malkin skidded and was swept off his feet into the flood. He would surely have drowned in the horrible muck, had not Thyllan, who was further downstream on the edge of the water, grasped him by the tunic as he whirled past and hauled him out.

Malkin made quite a spectacle in the yellow light and the vapour that had come up from the sea. His fine robes of office hung lank and stained, the once-white fur at his throat was ratty and dripping, and blood ran down his face from his nose. The man burst into tears, his dignity completely gone.

Thyllan stared at him a moment in silence, then turned away and continued picking his careful path along the side of the sewer. To some it seemed that he had taken over the leadership of their little group.

They continued without further incident, eventually reaching a place where iron rungs climbed the side of the tunnel to a circular porthole on the top. Beyond this inspection point the passage plunged down and was full of water. A guard climbed up, drew back the well-greased lever and the lid fell open.

'Just a few minutes more!' Mendark said. 'Ah, Orstand, if only you were here.'

Tallia felt an overwhelming sense of relief. For the last five days she had lived with the dread of being taken and tortured. And there was Lilis to think about. Being an only child, Tallia could hardly describe her feelings for the waif. She loved Lilis more than she had ever loved anyone and knew what a dangerous emotion that was. If they could just get away from Thurkad, though, there was a chance.

They emerged on a stone jetty in a tiny cove between two parts of the massive wharf city, which here towered more than three storeys high – four platforms of tarred timber supported on piles half a span through, viciously crusted with barnacles. Nothing could be unloaded from a boat in Thurkad without the say-so of the wharf city, uneasy symbiont with Thurkad. And that was a right that the wharf people, the Hlune, guarded jealously.

The jetty, and the cove, were empty.

'Where is the boat?' cried Mendark in dismay.

Behind them, Thyllan brayed with laughter.

7

THE MARCH
OF FOLLY

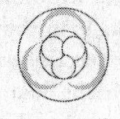

'*Kar-annnnn!*' Llian wailed, looking back as Tensor dragged him to the door. She was just a sad little bundle on the floor between the guards, one fist clenched, her hair red against the white marble. Blood had pooled on the tiles beside her.

'I won't go,' Llian muttered. '*I won't go!*' he screeched in Tensor's face, but he might as well have been talking to a rock. The hand embracing his hand was like stone, and Tensor's face was as dark and hard as obsidian.

Llian sagged down into a crouch and when Tensor jerked his arm he came up like a spring uncoiling, butting the Aachim under the jaw so hard that his teeth snapped together. Tensor staggered backwards then Llian ran, leaping over bodies and benches, to fall to his knees beside Karan. He took her hand in his and it was icy cold, yet under her eyelids her eyes flicked back and forth. She lived! Llian took her in his arms and kissed her eyes, as gentle as a butterfly at a flower.

Tensor hauled Llian up by the collar and shook him, his face to Tensor's staring face. The potency had hurt the Aachim terribly. His whole body was wracked with tremors that he could not control, while blood leaked from his mouth to drip through his black beard. Then his granite hand clamped

Llian's wrist again, Tensor's eyes looked through Llian's eyes into his skull and turned everything there to mush.

The doors of the Great Hall crashed shut. Tensor scanned the street but it was empty. Llian was once more in his thrall, powerless to disobey, for the Aachim's power over him was irresistible. They went down the steps into the dark and the driving rain, and the few people on the streets hurried by with lowered heads, too immersed in their own woes to look his way. They went in haste through the wet streets of Thurkad and were not challenged, for death and doom were written all over Tensor's face.

That was an ugly night, one of the worst, and the first time that the violence and horror of war had really been brought home to Llian. It quite shook him from the romantic view of the Histories that his training had given him.

Only a few blocks away from the Great Hall a battle had been fought in the street, the dead greeting them all the way. Just in front of Llian, a tall young man was dragging himself along the gutter, moaning. Something trailed behind him, catching on the cobbles. It was his leg, completely severed, attached only by the seam of his trousers. His blood spurted into the flooded gutter.

'Help me,' he cried pitifully as they passed, his once handsome face a mask of pain.

Llian stopped, not knowing what to do, only that no one could pass by such a tragedy.

Tensor was unmoved. 'He will be dead in five minutes, chronicler,' he said roughly. 'And us too, if Yggur catches us.'

Even as he spoke the young man slumped face-down into the gutter and the flow from his stump ebbed to a trickle. Tensor jerked Llian's arm, hurrying him on, though after eight or ten steps he fell to his knees crying 'Shazmak! Shazmak!' at the stones of the road.

Llian stood by, still held by the wrist. Glorious, beautiful Shazmak lay in ruins, its people slaughtered. Tears coursed down his cheeks. What a waste. 'Karan! Karan!' he cried.

Tensor gained control again and they hurried on. 'Forget her, chronicler! She can't survive.'

Shortly they passed by a row of terrace houses all in flames and to Llian's horror someone leapt from a high window, screaming and trailing flame like the wedding train of a princess, to crash into a manicured rose garden. The scream was cut off; the flames lingered. Looking up, he saw other stick-figures at the windows with the flames roaring yellow behind them, then Tensor dragged him on. When Llian closed his eyes he could still see the burning rose bushes.

'We're being followed,' said Tensor a while later. Llian was indifferent, numb. Tensor wrenched him around a corner and pressed them both against the wall. A waif-like figure went past, looked around then stared up the alley. Tensor raised his fist. Llian was roused from his torpor. There was something familiar about the way it walked.

The child stopped, then began to step cautiously toward the alley. Llian could feel a pressure in his skull as if Tensor was willing her to come to him. The same urge gripped Llian too – another aspect of Tensor's power over him. Now he realised who it was. Another few steps and Tensor would smash her to the ground.

'Lilis!' he screamed. 'Get away! Go back!'

He lunged at Tensor so hard that the Aachim's head struck the wall with a thud. He went into a fit of trembling, slid down the wall and Lilis darted off. Before Tensor recovered, she was gone. Llian ran too, but had not gone ten steps before he was cuffed across the head, knocked down on the wet cobbles.

'So much honour,' sneered Llian on hands and knees, 'to lie in wait for a child.' He spat on Tensor's boot.

Tensor dragged him up effortlessly and Llian's only defiance was over, the iron control back stronger than ever. 'Come,' Tensor said, tightening his grip.

In the western part of the city they stopped at a secluded villa set back from the street. It was surrounded by an iron fence and a dense thorny hedge spotted in red berries. Tensor pushed on the tall gate with the flat of his hand, the latch gave a double click and the gate swung open. He knocked once on the door, which was opened by a woman about Llian's height, with bright red hair. Other Aachim stood behind her. Llian slumped on the veranda, too dazed, shocked and weary for rational thought. The breaking of the Conclave was imprinted on his mind. Whenever he closed his eyes he saw that final scene again – Karan's mouth wide in horror, her hair standing up in a red halo as Tensor worked his potency and killed Nelissa stone dead.

'Malien . . .' began Tensor, for the first time showing his distress. 'I never thought to see *you* here.' He held out his arms.

'I came west to visit my son,' she said, stepping back to avoid him. 'Just today I learned that I am too late.'

'Too late!' he echoed hollowly. 'My son, my son! Ah, Malien, I have not borne such evil news since Tar Gaarn fell.' He swayed in the doorway, the light catching the tears that quivered on his lashes.

Malien, a mature woman of austere beauty, looked up at Tensor. Something about her, other than her hair, reminded Llian of Rael, who had drowned in the escape from Shazmak. She resembled Karan too. He'd heard Malien's name before – at Shazmak, he supposed. Her features were not unlike Karan's: pale skin, rather round face, grey-green eyes; though she was older. That brought the image of Karan back again, lying pale and cold between her guards, her would-be executioners. Llian choked.

Malien glanced at him. Her face set rigid, utterly without expression. She put a small hand, with beautiful long tapering fingers, on Tensor's arm and drew him toward her.

'Come within,' she said in a low voice. 'Evil news needs be shared, though I think we few will prove insufficient for yours.' She inspected Llian. 'But what is *this*?'

Llian started, then he remembered the Aachim habit of referring to the other human species as things, at least until some kind of relationship had been established.

'It is a treacherous Zain,' Tensor replied. 'I may have a use for it, if matters turn out a certain way. I don't think it will cause any trouble now.'

Someone escorted Llian to a small room at the back of the villa and shut the door, though courteously. There was no light. He lay down on the floor in his wet clothes. That became uncomfortable for the house was cold, so he got up and, trying the door, found it unlocked. He went quietly up the hall. Beyond, in a long, high-ceilinged room, on a precious wool carpet, Tensor stood dripping, telling the tale of the Great Conclave.

'. . . Shazmak is taken and ruined, Faelamor said, and all our people dead.'

The Aachim were statues, expressionless as slabs of marble in a quarry, so great was their grief. It gave Llian the opportunity to examine them. Aachim, this different, long-lived human species, originally from the world of Aachan but marooned here on Santhenar after the Forbidding. Many were tall, but could have been mistaken for old humans like himself, for the obvious differences, such as the little round ears, the ridge across the top of their skulls, the vestigial tail, were concealed by hair or clothing. Where necessary they hid their yellow or green, oval-pupilled eyes with glasses. The exceptionally long fingers were harder to disguise.

Llian knew most of them from his stay in Shazmak. Blase was tall with dark-grey hair hanging in ringlets about his shoulders and a great arching plough of a nose. Beside him stood two women, tall Iennis with close-cropped hair and a golden ring around her small ear, and Thel, an engineer, compact and powerfully built. Next to her was a slender young man of Llian's height with a spiky shock of black hair.

His luminous yellow eyes had elongated pupils like slots in a door. Llian had not met him before.

Next were the twins Xarah and Shalah, quite small women, the first with yellow hair and a pale, freckled face, her sister a darker version. They were the youngest of all the Aachim. Standing apart from them was a fine-boned man with arms and legs as slender as a child's. He looked fragile, his face sagging in grief. This was Trule. The news had quite broken him.

Malien broke the silence. 'How did this come about, Tensor? How could Shazmak have fallen?'

'They were *Ghâshâd*!'

Even Malien let out an involuntary cry of fear; the other Aachim wailed. 'Ghâshâd,' she repeated, needing to sit down. 'Where have they come from after a thousand years?'

'No one knows,' said Tensor. 'I only heard the news last night. Yggur found them and made them his servants, the Whelm. But now they have rebelled, *or been turned*, back to what they were before.'

'Who showed them the way in?' Malien's voice was hard as metal.

'It is a long tale, Malien. Karan came to Shazmak two months back, with this chronicler who now spies on us.' He gestured at Llian. 'Then they fled again with Rael's aid.'

The mention of Karan's name brought tears out of Llian's eyes. He desperately wanted to run back to her, even tried to take a step toward the door, but Tensor's control over him was as tight as ever.

'So I've heard already,' said Malien, barely controlling her anger, 'and that in chasing them you captured Faelamor and sent her prisoner to Shazmak. The most powerful woman on Santhenar, with all the Faellem behind her! How could you do such a senseless thing?'

'We came upon her, watching as Yggur's Whelm killed our own people. I was sure that she was in league with them.'

'A more unlikely alliance can hardly be imagined,' Malien

said in cold fury. 'I see it now – Faelamor corrupted Shazmak from within, like a termite.'

'Faelamor said that Karan betrayed us.'

'I cannot believe that,' said the young man with the spiky hair.

'Nor I, Asper,' said Malien. 'Where is Karan now, Tensor?'

'She fell at the Conclave,' Tensor said sombrely.

'You abandoned her!' Llian shouted. 'She was still alive!'

Malien's face was anguished, but her voice, when she turned back to Tensor, was frigid. '*Is this true?*'

'Yes,' said Tensor, 'but she could not have lived.'

Malien struck her breast with her fist, then the Aachim made a mourning circle around her, close but not touching, while Tensor stood with his clenched fists hanging at his sides. Finally the circle broke apart.

'And what did Karan say to Faelamor's lies?' hissed Malien.

'She said that Faelamor seduced Emmant and that when he left Shazmak he showed the Ghâshâd the way in. But to that Faelamor said –'

'Faelamor said, *Faelamor said* –' her voice rose in fury. 'You preferred *her* word to Karan's? Tell me it is not true.'

'Karan kept the Mirror from us, even deceiving the Syndics.'

'Bah!' said Malien. 'Faelamor is a prodigious liar. To the Faellem, truth is the weakest illusion of all.'

Llian was fascinated by what he was learning about the Aachim, and Faelamor too. All this he would use in his *Tale of the Mirror*, which he hoped would one day be among the Great Tales.

Llian was a master chronicler and a teller too, the youngest to have achieved both honours in many a century. This was just as well, since he was clumsy and inept at most other things. The Histories were his life, as they were vital to the culture of Santhenar. Every family kept its own records and everyone yearned to be mentioned in the Histories of the world, or even, impossible dream, in one of the Great Tales. To add another to the twenty-two Great Tales was a wonderful dream.

'There was truth there,' Tensor went on, rousing Llian from his romantic fancies, 'though whether it was *all* truth, maybe not even the Syndics could have told. I realise now that Faelamor is a foe beyond me.'

Malien's reply cracked like a whip barbed with iron. 'Your folly that you would not see what every Aachim knows. Our folly for allowing you your way. *Why* did you send her there, defying all advice? You have destroyed our world and our life, and made us outcasts. You must take a new name. Call yourself til-Pitlis – lower than even Pitlis of accursed memory.'

Pitlis had been one of the greatest Aachim leaders of all time, Llian recalled, and the architect who had designed Tar Gaarn, their greatest city. But he had been proud to the point of folly and would not listen to advice. His foolish alliance with Rulke the Charon led to the fall of Tar Gaarn and the utter ruin of the Aachim. Even now, more than a thousand years later, they had never recovered from it. Llian knew the *Tale of Tar Gaarn* well.

'I am dreadfully afraid,' Tensor said. 'Look at this!'

He brought a tubular black metal case out of his pocket and slid something from it that uncoiled into a flat sheet of its own accord. The Aachim surged forward to stare at the precious artefact – the Mirror of Aachan. They had not seen it since Yalkara the Charon stole it from them at the fall of Tar Gaarn.

It was made of a single brilliant leaf of black metal. On one side the edge was raised to form a frame, within which was set a flexible material as clear as glass. That enclosed a shiny fluid metal, like jellied quicksilver, which the light caressed with a thousand ripples and swirls of luminosity. The border of the frame was written with finest silver characters, glyphs that even to Llian's educated eye were unfamiliar. Impressed in the top right-hand corner was a symbol, three golden bubbles grown together, enclosed by touching crescent moons in scarlet, all set within a circle and infilled with fine silver lines twining and intertwining.

Tensor held the Mirror up so that its face caught the lamps. Someone gasped – fragile Trule, Llian thought. The Aachim stared at the Mirror as one. The scarlet moons caught the light and, for an instant, flames burned there. The surface of the Mirror shimmered as if about to burst with light. Llian felt his scalp prickle.

Tensor fingered the symbol. 'The Mirror is transformed – Yalkara's work.'

'I don't like the look of it,' Asper said in an awed whisper. 'What can it mean?'

'I don't know. And since you will ask, I have no idea what she did to it.'

'In which case I wonder why you spent so much time chasing it,' Malien said acidly.

'Is this the end?' interrupted a man standing in the shadows. Clean-shaven, craggy of face and woolly of hair, he was quite the tallest person Llian had ever seen, Aachim or otherwise. 'Had not even the Conclave an answer?'

It took a long time for Tensor to respond. 'It is profaned, Hintis,' he said in accents slow and drear. 'Faelamor had another shock for me. Surely she planned it.'

'She is a cunning one,' said Hintis, shaking his woolly head.

'Her lieutenant Maigraith suddenly appeared on the balcony,' said Tensor, his face frozen in remembrance, his lips drawn back from his teeth. 'How arrogantly she stared down at me. I felt she sneered at my agony. And her eyes were Charon eyes, that I had never thought to see again. I could not bear it. All the world was against me.'

'You struck her down!' cried Malien. Her eyes shone as she looked up at him. 'That was a bold stroke!'

'Ahhh! If only I had. I was sure that Faelamor and Maigraith conspired against me.'

No one spoke. The eyes of the whole room were on him. Llian crept closer but no one noticed or cared.

'I had no courage left. I used the *hakasha ka-najisska*

against Nelissa. She is dead and the whole meet laid low.' Tensor's huge hands fell against his sides. 'It was awful. I can still feel it ringing in my skull.'

'*You violated the Great Conclave?*' cried Malien, trembling in her rage. 'You struck down our defenceless allies with a forbidden spell that has destroyed more of the Aachim *than ever it did our enemies*? That potency was created for one purpose only, and even there it failed.'

For an instant Llian thought that she was going to strike Tensor, then she whirled and ran out of the room. One by one the others followed, their heads hanging low, until only Tensor remained, still dripping on the carpet.

Llian stood against the wall, staring, ignored. He could hear the other Aachim speaking among themselves, but not what they said. Then they came back, one by one, Malien last of all. Llian might have been part of the furniture.

Malien walked right up to Tensor. 'My feelings for you are expunged!' she said bitterly. 'As though we never met. I have forgiven your follies over and over again, but I cannot allow this . . . *corruption*! You have profaned everything we ever had or made together. I cleave you from me forever.'

So saying, she took the front of her blouse in her hands and rent it asunder, baring her breasts, then cast the rags of silk on the ground at his feet. She tossed her red hair so that it covered her face, turned and walked slowly away.

Tensor shrieked, a piercing wail of agony. The glass lamps on the walls shattered, tinkling on the floor. He fell down on his face and slowly drew in his legs and arms, balling up the torn silk in one hand. The other Aachim followed Malien, so stiffly that they might have been going to a child's funeral.

The pressure of Tensor's will, which had sapped Llian of free choice ever since the breaking of the Conclave, vanished. He was free, if he had the courage. He crept to the door. There was no one in sight, nothing to stop him from just walking out. The front hall, as he edged down it, was dim. The door opened easily under his hand. He slid through and stood on the veranda, looking for the path and the gate through the hedge, wondering how to find his way back to the Great Hall through the foggy dark of an unknown city at war. He hesitated too long.

Click-click! The sound was clear even over the rain on the slates, water running in the gutters, wind in the eaves. The hairs on the back of his neck stood up. It might have been a sentry at the gate but he did not think so. A shadow congealed out of the gloom. Forward or back? Either choice was doom-laden. The shadow blended into the dark again. Surely he was invisible against the door. He edged backwards.

Something thudded into the door frame. Llian tried to dart back inside but was brought up sharply, caught by the sleeve. He struggled, before realising that the spear had gone through his coat.

He wrenched the sleeve free but before he could move something struck him hard, a pain as sharp as ice seared through his right side and he was pinned against the door. The lights went out inside the villa. Llian cried out, then a warm hand went over his mouth and Malien said, 'Shut up!' in his ear and wrenched out the spear. Llian screamed. She hurled him back through the door, banging it shut. Another spear shook the door.

His cry had quite transformed the Aachim, who were at the doors and windows so quickly that he did not see them move, lowering metal shutters and clamping them in place. Malien, still without her blouse, struggled with the long bolts as something struck the door a blow that shook the walls. Another blow forced it partly open against Llian's shoulder, then Tensor threw himself at the door, it crashed shut and they forced the bolts home. Malien caught Llian under the arms, dragging him back to the main room.

Llian tottered, sweating but freezing cold. Someone held him up while Malien tore off the bloody shirt. Abruptly his legs folded up under him and they laid him out on the floor. Malien's breast and side were bloody with his blood.

'Are we secure?' she yelled.

'Almost,' someone shouted.

Tensor ran up. The spear had cut a deep furrow under Llian's right arm between the seventh and eighth ribs, angled through the muscle and out the back. Blood was pouring down his side.

'A bad flesh wound, no more,' Tensor said. 'Bind it tightly and bring him.'

He disappeared. Llian closed his eyes and drifted away. The wound throbbed and pulsed. Something burned, his eyes flashed open and he beheld Malien sponging him with a steaming cloth. The heat felt good on his skin. He closed his eyes again, barely following the progress of her ministrations: the cleaning of the wound, the ointment, the pads. Cloth ripped in his ear – his shirt – and she bound the wound so tightly that he could not take a deep breath. Then he was lifted up and another shirt put on him – it was soft as silk, one of hers evidently – and wool garments over that.

'Who are they?' Llian groaned.

'The spear had Whelm markings on it,' she grunted.

Now the doors were being attacked with axes or mattocks. Someone, the very tall Aachim, took Llian up again. He felt himself being carried down a long set of stairs.

'Burn it,' he heard Tensor shout.

Llian's eyes fluttered open. He saw a torch flung into a pile of waste timber and oil-soaked rags, already prepared. Yellow flames licked up.

They continued down the steps, through a trapdoor into a cellar. The trap slammed shut. Through the cellar they went, crammed with barrels and cheeses the size of wheels, then into a wet tunnel. The engineer, Thel, hacked wedges out of a cheese with an axe and passed them round. Tensor had a huge pack on his back and the others the same. He watched everyone through, pulled a lever, the keystones fell and the roof caved in for three or four spans. Earthy air rushed past. When they could see again, nothing was visible but a wall of earth. A few minutes' walk away they emerged through a featureless door into another cellar then out into an alley like thousands of Thurkad alleys. The rain pelted down.

'Xarah!' Tensor said to the young woman with the mustard-coloured hair. 'You will go to our secret refuge and wait. If any of our people come –' he put his lips to her ear and Llian did not hear the rest.

Xarah darted a glance at her sister, who stared back at her, frozen-faced. 'I can't spare both of you,' Tensor said. Xarah nodded, embraced her sister, then with a show of reluctance turned away. Shalah watched her out of sight, wiping her eyes.

Llian had come from the Conclave with nothing but the wallet on his belt that held his purse, journal and the notes for his *Tale of the Mirror*, which he carried everywhere. Tensor flung a cloak over Llian's shoulders. Llian pulled it around him with one hand, Asper did the other side for him and pulled the hood down.

They went out into the black of night. The wind still flung rain at them from the south. There were sounds of battle from there too. Then they were off via a secret way, a concealed door in the city wall, well inland from the harbour. But evidently the secret had been discovered, for when there were still two to pass through a voice challenged them.

'Who goes?'

Leaping forward, Tensor struck the guard down. He barked a command and the Aachim scattered. Llian knew a few moments of jolting agony as the man who carried him sprinted away into the dark. There were shouts and what seemed like the whiz of an arrow past his ear. His bearer slipped in the wet, dropped Llian and landed on top of him. Pain flared, obliterating his consciousness.

The rest of the night was torn to fragments with each shred of wakefulness containing only one sensation, the fire in

Llian's ribs. But now it was morning, he could tell without even opening his gummed-together eyelids. His side throbbed. From the pounding he knew that whoever carried him was almost running. Just then the man stopped, thumping Llian down on cold ground.

Llian opened his eyes. The sky was growing light, just visible through interlacing branches and narrow leaves. They were well out of Thurkad. He'd never find Karan now. He sank back into misery, into a dream that was no better.

Thirst roused him. His hand grasped snow. Fingers pinched it up, pressing it into his mouth against a dry tongue. He tried to move his other arm but it hurt too much. His whole side was burning, and his shoulder, and the muscles of his back.

Away to the left the tall Aachim was standing against a tree staring down a rough track. His chest still heaved. Llian did not remember his name.

'Hey,' he cried. His voice was feeble, a ghost on the wind. Nonetheless, the man looked across at him before staring back down the path.

Llian tried to sit up but could not. Rolling onto his good side, he levered himself to his knees. Blood trickled down his belly. He forced himself upright, staggered a few steps to the nearest tree and promptly fell down again.

'Kwoit!' said the Aachim.

Llian puzzled at this as he prised himself off the ground. Perhaps he meant 'Quiet!' Llian slumped against the knobbly base of the tree and rested his chin on his knee. His head was spinning. Where was he? And where were the other Aachim?

In the growing daylight Llian saw that he was just to one side of a steep, rather overgrown path, but the trees closed off the view beyond. The Aachim kept to his watch, motionless as before. A morning breeze whispered in the treetops; light snow began to fall again. Eventually the man seemed satisfied and picked up a big pack.

'You wook?' he said to Llian.

Llian frowned, then placed the accent. The man was from the far east, presumably the Aachim city of Stassor. 'I think I can walk,' he said at length. 'If you don't go too fast.'

The Aachim turned up the slope. 'Come,' he said.

Llian stood upright with the aid of the tree, felt for his wallet, which still hung heavily from his belt, and followed. Soon the path became too steep and he had to sit down lest he faint. The Aachim heaved him over a big shoulder and they continued.

Llian's head whirled again and for the rest of the day he knew only a confusion of jolting, painful travel, intermittent rests on snow that grew ever deeper, and the heavy breath of his porter. Finally the man stopped, propped Llian against a tree and disappeared.

Llian again tried to ease his thirst with handfuls of snow. It made his teeth hurt but the thirst was unabated. He leaned back and endured. He could do nothing more. There was nothing to be seen but snow and wind-writhen pines, and stark outcrops of shiny grey schist feathered with lichen.

It was not so cold, nothing like the journey to Shazmak had been, but Llian's feet were frigid blocks. His body could not seem to make any warmth. Snow continued to fall. He had no idea where they were. At dusk, which at this time of year was around five o'clock, the Aachim unwrapped a packet and shaved slices off the black lump inside. He shook the slices onto a broad leaf, which he presented to Llian.

'Thank you, Hintis,' Llian said. The name had come back to him after a struggle. He must indeed have been in shock to have forgotten a name, for it was part of a master chronicler's training to remember things spoken or read, perfectly. He gnawed at the black slice. It was a kind of pickled meat, hard, hot and spicy, and before he'd finished the first slice he felt sweat break out on his forehead. Another handful of snow cooled his burning mouth. The meat was delicious. He took a second piece.

'Where are the others?' he enquired with his mouth full.

'Don't know,' Hintis replied in his thick accent. Then, evidently to forestall Llian's next question, 'They will find us!' He shaved another edge of the black lump, cut the slices into neat strips and ate them one by one with the point of his knife. For the second course they had chunks of flaky cheese. When the meal was finished Hintis said to Llian, 'Sleep now, I watch,' and walked away into the gathering night.

It was too cold to lie down. Llian sat on a pile of sticks, the best chair he could make, leaned back against the tree and closed his eyes. The night was still, overcast and dark. There were no insects to annoy him. The irregularities of his seat were only a minor irritation.

His side flamed. Having dozed most of the day, now he could not sleep. Once there was rustling from the forest some distance away. It might have been Hintis, or just a forest creature. He ached for Karan, but she was lost. He had failed her. The miserable night passed more slowly than any he had ever spent.

Yggur did not have enough soldiers to completely encircle Thurkad – it was too large and there were too many ways out, especially through the rugged hills on the north side. But not far away, a company of his finest troops lay watching, waiting for their Whelm scouts to come back, alerted by signals that someone important had slipped through the net.

Finally one of the scouts appeared, a woman swathed in coarse grey robes and baggy hood. The Whelm were slow, clumsy, but for all that, dogged and relentless. Yet they had a weakness, one that Karan had identified in her long pursuit by Idlis. Originating in the frozen south, they were oversensitive to the sun and had to protect their eyes with slitted shields, their skin with all-enveloping robes.

The scout's name was Yetchah – the woman who had followed Llian from Chanthed last autumn. She was young, more attractive than the other Aachim, her eyes huge but

103

black as midnight. Her coarse black hair hung in irregular hanks, hacked off with a blade. Yetchah saluted the captain of the company, looking very satisfied. He waited for her to speak, knowing that the Whelm could not be hurried.

'It is our enemy, Tensor,' she began. 'The Aachim who fled from the Great Hall of Thurkad the night before this night. He carries a great prize, the Mirror of Aachan itself. There are another eight or nine with him but they do not appear to be heavily armed. To take him would be almost as great a deed as the capture of Mendark the sorcerer.' She spat his name through fleshless grey lips.

'Then let us make a plan. What do you know about these Aachim, Yetchah?'

They huddled close to the fire, talking softly and tracing routes on a map with their fingers. Finally the captain nodded.

'Signal the other squads. We will try to drive them up this ridge, for there is a precipice on the other side. If we can corner them there, they will have to fight or surrender. And if they fight – then we are five to one, and better armed!'

Woken by the sound of voices, Llian saw two more Aachim: tall Iennis with cropped black hair, talking to Hintis, and a smaller woman with red hair – Malien surely.

She turned; it was Malien. She was explaining something to the others with her hands, pointing to the forest, then Hintis nodded and set off in that direction. Iennis began to remove things from her pack. It was just coming dawn.

Malien squatted down beside Llian and looked him over carefully. 'How are you this morning?' she asked with a smile that reminded him of Karan.

He was cold and hungry and cranky. His side throbbed. He gave her a pallid smile. 'Sick,' he said.

She unfastened the green silk shirt. 'What's this?' she asked, sighting a jade amulet that he wore about his neck.

'Just a keepsake my mother gave me, before I was sent away from home.'

'Sent away!' She raised an eyebrow. 'Were you a trouble-maker?'

Llian managed a laugh. 'The reverse, actually. I was a clever child, and came to the notice of Mendark, who offered to sponsor me at the College of the Histories. I was only twelve.'

'Chanthed is a long way from Jepperand, where the Zain live,' she said, sitting back on her haunches and frowning at the amulet.

'Too long! My parents were poor and it was an opportunity that would never come again. I went to Chanthed sixteen years ago and haven't been back. I wish I could go home.'

Malien seemed struck by the amulet, though Llian knew its value was only sentimental. 'There seems to be some kind of a charm on it,' she said. 'Is your mother . . .?'

'No! Faelamor did something to it so that Emmant could trap Karan with it. It's tainted now, but for all that I could not throw it away.'

'I'll have a look at it. I can remove the charm at least.' Malien slipped it over his head. 'Now, let's see to your wound.' She inspected the bloody bandage and the stains down his side. The bandage was glued to the wound with blood.

'Does this hurt?' she asked, touching the wound and several places around it. Llian was hard-pressed not to scream. She frowned again, ginger eyebrows almost meeting above her nose. How like Rael she was!

That brought back a whole cascade of memories. Llian wondered if they were related. She could have been an older sister. He did not know how to tell the age of the Aachim.

Malien sat back on her haunches, pursed her lips and gathered sticks for a fire. Iennis spoke a warning but Malien shook her head and struck sparks into the tinder. The first sparks caught, growing into a little yellow flame, then to a small, almost smokeless fire. A pot began to trail steam.

Washing her hands, she soaked off the bandages and cleaned the wound. 'You were lucky,' she said. 'The spear just opened you up along the side and poked a little hole through here. It's a good clean wound, a little red but not poisoned.'

'It hurts like blazes,' said Llian, sweating.

Malien laughed. 'Of course it does,' she said, 'though many have endured far worse with no complaint.'

'I can tell you a thousand tales of heroes too stupid to feel pain,' Llian muttered, looking more like a sulky schoolboy than a great chronicler.

Malien shook red powder onto the gash from a small ebony vial, stoppered it again and then took up a needle and thread.

Llian was alarmed. 'What are you going to do with that?'

She showed her perfect teeth in a cheerful grin. 'I'm going to sew you up, chronicler. You can write a new tale. Call it *The Thousand and First Hero*, or *The Boy Who Screamed*.' She laughed.

'No!'

'It has to be done.' She went two steps to the fire and warmed her hands. The needle passed through the flames. She threaded it without looking, tested the point with the tip of a finger, then put it to the flame again, careful of the thread. 'Though, if you prefer . . . I could leave it to Tensor.'

'No! – I mean, do it then!'

The wound took a lot of stitches and it was not just the pain of it, or the sight, or the anticipation. As she drew the long bloody thread through his flesh it made a most unpleasant raspy ache, a horrible feeling. Slowly the gape drew closed, the skin puckered up into ridges around the black stitches, and Malien put two more stitches into the neat slit in his back where the spear-point had come out and pinned him to the door. Then she bandaged all up and helped him on with his shirt and coat.

'Maybe I should bind your arm to your side,' she said thoughtfully, 'in case you burst the stitches.'

'No!' Llian repeated, but she did it anyway.

Just then Tensor appeared with the rest of the Aachim, running up the hill with their heavy packs.

'Come on!' he shouted. 'We are pursued.'

The fire was stamped out and covered with snow, Tensor glanced at Llian, nodded and they were off. All that night they ran but they could not shake their pursuers, who hunted them as tirelessly as a pack of hounds. Llian slowed them greatly, whether he ran or was carried. Just after dawn Tensor called a brief halt for breakfast.

'Who are they?' cried the woolly-haired Hintis in his difficult accent, gulping water and bread.

'I very much fear that there are Whelm among them,' said Tensor, 'to have tracked us so easily through the dark.'

'Whelm or *Ghâshâd*?' Hintis bared his teeth. 'Where did *they* come from after all this time?'

'That is a question we would all like an answer to,' said Malien.

'Then I say we stop and lie in wait for them. Let us tear the truth out of them to avenge Shazmak. It is like a thorn in my breast running before *them*.'

'Indeed we will avenge Shazmak,' said Tensor softly, putting his arm around Hintis. 'But the master first, then the servants. Would you jeopardise that?'

'This Zain of yours slows us unbearably,' scowled Hintis, 'and there is a stench about him that I can't abide, something that niggles at me. What say you I dash his brains out against yonder rock? Then we will show the Whelm our legs.'

Llian blanched, but his fate still had some way to run, for Tensor said, 'You must endure him, Hintis, for I need him. Endure, as we Aachim have always done, for as long as it takes.'

Hintis spat right next to Llian's boot but said no more. They raced up a steep ridge, that grew ever steeper and fell away to right and left into country so precipitous that it could only be climbed down, and any climber would be defenceless.

'I don't like this,' gasped Malien as they clambered among

boulders and fallen trees. 'They are driving us into a trap. Where does this way lead?'

'I don't know,' Tensor replied. 'This country is foreign to me.'

'Well, if they have enough troops they can be right around the bottom of the mountain before we labour to the top.'

'A few squads spared from the war cannot keep us from our destination,' said Tensor, swinging the labouring Llian over his shoulder and striking out up the hill faster than ever.

Shortly they reached the top of the ridge, emerging out of forest onto a dome covered in heath and spiky grass, all littered with cracked rock. No refuge here! They ran across the clearing then stopped abruptly. Ahead the ridge was cleft by a gorge hundreds of spans across; beyond which they saw a cliff of black rock four or five spans high, and below that a steep scree slope, the latest of many landslides, running all the way down to a rushing river. Looking down they realised that their side was much the same. They were trapped.

The Aachim looked at one another. No one spoke.

'Do we die here, like *this*?' said Tensor. 'We can take many of them with us.'

'I have no stomach for it,' Malien replied. 'I will go over the cliff first and take my chances with the landslide and the river.'

As she spoke, soldiers appeared on the other side of the clearing. Tensor looked down again. 'Who will volunteer to try it? You, chronicler! Make up for all the trouble you have caused us.'

So saying, he slashed the bandages that bound Llian's arm to his side.

'What are you doing?' Llian cried.

'Throwing you down the cliff. If you survive, run across the slope or the landslide will catch you. Ready?'

No! Llian squeaked, then Tensor held him out and dropped him over.

8

DREAM SHARING

L lian fell like a stone, grazed a buttress of black rock and crashed onto the steep slope below, skidding and sliding down on his backside. A searing pain told him that the wound had torn open again, but soon he was too terrified to feel it, for the slope began to move under him. Scrambling to his feet, he took a step and fell over again. He sprang up, scrabbling on hands and knees, the broken rock crackling all around him.

Suddenly he was sliding down, terribly fast, out of control. He looked up and the whole slope seemed to be moving above him, a flood of rock. What had Tensor said? *Run across the slope*. Then he understood. The landslide was shaped like a fan – if he could stay upright and move fast enough he might be able to keep out of its path.

He found that to be easier said than done, for as soon as he put any weight on the scree it slipped under his feet, unbalancing him and throwing him down. Time after time he came to his feet only to fall again. Once he rolled over and kept rolling, falling faster and faster, pebbles smacking him on arms and face and hands, knowing that beginning to move above him were bigger rocks that would grind him to pulp.

Then Llian's feet found a purchase, he stayed upright and

found that it was much easier to keep his balance if he ran. So Llian ran until the stitch in his left side hurt almost as much as the spear wound in his right, until blood from the wound ran down to soak the waistband of his trousers. A rock the size of a grapefruit smacked him behind the knee, collapsing it and sending him skidding down the slope. Forcing himself up, Llian saw a boulder bouncing right at him. He threw himself flat, the rock went over his head, then Llian scrambled out of the way of the ones following, put his head down and ran as fast as he had ever run.

The landslide was now a smashing, crackling roar in his ears, a wild animal thing at his heels. Ahead Llian saw a little cusp between this slide and the next one further round the hill. He dived for it, landed just short on his injured side, shrieked soundlessly and clawed towards it on his hands and knees. The landslide battered at his legs, trying to drag him under. He swam over the rubble, gained the cusp and threw himself head first over it onto the next scree slope. Llian rested on that dangerous perch for a moment, afraid that it would also begin to move, then when it did not he picked his painful way down to the river.

Behind him the other Aachim leapt over the cliff, one after another, plunging feet first into the river of rubble and coming up running, roaring with glee amid the danger. They made it look so easy, all save the third-last, the delicate, sad-eyed Trule. He landed awkwardly and his ankle went right over, breaking with a crack that Llian heard over the roar of the landslide. The pack pulled Trule down, he fell into the slide and did not get up again. After that came Malien, and last of all Tensor, running the slide expertly all the way to the bottom and skidding to a stop beside Llian.

'Trule?' he asked.

Malien had gone as close to the end of the landslide as she dared. 'Alas, he is dead,' she said softly. Tensor bowed his head. They all did, for a minute: yet another Aachim fallen.

The landslide rattled into silence. Heads appeared over the top of the cliff. Half of the rubble was gone into the river now, leaving a steep bare slope below the cliff, too dangerous for their hunters to do what they had done, even had the Aachim not been waiting at the bottom.

Tensor turned and approached the river. They had gained half an hour at the most.

Their pursuers were cunning and hard as iron. They followed all through the day and the succeeding night, never getting close enough to attack, but never being far away either. Once Llian actually saw them, a dark band at the bottom of the range he was just cresting. The snow had stopped though it still lay calf-deep on the hill, and it was impossible to move without leaving tracks. But that was all he saw, for the torn-open wound became infected and he spent the day in a fever where all he remembered was pounding, pounding and the anxious faces of Malien and Asper staring down as they did things to his side.

By late in the afternoon of the following day the Aachim had crossed the range of hills and passed into the tall trees of Elludore Forest. Before the trees closed off their view they spotted their foes again, seemingly closer than before.

'Are they more tireless than we are?' Tensor cried, his dark face darkening. 'Away!'

One Aachim threw Llian to another, who hurled him over his shoulder and they ran. Here the snow was less, just a veneer of white, and by nightfall it became patchy then disappeared completely. They continued all that night, stopping neither to rest nor even to eat, walking up streams and across rocky outcrops, doing everything they could to throw the enemy off. The following morning, to Llian's terror, they swung across a steep gully on a vine.

'Never fear, chronicler,' sang out Malien with a merry laugh. 'You go over the easy way.'

So saying, she seized the end of the vine and bound him

to it, hand and foot. Another Aachim drew him back then pushed, a great buffet in the back. Llian swung out across the ravine, but unfortunately with not quite enough force to be caught at the other side.

He let out an undignified squeal as the pendulum swung back and forth finally coming to rest, leaving him suspended over the creek. Below were small pools and threads of water, a long way down, surrounded by boulders big as horses. It wasn't really that far, but a fall would have broken every bone nonetheless. The Aachim roared with laughter, even Tensor, and they hurried to get a line on him in case the enemy were still close behind.

'Ah, it does me good to hear you squawk, chronicler,' said Tensor, wiping his eyes as he caught him and swiftly unlashed the cords.

They stopped at dawn for a hasty breakfast of shaved meat, hard bread, flaky cheese, dried fruit and water, then pressed on in the same way.

By nightfall even the Aachim were exhausted and had to rest. Tensor sent the watches far out into the forest. They were changed every few hours, but they saw nothing and heard nothing, so a small fire was dared for their comfort and to heat water.

Another day and another night they marched, and the morning after, when they were relatively certain that they had lost their pursuers, they stopped by a rushing river to eat, to bathe and to sleep. When the bandages were removed Llian found that his wound was beginning to heal, though there was still an angry red welt along the ridge of stitches, and a thicker lump where they had been redone while he was in the fever. Asper, who was a healer, bathed the wound and dabbed more of the red powder on but did not bandage it. Llian was too tired to care. He washed his feet and hands, gulped down hot tea and bread, fell on his couch of bracken and slept.

But he did not sleep soundly. His dreams were pregnant

with foreboding, a nameless, bodiless dread of approaching cataclysm. He slipped into blessed dreamless sleep for a while, but that twisted into another nightmare where he dreamed of Rael in his room in Shazmak, playing a threnody to someone that Llian could not see. The scene shifted and Llian realised that Rael was playing to Malien, a warning about Tensor, and about Llian himself. Llian was an engine, the dream warned, a bringer of doom to the Aachim. Then Rael was dead, drowned white, but still he played, and when he sang green water and clotted weed came out of his mouth. That dream faded, another horror jerked him awake and Llian was too afraid to sleep again.

Several of his companions were wrapped in their cloaks, asleep. Llian took a mug of tea, strong and bitter from long stewing, and a crust, then wandered down to look at the river. As he picked his way along the bank through tall trees, some undercut and fallen to expose their twisted roots, the sounds of two people in a fierce argument came to him.

'– never agree!' was said with vehemence. It sounded like Malien.

'Then what would *you* do? Do not reject my plan unless you can put a better.' The rumble was unmistakeable – Tensor!

'I would go back to Stassor, whence I came. Would that I never allowed you to drag me from my home.'

'Then go, though I will miss you sorely.'

'Ha!' she cried. 'Our partnership failed long ago; I have cast you off. Never did I mean a tithe to you of what your own schemes and follies did. I disgraced my family and my house when I bonded myself to you. How Elienor would have wept to see the way her line is ending.'

'Elienor would weep,' said Tensor in brittle tones, 'and then she would get up and strike back to preserve her family and her people.'

'Ahhhh!' she cried. 'Get away from me. Never approach me again!' She flung herself down upon a boulder, wrapping her arms around the smooth rock and pressing herself against it. Tensor stalked away.

Llian stood among the trees, watching Malien. She did not move. He crept down across the gravel, trying not to make a sound, but when he was a few steps away a pebble slipped underfoot and he fell on his knees with a grunt of pain.

'What do you want, teller?' she asked, without looking up.

He did not know what to say. 'Who was Elienor?' he asked eventually.

Malien sat up. 'You, a master chronicler, ask me that?'

'Even our own Histories have many gaps. But where I studied, at Chanthed, there was nothing about the Aachim for the last thousand years.'

'Elienor,' she said softly, and her eyes took on a faraway look as she reflected on that ancient tale. 'She lived and died long before that, before my ancestors came to your world. She was the founder of my line, and Karan's too.' She stared at his face. 'We both carry . . . carried her name.'

Her words struck him like a spear in the chest. His wound sang out as though that spear carved him afresh. Tears like stars of frost formed in his eyes but did not fall.

'Karan *is* dead? How did you learn of it?'

'From what Tensor said it seemed . . .' Malien broke off at the look on his face. 'Hold! I was not there, but you were. You saw as much as he did. You did not see her dying?'

'No! When I held Karan I saw her eyes move under their lids but she lay on the floor as still as death, and she was icy cold.'

'That is what the potency does, but most of your kind would survive it if they were healthy. It hurts us Aachim more than it does the folk of Santhenar. That is one of the reasons why it is prohibited. Karan only being part-Aachim, it might affect her badly or only a little.' She was struck by a curious thought. '*How is it that you were able to see?*' There was a ragged edge to her voice.

'I don't know. When Tensor used the potency, the pain

was awful. I went blind, but only for a second. I felt something close in my head, like a gate. Then it opened again, the pain had disappeared and I could see.'

She took his face between her hands and looked into his eyes, long and carefully. When she released him the edge was gone. 'Take heart. Though Karan has Aachim blood, I do not think it would have killed her.'

Little comfort there, but better than none. 'Tell me about this potency of Tensor's, he said. 'Why is it prohibited?'

'We have used it just twice before. Each time it did us more harm than our enemy.'

'Where did it come from?'

'We made it after the Forbidding closed the way back to our own world. When we realised that Aachan was lost to us, we rebelled against being the slaves of the Charon. Trying to make a weapon that would be proof against them, we developed a mind-blasting spell, a "potency".

'The first time it was used was a disaster. Ten of us (I say "us", chronicler, though you realise it was more than two thousand years before I was born) waylaid Rulke. He would not accede to our just demands, so one of us blasted him with the potency while the others stood back with their own spells, just in case. Rulke was badly hurt, but we had not reckoned with our own sensitivity to the spell. It triggered all the other potencies, setting off an uncontrollable reaction that left four of us dead and the others brain-stormed and helpless. Rulke recovered before we did and made a brutal example of the survivors.

'But we are slow learners, Llian. We devised a better potency but by then Rulke had a defence, his Gift of Rulke that he gave to your Zain ancestors. The Gift reflected the potency back on those who made it. That was much later, at the beginning of the Clysm. Many of us died that day and the potency was outlawed. And even now some of us don't like the Zain overmuch,' she said, but smiled to show that she did not hold to the prejudice.

A sound like a horn came faint on the wind. Malien jumped up and began to gather things into a leather bag.

'Elienor!' he said.

'No time for that tale, or any of the tales about her,' she said, pulling the drawstring tight.

'Who was she? At least tell me that, as we walk.' He used a little of his *voice* on her, that seemingly magical ability of great tellers to move their audience – in this case, to make her want to tell him what he wanted to know. Malien gave him an amused look, but answered anyway.

'She was the one who gave the warning when the Charon appeared out of the void and took our world away from us. She rose up from the slaughter, the only one of her family to survive. Were we more like her, the Charon would have been cast back into the void and we would be masters of beloved Aachan still.'

They were scrambling up through the tangled roots of fallen trees. 'She struck Rulke a killing blow, one no one else could have survived. No other Aachim ever laid weapon on him, or even dared, yet Elienor was the smallest and most timid among us. How we have declined!'

'How did the Charon take Aachan? How did they come to be in the void, and how did they get out of it again? The Histories are silent on such matters.'

'Another time, chronicler. Each of your questions would take a night to answer.'

He subsided, greatly dissatisfied.

'Why do you not sleep?' she asked as they neared the camp. 'The march just completed is nothing to what lies ahead.'

'My dreams were terrible. I was afraid to go back to sleep.'

'What dreams?'

'Awful dreams. I can't remember anything about them.' A fragment came to him. 'Except . . .'

Malien sprang up an outcropping of sandstone that was shoulder high, and onto the terrace above. The outcrop, crusted with lichen, moss-covered at the bottom, was like a wall across Llian's path. There was a seep at the base of the rock. Water began to puddle around his feet. He scrabbled at the sandstone.

Malien reached down lazily to pull him up by his good arm. She smiled as though she liked him.

'Except?' she said.

'The only concrete thing I remember about my dream is that you were in it.'

The smile disappeared. 'I, in *your* dream?'

'Yes, and Rael too.'

Malien frowned, looked at him slantwise from her grey-green eyes, then strode ahead. No further word was spoken. Soon they reached the camp and found a smokeless fire and a hot drink but, whatever the horn signal had been, no crisis.

Llian slept the afternoon away and did not dream. That night they were off again and he had no chance to question Malien further.

Their pursuers had drawn near again, so they spent two days hiding in the forests of the northern part of Iagador. Then fortune favoured them with foul weather, wind and later sleet and driving rain. Under its cover they fled north, walking night and day (almost at running pace for Llian) through the roughest country they could find. They waded waist-deep through freezing swamps and shallow rivers, clambered up rocky gullies and down jagged cliffs, fought their way through thorn forests. By the end they had reached uninhabited places where the mountains ran right down to the sea.

One day they came to a foaming torrent, a cataract set in a deep gorge like the mighty River Garr of Shazmak, only smaller. Crossing that was a hazard which took all day. Afterwards Tensor climbed to the highest point of the ridge, looking down to the coast. There was a sizeable town at the mouth of the river far below. North of the town the mountains drew back from the sea again.

'This river must be the Gannel,' he said, 'and that is the town of Ganport. Good progress, in this country, but we must do better.'

They moved in single file, winding up the mountain track, the last of them dragging a branch to smear their prints into the mud. It was raining again and it grew heavier as they neared the top, mixed in with drifting bands of mist.

At the summit the rain stopped momentarily but they looked up through the treetops to leaden skies, a deluge waiting to burst down on them. The trees here were twisted by the gales into eerie shapes and the wind sang in their leafless branches. The ground was broken by arching oval outcrops of grey granite. They splashed out of the trees into an alpine bog meadow, where the moss grew in mounds like giant cushions among the mushroom shapes of the granite, and the water underfoot was the colour of beer.

Asper stopped suddenly. The most cheerful of the Aachim, even he looked depressed. 'I feel like I'm running on a treadmill to nowhere,' he said, wringing the water out of his hat.

No one answered. After a fortnight on the road, their spirits were as sodden as their clothes. Even Tensor was worn out from the slog up the mountain in the mud. Llian fell down on a moss cushion.

'I say we rest here,' said Malien, 'unless you want to kill your prisoner, and the rest of us too. We cannot run forever.' She jerked a thumb at Hintis.

Hintis was suffering worse than the others, as if his extreme height robbed him of stamina. He sat with head hanging between his legs, breathing in quick ragged breaths that gurgled in his chest. His frizzy hair hung lank. Tensor looked impatient, but Hintis rolled over and lay on his side in the slush. 'My chest burns,' he said hoarsely.

'We'll camp here,' Tensor replied.

They found a campsite back between the trees, where a

great curving plate of granite sat like the cap of a mushroom on three smaller outcrops. The space underneath provided shelter of a sort, though the ground was wet and the sleety wind blew right through. Malien dosed Hintis and the rest of them with medicines from her pack. There was enough dry stuff caught in the crevices of the rock to kindle a fire, but though they built it up until the rock shadows danced like dervishes, Llian could not get warm.

He dozed on the ground, wrapped in cloak and blanket. His dreams were haunted by ghostly voices calling out to him, holding out welcome cups and begging him to drink, but each time he reached for the fragrant liqueur it vanished in his hand. Later he dreamed he was back in Thurkad, dragging a severed leg along the gutter, begging for help, but no one would aid him.

Llian woke thrashing. The fire had died down and the Aachim were sleeping, all but the sentries out in the forest. What was that? Something had fluttered just at the edge of his vision. It was gone. No, there it was again, a white thing flitting from boulder to boulder. The hairs rose on his arm, but as soon as he looked directly at it, it vanished.

It was a waste of time trying to sleep – he was wide awake now, cold and depressed. Llian tugged soggy boots onto numb feet, dipped a mug of stewed prune tea from the pot and wandered away from the firelight toward the moss meadow. The clouds had thinned, outlining the full moon. It was yellow, barely any of the dark side showing, and gave just enough light to guide his way among the boulders. The mountain air had the faintest whiff of brandy.

He sat on a rock, sipping the sweet tea, the mist thickening his eyelashes, and took stock of his miserable life. He had lost Karan, Tensor was dragging him to a horrible doom and he was helpless to do anything about it. Through the racing clouds he glimpsed the scorpion nebula, a red-shadowed ill-omen that had first appeared the night of his *Tale of the Forbidding* last summer. He shuddered, then cloud covered it again.

Once more something flickered at the edge of vision. That was strange, for it was totally dark now. At the same moment he was prodded in the back and he leapt off his boulder, stifling a gasp.

'Calm yourself, chronicler,' came Malien's amused voice. 'Our enemies are far away.'

'Your enemies!' he said bitterly. 'Mine are all around me, taking me away from everything I ever cared about, to use me and throw away the rubbish afterwards.'

'Think of it as an opportunity to see what no other chronicler has ever seen and tell tales that no one has ever told.'

'I did, before I realised that I am a hopeless, useless failure, and better off dead.'

'Pah! Of all human emotions, self-pity is the most contemptible. Get up and make something of yourself.'

Her words were like being whipped across the face. Llian's rage flared, such that he could have ripped boulders out of the ground. He struck back, intending to hurt. 'Then I am contemptible,' he said softly. 'But not so contemptible as you Aachim, whining and wringing your hands about lost Shazmak and every other setback. Look at your own Histories! You are attracted to hubris like maggots to dung. You give power to fools and then follow them blindly into the abyss, because you are too proud and too afraid to cast them aside and think for yourselves. And now you are doing it again. Only days ago you wailed and cursed Tensor for his folly, yet already you are closer to him than a leech on a dog's balls.' He stopped suddenly, shocked at his crudity.

'Yes,' said Malien, 'we have two fatal flaws and you've put your finger on them. We are overly proud, but our courage falls short at the sticking place. That is why we lost Aachan. That is why we fail, in the face of an enemy who never gives up.'

'Well, I won't give up either. I *will* make the tale my life

120

again. Nothing will stand in my way. Nothing else matters anymore.'

'Never say that nothing ever matters, chronicler. Your people . . .'

'Sort out your own affairs before you lecture me! Nothing matters now but the tale.' He brushed past her, splashing through the bog, trampling the delicate cushion mosses, into the black and ghost-ridden night.

Malien watched him go, shivering, uneasy. Still, what harm could a chronicler do? It was the end of her watch, so she went back to the fire, the hot prune tea and her blankets.

Eventually Llian's rage died down but the resolve only grew stronger. He had drifted too long. He would use this opportunity, that other tellers would have killed for, and do whatever was necessary to follow the tale.

A spectral something fluttered on the edge of his vision again and suddenly he realised what it was. This was Tisane Mountain – there had once been a monastery here, famous for its waters and its brandies, filtered through purest moss peat. But the plague had come to Tisane, hideous eruptions of black boils that burst with a vile stench, slaying half of the brothers and sisters within a week. The rest took a vote, locked themselves in the distillery, even the ones who voted against, and burned it to the ground with barrels of their finest brandies. The place reeked of spirits for weeks afterwards and had been haunted ever since.

A ghost drifted up to him, a pretty young woman in tunic and cap. She held out a goblet; the tang of cherry brandy was overwhelming. Llian reached out for the cup and suddenly the place swarmed with lonely spectres, each whispering the delights of its own liquor, desperate to attract his attention. They had not had a customer in centuries. But they were shades, while blood ran through his flesh. Each time he touched a cup it vanished and the spectre with it. The miraculous cordials were gone forever; their customers as well. The air reeked of spirits and regret.

Harmless ghosts! Llian thought, sighing for the brandy. He turned, stepping light-footed through the shades and the mosses back to the camp. He felt that he had found himself again.

After that they literally ran for a day and a half. At the end of it they stopped for three or four hours to rest, to sleep briefly, to argue about the next course, but Llian was too weary to listen. As soon as they stopped he fell to the ground, clutching his heavy cloak around him, and slept where he lay.

Then they were off again, running and running until it seemed that he had never done anything else, had never felt anything but the thud of blistered feet against hard ground, the shock travelling all the way up to the back of his head, had never taken any breath that was not a gasp and a burning in his good side, and a throbbing in his injured side even though it was healing well. Llian grew stronger every day but he was never anything but exhausted, for as time went on the Aachim seemed to lengthen their stride, taking a grim pleasure in the flight and the pain.

The weather was still miserable: rain, wind and sleet, and at first they made slow progress. Some days went by with only four or five leagues added to their tally, no more than an army might have achieved on a good road, though not the rugged way they went. But by the time the wind turned around to the west, bringing warm clear skies with it, their pursuers were far behind. Perhaps there was no longer any pursuit, and in the tall forests at the foot of the mountains there were days when they made twelve leagues, and once, fifteen. If it had not been for Llian they would have gone much further.

This day they held a conference – whether to go back into the mountains to hide or head east across the sea to Lauralin. Tensor did not speak at all yet it seemed that he had a destination in mind. In the end they did neither, just kept on.

In their race north, Llian had no time for anything but running and sleeping, and at the end of each day he fell onto his bed of bracken or boughs and slept – too drained even to dream. Only once did he have that dream again, or at least wake knowing that he had. It was on the night before they were to reach Siftah, a fishing town on the north-eastern tip of Meldorin. Where was there to go after that but across the sea?

They had come down to the coast again, and for want of a better camp had installed themselves under the overhang of a low cliff, too shallow to be called a cave, which was open on either side to the rush and ebb of the wind from the sea. The damp wind made it unpleasant, though it was not really cold – not to someone who had walked to Shazmak in the winter.

A screen was woven of dry sticks and hung in front of the fire, enough to conceal a small blaze from view. Llian sat motionless inside the niche, while Aachim prepared food, and other Aachim made camp. Malien inspected his wound for the last time, for it had healed to a scabby pucker along his side.

Llian pulled up his shirt, once Malien's silk shirt, now sadly stained and coming apart at the shoulders.

'And does it yet trouble you?' she asked, still squatting before him.

'A little, when I stretch or move suddenly; and after a long day.'

'That is all? Then you are fully healed. My ancient bones feel as much every day.'

'Ancient! I thought that you Aachim lived practically forever. I know that Tensor has.'

'Some do, if accident or disease don't prevent it,' Malien said.

'How does that come about?' Llian wondered.

'I don't know. We just live for a long time.'

'As do the Charon and the Faellem,' Llian reflected, 'and

those masters of the Secret Art, like Mendark and Yggur, who have learned how to lengthen the brief lives of us old humans.'

'Just so. But the span of *my* line was never that long and I have passed my midpoint. I can't say that it troubles me.'

'How old are you then?'

She stared into his eyes so intensely that even Llian became embarrassed and looked away.

'In my culture, as in your own, that is an ill-mannered question. Even from a prying chronicler.'

'I'm sorry,' said Llian, mortified to realise that his cheeks were hot.

'But I will answer it, against a time when we Aachim may exist only in tales such as yours. I have lived more than two of your life spans, and if I will it, and fortune allows, I might live another two. That is enough.'

'Have you children?'

She looked up at the waning moon. 'Only one, so far. I doubt that I have the heart for another.'

'I would have thought –' Llian broke off.

'Is there no end to your curiosity?' she said, but she was smiling. 'We Aachim are different to old humans in many ways, Llian. In fertility too. It is not continuous, as in the women of your species. I have had three brief fertile periods in my life, the last being thirty years ago. I may have one or two more. Ah, my son!'

'What happened to him?'

'I should ask you that. You saw him die.'

'Rael!' The back of his neck came out in goosepimples.

'Rael,' she echoed.

'H-he was helping us escape from Shazmak.' Llian had to force himself to speak without stammering. 'He delayed, cutting the rudder of the other boat so that they could not follow us. Then, when he tried to get aboard, the current was too strong. It pulled him under.'

'He was a powerful swimmer,' she said. 'Maybe it was his way of escape from an impossible dilemma.'

'I remember . . . just before we fled. He looked so sad. *Alas!* he said to Karan. *You have your other house and your unspoken purpose to comfort you. For me there will be no return.*'

'Karan cared for him so much.'

'Theirs was a great friendship.'

'Rael was the noblest person I ever met,' said Llian.

'Ahh! No greater sorrow! I cannot talk about him to you. Come with me.'

He followed her over the rocks down to the water. She stood in the cold wind at the sea's edge, where the crashing waves meant that there was no chance of being overheard.

'Tell me about the dream,' said Malien. 'Have you had it since?'

'Just once. It was a very brief dream: Rael was in his room in Shazmak. He played music for me there one day. But in the dream he was playing a melancholy song to someone I could not see. Then it changed, to a terrible warning, I saw you there and –'

'*That is my dream!*' said Malien, covering her face.

'Your dream?'

Malien's hand slid down. She went all remote, closed up, and Llian thought he must have touched on a taboo. Then evidently she realised that some explanation was owed. 'I can hardly speak of it to an outsider,' she said in a whisper. 'It is one of our greatest intimacies.' She looked him in the eyes and hers were wet.

'Sometimes we Aachim, if we have been very close, can still share communion for a while after one has died. *But how can it have come to you?*'

'He was playing to you,' Llian said. 'A warning. You were as still as death; I think that you were weeping. That is all. It was the same both times.'

She shivered; her face froze. '*Dream sharing!* Doom! Doom!' she whispered, then walked away up the shore.

He did not see her again that day and she did not speak to him at all for a week, though several times he caught her staring at him as if she sought some sign in his face. And he knew what she was looking for, the stigmata that would show that the Gift of Rulke was developing in him. He grew deadly afraid, and knew just how fatally he had erred when he hesitated in the doorway back at Tensor's villa in Thurkad. What would they do to one who bore those marks, in this of all times?

9

IN THE WHARF CITY

It was the first day of endre, mid-winter week, by tradition a cursed, haunted, ill-omened time when sensible citizens stayed indoors and made no decisions. Only three days to go till hythe, mid-winter day, the ugliest day of the year.

Mendark and his company hid back in the tunnel for some hours, until Tallia, after much searching, found a labourer on a nearby wharf to tell them what had happened. Their boat, in fact every stray boat in Thurkad, had been impounded by Yggur's troops during the night. They had left their departure a day too late.

Mendark could scarcely speak, so great was his rage and fear. 'This came about because I did my duty,' he choked. 'I'll have to beg the Hlune to take us in. What a humiliation! What if they refuse me?'

He paced back up the tunnel, splashing heedlessly through the stinking water, then came running back to where Tallia stood talking to Torgsted. 'Tallia, I must have a boat *tonight*. Get to work and find one. Torgsted!' He lowered his voice. 'You have always been loyal – what I must ask you now will test you to your limits. Keep an eye on Thyllan for me. If it comes to a break, are you prepared to go with him and keep watch for me? Pretend to betray me? I know how much I am asking.'

'I'll do it,' Torgsted said vehemently. 'However long it takes.'

Mendark shook his hand, then turned to the rest of the group, who were perched uncomfortably on a slime-hung buttress some distance away. 'Well, it can't be put off. Come on.'

They followed him into the massive wharf structure. It was as big as a city, three and four and sometimes even five storeys high, and nowhere less than a thousand paces wide. The labyrinth of the wharf city stretched around the shore of Thurkad for more than a league, slowly sinking into the mud of the harbour, forever built anew on top of the old.

It was near midday. Mendark led them into a maze of huge, tarred timbers, most divided into wood-walled warehouses and cells, and all dripping from top to bottom. Almost immediately they were accosted by two of the lanky Hlune, the toga-clad, sharp-featured, mud-complexioned people who ruled the city within the wharves and controlled everything that was loaded or unloaded there.

The first Hlune, distinguishable as a woman by the absence of pigtailed chin-whiskers, gripped Mendark's arm. He stopped at once. She looked gravely discomfited, shaking her head from side to side and making a clucking sound like a hen on a nest. Hlune speech was punctuated with a variety of such sounds, which made it hard to follow.

Mendark looked her in the eye, speaking in a richly resonant voice, unlike his normal soporific tones. 'Honourable Hlune! In the name of our long alliance and mutual interests, I beg refuge for myself and my people. Just one day.'

She stared at the group, still clucking, and her eyes grew wide in alarm. Then she let out her breath in a plosive pop. 'Refuge, *now*? No, no, *no*!'

She swung around to the man, who was clicking his teeth together nervously. His eyes darted over Mendark's shoulder. 'Come quickly,' he cried, grabbing Mendark's arm and dragging him into a bare room, just a cube of black timber. 'Hurry, all of you!'

The walls were made up of slabs that barely touched, the wood crumbling with rot. The floor slabs were awash with the rising tide. Dark rainwater leached through the tarred ceiling onto their heads.

'Stay here,' the man hissed when they were all inside. 'Do not open the door!'

'Put this on, Magister,' the woman said, handing him her hood. 'Come with me.' Mendark pulled it down and followed her out.

Peering through the cracks in the wall, Lilis saw Mendark hurried off by the woman while the man stood guard outside. 'What's happening?' she asked Tallia.

'We're in bad trouble, child,' Tallia replied. 'Yggur has shut the city up tight; we don't have any way of escape. Taking us in can only make things worse for them.'

Lilis pressed her new pack to her chest, afraid that it would be confiscated. 'What will they do?'

'They may refuse us. Mendark can be very persuasive though, and he has done business with the Hlune for a long time. Let's wait and see.'

Finally Mendark was led back. 'Phew! I was quite worried there. They have agreed to give us refuge for a day. That should be enough.'

Tallia thought he was putting on a very brave face, but she said nothing. They were taken to a better room, a chamber high up, and for the Hlune so luxuriously appointed as to have beds, though they were dreadfully dank. When the escort was gone again, and the door shut, they held council.

'The Hlune offer us sanctuary, not exile,' said Mendark. 'We must make what plans we can. What is your view, Malkin?'

Malkin was the leader of the group of merchants and lawyers, but after falling in the sewer the man was far gone in misery. His fellows, though now they felt nothing for him but contempt, deferred to him and kept their silence.

Thyllan was not shy. He flung out an arm at Mendark, his face red with wrath. 'How many times did I warn you of this man? He was Magister for a thousand years and look at the result! The treasury is bankrupt, our armies debauched and Thurkad lies crushed beneath Yggur's boot. Now the Conclave, our most precious tradition, is violated by *his friend*, Tensor.'

Tallia made to interrupt the theatrics, but Mendark closed his hand on her arm. 'Let him speak,' he said.

Thyllan continued in a booming voice, more suited to addressing a rally than their shabby little group. 'Hear me! Out of ruin I see a ray of hope, if we have the courage to seize it. The past is dead, but I see the way into the future. The Council holds secrets that have not been used for a thousand years – *the Proscribed Experiments*!'

'The Council swore never to use those powers again,' cried Mendark, looking alarmed.

'The oaths of that Council are not binding. The past cannot fetter the present, for no one can see the perils of the future, or the needs. We must use what secrets the Council preserved against such a crisis. We have nothing else.'

Tallia was watching the rest of the room, trying to gauge their reactions. It was going badly. Just as Thyllan had swayed the Conclave, making Mendark appear old, weak and selfish, so did he here. He was a dangerous opponent, and if he convinced the guard they would be in deadly danger.

'The old Council is broken!' Thyllan roared, striking the wall with his fist. 'We must cast out the traitor and forge a new one. And we must have a place of safety from which to build our strength. Somewhere nearby, difficult to conquer, easy to defend. We will go to Nilkerrand, across the sea.'

The merchants stirred. Whatever their failings, they were not fools. Their interests were the interests of Thyllan; their lusts his lusts. Even Tallia felt a twinge of admiration for the man, who could rise from the bed where he lay witless and, in less than a day, without a single retainer and in wretched sanctuary under the nose of his foes, plot the conquest of his world.

'*Nilkerrand!*' Mendark said. 'And you call *me* a fool.'

Berenet twirled his mustachioes, staring at Thyllan with an enigmatic smile. Impossible to tell what he was thinking.

'But first,' Thyllan cried out, 'we must discard the dross from the old world – the treacherous Mendark, who shall be known as the Old Fool. What say you?'

'This is not legal,' Mendark said weakly. 'The Council may not be dissolved while its purpose remains incomplete. This pathetic remnant cannot even empower you as Warlord. But what do *you* know of honour, of our ancient codes? The only law –'

'Law has failed,' Thyllan interrupted. 'We must draw strength from our own ideals to remake the world, and finally, the laws that bring us harmony.'

'Follow him at your peril,' Mendark said to the group. 'His reign will be as brief as snow in summer. Support this folly and you set back our cause –'

'*The old fool!*' Thyllan sneered. 'The one who was Magister for an age, the age that Thurkad fell. The one who *did nothing, knows nothing*, and has *nothing to offer* but the delusions of the past. Better to try and fail than to die knowing we were afraid to try.' His voice was ripe with disgust, so that even Mendark's personal guard looked troubled. 'Cast him out!'

The vote was tallied, and the merchants took side with Thyllan. Tallia and Berenet abstained from the farce but Mendark's guard turned their coats, all except Osseion. Torgsted joined the rebels, though Tallia hoped that he followed Mendark's plan. So it was settled. Illegal though it was, the Council was dissolved and reformed, with Thyllan as Magister.

Mendark turned to his little group, who were huddled together, shocked at the sudden reversal. He was remarkably calm. 'Well, nothing more we can do. You have no objection if we go our own way?' he asked Thyllan.

'Begone!' said Thyllan, 'or feel my *wrath*!'

Mendark smiled, and Tallia suddenly realised that he was up to something. Berenet and she took up one of the chests and Osseion the other.

'Put them down!' Thyllan ordered. 'Guards –'

Mendark raised a clenched fist. Thyllan went pale and clutched his head, unable to complete the sentence. 'Better get back your strength before you take me on,' Mendark said grimly.

He led his little group – Berenet and Osseion, Tallia and Lilis – outside. Thyllan's curses followed them. 'That went better than I had hoped,' Mendark said with a chuckle, as soon as the door closed behind them.

'You intended to break with them?' asked Tallia.

'Safeguarding that lot was like carrying a corpse on my shoulders,' he said, dripping scorn. 'Let them go to Nilkerrand! I've got other things to worry about.'

'The Council!' said Tallia.

His good humour vanished. 'What am I to do? Orstand can never be replaced. I can't do it on my own.'

'You have me,' said Berenet, a pleading tone in his voice. 'We can form a new Council.'

Tallia snorted. Mendark glared at her and tried to smooth things over. 'The Council is more than a title. The experience lost these last few days can't be replaced in five hundred years –'

Berenet turned away abruptly. As he did so a Hlune guard came marching up. She listened silently as Mendark explained what had happened, her mouth curving further down with each word.

'What you want?' she snapped at the end.

'I beg sanctuary anew for myself and my companions,' he said patiently.

The woman pointed back into the room they had just left. 'There is your sanctuary,' she said.

'No good,' said Mendark. 'They are my enemies now.'

'You begged us to take them in. You must stay with them.'

'I cannot!'

Her brown eyes flashed sparks at him. She stamped her flat foot on the wet deck, making a fishy slap. 'Go back inside,' she cried, but Mendark did not budge. A swarm of children appeared out of the gloom, thin grubby urchins with staring eyes. Seeing herself in them, Lilis clutched Tallia's hand.

'Are they going to throw us out?' she whispered.

'I don't know, Lilis.'

The guard glared at Mendark. He was immoveable. Finally she gave a warbling whistle and another Hlune appeared. The two chattered together, their speech punctuated by tongue clicks, cheek pops and nasal honks. The second Hlune shook his head, then the woman led Mendark away by the sleeve while the others waited.

An anxious half hour passed before she returned alone. 'Come!' she hissed.

They were taken on a long, exhausting walk, up and down again, hauling the chests as well as all their other gear. The new accommodation reflected their lowered status – a bare room just above the high-tide level, and the water stank. Mendark was waiting there.

'They are not pleased!' said Tallia.

'During my time as Magister, not all of my dealings with the Hlune were happy ones,' said Mendark. 'I had to threaten them. Now we must really be on our guard. They are terrified that Yggur will burn them out. It will not take much for them to betray us. And Thyllan knows that without a treasury his plans are hollow. Tallia, come with me.'

She followed him outside, just out of earshot of the watching Hlune.

'What are you going to do, Mendark?'

'I don't know,' he said, looking haggard. 'You do *your* job – find us a way out. Have you gold?'

'Some,' she replied. Then, realising that the hire of a boat now might cost a hundred times the normal tariff, 'Though perhaps not enough.'

'Take this. It is the one commodity I still have in plenty.' He took a purse from inside his robes. 'Take the scruff with you, and if you get the chance, leave her behind.'

Tallia slid the purse into her pocket. It was the weight of a half-brick. 'Your generosity is limited to Thurkad's gold,' she said, turning away.

Before she'd gone ten steps a furious guard put her upraised hands against Tallia's face. 'Where you going?'

'Into Thurkad,' said Tallia politely.

'Go back!' The guard fingered her knife.

Tallia put her hands up and backed inside. 'You heard?' she said to Mendark.

'I'd better speak to her,' he sighed.

It took much argument before the Hlune were convinced that the only way to get rid of the unwelcome guests was for Tallia to find a boat. By then it was late in the afternoon.

Now Tallia and her little shadow were waiting beside one of the main support piles of the wharf city, a trunk so big that they could not have linked hands around it. They could go nowhere without an escort but the Hlune was slow in coming.

'Have you been in here before?' Tallia asked the waif.

Lilis shivered. 'This is a forbidden place. Once I came with a message, though only to the bottom of the steps.'

'Are you afraid?'

'On the streets we're always afraid. But not now, not with you.'

'Well, I am.'

'You?' In Lilis's mind Tallia was all-powerful. 'Everyone says how clever you are.'

'Oh? What do they say?'

'That you are the best fighter in the world. That you can beat armed men with your bare hands.'

Tallia chuckled. 'That's just bar talk. I can defeat one or

two; perhaps even three if I am lucky, or if they are unskilful or drunk. More than three, I would be just as helpless as you.' Lilis did not reply to that, only held Tallia's hand more tightly. 'And I prefer not to fight at all, if I can help it. What else do they say?'

'That you can do magic even better than the old Magister.'

Tallia laughed aloud. 'I bet they don't say *that* in front of Mendark. That's not true at all.'

'You *can't* do magic?' Lilis sounded rather let down.

'I – I can, Lilis, and if things come to a tricky pass you may see some of it. But we don't use the Secret Art if there's any other way, and we don't talk about it at all.'

'Oh!' said Lilis.

'Now we have to find a boat and a great sailor.'

'I don't know any sailors,' said Lilis, smoothing her hand along the rough surface of the pile. 'I kept away from the wharves. Sailors frighten me.' There was a long silence. She examined her fingers, which were brown with dust. 'But there are people who can find anything, if you can pay them.'

'I can pay, but are they trustworthy?'

Lilis shrugged. 'Perhaps.'

'Have you ever heard of a boatman called Pender?'

Lilis shook her head.

No, why would you have, Tallia thought. Pender came from Narne, a long way away. He brought Karan and Llian here, and did a remarkable job by all accounts. An outsider, an outcast – that's what we need.

Just then the escort appeared, looking very edgy. 'Very well,' Tallia said aloud, 'take me to these people of yours, Lilis.'

The light began to fade. It was still raining. Lilis and Tallia were now crouched at the edge of the wharf city beside an old stone dock, long abandoned and built over. Tallia wore grey robes, and had lightened her face and hands, but was otherwise undisguised.

They were waiting for the dark. The waterfront was one of the most closely watched places, and Tallia would certainly be on Yggur's list. She might have gone veiled, as some of the peoples of Faranda did, but they were few in Thurkad at any time, and the veil now would be an invitation to look beneath. She did not want to use illusion either – Yggur was a famous master of the Secret Art and no doubt had minions trained to sense such things. If he did, it would be like walking around at night with a torch on her head. Better the dark and the alleys, and her excellent guide. And the weather was in their favour, cold and rain and wind an incentive to the guards to be a little less thorough.

'I'm frightened,' said Lilis. 'Look, there are guards here too.'

'I see them now,' said Tallia, blessing the child's eyes, which were even keener than her own. 'We'd better try another way.'

They found every way out of the wharf city to be guarded as thoroughly as the first. 'Yggur must suspect that we're here,' said Tallia. 'Do you know any secret paths up into the city, Lilis? You know the streets better than I do.'

'There are sewers and stormwater drains and old smuggler's tunnels,' said Lilis.

'Take me to one that goes further up the hill. One that no one knows about. Maybe it's not so well guarded away from the waterfront.'

Lilis's cold little hand took Tallia's warm one and they followed a wandering way until it was completely dark. Lilis stopped by a stinking drain. 'We go up here, a long way. It comes out behind an inn – The Mother Pearl, a smugglers' place.'

'Good, I'd like to keep to the back streets. I don't think Yggur's patrols go in there yet.'

'Probably too afraid,' said Lilis, shivering.

The drain was a waist-high, stone-lined channel that had been paved over long ago. It stank of every rotting thing that a city of a million people could generate. Lilis, who had left her new clothes and boots behind, splashed off. Tallia followed cautiously, over broken stone slimy with weed. By the time she reached the other end she was soaked in stinking water to the knees. Lilis showed Tallia how to wriggle out through a rusty grating and put back the rubbish caught there so that the gap was not evident.

Their trip through the alleys to the back of the inn was uneventful since there were enough people on the streets for them not to attract attention. But when they arrived they found no sign of life – no lights, no sounds and the back door was barred. Lilis went carefully around the front, coming back almost at once.

'I saw a watcher just down the street. The door is closed with boards, and there's black writing on the wall. I couldn't get close enough to read it.'

The inn must have been shut down. Doubtless, most such haunts were closed and the others watched, all those that Yggur knew about. Tallia edged back up the alley. But there was another curious thing to think about.

'You can read?' she asked Lilis.

'A bit,' said the child. 'Street signs and posters. Sometimes I help if there is a letter to be ciphered.'

They were now clambering through the labyrinth of rubbish-choked alleys behind the waterfront promenade, a roundabout way to get to their next possibility. The few burning street lamps were surrounded by foggy haloes. The people on the streets had a hungry look.

'Is that common among you?' asked Tallia.

'What?'

'Being able to read?'

'No,' said Lilis, 'but a few of us can. I'm the best. My father had a book. He used to read me stories and show me the letters and the sounds they made. I dream about that book, almost as much as I do about him.' She sniffled in the dark.

'What happened to your father and mother?'

'My mother got sick and died. I don't remember her. I lost my father. I *lost* him.' Her voice was full of grief and melancholy and childish guilt.

'How could you lose your father?'

'We came to Thurkad when I was five. We were walking along looking at the ships. I had a toy, a little wooden bear. I dropped it in the water and it floated away. He jumped in after it.'

Tallia could imagine the rest. It was too pathetic. 'Oh, he drowned right in front of you!'

'He was a very good swimmer!' said Lilis scornfully. 'He got it, and all the people were talking about him. Then some men came up, sailors or smugglers. They hit him on the head and dragged him off to their ship, and sailed away. He never came back.'

'They *pressed* him? Here, in Thurkad?' Tallia was incredulous. 'And no one did anything?'

'Hist!' said Lilis, her head darting this way and that like an animal on a scent. She took her guide duties very seriously. Darting at Tallia, she pushed her hard towards the shadows. 'Get down!'

They crouched down. Nothing happened for ages, then a pair of guards appeared, walking quickly down the centre of the street. They kept looking over their shoulders. Near the other end of the lane something splattered against one of the soldiers' helmets. They went into a defensive crouch, spears at the ready, but nothing further happened and shortly they disappeared in the mist.

'They're just as scared as we are,' said Tallia as they set off again.

'Good!' said Lilis.

'So no one did anything after your father was taken?' Tallia asked.

'I didn't know anyone. No one would speak for me. I had nothing but my clothes and my little bear. I cried for a day and a night and another day. I slept in a barrel in the alley.'

'Does that happen often?'

'The press-gangs? It happens. Especially to sailors and people who can swim. I'm sure he must be dead, else he would have come for me. Seven years he has been gone. Seven . . . years.' Suddenly she was crying, great choking sobs, weeping for the whole world that she had lost.

Tallia took her in her arms, sat down on a wet flagstone and held Lilis tight while she sobbed and sobbed until it seemed her little frame would just dissolve away with the tears and the heartbreak. Eventually the sobs gave way to great shuddering gasps, and these to a trembling, then all at once she stood up.

'I am twelve and a half. I have no father. There is no one but me. Come, The Student Prince is still a long way.'

Twelve! thought Tallia. I thought you were much younger. Well, you have me now. If he *can* be found he *will* be. 'What was your father's name?'

'His name was Jevander but I called him Jevi. He had another name too, but I don't remember it, our family name. I just called him Jevi, and he called me Lilis.'

'What was he like?'

'Gentle and kind. He was hardly ever cross with me, even when I was very naughty. I remember one day –'

'No, I meant – what did he look like? Was he tall or short, what colour was his hair, that sort of thing.'

Lilis did not speak for a long while, though her face was alive with memories. 'His hair was like mine,' she said eventually. 'And his eyes. I can remember him holding me up to a mirror so that my face was beside his, and saying how alike we were and how lucky we were to have each other. He often said that. I don't know if he was tall or short. He always seemed big to me. But he wasn't fat.'

Tallia took her hand and they walked slowly along without further speech. Twice more they had to slip into the alleys to avoid patrols. Tallia felt strangely uncomfortable, sneaking about in her own city. The Student Prince turned out to be a two-storey affair of drab-grey stone, announced by a cracked signboard depicting an androgynous youth with cropped hair sitting dejectedly on a thick tome. Other books were stacked haphazardly before the student and a flask teetered on top.

Lilis looked both ways but there was no one to be seen. The door was closed, but opened to Tallia's gentle knock and after a careful inspection they were allowed in to a dark room that was nearly empty. The room was lit by a small fire. They took a table right beside it. Tallia sat down with a great outrushing sigh.

'Are you hungry, Lilis?'

There was a despairing look in the child's eyes as she shook her head. 'I have no money. In Thurkad if you cannot pay, you cannot eat.'

'Nonsense! You work for me now, my little guide, and guides earn ten times the price in time of war. Order everything you want, for there may be a long march on short rations after this.'

Tallia debated whether to tell Lilis about the ransom money from the people she had rescued, but decided to keep it for a safer time. They ate well, but did not find what they were looking for, and eventually went back out onto the cold street.

As they turned the corner, a lamp was unshuttered in an upstairs room across the street from the inn. The front door opened and the watcher slipped into the street, following like a ghost.

They searched into the night, at all the haunts that Lilis knew about, but did not find anyone who could provide a boat. Most places were closed, boarded up, while several had been burnt to the ground. Everyone was in hiding, and perhaps the news had got around that Lilis was no longer one of them, no longer 'of the streets'. Tallia began to despair. They would never find a boat. What was she going to say to Mendark?

Lilis looked over her shoulder again. She'd done it a dozen times in the past few minutes. She began to walk faster, tugging at Tallia's hand. Tallia could not resist the urge to look, but saw nothing. She was becoming infected with her guide's unease. Her city was not hers anymore, and she did not like it.

'What's that?' whispered Lilis. They were now creeping through a mean alley not far from the wharf city. She cocked her head.

'I didn't hear anything.'

'I did. There's someone behind that fallen-down arch.'

Tallia felt for her knife. 'Lilis,' she whispered. 'Get ready to run.'

Lilis said nothing.

'Lilis, listen to me. When I say the word, run and hide.'

'I'm your *guide*!' Lilis said fiercely.

Tallia did not press it. 'Very well; pretend that nothing has happened, but keep your eyes open.'

They continued. 'Someone's behind us,' said Lilis. Then, a few minutes later, 'They've gone – I think.'

'That might be worse,' said Tallia, glancing over her shoulder. The drifting mist made it impossible to tell if anyone was there. The alley seemed to run forever. There were no lamps here, and though the buildings hung over the street, every window was shuttered, shedding only stray bands of light. 'Do you know any other way out of here?'

'No!' said Lilis in the barest wisp of a voice.

A shadow crossed the end of the alley in front of them, then another.

'There's someone behind us again,' said Lilis.

'Ahead too,' Tallia muttered. 'It might be nothing. And then again – Lilis, if I am taken, make sure to run all the way to Mendark, because no one else will be able to get me free.'

Lilis did not answer, but Tallia could imagine the look on her face. Back on the streets, but no longer accepted there, her life would be brutally short.

They kept on. The mouth of the alley was illuminated by a lamp in the street beyond. Two guards appeared, staring in their direction.

'Hide!' said Tallia.

Lilis slid behind a heap of smelly refuse. Tallia crouched down in the darkness, praying that the guards would be gone before whoever was behind caught up.

The sentries moved into the alley, muttering and prodding the shadows with their spears. It was a determined search; no option but to attack first. Taking the chance that there were only two, Tallia exploded out of concealment. The first guard was poking around behind a water barrel. She landed behind him, thrust one long leg between his legs and with a tremendous heave up-ended him into the barrel. He flailed on the rim before she slammed his legs upright, plunging him head first into the water.

Tallia snatched up the fallen spear, whirling as the second guard thrust his weapon at her, lightning fast. Weaving out of the way, she stabbed the butt end of her spear into his belly. He gave a winded cry and doubled half over. It turned out to be a ruse, for he lunged, driving his spear into her thigh with a piercing cold pain. Tallia whacked desperately with her spear butt, catching him at the base of the throat. He dropped his weapon to stagger around, choking. She wrenched his spear out, cursing her carelessness. It was a deep gash, blood pouring out of it. So much for my boasting, she thought ruefully. I could bleed to death here. She tried to staunch the flow with the heel of her hand.

Behind her the other guard was still thrashing in the water barrel. He got one foot against the wall and managed to tip the barrel over. Her assailant was beginning to recover too, feeling around for his spear. Tallia watched him helplessly, then something shot through the light and struck him on the temple, sending him sprawling senseless in the muck.

Lilis was beside Tallia in an instant. 'What was that?' Tallia moaned.

'Half a brick! Are you all right?'

'No, I'm not.'

She hacked off the trouser leg and pressed a pad over the wound while Lilis stood by the two guards, prepared to defend her with a spear. The man from the barrel flapped listlessly, too far gone to offer any threat.

'Come on,' said Lilis, trying to support Tallia. 'There's someone coming the other way.'

The cloth pad was already saturated. 'I've got to get a bandage on,' Tallia groaned.

'No time!' said Lilis. 'Quick, lean on my shoulder.'

Lilis led her out onto the street and immediately back into the shadows of a lane not much wider than Tallia's shoulders. Tallia could feel the blood pumping out of her leg with every step. Someone shouted behind them. Looking back she saw a bony rat licking her blood off the cobbles.

Lilis dragged her up another lane, no wider than the first, across a courtyard, through a broken stone wall and into an overgrown hedge which showered them with icy drops.

Tallia felt quite dizzy. 'Stop! I can't go any further.'

'I have stopped,' said Lilis.

It was absolutely dark under the hedge. Lilis cut Tallia's trouser leg to strips and bandaged the wound by feel, pulling the bandages tight until the flow stopped. Tallia lay back in the mud, wondering how they were going to get home again. Endre was living up to its reputation.

The short trip back to the wharf city was one of the worst nights of pain and terror she had had in her life. She staggered the whole way, leaning on Lilis's shoulder, which was about the height of her waist. After crawling down the drain, eventually they did get back inside the wharf, not long before dawn. Lilis was a white-faced, red-spattered ghost, barely able to walk.

Just inside, Tallia collapsed. A mob of Hlune appeared out of the darkness, silently staring. Lilis drew Tallia's long knife and stood over her, waving the blade at any who came too near. 'Call Magister!' she screamed, and kept repeating that until a message was sent. Tallia's leg was scarlet from one end to the other. Finally the messenger reappeared with Mendark and Osseion.

Mendark inspected the wound, then Osseion lifted Tallia in his arms and carried her back to their cell.

Tallia woke to find the wound had been stitched and was being bandaged. 'Where's Lilis?' she whispered, looking around frantically.

'Sleeping,' said Osseion, pulling the bandage tight while Mendark held a dressing. 'Ah, what a brave, loyal friend you have there. No one could get near you until we arrived.'

'But you failed!' said Mendark. 'What are we going to do now? We're trapped!'

Mid-winter week dragged on endlessly – miserable days of foul weather where Tallia lay helplessly in her hammock waiting for her wound to heal enough so that she could walk. Berenet had gone out into Thurkad the night after her injury, but with no more success than she'd had. Since then he had not been able to get into Thurkad at all, for all the secret ways were watched now. The Hlune were incredibly hostile. Mendark expected to be thrown out onto the street at any moment.

Three days later Tallia was able to walk, though very painfully. 'I can't just sit here and let us be taken,' she said to Lilis. 'Do you know any other way at all?'

'Today is hythe, mid-winter's day,' said Lilis with a shudder. 'The worst day of the year.'

Tallia was not superstitious, but she did not like the idea either. 'I know, but I have to try.'

Lilis thought of one or two forgotten smuggler's tunnels that were worth trying, so with their stone-faced guide they set off for one last attempt. The trip was fruitless, for both ways were now watched by Yggur's guards. Tallia knew that her leg was not up to the job anyway.

After midnight they turned back, but halfway home saw an orange glow in the distance and heard the crackle and roar of fire. As Tallia began to hobble that way, a child ran out and spat on Lilis's boot. An old woman cursed them from a doorway, making warding signs with her fingers. The Hlune were a deeply superstitious race – no doubt that was why Yggur set his fires this day. A pair of Hlune with spears forced Tallia away.

They were escorted back to their room at spear-point, and every step of the way they were spat upon and abused. Near the doorway a jellyfish splattered against Lilis's jerkin; Tallia was struck on the back and head by rotten vegetables. Lilis was shaking with terror by the time they reached their room. Neither Mendark nor Berenet was there so they cleaned themselves up and Lilis went to bed. Tallia sat up in a chair with a blanket around her. Sometime later she was woken by Mendark, shaking her violently.

'Tallia, Tallia!'

Tallia wanted to tell him to go to blazes, but of course she did not. She pulled the blankets back up. 'I'm listening.'

'There was a fire earlier,' he said, very agitated.

'I saw it,' she said. 'Did it do much damage?'

'Considerable – it was a warning! The Hlune are hysterical with fear. Yggur knows we're here!' He twisted his stringy beard in his fingers.

'Are you sure?'

'I'm sure! He is threatening to burn the whole wharf city if they don't give us up.'

'It could be just an idle threat. How can he know?'

'Yggur doesn't make idle threats.'

'What do the Hlune say to him?'

'They deny ever seeing us, of course, and threaten to burn Thurkad in retaliation.'

'Would they?'

'Oh, they can be ruthless. But if I were Hlune, I would be going through the easier options first. I am no further use to

145

them; better to betray me and get back to business.'

'Loyalty must still count for something.'

'We've tested its limits. Find a way out, damn quick, or we're finished.'

That night Tallia was woken by voices just outside the door. It was Mendark, speaking to one of the Hlune, and Mendark was uncharacteristically humble.

'Please,' he said. 'Just a few more days.'

'No!' The Hlune's voice was rather like the honking of a gander. 'The fate of our city lies on the toss of a coin.'

'Perhaps,' said Mendark, dropping his voice, 'if I were to offer a little more compensation for your inconvenience . . .'

There was a long silence, so long that Tallia wondered if they had moved away. Then she heard a dull clink and the man honk-honked. 'I'll try to sway them. We want to help you, but Yggur is not predictable. Our city cannot be risked, not for all the gold in your chests.'

'*How long?*' cried Mendark, then realised that he was shouting. 'How long can you give us?' he whispered.

'Three more days. If you cannot find your way out by then, we will have no choice but to put you onto the street.'

'Three days!' Mendark gave a cry of despair.

Tallia eased her leg over the side of the hammock. It hurt terribly. Though it was impossible, she had to try again.

10

ARTICLES OF WAR

Dolodha climbed back up the shaft. Her tatty robes were saturated. Yggur was waiting on the floor above the basement where the cage had crashed, peering down into the gloom.

'The lower door is jammed,' Dolodha said, shivering. 'They're trying to free it.'

'And Mendark?' he asked in a deadly voice.

'He's got away!' She bowed so low that her hair swept the floor. 'A secret door. Two drowned but the rest escaped.'

Yggur raised his fist and she skipped sideways out of the way, right into the path of Vartila, who cracked her hard over the ear with her rod.

'Bad tidings!' Vartila snapped as the girl crawled off, blood running from a cut ear.

Maigraith expected Yggur to curb the Whelm, but he said nothing. She caught the messenger by the shoulder, intending to help her. The girl kept darting her head away as if expecting more punishment. Her thin body knew only obedience. 'Stop!' Maigraith shouted. Dolodha froze. She was dazed, appearing to be suffering from concussion, but as soon as she recovered she insisted on going back to her post.

Yggur climbed down the shaft into the basement. Shortly he returned in a cold fury. 'Gone!' he raged. 'A secret tunnel that we failed to find. The scryers will pay for this!'

'I'm sure they did their best,' Maigraith said softly. Yggur's rage after finding the simulacrum of Mendark had been terrible. She did not want to see it again.

'That isn't good enough!'

Maigraith began to feel most uneasy. What had she gotten herself into? 'Yggur,' she said, running beside him again, 'that poor messenger was treated very unfairly. Do you . . .?'

'She knows my Articles of War!' he said curtly. 'They are read every week. Succeed and you are rewarded! Fail and you are punished! What could be fairer?'

'How did she fail?'

'She bore bad tidings. Her group let me down and they must all suffer for it. And next time everyone will try harder.'

By the time they returned to Yggur's fortress it was morning. Maigraith, exhausted, lay down on a couch while Yggur paced back and forth. Try as he might, he had not been able to trace Mendark's escape way. 'Where can he have gone?' he said wildly. 'Can Mendark have got out of Thurkad already?'

'I think not,' said Zareth, stroking his chin-plaits. 'Though . . . he might have had a small boat hidden.'

'Find out!' Yggur raged. 'Has he got free? By land or by sea? Or is he still in the city, holed up somewhere in the slums, *or the wharf city*? Should I try to burn him out? What say you to that, Zareth?' Yggur spoke with mischievous intent, for Zareth was Hlune, of that race which dwelt within the wharf city and controlled all seaborne commerce with Thurkad.

'My advice is not impartial,' Zareth said calmly. 'But you must know this: we Hlune have prepared defences against fire, for it is our greatest fear. They may not succeed, but if the wharf city goes, be sure that Thurkad will be razed to the ground.'

'The whole city is a fire trap,' said Yggur. 'I'll send embassies to the wharf city, and to that monster S'Courcy too, to cajole and threaten. We'll find him!'

'Faelamor is sick,' said Maigraith, feeling duty neglected. 'I must go to her.'

'Good idea.' He shouted orders and two Whelm accompanied Maigraith up the stairs. 'Don't let her die. There is much she can teach me.'

She found Faelamor much as she had been before – quite apathetic, lying asleep or, when awake, staring at the ceiling. Occasionally she rose to stumble around the room for a few minutes before collapsing on her bed again.

When Maigraith returned to Yggur's command centre he was still working furiously. He had not slept for days and was by now an automaton, totally obsessed with the hunt for Mendark and the securing of the city. Maigraith found this obsession disturbing. Nonetheless she sat beside him, saying nothing as he issued orders for the control of Thurkad and the punishment of those of his servants who had failed.

Finally, that afternoon, he looked up and noticed Maigraith slumped in a chair, desperate for sleep. 'I'm sorry,' he said, not even smiling. 'I cannot rest until my enemy is taken. Dolodha!'

The messenger, a drab bundle on the floor, sprang up. The side of her head was swollen and her split ear scabbed with brown blood.

'Show Maigraith to my apartments,' he said. 'Make her a bath and a bed. Attend all her needs.'

Dolodha led Maigraith away through long corridors to a large door that was guarded by two Whelm. Dolodha relayed the orders; they were admitted inside. A bath was run.

'It's cold!' Maigraith exclaimed, testing it with her toes. She was by no means accustomed to luxury, but a cold bath in winter was less than she expected.

'You want a *hot* bath?' whispered Dolodha, with such astonishment that Maigraith did not insist.

'This will be adequate,' she replied curtly, and was in and out in record time. Her dirty clothes had already disappeared. She put on the robe that Dolodha held out for her and was shown to a large though spartan room that quite clearly was

Yggur's. Maigraith was dismayed. Whatever the relationship with Yggur might eventually turn out to be, this was impossible.

'I can't sleep here!' she said.

Dolodha shrugged, continuing to turn down the bed. Maigraith went to the main door and opened it. The Whelm guard outside barred her way.

'Let me through!' said Maigraith.

The man shook his head. 'I have no orders to allow you out until the morning.'

'Then go and tell Yggur it is not my wish to sleep here.'

'I cannot leave my post!' he said woodenly.

Normally Maigraith would have hurled him out of the way, but the past days had drained her dry. She stumbled back to the bathroom to sit down on the edge of the bath.

'Bed is ready,' said Dolodha, standing beside her.

'I can't sleep there,' Maigraith repeated, looking through the other rooms.

'Master has given orders,' said Dolodha fretfully, touching her scabbed ear.

Maigraith had no wish to see the girl punished again. She tore the covers off the bed, to Dolodha's distress, and curled up on the floor of the living room. Her last sight as she drifted off to sleep was Dolodha standing watch, frozen-faced, in the doorway, and the girl's red and bloody ear – only the first punishment for the failure of her group.

She woke in the morning, realising that her worries had been ground-less. Yggur had not come up at all. Dolodha lay on the floor asleep, but the instant Maigraith rose she ran to fix breakfast.

Afterwards Maigraith went to see Faelamor again, whom she found too listless to speak. Maigraith spent the morning sitting beside her, preoccupied with Faelamor's declining health. What if she died? In spite of her feelings about Faelamor, the chains of duty and obedience were still strong. Her life would have little meaning without her liege.

Following Mendark's escape from the citadel, Yggur was so frantically busy that Maigraith barely saw him. Confined as she was to the fortress, surrounded by Whelm that she could never see without the horrors of her previous torment rising up, she began to brood and to think that she had made a fatal mistake by coming here.

She spent most of her time in Yggur's command centre, watching him, though they seldom exchanged more than a few words. What did he want from her? He was so preoccupied, so turned in on himself that it was impossible to find out. What did she expect of him, for that matter? A companion, a friend, *a lover*? Faelamor had never allowed her to have a friend in all the time Maigraith had served her. Duty had been her only friend and Maigraith had no idea how to begin with Yggur.

'Yggur,' she said tentatively that afternoon.

He turned a blank face to her. His hands shuffled the despatches on the table, impatient to get back to work. The officers and servants watched her, as still as insects. She stared into his sunken eyes, becoming more confused, more self-conscious every second. He had vital work to do and she was an unwelcome interruption.

'Nothing,' she said, then crept back to her seat.

A dozen more times she tried to speak to him, but never managed to get out what she wanted to say. His face went blank whenever he looked at her. She could glean no idea of his thoughts, and this inhibited her from speaking her own lest she totally misunderstand him.

Maigraith fell into a fit of brooding, a smouldering resentment. After starting out with such timid hopes, and having those hopes dashed, then raised when Yggur said he cared for her, the past days had been terrible. He said not one kind word to her, nor even a harsh one – Yggur totally ignored her. Maigraith tended to hide her feelings rather than speak them, and finally they would burst out in a blaze of fury. If this was what friendship was like, she was better off alone.

Then I *will* be alone! she thought furiously. I'm not going to hang around, begging like a puppy. I will leave this very day, if he will allow it, and if he doesn't I will create such fuss and fury that he will wish he had never met me.

'Damn you!' she shouted, shaking her fist at him as he went into yet another meeting with his generals. 'What are your plans for me?'

The blood rushed to Yggur's face; the pen in his hand gouged the paper. Abruptly he rounded on his soldiers and servants. 'Out!' he roared.

When the room was empty at last, he said softly, 'Be so kind as to keep your personal problems to yourself when I am working.'

'I will, in future,' she raged. 'I'm leaving!'

'Leaving?' He looked puzzled.

'You won't talk to me. I'm like a prisoner who is never told what she is in prison for. I was better off alone.'

'What do you want to talk about?'

'Anything!' she screamed. 'What are your plans for me?'

'I do not presume to have any plans for you,' he said quietly. 'Your company is – it pleases me. That is all.'

'What about *me*? I'm not your puppet, to grin when it pleases you and say nothing the rest of the time.'

He just stared at her, uncomprehending.

'By allying myself with you I go against Faelamor and everything she has worked for. I can't do that on a whim. I need more!'

'Maigraith . . .' he began, then froze. 'I . . . I can't . . .' He spun around, his back to her, letting out a muffled groan. When he turned back, his face was a mask of control. 'Come with me,' he said, and led her up to the top of the old fortress and out onto the battlements. Sleety wind blasted into their faces.

'I can't . . .' he started to say, then turned and paced away from her. 'Perhaps you *should* go. I don't have anything to offer you. I . . . I know myself, Maigraith, and what I know is not very . . . likeable. You know my history!'

She followed him. 'You were young, brilliant,' she said. 'You had everything. Then the Council – Mendark! – begged you to help them in their quest to banish Rulke from Santhenar.'

He shivered with the memories. She extended him her hand. 'You worked the Proscribed Experiments for them,' she continued, 'but Rulke was too strong. The Council broke, abandoned you, then Rulke possessed your mind and drove you mad, before he was finally imprisoned in the Nightland.'

'I feel it still,' he said, eyes staring into the past. 'The pain of possession, the terror of it happening again. Revenge on those two, Mendark and Rulke, has driven me ever since I woke from my madness. I remade myself into a machine. I am empty inside, Maigraith. A shell that contains nothing but hate and fear.'

This confession struck Maigraith more deeply than anything he had ever said. His whole body was quivering. She could feel it through his hand. 'You are not unfeeling,' she said, 'else you would not be hurting now. You care, and I care for you for knowing it. I also hurt inside – you know why.'

He clutched her slim hand in his hands, enveloping it completely. There were tears on his lashes.

'Maigraith,' he said. 'You are good for me. I don't know if I can do the same for you – I am frozen over.'

'I don't need much,' she whispered, walking beside him. 'But I do so long to be shown a little kindness.'

'Has no one ever treated you so?'

'My first teacher,' she said, 'but that is long, long ago. She would be dead for ages, poor Hana. And Karan – she tried her best to be my friend but I drove her away, abused her cruelly and let her down when I should have been a friend to her.' She looked up at his dark visage through mist-thickened eyelashes. 'I am well suited to you. I am cold inside; timid. I can't bear people to see my feelings. But perhaps . . .'

They walked along the length of the wall, through an empty guardhouse, and turned onto the next section. Suddenly he stopped and gripped her arms at the elbows.

'Perhaps? Are you making an offer? Speak plainly – I cannot abide talk that goes nowhere.'

'I am afraid to speak plainly in case I am mistaken,' she said. '*But I will!* I am making a suggestion that might become an offer. If you are willing.'

'Perhaps you and I could teach each other something?'

'Yes!' she whispered.

The wind whirled out from the other side of the guardhouse; a freezing blast. Maigraith, shivering, drew closer into the shelter offered by his big body. Some emotion rippled across his face; a struggle taking place. 'Would you . . .?' he whispered into the wind, moving his hands out then springing them back again.

'What?' she asked softly.

He shouted it across the battlements. 'Would you – embrace me?'

He spread his arms. Maigraith edged towards him. She put her arms out, sliding them under his. They stood in that awkward pose for a minute, close but not touching, then some inhibition broke in Maigraith. Sighing, she squeezed him tightly, and Yggur folded her in his arms.

They talked, when Yggur had time over from the war and his obsessions. They walked on the rooftop late at night, when all the work was done, or in the pre-dawn hours before it all began again. They touched, but only hands or arms. Occasionally they hugged. But that was all. Their relationship could not advance beyond that. And at every step she had to coax and cajole, for he knew even less about the matter than she did.

However, after a day or two Yggur fell back into his obsession with Mendark. Since taking Thurkad, things had not gone well – there were rebellions all over his realm, and quelling them stretched his resources and armies to their

154

limit. He was sure that Mendark was in the wharf city, but did not dare invade that trap.

'I'm sorry, Maigraith,' said Yggur. 'I – since I came here I've begun to lose control. My powers are less than they used to be. My sorcerous tools barely answer me here – as you saw when we tried to scry Mendark out. I must remake them to suit the aura of this queer place, but what then? And what happens once I leave?'

Almost a week had gone by since she had arrived here. Maigraith suddenly knew that their friendship was going nowhere; that though a part of him wanted more, it was all too hard. He was incapable of going further. Having come so far herself, Maigraith could not contemplate their relationship freezing at this point.

Yggur was too repressed, too fearful, too narcissistically bound up in his own torments. Unless she did something dramatic, they would fall apart as inevitably as the petals dropped off a flower. And having gone through such agonies, and having found a friend, even such an inadequate one as Yggur, Maigraith was not going to slide back into her previous desolate state.

She wished there was someone she could go to for advice, but the idea of asking any of the Whelm was laughable, and poor Dolodha – no less preposterous. There might have been many ways to lift their relationship out of this abyss, but only one occurred to her.

'There is nothing for it,' she said to herself. 'I will have to take him to bed.'

That was an unthinkable step for her, for in all her long life Maigraith had never lain with any man, nor indeed ever had the urge to. She knew no more about the act than was told in the classics and the manuals of animal husbandry that she had studied during her schooling. In short, she knew everything that could be written down and nothing that needed to be understood.

Her objective, once stated, was not so easily achieved.

Maigraith was as innocent of the art of seduction as a new-born babe. Moreover, even had she known such arts, the idea of actually employing them was mortifying to contemplate. Her oblique suggestions glanced off him like paper darts off armour – he simply did not get the message at all.

Forced to become bolder by his lack of response, she began to drop hints about the ways of a man and a woman together. He looked at her so blankly that Maigraith began to wonder if that part of him had not been destroyed in his earlier troubles.

Mid-winter week was finally over. Today was the first day of Talmard, the last and coldest month of winter. Another night approached. They sat down to dinner, late, and Maigraith called for wine. She intended to drink as little as possible, for wine had had disastrous consequences for her once before. But she poured for Yggur with a heavy hand, topping his bowl whenever it was half-empty. That was not often, for he was abstemious as a rule, but after he had taken a couple of bowls she felt that she must speak now or not at all.

The words stalled in her mouth, the first few times she tried to speak them. Rising to top up his already full bowl she knocked her chair over backwards.

He put his hand over the bowl. 'Enough!' he said curtly. 'What is it you want of me?'

It exploded out of her, as her repressed feelings tended to do. 'I want *you!*' she cried, her face as red as the wine in the bowl. 'Will you not come to bed with me?'

Yggur's mouth fell open in astonishment. 'Bed?' he said.

Maigraith was mortally embarrassed. Had she made the worst mistake of her life? But to back down now would be far worse than going on.

'Are you not . . . *capable?*' she asked delicately.

He frowned, seeming to be trying to recall what the word meant. 'I am a man,' he said. 'I am capable. At least, I used to be.' He looked up at her. 'I have not wanted to for a long, long time.'

'Oh!' she said, unsure what he was telling her.

'This is something that you need?' he asked.

'I have needs,' she said ambiguously. 'I thought . . . if we were to embrace each other . . . intimately . . . it is a bonding of the body and the soul. It would be good for us both.'

Yggur contemplated the idea. 'But we have not so much as kissed.'

'We have not,' she replied, staring at his mouth. 'But I would like to.'

'Come here.'

Suddenly their roles were turned about. Maigraith did not even know how to kiss. She moved toward him very tentatively and found that the kiss was not unsatisfying, though his thin lips were hard and his beard scratchy. After a few seconds they separated. She rubbed her mouth with the heel of her hand, looking at him wonderingly.

'If you would care to go up,' he said, 'I will follow directly.'

Maigraith bathed, undressed, then slipped into Yggur's bed. The rough sheets set her naked flesh afire. She had given herself into his power. What was going to happen to her now? What would he require of her? And what would he do if she did not come up to his expectations?

Yggur reappeared, smelling of the bath. He snuffed the lights out one by one.

'Leave a light burning, if you please,' she whispered.

'Oh!' he said, but left the lamp beside the bed. He stood there for a moment with his head bowed, then abruptly slid off his cloak and slipped under the covers.

He lay still for such a long time that she was afraid he had gone straight to sleep, but when she finally touched him he rolled over and embraced her awkwardly, barely touching.

The wire frame of her glasses dug into her ear. Maigraith took them off and the light caught her carmine eyes. His own eyes showed shock and dismay. He clutched at her, his chin resting on the top of her head, and for a moment there was a look of horror in his eyes.

Yggur knew more about Maigraith's heritage than she did herself, for while he had held her prisoner in Fiz Gorgo last autumn, she had been unable to take the drug that Faelamor had given her to conceal the colour of her eyes. They had slowly begun to change back to that strange colour, indigo and carmine, that had identified her to Yggur at once. Only Charon, or those who had much Charon blood in them, had eyes of such colour.

That had not seemed to matter in Fiz Gorgo, but now, with the Mirror gone and the Ghâshâd returned, and turmoil beyond his control everywhere in his realm, it mattered more than ever. Just to look into Maigraith's eyes reminded Yggur of his enemy, the greatest Charon of all. Yet he knew that the Charon blendings had been ruthlessly hunted down after the fall of Rulke. *Who was she?*

She lay in his arms for some time, wondering about his unnatural stillness. Finally she put her lips right against his ear. 'Yggur,' she whispered. Her hot breath roused him.

Maigraith found their lovemaking a strange affair, for he kept moving so that she always had her back to the light. The business was soon over, and scarcely satisfying to either of them, but she had not expected much from it. However, the embrace, the sense of being held in his arms and of being one with him, was a new and wonderful thing for her. Rolling over, she looked into his eyes, smiled dreamily and fell asleep.

But as she did so, the lamplight shone in her eyes again, making them glow carmine, and Yggur felt a spasm of terror. Charon eyes! He wanted to leap out of bed and run all the way back to his swamp-bound fortress, to forget everything about the Mirror, his empire and his long-planned revenge. But he could not.

He gazed down at her face. Maigraith was indeed lovely, for in repose the downcast look that always marred her features was gone. He stroked her slender throat, then the image of those eyes came back and he felt an overpowering urge to dig his thumbs into her windpipe and rid himself of the menace that she represented. But he could not do that either.

He laid his head down on the pillows and groaned. In her sleep Maigraith reached out and held him to her, but Yggur did not sleep all night.

PART TWO

11

A CASE OF AMNESIA

Long she lay there, too weak to be anxious; safe in her lassitude, enfolded tightly in warmness, unusual but pleasant. Drifting, dreaming, all fears and terrors, all memories gone. Nothing left but ghosts of long ago. She was walking in the snow, in the moonlight, watching the creeping stars, the bloodstained moon. Calling excitedly as a meteor spark carved the sky. The cry of a mountain cat soared on the wind. She gripped the huge hand more tightly, despite the danger feeling utterly safe, protected, held.

Later, a familiar old room, the fire crackling, the crook of one big arm enfolding her. The wind sobbed outside, coming down the chimney with gusts of flame and smoke. She snuggled up against her father's chest, eyes closed, surrounded by the rumble of his voice, living the tales of ancient days, pictures so clear that they might have been painted on the inside of her eyelids.

A red-haired girl was walking in the snow. Was that her, or another of his winter-night stories? She sighed an inward sigh, then the pain in her head came back. A terrible ripping pain, steel barbs being drawn through her forehead. Pain that was the echo of earlier pain. Oblivion.

At last a faint creaking penetrated her semiconsciousness. She did not stir; could not even will it. The silence resumed its timeless beat. She dreamed again. Or relived. *Or lived!*

Creak-squeak – there it was again! Wood on wood, she realised. It surprised her, that she had passed from dream to thought, was able to think, had an identity. Creak-squeak. A little thread of curiosity tugged at her and she woke at last. She opened her eyes cautiously, lest she betray herself, though she could not have told why.

The room was small and dark. The wall beside her was stone, the smooth blocks gleaming with dampness. Her eyes roved along the wall. The part of the room that she could see was empty. No; beyond the foot of her bed a fire burned smokily in a little grate. On the mantelpiece above, a thick stub of yellow candle gave off a guttering light. Beside the candle was a large round green pottery flask. On the other side of the fire sat an old man. He had his feet on the wall and rocked back and forth, the chair creaking. The old man was dressed in dark, shabby clothes and brown boots. His short beard was grey; his hair grey and thin. Only the side of his face was visible.

Creak-squeak. The old man stirred in his chair. He looked to be studying a map drawn on bark paper. She closed her eyes and lay still. The chair scraped along the floor. The old man grunted, then liquid gurgled. She opened an eye cautiously. He poured the remainder of the flask into his bowl, replaced the flask on the mantelpiece and, settling back in his chair, sipped from the bowl.

She closed her eyes again. A single droplet of memory came back – a great meeting! There had been chains on her ankles. Moving one foot under the covers she touched the other ankle and winced. It was still tender from the shackles. Karan! she thought. *That's me!* Then came a gush of remembrance – a messenger bursting in: Yggur at the gates, the armies of Thurkad destroyed. Another trickle: Tensor mad, desolate, despairing, putting out his fist. Then nothing, absolutely nothing.

How had she ended up in this damp, shabby room? Who was the old man who sat at the end of her bed? Her head ached desperately. The Mirror was gone! Taken far away. All that she had suffered, all those who had died because of it, had been for nothing.

No, it was not her responsibility anymore. *I can go home*, Karan sighed. The memory of her battered, time-worn Gothryme appeared, pink granite walls glowing in the afternoon sun. Home at last! A mist began to rise inside her head again, the image faded and gratefully she abandoned herself to the darkness.

There was pain in her head such as she had never felt before, in the splinters of time that made up her awareness. Pain like aftersickness, but far worse. Between the pain she was wracked by nightmares more real than life, more violent, more horrible. Better the pain than the nightmares. She cried out; shrieked, sweated, burned, then sank back into the ocean of pain.

All she could smell was red iron. Red behind her eyes. Blind-red. There was shouting and crashing. Her fingers caught a thick stickiness, skinned like boiled milk, and brought it to her nose. Blood! She lay in a puddle of congealed blood. Now the hairs on the back of her neck rose, as though someone stood looking down at her. Chilly fingers touched her throat. Gathering the dregs of her strength, Karan screamed out her agony and her terror.

A long time later she bobbed to the surface again, sensing movement in the room. A flare in the dark. Cool on her brow. Cold rasping her face, her neck, her back, sponging all of her. Dark.

Shrieking, sweating, burning. Lips aflame, gullet searing. Choking, retching, gasping. Darkness darker than dark.

Much later Karan was awakened by a presence looming over her. She lay unmoving, willing him away, and the old man resumed his chair by the fire with a scrape and a creak. Opening her eyes, she saw that another candle stub flickered in the puddle of wax on the mantelpiece. She turned her head, the movement hurting only a little, to inspect the other side of the room. The wall had once been rudely plastered though most of the plaster had fallen off long ago. The door was made of thick planks and securely barred.

'Karan! I thought I'd lost you yesterday.'

Karan started. The man lowered his boots onto the hearth with a thud, then stood up. She shrank back into the pillow. He was old though not ancient, shorter than middle height, with a big chest and shoulders. Up close he was vaguely familiar. He looked of no account; sounded it too, with his slow country voice and his broad face tanned to leather. Once he would have been nothing to her, but now she felt so weak, so shattered in self-confidence and worth, that he represented a great obstacle and a threat. She did not know what to do.

'Who are you?' The syllables rasped her throat like a bladder full of sand.

'I am your healer. Your guardian for a time,' he replied.

'My gaoler!'

He shrugged. 'As you will. Without me you would be dead. But I am no friend of Yggur. I do my own business. My name is Shand.'

What is your business with me, Shand? she wondered. The name was vaguely familiar. Had Llian mentioned him at some stage? *Llian!* Instantly Karan felt such a tightness in her chest that she could hardly breathe. What had happened to Llian? She jerked herself upright in her bed and a barbed spike seemed to plunge right through her temple. Slowly Shand came into focus again. 'Where's Llian? Is he . . . He's not . . .' She could not bear to say it.

Shand leaned over her. 'Llian?' There was an edge to his voice that she could not identify.

How bright his green eyes were, how penetrating. He did

not look of no account now. Suddenly she felt afraid of this stranger.

'We came to Thurkad together,' she said. 'We travelled together for more than a month. He saved my life. I must know where he is. Please.' She put her hand on his wrist.

Shand looked annoyed. 'Thurkad is in chaos. Pointless to look; impossible to find.'

She snatched her hand away. The life was coming back into her green eyes, the colour to her pallid cheeks. Shand bent down, and what he saw in her eyes appeared to move him.

'Almost impossible,' he said, more kindly. 'There has been great bloodshed, great destruction. Yggur holds most of the city now. Half the population of Thurkad are refugees. But I will try.'

He pushed her gently but quite firmly back on the pillow. 'Just now you need rest more than anything. Lie down.'

'Someone must know where Llian is.' Tears came to her eyes. She had no strength to wipe them away. 'But don't tell him about me.'

'Him?'

Mendark! she thought, sitting up again. The name had come back to her, driving her into a panic. I remember *him*. 'Mendark! Say nothing about me, if he asks. Mendark is my enemy.'

Shand sighed. 'You don't have to worry about Mendark. He's trapped in the Old City.'

'Please,' she whispered.

'I'll ask where I can.'

The pain in her temple was excruciating. It was impossible to think. Karan's arms were trembling from the effort of holding herself up. She flopped back down, suddenly realising how weak she was.

'Where . . .' She scarcely had the energy to speak. 'Where am I? What happened to me?' The room wavered before her eyes. 'What do you mean to do with me?'

'I don't know what happened to you,' Shand replied in

the soft voice that was somehow younger than his weathered face. 'When I found you, you were in great peril: delirious, dying. I brought you here to safety. There will be time later for questioning, and answering.' Taking her limp wrist in one hand, he put the other over her eyes. 'Sleep!'

The warmth and the dark were so comforting that her fears slipped away. With a little sigh Karan slid into sleep and did not even dream.

Shand stood looking down at her for a moment, then when he was sure she was asleep he quietly unbarred the door, locked it behind him and made his way out onto the street.

When Karan woke again it was morning, a pale grey light slanting across the room from gaps below and above the door. The old man was not there. The fire had gone out and the room was frigid. She sat up slowly. The room swirled. After the dizziness had passed she eased her legs out of bed and stood up, leaning on the edge of the bed for support. Her feet cringed away from the cold stone. She looked down at herself. Her only garment was a worn grey shift, more like a singlet in length. Once Karan's form had been inclined to roundness; now she was shocked to see that she was gaunt, as if she had woken in someone else's body. The bones of her hips protruded; her legs were thin, her ribs outlined against the shift. How long had she been unconscious?

She had forgotten the latter part of her journey to Thurkad, erased it from her mind, and did not know that she had lost all appetite at Sith, weeks before the Conclave, and since then had taken just enough to sustain herself.

Her clothes were nowhere visible, so Karan wrapped a blanket around her. Step by cautious step she made her way along the edge of the bed then across to the fireplace. There she sank onto the chair, shivering, staring at the ashes. After a while she realised that she was ravenously hungry, a hunger so intense that she was almost ill as soon as she became aware of it. She could not find anything to eat, though a half-full water jug sat on a chest beside the door.

Cracking the ice on the top with her finger, she gulped the water. It was so cold that it made her teeth ache, and as it hit the pit of her stomach she doubled over with cramps and lay retching and gasping amid the ashes. Eventually the spasm passed but Karan was too weak to move.

The lock clicked. The latch lifted. Shand's grey head thrust through the door. His back was bent under a large bundle of firewood – panels from a front door, charred on one side, blistered green paint on the other, smashed to splinters on either end. There were smaller pieces in complementary colours, mouldings and bits of fluted architrave. It had been someone's home. That made her heart ache again for Gothryme.

Karan looked up dully. There was ash in her hair, a black smear on one cheek. He took her small hand. It was very cold.

'Why didn't you get back into bed, little cinder girl?'

'I couldn't,' she whispered. 'I'm starving! How long have you held me here?'

'I haven't *held* you here, as you put it,' he said with a trace of irritation. 'I found you three days ago in the Great Hall.'

'Great Hall? I don't understand,' she said, as Shand lifted the lid of the chest and rummaged inside. The recollections of the previous day were quite gone. 'No. Yes, Nelissa! Arbitrating? Is that the right word? The Mirror. A messenger . . .' She trailed off, confused. It was as if her memories had been rent into fragments and mixed together like shreds of paper in a basket. Nothing seemed to connect to anything else.

The lid of the chest banged. Shand came back with half a loaf of stale grainy bread that might have been made from flour swept up from the floor of a mill. It was full of husks and hairs, grit and little dark pellets the shape of mouse

169

droppings. There was also some dried-up cheese with flecks of mould inside the cracks, a couple of onions and, from a chipped brown jar, scraps of pickled vegetables so soft and colourless that they might have been left over from the impeachment of the last Autarch of Thurkad. He cut the food into pieces on a metal plate and put it in her hands. The blanket had fallen to one side, exposing small feet and slender ankles. Shand bent down and tucked them back in. He did not look threatening today, just worried.

'I'm sorry,' he said. 'It's hardly fit to eat but all I could get. I picked a poor time to come to Thurkad. Eat only a little at a time otherwise you will be sick. Your stomach is unused to food.'

'My stomach is unused even to water,' Karan said ruefully, taking up a piece of the brown bread. She inspected the morsel, picked out the most suspect particles and nibbled at what remained. 'What happened to me?'

Shand explained what little he knew of the ending of the Conclave. Karan struggled to remember, but there was nothing there apart from the names, a few islands of memory in an infinite sea.

He made a nest of kindling in the fireplace and in barely a minute the fire was blazing, filling the room with the smell of burning resin.

'How came I here then?'

'I went to the Great Hall – I hardly know why – and found you, barely clinging to life. I carried you here.'

Karan looked down at her plate, selected a fragment of pickled root. 'What happened to the other people at the Conclave?' she asked, gnawing the sour, fibrous and tasteless vegetable.

'I don't know and I can't find out. Yggur holds most of Thurkad, and soon he will have it all. Mendark is still defending the citadel, but it must soon fall.'

The names meant nothing to her; she had forgotten them again. 'What about . . . Maigraith?'

'I don't know her. Perhaps she is one of the unidentified dead.'

Karan shook her head, which still hurt. 'I would surely know it.' Then she regretted speaking. Shand might work out that she was a sensitive and sell her to whoever would pay most for her talent. That was a common fate of sensitives, especially in wartime.

'Perhaps she fled from the war,' he said.

'Perhaps.' She hesitated. 'Did you learn anything about Llian?'

'I spoke to one of the people who took away the dead. He was not among them.' Shand poked the fire with the end of a billet of wood. It spat little sparks back at him.

'Why did you bother with me, Shand? I keep asking, but you do not answer. Where have you taken me?'

'We are in an old part of the city,' said Shand. 'So labyrinthine and poor that none come here except those who can find nowhere else to live. Even Yggur's armies have kept out, though that will change after the citadel falls. You're not safe here – you stole his Mirror!'

'How long do I have?'

'No way to tell. Perhaps only hours.'

Karan's head lay on her arms like a great slug. She realised that Shand had been talking for some time, but she had not heard a word. She closed her eyes. Shand lifted her easily and carried her to the bed. She crawled within, still wrapped in her blanket, and fell into sleep.

Shand laid down his map and automatically reached for the wine. No! he said to himself, but a minute later had it in his hand again. Settling back in the chair, he put the flask to his mouth. The fortified drink was a comfort but there was not enough left to give him what he wanted – hazy oblivion, temporary absolution for his sins.

You're a fool, Shand! You should have stayed in Tullin where you couldn't do any harm.

He had once been one of the great, matching power and wits with the leaders of nations, but a personal tragedy had caused him to abandon all that. A long time ago he had retired to the mountain village of Tullin, about as far from the seats of power as it was possible to get. There for many years he had chopped wood and done chores at the inn for his living. Then one day the world had come to Tullin.

Late last autumn Llian had appeared there, sent out of malice on an errand he was ill-suited for: to find Karan and the Mirror of Aachan and bring them safely to Mendark. Shand could shut out the world no longer, but he found that the power and strength he had once taken for granted were gone – he had grown old.

He was in trouble now, helpless and afraid. The power that had frightened the Whelm away from Llian that night in Tullin had just been show, like a lizard puffing out its frill. All show, and if his enemies saw through it he would be as helpless as Karan on her sick-bed. He took up the map again. Shand had always been fascinated by maps and spent his spare time studying and making them, but he could not concentrate and laid it aside in favour of the wine.

As he sipped, he stared into the flames, musing. He had known Karan's father, Galliad, well. *Look out for the child, if something happens to me*, Galliad had said long ago.

Shand had laughed at that. Galliad had been a capable, clever man. 'What could possibly happen to you?'

'I have enemies but few friends. That does not bother me greatly, for myself. I have had a long life. But Karan is special.'

Shand had smiled and Galliad did too. 'Yes, every child is special but she is very special. She is sensitive, but she is more than just a blending of human and Aachim, as you might think. I will tell you the story sometime. If anything happens to me, keep an eye on her. I ask no more than that.'

Soon after Galliad had been killed in the mountains and Shand had never learned what he had to tell about Karan.

Her mother took her own life and the child went to her mother's people. Later Karan had disappeared, and though he eventually traced her to Shazmak, his oblique enquiries received the curt response that she had come back to her own. And there Shand had left it, returning with some relief to his own life.

Then, two months ago, Karan had appeared near Tullin, a grown woman, hunted by the Whelm, and he had done less than he should have to help her. He felt ashamed and responsible for what had happened afterwards. He had to amend that, no matter the cost to himself.

There came a racket down the hall. Shand jumped. A random act of violence in this war could wipe them both out. Karan groaned in her sleep. He sprang out of his chair, but it was just another of her nightmares. He put the bottle away and sat beside the bed, stroking her brow until she grew calm again and her eyes ceased their racing.

Karan the woman was not so different from the child he had met long ago. She was nothing like her big dark father and not much like her beautiful blonde mother, who had been as petite and fragile as a bird. Karan was striking too, unusually so, for she threw right back to a minor branch of the Aachim of old. She was small, pale of skin, her eyes the deep green of malachite and her hair as red as sunset. She was round of face, with wide high cheekbones and delicate features.

Shand went back to the bottle and the fire, remembering what he had seen in the Great Hall. The violence that had been done there shocked him, seasoned to war though he had once been. He'd walked among the bodies, finding several that he could rouse with a touch and a tot from his flask, and sent them staggering out into the rain. Shand had been about to follow them, for the sounds of war were all around and he was afraid of being trapped, when he saw the bundle against the wall with the unmistakeable hair.

Karan! What was she doing here? He was faced with the result of his dereliction in Tullin, not just for Karan but for the whole world. She was still alive, but for how much longer? What could he do? He had not been in Thurkad for many years. Most of his old contacts were dead. How would he ever find the surviving ones in this chaos?

Throwing Karan over his shoulder, Shand went out into the rain, walking the alleys for hours, trying to find a place to hide. Every door was locked and no one would let him in for any amount of money. In the end, afraid that Karan was dying, he smashed the lock of a shabby tenement with his staff, forced his way in, found an empty room, paid the terrified landlady a week in advance and set to work, to bring Karan back to life.

A door slammed nearby, bringing Shand back to the present. Outside, the war continued as deadly as ever. He had hidden from himself for too long. He was old, with nothing but his rusty wits between them and the enemy. Just carrying her here had shown him how feeble he was. He took up the bottle again.

Karan woke with an effort, like swimming upwards through a lake of mud. She realised that it was not the whole room shaking, merely her shoulder.

'Get up! They're looking for you. We've got to go *now*!'

She sat up, staring at Shand, who turned away abruptly, busying himself in the far corner of the room. What did he want from her? Experience had taught Karan that most people wanted something. Was there a price on her, or did he want to make use of her sensitive talents?

Shand looked up from his packing. 'Come on, come on,' he said roughly. 'There's no time for dreaming.'

'Where are my clothes?' she said crossly. 'I can't go out in a blanket.'

He stooped, reached beneath the end of the bed and pulled out a small cloth bundle. 'That's all you had. Hurry!' He unbarred the door and stood there, listening intently.

The bundle was tied with a knot. She fumbled at it with

174

strengthless fingers. The door clicked. Shand was gone. She felt, suddenly, very afraid.

Karan heard shouting down the hall; then fists beating against a door. Her scalp crawled. To her surprise the knot came apart; she hadn't known that her fingers were still working on it. She shook out the bundle. Her familiar baggy green trousers fell out. Dropping the blanket, she pulled the dirty shift over her head and drew the trousers on. Just doing that exhausted her.

The shouting and banging resumed down the hall. Karan listened with mouth agape as a door was assaulted, seemingly with an axe. Soldiers were searching the building. The axe crashed into the door, one, two, three, four smashing blows, then a scream so high and piercing that it hurt her ears. She burrowed under the covers but nothing could block out the sound.

RAT CITY

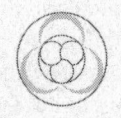

O utside, all was silent again. Karan looked down at the rag in her hands – her faded olive shirt. No boots, no undergarments, no hat, no coat. The shirt must have been torn off her – it was rent right down the front. How could she go out in that? And it had been washed hastily or carelessly, for it was mouldy and had a bloody stain down one side.

She put the shirt on with a shudder. Outside the screaming began again. At that moment Shand leapt through the door. 'Where are the rest of my clothes?' she demanded.

'I don't know – don't ask stupid questions! Quick, get your boots on!' He ran back and forth in a panic, picking things up and throwing them down again.

Bending down to look for her boots, Karan felt so weak and dizzy that she almost passed out. She had to cling to the side of the bed to save herself from falling. 'I have no boots,' she said, remembering that she had been taken to the Conclave barefoot and in chains.

Shand cursed. 'Then you will have to go without!'

He dragged her through the door. Helpless as she was, his coldness and anger struck her. Outside, the warmth she had brought from the bed was gone instantly. Halfway down the gloomy corridor they passed a splintered door and looked into a room as shabby as their own. A woman clutched a dead child to her breast screaming uncontrollably. Shand dragged the staring Karan away.

At a corner he put his head around cautiously, then ducked back. 'Guards!' he said, jerking her arm so hard that her head spun.

'Where . . . going?' Karan asked thickly. She could feel her head lolling on her shoulders; feel the madness not far away.

Shand dragged her the other way at a fast walk, then down a narrow stairway. 'To the cellars,' he said.

They went through a door into darkness. Shand lit one of his candle stubs and picked his way through a filthy storeroom to a damp basement that looked empty but for rows of barrels. 'All these places have their bolt holes and their ways out,' he said, walking along the wall holding up his light. 'In the olden days they used to store water for the whole building here.'

Karan sat on the floor while Shand worked. She felt a little better now. 'How did they get it in?' she wondered. Ever since her days in Shazmak, Karan had been keenly interested in matters of plumbing; she was always looking for new ways to improve Gothryme. Home – the thought dropped her into a well of loneliness and longing.

'I'm looking for a trapdoor into the alley,' Shand continued. 'I saw it from outside yesterday.' There was a fresh uproar, not far away. 'Farsh!' he swore. His hand shook, splashing warts of hot candle wax on his nose. He dashed them away. 'Quick, put your back to the door.'

Karan did so, feeling around in the dim light for bolts or locks. There were none. She sagged against the door, watching Shand running back and forth with his light, knowing that they must be caught and it would be worse than if they had stayed in their room. Since they were running away, they had to be guilty.

'Here it is,' said Shand, holding his light up to the wall.

Karan's brief hope was dashed as she felt the door move behind her. She braced herself, her feet slipping on the slimy floor. Over at the wall Shand was struggling with rusty bolts.

177

'Door's stuck,' she heard distinctly from the other side. 'Don't think anyone's been in here in a long time.'

'You want to explain that to the Whelm?' another man rumbled. 'Get it open!'

Karan felt the panic rising. She wanted to lie down on the floor and scream out her terror.

'Hold it!' hissed Shand.

There was a tremendous smash in her ear and something stung her cheek. An axe blade was protruding through the door beside her ear – a couple of fingers the other way and it would have gone into the back of her head.

Karan moaned, staring at the blade. Shand snuffed the candle. The axe was wrenched out, then the door smashed open so hard that Karan was sent flying across the room. Fireworks went off behind her eyes. Someone sprang through the door and another followed him.

'There's someone in here,' shouted the first man. 'Quick, the lantern!'

The light dazzled her. She lay where she was, too dazed to move.

'Doesn't look like anyone on the list,' the first man said, 'but we'd better take her in anyway. Go and check behind those barrels.'

He bent over Karan and lifted her head up. She gave him a vacant stare.

'Name!' he demanded. He was the hairiest man she had ever seen, his face almost completely obscured by a matted brown beard. Karan was terrified.

'Mellus,' she squeaked, a name like one of her middle names.

'Where from?'

'Go –, Go –' Gothryme almost came out, despite herself.

'Where?'

'Goss – Gossior,' she choked. 'Across the sea.' With her blend of accents, Karan knew that she could have come from anywhere.

Just then there was a scuffle down near the barrels. The light went out. The soldier let Karan fall and ran back that way. There came a meaty thump. They'd killed Shand – she knew it. A shadow appeared behind her.

'Come on,' said Shand. He picked her up, carried her over to the wall, felt for the trapdoor and lifted it up with one hand. Awkwardly he heaved her up with the other. 'Get hold! Stick your head out and see if anyone's looking. Quick!'

Karan put her head out into the rain. 'Can't see –' she said.

Shand thrust her through, a great heave on her backside, and she fell into the wet alley. He followed, grunting.

'What did you do?' she asked, picking wood splinters out of her cheek.

'Whacked them with a barrel stave. I feel better already. Come on. They'll be after us shortly, and they've seen your face now.'

They emerged onto the street beside an anonymous grey stone building. Black clouds overhead promised more sleet. The wind clubbed Karan in the back, striking through her shirt like cobweb. The cobbles were coated with slush and ice. She staggered along, holding her shirt together at the front, weeping with the cold and the pain. The street was nearly deserted. Those few who had been forced outdoors hurried past with heads low and eyes downcast: three pinch-faced men in maroon gowns and hoods (unlikely that Yggur would tolerate *that* cult); a boy with a basket of scabby vegetables; an old woman, limping.

Karan stubbed her toe on a broken cobble, slipped and fell on her face in the freezing slush. To lie there hurt less than to try to get up. Shand heaved her to her feet. Swaying, she saw that her toe was pouring blood onto the grey snow. Shand was off again. Karan staggered after him. She had never felt so weak.

'Shand!' she called, a little squeak of a voice.

He turned back, almost running. 'I can't go on,' she said.

He put his arm around her waist, holding her tightly, almost lifting her off the ground. They rounded the corner of the building. Straight ahead were four soldiers, interrogating a middle-aged man. Shand hesitated for a second, but a soldier beckoned. Karan had no courage left.

'Be yourself. They are only soldiers,' he said under his breath. 'Say nothing. Pretend you are dumb or witless.'

That won't be difficult, Karan thought. But these were veterans, tough and old. There would be no fooling them. As they approached, Shand put her down. She stood in a puddle, trembling as in a fit.

One of the guards, an unshaven giant with a bandaged shoulder, twisted the man's arm behind his back and pushed him to his knees in the slush. For a horrified moment Karan thought that they were going to execute him on the spot. The prisoner evidently thought so too, for he put his free arm up over his head in a pathetic attempt to protect his neck from the sword. His expensive coat tore at the shoulder, showing a white flag of stuffing. He gabbled out something, one of the soldiers laughed and the prisoner was hauled away at spear-point. The giant gestured them forward.

Shand spoke to the guards in a deferential way, tugging at his beard while pointing back the way they had come. He had a trick of making little circular gestures in the air as he spoke. The soldiers turned to look that way, then back at Karan. She stepped forward a half-pace, sure that the guards from the cellar would come running any minute; equally sure that she would be sick if it lasted much longer. Surely that would show them that I am harmless, she thought ruefully. It wouldn't have mattered if the guards had questioned her, for she had forgotten it all again.

Shand said something to the soldiers and they laughed. Karan bent and poked her bloody toe. The foremost guard hauled her upright, staring at her as if committing her face and form to memory, then she realised that her torn shirt was gaping open to the waist. She pulled it together hastily, someone chuckled, her stomach heaved and she retched into the slush at his feet. The soldier stepped back hastily, gesturing them on. Shand put his arm around Karan's waist again and led her away.

'That was a near thing,' he said, with strange cheerfulness. 'They're definitely looking for you. But of course they were looking for a woman with red hair.'

Karan stared at him as though he were mad, then caught a strand of her hair and pulled it in front of her face. It was the colour of soot. Her beautiful red curling hair, her only vanity, was a lank ugly black. Tears burned her eyes. She began to weep and once started could not stop.

Several times more they encountered soldiers and were questioned, but each time Shand talked his way through. Eventually, after many rest stops, the last in a part of the city so squalid it was impossible to endure the stench for a minute, he dragged her out of a lane to the top of a narrow, steep stair. There was water at the bottom. Without a word Shand began to descend the steps. Had he not been there, Karan would have lain down in the muck and never got up again. Her toe had stopped bleeding at last, had even stopped hurting, her feet were so cold.

'Where are we going?' she gasped, falling down on the top step.

'Hurry! We can talk later.'

A shout came from behind them. Looking back, she saw soldiers at the other end of the long lane. 'Halt!' one shouted, then they broke into a run. To Karan's right was a blank wall; to her left a narrow alley ran between decrepit warehouses. She forced herself to her feet, stumbled down the alley a few steps, hesitated then ran back, crying with frustration. Where once she would have made the right decision instantly, now she could not make any. There seemed to be nothing inside her head.

'We can't get out that way,' cried Shand. 'Quick, down the steps.'

Karan froze in indecision. Shand heaved her over his shoulder and literally ran down the stairs, skidding on the steep treads. At the bottom he slipped on the slimy step, dropping Karan into the water. It was numbingly cold. She raised her hand; he hauled her out and propped her against the stone rail. His breath came in wheezing gasps.

They were surrounded by the massive, decaying piles of the great wharf city, stretching in all directions beyond sight. The sight of it made her skin creep. Karan had been lost on the waterfront of Thurkad once as a child. She had wandered into the wharves, with their strange inhabitants peering at her from behind every pile, saying nothing. It had only been a few hours before she was found again, but she had never forgotten the sight of it, or the stench, or the mad terror of her mother when she recovered her.

The steps ran down steeply between two stone abutments and continued beneath the water. Only ten spans away, partly submerged, was the lowest platform of the wharf, but directly in front of them it was gone – rotted away or sunk in the mud. Shand jumped up, probing the dark water with a stick.

'Come on,' he called. 'We can get across this way.'

He stepped in, feeling in front of him like a blind man. The water came up to his thighs. Someone shouted behind them and Karan started. A soldier stood at the top of the stair, pointing at them. Shand seized her wrist again and hauled her out of view as arrows thunked in the timbers above their heads.

Keeping the line of piles between them and the end of the steps, Shand led Karan into the wharf. The deck was warped – one minute the water was up to their waists, the next just a film on the slimy surface. Inside it was dark, humid and ripe with the smell of salt water and rot. Chinks of light slanted down here and there, spotlighting curtains of algae or brown fungoid growths.

There was a gentle splash behind Shand. He called out. 'Take care, the deck's all rotten here.'

He moved slowly forward, probing the dark water. The platform felt spongy underfoot. In one place it broke under his weight and he had to flounder backwards to safety. He looked over his shoulder for Karan. She was nowhere to be seen. Where had she been standing? Across there, where a ray of light shone down on the water. Shand picked his way across the crumbling deck but could not see her. Then, remembering that faint splash, he looked down.

The water was clearer here. Karan was below the surface, drifting with her arms wrapped around her body and her knees tucked up, revolving slowly. Her eyes were open and staring, but she made no attempt to help herself. Shand prodded her in the side with his staff. She seemed surprised, then caught hold of the stick, and even after he pulled her out and she lay on the decking streaming and shivering, she still clutched it. He examined her carefully but there was no sign of any injury and she said nothing.

Increasingly worried about her state of mind, Shand went more carefully and always held her hand. In this fashion they made their way steadily into the heart of the great wharf city.

'Where are you taking me?' Karan asked dully, as they rested on a fallen beam. She began to shiver convulsively. Her feet and hands were bloody from the shells and barnacles that covered every surface; in the dim light her face was a ghastly green.

'There are places in the wharf city where not even Yggur would follow us. However the people who live here, the Hlune, will tolerate us for a time, if I ask it of them.'

'They must,' said Karan faintly, 'for I cannot go another step to save my life.'

'You'll have to. We're yet on the inner fringe, where only

the most degraded ones live, for the waters are putrid with the wastes of Shazmak. Sit here! I'll find somewhere for you to hide while I negotiate with the Hlune. I won't be long.'

So saying, he took off his pack and laid it at her feet on the platform, which at that point was above the level of the water and relatively dry. He set off, soon returning.

'There's a place nearby that'll do for tonight.'

Karan limped after him, leaving smears of blood on the timber. After a minute they found an empty storeroom, a space about five paces by four, enclosed with planks and having a rude plank door. There were others like it nearby. The wharf city contained half the warehouses of Thurkad, though these ones had subsided below the high-tide level long ago and were no longer used.

They went in and Karan sank down on the wet floor. It was quite dark inside, Shand just a shadow moving about. She began to doze off but he shook her awake.

'You can't sleep yet, and not on the floor at all – the tide will come up in a few hours. You must try to avoid the water here; it's full of the foulness of Thurkad.'

Too late, she thought. He felt around the walls and identified shelves, planks of raw wood. They were covered in a brown growth that powdered under the sweep of his hand, filling the air with choking dust. On one shelf he made a bed with blankets then lifted her up. Karan wrapped the blankets around her, breathing shallowly, her mind numb, her belly empty, her feet hurting. She was faint from hunger. Shand shrugged the pack onto his back and turned to the door.

'Shand,' she squeaked, close to panic. He turned. 'Don't go!'

He stood with his hand on the door frame. 'I must. I won't be long.'

'Please, I feel like I'm going to die. I'm so cold.' Her teeth chattering, she slid off her perch, landed on her feet then crumpled to the floor.

He ran across, thinking that she'd relapsed into madness. Her hand was icy; she was shivering in spasms, on the edge of hypothermia. 'Shand, you're a fool,' he said to himself. 'Look what you've done to her.'

He stripped off her wet clothes, dried her and chafed her limbs until the shivering stopped, then wrapped her up in all the blankets they had. She sighed and opened her eyes.

With a knife as long as her forearm Shand shaved wood off one of the beams into a pot. He chopped food into tiny pieces into a smaller pot, filled it with water and balanced it over the first pot on a pair of spoons.

'More!' came a whisper from Karan's blankets, whence only a pair of eyes could be seen. 'I'm starving to death.'

He cut another onion, crumbled another piece of bread into the pot, struck sparks into the tinder expertly, blew on the tiny glow and in only a minute there was a lick of flame in the fire pot. That was such a cheering sight that Karan crawled over to the fire, warming her hands and feet at the small blaze.

'Now let me have a look at your feet.' He cleaned the long gash on her toe, dabbed a waxy salve on and bandaged it. 'How could I have forgotten that you had no boots?' he said to himself, shaking his head at her tattered feet. 'To drive you so through the snow. How feeble my wits have become.'

He worked carefully, neglecting not the least scratch. Karan was silent all the while – grateful for his attentions, but scarcely noticing what he did. She was lost in the past, reliving childhood nightmares about being trapped in the wharves of Thurkad.

Though he twice replenished the fire pot there was not enough fuel to boil the stew, but it was soon hot enough for Karan. Shand lifted her back up onto her bunk, quenched one of the spoons in the pot and passed it up to her.

'Eat it all, if you can,' he said. He threw the coals out the door into the water, washed the fire pot and repacked it.

The stew was watery and had little flavour, but Karan

didn't care. She spooned down the hot mush until her belly was so full that it hurt. A delicious warmth began to spread through her. The cheese had melted into a stringy lump at the bottom of the pot. It was rubbery, with a strong smell and a rich ripe flavour.

While she ate Shand watched her and, finally, was satisfied that she was well enough to be left alone. 'Now I must see the Hlune or there will be trouble. We are trespassing in another country, Karan, and the owners are jealous of their privacy. I hope to be back before tomorrow, but I'll leave the rest of the food, just in case. No soldiers will come down here, *not yet*. Stay inside! Sleep.' He went out, closing the door behind him.

Soon the pot, which had contained enough for two hungry people, was empty and still she wanted more. Even her feet were starting to warm up. Karan lay down on her side, curled up and tried vainly to sleep. There were too many distractions. She was afraid of the dark and the fierce, strange people that dwelt here. The rough planks pressed against her hip, on which it seemed there was no flesh left. The dust rose with every movement and drifted in the air, making her sneeze, her nose run and her eyes water. It was very dark, only a few pale-greenish chinks coming in through gaps in the wall, high up. Later they faded too, as darkness fell. But the place was unexpectedly noisy.

Karan lay with her eyes closed, making a catalogue of the noises. The longer she listened the more there were. There was the constant lap-lap of wavelets beneath her, though this place must be a long way from the seaward side of the wharf. The wharf creaked constantly, a dozen different kinds of sound, from low, barely perceptible vibrations that seemed to be the whole structure shuddering like a great organ pipe, to smaller local shivers and shakes, creaks and groans. The water rose and fell gently beneath her with the swell from the sea, and over the hours the tide came flooding in until it rose up through the slotted floor of her little room.

Several times a heavily laden wain rumbled across the wharf platform far above. Children leapt from beams into the water at their play – they must have been quite close – and the vermin that were everywhere in Thurkad skittered across the timbers, squeaking and scratching. The rats were so bold that she had to constantly chase them away from the food bag, finally tucking it under her blankets.

And one time the whole structure shuddered wildly, with a rending of timbers and a wailing that continued long after the shaking had stopped, as one of the ancient foundation piles, rotted beyond its capacity to bear, collapsed and all that it supported fell with it. But by then Karan was asleep.

Early the following morning she was woken by a thunderstorm over the city. The pitch blackness of the night was riven by blue-white flashes that came in through every crack and gap in the structure, and the light made her look sicker than ever, though only the rats staring at her an arm's length away could see it. Karan kicked out and they scurried away, but later dreamed that they were creeping under her blankets.

The thunder sent little sympathetic shivers and shudders through the wharf, and the pegs of ironwood that held it all together slipped and squealed. Then the rain came, pelting down like the roaring of surf upon a lonely beach. It trickled down the massive beams and posts and piles, running across the platforms and floors and all the layers of the wharf, until eventually it seeped through the gaps in the roof of her cell, sometimes overflowing in a continuous stream, at other times falling in a dark curtain over the length of one warped plank.

No use huddling there under the drips. She must have slept better than she'd thought, for Karan was no longer sleepy, and standing did not exhaust her quite as it had the previous day. Her toe was sore and red, though the other scratches were healing. She was starving again. She ate an onion and some bread, both showing suspicious gnaw marks, and looked for a drink.

Over in the corner water was dripping into water, where

a pipe diverted run-off into a rainwater barrel. She reached in to scoop out a hand of water and her fingers sank into a mat of fur, a pulpy decaying mess of flesh and brittle bones. A loathsome smell came up. She dredged it out, holding it as far away as she could. It was a rodent, rather larger than a rat, and so rotten that the flesh was weeping from the bones. She flung it away then went outside to wash off the putrefied, jelly-like stuff that clung to her fingers. Back inside the smell was ripe, and the floor under her bare feet now felt so unpleasantly slimy that she had to abandon her refuge.

Her clothes, which Shand had spread out to dry the previous night, were still wet and covered in mud, just like her. Salt itched in her armpits. Nearby, the rainwater showered off the edge of a huge beam. Karan got under the shower, so cold that it took her breath away, and scoured herself with her shirt until her skin was pink and tingling. She scrubbed her hair with her fingers for as long as she could stand the cold water, and though a little of the dye came off, the colour of her hair seemed to be unchanged.

Then she sat down on the decking and washed her clothes in the dark water. The bloodstains on her shirt had faded a little. She hung the garments up on long splinters thrust into cracks between the planking, though with little hope of them drying in the cold humidity of this place.

The tide was rising again, the water ankle-deep already. She found a roost that was above the reach of the tide, and dry as well. There she perched, completely wrapped in the blankets, only her face peeping out, munching the last of Shand's bread. Her skin glowed from the cold and the scrubbing. The coarse wool irritated her sensitive skin, her feet were blue, yet she felt better than she had at any time since she had come to Sith and found no one there to take the Mirror.

The Mirror! That was the past, ancient history. Another Karan entirely. Whatever had motivated her to carry it so faithfully and for so long? She had no idea.

A long time she sat there, slowly growing warm again,

and even dozed a little. When she woke the slanting light told her that it was mid-morning. Shand had been gone almost a day, longer than he had said. Something must have happened to him.

Getting down from her perch, Karan padded across the decking, peering each way as far as she could, which was not far. There was nothing to be seen. She filled the pot from a dripping plank and drank her fill. The water was good, though with a tarry taste.

What if Shand never came back? She had no money, no food, no shoes. Yggur held all the city. She knew nothing of the people that lived within the wharf, except that she feared them. What would they do with her if they found her?

She felt the vaguest unease, just the faintest tickle of danger. Karan would have ignored it once, but it set her to wondering what had happened to her sensitive abilities. After her horrible experiences on the way from Shazmak to Narne, Karan had closed off her talent, suppressing the memories, and since then she had not been able to find either again.

Almost as she had those thoughts, a figure materialised in front of her. It was tall and lanky, clad in a single piece of dun-coloured fabric looped around its waist and knotted at the shoulder. The face was partly obscured by a head bag, a crumpled mass of cloth that sagged down to the shoulders on either side. Just the jut of a big thin nose was visible, a wispy pigtail on the chin, a bony hand. The long arm reached out, the hand took hold of her blanket and jerked. Karan grabbed the blanket before her nakedness was exposed and pulled it around her.

The figure made a deep noise in its throat and reached out again, this time taking hold of her arm. Surprisingly, its hard fingers were warm against her skin. It pulled her effortlessly. There was no point in resisting.

13

A VAT OF JELLYFISH

Karan had no idea where she was being taken, though it must have been towards the sea, for she became aware of waves breaking against the platform underneath. Eventually she was led into a large room, a meeting chamber almost ten spans across and six high. The light of the lamps struck her blind for a moment, though they were not very bright by the standards of the outside world.

The room was lit by a myriad of tiny lamps and stank of fish oil, raw and rancid, burning and burnt. People like the man who had brought her here – tall and long-limbed, with huge flat feet and hands, and skin with the granular texture of sand – crowded the chamber. All were talking furiously about the war and the fall of Mendark. They must be the Hlune that Shand had gone to see. They were congregated on a large ironwood platform that comprised about a quarter of the room, built out from the far wall above the level of the high tide.

Swathed in their togas, the men and women looked quite similar. The men were distinguishable only by a greater breadth of shoulder and by whiskers twisted into a rat's tail below the chin, the length of the tail seeming to be proportional to the status of the man. The women wore their hair in a long plait at the back, rank being denoted by the number of subsidiary braids at the bottom.

In the centre of the platform, on matching carved chairs of red cedar, sat two elders, a man and a woman, both naked to the waist. They looked better fed than the rest, though not fat. The woman's plait was flung over one shoulder, a hundred braids spread like a fan between her breasts, while the man's chin-whiskers were plaited down to his navel.

Her captor conveyed her to the base of the steps that led onto the platform. There he stopped, still gripping her arm tightly. The wait was nerve-racking. Just to stand was exhausting and Karan's head throbbed almost as badly as it had on her first wakening.

One time a Hlune messenger ran in, his robes flying, and leapt up high on the platform. He skidded on the damp wood, recovered, then burst out in furious chatter in which several times Karan heard Mendark's name.

Both elders rose from their cedar chairs, looking grave. The other Hlune gathered around them but now, in the chorus of voices, Karan could not make out anything at all. Finally the messenger was despatched with instructions, the elders sat down again, the man nodded to the woman and she put her hand out in Karan's direction.

Karan was brought before the elders, but again the process was delayed by a messenger. Hlune language seemed to be the common speech of Meldorin, but they spoke so quickly and with such a strange accent, punctuated with tongue clicks and cheek pops, with clickings of the fingers and rapping on kneecaps, that she could barely comprehend one word in a sentence. She did understand, however, that Thurkad had fallen and the Hlune were terrified that Yggur would torch the wharf city to drive out any enemies who might have taken refuge there. Several times she heard them exclaim, 'The horesh! The horesh!' which she took to mean, 'The burning! The burning!'

That was their most deadly fear. Long had they lived within these multi-storeyed wharves of old Thurkad in an uneasy partnership that suited them, and Thurkad too, but never before had the city been taken and they did not know what to expect.

While she waited, Karan examined her surroundings. The ceiling was held up by huge beams of ironwood, the intensely hard and durable wood that made up the skeleton of the wharf. Here the ironwood was smoothed and polished so that in the light of the lamps it had the look of priceless red-black ebony. The roof of the chamber, and the walls, were panelled with red-brown cedar wood down to the high-tide mark. Below that the room was also panelled but in timber of a paler brown, heavily varnished against rot.

Now she realised that there were another, smaller folk here as well. They were her size, with paler skin and more regular, pleasant features than the Hlune, with slender shoulders but round jutting buttocks. These people appeared to be a toiler race for they ran back and forth all the time she was in the room, bearing food and drink, carrying messages, moving furniture or simply cleaning and repairing. They were dressed alike, men and women both, in just a winding of drab cloth that covered them from hip to knee.

Karan caught the words 'red hair', and realised that it was her turn at last. There followed a lengthy debate as to whether she was the one that Yggur sought. The elders inspected her carefully, especially her black hair, and rubbed a few strands between their fingers, remarking at the stain that resulted. That provoked more chattering, then the woman gestured and the blanket was stripped away. Karan stood naked under their gaze, red with mortification. Evidently they were satisfied about her identity; Karan was beckoned to one side while the elders held a long discussion.

'What's happened to Shand?' Karan interrupted. The elders ignored her.

'Shand, yah!' said an old Hlune woman whose hair was done in many braids. She nodded vigorously, showing her toothless gums.

'Where is Shand?' Karan asked again. 'What's happened to him?'

'Shand, yah!' the old woman repeated. No one else took the slightest notice.

The debate continued, fast and furious. Karan hardly cared, the cold had made her so lethargic. Her blanket had disappeared. She squatted down, concealing her nakedness as best she could, not that anyone showed the least interest in it. Karan could feel the madness, never far away over the past few weeks, rising to the surface again. If she stayed here much longer it would burst out and drown her, wash away all the memories yet again, leaving her empty and defenceless. She realised that today was the first day of endre. Things could hardly get better until after hythe.

She was just about to lie down on the floor and give up when the elders came to a decision. Orders were honked out, the man who had brought her here gripped her arm then led her to a small room nearby, there presenting her to a group of the smaller people.

'You stay,' he said. 'Work hard and Telt will feed you. No work, no food!' Then he hurried away.

Karan wanted to burst into tears, she felt so humiliated and abandoned. The toilers, the Telt, clustered around, staring at her in the dim light. They did not know what to make of her either. Physically she was like them, and her hair was a sooty, uniform black much like theirs. But her eyes were green, her nose narrower, her hands and feet smaller and more slender, her features more delicate. She was like them, and yet unlike.

'Where's Shand?' Karan whispered weakly.

'Chard!' exclaimed a young man with very black eyebrows. 'No chard! Work!'

'Not chard,' she said. '*Shand!*' But the name did not seem to mean anything to them.

One of them touched her – his hands were also warm – and exclaimed: '*Caudid!*'

Cold! She was freezing, shivering convulsively. Someone

flung her a piece of drab cloth. She wound it around her hips the way they wore it, and that seemed to solve the problem of her identity for them, though it did little to warm her and it smelled mouldy. Now the young man, no taller than her, led her to the corner of the room and with gestures set her to work. They must think I don't understand their speech, she thought, for they said nothing more to her all the while.

On the platform in front of her was a large barrel, full of something like small jellyfish, though tougher and more leathery than any she had ever seen. They were coloured the palest aqua, with stubby tentacles that had tiny purple spots in rows along them.

Her job was to pick a jellyfish out of the barrel, cut off the tentacles which she must put to one side, hollow out the body and stuff the cavity with a mixture of aromatic herbs, then pack the creatures in layers in a smaller barrel, interleaved with layers of salt and another pungent, coarse-leaved herb. Finally the barrels were topped up with clean sea water brought in from outside in special barrels, and the top hammered on. That was the easy half of the job.

When each barrel was full Karan began again on the tentacles. She had to scrape each with the back of a knife until the stinging spots were removed, then slit the tentacle down the middle and flatten it by pressing and beating, for the flesh was tougher than it appeared. When the flattened tentacles formed a large pile she must feed them one by one into a press, placing each across the previous one, and finally heaving down on the lever until it would go no further. A quantity of thick jelly oozed out of the bottom of the press, and this was caught in large oval bladders, sealed and sent away. The other product of the press was an opaque, rubbery, layered brick which she shaved smooth with a knife and stacked in a corner of the platform.

As soon as she started on the tentacles Karan saw why it was a job for the lowest of the low. They were tough, more like rubber than jelly, and the stinging spots almost impossible to scrape away without being stung. And she was, repeatedly, until her fingers were so swollen and painful that they could barely hold the knife.

After some hours of this the others suddenly stopped work, climbed up to a rotting platform above the water level and began their evening meal. Karan went to join them, rather tentatively, for she did not know what was expected of her, but one of them, a woman taller than the others, gestured her back to her pile.

'You not work hard,' she exclaimed, shooting out her arm so hard that her breasts jiggled. Her belly was big in the middle stages of pregnancy. 'No work, no eat!'

Karan splashed miserably back to her corner. The pile of tentacles still to be done was enormous, and the tide had risen so that she was standing up to her knees in cold water. Her fingers were swollen like fat little bladders. Climbing up on a bench out of the water, she bent down and picked up another tentacle. Her face was as white as a cloud, and once she almost fainted, only saving herself by dashing sea water into her face.

By now she was desperate with hunger and thirst. Even the brown sponges that grew on the piles were beginning to look edible. And what had happened to Shand?

Well, whether Shand returned or not she could not stay here. In this society the small ones were low, and she, a stranger, an oddity, the lowest. She would submit to that while she had to, but not an instant longer.

Hours later she finished the job. The tide was at its highest now, almost up to the level of the bench, so she dangled her legs over the side and washed them clean. Her back was locked from bending over so long, her legs spattered with jelly, her feet swollen from a myriad stings. But it was not as bad as the swamps and leeches of Orist. She could bear it, for there was no enemy here. They wanted nothing from her but hard work and Karan had been used to that at Gothryme.

Karan realised that the others had finished their work and were gathering on the platform again. An oil stove glowed underneath an urn. The stove smoked, filling the air with the reek of half-burnt fish oil, but before the water boiled someone pointed to the oil level and pinched out the flame. The pregnant woman scattered dried herb – the coarse, large-leaved kind that was used in the jellyfish barrels – on top of the water in the urn and stirred it gently until the water became the colour of dead grass. Wooden mugs of tea were handed around. Karan went forward tentatively and, after a moment's hesitation, she too was given a mug. How grateful she was for it!

She took the mug in numb fingers and put it to her lips, allowing the steam to drift over her closed eyelids. The tea had a rank odour. The mug grew warm between her fingers. She took the smallest little sip. The feel of the hot liquid in her mouth was indescribably wonderful, the only warmth she'd felt all day, though the taste was indifferent, like wet straw. Karan drank it slowly for the warmth.

The others were eating thin slices cut from the compressed bricks of jelly tentacles, taking them raw. The idea was nauseating but she must eat. Karan reached for a slice of the *pan*, as they called it. But the man with the knife gestured her away, pointing toward the small heap that she had made, by which she understood that she must eat from her own pile.

Karan sat down by herself, cut a slice from a brick with her knife and nibbled at it. It was slimy, with a soft texture rather like rotted cheese intermixed with strings and layers of rubber, but it had no taste. She chewed her pan mechanically, swallowed and took another bite. A blinding pain struck the tip of her tongue. She spat the mess back out on the floor, poking through it with a finger, and there in the middle was a purple stinging spot that she had missed. In the slice that she'd cut off there were more – when she held it up to the light – tiny spots that were barely visible. Every eye in the room was on her but the Telt soon turned back to their own dinner.

Karan cut a slice from the other end of the brick, examined it carefully, and put it in her mouth. She chewed and bit into something so foul that she instantly threw up.

A young woman, her hair so glossy that it must have been freshly oiled, took the remains of the slice from her hand. She spoke rapidly, but all that Karan caught were the words 'foul-jelly'. Karan looked blank. The woman went across the room to come back with something in her hand, a small jellyfish that had been put to one side. She showed it to Karan, shaking her glistening hair, which had an overpowering aroma of fish oil. The jellyfish was almost identical to the others, except that the colour was pale grey instead of pale blue. She put it under Karan's nose – it was not rotten but a sickening smell came from it.

'Foul-jelly,' she said again, putting it to one side.

Karan threw the remains of the pan in the water. The woman inspected another of the bricks, sniffed it and handed it to her. Karan thanked her with her eyes but by now she had lost all appetite.

'I am Karan,' she said. 'What is your name?'

'Karan!' the woman said, tinkling with laughter. 'I am Cluffer.'

Cluffer touched the tip of her nose to Karan's, took the mug from her swollen hand and filled it again from the urn. Karan carried it back to her workplace, nursing the hot fluid, savouring the rest and the quiet for however long it lasted.

Sometime later, work was finished for the day. Over in the corner the man with the black eyebrows was embracing Cluffer with a passion that Karan had rarely seen in public, burying his face in her hair and sniffing as though she wore a rare perfume, while she caressed him from head to foot. The others looked on with smiles and words of encouragement.

It must have been well after midnight. 'Come!' said another young man to Karan. 'Time to sleep.'

The Telt, who numbered about ten, went out in a group.

Karan followed them to their living quarters nearby. This room was sparse in the extreme, a mere box with a wide communal sleeping platform high on one side. The platform also served for eating and working, though it was unfurnished but for some blocks of wood for stools and a shelf that held ironwood carvings.

They washed themselves in sea water, hung up their loincloths, climbed up on the platform and bedded down together, covering themselves with blankets made of long strands of oiled seaweed roughly woven together. Karan sidled toward them but it was soon made clear to her that she was an outsider, not one to share warmth with. Cluffer, who had helped her earlier, picked up one of the blankets and pointedly carried it over to the farthest corner of the platform.

Karan curled up on the cold platform, wrapping herself as well as she could, but she still shivered all night. That night was one of the most miserable of her life. She would have fled, had there been anywhere to go, had they allowed it, but in her present condition she knew she would not last five minutes on the streets of Thurkad. What a come-down from her strength and independence of a few months ago! No, she could do nothing but remain here and hope to find Shand again, hope that when she did there was somewhere to flee to.

In the early hours there came a muffled giggling from the other side of the room. The seaweed rustled, then she heard more giggling and other kinds of movements. Someone laughed aloud and, in her misery, Karan was sure that they laughed at her. She groaned. The giggling stopped at once and it went quiet again.

Up to this point there had been no room in her head for anyone but herself. Now, lying on the damp planks, the weedy blanket hugged around her, her heart began to ache for Llian. She had hardly thought of him these past days, except in those brief conversations with Shand. Had he really left with Tensor? Had he gone willingly, or captive? Why would Tensor want him? Where had Tensor taken him?

The blankets provided no warmth at all. Karan brooded about Llian, remembering the many nights they had spent together on that trek through the mountains to Shazmak, and escaping afterwards. The nights had been much colder than this one, and once, she remembered, they had been near to freezing to death. Though then they had been well-clad and had the warmth of each other too.

I had meat on my bones then. You corrupted me, Llian, weakened me. I came to depend on your being near. How I long for you now, for the warmth of you. Once I would have lain here alone and damned the cold, dared it to touch me. How I long for your beautiful voice, the best part of you. What a fool I am to have sunk for a fool such as you.

Yet you taught me about loyalty – at the end you were the only one to believe in me. I saw you trying to defend me. What a sight – a sword in your hand. It might as well have been one of these jellies. She laughed at her warped humour.

Well, Llian, wherever you are, I will find you, and extract you from whatever disaster you have got yourself into, and take you home to Gothryme. You can write the rest of your tale there. That will be my only goal and purpose, and nothing shall distract me from it.

That decision marked the beginning of her mind's recovery. The night passed, as even such nights eventually do, and the pitch black was replaced by the pale-green gloom of day. Karan woke bewildered, having no idea where she was or how she had ended up lying naked in a pile of seaweed. It was not until the Telt stirred, soon after dawn, that the memories began to come back. For a while she wondered if she was going mad again.

For breakfast they ate jellyfish cake and several kinds of cooked weed. One was soft and grey like her blanket, another fleshy and leathery brown, a third like lettuce but with little bladders that popped in the mouth.

Karan expected to be summoned back to her vat. But instead they drank more weed tea, then some of the Telt wandered off, while others lay down on the platform staring up at the ceiling or down into the dark water. One or two played on hard little wooden pipes. Often she caught their eyes on her. Once, when she was shivering with her head in her hands, ravenous and wracked by stomach cramps, her fingers and toes throbbing and her head too, so pale that her skin looked transparent, Cluffer sat down and put an arm around her shoulders. Again she seemed surprised at how cold Karan was and came back with a big wooden mug of tea even though it was not teatime. Karan was grateful for the warmth of her shoulder and hip and thigh, but more grateful still for the tea.

During this rest time two or three of the Telt took down partly completed carvings and worked at them carefully. The carvings were mostly of the beasts of the seas, but usually the small, subtle and insignificant ones, like the small pipefish that cleaned the piles of the wharves. There were also carvings of themselves, all the ages of them, from newborn babies to withered crones, but none of the Hlune.

Several days went by, and each was the same as the one before: she would rise soon after dawn, sometimes with no memory of the previous day; eat jellycake and weed, drink straw-flavoured tea; sit for a while, reflecting, or walk around, though not too far, else she was sent back by the Hlune; then go to the preparation room to clean jellyfish from midday till midnight, until her back throbbed and her fingers were numb. If this was the price of food and shelter she would pay it no matter how it pained her, and no shirking, though she was wracked by cramps the whole time.

At the end of each day she washed herself in the chill sea, and her loincloth too, otherwise by the morning the stench would be unbearable. She ate more jellycake and drank more tea, lay down in her nest of weeds and shivered until the dawn. And often in the night, and sometimes even during the day, she would hear that tinkling laughter and imagine that they were laughing at her.

Hythe came and went unnoticed – no worse than the previous days, but no better either. Karan made several attempts to recover her sensitive talent, but where she had once been able to sense danger instinctively, had been able to make sendings almost at will and occasionally even link and speak into the mind of another, now there was nothing in her head at all. Her talent had never been reliable, and using it gave her terrible aftersickness, but it was better than being without it.

Four days after her arrival, in the afternoon of the day after hythe, Karan was working away quietly at her vat, feeling desperately ill, when she became aware that the incessant chatter of the Telt had stopped. Looking around she saw a deputation of the Hlune staring at her. They called Cluffer's lover over and spoke long and fiercely to him. Voices were raised, the young man shouted back, spun around to his people and a series of questions tumbled out so rapidly that Karan had no idea what he was asking.

'No!' said Cluffer abruptly.

The young man turned back to the Hlune, throwing out his arms. To Karan's astonishment the other Telt also spread their arms and made a line across the room between her and the Hlune. A furious argument ensued, clearly about her, then the leading Hlune stamped a big flat foot.

'Tomorrow!' he said ominously. He whirled and disappeared, the others following.

The Telt looked at each other and at Karan but did not go back to their work. Instead they lit the urn for an unscheduled tea-break, and when it was ready they called her over to join them even though her work was not nearly done.

'What was that about?' Karan asked the man beside her.

'Guest-right!' he said, but would say no more.

Karan drank her tea in silence. This was an alarming development. For the rest of the day and all night she expected the Hlune to appear in strength, to cast her into the streets of Thurkad, or betray her to Yggur.

14

A ZEALOT'S REWARD

Sixty leagues away, a meeting was taking place in Shazmak, the magnificent Aachim city now occupied by those former Whelm who had become Ghâshâd. They had been the servants of Rulke in ancient times, until he was taken by the Council and put in the prison of the Nightland.

The Ghâshâd milled around like mechanical sheep in the vast meeting hall, a cavern whose roof was an oval dome supported by curving walls. The great iron doors at either end were shut fast. The walls were covered in murals of the world of Aachan: iron towers on icy crags; mountains crusted with sulphur, yellow and red; black-leaved, tormented jungles. The dome was painted as an alien green sky with a sullen orange moon glaring down.

The floor sloped as in a theatre. Down the lower end was a dais on which stood a semicircle of high-backed wrought-iron seats, most of which were occupied by Ghâshâd. Just off the centre of the semicircle was a pedestal of stone, around which spiralled a black iron stair of twenty steps. The pedestal was topped by a dock of iron lace, surmounted by a railing of veined red marble. Karan had stood there during her trial some months ago.

A squat, stout man addressed the Ghâshâd. His name was

Jark-un. 'Thassel has come from Thurkad with tidings of the war,' he said. 'Disturbing tidings.'

Thassel, a skin-and-bone man even among the other stick-figures, stepped forward. 'Thurkad must have fallen by now,' he began in gravelly tones.

'Three days ago,' said another, an old woman called Quissan. 'We had word by skeet just yesterday. But no more than that, so we anxiously await your tale.'

'Our enemy Tensor fled north from Thurkad nine days ago. He has the Mirror of Aachan. He used a terrible potency, killing many people.'

'That wakes a disturbing memory,' said Jark-un. 'A danger to our master.'

'Indeed it does.' They listened in silence while Thassel finished his story.

'So,' said Jark-un at the end. 'This was a wonderful thing that we did, seizing Shazmak for our master. But what are we to do now?'

'I, too, am confused,' said another.

'Our master needs us,' said a smaller, younger Ghâshâd, an albino with pink eyes. 'I can *sense* his troubles.'

'But we cannot reach him, Rebban!' cried the old woman, Quissan, in a passion. She clenched her fists and smote her breast. 'What does he require of us?'

'We don't know,' said Jark-un. 'We just don't know.'

'We don't even know if coming here was the right thing to do,' said another, a younger woman with black hair shaven to stubble and a wild look in her eye. 'Were we right to have cast Yggur off? Maybe we were meant to serve our true master through serving Yggur.'

This was a discussion that they'd had almost every day since taking Shazmak, but there was no way to resolve it.

A tall man with a scarred face spoke up. 'I would hear again *the awakening*,' he said. 'Would that I had been there.'

Jark-un sighed. 'Sometimes I wonder if you were ever meant to come with us, Idlis. Tell it again, Rebban.'

'We did our work well,' said Rebban, 'that night in the forest near the town of Narne. Karan was so afraid that she began broadcasting her fears without even knowing it. But when she made a link to Maigraith – and what a powerful link it must have been, that the master could catch it from the Nightland – ah, what a glorious moment! We all cried out as with one voice: "Oh, perfect master! At last! At last!" '

He spoke as a teller would have, precisely the words and the tone that had been used that night. 'And then *he* called. The master spoke to us for the first time in a thousand years.

'Oh, faithful servants,' Rebban's voice was now a vast, foreboding boom. *'The crisis approaches, and so much to do. Listen, and obey. Already the link fades. Do you remember yourselves?*

'Now we remember. We are Ghâshâd, master.

'I have an enemy, Ghâshâd!

'We know him, now.

'Torment him. Goad him. Drive him to folly. But do not harm him. Call together the Ghâshâd, and when the opportunity comes, seize it!'

'That is all,' gasped Rebban and fell down panting with the strain. His skin was blotched red all over, the colour even visible through his hair.

Idlis's eyes had grown moist as he listened, and his coarse hair stood up on his head. 'I weep to hear the master's voice,' he cried, bowing his head, 'though I have heard it many times now. Oh, perfect master!'

'We seized the opportunity, but did we do the right thing?' asked Quissan, irritated by his fanaticism.

'I don't think we did,' said the young woman with the shaven head. 'What use is Shazmak to the master? It's a hiding hole, not a fortress to strike at his enemies from. It's too far from anywhere. The master would not cower here like the cowardly Aachim.'

'There are several things we must do,' someone else said.

'First we must try to scry out Tensor's path and his purpose. Likely we will fail, but we must not falter, for this potency hurt our master badly in ancient times. We must find a protection against it.'

'That is one thing we can do,' Jark-un agreed. 'Let us form the *circle* and begin the sensing and the scrying at once, though I am afraid that the distance will defeat us.'

'There is another thing,' said Idlis.

They did not pay him much attention, for Idlis was the least of them and known to be something of a zealot, but after their other business was done, to no avail, Jark-un came back to humour him.

'What is this idea of yours?' he asked.

'I am thinking of the woman, Karan of Bannador, that I hunted before,' Idlis replied. 'Is it known what happened to her?'

'I did not hear,' said Thassel.

'She is a blending of human and Aachim,' Idlis replied. 'That is how we found power over her before. And she is a sensitive too, for we tracked her through her dreams. *And she can link* – that is how our perfect master found us. We must track her down again, use our power over her and force a link through her so that we can speak to our master again. That is the only way to find out what he requires of us.'

The room was silent, then they let out a harsh roar like a flock of crows cawing, and lifted Idlis onto the dais. 'The least of us becomes the greatest!' cried Jark-un. 'We will hunt Karan down and *compel* her, and Idlis shall lead us to her.'

Greatly heartened, the Ghâshâd began to form their scrying circle anew.

15

NO ENTRY

After Shand left Karan he went straight to the Hlune, whom he had befriended of old. Despite his words to Karan, he was worried, knowing that after so many years the Hlune might not remember him. He was taken into the great meeting chamber and brought before the two elders. Shand tried to remember how to pronounce their names, as any mistake would be offensive. The man was Chraif, spoken with a coughing sound. The woman's name was Isout, spoken as two distinct syllables with a stop in between, and the second syllable accented with a nasal honk.

The man with the long braided whiskers got up from his cedar chair. 'Shand!' he said, holding out his hand.

The woman nodded but did not rise, a worrying sign.

'I am sorry to have trespassed in your city, Chraif,' Shand began uncertainly, putting too much cough into the name. 'I was forced here by the war.'

'The war!' said Chraif tersely, resuming his seat. 'Everything is different now. How may we help you?'

'If you could offer a friend refuge for a day or two,' said Shand, 'it would greatly assist me.' He explained Karan's situation guardedly.

'This is a difficult time to be asking such favours,' said Isout coolly.

'I would not have, I'sout,' said Shand, pronouncing the name perfectly. 'But I had no recourse.'

Isout smiled, nodded to Chraif, and sat back.

'On the other hand,' said Chraif, 'you helped us sometime back, and we do not forget our friends. Your companion may stay here in safety for four days, but no longer.'

'Where is she now?' asked Isout. 'We are sorely pressed with the war.'

Shand told them.

'We will keep watch on her,' said Chraif.

With that worry taken care of, Shand did not go back to check on Karan. The wharf city was abuzz with rumours, among them that Yggur was looking for a sensitive with red hair. Besides, Karan had to learn to rely on herself again, and the sooner the better. He hurried back into Thurkad to find a way out of the city.

That would take a deal of organising; every day he saw people being dragged off by the guards. Thurkad was rigidly controlled by Yggur, and what before the war would have cost silver tars must now be paid for in gold tells, twenty times the value, if it could be done at all. Shand had gold but it was not unlimited. He set out to renew his contacts of long ago.

After tramping the streets for days, interrogated on every street corner by Yggur's blackfists, he was in despair. His old contacts were all dead or in hiding. Finally, when Karan's four days were nearly up, he gave up and headed back to the wharf city. He did not want to overstretch the Hlune's friendship.

He could not get in. All the paths were guarded by Yggur's soldiers and they were quite the most officious he'd ever met. There were other ways, of course, and after some searching he found one – a covered-over drain, though it was half a league away from where he'd left Karan.

Shand crawled down the stinking drain for half an hour but found the exit was guarded by equally watchful Hlune.

The instant he appeared, their spears came up at his chest. Their faces were hostile.

'My name is Shand,' he said. 'I have a safe conduct from Chraif.' In his anxiety he grossly mispronounced the name.

The lead Hlune scowled but held out his hand. 'Show me!' he said curtly.

'I have no paper,' said Shand. 'It was a verbal agreement.'

'All agreements terminated,' said the Hlune, prodding Shand in the chest with the spear. It was needle sharp; he could feel it pricking through his coat.

'But you can ask –' he began.

'Get out!' said the leading Hlune. The guards behind growled menacingly. They looked so agitated that Shand did not dare press them any further. He backed away and crawled up the drain again, sitting halfway along in the darkness trying to work out what had gone wrong. Why were they so changed? More importantly, was Karan all right?

He tried another way but met with an even more aggressive response, and had no option but to go back. Today was hythe, mid-winter day, a sleety, windy, utterly depressing day. By now desperately worried, Shand headed for the last contact on his list, feeling glum and useless and old. It was a cellar bar that had always been run by a plump woman called Ulice, but even twenty years ago she had not been young.

He checked the alley and gave the secret knock. Nothing happened, but he became aware that he was being watched through a spy-hole. Shortly the door bolts rattled and he was ushered inside by a child, to a parlour where a round table was set with a blue and white checked tablecloth. Shand took the offered chair and waited.

After a minute a woman put her head around the door, inspected him, then ducked away. Finally a very fat, white-haired old woman appeared, wheezing as she walked.

The old woman knew him at once. 'Shand!' Ulice beamed, flinging out her arms. Shand sank into them like a baker's fist into dough.

'Sit down, sit down,' she said, propelling him into the chair, bustling mugs out of a cupboard, and from the back, a flask of a kind that he knew very well.

'This is the very last!' She cracked the wax. 'The best batch of gellon liqueur you ever made. I've saved it these past five years, hoping that you would come by. Surely you haven't been to Thurkad without visiting me!'

'I'll send you another crate when I'm back in Tullin,' he replied. 'In truth, I've not been here for many years. My bones are old now.'

'They don't look it,' said Ulice, 'but let us drink for I will be gone when next you come. This is my daughter, Asrail. Do you remember her?'

Shand vaguely recalled a noisy girl with scabs on her knees and no front teeth. This quiet, brown-haired, buxom beauty was nothing like her, but a lot like her mother had been thirty years ago. He said so.

Ulice laughed. 'Lucky she looked down and thought she recognised you, my friend. That knock is years out of date. Here is the new one.' While Shand practised the new sequence on the tabletop, she continued. 'Asrail is more beautiful than ever I was and better with the customers too. But I see hard times ahead. This Yggur is a moral man, very bad for business. And the war – terrible!'

Shand sipped his liqueur, agreeing that the war was indeed a horror.

'But you did not come so far just to drink with me, old friend. What can I do for you? Whatever is in my power.' She spoke only the truth. Ulice's power was considerable and she could arrange almost anything – for a price.

'I need a boat and a rare good sailor for a day or two. Can this be done?'

'Of course, though this is the worst of times to ask. Every plank has been impounded to stop the Magister from escaping, but Mendark is too wily for them. He will never be taken! How long can you wait?'

'A few days only.'

Ulice frowned. 'Then you must come back tomorrow. I don't promise, but I think I can satisfy you.'

Shand was profoundly relieved, for Ulice never promised. 'What price?'

'A few tells, I should say, but your credit is good here, if you are short.'

'Tells I can manage.' He hesitated.

'There is something else. Spit it out, my friend.'

'Several things! I left . . . someone in the care of the Hlune but now I can't get back into the wharf city.'

'Someone?' she said sharply. 'Not Mendark?'

'Not Mendark!' he replied with an ironic laugh. 'So *that's* where he's hiding?'

'I can't talk about that even to you. A conflict of interest.'

'No matter! I must get back in, though, and meet with the elders. And I'd better see Mendark as well.'

'I will find a way for you to do both. That is all?'

'One final matter, but it is highly confidential.' She said nothing to that, of course. All her clients' affairs were confidential. 'A woman went missing from the Conclave, by name Karan Fyrn.' He hesitated; but then, Ulice must be told everything. 'She is a sensitive; rather special.' He described Karan. 'It is vital that I know who is looking for her.'

'Get her out at once! Yggur has already taken a good number of the sensitives in the city. And broken half of them.'

'There could be others looking for her as well.'

Her old eyes scanned him, reading all his secrets. 'I will enquire,' said Ulice. 'Now, if the business is done –'

'It is,' said Shand. 'Ah, it is good to see a friend again. I have been in despair this last week, but you have given me hope.'

'That is well, for you were my very first customer, Shand. You took me on when no one else would and I do not forget that!' There were tears in her eyes.

'Those were the days,' said Shand, feeling sentimental too.

'Come closer to the fire and bring your bowl with you. This will be my farewell, old friend, for my heart is giving out and it is time to pass the business down. Let us finish the bottle and smash the glasses in the fire afterwards.'

In the early hours a Hlune pushed his way in past Osseion and shook Mendark awake. 'Come. A visitor!'

'Who is it?' Mendark asked irritably, for he had been lying awake for hours in a lather of depression and hopelessness and had just got to sleep. The Hlune did not reply, only kept tugging at his arm, an irritating habit that he had to endure in silence.

'Well, bring him in then,' Mendark said, grimacing.

The Hlune continued to pluck at his sleeve until Mendark gave up and followed him out into the night-dark wharf. Several times they encountered other Hlune who gave Mendark foul looks. Once a rotten onion came hurtling out of the dark to splatter on the wall right next to him with a disgusting stench. They walked for ten minutes along a right-of-way through the wharf city, used by ship's crews, suddenly coming to an open space at the outer edge of the structure. The nearest navigation light was some distance away, leaving the deck dimly lit. It was windy here; rain spat at him. On a plank bench a shadowed figure sat, indistinguishable in weathercloak and hat.

The man stood up and took off his hat. He was short but well-built, with iron-grey hair and a grey beard a few weeks old. Mendark was quite taken by surprise.

'Shand!' he cried. 'Things must be worse than I imagined if the war has reached even to your retirement village. What reminded you of your dereliction? Are *you* not provided for?'

Shand ignored the sarcasm, the venom. 'No wonder you are cast down for the second time in weeks, if this is the way you treat your allies. As it happens I told Tallia, when she came to Tullin a couple of months ago begging my assistance in your name, that I would come to Thurkad. Here I am.'

'If you come to counsel me I'm not interested. It's much too late for that.'

'I do not. I come merely to talk, to tell you what I know and learn what you have to say. Or not. Please yourself.'

The Hlune reappeared, carrying a small brass urn and burner on a tray with bowls and tea-making equipment. He put it down beside Shand then stepped back into the shadows. Shand wet the wick with spirits, struck the flint at it until there was a small flame and turned up the oil. Blue flame turned to smoky yellow, shadow fingers danced on the wall, then he returned to his bench.

'How did you know I was here?' Mendark asked, looking around fearfully as if his secret was revealed.

Shand chuckled. 'I'm not going to give away my sources. Where else could you have gone without a boat?' He was quite different from the scared old man of a few days ago. He was back in control again.

'Very well,' said Mendark. 'I will humble myself. I do need your counsel, if that is what you are offering. In a thimble, this is the situation and it is a disaster in every respect.' He told the sorry tale of the Conclave, the war and his own troubles since. Shand listened in silence.

The flame guttered in the breeze. The stench of burning fish oil was very strong. Mendark squatted on the decking, fidgeting, looking out to sea and waiting for the urn to boil. At last it bubbled and he flung in an overgenerous hand of weed. He stirred the pot with his bowl, holding it by the rim so as not to scald himself, then scooped out a bowl for Shand and another for himself.

'I don't know what to do,' Mendark cried abruptly. 'I can't find a boat, and tomorrow the Hlune are going to throw us out on the street. Shand, I don't know where to turn!'

Shand took a sip, finding the tea too hot and too strong, and put the bowl down carefully on the deck. He was silent. All this trouble might have been avoided had he acted when

213

first Llian begged him for help, back in Tullin at the beginning of winter. Shand could guess why everyone wanted the Mirror of Aachan. It was not apathy that had prevented him from helping then, or world-weariness, or the futility of striving against the twists and turns of fate. Those meant less to him than the awakening of bitter memories that he had hidden from, an age ago.

'I wonder if Tensor might not have gone north,' he said.

'North?' barked Mendark. 'East is where their other cities lie.'

'Would the other Aachim welcome one who brought only strife and the probability of ruin? No, Tensor is an outlaw now, without duty or honour. Tell me more about Llian.'

'What's that got to do with my problem?' Mendark said, balling up his fists.

'Humour me,' said Shand. 'We'll get to you in time.'

'Well, in one day he undid all his good work of the past months.' Mendark ran through the tale of Llian's misadventures in the citadel cellars before the Conclave, the fruitless search through ancient files for any document that could shed light on what had happened at the time of the Forbidding, the abortive rescue of Karan and her subsequent recapture by Thyllan.

'Unfortunately, Karan was lost after the Conclave,' said Mendark. 'I could have used her.'

Mindful of Karan's fear of Mendark, Shand did not enlighten him. 'Why would Llian go with Tensor?' he wondered.

'Go with him! Llian was terrified of him and with good reason.' Mendark told how Llian had defied and humiliated Tensor at the trial in Shazmak.

Shand was astounded. 'More to him than I thought.'

'More fool! Anyhow, let us apply ourselves to the larger question. If Tensor did go north, why? And where?'

'Anywhere is good enough if you seek to trifle with the Nightland, for it touches all places equally.'

'I can't search half the world.'

'Then go to Zile, to the Great Library, and speak with Nadiril the sage.'

'You're right; I've even been thinking that myself. Where else can what I need be found? Who better to know than Nadiril? I *will* go to Zile – if I ever get out of here.'

Mendark's tea had grown cold while they talked. He threw it down on the deck and took another. The previous had been a straw colour but this was red and very strong. He sipped, grimaced, sipped again.

'Tell me about Faelamor,' said Shand. 'Her reappearance disturbs me greatly.'

'What she said at the Conclave had the ring of truth,' said Mendark, staring into his cup. He told that story, of the fall of Shazmak and Faelamor's advice about the Mirror, that it held no power at all, only secrets. 'I was absolutely convinced.' He looked up at Shand, scratching his straggly hair. 'But she is master of all forms of illusion. The tale she told about the fall of Shazmak was a lie. It was she who betrayed Shazmak, not Karan. I've checked the details of both stories.'

'The Mirror disturbs me!' said Shand. 'When it was lost I'd hoped that it would stay lost forever.'

'You know about it?' Mendark asked, intrigued.

'Indeed,' said Shand, 'though I don't propose to tell *you*, so don't bother to ask.'

'No more than I would expect of you,' Mendark sneered, but it was a half-hearted effort. His own problems were too immediate. 'It is hard to come down to this, Shand, begging for shelter in these stinking wharves.' He looked haggard and old.

Shand stared at him unblinking. That is how your subjects have always managed, he thought. And you have a fortune to ease your passage. Yet, you are better than the alternative and I will help you if I can. 'How did it happen? You always have an escape route.'

'For my faults, none of which I am blind to despite what you think of me, I do love Thurkad. I would not abandon my city while there was any chance to save her. But I fought one day too many and my boat was taken. Tallia and Berenet are taking terrible risks looking for another boat and a reliable sailor. Every time I send them out I dread that they won't come back. *I'm desperate!*'

'Well you might be. Perhaps I can help you there. But now I must go.' Shand cast the dregs over the side, put the bowl down beside the urn and walked away. The sky was just beginning to grow pale in the east.

'Shand,' cried Mendark unsteadily, running a few steps after him. 'I've got to have a boat. Can you do anything?'

Shand stopped, grimly amused. This was a turnabout, the great Magister running after a village woodchopper. 'I'll try,' he said.

'Where will I find you?'

'I'll find you, at need,' Shand said over his shoulder. He walked off.

Behind him, Mendark went slowly back into the wharves.

Shand was not quite as carefree as he made out. A day and a half had gone by since his first meeting with Ulice and he still had no idea what had happened to Karan. He had sent three messages to the Hlune elders but none had been acknowledged; presumably they hadn't been received. The Hlune allowed him access to the public right-of-ways through the wharf city, but not inside, and none of the guards had any interest in his problem. The news that Yggur was hunting down all the sensitives was particularly alarming.

It was growing light when Tallia and Lilis returned, having once more failed to get out of the wharf city. Lilis was too tired to eat, but she washed herself carefully with a tiny amount of fresh water and crawled into her hammock. She humped around a few times, pulled the blankets around her ears, smiled sleepily at Tallia and was instantly asleep.

Tallia pinched out the light and left her there. Lack of sleep had made her thoughts muddy; she needed to talk to someone to clarify them. Osseion, cheerful as always, was standing guard outside their room. His shoulders were broader than the door and he had to bend his head to get inside. She asked where Mendark was.

'He was called away to see a visitor – he went toward the south-west side a couple of hours ago. Any luck with the boat?'

'No! I'll go and find them.' She set off and said to the first Hlune she saw, 'Take me to Mendark, if you please.'

The woman shook in rage. 'Go back inside,' she hissed.

Tallia's leg was incredibly painful. She was in no mood to be trifled with. *'Take me to Mendark!'* she roared, shaking her fist in the woman's face.

The guard gestured to another Hlune. They spoke together in whispers. The woman then took Tallia's sleeve and led her on a labyrinthine passage through the wharves, finally emerging onto a rainy deck on the seaward side. It was windy here, only partly shielded by the upper levels from the spitting rain. Suddenly Tallia caught sight of a vaguely familiar figure turning a corner up ahead. In the dim light it was more a matter of posture and rolling gait.

'Shand?' she cried, limping after him.

The figure turned and it *was* old Shand, whom she had not seen since Tullin. He laughed and held out his arms.

'What a pleasure it is to see you again,' she said. 'I thought you had decided not to come after all.'

'I nearly didn't, even though I'd promised. But here I am! And what a disaster!'

'Yes, Mendark must be losing his wits. When can I talk to you?'

'Right now, if you like. Have you breakfasted?'

Tallia had not and she was famished.

'There's a place up the hill that still has good food, if you dare to go that far.'

Tallia looked uneasy. 'Every way is watched.'

'I know a secret path,' he said. 'You're after a boat?'

'Desperately!'

'Well, I might be able to help you. There are fortunes to be made in this war, for those bold enough. I've also been looking for a boat these past few days and I've found one. I'm going to meet the fellow now. Come with me.'

'How did you get in here?

'A contact.'

'Can I ask you a personal question, Shand?' she asked as they walked.

'Of course, though I won't guarantee to answer it.'

'When we first met in Tullin and I asked why you had not helped Karan, you made an excuse about being too old. Yet here you are, right in the middle of the war.'

He paced steadily beside her. 'I'm a fool!' he said after such a long interval that she was afraid he wasn't going to answer at all. 'I could have prevented all this, but I was afraid of waking the past. I love my life in Tullin, chopping wood and serving in the inn, and when all the work is done, sitting in the sun on the veranda with a mug of wine. I *am* very old, you know, too old for this.'

Near the edge of the wharf city they climbed off the right-of-way, went down steps right to the water, passed through a cleverly concealed door and, after a lengthy walk underground, emerged in the alleys of old Thurkad. Soon Shand stopped outside a brown door in a stone wall. No one was looking; he gave a triple knock then four single raps, and the door creaked open. A scrawny old man inspected them carefully, especially Tallia, finally allowing them in. Steps led up and down. They were conveyed to a basement hall, through two more doors and into a large, low room with a fire in one corner. The room was smoky, dark and warm. There were many small tables but few were occupied. Shand spoke to the barman, a scarlet-faced sot by the look of him, who shook his head.

'He is not here yet,' said Shand. Then to the barman again, 'What is the menu today?'

'*Horlash!*' said the barman. 'Horlash today, horlash tomor-row, horlash till the end of time.' Horlash was a red spicy stew of seafood and vegetables, its ingredients varying according to what was cheap at the markets.

'Then bring us two servings, with bread and hot wine,' said Shand, walking over to the fire and holding out his hands to the blaze.

Tallia sat down at a table beside the fire. The horlash came, large bowls nearly full. It smelled wonderful, though she ate the whole bowl without tasting it, too immersed in her problems.

'The war has turned Thurkad upside down but you see some places are already back in business,' said Shand with his mouth full. 'Here, anything can be arranged if you can pay the tariff.'

'What is this place?'

'No Name!'

'Pardon?'

'It's called No Name. Always has been. It has been here for half a dozen lifetimes.'

'What contacts you have!' Tallia said with admiration. 'I've been in Thurkad ten years and never heard of it.'

'*Had*. They are nearly all gone now. I've been out of bus-iness too long.'

Tallia mopped her brow, took off her coat and hung it over the back of the chair. Two stone goblets of steaming wine appeared: dark red, sweet and aromatic with cloves and curls of cassia bark.

'One of these in your belly and you'll be hot for a week,' said the barman, with a casual leer at Tallia's bosom. She gave him a cold stare, he went even redder, swiped at the table with his cloth and slouched back to the bar.

Even Shand's goblet was still half-full when a fat man came in, took a drink and followed the barman's pointing finger to their table. He looked them over carefully before pulling up a chair.

'Pender is my name,' he said, staring at Tallia and frowning. 'I know your face.' She said nothing. Shand sipped his wine.

'Two years ago, it must be, eh! You came to Sith with the Magister. I was unloading at the passenger wharf. They ordered me out of the way. You were wearing crimson and black. I thought you were his *dolicha*, his concubine.'

'This is Tallia bel Soon, once of Crandor, and now Mendark's chief lieutenant,' said Shand sternly.

Pender was not easily embarrassed. 'Crandor! There is a place! It would cost buckets of gold if you want to go there, eh!' He rubbed bristly jowls, smiling with the kind of dreamy greed generally associated with winning the Thurkad lottery.

'I am Shand,' said Shand. 'First, my business! It will take two days, beginning tonight, if you can manage that.'

'I can,' Pender said.

'And immediately after that, Tallia has a commission that will make your fortune.'

Pender positively glowed. 'Where do you want to go?'

'I –' Shand began, then changed his mind. 'No, settle Tallia's first, she needs to get back.'

Tallia was in no hurry to return but evidently Shand's business was private.

'Where can I take you?' asked Pender.

'Zile, and possibly further,' she said.

Pender grunted, his eyes narrowed. The greed was internalised. 'Just you?'

'There are others.'

'The Magister perhaps?' Despite his recent overthrow, Mendark had held that position for so many lifetimes that the title was not readily transferable to another.

'Perhaps,' she said.

He calculated. 'A month there, a month back. No doubt there will be a lot of waiting around, earning nothing. Supplies for . . . about how many people?'

'Say, five or six.'

'Six, plus myself and crew. I must pay ten times over the

rate at the moment. Supplies alone will cost ten tells.'

'No doubt you'll buy most well away from Thurkad, at not much over the normal rate.'

'Some maybe, though who knows where the war will be in a month, eh! And spare canvas, cord, spars . . .'

'I understand all that,' said Tallia, tapping the table impatiently. 'Name a figure!'

'A two of hundreds to Zile,' said Pender in a gust of words, as though if he said it fast enough it would not sound so outrageous. 'Tells, that is.' Then, growing bolder at her lack of reaction, 'Double that if the Magister comes. Plus all damage, tolls, customs charges, bribes and other expenses will be to your account. After Zile we'll negotiate again.'

'We could buy our own boat for that,' said Tallia. The figure was higher than her most pessimistic expectations.

'Before the war you *might* have, if it were old and rotting to pieces,' exaggerated Pender, 'but now, my little skiff would fetch that price. And who would you have crew it? I give you the best. Besides, if we are caught I lose my head, a precious thing, eh!'

'Remarkable!' said Shand ironically.

Pender glared at him. 'Anyway, I will have to find a bigger boat on the way. Mine is too small for the stormy gulf. That will take your entire fee and every grint of my savings as well.'

'Let me consider,' said Tallia. 'Five minutes, if you please.'

Pender took his drink and waddled back to the bar.

'Is he reliable?'

'He's all we've got!' said Shand. 'But I gather he's more reliable than most and, as a sailor, one of the best.'

'I had heard that, too. And the price?'

'It's a scandal, but you don't have any choice. Today, boats are scarce as donkey eggs. Besides, even if it were a thousand tells Mendark would scarcely notice, given the riches he has secreted across Meldorin against such a time as this. Yggur will find the Magister's coffers as bare as Shag's Rock.' He referred to the guano-crusted pinnacle guarding the entrance to the harbour of Thurkad.

'I know. I hid a lot of it myself these last few years.'

'A little of it. He has been putting it away for more than a hundred years.'

'Oh!' Tallia actually looked surprised. 'One last thing. We've worn out our welcome. I don't suppose you could consider letting us go first?'

'I don't suppose I could,' said Shand. 'My business is urgent. I dare say the Hlune will be more accommodating once they know you're going.'

'Well, thank you for your help.' She waved at Pender and drained her goblet.

'Agreed,' she said. 'We meet at the north-eastern corner of the wharf an hour before dawn three days from now. Half the fee then, the rest in Zile.'

'A quarter now, a quarter then, and the rest in Zile,' said Pender. 'There are a lot of expenses.'

'Very well.'

He held out his hand, which she crushed to seal the contract. Pender winced. Tallia counted out a quarter of the fee in her lap and passed it to him. Shand stood up and she embraced him. 'I hope we meet again,' she said. 'Thank you.'

'We will,' said Shand. 'Go back the way we came.'

When she had gone Shand and Pender sat down again. The waiter refilled their goblets.

'You can trust her,' said Shand.

'And Mendark?'

'Make sure your interests always coincide.'

Pender grunted. 'Now, what can I do for you?'

'I want to go north tonight, as soon as it is dark.' Shand pulled a map out of his pocket and they huddled over it, talking winds and currents and tides, where supplies were to be had in the war, and many other things. Finally, their bowls empty, Shand nodded and they shook hands on the arrangement.

'And your fee?' he asked.

'Two tells,' said Pender absently.

Shand handed over the fortune at once. He had expected it to be more. Now all he had to do was get back into the wharf city and find Karan. But Shand had his confidence back – he knew he could do it, now. First, better make a last call on Ulice.

A SEA OF TROUBLES

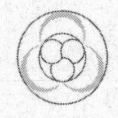

Berenet oiled his stone and glided it down the sword blade yet again. The wait had been nerve-racking in the extreme, the Hlune so hostile that Mendark feared betrayal at every moment. No one had been allowed out of the dank room for days. Mendark started at every creak and groan of the wharf structure, every footfall outside the door.

'What if Pender doesn't come?' he muttered, pulling at his hair. 'What if it's a trap?'

'Then we'll take a good few of them with us,' said Berenet. As natty as ever, he seemed unfazed by the week in close confinement, though he sharpened his sword unceasingly.

'Will you put that damned thing away!' Tallia shouted.

Berenet looked up at her from under black brows and rasped the steel up the other side.

On the third morning after Tallia's meeting with Pender, the door was thrown open before dawn and six grim-faced Hlune ordered them out. They were led on a labyrinthine passage through the wharf.

'Where are they taking us?' Lilis whispered.

'To a boat, I hope,' said Tallia, though she rather thought they were being led to their deaths. Finally they reached the seaward side of the wharf, where the wind howled in their faces. It was just getting light.

'Go down!' said one of the Hlune.

Far below the waves crashed violently. 'Down?' said Mendark, like a man required to walk the plank.

Lilis peered over the edge. A none-too-secure wooden ladder extended several storeys below, to a little jetty stepped off the wharf city.

'Move! Your boat is coming!'

Mendark looked all around. There was no sign of a vessel in the white-capped waters. A crowd of Hlune had assembled in the gloom, a thicket of spears in their hands. He bowed to the Hlune and held out his hand but the toga-clad figure dashed his arm aside. The man's face was as dark as the stormy seas.

At that moment a galley appeared, cruising along the edge of the wharf city. They retreated into the shadows until it was gone. They've betrayed us, Tallia thought. She glanced at Mendark. He was past reacting.

'The ladder looks a bit suspect,' said Tallia. 'Let me go first.

She climbed down carefully, her cloak writhing and crackling in the wind, and her little shadow followed her. Just as they reached the bottom a wave burst over the jetty, sweeping Lilis off her feet toward the edge. Tallia stretched and grabbed her, holding herself with one foot hooked through the lowest rung. They held onto the ladder while the others crept down.

Lilis braced herself against the wind and pulled the hood close about her ears, squinting into the spray. Still no boat! Tallia was sure that Pender had taken the money and informed on them; that this was a trap.

Behind them the massive piles of the wharf city stretched in lines like temple pillars. Here, on the seaward side, even the lowest deck was high above the water. A freezing, sleet-laden south wind howled through the piles, coating everything in a crust of grainy ice. It had been blowing for days down the whole fetch of the Sea of Thurkad, driving the waters up into wild, crashing waves as high as the masts of a small ship. Another wave broke over the jetty, wetting them to the knees.

A second galley appeared, cruising at the limit of visibility, then disappeared into the mist.

'They've abandoned us,' said Berenet, wiping the water from his face. His mustachioes hung limply, dripping with water.

Lilis was the least concerned of any of them. She had her new boots, her warm clothes, a full belly, and that was more than she had been able to hope for in the last seven years. Tomorrow was too far away to worry about.

A funny-looking, shabby boat appeared out of the rain. 'That's it?' Mendark said incredulously. It was not much bigger than a skiff, with a little stubby mast. Pender was upright at the tiller, shouting towards the wharf, though the wind took his words away.

'We're going to Zile in *that*?' Mendark repeated, appalled. He looked up. The spears were angled down over the ladder. He gestured behind him and the others came up to the edge.

Lilis, who had a healthy fear of boats, grew afraid. The boat approached, backing up on its oars. The nearside pair were shipped just in time, as the side of the boat crashed against the jetty. By the light of the lantern she saw a name painted on the bow, *The Dancing Goose*, and a rudely carved figurehead that might have represented that species, orange of beak and wild of eye.

The figure at the bow flung a rope. Osseion caught it and took a half-turn around a pile, swaying back and forth to keep the tension even as the boat rose and fell. Another rope was flung from the stern; Berenet looped it twice around a post and tied it with a lubber's knot as Mendark, Tallia and Lilis scrambled in. Berenet jumped, landing on the piled bags. Something smashed inside. Last of all Osseion sprang in, the oarsmen took up their oars and pushed the boat away.

A crewman heaved at Berenet's rope, thinking it caught,

but it was tied fast. Suddenly they were in deadly peril. The water shrank down in advance of a huge wave and the rope began to lift the stern up out of the water. Lower sank the bow. Even Lilis knew that the following wave would swamp them or dash them to pieces against the side of the jetty.

Pender leapt up, knife in hand, to slash the rope free. The stern crashed down; the wave flung them into the side of the jetty. Someone shrieked. There was a creaking and a cracking of timbers until it seemed the boat must capsize. Water gushed in through the side, then the surge spun them around, past the jetty and beneath the wharf city into quiet water, the mast rattling against the high platform above.

The rows of great piles, faintly outlined in the gloom by patches of phosphorescent weed, stretched beyond sight. The oily water rose and fell. Drips cascaded down from above. The crew shipped the oars and manhandled their boat further under the wharf. In a place where the piles were thickly clustered, supporting some great structure above, the crew baled the water out. Pender calmly lit a lantern, stepped to the middle of the boat and took Berenet by the front of his coat.

'You incompetent fool!' he cried, shaking him. 'You nearly killed us all.'

Berenet tried to push him away. The beautiful coat tore down the front. 'Damn you,' he screeched, 'you'll pay for that.'

'*You'll pay!* Look what you've done to my new boat!'

'Call this a boat!' Berenet sneered. 'You couldn't sail it across a bathtub.'

Pender was used to insults but he was inordinately proud of his new vessel. 'It's got too much ballast,' he roared, and as the boat rolled in the swell he tipped Berenet neatly over the side.

'What the hell are you doing?' cried Mendark.

Berenet disappeared under the oily water, then surfaced, spluttering and swearing.

'Damned fool,' said Pender. 'I won't have him. Swim to the ladder,' he shouted, pointing. Berenet thrashed toward the nearest pile.

Mendark lurched forward. There was a long gash across his forehead.

'Do you want to sail to Zile, *or walk*?' Pender asked icily.

'You'll regret this!' Berenet screamed as he pulled himself up a decayed plank ladder.

'Pick him up!' Mendark said furiously.

'Damned if I will!' cried Pender, staring him down.

'We all go or none,' said Mendark, but his voice cracked as he spoke.

'As you please,' Pender replied. 'I'll refund what's left of your advance, of course. Chert, bring my strongbox.'

'Perhaps,' said Mendark in a low voice, 'we can negotiate.'

'I say who travels on my boat,' said Pender, 'and he doesn't!'

Mendark wiped blood out of his eyes. His bluff had been called. He was not prepared to do the same, especially for someone under suspicion of treachery.

'Pull me across,' said Mendark.

He clung onto the ladder for a moment, speaking in a low voice. Berenet pushed him away, shouting, 'Hennia was the traitor, you fool! I'll never forgive you for this.'

Mendark froze. 'Hennia? Why didn't you tell me?'

'I wasn't sure until she left us, and then there was no point. I do not accuse without evidence, *unlike some*!'

Mendark glared at Tallia but she was lying on her back, blood running from her nose. He tried to climb up the ladder, speaking urgently. Berenet pushed him away with his foot.

'It's too late, Mendark! I served you faithfully and you judged me on hearsay, and *hers*!' He spat in Tallia's direction. 'I'll do everything in my power to bring you down.' He dragged himself up the ladder with a face that would have curdled beer.

Mendark dropped back into the boat. The blood on his

cheeks looked like the war paint of a savage. 'You had better be worth your price,' he said coldly to Pender.

'I am,' said Pender just as coldly. 'Sit down, eh! Hey, Chert, get that gear tidied up.'

The shorter of the two sailors, a solid, short-legged man with muscles bulging through his jerkin, made signs with his fingers to the other. They stowed the packs and the chests. The passengers huddled in the covered area at the bow and took stock of themselves. Osseion had three fingers badly lacerated and crushed between the side of the wharf and the boat. Tallia looked dazed, with a welt on the side of her head and blood all over her face. Lilis had fallen under Tallia; apart from a bruise on her chin she was unhurt.

Mendark lifted Tallia awkwardly, with her head back; there came a gurgling sound in her throat. Lilis hopped up and down, tears on her cheeks, thinking that her friend was dying.

'She's choking, you fool.' Pender thrust Mendark roughly out of the way and pulled Tallia toward him. She slid off the seat onto her knees, then he put his fingers in her mouth to free her tongue. She began to choke and cough up blood onto the bottom of the boat.

'Water!' Pender shouted. Osseion passed a full dipper across, his mashed fingers leaving red streaks on the side. Pender turned Tallia's head sideways and gently washed her face clean with his thick fingers. He lifted her back on the seat, inspecting her with the lantern.

Cleaned up, they saw that she was not hurt that badly after all. Her nose was swollen, the bone possibly cracked, and the left side of her head was bruised and bloody in two places. Tallia opened her eyes. Lilis exclaimed her relief.

'Oh!' Tallia said thickly. 'What happened?'

'Rest now,' said Pender.

Mendark helped her to the covered area at the bow, onto a folded canvas. Pender turned to Osseion, who sat stoically at the end of the seat, staring at his lacerated fingers.

'Hey, what's your name?' Pender said to Lilis.

'Lilis.'

'Well, Lilis, get the dipper and bring some water from that barrel. No, look, there's a tap. Good. Wash his hands and clean all the muck out of these cuts. Can you do that?'

Lilis was afraid of Osseion, for he looked so big and fierce, and his bare arms were scarred to the shoulders with clan markings. 'Yes,' she said in an insignificant squeak and set to work, looking all the time back at Tallia. The fingers were rent to the bone from the barnacles, but not broken, and they were soon salved and bandaged, and Mendark's head too.

'Now let's see what damage the *Goose* has taken,' said Pender. 'Hey!' he shouted to the crew. 'Put her up over that beam so I can get a look underneath.'

They rowed the boat hard onto a beam that was just awash, then got a line onto a pile and heaved until the warped planks rode up out of the water. Pender stripped down to grubby underwear and slid into the oily water, inspecting the damage with care. Lilis, leaning over the side, was awestruck by the vast globe of his belly and his mighty hams.

The side of the boat, near the gunwale, was splintered and broken. Further down, below the waterline, the hull was sound but some of the planks were sprung and threads of water trickled in, even in the calm conditions. Pender frowned.

'Chert! Cut me a bit of canvas, this size.' He made a shape with his hands.

While that was being done, Pender worked from the inside with hammer and chisel, levering the planks back in place as best he could. Mendark was up and down a dozen times, staring every way, agonising about the time the repairs were taking. Finally the canvas was tarred and nailed down over the planks from the outside, and the cracks tarred on the inside too. A green, misty light began to spread around them.

'It'll hold for a while,' Pender said, rubbing the stubble on his jaw. 'But it's going to be a big risk at sea in this weather . . .'

'Come on!' said Mendark, looking panicky. 'Every minute puts us in greater danger.'

'Then move!' said Pender. '*Up front!*' he shouted. 'Bale with this,' passing a wooden bucket forward.

Just as they started to move, a tall figure appeared at the top of the ladder Berenet had climbed.

'Stop right there!' Thyllan's voice was strangely muffled.

Mendark stood up. His former guard were behind Thyllan, armed with spears. Someone that might have been Berenet lurked in the background.

'You! Fatso!' Thyllan shouted. 'Row across.'

Pender stared back at him but did not move. The guards raised their spears.

'Don't,' said Mendark to Thyllan, 'else I turn your brain back to the jelly Tensor left you in.'

Thyllan raised his hands. 'Let's be reasonable. All I want is the boat and the gold. You've got plenty more hidden away.'

Mendark looked across to Tallia for help, but she was so dazed that she hardly knew what was going on. 'And me dead,' he said.

Pender, who was standing directly behind Mendark, said something in his ear. Mendark jerked.

'Hurry,' Thyllan shouted. 'Or I put a spear through the child.'

'Means nothing to me,' Mendark shouted back.

Lilis went as still as a post. 'Get behind me, Lilis,' said Osseion, and she crept into shelter gladly, peering out between arm and body.

'Row across,' said Pender to his sailors.

'Leave those oars alone,' Mendark cried, but already they were moving forward.

When they touched the pier, the sailor called Chert held onto the pier while Thyllan came tentatively down the worm-eaten ladder.

'Get a rope onto that ladder, Chert,' said Pender softly.

'You, big fellow, take his oar and get ready to row like blazes.' Osseion slipped into the seat, gripping the oar with his bandaged fingers.

'Pass the chests up,' said Thyllan, looking up the ladder anxiously.

'What's the matter?' asked Mendark. 'Are you out without authority? I'll throw the gold overboard before I hand it to you.'

Thyllan called his guard. They made a chain down the ladder, the sixth guard climbing into the boat.

'Come on, hurry it up!'

The guard heaved at the first chest. It was immensely heavy. He got it up knee-high, then just as he did so Chert, still holding onto the pier, rocked the boat violently. The guard overbalanced, dropping the corner of the chest on his foot. He shrieked.

'At the oars, *heave*!' cried Pender, and they thrashed the water on either side. The boat leapt backwards; the rope tightened, ripping the bottom half of the ladder off the pile. Thyllan and the guards clung desperately to the ladder. 'Harder!' Pender roared. The wormy wood snapped at Thyllan's feet. The guards plunged into the water where, dragged by the boat, they flailed helplessly under the weight of leather armour.

Chert heaved the injured guard after them, slashed the rope and the rowers pulled away. By the time Thyllan scrambled up the ladder and snatched a javelin they were safe behind the clustered piles of the wharf.

The Dancing Goose had just emerged from the shelter of the wharf when there came a cry from the bow, 'The blackfists!' and a crossbow bolt slammed into the pile beside Pender's head.

A long low dark galley was racing out of the rain at them, moving swiftly under a bank of rowers. Pender did not hesitate. 'Back!' he cried.

The boat spun on the crest of a wave and shot beneath the wharf again, into the stillness and the dark.

'Now what?' Mendark groaned.

'We'll have to try and outrun them,' said Pender.

'Outrun a galley?'

'There's a good chance in this wind. Best we've got, anyway. If we're not away in the next ten minutes, we'll never get out. Ready?'

Mendark nodded doubtfully, though he knew they had no choice. Pender directed the boat in a zig-zag course beneath the wharf city, out to another edge. It was quite light now. There was no sign of the patrolling galley. The two silent crew unlashed the top half of the mast and put it up. They took up their oars. Pender eased the bow out; still no sign. A little further.

'Go!' he said.

The crew strained at their oars. The boat moved sluggishly, wallowing in the big seas until it gained way. The sail went up in jerks. Just then the galley came fast around a corner of the wharf, a few hundred spans away, heeling over, the foam hurled away from its plunging bow. The lookout pointed and it altered course fractionally.

Mendark cried out. Lilis crept under Tallia's long arm. Pender had the sail up at last. The canvas belled out in the wild wind, rolling the boat over dangerously. The oarsmen shipped their oars, the tiller went over and they began to gather speed with the wind directly behind, flying straight toward the galley, which was skimming along the edge of the wharf.

'Get your heads down,' shouted Pender.

'No chance,' said Mendark, anticipating what the enemy would do. 'As we cross in front they'll spin around and come broadside on to ram us.

Pender turned slightly from the wharf and the galley began to turn as well.

'We'll never make it!' Mendark cried.

It was clear that they would not, though still Pender persisted with his course.

'*Heads!*' he yelled.

At the last possible instant he flung the tiller over hard and the boat shot into the narrow space between the other vessel and the edge of the wharf, shattering the oars all along that side of the galley. For a moment the air was full of shards of oar and rowers flung off their benches, then they struck the galley a glancing blow near the stern, scraped the other side along a wharf pile, sending a stinging shower of barnacles and tiny mussels into their faces, and suddenly they were free and fleeting east down the harbour faster than the little boat had ever gone.

Behind them the galley listed sharply, a host of hands grasped for the wharf, the weight pushed the gunwale under the water. The galley swamped and disappeared beneath a wave.

Thank you, Shand, thought Tallia, looking up at their fat captain. Trust you to find the best.

'They were waiting for you,' said Pender. 'Twice the fee would not have been enough had I known.'

'Well, you accepted the contract and you're bound to take us. But I take the point. Get us safely to Zile and I'll pay you double,' said Mendark, now appreciating what his captain was worth. 'Ah, poor Berenet,' he sighed, with a quite uncharacteristic show of sympathy. 'That was a bad thing.'

Lilis sat up, shaking barnacles off. Tallia stirred on her canvas. 'Where *is* Berenet?'

'Pender threw him overboard,' said Osseion soberly.

'Well rid,' said Tallia nasally. 'I could swear I saw him talking to one of Thyllan's people late last night.'

'He was spying for me!' said Mendark, barely controlling his fury. 'I once thought that he might be Magister after me. He had such promise.'

'I never saw it,' said Tallia under her breath.

'Just shut up, Tallia!' Mendark cried. 'He said that Hennia was the traitor and I believe him. I've turned a friend into an enemy because of you.'

'That was him at the top of the ladder,' said Lilis.

'He's in good company then. *And* he knows where some of your treasure is hid, Mendark,' Tallia went on.

'Enough!' yelled Mendark. He fished curls of willow bark out of the medical bag and passed them across. 'Chew this. It might make you a bit less shrewish.'

She took the medicine silently and pulled the canvas sheet up to keep out the wind and spray. Her nose was so swollen that she could not breathe through it. She closed her eyes and tried to sleep through the crashing of the boat, but she could not. Mendark's words had to be considered. Hennia the traitor after all? She went through the evidence in her mind and it fitted Hennia better than it had Berenet. Had she misjudged him; been blinded by his appearance and his manner? It began to look all too likely. What would the consequences be?

Lilis got up and went forward. 'We're not free yet,' said Pender. 'With this wind they could still catch us before the Heads. Hey, come away from there,' he called to Lilis, who was stretched out on the bow near the figurehead.

'*The Dan-cing Goo-se,*' she sounded, sliding feet first back into the boat, smiling to herself.

'Mendark can't afford to lose anyone else,' Pender said sternly, pointing to the seat.

They crashed and wallowed through steep ugly waves, east then south then east again, racing toward the Heads and the dubious safety of the Sea of Thurkad. Now they were heading due east, sliding along the crests of the swell. It was overcast, a grey day with a wild wind. Sometimes the waves threatened to break over the side and swamp them. Somehow Pender was always able to anticipate this, though as they dropped into each trough the spray burst in their faces. The wind howled in the lines. Sleet began to collect on every surface, icing their hair and beards.

'We're taking water!' cried Chert and began baling furiously with a canvas bucket.

'How bad?' yelled Pender.

'Can't tell with all this spray.'

'Keep an eye on it then.'

The seas changed direction as they came around a point. A squall blotted out the view. Sleety rain lashed them for a minute or two then the squall passed. The day seemed to be growing darker. Suddenly a light flashed high ahead. Mendark groaned.

'What's that?' he cried.

'Lighthouse on North Head,' shouted Pender over the wind. 'They're signalling!'

'What does it say?'

'Can't read it. You can guess as well as I can, eh.'

'Yes,' Mendark said gloomily.

'With luck, he hasn't any boats outside in this weather. Here you!' Pender yelled at Osseion.

'Osseion's the name. What can I do?'

'Osseion, eh!' said Pender. 'Keep lookout behind.'

Osseion stood up, braced himself with his good hand and peered into the gloom. 'Nothing yet,' he said.

'The buggers! Look sharp, mind.'

Minutes passed. As they moved down harbour the angle of the swell changed progressively. Now they were sailing directly into it.

'There's the Heads,' said Mendark as they climbed a great wave.

Closer to the sea, the swell came directly from the east and grew higher and longer, so that in the troughs they were almost becalmed. In this way they progressed, rising and crashing down again, angling across the waves lest the impact tear the weakened timbers apart, at the top the wind catching them with a jerk and in the trough dying away almost as suddenly.

'There's a light flashing behind us,' cried Osseion as they teetered at the crest of a huge wave. 'Gone now.'

'Can you see a boat yet?'

'No!'

'Then perhaps they can't see us either.' Pender glanced up at the grey sail, the colour of the water. 'Won't be long though.'

The lighthouse was signalling again, perhaps repeating the message. Now, to their dismay, the clouds parted and a misty sun illuminated the Heads to north and south, the white-crusted spike of Shag's Rock, the violent sea and the grey light-tower.

'They'll see us now!' said Pender, and as they climbed the next swell Osseion sang out.

'I see them! One, two, three.'

They looked where his finger pointed. There, lifted high on the crest of a wave, was a black galley just like the one that had attacked them before. Behind it, two more. They were not much more than a sea mile away.

'Three!' said Pender heavily, 'and coming as fast as a storm.'

The boat crashed down into the trough, the mast gouging great curves in the sky, the planks groaning. Tallia's head felt like a dropped pumpkin. She swayed on her feet.

'Watch it,' said Mendark sharply.

She sat down suddenly, holding her head.

'Are you hurting?' asked Lilis, putting her cold hand on Tallia's forehead.

Tallia wiped a few tears across her cheek. 'Very badly,' she said. 'But I'll be all right in a while.'

They rose up the next crest. At the top the wind flung them over so hard that the packs fell into the sloshing bilge. 'It's coming in faster now,' Chert yelled as they restacked their gear. 'Nearly too fast for me.'

'Tallia, get up there and bale! Osseion, see what you can do with this.' Pender heaved him a large dipper. 'There's a pot under the seat, Lilis. Mendark, what are you good for? A fog or a mist would do nicely right now, eh!'

237

'That's beyond anyone in this wind,' said Mendark, looking as bleak as the water. 'How far to the sea?'

'Best part of a league. Just a bit too far, eh! Well, can't you blast them apart with fire from your fingers, or bring Leviathan up from the depths to smite them with his tail? Surely some of the tales must be true!'

'Leviathan needs be nearby; I can't make one from a sardine,' Mendark replied.

Pender was not suppressed. 'I heard tales of the *great* magicians who could destroy a ship with a single blast.'

'Tales are all they are,' said Mendark. 'A blast of *what*? The Secret Art cannot disobey the laws of matter and energy. A ship is cunningly made to withstand the wild storms and seas of the Great Ocean. How can one mind call upon greater forces than that, how shape and focus them? My head would need to be as big as your Leviathan. You know not of what you speak.'

'Then what *can* you do?'

'This is the limit of my power, and none of us has greater, as a man can never run as fast as a horse. If that boat had a fatal weakness, say a single peg that, being loosened, would cause the parts of it to become unseamed, and I knew well that weakness and that peg, I might be able to work it loose to sink the ship, though it would cost me dear in pain and aftersickness. No more can I do, and if it were otherwise we masters of the Secret Art, were we so disposed, would long ago have enslaved every other being on Santhenar. Besides, far easier for the mind to design an engine of destruction and the hands to build –'

The boat left the water for a second at the crest of a wave, then smashed down again, hurling him off his seat. Mendark climbed back on, wiping his face.

'What about a blast of fire? Surely even *you* can make fire, burn them!'

Mendark tried to match sarcasm with sarcasm. 'Most of the magical wonders you gaped at in your cups were just done by illusion, by *seeming*. They were not *real*. To make *real* things move or change or break requires real work, and much of it. Yes, I *can* conjure fire from my fingertips but it still won't burn wet wood. Now if only they had a barrel of naphtha on board, you would see a blast to light up the whole of Thurkad.' With that thought Mendark looked longingly back in the direction of the pursuit.

'A charlatan and a fraud!' Pender muttered under his breath. 'I knew it all along.'

'I need something to work with,' Mendark went on unhappily. 'Anyway, they're still too far away. I have to see them, *know them*, before I can do anything. Tallia may be able to confuse them; she has more skill with illusion than I.'

'Well, get the hell up the front and bale,' Pender yelled and, as Mendark swayed forward, 'Pox-ridden bastard of a mule and a goat, you are as useless as Llian of Chanthed. Tallia!'

Osseion was baling furiously with his dipper. White teeth flashed in his dark face as Tallia passed him on hands and knees, astounded at what Pender could get away with even in this desperate situation. Lilis glared at Pender, furious at the insult to Llian, her first friend, but Pender was oblivious of his crime.

'What can I do?' Tallia asked, clinging unsteadily to the side. The spray had started her head bleeding again. Lilis stopped baling long enough to wipe the blood away with her hand.

'Anything that will hide us or confuse them, even for a couple of minutes,' said Pender. 'They're coming on too quickly. I thought the seas would slow them more out here.'

'Lilis,' said Tallia. 'Come here! Hold me steady.'

She stood up and tried to do something with her fingers. A double wave corkscrewed the boat, flinging them both into the bilge.

'Can't you do it sitting down?' Pender wondered.

'I've got to see them clearly.'

'Leave it then. I don't want to lose you over the side.'

They pounded on through a swell that grew higher and ever higher still, though less steep and further apart as they approached the Heads.

'What's that,' cried Lilis, who was facing south as she baled. 'More boats, Pender. Another two!'

'Farsh!' swore Pender. 'Farsh, farsh, *farsh*!'

'They're closer than the others,' she went on.

'And coming faster with the wind,' said Pender, standing up at the tiller. 'But the seas will slow them when they cross between the Heads. If they're not careful they'll swamp. How is the water?' he shouted, though there was little need to ask.

'Gaining,' came the reply. 'I can feel a crack opening and closing with each wave.'

'Well, bale faster then!' He turned to Tallia, who was plying the dipper absently, her forehead wrinkled and her eyes mere slits against the spray.

'I think we're caught,' he said, almost conversationally. 'They'll get to the Heads first.'

'Can't you dodge through like the last time?' asked Lilis, without stopping. She closed her eyes as the spray smacked her in the face. Her pale hair was running with water.

'They'll expect tricks now. Doubtless they want Mendark and Tallia alive, but they'll fill the rest of us with arrows at close range if we try to break through. There's just too many of them, child.'

'Keep going,' said Tallia, gritting her teeth. 'I might be able to do something yet.'

The wind here gusted westerly, flattening the swell a little and helping them more than it did the galleys. Now they were but half a sea mile inside the Heads. The two boats from the south were a bit further away, rolling and labouring in the great seas between the Heads, moving directly towards Shag's Rock to cut them off. The other three were still gaining.

'What about there?' cried Tallia, pointing to the narrow channel that now appeared between North Head and the Rock, a tiny gap in the wild surf breaking from the sheer northern tip of Shag's Rock all the way up to the rock platform at North Head.

'The Gap? Not in this weather. It looks wide enough from here, but the reef goes nearly all the way across. There's just a slot of deep water against the cliff. The tides race through there, eh! Unless you approach it perfectly, the current and the surge and the wind will push you onto the Rock.'

'Can you swim, Lilis dear?' asked Tallia, touching her on the shoulder.

'Of course. My father taught me,' she said, baling away with her good arm.

'I can keep myself afloat,' grunted Osseion, 'if it's not too rough.'

'I can't swim a stroke,' said Pender. Everyone looked at him in astonishment. 'That's why I'm such a good sailor, eh!'

He looked back. The boats behind were almost close enough to shoot arrows at them. The ones to the north were crawling towards the Rock. Pender caught Tallia's eye.

'The reef coming out from North Head has two prongs that almost touch the Rock,' he said, pointing. 'See them there! After the first there's a patch of clear water where the tide sometimes makes a whirlpool, and beyond that is the second prong of the reef. The channel is wider there, eh! Beyond that there's a lagoon before an outer reef that runs from the outside of Shag's Rock across to the seaward side of North Head. The channel through that is just a slot, narrower than this boat, so we can only get over the outer reef on the crest of the swell. It might be possible, but the timing would have to be perfect, eh!'

'And you know it well?'

'I used to sail the Gap for a dare when I was young. Though never in seas like this.' He paused. 'Or a boat this big.'

'How did you never learn to swim, growing up in boats?'

'Just never did. Always panicked in the water when they tried to teach me. But I've survived two shipwrecks.'

'Could you take us through from the shape of the cliffs, ignoring the sea?'

'I might, with a lot of luck. You can change the sea?'

'Of course not! But I might be able to make it look different for a moment, enough to confuse them. But as Mendark said, to work illusions you have to be close.'

'Water's steady,' Chert sang out from the bow.

The enemy behind was very close now, within bowshot, though there was little risk of being hit in these seas. The other two boats were crashing through the swell midway between the Heads. The end was just minutes away.

Pender squinted southwards. 'They're going too hard. There must be a big price on you.' He was looking at Mendark as he spoke.

'It's big!' said Mendark.

'They'll swamp!' Pender said, standing up at the tiller again. Almost as he spoke the first and faster boat lurched, oars waved in the air and it stopped dead in the water. A massed cry was heard above the wind. The second boat slowed, swerved around the first, its oars flashed backwards for a moment then it slowly continued. 'No, they're safe. A bold captain but a skilled one. See, they're baling the water out now. For a minute I thought we might have squeaked past, if there was just one. They're coming on again.'

'No chance of getting past to sea?'

'No. There's nowhere to go now. The others have spread out to block us going north-west, not that there was any chance there. Surrender, the rocks or the Gap are our choices.'

'The Gap then,' said Mendark heavily. He looked at the others. 'The Gap,' they said.

'Lilis,' said Tallia, 'can you swim a hundred spans?'

'Easily,' she said proudly. 'I used to bathe in the sea.'

'What about your shoulder?'

Lilis still wore her arm in a sling. 'It doesn't hurt anymore.'

'Good. Here are two tells. Put them somewhere safe. I want you to jump out and swim to shore now. Head for that little beach, go down . . .'

Lilis pushed the hand away. 'You did not leave me. I will go through the Gap.'

They went back to their tasks, everyone but Pender baling furiously, and even reduced the water level a little. The wind had come further around to the west, though the vessels behind still gained. The seaward boats were cutting through huge seas, quite slowly now, approaching the southern end of the Rock.

Now, as they neared the Gap, Pender pointed out its features to Tallia.

'Shag's Rock has cliffs all around, and except in the Gap, a rock platform surrounds it. See, there are the inner reefs running from North Head, where the waves are breaking. We have to get through there, right against the cliff.'

He pointed, but all Tallia could see was a great wave bursting right across and no channel at all. The rain congealed to ice on her spine.

'And there, you can see the lagoon and the outer reef running back to join with the headland further south. We can't see the slot through the outer reef from here, the breakers are too big. Ah, they're coming right over the reef. It's a wicked passage.'

'You will get us through though, won't you?' came Lilis's piping voice.

'I don't know that I can, child,' he said heavily. 'In five minutes we might all be dead.'

Now they were passing the Gap, a hundred spans out and heading directly toward the outer boats that were waiting, blocking their path to the open sea. The pursuing galleys were not far behind.

'Let them think that we'll try the same manoeuvre as before,' shouted Pender.

the better. But we can't get across the bar until the swell falls.'

'So Yggur's troop galleys won't come either?'

The sailor spat over the side. 'Fair-weather craft, those. We'll be fishing a good day before they dare to put their noses out of port.'

Shand nodded and fell in beside Karan again. 'One tar. That's much better. Let's get out of this wind.'

They watched the waves breaking around the southern headland for a while, then turned back to the town, to a different and more agreeable inn. The next day the gale had blown out and it was a cold sunny day, but the swell had not abated. They walked along the harbour for an hour or two, Karan bought a comb and a little flask of lime perfume, they drank coffee at a quayside table, replenished their supplies and, when in the early afternoon it began to rain, returned hastily to the inn. Karan caught up on her sleep while Shand spent the afternoon with his maps.

The following morning was cloudy and wet, but the dangerous swell had fallen. They took ship on one of the larger vessels, not the one they had seen yesterday.

'The redhead!' exclaimed the captain, as they climbed the plank. 'How was your bath?'

'Does everyone in Ganport know about my affairs?' cried Karan in vexation.

The captain, a thick-bodied woman with a pox-scarred face, snorted. 'It's a change from talking about the weather and the fishing. Besides, anyone who goes one up on old gooseface has our favour, grasping old turnip! Come aboard. My name is Tessariel but everyone calls me Tess.' She was clad in heavy waxed canvas: trousers, coat and hooded cloak. Even her canvas boots were waxed against the wind and the rain, and her garments rasped together as she walked.

Karan felt an overwhelming relief as they left Ganport behind, though soon she was more preoccupied with her stomach, for the sea was still wild. Their boat, which led out saw the unruly red strands peeping out from under her scarf. 'Not while the bamundi are running. Maybe in a week or two, if there is fine weather.'

'Surely there are other boats capable of crossing the sea?'

'There were,' the man agreed, 'but most have fled north from the war. We fishers are all following the bamundi now. Look at the waves – you need a sound boat and a good crew at this time of year. Wait a week or two.'

Shand persisted. 'What would it cost for passage to Grane-wys?'

'Now? Five gold tells would hardly be enough. But after the bamundi season, maybe a tar each. We don't have many passengers though.' He turned back to mending his lines.

Shand and Karan walked on. 'Five tells!' she said. 'That's a fortune.'

'Enough to keep us on the road for a year or two,' he agreed. 'Our need must be really desperate before I would pay that.'

She stared at him in astonishment. 'You would pay *five tells* for me? You *have* five tells! Where did *you* get such wealth? I didn't see . . .'

'Hush. Never talk about such things on the road. I told you that I was not always what I am today.'

'Let's continue on up the coast. There will be other towns, other boats.'

'If we get that far! Wait a minute.' Shand turned back to the fishing boat. 'Do you go out to the islands?'

'Of course. That is where we are based, as a rule.'

'What fare?'

'A tar for the two of you, since we go there anyway, and at our own pace. But you might have to haul on a line if the fish are running well.'

'And when will you go?'

The man looked at the sea. 'Perhaps tomorrow. More likely the day after. It's not the sea that bothers us, you understand. We fish for bamundi in any weather, the wilder

319

Lilis still wore her arm in a sling. 'It doesn't hurt anymore.'

'Good. Here are two tells. Put them somewhere safe. I want you to jump out and swim to shore now. Head for that little beach, go down . . .'

Lilis pushed the hand away. 'You did not leave me. I will go through the Gap.'

They went back to their tasks, everyone but Pender baling furiously, and even reduced the water level a little. The wind had come further around to the west, though the vessels behind still gained. The seaward boats were cutting through huge seas, quite slowly now, approaching the southern end of the Rock.

Now, as they neared the Gap, Pender pointed out its features to Tallia.

'Shag's Rock has cliffs all around, and except in the Gap, a rock platform surrounds it. See, there are the inner reefs running from North Head, where the waves are breaking. We have to get through there, right against the cliff.'

He pointed, but all Tallia could see was a great wave bursting right across and no channel at all. The rain congealed to ice on her spine.

'And there, you can see the lagoon and the outer reef running back to join with the headland further south. We can't see the slot through the outer reef from here, the breakers are too big. Ah, they're coming right over the reef. It's a wicked passage.'

'You will get us through though, won't you?' came Lilis's piping voice.

'I don't know that I can, child,' he said heavily. 'In five minutes we might all be dead.'

Now they were passing the Gap, a hundred spans out and heading directly toward the outer boats that were waiting, blocking their path to the open sea. The pursuing galleys were not far behind.

'Let them think that we'll try the same manoeuvre as before,' shouted Pender.

Something struck the mast of the boat, quivered there for a moment then fell into the bilge. It was a long arrow. Several others whirred overhead as they sank into a trough.

'Stop or be killed,' came a shout from behind.

17

ABANDON SHIP

The dipper rattled against the bottom of the boat.

'Stop baling,' screamed Pender. 'Get down!'

Tallia held her breath. They were right past the Gap; Pender had left it too late.

'Now,' he shouted, flinging the tiller across. 'Hang on tight!'

The hands leapt to their work, the boom swung across, the sail filled with a crack. They drifted closer to the surf breaking over the inner end of the rock platform. Closer, closer. Lilis made a little cry. In seconds they would smash on the rocks. Then the gale gave them a great thrust like a kick in the back and they shot off at right angles, straight for the Gap.

Tallia reached into her mind to release the illusion that she had designed. Her head felt as if it was going to break apart. Suddenly the whole world went misty, the breaking seas smeared into a blur. Pender jerked and stared around him, wild-eyed. Tallia's iron fingers gripped his arm. 'As you *know* it to be,' she said into his ear.

The boat flew past the cliff so close that the end of the boom almost touched, flying faster and faster with the great wind funnelling through the Gap. A flight of arrows gone wild struck the rock high above their heads. She stole a glance over her shoulder. The galleys were already turning towards them, less than a hundred spans away.

They approached the first reef, sinking down in a trough, the cliff at their right shoulders, to their left the black rocks rising like teeth out of the concealing foam. Tallia gasped, fell down and the illusion faded for a second, replaced by wild waves all around. It came back as they blasted through the whirling water, the surge pulling them one way, the tide another. Across the edge of the whirlpool they raced. It flung them sideways with a sickening lurch, they shot past the second reef on the rising swell and into the relative calm of the lagoon, racing toward the invisible gap in the outer reef and the wicked surf breaking along it from one end to the other.

'Pray,' yelled Pender, spilling wind to cut their speed slightly, to synchronise their passage with the bursting waves.

Behind them the three galleys were approaching the first channel in a line. The other two were no longer in sight.

'Down, they're shooting!' shouted Osseion, who was keeping watch again.

They ducked and another flight of arrows sang by. One went straight through the sail, splashing into the sea in front. Behind them the first galley tried to follow where they had gone safely, but with oars thrashing it had to pass further from the cliff. It ran full tilt onto the concealed rocks, shattering into planks and oars and screaming sailors that were soon swallowed by the boiling sea.

Tallia's illusion vanished. The second galley, close behind, swung to avoid the first and smashed on the reef as well, taking the bottom out. It capsized and sank in seconds. The third spun on its oars at the last moment, pulling furiously away, but the funnelled wind and the racing tide pushed it sideways into the Gap. The bow struck the cliff and the stern the reef, it broke in half and disappeared. An oar spun round and round in the whirlpool, then the cliff cut off the scene.

'There,' cried Pender. 'See it – the Slot!' It was the place where he had driven his dinghy through as a child. Ahead the surf raged; they rose up on the swell, up and up, then began to slide down again. Down they sank until the outer reef seemed to thrust up from the water toward them. He made a minute adjustment to the tiller and the lines, then cried, 'Ah, no!'

A huge wave was bursting along the reef in a roar of foam, coming towards them at just the right pace to drive them sideways onto rock. Pender jerked on the lines, spilling a little more wind from the sail, adjusted the tiller again. The sea seemed to suck them down, the rocks sliding by on either side, the boat began to rise again and then they were through the Slot.

Not quite! With a wrench that hurled them all into the bottom of the boat the keel struck the reef. Timbers shrieked; the boat spun around, right into the breaking wave. Foam exploded over the bow. For a moment it seemed that they would drive straight down to the bottom, then the bow was flung up with a tooth-snapping jerk and the wind blew out the sail. The boat rode up over the surf, bobbed on the huge swell then drifted into the lee of Shag's Rock.

Pender put up a small sail and they wallowed their way north, baling for their lives. 'It's still not over,' he said, when they had reduced the water level and repacked their scattered gear. 'I'd say we've lost part of the keel, though she lifted at the last moment and saved the rudder. Chert, take the tiller – I'll have a look at that leak. Hey you, come 'ere.'

Chert stumped back. His thighs were massive, the dingy canvas trousers making a rasping sound as he walked. He dropped onto the seat, thumping his feet down next to Lilis. His stubby toes were webbed, his feet as red and cracked as a peasant's. Lilis inspected them in uneasy fascination. Chert grinned, poking her in the belly with one battered toe. She slid away down the bench and he laughed aloud.

The unnamed sailor, whom Pender addressed only as 'Hey you!', bent down over the crack in the boards. He was an extraordinarily ugly man with an empty eye-socket and the corresponding ear reduced to a tiny flap below the earhole. He laughed a lot, showing yellow teeth as big as thumbnails, but he never spoke. His tongue had been cut out.

'The boards are badly sprung,' Pender said, straightening up. 'I can't do much about that here. But there's a crack I can plug. Hey you, put your big ugly foot right there! She's *The Lame Goose* now, eh!'

Pender set to with his tools and his tar pot, and in half an hour had made a temporary repair. Shortly they began to feel the pull of the wind again as they drifted beyond the protection of the Rock. He stood up, wiped his hands and turned back to the tiller. 'It's no good,' he said, jowls sagging. 'We'll have to find another boat, and damned quick too. That'll be to your account, of course.'

'Of course,' said Mendark, too shaken to debate the matter. 'Where do you have in mind?'

'Ganport is the likeliest and that's forty leagues and more. Best part of a day the way the *Goose* is sailing now, even if the wind holds. Trouble is, I don't think she'll last that long.'

'What's the matter with her?' Lilis wondered.

'We hit too many things too hard. Every time we crash over a wave . . . like that, it shakes the planks a bit more. The poor old *Goose* is coming apart, child.'

'Maybe we'll still have to swim,' Osseion interjected.

'Not as hard as them back there, I hope,' said Tallia. 'There were at least a dozen people on each of those galleys.'

'Are they all drownded?' asked Lilis.

'Drownded!' Pender smiled. 'Probably not. Those that were carried into the lagoon, most of them I imagine, could get out easily enough over the rock platform. And help is close. Look, the lighthouse is flashing now!'

'They're signalling to Yggur,' Mendark broke in. 'We're not safe yet.'

'Not near,' Pender agreed, 'but we've got a lead of a few hours.'

'Well, I'd like a sleep if we can rest from baling for a while,' said Tallia. 'I had none last night.'

'One baler should be enough for now,' said Pender. 'I'd better put a bigger sail up. At least make the lighthouse think that we're in good repair.'

They hoisted up a sail almost as large as the one that had blown out. The boat picked up speed at once, though it sailed with a list and more sluggishly than before, as if something was dragging underneath. There were no other vessels visible on the white-capped water. The wind moved back to the south, bringing another flurry of sleet. They pounded through the waves until the still-blinking light on the tower had disappeared in the rain, then reduced sail once more.

The passengers huddled under their canvas. They were all saturated, feeling their injuries keenly now that the excitement was past. 'I'm sorry the illusion didn't last any longer,' said Tallia. 'I couldn't hold it. My head was bursting.'

'You didn't need to. I hadn't thought that their oars would prevent them getting through. But I'm sure it saved us from that first flight of arrows. Lucky that none of them ever played there as children.'

'Lucky,' said Tallia sombrely. Lilis snuggled up close, her head on Tallia's breast. 'I knew we would get through,' she said sleepily, and slept.

Tallia did not sleep and knew after the first few minutes that she would not. Her head felt as though it had been banged repeatedly against a rock, and every lurch and shudder of the boat made it worse. She endured it for some hours, then finally disengaged herself from Lilis, pulled the canvas back over her and stood up. The others were sleeping, even Mendark.

'I need something to do,' she said to the shadow that was Pender.

'Nothing to do,' he said, 'except sail and eat.'

'Let's eat then.' They shared bread, cheese and pickled

meat, with strong mustard and slightly salty water from the barrel lashed down in the middle of the boat. It was sleeting again.

'Where are we now?' she asked later on.

Pender looked up to where the sun should be. 'We might have made thirty sea miles. Twelve leagues or so. Good progress with half a boat but there's a long way to go, eh.'

'Can they catch us?'

'A fast boat could.'

'Anything we can do?'

'No. But as long as they don't find us before dark, they'll expect that we're still well ahead. They don't know that we're lame.'

'Doesn't help us much if they're ahead,' said Mendark gruffly from the canvas.

'We're making water again,' said Pender. 'We need two baling now,' he called to the other end of the boat.

The Sea of Thurkad here was about thirty leagues wide and they were sailing about a league out. Pender turned in toward the shore, where the wind was less, ran in as close as was safe, then north again. 'Less to swim, and less strain on the *Goose* too,' he said.

'I'll take a turn,' said Tallia, anxious for any kind of distracting activity. She had never been a good sailor and was feeling seasick. Going to the middle of the boat, she took a bucket and began to bale methodically, and even after an hour would not take a spell.

So the hours passed. The wind abated; Pender felt bold enough to put up a larger sail, a grey one that blended into the rain and the sea. A gull perched on the top of the mast, calling to its mates. They pounded on.

'How far now?' Mendark asked Pender that night. They were baling three at a time now and only just holding it steady. A full moon darted in and out of the clouds.

'Three leagues, I guess. We've done better than I hoped.'

Just then the boat struck something in the water, lurched, listed and the sea began to gush in.

'What's that?' cried Lilis, waking with a start.

'A log,' said Pender. 'She's finished! I'll try to put her on the rocks.'

He turned the boat toward the gloomy shore, a hundred spans away, where a rocky ridge ended in a narrow platform of steeply dipping shale. 'No! Keep baling, you fools,' he shouted, as they gathered their gear. 'That'll be no use to you in the water.'

They hurled water out of the boat, Osseion put his huge foot on the largest leak, the shore drifted closer, they limped around the end of the point into a gutter between two boulders and felt the bottom grate on rock.

'Get your gear out quick!' cried Pender, trying to keep the boat steady against the shore with an oar. It was relatively sheltered but there was a strong surge from the waves breaking on the point. Chert jumped out and jerked the bow rope taut, they climbed onto the slippery shale and made a chain to pass the gear up the shore. Soon everything was ashore except for two very heavy chests.

'How are you going to carry those to Ganport?' asked Pender.

'How are we going to buy a boat without a fortune?' Mendark replied. 'Get it onshore.'

Between them they manhandled the chests across the rocks, which were dangerous with barnacles and razor clams, to the base of the ridge. In the meantime Pender took an axe and with quick strokes brought the mast down into the boat. 'Give us a heave,' and they all strained. The boat was stuck, then a surge lifted it and it slowly slid down. The figurehead disappeared beneath the water.

'*The Dancing Goose* is dead,' said Pender sadly. 'I only had her for three days.'

It was raining again. 'We'd better find somewhere to camp,' rumbled Osseion.

They scrambled up the ridge to a sheltered fold concealed from view of the sea. Lilis and Tallia gathered wood for the fire, Chert and the mute sailor heaved the chests up while Mendark, Osseion and Pender set up the camp. They had no tent but Pender soon rigged shelters between the trees with canvas and rope. The fire eventually caught and they piled wood on until there was a blaze big enough to cheer even Mendark.

Tallia looked around their little group – Lilis covered in bruises and her arm in a sling, Osseion with the bandages on his fingers all bloody, Mendark bearing a great gash across his forehead. Her own face was bruised black and her nose throbbed.

'Let's eat,' said Pender. 'Tomorrow might be worse.'

18

MUD AND BLOOD

After dinner, Mendark and Tallia went away from the campfire to make a plan.

'You and Pender must go to Ganport,' he said. 'Go before dawn and in all haste. Can you get there tomorrow night?'

'I imagine so,' she replied. 'He said it's about three leagues.'

'But that was by sea – it'll be a lot further on foot.'

'Still possible, unless there's a bridge out. A long day's walk for Pender though.'

'If he wants a new boat badly enough he'll manage it,' said Mendark. 'And if he doesn't, I dare say that you can find someone else in Ganport.'

'We'll get there,' said Tallia. 'You'll stay here then?'

'Yes, my leg is still painful. How's yours?'

'It hardly troubles me at the moment, though I haven't done much walking lately.'

'No chance of you getting back tomorrow night?' At her incredulous stare he added, 'Late?'

'Hardly. Don't ask what isn't possible, Mendark.'

'All right, but we'll keep watch, tomorrow night and every night. Now, here's the signal . . .'

They agreed on that and several other matters, then Mendark went on, 'If you don't come by the third night, I'll know that something is badly wrong. I'll hide the chests and come down after you. What else? You have my seal?'

She nodded.

'Use it cautiously,' Mendark said, 'if you must use it at all. Ah, the boat. Make sure it's a strong fast one. He'll want to buy some old tub to carry cargo up and down the channel. Nothing matters but that it is fast.'

'There aren't likely to be too many boats for sale, even in a fishing town like Ganport.'

'If you offer enough you'll find plenty. So much money only comes once in a lifetime.'

That illuminated an aspect of Mendark's character that Tallia didn't much like, but she said nothing. After settling it with Pender, Tallia took some more willow bark for her headache, which proved ineffective, and they all turned in.

Tallia and Pender left before dawn the next morning. Lilis waved goodbye and went back to the fire looking very forlorn.

'What's the matter, kid?' asked Mendark without much interest.

She straightened up and wiped tears away. 'Nothin',' she sniffed.

'Good! Well, get some water on, I need a hot cup of chard.' Mendark walked back to the fire and rubbed his hands together over it. It was still windy and cold.

Lilis emptied the dregs and ash out of the big water pot and stood at the edge of the firelight uncertainly.

'What's the matter now?'

'I don't know where the water is.'

'Then *ask*! Osseion fetched it last night.'

Lilis had not spoken to Osseion in the days they had been together. He looked far too dangerous, with his scarred face and arms. But he seemed a lot less fierce than Mendark now.

'Hurry up!' Mendark was particularly irritable in the mornings.

She went silently to the shelter and peered in. The firelight threw dancing shadows inside. 'Er . . .' she said. Osseion had not stirred when Pender and Tallia left, but he was sitting up now, scratching his head. He smiled. 'I have to get the water but I don't know where it is,' she said.

'I'll show you.' He reached for a boot with his bandaged hand. 'Ahhh!' he cried, staring at his fingers.

'What's the matter?' she whispered.

'Such a pain!' He sat still for a moment, wringing his hand, then said, 'Help me with my boots.'

She was glad to have something to do. The gigantic boots were wet and heavy; it was hard work getting them on the vast broad feet. She tied the laces and Osseion levered himself to his feet. She didn't come up much past his waist.

'Down this way. It was quite near the sea that I found water.'

The sky was just beginning to grow light, though not enough to be of assistance, and down in the gully it was black as molasses. They found the pool by almost falling into it, a jagged-edged depression in the shale at the foot of a steep slope, fed by little threads of water running down over the rocks. There were other small depressions and ponds above and below, most covered by ice.

Lilis filled pots and buckets, then washed her face and hands in the icy water. Osseion took the biggest vessels and they headed back up the hill. When they reached the camp he sat down, clumsily peeling the bandages from his fingers. They were very swollen and one, the middle finger, was almost purple.

Mendark came over. 'That's not good,' he said after a brief inspection. 'I should've attended it last night. It'd better not get any worse.'

Tallia and Pender had made good progress, though the track was steep and muddy. Pender whinged continuously about his blistered feet and the stupidity of walking when one could sail, all of which Tallia bore with fatalistic good humour.

In the mid-morning they stopped briefly for a drink and

a spell. Though it was cold, Pender was dripping with sweat.

'You'll be a lean hard shadow of yourself when we get there,' she said with a chuckle. She felt cheerful, though her head still ached and her thigh was throbbing.

'I'll make it up,' he grunted. 'Plenty of places to eat in Ganport.'

'Do you know it well?' she asked.

He laughed harshly. 'Haven't you heard?'

'Heard what?'

'I used to have my own little ship, taking cargo up and down the sea, eh! And sometimes further – into the great ocean up Faranda way, and even down into the Sea of Mists.' He drained his drink.

'Let's go,' she said.

'Made a lot of enemies. The guilds in Thurkad and here, mainly. They don't like outsiders taking their profit, eh! I had the right warrants, the right papers, but I could get no cargoes except those that no one else would take. Stinking hides; dead bodies once; poisonous quicksilver; oil of vitriol. I did not thrive but I survived, eh!'

He paused while they negotiated a bridge made of a single plank across a rushing creek. The timber sagged underfoot, trying to slide them into the water.

'I was *better* and cheaper, and occasionally I had good cargoes – wool and oil. Once I even carried spices.'

Now they were trudging up a steep path through grizzled pines. Pender was breathing heavily, making hard work of the mud. When they reached the top he sank down on a slab of cut stone. 'My feet hurt,' he said again, taking his boots off to rub blistered feet.

Tallia looked around. Other squared stones lay all about, and a broken column behind them. The remains of a roadside temple, or a way station built in more prosperous times.

'You'd better bandage those or you won't be able to walk,' she observed. 'Why don't we have an early lunch? I'll get it ready.'

She sawed slabs of bread, clapped lumps of pickled meat and cheese inside, smeared on mustard and passed one across to him. 'Same as yesterday.'

He gulped his down in a few great chunks then looked around for more. She handed him the loaf. 'I was in Ganport,' he went on, 'picking up a cargo of oil from a ship that had to dock to have the rudder fixed. A cargo for my best customer. I went to the tavern that night to celebrate, but when I got back the guard had gone and my boat was blazing. It burned away to nothing in a few minutes.

'I knew that the guild had done it but I couldn't do anything about it. The owner came looking for me. I ran and never went back; ended up paddling the Garr in stinking Narne, still doing what no one else would. *But no more!* I'll do anything to get another ship. *Anything!*' he said, stuffing in the last of the sandwich.

'Surely the owner would have got his money back from the brokers!'

'That may be so. I couldn't afford to wait and see.'

They continued in silence for most of the afternoon, at dusk reaching a broad river, the Gannel. There they sought out a ferryman's hut and were rowed across. On the other side the path continued downstream, several hours' walk before they arrived in Ganport.

As they trudged down the dimly lit streets, Tallia ran through her options. Mendark had asked her to keep an eye on Pender, but at the same time he did not want to reveal the identity of his factor here.

'Why don't you go down to the waterfront,' she said. 'I'll make my own enquiries. Let's meet for a late dinner. Where do you suggest?'

A seedy-looking inn, The Four Fishes, was just down the street. Another, The Gannel, equally seedy, nearby.

'None of these,' he said at once. 'These are towners' places. No sailor would go in there. No food worth eating, and none at all, late. Down on the waterfront,' he pointed. 'The Flying

Bamundi used to be the best and it was always open. With luck, I'll meet you there in a couple of hours.'

He limped off in that direction with his rolling fat sailor's gait. Tallia pulled her hood up and went another way to take care of her own business.

Back at the campsite, the following morning started badly. Lilis was woken by someone gasping and crying out in pain.

'What is it?' she called, jumping up and stumbling around in the dark.

'My hand,' cried Osseion. 'It feels like it's going to burst.' He lurched out of the tent to the fire, tearing the bandages off.

The middle finger was swollen to almost twice its normal size, the skin shiny, black and drum-taut. Mendark came blinking into the light, took one look at it and said, 'It'll have to come off.'

'No!' cried Osseion, looking terrified.

'Come now, Osseion! I remember the day that you led the storming of the walls of Tarjidd, and when the battle was won you came out with an arrow broken off in your shoulder that you didn't even know was there, and so many other wounds that it took six hours to patch you up again.'

'I – ahh!'

'It's the finger now, or the hand in two days,' said Mendark with steely voice. 'A finger more or less is nothing, but a hand . . .' The pause made his words very ominous. 'With one hand you won't be any use to me. Lilis, rouse out those sailors to hold him down.'

She went to the other shelter. It was empty.

'They're gone!' she shouted across the clearing.

Mendark cursed long and fluently.

'Not in front of the child,' said Osseion, staring at the finger.

'Lilis, hold his arm down over here.' Mendark pointed with his long knife to a log then thrust the blade into the

258

coals. Osseion put his slab-like hand down, palm upwards, with the middle finger extended onto the log.

Lilis gripped his wrist with her little hands and pushed down with all her weight. The finger looked like a black pudding in the firelight. Mendark withdrew the knife, flinching at the heat of the handle, inspected it carefully and put it back. He found a rag in his pocket, wrapped it round the handle and drew the knife out again. The blade glowed orange. He held it above the finger, judging the place.

'Do it then, damn you!' Osseion choked.

Lilis was staring in horrified fascination. The knife hovered above the finger, moved fractionally, touched with a wisp of smoke, then Mendark thrust down with all his strength.

Osseion bellowed and his arm jerked so hard that Lilis was flung into the air, to land on her bottom a span away. Osseion was staggering around, dancing and shaking his hand in the air. Mendark stood well back, the smoking blade hanging down.

Lilis came softly back to the log. They all looked down at the finger. There was a stench of burned and rotten meat in the air. She thought she would be sick. Mendark reached down and with a swift movement flung it into the fire. Osseion held out his hand, which Mendark inspected carefully. The finger was gone neatly and the stump seared, scarcely bleeding.

'I think we've saved the hand,' said Mendark. 'Leave it unbandaged for the time. I've nothing that will ease the pain save willow bark, and I think this is well beyond that.'

'I'd sooner the brandy you've got in the chest,' said Osseion, whose face had gone almost as pale as Lilis's.

'I'll make the breakfast,' said Lilis, busying herself on the other side of the campfire.

'This other news is grim,' said Mendark when they had their plates of honey-sweetened porridge on their knees and big mugs of hot chard beside them.

Osseion said nothing. He ate clumsily, holding the spoon

between finger and thumb, inspecting the space between his fingers over and again. He shuddered occasionally, then as soon as the porridge was finished he took his mug, went back to the shelter and lay down inside.

Mendark was left with Lilis. He glared at her across the fire, this tiny, skinny, silver-haired waif with her big intelligent eyes. He seemed to want to talk. She looked up, caught his eyes on her and looked down again. She didn't want anything to do with him. He was all-powerful and she was nothing.

'Grim news,' he repeated, clearing his throat. 'What should we do now?' He wasn't expecting an answer, just wanted an audience for his own musings.

She held up three fingers. 'Warn: hide the gold. Tway: move the camp. Thray: keep guard in case they come back. Fahr,' she said, holding up another finger, then stopped, looked dismayed. 'Maybe they go to the town, tell the enemy. Maybe Tallia is trapped. Maybe ships come.'

Mendark was impressed but it didn't really help. 'Whatever happens we are just three, and a poor useless crippled three at that.'

'You're a mancer,' she said more boldly than she felt. A month ago she would not have dared to look at him. 'I'm good at guiding and hiding and –' she broke off abruptly. 'He's big and strong,' she said, pointing to the tent. 'We're not helpless.'

He fixed a keen eye on her. 'Go on! What else are you good at that you don't want to say?'

'Nothing.' They had tried to train her as a pickpocket, but though her fingers were clever she lacked the will for it. 'My father taught me that it is wrong to steal.'

'Normally it is, but not when you are starving. Not when you steal from an enemy.'

She did not answer. Lilis did not want to talk to him at all – she was afraid that he would trick her with words. But her life was doing what other people wanted, so she sat looking down at her grubby feet and listened. She wanted to go down to the rockpool to bathe and wash the new clothes that she had been wearing for days. And she kept seeing the black finger smoking on the log and the agony on Osseion's face. He had been kind to her.

Lilis realised that quite a while had gone by. 'I have to wash,' she said. Mendark did not answer.

She got her pack and went barefoot down the hill. On the way back she came upon Osseion standing on a high rock outcrop, staring seawards. The two chests were open and Mendark was labouring off into the trees with a heavy leather bag in either hand. She went to help.

'No!' Mendark said sharply. 'I'll do it.'

Lilis shrugged. It was his gold. She looked in the chests. One was already empty; the other had two or three bags left in the bottom. She hung her clothes over a bush to dry and sat down by the fire again.

The previous night Tallia had waited at The Flying Bamundi but Pender did not appear. This did not unduly worry her. She ate a hearty meal of grilled bamundi seasoned with precious pepper and lime juice, drank half a bowl of an indifferent yellow wine and went to her bed where she slept soundly and long, waking to find her headache gone. Downstairs she found Pender, bloodshot and bleary from a night in the inns, tucking into a huge breakfast.

'I spoke to Mendark's factor,' she said quietly. 'He will contact me if he learns of a boat. But we must be very cautious. Yggur has spies here, and one of his boats came in the night before last, though it stopped only briefly.'

'Yes, I heard that too. But they do not love him here and I think that our gold is better than his promises or his threats. There are several vessels that might be for sale, for a fortune.'

'What sort of a fortune?'

'Many hundreds!'

'Tell me about them.'

'The first is a fishing boat, a fair size but very old. I know the captain. His leg was crushed loading barrels a month or two ago. He cannot manage and neither the son nor the daughters care for the sea. He was looking for a sale even before the war, but he is greedy.'

'How greedy?'

'A seven of hundreds. Too much for such an old boat, even at a time like this, for it has the worm in it.'

'And the other?'

'The second is an old cargo vessel, rather like the one I had once, though bigger. It's slow but solid, very well built. It could go anywhere, even to Crandor.' His eyes gleamed at the thought.

'Why is it for sale?'

'The owner was killed in Thurkad when the war began. The family have to sell.'

'Hmn. And you like it, eh?'

'Yes, though the price is tremendous – a nine of hundreds and a fifty.'

Tallia rubbed her chin thoughtfully. Ganport was not Thurkad, but still Pender was doing very nicely out of Mendark. 'Expensive and slow. Neither is quite what we want. Anything else?'

'Not that I would touch.'

She left it at that and spent the day in the inn, keeping out of sight, and when she did go out briefly she used a minor illusion to make herself look older, shorter and shabbier.

That night Mendark's factor visited her, a tall lean man with a black-beard shadow and very hairy arms. He wore a dark brown robe with a leather belt and the sleeves rolled above his elbows. His sandals were down-at-heel.

'I have found one that would suit entirely, if you are game to take it on,' he said, speaking low even though the door was secure. He leaned across the table and gold flashed in a front tooth. 'It is a smuggler's boat; well built, roomy and fast. And a good price too – a very good price.'

'What's wrong with it?' she asked.

'It was used for smuggling ... certain oils and herbs. Illegal things. The captain and crew were executed, the owner expelled from the guild and the boat confiscated by the Customs Master. Its name is black in every port in Meldorin, and even beyond. In times past they would have burned the boat as well.'

'It sounds ideal.'

'There'll be trouble everywhere you go. Delays, excuses, endless questioning.'

'As long as it gets us to Zile, that's all that matters. Who is selling it?'

'The Harbour Master, on behalf of the Customs House.'

'Then they can make out new papers to minimise the trouble. When can I see it?'

'In the morning. Go to the Harbour Master's office.'

When Pender returned and heard her news he was not pleased. '*Black Opal!* I know all about her. No!'

'Is she not what we need?'

'She's a wonderful boat, they say, but the trouble would not be worth it.'

'I'm going to look at her in the morning, at seven.'

'You'd better find yourself a captain and crew then,' Pender said ungraciously.

'Just come and look at her, Pender.'

'You can change the name but you'll never get rid of the reputation. Every port you stop at you'll be harassed, searched, delayed and maybe even held in the watch-house for a week or two, just to show that they don't like your boat.'

'Well, we won't stop then. We'll go straight to Zile.'

Pender rolled his eyes as though to say 'such idiocy'.

Despite all her arguments he would not budge. 'In that case you will need to return the greater part of your fee,' she said coldly, turning away. Tallia slept very badly that night.

It was still raining and windy when she headed down to

the port in the morning. *Black Opal* was tied to an old jetty behind the Customs House. She was painted black, with blue and red and gold trim, a handsome boat about seven or eight spans long. Tallia spoke to the Harbour Master and went aboard, and as she did so Pender appeared, red in the face and breathing hard. She waved and he climbed aboard.

'Since I'm here anyway I may as well have a look,' he said, without sincerity. She deferred to him and he went over the boat with absolute thoroughness, though with an ill grace. When they were finished and back on the wharf in driving rain, she could see in his eyes that *Black Opal* was a good boat.

Tallia went to the Harbour Master's office. She was a small dark woman with swept-back black hair so tightly coiled that it looked like a breaking wave foaming over her head.

'The price is set at six hundred tells,' she said, opening a ledger and closing it again without looking inside. 'It has been set by Customs and I have no authority to negotiate. It is a fair price, considering her reputation. She's a sound boat, worth twice that were she not encumbered. Are you interested? I should warn you that Yggur's representative has already asked about her.'

'Only asked?'

'Perhaps he lacks authority for such an expenditure. But surely in a few days –'

'How long to have the papers drawn up?'

'They could be ready for stamping and signing after lunch.'

Tallia thanked her and went out. Pender was sitting gloomily on the veranda, watching the rain. 'You are not willing to buy her?'

'No, for all that she's a wonderful boat, worth a ten of hundreds except for her name. It will be hard enough for me to start again without that handicap. Anyway, I don't have the money.'

'Then here is a compromise. Mendark will buy her and

you will captain her to Zile. After that, if she is too much trouble, we dispose of her and Mendark will bear any loss.'

'And my fee?'

'It should be less, since you are not the owner. But you have done us well so far, and lost one boat already. I say it stays the same. Can you agree to this?'

He put out his hand, looking much relieved. 'But she will cause us a lot of trouble.'

'Let's get it done.' They went inside. 'I will take it,' said Tallia.

'What name?' said the woman.

'I . . . Name of the boat?'

'What name on the papers? Do you buy on your own account or on behalf of another? If on account of another I must see a warrant for you to act as their agent. Be warned that there are severe penalties for false swearing.'

'My account,' said Tallia. 'I am Jalis Besune, formerly of Thurkad.'

'You have papers?'

'At the inn.'

'You will bring them for the signing.'

'Indeed,' said Tallia, heart sinking with the realisation that she would have to forge them.

Tallia paid the six hundred tells, Pender looking casually sideways to see how much more the bag contained. She received a magnificently sealed and embossed receipt, and they promised to return in the afternoon.

'Now,' said Tallia as they went down the steps. 'Get that name painted out. Call her . . . call her *The Waif*. That's a more modest name. Buy paint enough to repaint her on the way. How long to get all the supplies we need?'

'To Zile?'

'Yes.'

'She's been stripped bare: tools, rope, stores, the lot. Look at the sails – they've practically got holes in them! Tomorrow night, with a lot of luck.'

Tallia pursed her lips. 'So long? Mendark will be fretting already. Make it tomorrow then. To go by dusk.'

They were walking down the road back to the inn when Tallia caught sight of a familiar figure turning into an alley. That squat body and lumbering walk were unmistakeable. 'Hey, isn't that Chert?'

'*Farsh!*' cried Pender, and shouted, 'Hoy!'

The head flashed around, then he darted up the alley. By the time they reached the entrance there was no sign of him.

'I don't like this at all! Who were your men, Pender?'

'Hard workers, but no more honest than they need be. Do I trust them? Not an ell.'

'They've probably informed Yggur's agent already,' she groaned.

'With all that gold back there? More likely they're collecting a band of cutthroats to sail up and take it.'

'Mendark can take care of his,' she said, not totally convincingly. 'I'd better get back.'

'You can't go until the papers are signed. Down at the port you will find someone to take you, but the price . . .'

'Will be high,' she finished. 'I'll see you back at the Harbour Master's for the signing. You must meet us at the camp by tomorrow night, whatever the state of the supplies.'

Tallia went back to the inn and sent a message to Mendark's factor, but he was out and she was forced to go herself to buy ink, pen and paper of suitable quality. She spent the next three hours working carefully, forging papers that stated her to be Jalis Besune, formerly of Roros in distant Crandor (for her accent and looks were difficult to disguise completely) and these last five years a Thurkad spice merchant (a trade she had some knowledge of) with a warrant from the Magister. She embossed her personal papers by hand, working from the back with the blunt end of a needle, an agonisingly slow task, rubbed down the embossing with the end of a bottle to blur it, conscious that it was an indifferent job, signed and dated it, and sealed both documents with black wax and the Magister's seal. Then she spent a further precious hour ageing the documents with dust from the windowsill and finally put them in her wallet along with a sprinkling of cloves and a shred of mace.

The boat's papers were not ready when she returned, and by the time they were finally completed, signed, sealed and stamped it was dusk, well after the time she was to be at the waterfront to catch her boat.

'Your papers, if you please,' said the Harbour Master.

Tallia handed them over and the woman checked them carefully, even holding her personal documents up to the light to check the embossed marks. Her nose wrinkled, she sniffed. 'Cloves!' she said. She ran her finger over the black wax seal and said, 'You have important friends!' then nodded and passed the papers back. She rolled the boat's documents, slipped them into a cover of waxed cloth, tied the end with its cords and handed the package to Tallia without a smile. 'Fare well,' she said.

Tallia retrieved her pack from the inn, wanting to run but knowing she mustn't attract any more attention. It was dark by the time she reached the waterfront.

The master of the boat held out his hands, palm upward. 'Too late,' he said. 'The bar is very dangerous in this sea. I don't dare it in the dark.'

'Cancel!' Tallia said furiously, knowing that Chert's gang could already be on their way.

She went back to the inn but Pender was not there. What could she do? Mendark was far from helpless, but if a gang came on him in the dark a lucky blow could finish him as easily as any. No way to get there before morning, even if she walked that track all night.

Finally Pender came in. She gave him the papers and explained the situation to him.

'Well, Chert is a disorganised rogue. Unlikely he would have been able to get away today.'

'But in the morning –'

'Let's wait till then, eh! Maybe the weather will be too rough for him to get out tomorrow. It often is here.'

In the night it stormed, with wild winds and heavy rain. Tallia went to the waterfront at dawn but there was no one about and the sea looked as rough as before. Then, just as she turned away, she caught sight of a furtive movement at the other end of the harbour. Pulling her hood over her face, she strolled casually down that way. Fifty paces back she stopped, sheltering from the driving rain beside a fishing boat on a slipway. Part of the hull had already been scraped down, barnacles and worm tubes crunching underfoot, though there was no danger of anyone hearing in the wind and rain. Yes, there was the man she'd noticed, standing between two boats and peering at another, further down the bay.

From where she stood Tallia could not see anything unusual, so she clambered up onto the deck of the boat. Cold rain lashed her face; as she pushed back her hood to see better a pool of water ran down her back, though it only added to the chill that was already there. A group of people were readying a small boat for sea, and even as she watched the sail jerked up, the ropes were cast off and the boat moved sluggishly away from its mooring.

It came past quite close, drifting back into shore. Tallia slipped behind the wheel-house. A hairy, brutal-looking man shouted and struck the fellow at the tiller in the side of the head. The boat swung sharply then headed out to sea. As it passed Tallia saw Chert clearly, hauling on a rope, then the boat vanished in the fog and the rain.

The watching man turned, heading back past her boat at a fast walk. She did not see his face. He went on board one of several vessels that were moored close together, all flying the flag of Yggur's navy. Immediately a woman jumped onto the wharf and ran in the direction of the nearest inn.

Tallia sprinted to her own inn. In the driving rain, that would not attract any attention. By the time she reached it her thigh was aching. Pender was already gone, no one knew where, so she left him a note and, by now very afraid, headed up the muddy track to the campsite as fast as her leg would allow her.

19

FIRE ON THE WATER

Mendark had confidently expected the boat the previous night and when it did not arrive he began to fret. Several times they had seen flags flying the blackfist insignia, far out on the sea.

'They've been captured,' he said.

'Give them another day,' grunted Osseion, more withdrawn than ever. He often took his hand out of his pocket, staring at the place where the finger had been. The loss of it seemed to have sapped his confidence in his own strength.

'Can Yggur's power stretch so far, so soon?' Mendark agonised.

'Wouldn't take much power to drop a bag over her head in an alley,' said Osseion gloomily. 'No point staying here.' But he remained on his log, a vast melancholy shape against the leaping flames.

Lilis was shocked at how quickly they seemed to have given up. This was what her life had always been. She had not lost an empire, or even a city, though one by one her new friends went away and did not return.

'I will keep watch,' she said to their downcast heads. She pulled her oilskin tight about her, for it was drizzling, took a mug of chard and a slab of cheese and went down the ridge to a tall outcrop of slate. Climbing its sharp jutting sides, she settled into a crevice on top. From there she could see up and down and nearly across the sea, when it was as clear as now.

She sat on her rock for some hours, watching the reflections, the patterns of wind on water and the boats on the sea. Once a vessel came angling in close to their ridge, to Lilis's alarm, but it merely fished up some crab or lobster pots and put them back again. The boat moved off to the north and soon disappeared. Lilis nibbled her cheese. The weather was wet and windy but she did not mind, warm in clean clothes and dry boots. She still could not comprehend how the miracle had come about.

The bitter chard was cold now. She hated chard anyway. Lilis tipped it out, watching it trickle down the rock. Her bruises from the beating were gone, though the memory remained and her shoulder still ached sometimes.

The sun set behind her, just an outline through the clouds. Suddenly it was cold. She wanted to go to the fire, but she'd better keep watch a while longer. Mendark had thought the hard cheese very poor fare but it tasted good to her and she gnawed away until the whole piece was gone. More boats passed, the last sun catching their sails, and the light began to fade.

A dark shape appeared below her. 'Lilis child, where are you?' It was Osseion. He had something in his hand.

'Up here!'

He looked up, startled, then smiled when he caught sight of her pale hair against the slate.

'I brought you something to eat – put some meat on your bones.'

She scrambled down. He had a huge sandwich in his gap-fingered hand, slabs of bread as big as his foot, fried in dripping and filled with hot pickled beef, onions and melted cheese. Osseion sat down with his back against the outcrop, Lilis beside him, cross-legged on her oilskin.

'We're a grim old pair, eh!'

She munched her sandwich, having nothing to say.

'What are you going to do when we get to Zile?' he wondered.

'Don't know. What are *you* going to do there?'

'I'll sit around waiting while they talk and when they're done we'll be off again, I expect. I'm just a soldier – and that's about all I'm good for.'

He broke off. A boat had appeared from the direction of Ganport, sailing slowly.

'What are they doing?' asked Lilis.

'Searching for us, I'd say. These bluffs must all look the same in this light.'

'Could it be Tallia?'

'Don't think so. Old Pender would know the place at once. Could be the blackfists,' he said, 'or that scoundrel Chert. Better run back and tell Mendark.'

She took a big bite of her sandwich and jumped up.

'No hurry!' he said. 'Even if they find the place it'll take a good half hour to get here. I'll watch.'

She ran up the track. At the camp Mendark was doing something to one of the chests. 'They're coming,' she cried with her mouth full.

'What?'

'Osseion thinks it's the enemy.'

'Have they landed?'

'No, still looking for us.'

He finished what he was doing, went to the shelter and came back to sit, apparently unconcerned, by the fire. Lilis ran back down to the rock.

'What did he say?' Osseion asked, staring down at the sea.

'He just went and sat down by the fire.'

'He knows his business, don't worry.'

'I do worry. Where's the boat gone?'

'It went past, around that bluff.'

'Look, what's that?'

'Where?'

272

'See, just on the far point!'

'You've got good eyes, girl! Looks like they're being followed. But is it our Pender or the enemy? It's pretty small – I think Pender will come in a bigger boat than that. Another couple of minutes and we'd never have seen. Just keep an eye out – I'll go and have a word with old Magis.'

Lilis looked down again. It was almost dark now. Rediscovering the sandwich, she took another huge bite. The meat was still warm inside. What a pleasure eating had become. She finished the sandwich. It grew dark. Osseion did not return. What was Mendark planning? If only Tallia were here.

Tallia was still hours from the camp. The path was treacherous and in places little landslips had carried it away or buried it under mud and rock. The plank bridge of two days ago was gone, washed out in the night deluge with no sign that it had ever existed, but for the path ending at the torrent. She had to climb up the mountainside to find a way across, an old trunk long fallen and green with moss. The climb, the precarious crossing and the slipping and sliding descent took the best part of two hours. When she finally rejoined the path she wanted to run, knowing that it was a four-hour march from here and almost dark already. But that would be foolish. She continued at a fast walk, feeling events slipping out of control.

Finally she was labouring up the last muddy slope, the thigh wound of a fortnight ago now very painful. The trip had been much slower than she could have anticipated, the track a quagmire, the previously dry gullies now dangerous cascades. As she reached the top she saw flames far down on the shore. It looked like a burning boat. Surely not Pender? He could be there by now. Shouting came on the breeze, then died away.

She hobbled across the crest and down into the gully that descended to the rockpools and the bay, sliding and skidding on the muddy path. Up the next ridge she pounded. The going would be quicker down the ridge. She felt quite exhausted.

Tallia felt her way down through the scrub between the jutting outcrops of slate, like standing stones, that marked the crest of the ridge. The shouting came again, reached a crescendo and stopped.

Eventually she reached the camp. The fire was still burning. The shelters were standing. The camp was empty, though. Tallia circled the clearing cautiously, then entered. There was nothing of value left in the shelters. The chests were gone. She tripped over a log, only it was not a log but a body. She turned it over. It was the unnamed sailor – the mute.

Something lay on the ground near the fire: Lilis's pack! Scattered on the ground were her spare clothes, soap, comb and other possessions. Nothing would have induced her to leave them behind. Tallia gathered them up and tied the pack to her own, trying to reconstruct events. Now really worried, she headed carefully down to the water.

Pender too had had a frustrating day. At every step he had suffered delays; deliveries not made on time, not made at all, or not what he had ordered. The merchants and ship-wrights of Ganport were surly, stiff-necked and used to doing things at their own pace, not at the urging of some fat upstart from Thurkad, as he was told more than once. It was also evident, though they did not say so, that *The Waif* was a large part of the problem.

Twice Pender cancelled an order in fury and took it to another merchant who turned out to be equally obstreper-ous, and so by the middle of the afternoon all he had received was the fresh food and vegetables and two barrels of water. The remaining barrels he had sent back because they were foul. None of the preserved foods had come, the spare sail and cord and spars he had ordered were not nearly ready, nor the bolts of canvas, nor the barrels of pitch . . . The list was endless. He had received none of the myriads of tools that were needed to operate, maintain and repair the boat. There was no hope of being ready today, or even tomorrow.

He had the same problem with sailors, for *The Waif* needed a crew of six for the open sea. Eventually he found four, including one reliable chap called Rustible, who had sailed with him years ago. Rustible was a rather square man of about forty years, all his exposed skin sunburnt to the colour of a brick. The top of his head, completely bald, was the same colour, framed rather incongrously by frizzy blond hair that stuck out like wool from the level of his ears. Blubbery lips made his speech rather hard to follow.

Another two sailors came recommended and one was unknown. Pender had two other names but they had not yet been found.

Late in the afternoon Pender went back to the inn for a hasty lunch and received Tallia's urgent note. He crammed the rest of his fish into his mouth, thrust the bread into his pocket and ran down to the boat. Rustible was standing at the dock, shouting and waving his arms, the raindrops flying from his thick lips. A man and a woman, twins in the sag of their jowls and the spread of their buttocks, were standing by a dray laden with folded sails. One sail was unfolded, spread right across the dock.

'Look at this rubbish,' Rustible shouted, spitting on the sail at his feet. 'Liars, cheats, thieves every one of you!' The cloth was old, worn through in several places, and parts were moth-eaten.

The woman held up her hands. 'The fool has sent the wrong one,' she said. 'I'll take it back. But the others are good.'

Pender climbed up on the dray and flipped open the next bundle. It was the same cloth as the first, carefully folded so that the blemishes did not show.

'No good,' he said. 'Take them all back!'

'We have worked all day,' said the man.

'*No good!*' shouted Pender, heaving it into the harbour. 'The order is cancelled.' He gestured with a thumb to Rustible and they went on board.

The wind had come up during the day and conditions were so rough that the Harbour Master warned him against sailing, but Pender slipped anchor and departed. It was a very rough crossing of the bar, though not dangerous for him in this boat, and before moonrise they were on the sea heading back south. The winds began to abate at nightfall but both wind and current were against them. They had to tack across and across, hard work as they were shorthanded, and made less than a league headway in the first hour.

They were still leagues out when Rustible cried out, 'Look there!'

Something was burning on the shore, flames leaping as high as the trees. 'What's going on?' Pender said. 'I don't like this at all.'

He stared at the blaze, trying to untangle all the possibilities, but could not make it out. Pender took careful bearings on the location, though he knew where it was – the rendezvous point.

Rustible shivered. 'Maybe we'd better go back.'

Pender was not a brave man, but he was an honest one. 'I told Tallia that I would be there tonight and so I will be.'

Eventually he mastered the unfavourable winds and currents, overshot the point and drifted slowly back. The moon came out as he edged the nose of the boat around the point. A few coals still twinkled on the shoreline. Further up the hill the campfire was bright. There was no signal. He did not dare give one now. What had happened?

Pender decided to sail straight by as though he was just another passing boat. He did so, coming in as close as was reasonable. 'No signal!' he muttered. 'What's happened? Poor little Lilis.'

'What are you going to do?' asked Rustible.

'Nothing we can do but be ready. We'll wait offshore. I don't dare take on a bunch of armed men.'

At the campsite, tense minutes passed. Lilis stared into the dark from the top of her rock, chilly now in spite of her new clothes. She was watching for Pender's signal but nothing came. Eventually Osseion relieved her. Afraid of enemies creeping in the dark she sat by the fire, holding her precious pack in her arms.

A pot of soup was simmering on the embers. She filled her mug and waited. And waited. The stars drifted, the scorpion nebula flared; the empty mug fell from her fingers onto the grass. Lilis slept and dreamed.

Osseion came back to warm himself beside the fire.

'No sign?'

'Nothing, but I don't think it'll be long now.'

Mendark twisted his beard in his fingers. 'But who will come first?'

Osseion went back to the lookout with a big mug of soup.

'Urchin!' Someone was shaking her hard. Lilis blinked awake. 'Time to go. Get up!' She was lifted bodily and set on her feet.

'What?' She wanted to lie down again, then suddenly realised where she was and who she was with. She followed Mendark into the trees to a place with a good view of the clearing. He crouched down; she squatted beside him.

'What are we waiting for?'

'Shhh! I have to *see* them.'

'Is Osseion coming?'

'He has something else to do.'

The night was still. Nothing happened for a long time. Lilis began to ask another question but Mendark jabbed her painfully in the ribs with an elbow. How hard and bony he was.

A wild dog barked some distance away, though when she thought about it, the sound seemed not quite right for a dog. The moon, a few days past its full, came over the trees and shone down on the campsite, the shelter, the fire and the two chests beside it. Shadows in the tents looked like people sleeping. Lilis's pack lay beside the chests where it had fallen while she slept.

'My pack,' she whispered urgently.

'Quiet!'

'But everything –'

Cold fingers clamped over her mouth and a voice fiercer than she had ever heard on the street said in her ear, 'Damn your pack, *be quiet*!'

Lilis choked down a sob. A stone clacked down the hill. Silence fell. A shadow appeared on the open side of the clearing, then blended back into stillness.

Shadows flitted across the camp to the shelter. Arms were raised, then plunged. One man hissed and others ran to the shelter. Lilis saw a hasty conference, black against the white moonsplash, then the shelter was ransacked while another two tried to open the chests. Mendark said something under his breath, then slid into the darkness. Someone picked up Lilis's pack, emptied it on the ground, pawed briefly at the pile and turned away.

Two of the intruders tried to lift a chest but it would not budge. They heaved. The handles broke off. A knife was thrust between catch and lid. It snapped. They had no more success with the other chest. Finally someone hacked down a couple of saplings, bound them to make a litter and the chests were hoisted up.

Just then there was a cry from down the hill and a flame leapt high. The two litter-bearers collided, the chests fell, someone shrieked. More shadows appeared and began to struggle together.

Right in front of Lilis two figures did battle in the moonlight. One was armed with a long staff with which he parried the knife slashes of the other. He swung the staff wildly, the other ducked and cut upwards with the knife. It must have caught the first man's arm, for he gave a yelp and shook his hand. Then he turned and fled in a crouch, running right at the flimsy shrubs behind which Lilis crouched.

She did not even have time to duck before the fellow crashed through the bushes and trampled right over her. A sandalled foot caught her shoulder, tumbling her on her back. The man tripped, thumped into the ground then scrabbled away on hands and knees as the one with the knife charged after him. Lilis did not dåre to move, for she lay in a tiny patch of moonshadow and it was bright all around. A big foot smacked the ground beside her ear. Moonlight touched the knife in his hand, a long sinuous blade like a kris, then he disappeared in the shrubbery. The crashings and scufflings went on for some time afterwards.

Lilis rubbed a throbbing shoulder. It was the one that had been dislocated before. She put her arm back in the sling.

'Urchin?' Mendark whispered from somewhere to her left.

'Here,' she whispered back.

'Come on – this place is more dangerous than I thought.'

They went quietly down the hill toward the pools. Several times on the way they had to hide at noises in the undergrowth. They crossed the water, climbed the rocks on the other side and waited.

From there Lilis could see a burning boat over on the point. As she watched a flaming bundle arched through the air and crashed onto a smaller boat halfway round the inlet. The deck was briefly illuminated before the fire was flung overboard and died in the water.

'Too bad,' said Mendark, without particular regret.

Someone shouted, evidently from that boat, and there was an answering shout from up the hill. The melee up there continued, then clouds covered the moon and silence fell.

They heard a deep, characteristic chuckle. 'I feel better now,' said Osseion, who had found them in the dark without a sound. 'Four-fingers isn't as useless as he thought – Yggur has one less boat tonight.'

'Pity about the other one,' said Mendark.

'Ah,' said Osseion. 'But while the guard was searching for me I cut the painter.'

'That was clever,' said Lilis. 'What do we do now?'

'We keep quiet,' Mendark replied, though without heat.

'How do you think it's going up there?' Osseion wondered.

'It looked as though Chert's gang was getting the better of the blackfists.'

They each kept to their own thoughts until the moon returned, shining brightly on the water. There, just below them, the skiff was drifting along the shore with the wind. It grounded on a rock, twirled around slowly and stuck just below them, a silver spear in the moonlight.

Mendark cursed.

'Do you want – ?' began Osseion, checking the moon, which now rode high in a clear patch of sky.

'No! They'll see you and know that we must be hiding nearby.'

'It's right where Pender is to come.'

'If he's coming!' Mendark said darkly.

Lilis spoke up. 'I could creep down and push it away. They'd never see me. In Thurkad I –'

'No,' said Osseion.

Mendark stared at her small sharp face. 'Yes, go!' he said. Osseion took a sharp breath and banged his injured fist against his knee.

Lilis was quite afraid as she slipped, a dark-clad shadow, out of the scrub onto the rock platform. A low voice carried clearly across the water.

'There it is! Run, before it drifts off.'

She scuttled along a gutter and, taking advantage of the cover of boulders, zig-zagged across to the boat. Lilis was afraid that it would be stuck fast, but it moved to her furious heaves and she waded in after it. Soon the water was up to her chest. So cold! She slid off a boulder into deep water and swam. The sling was a hindrance so she took her arm out and found that it was not needed anyway.

The wind kept pushing the boat back to shore. Lilis wasn't strong enough to move it out into the bay where there might be a current. She peered around the stern. A tall man was walking briskly along the platform. He stumbled and cursed.

Lilis kicked furiously. The boat glided out, then slowly drifted back again. She kicked again; the boat crept out a few spans. Now the tall man was close. He waded into the water, the moon showing him clearly: a lean man with a short black beard.

He slipped, recovered and reached out, but the boat was just too far away. He extended his arm. Just then Lilis's feet touched rock. She pushed hard, the boat moved away from the man's outstretched fingers and he fell with a splash into a deep gutter. He began to shout and thrash around, evidently not being able to swim.

'Help!' he roared.

Lilis kicked mechanically but it did not seem to make any difference. The cold had crept into her very core, until every action took on the slowness of a dream.

The tall man, after splashing and yelling for some time, eventually dragged himself back onto the rocks. By the time help reached him the boat had drifted around the curve of the shore, caught the gentle tide and began to move out into the bay. The second man cursed the first, cuffed him on the head, took off his own clothes and boots and swam clumsily out, thrashing and gasping. Eventually he reached the boat and heaved himself over the stern, swearing at the cold and his useless mates.

Lilis sank down into the water, clutching the rope. She was terrified, but not game to let go. She did not think she could swim back from here against the current. Her teeth chattered uncontrollably.

A weasel head thrust over the bow, a hard hand gripped her upraised arm. She was hauled easily out of the water and cast on the floor of the boat.

'What's thith, hah!' lisped an unpleasant nasal voice. He

laughed, revealing a dark cave full of rotten teeth. 'One of Mendark's little raths. We'll thee about you thoon.'

The moon shone down full. Lilis averted her eyes from his wiry, hairy nakedness. She was shivering convulsively. The man found a pair of oars and began to row the boat with much splashing and a continuous stream of oaths. After a while she stirred but a filthy foot stamped on her ankle.

'Lie thtill,' he snarled, 'or I'll batter you. There'll be no more trouble tonight.'

The keel grounded on the point. Someone grabbed the painter. The hairy man dragged Lilis over the side.

'What's this, a child?' cried the tall man who had fallen in.

'Yeah, pocthy little brat,' said the hairy man. 'There'll be fun later!' He tied her arms with rope and shoved hard, so that she fell down on the sharp slate. 'Lie down! Don't move.'

Lilis was gripped by a deeper, blacker cold, a paralysing, petrifying terror. Mendark and Osseion did not know where she was and she did not think Mendark would care anyway. These cutthroats (for she had no doubt that these were not Yggur's people) could do anything they wanted with her.

'Ficthed them other thcum, eh!'

'Yeah!' said a third man, appearing out of the scrub. 'The dahls will be wailing back in Thurkad tonight. How many did we do?'

'Three, out of thicth or theven. Retht are thtill running.'

'Who'd we lose, apart from Ban?'

'Torquil, and the fellow who burned up. Forget hith name.'

'Don't matter now. His goose is well and truly cooked. Ha!' The wit was emphasised by a bray of laughter.

'Ah, but Torquil wath a good man. A good friend.'

'Gold is a better friend, and our shares are double now.'

20

NORTHWARD BOUND

I t was late in the afternoon of the day following the dis-
agreement between the Hlune and the Telt. Karan had
hardly slept for worrying and when she finally did doze her
dreams were wracked by nightmares. After she woke she
could not remember them, but felt on edge.

The day had been no better. It was very cold, snowing
above. The stinging spots had been unusually virulent today
and her swollen fingers particularly clumsy. Her feet hurt
too, and she was ravenously hungry, for the *pan* still cramped
her stomach, so she took as little as possible and kept everything at bay with her work.

A group of shrouded Hlune appeared in the opening that
passed for a doorway. They looked angry, in so far as their
faces showed any emotion, but resolute. Karan stood up,
clutching her knife, sensing that this time they would prevail.
The Telt laid down their tools as well, and Cluffer went
forward. An angry argument ensued. Karan could still not
follow their rapid speech but it was clear her sanctuary was
over. She heard Yggur mentioned several times and deduced
that she was to be handed over to him.

Once again the Telt made a line across the room between
Karan and the Hlune, whereupon the leading Hlune snapped
his fingers and they all drew stubby knives.

Cluffer went rigid in alarm. 'You break the covenant,' she said clearly.

'We do,' said the Hlune, 'if you will not give her up.'

Cluffer turned to her people, looking as if she was walking to her doom.

Karan's heart was wrung. The Telt so poor, yet so loyal to their uninvited guest. It was a greater sacrifice than she could allow. 'No!' she said, 'I will go.'

Cluffer shook her head miserably.

'Guest-right!' said Karan, holding up her hands. 'You cannot stop me.'

Cluffer looked ashamed and relieved at the same time. Karan went forward two steps, then stopped, glancing down at her swollen feet. What was going to happen to her? Yggur was not a kind man – she knew he would avenge himself on her for stealing the Mirror, then use her talent until she was a broken, useless thing. Her life was over.

She darted her eyes around for any way of escape, but there was none. The leading Hlune stepped forward, catching her elbow in a crushing grip. Karan looked into his eyes, but all she could see was the man's own fear of Yggur. They no longer had any mercy to spare.

Unexpectedly, she heard Shand's voice outside the door. Her heart leapt. Then his voice was overwhelmed by the clucking cries of the Hlune, and the clamour grew until it was like a riot in a hen-house.

A cry pierced the tumult, there came a vast rolling boom, then silence. Karan tried to wrench free, but the Hlune did not relent. Her arm had gone numb from the elbow down.

'Shand!' she screamed. 'Are you all right?'

Outside someone groaned. Karan was sure that they had killed him.

Shand appeared in the doorway, red-faced, panting but otherwise sound. The Hlune holding her arm sprang out of the way, crying out to his fellows outside the door. A honking groan answered him.

Karan sank to the floor, rubbing her elbow.

'Take her and go!' shouted the leading Hlune. He gestured to Karan's corner, then stalked away, the others sweeping after him.

The Telt went back to their places but did not resume work. Shand caught sight of Karan and a smile creased his old face. As he approached the smile disappeared, but the damage had already been done. Now that the danger was over Karan was furiously angry, for her abandonment, for the cold and the terror, but most of all for the loss of her dignity, at him seeing her half-naked and spattered in bits of jellyfish.

'You said you would be a few hours,' she said coldly. 'That was five days ago.'

The amused look was back. 'I did my best for you,' he said mildly. 'The Hlune have treated you kindly enough. They gave you food, clothing to replace that which you appear to have lost, and honest toil to earn your meals. You have neither been neglected nor harshly treated, nor made to do more than they do themselves. And they hid you away because I asked it; protected you from Yggur who is hunting you by name.'

'Were it not for the Telt I would have been given to him yesterday,' she said furiously.

He tried to conceal his shock. 'I hadn't realised that things had gone so far. But you weren't, and that is no mean favour for them to do a stranger, and an ungrateful one at that, in these times. For doubt not that their own miserable existence, as you see it, is under threat. Still, that is all over – we are leaving Thurkad now.'

'Leaving! How?'

Karan was not sure whether to be relieved or afraid. Her previous experiences with Shand had been hideous. She put down her knife, washed in sea water, then bowed to the Telt and thanked them for their hospitality. They smiled back at her. Cluffer laughed, though not unkindly, and embraced her. The Telt turned back to their work as Karan followed Shand out.

'A great deal has happened in the last week,' he said. 'I do owe you an explanation.' He was quite different from the cranky, anxious old man of before. What had happened in the intervening days to transform him so?

'The citadel fell about the time I left you here. Unfortunately for us, Mendark also hid in the wharf city and that changed everything. I went out to look for a boat and couldn't get back in again. I'm sorry! Now we are going.'

'I can't go anywhere like this.'

'I have clothing for you,' he said cheerily, 'and boots, and all else that I thought you might require.'

Soon they reached a place near the outer edge of the wharf and in a little neglected storeroom Shand retrieved his bulky pack, handing her a new one.

'In there you will find what you need for your dignity,' he said, 'if not for your comfort. Get ready now – a boat is coming as soon as it's dark.' He lit a candle and went out.

Expecting badly fitting rubbish, Karan emptied out the pack. But in spite of her fears, Shand had done well – there was almost everything she could have wished for. She found several pairs of loose trousers, the kind that she liked, as well as a heavier pair, and thick woollen socks. At the bottom were two pairs of boots, slightly too big (but an extra pair of socks would make up the difference), some soft shirts and a heavy one, a long coat and hood, woollen on the inside, waxed cloth on the outside, underwear so soft that it might have been made of silk, a knife, mug, plate, bowl, soap – bless him – and other items.

Karan dressed quickly in the warmest clothes, pulled on two pairs of socks and the boots. They felt wonderful. Hanging her loincloth over a spike on the wall, she took up her pack and went out. It was growing dark. The wind blew strongly from the south and waves were lapping at the piers. A small boat waited below, dark-painted and with a dark-blue sail; Shand was already within.

Karan stood at the top of the ladder for a long moment,

wondering what to do. The wind lifted the black curls away from the back of her neck. She did not have to go with him. She was weak, ill, penniless, hunted, yes! But she had been all that before. She could find her own way, if she had to. All she needed was a little coin.

'Come on!' Shand called tersely. 'This is no place to dally in.'

An angry response sprang to her lips but before she could utter it there came a familiar voice from the boat.

'Come quickly, eh! They're watching for you all around the waterfront.'

That reminded her of a previous departure. 'You brought me here,' she murmured, taking a small step toward the ladder. 'You said I would be safe here.'

'*Good place to hide,*' I said. 'But that is changed now, eh! So I take you away again, to a better place.'

'Away from Thurkad?'

'A long way.'

Karan made up her mind. The unknown was preferable to the known. Anywhere was better than Thurkad. She climbed down into the boat and they slipped away into the darkness.

The boat took them invisibly out of Port Cardasson, away from Thurkad through the great headlands into the teeth of a big swell.

Once they were out on the sea, Shand unshuttered his lantern. It was Karan's old boatman at the helm, and she was glad to see him.

'Pender,' she said, hugging him and kissing him on each of his fat, bristly cheeks. 'You're the first friend I've seen in ages.'

Pender squirmed, but nonetheless he was smiling. Karan had been kind to him and he was fond of her in his way. Wisely he did not reply, save to ask, 'What happened to your hair, eh?'

Karan scowled and jerked a thumb at Shand. 'Where are we going?' she asked.

'I can take you up the coast,' said Pender, 'but only while

the night lasts, for I must come straight back tomorrow.' And this time he meant it. 'I have another errand. Do not offer me money, eh! for I cannot go any further.'

'I have no money,' she said, 'not a single grint.' Karan turned to Shand. 'Did you bring anything to eat *this* time?'

Shand smiled. 'Pender did. He is a most reliable provisioner.' He pulled a huge sack out from under the seat.

'*The best dining is at a fat man's table,*' said Karan respectfully, reaching for the sack. 'But Pender, you have a new boat.'

Shand held the bag away, felt inside and brought out one or two small items that might have been pieces of dried fruit. He put them on the seat in front of her. 'Just take a little at a time, till you get used to it.'

'The other was a river boat,' said Pender. 'For the Sea of Thurkad I needed a bigger and a stronger one. And here she is, *The Dancing Goose*. And crew too, if your trip were not secret. And when I go to the ocean I will need one bigger yet. But first I must have the gold, eh!'

'I hope you get it,' said Karan. Then she scowled at Shand so fiercely that even in the dim light he was taken aback. She snatched the bag from him and emptied the contents on the floor of the boat.

'What did you eat this last week?' she asked coldly. Shand looked away. 'Well, *I* ate jellyfish. *Jellyfish!*'

'You ate *pidgon*!' cried Pender in astonishment. 'No wonder you look as gaunt as a herring.'

Karan ate for an hour in the starry dark: bread and cheese and onions and smoked meats; pickles and dried fruits and mushrooms; nuts, pastries, raw vegetables and every kind of fruit that was to be had in the vicinity of Thurkad. It was the biggest meal she had ever eaten and even Pender looked on in awe and admiration. Only one thing she did not touch, a flask of sweet wine.

'I'm not ready for that,' she said, putting it back, then lay back with her eyes closed.

'Are your wife and children still in Sith, Pender?' she asked sleepily, a long time after.

The topic was a sensitive one, but he answered after a while. 'Yes, I had word just two days ago. They are safe, living in the house of Dirhan, the Customs man. He is an old *friend* of hers.' The emphasis was a warning not to pry too deeply, and Karan recalled the coldness between Pender and his wife.

She fastened up her coat, put the hood over her head, snuggled her cheek against a piece of crumpled canvas and sighed contentedly. Her eyes drifted closed. Apart from a full-to-bursting ache in her stomach, which she would not admit, she was at ease. Karan slept, warm and well-fed and secure. The future, even tomorrow, was unknown but she did not care. The trust she felt in Pender would have astonished him.

The boat sped on in the starlight. Shand hunched down out of the wind and the spray, immersed in his own thoughts. Pender sat upright, one foot on Karan's pack, his hand on the tiller. The wind was steady at their back, the sail required little adjustment. So the night went. Once or twice they saw white sails in the distance but were never hailed.

They travelled quickly with the strong wind, fleeting east of north up the Sea of Thurkad for a good eight or nine hours, and a few hours before dawn passed the mouth of a large river where a cluster of lights marked a town. Forest came right down to the water. Another hour went by, then Pender turned sharply to the left and brought them fast round a rock platform shaped like a hooked finger, over which the waves rolled and burst, and back to a sheltered place, a tiny crescent of beach, where he grounded the boat on a gravelly shore.

'You've done well,' said Shand. 'That was the mouth of the Troix back there, was it not?'

'Yes, better than I expected, eh!' said Pender. 'We've come near enough to twenty leagues. That's the northern part of the forest of Elludore. You'll have hard walking for the next week.' He passed their gear over the bow to Shand and turned to his sail. 'Fare well.'

'Pender!' cried Karan, and he stopped what he was doing. The starlight shone on his forehead.

'Have you heard anything of Llian?'

He grunted an inaudible nothing and spat over the side. Karan waited, staring at him anxiously. Finally he spoke, grudgingly. 'Not a whisper. Wherever he went, it was not by boat.' He gestured to Shand, who was holding the bow steady. Shand pushed, the boat slid over the gravel, Pender pulled it into deep water with the oars, put up the sail and the dark craft was gone.

'Fare well!' they cried to the night.

Gravel grated under their boots. Shand lifted the pack onto her back. It felt very heavy, though all it contained was her clothing and a water bottle. She had slept for most of the journey and felt fresh, invigorated by the wind and the salt spray on her face, but there was no strength in her legs.

'I've no idea where we're going, or why, but let us go,' she said.

'We're heading north,' Shand replied, stowing the sack of food in his pack. 'Away from the war. Ah, it's good to be out of Thurkad.'

'I think so too. I never wanted to go there.'

Shand's eyes glinted, then he led the way into the forest. It was almost dawn; already the sky was lightening, and it would be a clear windy day.

'Who are the Telt, Shand?' she asked, a question that had been on her mind for days.

'It's a curious story,' he replied, threading his way through the trees. 'Long ago they used to dwell in the marshes and swamp forests around the edge of the bay, in huts built on stilts. But when Thurkad grew, the marshes were drained and the forests cut down. The Telt were slowly dying out from misery, for they are timid and could do nothing about their situation. The Hlune, a race of traders, offered them a place to live when no one else would – they offered them the wharves in return for a lifelong indenture.

'Each child has the choice to break the indenture at age ten. But few do, for there is nowhere for them to go and they cannot live alone. The Telt don't like the Hlune but they are necessary to each other.'

They walked slowly up a ridge of dark, layered rock, where the trees were puny and twisted from the wind, and by the time the sun rose found themselves on a bare knob which offered a view all the way up and down the coast.

'Stop!' Karan panted, sinking down on hands and knees. The big pack made her look like a tortoise.

Shand lifted it off. 'We'll rest here. That was a steep climb.'

'Too steep for my useless legs,' she replied, rubbing her calves, but soon she perked up. 'What's that place down there?'

'I have a map, if you'd like to see it.'

'No, just tell me.'

'It's the estuary of the Troix.'

Karan gazed about her. The forest beyond Troix, back in the direction of Thurkad, stretched to the limit of view. Northwards the mountains squeezed the coastal forest right into the sea, the rugged and uninviting path that they were to take. In the east the Sea of Thurkad, here at its widest point near forty leagues in width, was all white-flecked water and a few foam-encrusted islands midway across. The sea, Karan knew, ran north-west for a hundred leagues or so to the ocean.

In the opposite direction it extended in sweeping curves for more than two hundred leagues, steadily narrowing to Gnulp Landing, where an arrow could be shot from one side to the other, though the race was so strong there as to be virtually prohibitive of navigation. Beyond Gnulp, the channel opened out again into a chilly and fog-shrouded inland sea, the Karama Malama or Sea of Mists. Such was the Sea of Thurkad, that separated the island of Meldorin from the great continent of Lauralin immediately to the east.

Behind them in the west, though she could not see beyond the next ridge, Karan knew that the mountains ran virtually unbroken from the north-eastern tip of Meldorin south along the sea coast, then inland in a great sweep that enclosed the nations of Iagador, her own beloved homeland of Bannador abutting the mountains of Shazmak, back to the shore of the Sea of Thurkad beyond Sith, and south by east all the way to the Karama Malama.

There were a few sails on the water and a little patch of smoke near the town of Troix-on-Sea, but no other signs of humanity.

'What now?' asked Karan.

'Breakfast, if you can fit it in, then we march on until you are tired. There should be a path a little higher up. We follow it north along the coast at whatever pace you can manage.'

'Will there not be patrols?'

'There could be, though few people live in this country, only a few hunters and herders. It's too poor for farming. I think we're as safe here as anywhere.'

Karan thought of her father, waylaid in the mountains behind Gothryme, slain for a few coins, and shivered. At that, the faintest trace of her nightmare came back – a dream that she was being watched by a circle of Ghâshâd. That made her shudder though she could not quite remember why. She found a knife in her pack, tested the edge, hung the thong of the sheath around her neck and dropped it down inside her shirt.

'Breakfast then. I'm hollow as an old wineskin.'

Shand began to gather sticks for the fire.

'What about Llian, Shand? Did you find out anything about him?'

'There was a rumour that he went with Tensor . . .'

'*Went* with Tensor,' she cried out. '*Went!*' The very word, or the emphasis he put on it, infuriated her. 'No, I *will not* believe that. He may have been taken but he would not have gone willingly.' After a drawn-out silence, she said, 'Why *would* he?'

'Mendark said that Tensor took him,' Shand repeated mildly. 'Whether he went willingly or unwillingly, who knows?'

'You hesitated a moment ago. You have some private suspicion of Llian?'

'No. Not any longer. And yet . . . no, it is nothing.'

'I must know, if you have something against him. I *must* know.'

'At the beginning, in Tullin, I was worried . . . and now this. It disturbs me. But what is your concern?'

She looked down at her lap, where her fingers writhed. 'We travelled a long way together and endured much together. I already told you that. Naturally I wish to know what has happened to him.' Being a chronicler, Llian was fascinated by the unfolding tale of the Mirror. It was one of the first things Karan had noticed about him. Now Shand had raised an ugly suspicion – that Llian had gone with Tensor willingly to follow the tale.

'But you doubt him too?' asked Shand.

'*No!* Llian is my friend.' I am loyal to my friends, she thought, putting the suspicion behind her. I do not blather their weaknesses to the world. And I am secretive too. I would never tell a stranger, especially one as strange as you. 'My dearest friend,' she said emphasising the word in such a way that he could be in no doubt as to what she meant by it. Softly, 'Almost my lover. No passing thing, that.'

21

A CURIOUS BATH

An hour later they continued up the ridge, full of hot tea and porridge thickened with dried grapes, honey and butter. Karan had taken two full bowls of that, eating until she was stuffed, and shouldered the pack most reluctantly. In this steep country she could only go for a few minutes before needing a rest and, as soon as she began to labour, Shand called the halt. After about two hours they came suddenly onto a broad path which was well used, judging by footprints in soft mud. The path meandered across the slope of the hill to north and south. After a brief rest they headed down.

When they were out of the trees she noticed that the wind had come up and the sea was covered in breaking waves. Gritty particles of sleet peppered their faces.

'It's going to get worse,' Shand said, staring back in the direction of Thurkad. 'I'm glad we're not out on the sea now.'

'I hope Pender gets back safely,' Karan muttered.

In the mid-afternoon, Shand judged that they had covered a good league. Karan was beginning to stagger. 'Enough for today. Let's find a camp.'

The ground was steep and stony and off the path it fell into a tangle of deep gullies. Above them the slope continued just as hard. Shand pointed that way.

'Beyond the crest, I think, out of sight of the road. Can you go that far?'

Karan leaned against a tree, rubbing her cheek with cold fingers. She nodded, too weary to speak. At the top the ridge branched, the branches separated by a shallow gully.

'Look!' he said, indicating a patch of green at the foot of the grey rock. 'A spring. We'll camp just over the ridge, out of sight.'

The bottom of the gully was muddy but the spring clear and clean, so they filled their bottles and washed their hands and faces before the last steps to the top of the second ridge. A flat piece of ground covered in coarse grass and sharp stones, shielded by small umbrella-shaped trees, invited them to stay. Karan flopped on the ground, rubbing her feet as Shand busied himself with the campfire.

'My knees won't hold me up any longer,' she said. 'I'm sorry, I have to rest.'

'I'd sooner you did, otherwise you will be useless tomorrow. Besides, so much of my life have I spent on the track, it's no more trouble for two than it is for one.'

Nonetheless Karan was soon back on her feet, gathering branches and breaking them into lengths for later, then labouring back up from the spring with a pot full of water. Shand, down on his hands and knees blowing on smouldering tinder, was struck by the difference between her and Llian, who even in the best of times was a good-natured shirker. What on earth had she seen in him? But then, he reminded himself, Llian did have one notable quality. The tinder burst into flame. He fed it into a cheering fire and went to put the tent up.

Karan dragged a couple of logs over, inspected hers carefully for things that might bite or sting, and sat down close to the fire. Shortly she got up again, walked unsteadily to the tent, came back with a blanket, wrapped it around her and lay down on the ground.

'I'm too tired to sit,' she said, catching Shand's eye.

He grunted, continuing to prepare the dinner, a stew. The sun went down. Karan dozed. The stew simmered. Water boiled over into the fire with a hiss and a cloud of ash. A piece of wood exploded, sending sparks and hot coals in all directions. She sat up suddenly, beating tiny sparks off her blanket.

'What's that I smell burning?' she asked irritably.

Shand reached over to flick a red cinder from her black hair. 'It doesn't seem to have done much damage.'

'It hardly matters. It's ruined anyway.'

Shand was not going to be drawn into that topic. 'Dinner-time,' he said loudly, rubbing his hands.

This thought drove the other from her mind. Karan held out her bowl until it was filled to the brim with hot thick spicy stew, and said not another word until that was gone, and another half a bowl, and the bowl wiped clean with torn-off chunks from a round loaf of grainy bread. The stew was followed by a mud-thick, sweet yellow beverage that tasted of vanilla and cloves.

'What's this?' Karan wondered.

'It's called mil. They drink it in the east, where I dwelt when I was young. Younger, at any rate. You can buy the pods at one or two places in Thurkad, though generally they're stale. It's just the thing when you're cold and weary, but it can make you drowsy if you're not used to it.'

Karan quaffed her mil, heated water in the largest pot and scrubbed her hair until she could no longer hold her arms up. The water, when she flung it away ferociously, was grey, but her hair was as black as ever.

'Give it time,' said Shand. 'It doesn't look so bad to me. Anyway, it will grow out eventually.'

'Why should I care how it looks to you? It's my hair and it looks vile. The best part of me and you have ruined it,' she cried, kicking the other pot clean across the fire. Clouds of steam and ash belched up. The pot tumbled over the side of the hill, rattling and clanging, and she had to hobble after it. The clamour continued for what seemed a long time, then Karan dragged herself up the hill. The pot was now rather battered and had a broken handle. She put it down beside the fire and sat upon a stone.

'I did it to save your life,' Shand said.

'I'm sorry,' she said. 'I don't know what came over me. Please don't think I'm ungrateful.' She put her head on her arms, rocking back and forth. The firelight gleamed in her hair, traces of red among the black, though that could have been the colour of the flame. Karan sat that way for a few minutes, then got up unsteadily.

'I'm so very tired.' Without looking at Shand she limped around the fire, crawled into the tent and slept the night away.

Shand sat up late by the fire, drinking mil and yellow wine from the skin that Karan had refused, thinking and looking up at the stars, very watchful. Once or twice he went into the forest, listening for anything out of the ordinary. Though these lands were sparsely habited, he knew that it was never quite safe to be alone on the road. After midnight he rolled into his blankets and dozed until just before the dawn.

In the morning he was already up and had the porridge cooking before Karan appeared. The smell of it drew her out of her tent and she stood there in her shirt, bare-legged and rubbing her eyes. It was a miserable day, as windy as yesterday, blowing rain and sleet. She stared at Shand blankly, as though she did not know who he was or what he was doing there.

'Good morning . . .' she said, struggling to remember his name. She had often woken like this since the Conclave, sleep dragging her back to the state that Shand had found her in. Karan furrowed her brow, finally forcing the name into conscious space. '. . . Shand!'

She went down the hill to the spring to wash. She was only gone ten minutes but when she returned she looked her normal self again and came to the fire with her bowl and spoon and a cheerful greeting. On seeing the porridge pot she giggled and said, 'What on earth happened to that?' Then she remembered, 'Oh! Did I do that? I'm sorry.'

'No matter,' Shand replied, wondering whether she was really recovered at all. 'I can mend it. How are you feeling today?'

'Better, though my legs are quite sore.'

'We'll take it slowly this morning. And I am sorry about your hair.'

She shook down her hair. 'Perhaps I'm imagining it, but the black does seem to be fading. What on earth did you dye it with?'

He laughed. 'A dye made from the root of the myrtle flower, among other things. But a very poor dye it turned out to be, more brown than black, and the red still showing through. I did it again in a hurry with map-maker's ink. What a mess that made and what a fool I felt doing it, while you lay as if dead. I knew it wouldn't last. There are better dyes, but they require boiling. Anyhow, it served. With red hair you would never have gotten out of Thurkad.'

Karan was stiff early on, but that went away as soon as she warmed up, though her calves ached all day. She felt stronger than before and did not call a rest until the mid-morning, where they looked down on the sea from a high bluff. Karan suddenly rose to her feet with her hand halfway to her mouth.

'What's the matter?' Shand asked.

'There's a boat come in to shore where we landed yesterday.'

'It's a good place to land. There aren't many places as sheltered, in this weather.'

'It's flying Yggur's flag,' Karan said, feeling uneasy. 'Could he track our path across the sea?'

'You're the expert in that, I hear. I'd say not likely in this weather.'

'I know nothing about *scrying*,' she said tartly. 'That's one of the Secret Arts.'

'Well, he couldn't possibly know that *we* landed there.'

Of course you're right, Karan thought, but she could not get over the feeling that they had been followed nor could she relax for days after. And that thought led her back to Llian, but all she could sense was running, running day and night, and never stopping. She thought about Llian all the time now, a fruitless and miserable occupation.

Once more they finished their march in the mid-afternoon. That night she again scrubbed her hair with soap and hot water, though with no more result than before. She was not quite as weary and sat by the fire for a while after dark. Several times Shand caught her eyes on him, weighing him. Eventually she spoke.

'Why are you helping me? *What do you want from me?*'

'I have good reasons, but I don't feel like talking about them. Suffice it that Yggur was hunting you and I didn't see why he should have you.'

The next day they carried on as before. Karan's appetite was unabated. Midway through the third bowl of porridge Shand began to laugh. 'Slow down! If you keep on like this we'll run out of food long before we get to Ganport. There's none to be bought before.'

'There's plenty down there,' she said coolly, pointing to the sea, which was quite near, for that morning Shand had forsaken the main mountain path for an overgrown track that ran along the shore. It was a winding way, longer than the upper road, but easier here, where the rugged mountains came close to the sea.

The weather had worsened during the night, and an icy wind blew directly down the sea, blasting rain and bits of sleet at them through the trees, though fortunately the wind was at their backs. Late in the day Karan was sitting on a knoll rubbing her sore feet when suddenly she called out to Shand.

'Isn't that Pender's boat out there?' A vessel with small dark sail was sailing north, wallowing heavily, not far offshore.

Shand strained his eyes. 'It could be. It's got rather a list though. I can't quite say.'

'I'm sure it is. I wonder what he's doing back here?'

Shand felt no need to enlighten her. The boat picked up a shift in the wind and pounded away through the waves. 'With Pender, probably best not to know. His is a dangerous way to make a living just now.'

'I know. The sea is his life, and he's greedy for gold to have it back again. And why should he not?'

'He'll get it soon enough if this war lasts – if he keeps his head. A good sailor can ask whatever he wants.'

That afternoon, for their supplies *were* being used up faster than Shand had anticipated, they had gathered quantities of mussels, oysters and seaweed from the rocks, making a pot of chowder with wine and some wild garlic that Karan had discovered growing near the path that morning. While the dinner was simmering she went down to the sea and swam in the cold water, coming back blue and shivering violently.

'You'll kill yourself,' said Shand. 'Look, it's snowing up there. Don't be in such a hurry.'

'Only someone who has never been helpless could say such a thing,' she said curtly.

'No one knows more about feeling helpless than I,' he replied with such feeling that it shocked her, though clearly he was talking about another time.

After that she sat quietly while he put a blanket around her shoulders and fetched a bowl of chowder, and another after the first warming bowl was gone. When she had eaten sufficient she indulged herself in a small mug of wine.

That night was very cold, yet Karan scarcely noticed it, cosy in her clothes and blankets against the wild. The wind shook the tent all night, blowing sand and leaves against it, and a few flurries of snow, though not enough to whiten the ground. Around dawn the wind slowly abated, but the sky remained leaden with the threat of rain. There was an ugly sea out beyond the surf, with short steep waves bursting one against the other, as they began their daily trudge.

Each morning or each evening Karan swam in the cold sea, struggling out further each time, and one day she went so far that Shand lost sight of her dark head in the grey waters. Ten minutes passed with no sign of her and he grew alarmed, even contemplated throwing off his clothes and going out after her, though he had no idea where to look and was a poor swimmer. Then he saw her, a long way from the last sighting, stroking placidly along the front of the beach toward him. She swam all the way into the shallows, until she was lying in ankle-deep water.

Shand wrapped his cloak around her. She looked up at his grave face and said, 'I love to swim. I can feel it washing all the past away, renewing me. And the cold doesn't bother me.' As if to deny her words she gave a great, convulsive shiver.

Shand was wise enough to know when to say nothing, so he merely inclined his head toward the campfire. 'I'll make the tea then, shall I?'

On the ninth day of their journey they reached the Gannel River, a vast brown flood. By that time Karan had eaten all the food and was almost fully recovered, physically. Now they were making up to four leagues a day, good going through hilly country in the short winter days, especially as they had to stop before dark to fish and gather shellfish. In all that time Shand and Karan had hardly spoken, and whatever thoughts each had about the other they kept to themselves.

The Gannel was in flood from the winter rains and far too strongly flowing to swim, but Shand knew of a village along the shore where they might catch a ferry. They walked upstream for some hours until they found it, on the main path from the south. The village was a poor, shabby place, just a collection of huts, all mud in the winter and dust in the summer. They got a bowl of soggy noodles there in the mid-afternoon.

'The Gannel!' said Karan. 'There is a river, or at least a creek, near Chanthed with the same name.'

'It's the same river, and must be a very ancient one, for it has cut right through the mountains to get to Ganport.'

'Good. Let's go there.'

'What's the hurry? Can't abide my cooking?'

'Your fare is well enough but there are things I need to buy.'

'What things?'

'Oh well . . . A comb. A book to write in. Just *things*,' she repeated, her eyes flashing. 'And I'd like a hot bath.'

Shand was unconcerned. 'Ganport is not Thurkad, or even Tolryme, you know. I doubt if they run to books.'

Nonetheless he went off and found a little old man, bald as an egg, who led them silently down to a small boat tied under a shelter made of sticks. They stepped in and were rowed across. Standing on the mud of the bank, Shand put a copper into the old man's warty hand. He nodded and rowed silently back. They strolled along the northern bank of the Gannel, now among tall trees, now among reeds, continuing after dark on a broad path. Ahead the lights of a substantial town were visible.

Ganport was prosperous on account of the fishing and the trading, though the streets were almost empty as they reached the town. They saw occasional soldiers in the distance, troops in the livery of Yggur, but were not stopped. 'What does this mean?' Shand mused. 'Has the war come this far south already? They don't look like an occupying army. Let's be careful though, and not attract attention.'

The night was cold and clear and dark, the moon not yet risen but a hard frost already setting. They found an inn, by the name of The Four Fishes, that was drab, indeed almost seedy. Though Karan argued for a better-looking one up the street; Shand went into the first.

'It's less conspicuous,' he said.

The innkeeper was a tiny wrinkled old woman with a huge nose and no chin whatsoever. Her eyes stared in two directions at once and she was continually darting her head on its scrawny neck, looking rather like a goose gabbling about a fox.

'You will want to try our bath. The Four Fishes is famous for its bath, the best in all Ganporrrt,' she chirped, rolling her r's into a warble. 'The hottest water, the most luxurious balms and essences. It will bring the colour to your pasty cheeks . . . miz; would soften even your leathery skin, sirrr.'

Shand dismissed the bath but Karan was keen. The charge was almost as great as the cost of the room, their host clucking loud and long about the price of firewood and the wages of servants. Karan had to wait for an hour while sufficient water was boiled in a huge cauldron.

The bathing room was small and draughty, being a lean-to structure at the back of the inn with unrendered stone walls. The old woman flourished her broom at two louts who were hanging around and they slouched away with dark looks. Karan noticed the grass was worn away at one place, doubtless where they spied on the bathers through the wall. The bath, so called, was made of unglazed pottery so poorly fired that the rim was crumbling. It looked more like a well and had to be used standing up.

It was quite narrow at the top – a very pregnant woman or a very fat man might have had difficulty getting back out of it. There was a slatted wooden deck around it halfway up and a wooden plug which could be released by a chain. Karan inspected it with misgivings, wondering how clean it was, for the room had a dank smell and some of the slats were rotten.

'Very clean, very clean,' piped the cross-eyed host, darting her head vigorously, and to prove it swirled a mop about in the bottom and thrust it under Karan's nose. 'Clean, I tell you.'

The test was inconclusive, for the mop was so stained and threadbare that it showed nothing at all, though it smelled even more rank than the underfloor drain. Karan pushed it away and said weakly, 'Very well. Bring the water then.'

To her surprise, for the old woman looked as frail as a twig and there were several meaty young men serving in the inn, she carried the water herself, staggering in with a wooden pail in each hand and slopping water everywhere, so that by the time she reached the tub her buckets were only half-full. She banged them down on the deck, swayed, wiped her hand over her eyes, picked up the first bucket and spilled most of the water down the outside of the tub. Undaunted, she lurched for the second, but Karan, who could see that she might never get a bath at all, lifted it in for her.

'It's all right,' Karan said. 'You go and attend to your customers. I'll carry the water.'

The innkeeper rounded on her fiercely. 'Nonsense,' she warbled. 'We pride ourselves on our serrr-vice at The Four Fishes.' She tottered off with the pails.

Karan followed her out the back, found two more buckets in a smoke-filled out-house that doubled as the laundry and filled them after the old woman had departed. They made quite a few trips together, she steadfastly ignoring Karan. When the bath was half-full of steaming water, they filled it the rest of the way with cold.

'Soap?' said Karan sarcastically. 'Miraculous balms and essences? Restoratives for sallow skin?'

The old woman grumbled under her breath, weaved out and came back with a narrow-necked flask which she banged down on the rim of the bath. Pottery flaked into the water.

'Just this much,' she said, signing a tiny pool in the centre of her palm. Then she nodded to Karan, coldly wished her joy of her bath and with a last dart of her head staggered out of the room.

Karan sat down, took off her boots and socks, stuffed a sock in each of the largest chinks in the wall, undressed still feeling watched and turned to the tub. Then, on instinct, she plucked a straw out of the broom and thrust it through a third crack over the bath. She heard a cry, a crash as if someone had fallen off a stool, followed by a further yelp and silence. I hope the view was worth it, she thought, slipping nimbly over the rough edge of the tub. The water was splendidly hot. Karan inched her way down, supporting herself on her arms, reaching down with her toes for the bottom. By the time she obtained it the water was up to her chin. There she stood, luxuriating in the heat.

The flask contained an oily, corrosive-looking substance that might have stripped axle grease. It had an unpleasant odour. She poured a little into the palm of her hand, sniffed, shrugged and rubbed it into her hair. It did not lather, for her hair was full of salt. Karan ducked her head, washed it out and poured the whole contents of the flask over her hair. Foam began to drip from her hair and as she splashed it rose to spill over the rim of the tub. She scrubbed her hair over and over until even her standards of cleanliness were satisfied; until her head felt scalded and she grew dizzy from the heat.

On the way out she saw a long line of folk standing outside the door, and, thinking that they too were peepers, went by with her head in the air. Inside she related this to Shand in an indignant tone, but he only laughed.

'Don't be silly,' he said. 'They were waiting for their baths. Our host sells the hot water ten times over.'

'You mean the price I paid . . . you paid . . . *Sell the dirty bathwater!* The avaricious old cow. And to think I carried the water!'

'Why not? You had your bath. This way she earns three times the money and each gets their bath cheaper than the one before. Everyone is happy.'

'That's disgusting!' said Karan, taking a reckless draught of her wine bowl. 'In my country we would never bathe in the same water as a stranger. Well, I have the laugh on them all, for I pulled the plug when I got out.'

'You didn't!' said Shand.

'I did!'

'Lucky I've paid for our room already, or we would be out on the street.'

'Why is that?'

'You surely have made an enemy of the innkeeper. Now she must boil the water again and she will not forget what you have cost her. They nurse their grudges here, even more than they value money itself, for all that they are a grasping, greedy lot. Tomorrow everyone in the town will be talking about you. About the woman who threw away the bathwater. The woman who went to the bath with black hair and came back with red. Profligate, and suspicious.'

'*What!*' cried Karan. 'Are you sure?' She shook her tangles against the light. The dye, had she known, had been fading a little more with each wash, and now the hot water and the aggressive soap had taken the last of the colour away. It had not quite regained the magnificent smoky red that was its natural hue, but red it was nonetheless. 'Oh, Shand,' she said, and leaning across the table threw her arms around him and kissed him on his hairy cheek. Her elbow caught the jug of red wine, which slipped off the table and smashed, casting a scarlet lake across the carpet. All conversation stopped. Everyone in the room stared at her.

'Oh,' she said, lowering herself in her chair. Her face flushed to the hue of the carpet.

'Worse and worse,' said Shand gruffly. 'To further the insult you smash the crockery, ruin the carpet and display in public an unwholesome lust for someone old enough to be your grandfather.'

'Oh!' she said again, staring at him and putting her hand over her mouth.

'So it will appear to these folk, who have probably never been five leagues from Ganport, and know all southerners, especially those with red hair, to be utterly depraved. You'd better think of a story quick.'

Just then the old woman came into the room with a face as black as a cauldron, whereupon the customers at the bar clamoured to tell her of the latest scandal. Then their heads all swivelled around and stared at Karan, and the hubbub stopped again. Karan, whose face was almost as red as her hair, wanted to crawl under the carpet and die.

22

A FISHY TALE

'Oh!' Karan said for the third time. 'No, this is shameful, unbearable.' She looked Shand in the eye. 'Give me your purse.'

Shand put it in her hand under the table. She stuck it in her pocket and stood up. She walked slowly, but with dignity, across to the old woman, whose head bobbed furiously at her, though one eye still seemed to be staring accusingly at Shand. Karan put her mouth to the host's ear; the woman's face changed. She drew Karan through a doorway out of sight. Minutes passed. Shand sipped the dregs of his wine. A serving man collected the broken crockery and mopped the carpet with a grey cloth. A new flask of wine was brought. The attention of the room turned back to its own affairs.

The old woman came out again. Her face had resumed its look of wrinkled placidity. Karan followed, put her hand on the counter and said something softly to the host. Then she walked back to her seat and sat down. Shand looked at her quizzically.

'It's all over. Just a trifling incident, really. We are friends now, can you believe it?'

'If you can believe it, who am I to doubt?' he said dryly. 'Though I wonder if you realise how strong this wine is. What did you tell her?'

'You told me to make up a story.'

'Oh yes?' said Shand, quaffing his wine.

'It's rather silly. I couldn't think of anything at all, then my tongue just ran away.' She laughed. Karan seemed to have got back the mischievous humour she had once been well known for.

Shand frowned, then leaned back in his chair, bowl in hand. 'You'd better tell me.'

'In the filthy and squalid inns of vile Thurkad, I told her, where they put butter in the tea and do other things too unspeakable to mention, and where not even the Magister bathes more than once a year, where a night at an inn so magnificent as The Four Fishes, if there were such, which there isn't, would cost the stipend of a prince, there to my misery, and because of the war, I could find no room save at an inn disgraced by the name of The Flatulent Donkey. The room I had to share with a man and his wife, both of whom were dog trainers, and their seventeen hounds also, which lived up to the name of the inn, and neither the sheets nor the man nor the woman nor the dogs had been washed since the founding of Thurkad itself, so that there was filth on the pillows that you could scrape off with a knife, which I did before I lay down to sleep. Yet in spite of this and sundry other precautions I caught the terrible bloodsucking hair crabs of Thurkad, which creep and crawl about on the head and other parts of the body where hair abounds, though not in my case, and every touch of their innumerable feet sets up such an itching and every bite from their bristly and bloodstained snouts such a burning and a stinging and a throbbing and a prickling, that some people have been known to tear every hair from their heads, and the scalp as well, so as to be free of them, yet which nothing suffices to rid one of, save smearing each hair with bitumen brought all the way from the tar pits of Snizort, in the frozen south, and leaving it there for the space of no less than two weeks, after which time it can be washed away in hot water, and the petrified crabs, and generally the hair as well.'

As she paused for breath, the host rapped on the counter with a coin.

'You can't wash bitumen off with hot water,' said Shand. 'You need spirits of tar, or turpentine. But a droll enough story. I hope she appreciated it.'

'Oh, what I told her was more elaborate than that. I was quite astounded by my creativity. She even smiled at one point, though only after pointing out that I had used soap for ten people as well.'

'Hush now. I believe she is going to address the inn.'

'Cherished customers,' the woman trilled, eyes seeming to look at each one of them at the same time, 'my esteemed friend,' here she gestured to Karan, 'who has fled from the war all the way from Thurkad, most wicked of cities . . .'

'Aye, unholy!' 'Depraved!' 'Perverted!' 'Unspeakable!' assented the room, and while the clamour went on Karan continued in Shand's ear: 'And I said to her, after two weeks I came to The Four Fishes, jewel of inns, and washed away all the bitumen, but not wishing to risk infesting the esteemed customers of the aforesaid inn with even one dead louse I sent all the hot water gushing down the drains to the Gannel to feast the fishes, and for which loss of hot water I will gladly reimburse the honourable innkeeper and of course for all other damages ensuing from my excitement at discovering that the vermin were all gone, and a little more for your trouble.'

'H'm,' said Shand, lips twitching. 'That's why you're looking so pleased with yourself, is it? You suppose you got yourself out of trouble? I wonder what she is going to tell the customers?'

'Nothing, I hope,' said Karan, beginning to look anxious. 'Save that they may drink at my expense.'

Now the old woman was speaking again '. . . fled from wicked Thurkad with yon greybeard, her honourable grandfather . . .'

'Grandfather, ha! Vile old lecher!' came a single voice from the back of the room, near the fire.

The woman's head stilled for a moment, identified the interrupter. One of his eyes was bloodshot and there was a fresh lump on his forehead. 'Blegg, you scoundrel! Took your eye away from the hole a trifle late, did you? Throw him out, boys.'

Two stout lads seized Blegg, a pimply runt with ears like cabbage leaves, and threw him out the door.

'Honourable grandfather, she calls him, and who am I to question her word? Does she not look like an honest woman, a reliable, truthful, modest woman, to you? Does she not look just like any one of us?'

The customers, portly matrons and corpulent burghers all, heavy jaws slack, mud-coloured hair falling into their eyes, as one stared at Karan with witless hostility.

'She,' and here a tiny mottled finger described eccentric arcs through the air before settling on the shrinking Karan, 'tells me she came here wracked by the pangs of the Thurkad swamp fever that turns your very bowels to water. I will not disgust you with the details of that horrid pox which, though let it be said, only depraved and villainous people ever get. And see how sick and trembling she is, how scrawny and weak, how pasty her face, how yellow and glassy her eyes, like those of a dead fish, how ratty her hair, how . . .' at this point she hesitated, at a loss for inspiration, or perhaps having forgotten what she had started out to say; '. . . suffering the fever, as I said, and other infestations of the creeping, crawling, itching and scratching and tormenting kind which, to avoid shaming her before strangers, I will not mention . . .'

Her mind wandered again, her head bobbed and her eyeballs described separate circles in their sockets. Shand made a choking, snorting noise, inadequately muffled by his hand.

'So she apologises most humbly for committing, in her distress, and not at all because of the wine she drank, not at all . . . Though look you at how red her face grows, a sovereign indicator of the sot as well I know, who have had this inn for near to sixty year. Apologises for falling, not drunk, not a bit, over our tables and otherwise violating our customs. And, dear friend of mine as she will ever be, generously . . . Generously! See this tiny coin . . . Begs you to drink with her until this silver tar is utterly drunk up.'

She held up the coin so that the light fell on it, dropped it on the counter several times, listening intently to the ring, while again the room went disconcertingly silent, stared at it again, turning it over and over in her hands and finally testing it with her teeth. Satisfied at last, she nodded, slipped it in her pocket, glared at Karan and said again, 'Until this little tar is utterly drunk up. This tiny piece of silver.'

The room gave a ragged cheer and breasted the bar.

'She wanted another,' said Shand after a long silence. 'Remarkable, your friendship.'

Karan had gone silent and still. She was looking down and he did not realise for a moment that she was crying soundlessly, tears running down her cheeks and dripping on the table. Shand, thinking the lesson well learned, showed little sympathy.

'How could you be so naive, after all the travelling you've done? Anyway, tomorrow we will be gone and never return. Travel is full of little humiliations.'

Shand paused as a lout came by and saluted Karan with his glass. He had a mouth the size of a bucket with three teeth evenly spaced around its circumference. Around the room other customers, equally rum-looking, were waving, grinning or brandishing flagons at her in a horrible imitation of good cheer.

'And is there aught left in the purse for tomorrow, now that everyone in the northern half of Meldorin knows who you are and where you came from?'

She hurled it back across the table. 'It is not that much lightened,' she said savagely, 'and the colour was changing back anyway.'

Shand grunted. They sat there for a while, but the yokelish grinning and leering became so irritating, and Karan so morose, that they slipped quietly away to their room, to which after an interminable wait their dinner came, cold, overcooked and tasteless. When it was done Karan sat down in the only chair, staring blankly at the fire. Realising that the best thing to do was to leave her to herself, Shand went quietly out into the night.

He was driven back after midnight by a gale that came out of the south without warning. The room was dark. He lit a candle with a coal from the fire. Karan was curled up in a tiny ball in the big chair with her heavy coat pulled right up over her head, one hand hanging over the side of the chair.

Shand thought about waking her, but she seemed comfortable enough, so he took off his own coat and boots, bolted the door and crawled into what looked the less rickety of the two beds. He slept very badly, for his mattress was crawling with fleas, almost as many as in Karan's tale.

The next morning, for once, Karan was up before Shand. She had been down to the kitchen and ordered breakfast, which came after a wait of only an hour – lukewarm gruel and tasteless, too-sweet tea, even for Karan's sweet tooth. Neither mentioned the events of the previous night but Karan said sourly, 'That's the last time I'll let you pick the inn. Let's go!'

Shand forbore to point out that she had no money, while his might have to last many months.

'Go where?' he asked, scratching his flea bites.

'Serves you right,' she said. 'Anywhere but this inn.'

'All right, but put a scarf over your head. Please.'

Karan saw the sense in that. She wound a green scarf around her hair like a turban and crammed her floppy hat on top. They walked around the town for an hour, unpleasant in the wild weather, took a turn along the waterfront, and finally sat down on an empty jetty in the wind, watching the waves burst over the breakwater. Ganport was a large enough place for nobody to take any notice of them. Shand went off walking; Karan stayed where she was, feeling that she had reached a turning point, or at least a place where she must find some direction. Finally Shand came strolling back, whistling tunelessly.

'What do we do now?' said Karan, swinging her legs in the air.

Shand took a long time to answer. 'I'd hoped you could give me some guidance,' he replied.

Karan looked at him blankly.

'I know that you are a sensitive.'

'I *had* a small talent,' said Karan, 'though I did not use it overmuch. But it will be no use to you. It abandoned me on the way to Sith, or perhaps I closed it off – I can't remember. All I know is that it was not there when I needed it most, when Emmant came. I can hardly remember what it was anymore, though I feel diminished without it. But I always knew it was a precarious thing to rely on.'

'I was in Tullin at the beginning of winter, when Llian turned up,' said Shand, watching her closely.

At the mention of Llian her face softened and she looked away at the fire. 'Llian,' she said reflectingly, rolling the name around in her mind like a rare sweet; then she caught Shand's gaze on her and the mask went up over her face again.

'You made a sending the night he came to Tullin,' he went on. 'Even I caught it, and I am not sensitive. And even I knew that you made it to him.'

'How could you know such a thing? I was not even aware of his existence.'

'Were you not? Do you tell me that you never saw him at the Festival of Chanthed?'

Karan's cheeks went a delicate shade of pink. 'Of course I saw him *there*. But when I made it I did not know that he was in Tullin; how could I have?' Then another thought occurred to her.

'I see what you want from me,' she said, her eyes like a dog that had just been kicked. 'You sought me out and nursed me back to health so that I could find Tensor and get you the Mirror. I had hoped that you, at least, did not want to use me.'

'I don't,' said Shand mildly. 'When I took you away I didn't even know that Tensor had *been* at the Conclave. As I told you, I came hurriedly to Thurkad and spoke to no one on the way. Long ago I abandoned power and swore I would never take it up again. No, there were several reasons for helping you, but the strongest will do. I've put off telling you for a long time, vainly trying to keep the lid on the past that you and Llian broke open in Tullin. When I saw you lying there on the floor, with your little round face so white and your red hair all a-tangle, it took me back to the last time I saw you.'

Karan started.

'I last saw you at the burying of your father,' he said quietly. 'I knew your father well; in fact we were friends. You would have been seven or eight then, I suppose. You looked just the same.'

'Eight,' said Karan, the tears flooding her eyes. That misery was as near as yesterday. How she wanted to hear about her father. But he went on.

'I thought you were dead! But even dead, how could I leave you there? My life has been full of wrongs unrighted, not least when I refused to go with Llian to find you. Had I done so, none of this would have happened. What a friend I turned out to be! Time to make good. I discovered that you lived, so I put you over my shoulder and took you away: to bring you back to life, or bury you with decency. And on the way you came out of your coma.'

'I thought there was something familiar about you,' said Karan. 'But all that is behind me. Perhaps my talent will never come back.'

Shand turned the conversation to the more immediate issue. Knowing how independent and resourceful she had been before her illness, he felt constrained to put the matter delicately.

'Will you go your own way now or come with me?'

'Where would you go?'

'Anywhere. Wherever you wish.'

'I want to go home,' she said, looking wistful. 'Gothryme needs me and I miss it terribly.'

'I came through Tolryme on the way to Thurkad,' he said, referring to the town nearest her rundown manor.

She snatched his hand. 'Is Gothryme –'

'The war has not come to that part of Bannador yet, though the southern lowlands have suffered cruelly.'

'Tell me about Gothryme,' she interrupted, pathetically anxious. 'Rachis, my steward, is very old. He was quite vexed when I left with Maigraith to go to Fiz Gorgo. I said I would be back in two months, and that was half a year ago. I must send word!'

Shand said nothing, just stared her down.

'I can't, can I?'

'No!'

'Even then Gothryme was suffering from the drought,' she said miserably.

'There was autumn rain,' he said, 'enough for a harvest. They're not starving yet. But if the war goes on . . .'

'I just want to go home,' she whispered.

'You know you can't. You would be as big a danger to them as the war.'

'I know,' she said in a tiny voice. 'I have no choice in the matter.'

'Then you'd better come with me.'

'I have no money at all. How can you afford me? You, a poor old man who helps in an inn with no customers. Gothryme may not survive the war. I could end up a pauper.' Karan put her head in her hands, the rest coming muffled.

'I wish I were home more than anything, but for *Llian*. Maybe even more than him.'

'I was not always what I am today,' said Shand. 'Yes, I can afford you. That is . . . That is, ah –'

'What?' she asked anxiously.

'As long as you don't want too many hot baths.' He laughed, and after a moment she laughed as well, though only to be polite.

'Then I will come. My body is recovering, but inside I am empty and confused. I do need help and I've grown used to you.'

Shand made no remark at her grudging acceptance. 'We'd better get organised. I heard some disturbing news when I was walking a while ago.'

'Oh?'

'Gannish (that's the name of this country) capitulated to Yggur two days ago, though his armies haven't even crossed the border. And your performance last night has drawn attention to us.'

Karan looked panicky. 'We'd better run.'

'Indeed, but where? When the army gets here, they'll have a list of names and you will be on it. Sensitives are especially at risk, in times such –'

'You're not the first to tell me,' she said tartly.

'Then heed me! Yggur isn't the only one who would enslave you for your talent.'

'It can't be directed. It's quite unreliable.'

'They don't know that. And perhaps it can be compelled by one who is powerful enough. After last night you will be easy to find. Best to go across the sea, I think. The lands east of the sea are so vast and empty that you could hide there forever.' Pulling out his purse he spilled silver onto the planking, coins enough to keep her for months. 'You will need money. Take this.'

'I do, but I would not be beholden to anyone.'

'You are already – take it! Nothing could be more demeaning

than to have to ask each time you have a need.'

'I cannot repay you. After the war Gothryme may be ruined. Any wealth that remains will be needed to replant and rebuild, not for my trivial needs.'

'Living is no trivial need. Of all the things in the world I require, coin is not one.' She noticed that his eyes were moist. 'One day I may need your aid. If so, I will ask for it and you will repay me, if you can. If not, give it to someone who needs it, when the time comes. So the engine of the world revolves.'

Karan pushed the coins back across the splintery deck.

'When I want money I will ask for it. If there is indignity in that I will suffer it, for this is coin you have earned by your own sweat. And I will repay it in whatever currency you demand, when the time comes. That is no more than I would ask of someone who borrowed from me.' She changed the subject. 'I'm afraid, Shand. I couldn't hide from the Whelm, last time.'

'What did they really want, you *or the Mirror*? Shazmak will keep them busy for a time, and Thurkad. And Yggur! Your talent is valuable, but not so valuable that they would hunt you all that way.' Yet even as he said that, Shand recalled her father's words again. *She is very special. I will tell you sometime.* Maybe they *would* follow her that far.

'I would be happier across the Sea of Thurkad,' she said. 'I have a yearning to travel east and north; even to the shores of the Dry Sea.'

Shand looked up at her alertly, but let it pass. 'Then let us go to the Dry Sea,' he said, and was content.

They shrugged on their packs and strolled across to the fishing fleet in search of someone who could ferry them across the sea. There were a lot of boats in the harbour but no one wanted to take them.

'There is nothing over there for us,' said the second captain, echoing the first. He was white-haired and had no teeth, though his face was not ancient. He smiled when he

a fleet of half a dozen, was going by way of a crescent-shaped piece of rock called Horn Island, one of a group of islands across the sea. It was a long day's sailing, in this weather.

From their approach it looked inhospitable, for the eastern side was a smooth, steeply sloping curve of bare rock, with peaks at either end. But on the chart it resembled more a crescent moon with the tips of the crescent facing east, and a scattering of islets off the northern and southern tips. As they tacked toward Horn Island on that winter evening they saw snow glistening on the southern peak.

Karan wondered aloud why such a barren island was the base for the fishing fleet. Tess, overhearing, came across.

'There are few safe harbours north of Thurkad,' she said, gravelly voiced. 'Most all the ports on the western side of the sea are shallow, while those to the east are exposed to the winter storms. You saw how long we waited to go out across the bar. Horn Island is barren but has a magnificent harbour. More important, it is near to the deep channels where the bamundi run, and there is no finer fish in all of Meldorin, as doubtless you know. It fetches a great price. Though not this year,' she ended sadly. 'This wicked war! We'll sell little bamundi in Thurkad this year, or in the south, and the west cannot pay the price. And salt bamundi is not a shadow. Not a shadow.'

Karan did not respond at once. She was watching a small creature rather like a monkey, though with only a stub of a tail, running about in the rigging. Now it began to swing back and forth with one hand, staring at Karan with hard dark eyes as if weighing her up. The fingers of its other hand were twisted in the silky hair of its rump. The monkey gave a mournful chirp. Opening its hand, a clump of golden hair caught the breeze, drifting over the side of the boat.

'Pretty little things,' said the captain. 'The sailors bring them from the north. They pine for their forests though, and after a while they tear out their hair and waste away. Careful,'

321

she caught Karan's arm and pulled her out of the way. 'Don't stand underneath. They delight in crapping on visitors, filthy little brutes.'

Karan stepped smartly aside, losing interest in the monkey. 'I've never eaten bamundi. In Gothryme we can't afford such luxuries. The only fish I know is the pidgon, and that does not endear me to them.'

'Pidgon!' cried Tess. 'You exaggerate – you know less than nothing if you call that a fish. We would not even use the pidgon for a *runck*! Later you shall dine on bamundi; it is my duty to cure you of such abysmal ignorance. Ah, my bones tell me this will be a good night for fishing. Horn Island will have to wait, and so will you.' She went forward, shouting to the crew.

Lanterns were lit all over the ship. They sailed slowly south into the swell, while a canvas-clad sailor at the bow heaved the lead line, shouted the depth into the wind and heaved it again. This went on for some hours, the depths rising and falling, but never quite enough.

'We're looking for the deep channels,' said Tess, 'just clefts in the bottom where the biggest and the sweetest-fleshed bamundi run. But the channels are hard to find and the oldfellow bamundi, perverse fish that they are, bite only when the weather is wild. Even when you find a channel it is hard to get an anchor in it, and even harder to get it out again. I don't think we're going to have any luck tonight after all, though it is a prime night for bamundi.'

She hollered at the sounder, signalling enough. 'We'll sweep back to the north. Small bamundi are better than no catch.' And then in a great roar: *'About and out lines!'* and the deck was alive with running sailors. In only a minute they were heading north by north-east with the long lines, each with its eight or ten baited hooks, going over the side.

Karan watched until the first of the catch were hauled up, three fat fleshy fish, pale yellow on top, each the length of her arm, then went below to curl up in a hammock. She dozed fitfully, the wallowing of the boat making her feel dizzy, like the first onset of aftersickness.

Shand stayed on deck to watch the fishing. Small bamundi were hauled in steadily as well as one or two other types of fish and, just after dawn, to the astonishment of all, an octopus as big as the captain's head, with arms as long as her legs. The arms were wrapped many times around the lines and around a small bamundi which lay limp. As they hauled the octopus over the side one of the tentacles uncoiled gracefully and felt around in the air. The octopus was cream above but pure white below, with many tiny suckers on each arm and the faintest blue circles apparent within the cream.

'The bigger the *eight-arms* the tastier, unlike most fish,' said Tess with relish. 'You should wake your friend – she'll not see this like again. Indeed, in thirty years on the Sea of Thurkad I have never seen one this size or this kind.'

'Perhaps it crawled along the bed of the sea from the great ocean,' said Shand.

'Perhaps.'

Shand went below, thinking about the octopus, to shake Karan awake.

'Are we there so soon?' she asked dreamily.

'No; the fishing is just about done, but they have just pulled up an octopus, the biggest I've ever seen. Come and look!'

She climbed out of the hammock, rubbing her eyes, and followed him up the ladder in her bare feet. The crew were all gathered round the creature while one prodded it with a boathook, trying to get it off the line. The body sagged down, though it still held on with two arms. Other arms twined themselves around the rail. The rings, Shand noticed, had grown much brighter. The monkey was also staring at it, swinging back and forth above on a rope end, chattering away. Karan stared at the octopus with delight.

'Don't go too close,' Shand said in her ear as she edged forward. 'See that beak? It has a terrific bite. And they're quite strong when they have something solid to hold on to. In fact, I remember seeing a little one with blue rings like that once. It was on the north coast of Faranda, far from here, and its bite was deadly poison. I'd better tell Tess.'

He moved away. Karan, well back, was watching in amazement. She had never seen an octopus before.

The man with the boathook had succeeded in dislodging all but one tentacle from the line, but the last proved quite intractable. In frustration he dropped the boathook and tried to peel the arm off with his hands. Immediately another tentacle came out of nowhere, caught him around his wrist and pulled. The monkey swung overhead, chattering furiously and swinging its clawed hand at the octopus, then a tentacle came up behind to pluck it neatly off the rope. The octopus, its rings now an iridescent purple, pulled the monkey to its beak and bit it on the neck. The monkey screamed horribly then convulsed so violently that it flipped free and fell onto the planking. The sailor, still held by the wrist, slipped on the deck and was pulled towards the octopus.

Karan had her knife out in an instant, but the captain cried out, 'Stand aside,' and ran the creature through with a harpoon, in one side and out the other. The rings began to fade, it shuddered, the tentacles boiled and soon it hung limp from the rail. The monkey screamed for another minute, a bloody swelling grew on its neck, then suddenly it was dead as well.

Karan was too shocked to speak, though the sailors, to whom this seemed nothing out of the ordinary, heaved the dead monkey over the side very quickly, scrubbed the deck and went back to their fishing.

'Thank you,' said Tess to Shand, unwinding tentacles from the rail. 'In all my years I've not encountered a venomous one. What a pity. I have a passion for grilled octopus.'

'They're not dangerous to eat,' said Shand, 'as long as you take out the poison gland. I'll help you cut it up if you like.'

They starting dissecting the beast and talking animatedly

about great fish they had caught. Overnight the swell had died down; it was a clear day with not another boat in sight. Suddenly alarm bells rang in Karan's mind, so loud and shocking that she could not prevent herself from crying out, 'Aah, *help*!'

'What is it?' Shand said, jumping up with a bloody knife in his hand.

'They're coming for me!' Karan ran from one side of the boat to the other, peering out, literally shaking with terror.

'I can't see anything,' Shand said, after taking a good look around.

She calmed herself with an effort. 'It's nothing,' she began, then the red sun rising showed a dark galley coming fast out of the south directly for them. A slim sleek warship, and as it got closer they saw that the sail wore a black crucible on a white circle. Karan pulled the hood up over her hair; Shand stepped between her and the other boat.

Tess understood instantly. 'They're looking for you!'

'For her,' said Shand. Karan nodded numbly. 'Five tars to hide her.'

Tess took no time at all to decide. 'Into the hold. *Benn*; *Fenn*!'

Two sailors, who looked like brothers, listened to her brief orders then ushered Karan below. 'You!' Tess said to Shand, 'put this on!' She threw him a fisherman's smock covered in blood and scales. 'Start washing the deck.'

Shand put on the smock, pulled the hood up, threw his boots and socks into a basket and heaved a bucket over the side on a line. It came up brimming, banging on the planking. He splashed it over the deck and set to with a scrubbing broom.

Shand scrubbed, not too hard, but not taking it easy either, as the cutter pulled alongside. A man in the bow hailed them. They hauled their sail and crept forward on the oars until the bow of the cutter touched the side of the fishing boat, whereupon the man sprang lightly over the side. He was lean and hard, tall and dark-haired, a professional soldier. A man of authority, thought Shand, whose eyes would miss nothing. His chin-beard was woven into a plait ending in six smaller braids, showing that he was Hlune and an officer who had served with distinction.

'I am Captain Zareth,' he said to Tess, 'on a special commission for Lord Yggur.' He showed her a charter on parchment.

Shand was not close enough to hear what was said after that. The two walked together around the deck, Tess opening every locker, every door, the lean head checking everything, the chin-plaits swinging.

The hold was already packed with big square baskets full of gutted bamundi, carefully stacked to protect the precious fish from damage.

'Down here,' said Fenn, climbing down. He was stocky, with long golden curls and a mischievous grin. He passed baskets up to his brother, a leaner version of himself, until he stood in the bottom of a well, then carefully unloaded the precious fish from the lowest basket.

'In,' he said, picking Karan up as if she was weightless and popping her inside. He turned her so that her face was in the corner, space to breathe, pulled her arms up across her head and with a hearty laugh tipped the fish back in.

It became dark, the fish pressed heavily on her and distantly Karan heard the thud of the baskets being repacked. Cold water dribbled over her cheek and down the back of her neck. The timbers creaked. Something sticky began to drip into her ear. Drip. Itch. Drip. Itch. The hold slammed down; all light was gone.

Karan felt the vibration as the two boats touched. She wondered what had happened up on deck. Perhaps her sensitive talent was coming back at last. Her ear was so itchy that it set up a shivering irritation all over her. She had an overwhelming urge to sneeze. The boat rolled and a fish slid across her cheek, its rubber-lipped mouth coming to rest on her neck. As the boat rose and fell, it felt as though the bamundi was opening and closing its lips, kissing her throat like an unwanted lover.

Sandals thudded on the deck above. Lockers banged. The lid of the hold crashed back; she heard voices and feet on the ladder. The boat rocked again. Water dribbled out of the bamundi's mouth, running down inside her shirt. She could feel the sneeze building. She bit down on her tongue, too hard, and tasted blood.

'Empty those baskets. Tip them out.' The voice was only a few spans above her.

'No, not there.' It was Tess's voice. 'This is best bamundi. If you tip it in the bilge it will be ruined.'

'Get more baskets then, and hurry. I've many boats to search today.'

Tess shouted; someone came running down the ladder.

'More?' said Tess.

'Yes, more. All the way to the bottom. Unload them all!'

Karan felt a deep cold terror settle over her. She was going to be discovered and hauled back to Thurkad, and there was nothing anyone could do to prevent it.

23

ARRESTED FOR
FORGERY

The Waif was ghosting across the entrance to the ba
when Pender saw a boat drifting along the shore. H
watched as it was rowed clumsily back to the rocky poir
below the camp. They dropped anchor in the moonshadow
beyond the further point. A banner of cloud covered th
moon. Shortly a light blinked from the shore.

A minute passed. Blink, blink, flash, flash, flash, blink
The signal! Pender did not acknowledge it.

'Time to go,' he said to the crew.

Tallia crossed the slippery rock slope, passed between th
pools and headed up into the scrub, limping badly. Ther
she stopped, knowing that Mendark and Lilis should be nea
unless something had happened to them.

'Where?' she called softly.

'Here,' came Mendark's voice not twenty steps away.

Tallia eased between scrubby bushes. Mendark was sittir
on an outcrop. 'Where's Lilis?' she asked with a cold feelir
in her heart.

'Boat ran aground down there. She went to push it o
and didn't come back.' Mendark sounded defensive.

Tallia was speechless with rage. She spun around b
Mendark grabbed her by the shoulder. 'Don't be stupi

Osseion went to look for her, but I know where she is. They've got her on the point.'

'Chert's cutthroats! And you did *nothing*.'

'It only happened a few minutes ago. When Osseion gets back –'

'Now!' she cracked. 'Pender's out there too.'

'I just signalled.'

'Good. I'll go for her. If I flash, come and get us. You'd better get your *important* stuff,' she said with venom. On her way she almost ran into Osseion.

'They've got Lilis,' she hissed.

'Not for long.' All she could see of him was his eyes and his bared teeth.

'What happened?'

'Two boats turned up one after another. Chert's gang, then Yggur's sailors. I burnt Yggur's boat, then the two groups fought. I think Chert's mob had the best of it. They're trying to carry down the gold; or so they think.'

'How many?'

'Perhaps ten, in the two groups.'

They crept along the edge of the scrub to a point where they could see the boat. A man stood guard there. Someone lay on the rocks – Lilis! Several people were trying to heave two immensely heavy chests down the steep track.

The moon was bright now, with a crescent of the dark side showing, red and black blotches on yellow. 'We need a diversion,' said Osseion. 'Do –'

'Wait. When we begin, grab Lilis. I'll hold them off. No, if there's the chance, break the rudder first so they can't get back.'

Nothing happened for some time. Then they heard a thud as if one of the chests had been dropped, followed by a flurry of curses. Tallia grew impatient. 'I can't bear this any longer. Let's skirt around through the scrub.'

She moved away silently. Osseion followed. They got as close as they could get to Lilis. Tallia recalled that she still had Karan's lightglass in her pack. She fumbled it out, touched it to light and, with arm held high, flashed the signal in the direction of Mendark. There was no response. 'What's the matter now?' she muttered. 'I hope nothing's happened to Pender.' She flashed again, and almost at once it was answered.

'Gaspard, we need a hand!' someone cried from the track, then the guard at the boat ran that way.

'Now!' Tallia hissed.

Osseion bent down over a boulder half the size of a wheelbarrow. 'Give me a lift with this.'

She did so. Osseion staggered toward the boat with his load. Tallia hobbled to Lilis, who was shivering in great shuddering spasms. When Tallia cut the bonds, Lilis made a tiny cry.

'It's me, Tallia,' she said, picking her up. Lilis threw her arms around Tallia's neck and clung to her, weeping.

Tallia heard a mighty bang, then Osseion came back holding the rudder of the boat. His luminous smile flashed in the dark.

'There they are!' someone shouted. Yggur's sailors rushed at them over the ridge. Osseion casually swung the rudder at the first, clouting his assailant over the ear and sending him flying headlong across the rocks. The thieves came hurtling down the path. Tallia, with Lilis in her arms, was uncomfortably aware that they were outnumbered. They retreated toward the point, Osseion swinging the rudder like a scythe.

Just then there was a great smashing and rending of timbers behind her, and Tallia spun around to see that *The Waif*, running up silently, had rammed the smaller boat, stoving in the side.

'Osseion, take Lilis,' she cried.

Osseion sent the rudder spinning into Yggur's band, knocking two of them down. The thieves came at them from the other side, led by the lean hairy one, his lips snarled back over black gums. Lilis went rigid and moaned. Shocked,

Tallia handed her to Osseion, said, 'Go!' and stepped forward.

The man laughed evilly. 'A black rat thith time!' Then, realising that she was a woman, leered toothlessly, 'Double the fun – you're mine!' and swung his club at her.

Tallia swayed, ducked and before his swing was ended she kicked him in the jaw so hard that his feet were lifted right off the ground. He fell on his back on the rocks and did not move. She looked around. The other thieves hung well back.

Osseion handed Lilis into *The Waif*. The crew pushed the skiff off the bow. It began to sink. Tallia limped across the submerging vessel and climbed aboard *The Waif*. The sail swung and they moved away from the shore.

A melee began between the two groups on the shore, then *The Waif* was beyond range, heading back to Ganport in the quickening breeze.

'A good day's work,' said Mendark with a chuckle, good-humoured now that gold and boat and crew were restored to him. Tallia gave him a disgusted glare and went below to check on Lilis. She was sitting up in the sole bunk, swathed in blankets, a flask of hot water at her feet, but still shivering.

'I can't get warm,' she said with a wan attempt at a smile. Her skin was blotched blue and purple.

Pender came down with a huge mug and a slab of buttery bread. 'Hot soup is best,' he said. 'Smoked ham, pea and potato. Made it myself this evening in the galley, eh! We have a galley, Lilis!' grinning hugely. 'What a marvel! I will show you in the morning. Now, that was a brave thing you did.' He shook her hand.

Lilis took the heavy mug. Her hand trembled. She sipped. The soup was thick and rich and hot, almost unbearably delicious.

'He did not harm you, child?' Tallia asked.

'No.' She shuddered. 'But if you had not come –'

'Forget all that now. Look, here is your bag. I found it back at the campsite.'

'Oh!' said Lilis, her eyes shining. 'I thought it was gone forever.' She took the little pack, checked to see that everything was inside then tucked it in beside her like a favourite toy.

'Drink your soup. And then – to sleep!'

Tallia and Mendark stood at the rail, watching the sun rise. Neither had had more than an hour's sleep. 'I forgot to mention that there were three boats flying Yggur's flag when I left Ganport,' she said in a low voice.

'And how many others unmarked? *Pender!*'

Pender appeared at the bow, where he had been inspecting the timbers. Only his eyes were visible over a huge mug of soup which he sipped as he walked.

'Hardly damaged at all,' he said. 'What a wonderful boat!'

'You said there was a problem with our supplies,' Mendark began. 'I had been thinking that we should go by Ganport, but . . .'

Pender shook his head. 'Is a big problem. I have no spare sails, rope, spars or nails; no tools; no food but the fresh. The merchants of Ganport are cheats and liars – even the barrels of water were foul.' He swung around to Tallia. 'I told you that she was trouble, this boat. Now see where we are.'

'And maybe you still have enemies in Ganport.'

Pender looked sulky. 'They hate outsiders, for all that they live by trade.'

'The fault does not matter,' said Mendark hurriedly. 'Can these things be replaced elsewhere?'

'Problem is the sails,' said Pender, slouching against the rail to slurp the last of his soup. 'The ones we have are old, eh, and we have no spare canvas at all. If one tears, we're crippled.'

'It may be better to risk it here,' Mendark decided. 'Yes, get what you can today, while they still don't know that I have this boat. Once word gets back from the camp there will be no haven for us in the Sea of Thurkad. Tallia, go with

Pender and make sure that we get everything we need today. We must be gone no later than the mid-afternoon. Do whatever is necessary.'

A little later they were standing at the rail as *The Waif* sailed placidly north. Dolphins played in the waves nearby, following the boat and sometimes surfing on the little bow wave. The sun shone in a cloudless sky.

Lilis wondered aloud about the chests. 'Did Mendark put a *spell* on them or something?' she asked, big-eyed.

Mendark did not answer; he was deep in thought. 'No, Lilis!' said Tallia, smiling at the notion. 'The Secret Art is a serious and difficult thing, not to be used except at the greatest need. What Mendark did was this: he took out his gold and hid it in one of the pools, filled up the chests with rocks, weakened the handles so that they would break when the chests were lifted, and when the thieves came he made the chests seem even heavier. But that was not really a spell, just a *seeming*. That was why he had to stay behind and see who came, so that he could put it on them.'

Time drifted by. Lilis wandered away to the wheel-house, evidently not completely satisfied with the explanation. Pender was still eating, two thick slabs of bread filled with cheese and onions, green chutney dripping down his fingers. He gestured her to the canvas seat. Lilis sat down, swinging her legs.

'Pender,' she said after a while.

'Yes, Lilis?' He licked his fingers, wiped the crumbs off his chin and began to whistle.

'Did you ever meet a sailor called Jevi, or Jevander?'

Pender rubbed his stubble. 'Might have done. I've met thousands. What does he look like?'

'Like me.'

He stopped whistling and took notice. 'Who is this Jevi?'

'My father. I lost him seven years ago.' She told him about it.

'And you want me to ask after him? Jev-an-der. I'll look for him, child, wherever I go. Quite a few people to keep an eye out for, eh! Your father and Tensor and that wretched Llian.'

'Don't be nasty. You're no friend of mine,' she said furiously.

Pender looked hurt. 'Ah, child, don't say things like that. Llian . . . Llian . . . they say he is a wonderful teller.'

Lilis was slightly mollified. 'I know he is. He told me a tale. I will never forget it.'

'Told you a tale?' cried Mendark, who was walking past with Tallia. 'Why would he tell *you* a tale? He –' He broke off abruptly as Tallia's elbow gouged him in the ribs.

Lilis turned away to the rail and pulled her hood over her face. Tallia went across to stand by her side, looking out to sea. Lilis's shoulders were shaking. 'Are you all right,' she said. 'Mendark –'

'Of course,' said Lilis merrily and Tallia realised that she was shaking with suppressed laughter, with unholy glee.

'I have something that he will never have,' she said in a carrying voice, her laughter tinkling through the boat and across to where the dolphins were playing. One of them chose this moment to leap out of the water right next to the boat, grinning its dolphin grin. It smacked the water with its tail, splashing them to Lilis's delight, and was gone.

An hour later they drew up at the jetty. There were several boats at anchor, flying Yggur's flag, their decks crowded with soldiers.

'That's strange,' said Mendark. 'I wonder why they haven't gone ashore.'

'Look like they're waiting for something,' said Osseion, eyeing them with professional interest.

'Well, let's get the business over while we still can.'

Tallia and Pender went, together with all but one of their sailors, to each of the merchants in turn. At the cloth merchant they found that the sails had still not been cut.

'What cloth do you need,' asked Tallia, 'and how much?'

Pender pointed to a bolt of sailcloth. 'That's prime canvas. I inspected it the day before yesterday. Two would be ample. We will cut it ourselves.'

'What price?'

'Eighty-six tells the bolt, if they are full measure.'

'So much? What is full measure?'

'Forty spans.'

Tallia turned to the thick-bodied, sour-faced woman. 'That is your best price?'

Greed flickered in her eyes. 'Yes.'

'Good! Check the length, Pender.'

'No need,' said the merchant. 'The measure is good.' Tallia froze her with a glare.

Pender sang out the measurements.

'I make that one hundred tells and sixty-two tells and seven tars,' said Tallia instantly.

The merchant flicked her tally beads, frowning. 'That is correct.'

Tallia turned her back, counted the money and paid it. Lilis, hovering in the background, was profoundly astonished. She had not imagined that such wealth existed in the world, much less that Tallia should carry it around in her pocket.

'Rustible, have these brought to the boat,' said Tallia.

Rustible bent over the roll of cloth. Frizzy blond hair stuck out from the level of his ears like the fleece of a merino.

'No need,' said the merchant. 'I will arrange it.'

'At once,' Tallia said. 'Rustible, do not let the cloth out of your sight. And come straight back.'

In the same way they bought the rope, tar, tools and other supplies that were absolutely necessary. None of the excuses, lies, procrastinations or deceptions large or small had the least effect on her. Under Tallia's piercing glare the most tiresome, ill-mannered or downright obstructive merchants became cooperative. If the quality was to be had, she sent the goods to the boat at once. If inadequate, she went at once to another establishment. By lunchtime her bag of gold was almost empty but they had everything that they must have for a sea voyage of several weeks.

Pender then went with a sailor to finalise other purchases, while Lilis and Tallia sat down for a late lunch at an inn near the sailwright's shop. Afterwards they headed back to the harbour. Lilis had gone a little way ahead, not realising that Tallia had stopped at a silk merchant's booth. Suddenly she heard a scuffle, a cry cut off, and turned in time to see two men holding Tallia while a third cast a hessian bag over her head and bound it around her waist. They bundled her into a cart standing on the road and clip-clopped off.

Lilis was left staring, like the other passers-by, though they soon went about their business. This was a problem too big for her, but before Mendark could do anything he must know who had Tallia and where they had taken her. That was easy, for the cart went slowly across the length of the waterfront and up the hill to the Customs House, where Tallia, still immobilised in her bag, was carried inside.

Lilis ran back to *The Waif*, jumped down on the deck and crashed through the door into the cabin.

'Hey,' she cried, running smack into Osseion. 'Tallia . . .'

'What's the matter?'

'Tallia is arrested. They tied her up and took her to the Customs House. Quickly!'

Mendark came through the other door at that moment. 'Tallia, taken?' he said. He squatted down in front of Lilis. 'Tell me exactly what happened.'

She told him. He stood up. 'There's more here than it seems. Why Tallia? The forged papers, I suppose. They'll try to impound *The Waif* next. Pender was right about this boat. How many crew do we have on board now?'

'Three,' said Osseion. 'And me.'

'Where's Pender?'

'He hasn't come back. And something's going on. Yggur's soldiers have gone ashore.'

'Where?'

'Outside the Governor's palace.'

'Hmn! They can't know that I'm aboard. Well, keep careful watch. Osseion, you are in charge. Unmoor, sail around the point where you can't be seen and put down a small anchor. Issue what weapons we have. Be ready to pick us up. Watch for enemies from land and sea, especially if Yggur's boats start to move or anyone else approaches. If necessary, flee. I am told that Rustible is an excellent sailor. If you have to go, watch each night, on the hour, for my signal. It will come from the south point. Lilis, come with me. Have you money?'

'No,' she squeaked.

'Hold out your hand.'

She did as she was bid and he pulled coin from his pocket, copper and silver and a flash of gold, slid it into a little brown leather bag, tied the strings and put it on her palm. She stood there with her hand out, staring at it, then up at him. He folded her fingers around the bag.

'You have already proven yourself as one of my bravest,' he said. 'I do not forget that. There is a lot of money here. If I am taken, you will need it to find Pender and Osseion, and do whatever is needed to get Tallia and me free again. Or if we are killed or taken away, for you to live.'

'I might just run away,' whispered Lilis.

'You won't. Put it away and button up your pocket, and keep it hidden. You have a knife?'

'Yes.'

'Dare you use it, if you have to?'

She nodded, already seeing herself back on the streets, where both knife and money would soon be taken from her. Her thin face was absolutely stark.

'I can see what you are thinking, child, but I do not expect it will come to that. As you said back at the campsite, I am not defenceless. Now, stay close. Give me your hand.'

They went slowly up the road to the Customs House.

Despite what Mendark had said, he looked helpless, an old man with his granddaughter. Somehow, without notably changing his appearance, he had contrived to make himself look like a mild, kindly old gentleman. A well-dressed, possibly rich and influential gentleman.

They turned in at the Customs House, where Mendark puffed his way up the steps into a large room with a counter behind which people worked, checking documents. At the counter he leaned with both elbows, wheezed, slowly raised his head, looked across into the room beyond, turned to Lilis and shook his head.

A tall man came across, rubbing his eyes. He looked exhausted. 'What is your business, old sir?'

'I . . .' Mendark coughed, and it turned into a coughing fit so long that it was embarrassing. Finally he got his breath, wiping his red face and watering eyes with a piece of snow-white linen. 'Beg your pardon.'

'Are you all right, old sir?'

'Yes,' Mendark gasped. 'I would not trouble you, but this child has lost her guardian and thinks she may have come here. I do not think . . . She does not have . . .'

The man looked over the counter at the small child, also well-dressed and with unusual platinum hair. The black eye had faded to nothing.

'What is your guardian's name, child?' he asked wearily.

'Her name is Tallia. She is dark and very tall, and her hair is black.'

The man frowned, turned away, engaging in a long whispered conversation with one of the people at the bench. He came back and spoke to Mendark.

'The woman you seek is held here. She is charged with obtaining boat's papers using forged documents. A serious offence. A capital offence in wartime.'

'May the child see her?'

'That is no longer possible. She must go back to Thurkad for trial.'

'Thurkad! Is not Gannish a sovereign state?' Mendark asked.

'No more. As of midday today this territory is a province of Orist. The proclamation has just been made.' His expression showed that the change was none to his liking.

'What!' Mendark nearly choked.

'Our Assembly took the view that we could not win any war against Yggur; that resistance would be our ruin. We have lost our freedom but kept our lives. Yggur's guard is already coming for the prisoner. That will be them now.'

Outside the tramp of feet could be heard coming up the steps then along the veranda boards. 'The Assembly remains in power?' asked Mendark.

'Puppets!' the official spat. 'His troops will sail in, in a few days, then all orders will come from Thurkad.'

Tears welled up in Lilis's eyes and dripped onto the floor, though she made not a sound.

'I'm sorry, child,' the man said, flopping into a chair. 'We are a conquered people now. We must do as we are told. Wait here and you may see her as she is taken.'

The door opened; an officer and four soldiers marched in. The officer presented his credentials at the desk, cast a careful eye around the room but saw no danger in the decrepit old man and skinny child sitting beside the window. Lilis, looking up, found that Mendark's features had changed imperceptibly. While he still looked like that ancient gentleman, somehow he was no longer recognisable as Mendark.

The officer and soldiers went behind the counter and out the back. 'Aren't you going to do something to save her?' Lilis said fiercely in Mendark's ear.

'Indeed I am, very soon. Now do exactly as I say. Run across the point and wave to Osseion. He must bring the boat slowly into the port. Do not let yourself be seen. Come straight back. When I give the sign, run up to Tallia, crying, and throw your arms around her. Then cut her bonds with your knife. Clear?'

'Yes,' she whispered, dreadfully afraid. How could she possibly get through those soldiers? They would kill her, and Tallia too.

'Go. Don't run until you are down the steps.'

Lilis disappeared. Before the prisoners had been brought out she was back again, red-faced. 'The boat comes!'

'Good. Now we wait. When Tallia goes past, cry out her name.'

Shortly the officer came back, followed by two guards and Tallia, still with the bag over her head. Pender, sweating and looking as if he had already died his thousand deaths, followed her. The other two guards were right behind them. Lilis knew that it was hopeless. Pender's eyes looked at them without recognition. Mendark elbowed Lilis in the ribs.

'*Tallia!*' she wailed.

Tallia struggled, but the guards dragged her out the door and it banged behind them.

24

THE GREAT LIBRARY

'Are you ready, Lilis?' whispered Mendark, as the soldiers hauled Pender and Tallia away.

'Yes.'

'Come with me.'

They followed them down the steps and along the road around the shallow curve of the waterfront. *The Waif* was halfway along the bay, near the end of the first jetty, drifting imperceptibly along. Though a sailor was busily scrubbing the deck, a careful look showed that she was ready to sail instantly. Further down the bay, at the third jetty, Yggur's boats were tied fore and aft, the sails furled.

The soldiers tramped past the first jetty toward the second. Suddenly Lilis felt dizzy. The jetty scene in front of her went all blurry, the road seeming to take a turn down the second jetty. The soldiers stopped abruptly then began to mill about as if confused. Mendark stood up straight and caught their eyes, each in turn. Suddenly the officer spun on his heel and led the way briskly down the jetty.

'Go, *now*!' said Mendark, going pale under the strain.

Lilis scooted away, came up behind the soldiers, and gaped as the officer walked right off the end of the pier into the deep water.

'Tallia, stop!' she screamed. Tallia stopped dead as the

others marched past her and toppled into the water as well.

'Hold still,' Lilis said urgently. 'I have a knife.' She sawed through the tough cord, nicking Tallia's hand in the process. The bloody bonds fell away. Tallia wrestled with the bag. 'Our boat is coming,' said Lilis. Hearing a desperate wail, she looked down and cried out, 'Oh, Pender is drowning. I forgot poor Pender,' and jumped into the harbour.

Most of the soldiers were clinging to the piles, but Pender was going down for the last time, so gripped by panic that wavelets were washing into his open mouth. He was thrashing his bound hands so hard that she could not cut his bonds. His knuckle caught Lilis on the chin, snapping her teeth together. She bit her tongue as stars burst in front of her eyes. A wave smacked her in the face.

Lilis ducked under the water to come up behind Pender, but as soon as she touched his coat he twisted around, gripped her like a lifebuoy and sank, pulling her under. Bubbles gushed from his mouth.

They rolled slowly in the water, Lilis underneath. Pender was incredibly strong – she found it impossible to break his grip. Terrified that he was going to drown them both, she brought her knee up into his stomach. The remaining air exploded out of his mouth, she kicked free and bobbed up to the surface, gasping. Soon a brown-coated whale broke the water with his back and rolled, choking and wheezing. Lilis held on to the coat until *The Waif* drifted by and Osseion snagged Pender out of the water with a boathook. She was offered the comparative dignity of a rope. Clapping hands tightly to it, they hauled her up.

'Where's Tallia?' she cried, streaming and shivering on the deck.

As the stern of *The Waif* swung around, Tallia cast her bag aside and sprang on board. Mendark, who was hurrying down the jetty, waited till a rope pulled the stern up close, then he too leapt nimbly across.

'Go!' he said.

One of the newly hired crew pushed the boat off, the sails were set and they moved slowly out into the bay, gathering pace in the breeze. They had crossed the bar and were well out into the sea by the time the soldiers were rescued and Yggur's boats ready to give chase.

'Tallia,' cried Lilis, running to embrace her. Tallia lifted her high, laughing and crying, and Lilis wept a flood of tears onto her brow. 'Oh Tallia, I was sure they would take you away to be killed.'

'But for you and Mendark they would have,' said Tallia. 'They took me completely by surprise. But let us go and see to poor Pender.'

Poor Pender was already recovering nicely, though his fat face was blue and his eyes were haunted. When he saw Lilis he broke down and wept on her shoulder.

'Lilis, Lilis, I have no words for you. I will never forget. Never!'

'My art has a value after all,' said Mendark caustically, but for once Pender had no answer.

After she had changed out of her wet clothes, towelled herself warm and dressed again, Lilis went with the purse in her hand to Mendark, who was hunched over a collection of charts. He nodded absently, putting the purse to one side. At that moment, Tallia came in, drying her hair on a towel.

'What are you doing, Lilis?'

'Giving him back his money.'

'Mendark,' said Tallia sharply.

'Um?' He did not look up.

She tapped on the table, pointed to the little wallet. Mendark roused from his meditations.

'Oh! That is yours, child. Put it in your bag. You will need it one day.' He put the wallet back in her hand and turned away. Then, realising that in his preoccupation he had not thanked her, said rather gruffly, 'Thank you. You are indeed one of my best.'

343

'Come, Lilis,' said Tallia. 'Let us go out and look at the sea. There may be more dolphins.'

An hour later they saw two boats behind them, and Pender put on all sail. The slim vessel took off like a racehorse. Within another two hours they were alone on the sea, seeing no other sign of the chase that day. So they continued up the Sea of Thurkad, then west along the Sea of Qwale almost to the great ocean, and the weather was fair.

A fortnight later, after a slow but uneventful journey opposed only by wind and current, Mendark, Tallia and Lilis were sailing slowly up the long estuary of the River Zur toward the ancient city of Zile. The old channel of the Zur, that had sustained the city's trade for thousands of years, was choked with silt, not even navigable by their small vessel, so they had left *The Waif* in Framan, the new port ten leagues downstream, a vulgar place despised by the old aristocrats and even the common folk of Zile.

Pender remained in Framan to deal with all the bureaucratic obstacles that he still direly predicted. Osseion stayed there too, since Mendark felt no need for a guard here. Pender was in particularly high spirits, for Mendark had paid the double fare he'd promised, eight hundred tells. It was a colossal, staggering, unthinkable fortune, more than Pender could have earned in ten lifetimes had not the opportunities of this war come along. And another thing he had discovered: Mendark's name, even now, opened doors that had formerly been closed.

They were all recovered from their injuries. The three of them went on foot across the once great city of Zile, along avenues lined with massive columns, beneath arches of granite that had stood for two thousand years, since the time that Zile was great. But Zile had dwindled long since; the once bountiful lands around the Zur were dry and the irrigation canals crusted with salt. Most of its people were gone. Zile was left only with its ruins, its memories, and the Great Library, that wonder of the ancient world.

The Library swelled up out of the dust before them, a vast rectangle. It was the biggest building that Lilis had ever seen, and the most imposing, far greater that the baroque extravagances of the Magister's citadel in Thurkad. An old-fashioned, classical building, a rectangle of red marble with colonnaded walks on all four sides, it was four storeys high and many levels below the ground, and all very austere, almost unornamented.

'Where do it come from?' Lilis asked on the interminable walk toward it.

'It was the very first of the great libraries,' Tallia explained, 'for it was founded by the Zain even before the time of the Zurean Empire. It was first built by Larria the Zain, three thousand years ago, near enough. But that library was sacked thrice and burned once, and what we see here replaced it, built two thousand three hundred years ago when Zur was one of the richest empires on Santhenar and the Zain at the height of their power and influence. It once could boast that it contained the entire Histories of Santhenar.'

'Not any more,' said Mendark. 'The Library has fallen on hard times, and Nadiril is not what he used to be.'

'Who is Nadiril?' Lilis wondered.

'Nadiril!' Mendark rolled the word around in his mouth.

'He is *the librarian*,' said Tallia, emphasising the words. 'Some say that Nadiril the sage is the greatest librarian of all time. And he is a member of the Council of Santhenar, of which Mendark is Magister, or used to be when there was a Council. He is a very wise old man.'

'Too old,' said Mendark irritably. 'An obstreperous old man who hasn't attended a meeting in ten years. Time he moved aside. The Library needs young blood.'

'What do obstreperous mean?'

'It means cranky, like Mendark,' Tallia said crossly.

Lilis looked sideways up at Mendark's lowering brows, tightened her grip on Tallia's hand and edged closer to her.

'The librarian is expecting you,' the orderly said. 'This way, please.'

She led the way down a broad corridor, turned off it into a narrower one, down the steps to a narrower yet, and stopped outside a plain door. The orderly knocked once, ushered them reverently into a small room and closed the door behind. The room was spare, containing only a high bench the length of one wall, covered in manuscripts, a small hard pallet in a corner and a few shelves. It was cold.

Nadiril sat perched on a stool before the bench like some ancient and decrepit bird. The limbs extending from his grey robe were wasted, mere bone and sinew. The skin was drawn tight about the bones of his face, outlining the domed skull, which was blotchy and flaking like the skin of his hands. A few wisps of white hair still clung to the sides. His lips were grey and his eyes, when he looked up, were clouded, as though he stared into the well of time itself.

The grey lips broke apart in the ghost of a smile. 'Hello,' he said. 'Who is this?' His voice was like a breeze through cobwebs.

He unfolded himself from the stool. Mendark gave Tallia a significant glance, as if to say, 'The old fool has gone senile,' then Nadiril walked straight past him and creaked to a squat in front of Lilis.

'My name is Lilis,' she squeaked, taking a small step backwards, but thinking better of it she moved forward again.

'Give me your hand, Lilis,' said Nadiril. She extended her tiny hand and he took it in his bony claw and examined it carefully, first the palm side and then the back. He gave it back to her, searching her face. 'Why have you come to see me, Lilis? What would you ask of me?' Behind him, Mendark cleared his throat angrily.

'Tallia brang me,' said Lilis.

'Yes, but what would you ask of *me*? What do you need to know?'

'Can you find my father?' Her timid whisper was barely audible.

'Perhaps. Do you have a mother?'

'No,' Lilis said. 'She died.'

'I'm sorry to hear that. What else do you need to know?'

'Can you find my friend Llian?'

'Llian too! Llian the chronicler, from Chanthed? Careless child – what do you do with your friends?'

'They lose me. Can you find him too?'

'Probably. I will ask you about them later. Now I must attend to my guest. He looks *very* important.' He creaked to his feet again and turned away to Mendark and Tallia. Mendark was scowling but Tallia wore a secret smile.

'Mendark,' Nadiril said at length. 'When did you last come to the Library? More than five years, am I not right?' He held out a withered hand.

'Five years indeed,' said Mendark coldly. 'I came here with a young lore master, you may remember.' He spoke as if Nadiril's mind was as wasted as his body; perhaps testing him. 'Though he was not master then.'

'No need to patronise me, Mendark. Indeed I do.' The voice grew a little stronger. 'Llian of Chanthed, Lilis's friend. Well I remember *him*. I thought to bring him here once, but other matters got in the way. Would he come now, do you think? There is so little time . . .'

'I think he has gone his own road now. That is part of what we've come about.'

'Yes. We will come to that in time.' He turned to Tallia, who was standing quietly to one side, waiting in that still, patient way she had. 'You are Tallia bel Soon,' he said gravely. She inclined her head. 'How are your family?'

'My mother is well,' she replied, 'and working harder than ever. She is an engineer of mines,' she explained to Lilis. 'She knows how to pump the water out. A very clever woman.'

'I knew your mother's mother well,' Nadiril went on.

'Often she came here. A great scholar. We see so few from Crandor these days.' He held out his hand.

Tallia took the cold hand. 'My grandmother sometimes talked about you,' she said, looking into his eyes, for they were the same height.

That must have woken some long-forgotten memory, for Nadiril actually laughed, a low, rusty chuckle. 'I can imagine how she would have spoken,' he said. 'We had the greatest respect for each other, but we could never be friends. Still, that is past and she long in her grave. You have had a long journey and I see that you've not rested here in Zile. Come – we will sup together and talk of the new things you have seen.' He turned towards the door.

'The matter is most urgent,' said Mendark from behind.

'Doubtless. It always is when you come to me, Mendark. But it can wait. I seldom take bread these days but alone, and will not be denied. Besides, I know what you have come about. How could I not?'

They went out another door to a narrow staircase that spiralled up out of sight. 'Take my arm,' he said to Tallia. He took Lilis's hand with his other and they climbed slowly up and up, at last emerging on a broad platform overlooking the city. The breeze tugged at his robes but it was warm, the sun descending through a cloudless sky.

'I used to come here every evening and sometimes in the morning too,' he whispered, breathless from the climb. 'Just to look out across the city – to think, to plan, to dream. In the morning the sun would touch the western mountains with liquid fire while in the evening the flatlands of Zur were like a tapestry.

'But those dreams are not being dreamt anymore. Zile has grown smaller, and even the Library is falling into decay for want of the levies that were once paid as prompt as the rising of the sun. At a time when we are never more valuable, we are called upon less than ever. My own dreams will never be fulfilled, and my life is a struggle just to maintain what the past has given us. How can I pass on leaving all this untended? I *will not*, until I can hand the key to someone worthy.'

He paused but did not go on and Tallia, after a polite interval, walked away to look out over the city. The sun stood but a little way above the humps of the mountains. A trace of dust hung in the air; the sunset began to turn brick red. Even their brief passage had shown how the city was dying. Thousands of magnificent homes lay empty amid weed-filled gardens.

A cool breeze sprang up. Nadiril led them into an alcove where the south wind did not penetrate, and there a single servant brought them food. It was not the hot and spicy food that Zile was famous for but simple fare: bread, fruit, cheeses and green wine. Mendark and Tallia sat across the table; Nadiril handed Lilis to the vacant seat beside him. He removed the cheese platter neatly from Mendark's hand, offering it to her.

'This one is my favourite,' Nadiril said, pointing to a dark and malodorous cheese, a greenish shade of yellow with a brown crust. 'Though perhaps it will be too strong for you. I can barely taste it these days. Barely taste anything. Even eating has become a chore.'

'I will try,' said Lilis, her eyes shining, though not particularly at the thought of the food. She was thinking: *another friend! How blessed I am*. 'I can eat anything.'

'I suppose you can, child,' said Nadiril, whose all-seeing eyes could have related her whole history. He carved a substantial wedge and passed it to her plate with the flat of the knife. Vesicles in the cheese wept a pungent fluid. Tallia wrinkled her nose. He flicked crumbs from the knife and drew the platter closer. 'What about these others? This blue cheese –' he waved the knife at a rhomboidal lump, cream-coloured and veined as marble, 'is rather harsh at first, but what a creamy tang as it goes down! Shall I give you a small piece?'

'Please,' squeaked Lilis, hungry as a little mouse. They

had not stopped for lunch and now it was almost dinnertime. Across the table Mendark cleared his throat peremptorily and she said, 'After Tallia and *him*.' She would not say Mendark's name.

'Nonsense,' replied Nadiril. 'They are old, and used to waiting.'

Mendark scowled more fiercely than before and tapped with the point of his knife on the table. Tallia frowned, though probably at being described as old. Nadiril proceeded to explain each of the cheeses to Lilis: here a moist white goat cheese; another speckled with brown seeds like grains of rice, so hard that he had to use both hands to carve a piece; a third that was runny inside.

'This one is flavoured with chives and pepper,' Nadiril said, though when he cut it there was an overpowering smell of garlic.

'*Nadir* describes his state perfectly,' said Mendark out of the corner of his mouth to Tallia.

Finally a piece of each of the cheeses was arranged radially on Lilis's plate. Nadiril gave the platter to Tallia and took the oval fruit bowl. 'There is not much fresh at this time of year,' he said, though there were apples and pears and nuts of various kinds in addition to the dried foods.

'What is this warn?' Lilis queried, pointing to a dark-brown prune-shaped fruit that looked like a dog-dropping.

'*One*. What is this *one*,' Nadiril corrected. 'That is a date. Zile is famous for its dates. Try it; it is very sweet.'

Lilis took one gingerly, wondering if he was playing a trick on her, put it to one side of her plate and sniffed her fingers afterwards. 'And this?'

This was a large flat dried fruit, like an ear that had been cut off and left out in the sun. 'That is a dried gellon, the queen of all fruits. It has come from nearly as far away as Thurkad.'

'Gellon,' said Lilis, tasting the word. She still looked dubious. 'Where do it come from?'

Nadiril looked as though he was going to correct her again, coughed and simply said, 'It comes from the mountains near Chanthed. I expect that your friend, Llian, would like gellon. An old friend of mine sends me a crate each year, though I can barely taste it now.'

Lilis took a gellon and one or two other things, and the bowl was passed on. Tallia selected a date and ate it with gusto. Lilis nibbled carefully at the end of her own, found it good and, unconsciously looking around to see if anyone was watching her, as if she was back in her alley in Thurkad, reached out for another.

'Here, take a handful,' said Tallia, holding out the bowl.

Nadiril watered a cup of wine for Lilis, handed her the bread tray, and once everyone had enough he took for himself a minute portion of bread and cheese.

'Would that old friend by any chance be Shand?' asked Tallia as she peeled a quince.

Nadiril ruminated. 'Shand! Yes, that is what he calls himself now, though I can scarcely think of him with that name. He is one of the greatest . . .' he paused, looking sideways at his visitors '. . . map-makers I ever met – a dying art in these times. Do you know him? How is he?'

'I met him first in Tullin, at the end of autumn. He seemed well to me. I liked him a lot. And again in Thurkad, briefly, just after the events there. He helped me find a boat.'

'I saw him in Thurkad too,' said Mendark, clenching his jaw. 'Wandering around meddling and acting mysterious as usual. Old fool!'

'He found Pender for us,' said Tallia mildly. In spite of their brief acquaintance she thought of Shand as a friend and would not hear him slighted. 'You didn't tell me that you'd met him in Thurkad.'

'Shand is not the only secretive one,' said Nadiril.

'I see hundreds of people,' grunted Mendark. 'He told me nothing useful, including to come here.'

'Perhaps if you observed the protocols, the customs, the

courtesies, you might find others more cooperative,' commented Nadiril, and promptly turned back to Lilis, asking her in detail about her father, her life in Thurkad, and how she had met Llian. Finally the empty plates were taken away and bowls of roasted barley tea appeared, the brown grains floating on the surface.

Nadiril said nothing further to Mendark, who realised that he must wait on the old man's humour. After Mendark had drunk his tea he took Tallia's arm and they strolled away to look out over the town. It was growing dark now and the stars were coming out. The servant returned with lamps which he hung on brackets behind them, so that a yellow flickering light fell on the table.

At one point in her somewhat rambling tale Nadiril stopped Lilis. 'Do you tell me that you can read *and* write?' he said.

'I can read some things,' she said. 'Signs and notices and letters. My father taught me. And once I read a *book* when I was little. But I knew it already, for Jevi told me stories from it many times. I can't write much, just the letters, and my name and Jevi's, and a few things like that. There was never anything to write with, but in the mud. I wish I could write.'

'Why, child? What good is it?'

'Do you know what happens to street girls and boys when they are old enough, if they can do nothing?'

'I do,' he said gravely.

'I don't want that. I want to do clever things, like Llian and Tallia and you.'

'And Mendark?'

'He is too clever for me. I want to read the Tales. Llian told me one once,' she said, her eyes gleaming. 'It was wonderful. Even more wonderful than the ones that Jevi . . .' she broke off, feeling disloyal. 'I want to read books. You must have many books here, *hundreds*.'

'Indeed we do,' he said, not smiling. 'Perhaps a hundred of hundreds of hundreds. More than anywhere on Santhenar.'

He paused, then gave her a hard stare. 'What do you want to ask of me?'

She gulped, said nothing, turned away. 'I cannot,' she said.

'Come, child, of course you can. I am not so very fierce, am I?'

'I want to read and write, more than anything, but I cannot pay you. Nothing comes without payment.'

The eyes seemed to look right through her. 'You have no money at all?'

'I have some,' she said vehemently. 'But that is to find my father with. I will not spend a *grint* on myself until he is found.'

'Very well. You want to read and write. Come here and I will test you.' He took a slender book from the pocket of his coat, opened it at the first page and passed it to her. 'This is the *Tale of Tales* by Jadia Gerenji – an old tale of Zur. Do you know it?'

'No.'

'Read it to me.'

She read haltingly in her squeaky voice, stumbling over names and pronunciations, and after about five minutes reached the bottom of the first page. She turned the page.

'Enough,' he said. 'That will not do at all.' He fumbled in another pocket, looking very stern. 'Now, here is a piece of paper and here a charcoal pencil. Write down what you just read.'

She gave him a terrified look from under her eyelashes, bent her head low to the paper and began to write in a big childish scrawl. Ten minutes passed, the writing punctuated by muffled sobs and clenching of fists, and once she even banged her head on the table. At the end she passed the paper to him. 'Is that all?' he asked, glancing at the mess, the meandering lines of letters, smudged and stained with tears and crossings out.

'No, but the paper is used up.'

'Paper is very dear, child. For the price of this piece

you could eat for a week. This will not do.'

Lilis went so still she might have stared into the eye of a basilisk. Tears clung to her lower lashes, but did not fall.

'This will not do at all,' he repeated gruffly. 'I must teach you better. I will.'

'*You will*? she cried, seized his withered hand and kissed it. Tallia and Mendark looked around at the commotion. 'But how can I pay you?'

'Can you work hard?'

'No one will work harder. I will scrub floors, empty privies . . .'

Nadiril held up his hand and she stopped. 'Not enough. I would have you do harder work than that.'

'That is all I can do,' she said, tears forming again.

Now Tallia, who had been watching and listening from the wall, came over and sat down beside Lilis, enclosing her in her arm. 'Nadiril, you are unkind,' she said. 'Lilis, can you carry books and read books and write down the names of books?'

'Yes,' squeaked Lilis. 'But . . .'

'Good, because that is the work that Nadiril would have you do in payment. He needs you, Lilis. Am I not right, librarian?'

'I'm sorry, child. I am used to fencing with cranky old men like Mendark. I did not mean to frighten you. Tallia is correct. I need you, because you care and because you want to work hard. Will you work for me in exchange for my teaching and your keep?'

'I will,' she said softly.

'Good. Then give me your hand. Tallia, be witness to this contract.'

Lilis and Nadiril clasped hands. 'It is witnessed,' said Tallia. 'Should either of you have a grievance I will arbitrate it without prejudice or favour.'

'So you have settled your future,' Mendark said to Lilis as he came back to the table. 'I am glad.'

'Doubtless,' observed Nadiril. 'Is her future of no importance? Is she of no significance then?'

'Not as I see the future, but who knows? I cannot take on the burden of the whole world.' He spoke to Lilis. 'I do not wish you ill, child, but your place was never with us on our next journey.'

'I will be sorry to say goodbye,' she said, 'but I have found my place.'

25

ASHMODE

K aran desperately wanted to stretch, to sneeze and clear her throat. She huddled at the bottom of her basket, hardly daring to breathe.

'Come on! Hurry up!' she heard the officer shout.

Tess said something that Karan did not catch, for just then the boat rolled and a clot of sticky stuff oozed out of the fish's mouth into her ear. It began to itch abominably.

'Yes, more! All the way to the bottom. Unload them all!'

Karan started. What was the point in hiding? Surely he would hear her heart thrashing. She was tempted to cry out, 'Here I am – just get me out of this disgusting place.'

The rustling and the slithering went on for a long time. It was light enough now for her to see the wickerwork of her basket, which meant that the ones above her had been moved. In a flash of memory, Karan saw herself back in Fiz Gorgo with Yggur looming over her. What would he use her for?

Karan's basket creaked as someone stood on top of it. She shivered and went utterly still.

Shand finished scrubbing the deck and went back to cutting up the octopus. Just then Benn came running up the ladder. He looked worried.

'More baskets,' he bawled and the crew scrambled. 'We're in trouble,' he said to Shand out of the corner of his mouth as he went past. 'He wants the hold emptied.'

'I'm coming,' Shand said, finishing his work. He plucked a straw out of a broom as he got up, playing with it in his fingers.

As he climbed down the ladder he saw the chin-whiskered officer issuing orders. Even Tess's stolid face had begun to show unease. Though technically the sea was neutral territory, the whole crew would be punished if Karan was discovered, and their families too. Yggur already had a reputation for making examples.

The bottom row of baskets was exposed. Karan must be suffering agonies. Shand stepped off the ladder and wandered across, watching while the beautiful golden fish were transferred from one basket to another then carried up out of the way.

'What's that?' Zareth hissed, turning his head this way and that.

'I didn't hear anything,' said Tess calmly.

Shand had – a little mewling noise. The pressure was too much for Karan. 'Just the baskets squeaking as you walk,' he said, then 'Aah!' He slapped his ear and danced a few steps closer to Zareth, making the baskets creak under his weight.

'What's the matter with you?' Zareth asked coldly.

'Something stung me,' said Shand, rubbing his ear furiously.

Zareth turned back to the search. 'Open this basket next!' It was Karan's.

Shand moved forward until he was just two steps away from the officer, put the straw to his lips and blew. Zareth rubbed the back of his neck as if an insect had bitten him. Something fell on the basket. Shand held his breath and, as the man moved away, he nudged a sliver of wood down into the bilge. Zareth looked around irritably.

'Where is the rest of the fleet?' he asked Tess.

'Well to the east and south, I should think.'

'There is a reward for the red-haired woman. A gold tell, if we find her. Come on, open it up!'

'A gold tell!' Tess exclaimed, fiddling with the lid of the basket. 'What did she do, steal the great sceptre of Thurkad?'

'No disrespect, fisher!' Zareth flipped up the lid and took out one of the golden-skinned fish, holding it up at arm's length. 'This is best bamundi, you say?'

'Well,' said Tess, rubbing her jaw, 'those are a little blemished. The prime fish are over there. Fenn!' she called, pointing, 'bring that basket.'

Fenn banged the basket down on Zareth's sandalled toes, knocking the lid of Karan's hide-out closed at the same time.

'Stupid oaf!' Zareth swore, swinging his fist at the sailor, who took the blow on the ear without flinching.

Tess drew bamundi from the new basket, one after another, holding each up by the tail and describing in minute detail why it was prime quality. 'Enough!' cried Zareth at last. 'I've got work to do. I'll take it!'

The basket was refilled with the best fish and sent to the other boat. Zareth turned around, wiping his face. His brow was covered in sweat droplets the size of peas. 'Where was I?' he asked, looking confused.

'This one,' said Shand helpfully, pointing away from Karan's basket.

'No, it was that one, you old fool,' said Tess, striking Shand and pointing the other way.

There followed a furious argument, each pressing their own case, abusing the other with increasingly creative oaths. 'Shut up!' shouted Zareth, now drenched in sweat. 'Open them both!'

The baskets were opened, the precious fish unloaded into other baskets and carried up the ladder. Suddenly Zareth swayed and the blood drained from his face. There was a swelling on the back of his neck with a tiny blood blister in the middle. He sat down on Karan's basket, rubbing his neck.

'Dizzy!' he said, hanging his head between his knees. 'Aah!'

'Are you all right, sir?' Tess asked.

'The worst pain ... ever felt. Must be ... fish ... ate.' Zareth pulled his chin-whiskers. He stared around the hold vacantly as if he could not see straight. His cheek muscles twitched and abruptly he doubled over and threw up in the bilge. 'Seen ... enough!' He heaved himself to his feet, staggering to the ladder.

'Let me help you up,' said Tess.

'Can manage,' he said, crashing into the side. Tess showed him the way to the ladder, which he climbed like a drunken man. He staggered across the deck calling for his marines, groaned, hurled up his stomach all over the deck, slipped in the mess and almost went over the rail.

Tess ran to the side, calling to the other boat. She explained how Zareth had been taken ill. Two sailors bundled him over the side and the boats parted. As soon as they were gone, Tess seized Shand's hand and pumped it up and down as if she was trying to draw water from a well. There were tears of relief and exuberance in her eyes.

'If ever I am in a crisis,' she said, 'there is no one I would sooner have beside me than you. Was it the octopus venom?'

'On a toothpick!'

'What if you had missed?'

'I have another,' he said, feeling in his pocket with great good humour. 'Oops!' he said, frowning as he inspected the tip of one thick finger.

'You haven't ...' cried Tess, horror-struck.

'Just my joke,' Shand grinned and, taking the splinter out of his pocket, sent it spinning over the side.

Tess dealt him a blow in the back that doubled him over. 'Better see to your little friend,' she roared.

Boots thumped up the ladder, someone shouted from far away, then the fishing sounds resumed. Karan could only hear part of what was going on. Somehow she had escaped, though she didn't know how. It was a long time before anyone came to get her out. She supposed that Tess was making sure that the boat was not coming back. She felt abominably uncomfortable, slimy with fish dribble and panicky with claustrophobia. Her tongue hurt.

At last they came, the brothers Benn and Fenn, high-spirited as before, to liberate her from her smelly prison. Her leg muscles were so cramped that she could hardly walk. Once again, as she emerged squinting into the daylight, she was annoyed by the smile on Shand's face.

'What a sad little urchin you look,' he said, laughing as he flicked scales out of her hair.

'Travelling with you is a series of humiliations,' she replied, though this time she could see the funny side, and it was better than the alternative. She went forward to thank Tess.

Tess dismissed her thanks. 'We owe no allegiance to Thurkad, much less to the upstart Yggur. Lucky for you we met them before they went to Ganport. Had they known that the redhead left with the fleet they would have taken us apart, plank and nail. Now, what am I going to do with you? Why were you going to Horn Island?'

'To try and find passage across the sea,' said Karan.

'Is that all? I can take you there.'

'We cannot wait until after the fishing season,' said Shand. 'Our need is urgent.'

'I realise that. I will take you there at once.'

'Now?' said Karan and Shand together. 'What is the price?'

'Another tar, plus the cost of the basket of fish. Six tars in all.'

'Oh,' said Shand. 'Back in Ganport I was told five tells when the fish are running.'

'Five tells! Who told you that? A man with white hair and no teeth? P'seerol is a bit of a joker. No, six tars is a fair price. A good price.'

'I heard the soldier offer a reward of a tell,' said Karan

with an anxious glance at Shand. 'I would offer you the same.'

'No need,' said the captain. 'If I were a rogue I would take your gold and turn you in for the reward as well.' She considered. 'I'll put you ashore south of Granewys. That's fifteen leagues from here, more or less. Eight or ten hours, depending on the winds. It'll be after dark, but perhaps you would prefer that.'

'What if he comes back?' said Karan.

'The Sea of Thurkad is a big place; he could look for a month and never find us. Anyway, we fish the whole of the sea and go where we please.'

'He won't be coming back today,' said Shand.

They turned onto the new heading, east by north-east. Karan hauled salt water, washed herself and her clothes and donned clean ones. Then she went back to the hammock to resume her interrupted sleep and slept the day away.

Darkness was several hours past by the time they approached the rocky shore where they were to go their own way. 'This is as close as is safe,' said the captain, shouting for the anchor. Their gear was loaded into a tiny dinghy, the brothers Benn and Fenn handed them down and Tess herself rowed them to the shore.

'I'm sorry that we never had that bamundi dinner,' she said, embracing Karan with a crackling of canvas. 'If ever you come to Horn Island or to Ganport, come and see me and we will eat bamundi until we are fit to burst.'

'Thank you, I will. I will never forget what you did for me.'

The captain waved all that away. 'It cost me nothing. While we feast you can tell me your tale. That will be reward enough. Fare well.'

They heaved up their packs, suddenly heavy after days of inaction, and picked their way across the rock platform into the scrub.

It took two days of steady walking before they reached Granewys. They were not pleasant days for Karan, for she could not stop thinking about her narrow escape and the likelihood of further pursuit. She slept badly, waking to every night noise, and prey to fancies about being hunted. They did not have the comfort of a fire either – Shand was afraid to draw attention to themselves.

Granewys turned out to be one of the meanest towns she had ever been in, in both goods and spirit, just a decaying collection of hovels on the edge of the swamp that was home to every species of gnat, sand fly, mud fly and mosquito conceivable. The people were dirty, indolent and morose.

In Ganport they had bought a great bulk of smoked meat, smoked and salted fish, dried fruit and black flour, none of which had yet been broached, so that all they wanted in Granewys were fresh meats and vegetables and an extra pair of waterskins each. As soon as they found these they turned north, each with their own thoughts and longing for the solitude of the track.

The eastern coast of the Sea of Thurkad was quite different from the west, being low-lying, sandy and dry. Ahead of them the stony plains stretched treeless to the horizon, except immediately to their north, where a low range of hills bulged up like a chain of warts from the brown flesh of the earth.

'It was not always like this,' said Shand as they skirted the hills on the inland side, for the land along the coast was salt marsh or dunes, hard walking, and swarming with insects that bit or stung, and tiny flies that clustered around eyes and nose and mouth. 'This was fertile plain and thick forest, before the time of the Rifting.'

He choked, spat out flies like blackcurrants, and fell silent. Karan was so absorbed in her own problems that she did not think to ask what he meant. She had dreamed about the Ghâshâd again last night and could think of nothing but the horror of being hunted by them once more. Neither day nor night could she get away from her troubles.

They travelled north-west for four days, the land slowly rising and becoming drier as they went north and inland. For the first few days they sometimes saw people in the distance, driving their herds from one waterhole to the next, but not after that. The grass was thin, the grey stems rasping against their boots. The land was dotted with anthills that were taller than Karan. In the distance the purple smudge of the Jelbohn Hills grew slowly into a barrier across their path. Giant hunting birds wheeled in the air above: hook-beaked skeets that were used by the wealthy to carry messages, and other kinds, more vicious yet.

'It's hot!' said Karan, sitting down in the shade of an anthill and squeezing the last drops from her waterbag.

Shand unhooked one of the new ones and passed it to her. She took a sip and immediately spat it out again. 'Yuk!' she said, sniffing. 'It stinks.'

'The leather mustn't be cured properly,' said Shand. 'What's the other one like?'

Karan tested it. The smell nearly knocked her head off, and his pair were just as bad. 'What are we going to do?'

'Tip it out – we probably won't need them for the next week or two. Next place we come to, we'll get some new ones.'

Nonetheless it was an added worry and they were greatly relieved when on the afternoon of that day they reached the hills and found water without difficulty, one of many little springs at the base of the slope.

'This is the best time of the year here,' said Shand. 'There's plenty of water about at the end of winter. After that the rain fails and water's hard to find, except if a hurricane roars in from the Gulf of Rahdar. That's not something you'll want to experience either.'

They filled the clean skins then climbed a trail up into the lower part of the Jelbohn Hills. There, in a little sheltered valley surrounded by tall hills, they found a creek running into a pool but not out again, a moss meadow and tall trees growing up to the flanks of red limestone walls. They made camp by the pool and thought to rest for a while.

While Shand dozed in the shade, Karan climbed further up to be by herself. She sat beneath an overhanging shelf of sandstone, drawing on the rock with a piece of yellow ochre while she watched the skeets soaring, wishing she could fly away as easily from her worries. One of the birds hung on the air not far away, motionless but for its rippling wingtips, its long neck craned down, then it rocked from side to side, the vast wings thrust the air out of the way and it glided down toward the flat. Karan watched the bird all the way down, admiring how it subtly changed course with dips of one wing or the other. She lost sight of it among the brown shrubbery, then it reappeared, labouring under something that still thrashed in its claws. Halfway up, the hare, or whatever it was, struggled free, tumbling head over tail to smack into the ground with a puff of dust. The skeet wheeled, glided down and returned with the creature, now motionless. It flew right up past her, roosting so near that she could hear the rending and gobbling. Her life had not been much different, this last year.

The slenderest crescent of a new moon set and they sat around a little fire, the first they'd had since Ganport. It was good to be out of the incessant south wind and better to be beside a roaring campfire and eat hot food again, even if it was only another stew.

The wind shook the dry branches above them, a raspy rattle. Karan licked a trace of stew from the handle of her spoon, put it down on her gleaming plate and sighed. A chilly breeze curled into their enclosure. She hunched her small shoulders against it, drawing the collar higher, and sighed again. For the first time in a month she wanted to talk, to ask Shand about Llian, to gain some comfort there, and to hear him talk about her father too.

'How did you meet my father?' she asked tentatively.

Shand seemed to sense what she was going through. 'In

Tullin, at the inn, as a matter of fact. I must have met Galliad ... forty years ago, I suppose. He came through Tullin several times on that old southern path to Shazmak that you took last year. One time we were snowed in and he spent a week with us. We used to play at dice in the evenings. And later I went a-venturing with him down to Zile. I introduced him to old Nadiril, as I recall. That was after Galliad's first wife cast him off, but of course long before he married your mother. He was already old by our standards, though not for one of his kind.'

'Tell me about him.'

'His first marriage was to an Aachim woman, but it was not a happy one – indeed, the Aachim put every obstacle in their path that they could.'

'So for me and Rael,' said Karan, 'though we never got that far.'

'He suffered,' said Shand, 'but he was not bitter. He had a sharp tongue but he was generous in word and deed. Rather like you, actually.'

Karan smiled at the comparison.

'And you were the delight of his life, even more than your mother.' Karan's face closed up at the mention of her mother. Vuula had been very young when she married Galliad. Her family had hated him, which of course only made her the more determined.

Shand continued, 'All half-Aachim suffer, I suppose, because he was neither one nor the other and not really at home anywhere. That is a fault of the Aachim – their blendings are only half-accepted and half-trusted.'

'I never felt that when I was there,' said Karan.

'But you are mostly old human, and that is your life. I'm sure you never wanted to be Aachim.'

'No, I never did. But they treated me very kindly, as a guest and a relative.'

'Anyway, I'm sure that's why Galliad became a wanderer and a dabbler in arcane arts.'

'I didn't know *that*.'

'Oh, he was always looking for the key to some great mystery.'

'What mystery?'

'I don't know – he was secretive about that. Perhaps he thought that if he could offer it to the Aachim he would be accepted as one of them.'

'Emmant thought that too,' she said softly. 'But they never would.'

He fell silent, thinking about Galliad's words, that Karan was very special, and wondering what he had meant.

'I miss Gothryme so much,' she said. 'It's funny, because it came from my mother's family, yet whenever I think about it I see my father. He was always doing something with it – rebuilding the fireplaces or running water pipes around the house or fooling around with the privies.'

'The Aachim are the greatest engineers in the Three Worlds,' Shand remarked.

'You should see the stove in our kitchen,' she said dreamily. 'It's as big as a cart and heats water for the whole house. I have dreams about it sometimes. I've never seen one like it.'

'What else do you dream about?'

'Good dreams, you mean?'

'Mnn!'

'I often dream about Llian, about taking him home with me. But that makes me afraid. Afraid of losing him; afraid that he will be bored in my rustic little world. And –' She broke off, looking away.

'Yes?' he said after a while. 'What are you really worried about?'

'I hardly dare to say it,' she said softly. 'I am incredibly presumptuous, for Llian and I have never talked about such things. But, I want a child and an heir for Gothryme. Is that too much to hope for?'

'It's what keeps the world going,' said Shand. 'But you've plenty of time for that.'

366

'I don't know if I have.'

'Why so?'

She was silent for a time. Karan had never discussed such things before. She wasn't sure whether they should be spoken of, to *him*. 'The women of my family are not . . . very fertile. And their fertile time does not last long at all. My mother only had ten years. I'm twenty-four and I feel my time is running out.'

'Oh!' said Shand, and they both fell silent.

'I knew your mother too,' Shand said later.

'I don't want to talk about her,' Karan said sharply. She had mixed feelings about her mother. 'She must have hated me. Why else would she kill herself, leaving me all alone?'

'Despair makes us do strange things,' said Shand. 'I too have tasted that fruit.'

But Karan could not bear to listen. She walked away from the possibility of her mother, into the starry night.

After Jelbohn they continued north-east across a stony plain covered in tussock grass and saltbush that scratched at them as they passed. Here it was relatively arid, though once or twice on their trek there was a shower of rain, and one evening with a cold south wind they had sleet and snow, enough to coat the ground to the depth of a finger. That was to be the last defiance of winter. Subsequently the winds turned around to the west, warm humid winds that promised rain but seldom gave any. Water was a worry now; they were down to the foul skins before they found more.

The moon was near the three-quarter, and almost all of it the dark side. Once or twice Karan woke in the night from a bad dream to see Shand watching her anxiously in the dim light.

'What were you dreaming about?'

'Nothing, really. I just feel an awful foreboding, like everything I care for is going to be broken to pieces.'

'That's the trouble with caring for someone else,' said

Shand dismissively. 'Go back to sleep – we've got an early start in the morning.'

I've had this feeling every night since we got off the boat, she thought. Something's changing out there.

Beyond the plain was another range of hills and walking steadily they reached them in another three days. Passenar was the name of the place. Here, too, they were lucky with water. Just before they were forced to drink from the foul skins, a storm blew out of the west and drenched the hills with rain, so that every gully became a torrent. After that they found water in pools wherever they went. On the other side of Passenar they came onto another plain, covered also in saltbush and thorn thickets, and claypans now half-full of water, rich with small game. Then abruptly the scrub was gone and they began to trudge up a ramp of limestone and wiry grass.

They climbed over a little rise and suddenly there was nothing in front of them – nothing at all! The land fell down, cliff upon towering cliff, terrace upon terrace, slope upon slope, so far that it was like looking down from a mountaintop.

'Oh!' Karan cried, struck with wonder. It was vast beyond any imagining.

They were standing on the brink of a high cliff that stretched beyond the limits of sight to east and west. The cliff was at least a hundred spans high and there were grey blocks of limestone, bigger than houses, all along its base. Below that was a narrow shelf, falling off into a long steep slope cut by deep crevasses and gorges, broken by other cliffs, and finally stretching out to a cold, white plain which extended in all directions until it faded into the haze. A vast emptiness; a chasm as deep as an ocean, but there was no water in it.

'The Sea of Perion,' said Shand. 'The Dry Sea.'

Karan did not reply, only gazed out across that vast desolation.

Shand sat down on a hummock near the edge of the cliff,

watching her out of the corner of his eye. She was staring across the sea and, for the first time in a month, there was some animation in her face. She took a few steps along the cliff edge, a few steps back. Then she stopped, confused, and turned to look back the way they had come.

Shand sat patiently, keeping his eyes and his thoughts to himself, though he felt a twinge of excitement. It was almost as if, having come directionless all this way, he now waited for her to lead him. Lead *him*! If only she knew. Well, perhaps some day she would. What was it about her? Why was she the key to it all? He grew more sure every day that she was. And what was he doing here anyway, he who had sworn that he would never more become involved in the affairs of Santhenar?

Karan walked slowly back and sat down beside Shand on the thin grass, hugging her knees up under her chin, gazing over the sea.

'What is out there?' she asked at last.

'Mostly desert. In the west the whole of the great island of Faranda is arid, but for the west coast and the very north. To the east, most of Lauralin is savanna or desert, this side of the *Wahn Barre*, the Crow Mountains. Jepperand lies that way – the home of the Zain.'

'I know – I've been across Lauralin. Though further south than this.'

'On the other side of the *Wahn Barre* are the rich lands and forests of Crandor, a place half the size of our Meldorin Island. But to Crandor is a journey of four or five months.'

'And the Dry Sea itself?'

'It is a desert such as you have never seen. The bottom of the Sea of Perion lies two thousand spans below us. Two thousand fathoms I should say, since . . .'

'Two thousand spans! The great mountains of Shazmak can't be that high!'

'. . . and there, in the centre, it never rains – or rather, might rain only once in fifty years. In summer it is unbearably

369

hot, in winter miserably cold. The bottom is salt that is many spans in thickness. Nothing grows there, nothing lives, except around the shores, where there are seeps and brine pools, and on the tops of the tallest mountains, once islands in that most beautiful of all seas, on which snow falls in the winter.'

'It was not always so,' she said to herself.

'No! Before the Rifting, the Sea of Perion was a jewel. But that was thousands of years ago. There is a tale of it – the *Tale of the Rifting* – one of the Great Tales. You should have Llian tell it for you sometime.' Almost as soon as the words were out of his mouth he regretted them, but Karan continued dreamily rocking back and forth.

'I will,' she said.

'Then is the sea impassable?' Karan asked a long while later.

'No, not at this time of year, though it is rarely attempted.'

'What is out in the middle?'

'The islands that I mentioned, long chains of them. They form tall mountains now. On a few of them are ruined cities, from the time when they were real islands in a deep sea. Those that are tall enough have water, when the snow melts, and there are likely to be springs and seeps at the bottom. The largest mountains may even have water all year round, though it would be dangerous to rely on it. There may be water there one year and not the next. But on the plains there is nothing – neither water nor food nor shelter.'

'Might Tensor have gone that way?'

'He might. All the islands were inhabited before the sea dried up, I believe. That was in the time of Kandor, the third of the three Charon who came to Santhenar hunting the golden flute. It was he who built the Empire of Perion. His fortress city was on Katazza, the largest and tallest of the islands, and had the same name. The triple peaks of Katazza stand so tall that in good seasons there is snow on them for half the year. Sometimes you can see them from Faranda.' He ruminated. 'Katazza! It would make an incomparable

370

fortress, and an impregnable one, for someone who sought only solitude.'

'*Katazza!*' She started. 'Katazza.' Karan rolled the word around in her mind. 'Ka – taz – za.' There was something in the word, or the name. Not a memory – something stirred in her – her long-lost talent. She put her hands over her eyes and right there, with Shand watching, she tried to *sense* Llian out, to call his name across the distance that separated them.

Karan forced so hard that it hurt, with immediate and frightening results. For an instant she almost saw him – the figure in her mind was surely Llian, hiding behind a white pillar with two shadow figures creeping up on him the other way. 'Llian!' she cried aloud, then like a dream after waking it faded away and the more she tried the less was left of it. She forced harder, desperate to get him back, to find out what trouble he was in.

'Ugh!' yelped Shand, waking her to her surroundings.

'What's the matter?'

'*What are you doing, Karan*? I just got the most piercing pain in my head.'

'Sorry,' said Karan, realising that she had been broadcasting her emotions, a dangerous thing to do. Other sensitives could track her down that way – the Whelm had done it before. 'What do you know about Katazza?'

'A lot! What would you like to know? The Histories? The people?'

She dismissed such things with a wave of her hand. 'No! What's there now?'

'It's many years since my last visit, but the great towers of Katazza were still standing. Surely they will endure for another thousand years. Katazza Mountain is desert for the most part, but there is water too, and deep valleys where trees grow, watered by the melting snow. There might even be people – it's big enough – though there was no sign of any when I was there. I made my own map once, but I gave that away many years ago.'

Karan closed her eyes and walked slowly back and forth. She turned around several times then opened her eyes again. She was looking to the very centre of the Dry Sea. 'I *must* go out there. Can you take me?'

'I can, if that's *really* where you must go. Twice I've been across. It's a cruel journey though, even at this time of year. So, you think that Tensor has taken Llian there?'

'I don't know what to think. I might get there and find nothing, but I have to go.'

'Hmmn,' said Shand.

'What does that mean?'

'It is not a journey to be undertaken lightly. Out there we cannot afford *one* mistake or *one* accident. Even to be unlucky is fatal. We must prepare carefully; especially the new waterskins. There is, or used to be, a town ten or fifteen leagues to the east of here, a place called Ashmode. I think that is our best plan.'

'A town out here?'

'Why not? This land is fertile, and the rains come in the winter. There are herders, more than you might think, and farming in the river valleys, and mines aplenty. Salt and other minerals are harvested from the edges of the sea, traded right across Lauralin. Further east there are great cities, larger than Thurkad. And look!' He took her arm and led her back to the brink. 'Look down the slope. See the green! There are soaks and springs everywhere; underground streams gush out of marble caves like waterfalls and they can never dry up, for the water seeps all the way from the Great Mountains. It has to go somewhere.'

Still somewhat distracted Karan looked, and saw that the base of the cliffs, and the long slope beyond, was dotted with patches of green, dark and light, great and small.

'Further east,' continued Shand, 'there are rivers flowing down into the sea. Some have cut gorges greater than any you have ever seen. The greatest canyons on Santhenar lie on the southern edge of the Dry Sea, and down them flow rivers that have built their channels over the salt, making lakes of water that are nearly fresh. Some of the most remarkable sights of Santhenar lie along the cliff-bound shores of the Dry Sea – springs hot and cold that fountain twenty spans in the air; caverns that the whole of Thurkad would fit inside. There are wonderful caves at Ashmode.'

'Let's go,' she said impatiently. 'I'm worried about Llian.' Her fleeting vision of him had turned their leisurely trek into an urgent quest.

The town was three days' walk to the east, along the cliffs. Karan was pleasantly surprised when she got there. She had been expecting a seedy, frontier village like Granewys, but Ashmode turned out to be a large, spacious town looking over the Dry Sea, with gentle hills to east and west, and a small lake on the southern side, so deep that the water was blue. The town was built of blue-white marble, with great spreading figs and palm trees lining the streets. An old town, but prosperous for all its isolation, for looking down the slope she saw that the hillsides below the cliffs were terraced, making a vivid patchwork of green down for a league or more.

'What a lovely place,' she said, momentarily diverted from her urge to press on in search of Llian.

'Good! Let's find an inn.'

There were only two inns in Ashmode and the first looked so appealing, set with a view down the cliffs, and with broad verandas on all sides held up by marble columns, that they searched no further.

'It looks more like the mansion of a wealthy merchant,' said Karan.

'Well, wood is precious here and there is not the fuel to bake bricks, but marble is everywhere and easily worked. Maybe this place was built in richer times. Ashmode is, I think, a very old town. It may even have been here before the sea dried up.'

The inn was only half-full so they took a room each. 'First I'm going to have a bath,' said Karan, preparing to argue with Shand if necessary. He did not disappoint her.

'Another bath! How can you possibly need it?'

'In Shazmak we used to bathe every day, drought permitting,' she said rather primly. 'It's more than two weeks since I had one.'

'Every day! That's very unhealthy.'

'Pooh to you,' she said rudely, and went downstairs to ask.

The innkeeper was a tall bald man with a round scar on the top of his head, another on his cheek, a narrow scar on his throat, and a purple lump on his jawbone that looked as though it needed cutting out. His voice was a hoarse whisper. 'Of course we have baths, though the water is not hot today.'

Karan had her bath in lukewarm water, but she did not care. It was the first time she had felt clean since the notorious bath in Ganport. She washed her filthy clothes, hung them on a line and, clad only in trousers and shirt, for it was a warm sunny day, went back to the veranda. There was no one else there, although a few customers could be seen inside.

The food was different from what she was used to – spicy shreds of goat meat served on a sizzling hot plate with onions, huge lumps of grilled garlic, green vegetables she did not recognise and a mound of yellow rice. And with that, since she was feeling especially good, Karan ordered a mug of black beer. She had nearly finished the meal and was sitting back, picking at a last few grains of rice, sipping her beer and enjoying the view, the breeze in her hair and the sun on her toes, when Shand finally returned. Her hair flamed in the slanting afternoon sun. Lime-blossom perfume drifted on the air.

'I thought you must have gone on without me,' she said.

'I've been talking to the innkeeper about the Dry Sea. He crossed it many years ago.'

'Oh?'

'He was one of a party of twelve – three families. The rest died out there, women, children and men, and the sun near burned him to death. He's never got over it.' He signalled to a waiter.

Karan said no more, chilled by the words.

It took the whole of the next day for them to obtain the supplies that they needed – dried meats and fruits and other foods, enveloping desert robes and hoods to keep out the sun and the salt dust – and to have their boots repaired and make slitted eye covers to protect from salt blindness. By that time Karan was anxious to be on her way: the fleeting return of her talent had stirred up worries about Llian. She knew that he was in trouble that he could not get himself out of, and his restless curiosity would surely lead him into worse.

I know you're out there, Llian. I know it! The thought warmed her like the sun breaking through wintry clouds. And I'll find you. *Nothing will stop me!* She began to feel the return of that unquenchable will that she'd had before Narne.

'Do we really need these?' she asked impatiently, feeling the cloth of the robes that Shand was buying.

'Out there the sun burns all day every day. You can die of sunburn, you know, as well as ending up wrinkled and scabrous. Unless you want your face to look like mine, you need them.'

Karan shuddered theatrically. 'Horrible! I'll wear them. What else do we need?'

'Two new waterskins each, to replace the ones from Granewys, and something to keep the sun off when we camp during the day – as light as possible. Our tent is too heavy, with all the water we must carry.'

She bent down to look at a roll of cloth and her hat fell off. Her bright hair, which had not been cut for a year, sprang out in all directions.

The proprietor of the shop, who had been looking at them

curiously for some time, now edged a bit closer. Karan had not noticed. Picking the hat up, Shand crammed it back on her head.

'A length of this fabric might do,' Karan said, fingering a gauzy material that might have been used for a nightdress, though not a modest one, 'but we'd need to carry stakes to hold it up.'

'Too thin! Let's have a cup of tea while we think about it,' said Shand, abruptly gripping her arm and pulling her out of the shop. 'We'll come back in the afternoon,' he said over his shoulder to the shopkeeper.

'Stop it, you're hurting my arm,' she said angrily.

He did not let go, but loosened his grip a little. 'Come on,' he said. 'He was watching you a bit too closely for my liking.'

Shand looked over his shoulder in time to see the shutters of the stall clack down. The 'closed' sign went up and shortly the proprietor slipped out the back door, heading toward the town centre.

'You're imagining things,' she said, very annoyed, but just then another chill of foreboding touched her and she followed him across the road to the markets, a maze of little stalls to get lost in.

26

WOMEN'S AFFAIRS

S hand led her through the markets to a food stall with outside tables and benches, each with a sunshade made of palm thatch. 'Don't *ever* do that again,' said Karan furiously, jerking her arm free.

The waitress, a plump cheerful young woman with black hair and red cheeks, swabbed the table casually and stood back waiting for the orders with her arms folded beneath a splendid bosom.

'My friend will have radish tea with mustard and I will have cold mint tea with honey and cinnamon,' said Karan, with a malicious grin.

'*Radish tea!*' cried Shand.

The waitress gave an enigmatic smile. 'It's very . . . Ah, yes! Radish tea and mustard, very good for the old man. Especially old man who has trouble with . . . young girlfriend.' She laughed aloud. Karan was almost bursting at the look on Shand's face. 'Radish tea at once,' the waitress said, turning away.

'No, damn it!' cried a choleric Shand. 'I don't want radish tea, with or without mustard. I'm too old for that nonsense. Bring me sweet ginger tea and be quick about it.' He got up and moved to the other side of the table, giving Karan a savage glare. Laughter exploded out of her.

'Too old! Oh dear. Oh, I am sorry,' said the waitress, giving Karan a sympathetic pat on the shoulder. 'It must be very . . .'

'*Tea!*' roared Shand over Karan's giggles, and the waitress hurried off looking hurt.

'You found it funny enough when the laugh was on me,' said Karan, still smiling broadly, and after a moment Shand laughed too.

'I suppose I deserve it. It's been a long time since anyone made a joke at my expense.'

The teas arrived. The waitress crashed Shand's down in front of him, slopping it all over the table.

'Well, you did drag me across the road rather crudely,' Karan said. 'I don't like that sort of thing.'

'I'm sorry. We have to be careful not to attract notice.'

'Why would anyone be looking for us here?'

'Yggur has spies and agents all over Meldorin, and if he sets his heart on something, he never gives it up. I wish you'd keep your hair covered.' He sipped his tea, grimacing. 'Oh, this is horrible! What has she put in it? Here, taste this.'

Karan took a tiny sip. The taste was indeed vile. 'She's just used some desert herbs, I'd say, some women's medicine. She's only trying to help – me, that is. Here, put some more honey in it.' She sipped her own tea, smacking her lips loudly. 'Ahh, that's *good*.'

Shand drank his tea most ungraciously. 'Anyway, I have been thinking about this trip. There may be saltstorms.'

'Saltstorms?'

'Storms of wind-hurled salt dust. Salt can kill, if you breathe enough of it.'

'Salt can kill. Sun can kill. Seems like just about anything can kill out on the Dry Sea.'

'That's right, just about anything can. We need the tent, whatever the weight, and a fly that we can seal against the dust.'

'You'll have to carry it then.'

They drank up their tea and Shand went to the counter to pay. As he did so the waitress slipped onto the bench beside Karan and whispered something in her ear. She had a little package in her hand. Karan burst out laughing, shook her head, then something occurred to her and she whispered back. The waitress stared at Shand, at first puzzled, then amazed, put the package back in her pocket and ran off. Shand was idly watching the transaction from the counter. Karan went over to him.

'I have need of a tar, if you please.'

Shand took a silver coin out of his purse and put it in her hand. 'Shall we go?'

Karan's cheeks were a little bit pink. 'Just a minute. I'll meet you across the street.'

Shand shrugged and turned away. Shortly the waitress came back. She handed another small package to Karan, who gave her the tar, embraced her, then hurried after Shand.

'What was that all about?'

'None of your business. Nothing to do with *you*, at any rate. Women's affairs. Let's get going.'

Just then the afternoon sun flashed on the silvery wings of a large bird, a message skeet. It wheeled about the centre of the town, before settling down roughly where Shand knew the town hall to be. The skin on the back of his neck prickled. He looked across to Karan to see if she had *sensed* anything amiss. She was oblivious, whistling and tossing the little packet from one hand to the other.

'Women's affairs,' Shand said. 'How mysterious! Well, I have men's business to do.'

'Drinking, you mean,' she sniffed.

'If you like! Can you amuse yourself for an hour or two? We can finish the shopping this evening.'

Karan snorted. 'You're not the centre of *my* universe. I'm going to take a walk. I'll see you back at the inn for dinner.'

Shand could not have said why he kept the sighting from Karan, though he was well aware of her unsettling dreams and did not want to worry her unnecessarily. After they separated he headed in the direction of the town hall. Ashmode was isolated; likely they used skeets a lot for sending messages here. But on the other hand, maybe they didn't – the big carrier birds were notorious for being ill-tempered, vicious and almost impossible to train. Expensive couriers!

He wandered past the town hall and down the back, where he found stables and sheds. Outside the stable door a middle-aged man was vigorously shovelling manure from beside a watering trough.

Shand strolled by, put his boot up on the trough and refastened the laces. 'Nice day,' he said.

The stable hand was glad of the opportunity for a break, for he leaned on his shovel as though settling in for a long session. He was a big fellow with a quivering belly and a broad red mouth, a man who liked an ale and a gossip. 'One of the best,' he agreed. 'My favourite season, spring. Come far?'

'A fair way. Across the sea. I live near Thurkad.'

'Thurkad! That's a wicked place, I hear. And they say there's war in those parts.'

'Afraid so,' Shand said. 'Was that a skeet I saw a while ago?'

'Don't know,' said the man, caressing his belly. 'I was inside. But the mayor do use them.'

'Vicious things, skeets,' Shand replied. 'At least, so I'm told. I've never seen one up close. Like to, though.' He was lying; he knew all about skeets and how to handle them.

'Nasty! Mayor has a big cage around the back. I'll show you if you like.' He leaned the shovel up against the wall of the stable.

'The mayor won't mind?'

'Course not! Why would he? Anyway, he's away till tomorrow, gone fishing, so whatever the message is, it'll have to wait.'

Shand accompanied him around the back. As they crossed the gravel-strewn yard there came a furious screeching from a shed and a tattered young woman tumbled out, kicking the door shut behind her.

'What's the matter, Crace?' the stable hand asked.

Crace flicked blonde plaits over her shoulders and turned a furious face to him. The sleeve of her shirt was torn from shoulder to elbow. 'Damned bird! She's the meanest one I've ever handled. I can't get the message pouch off.'

'Can I see?' asked Shand, continuing his yokelish pretence.

'Put your eye to that knothole,' said the man.

Shand did so. 'She's a big one,' he said in awe. 'What do you feed her with?'

'Rats and rabbits,' said Crace.

Just then there came a frightful shriek and Shand sprang back hastily, falling over in the dust of the yard. The skeet began to tear at the wood around the knothole with beak and claw. Crace laughed. 'Do it again, old man, if you're game,' she said cheerfully. 'It'll tire her out.'

Shand put up his hands and backed away, pretending terror. He had learned what he wanted. The message pouch was marked with a black crucible on white – Yggur's insignia.

He headed back to the inn, rather thoughtful. Karan's dreams, the behaviour of the shopkeeper, the message from Yggur – it might all be coincidence, but Shand did not think so.

He reached the inn well before dark. Karan was not in her room, so he went to his own, lay on the bed and promptly fell asleep. Later he jerked awake, thinking that someone had called out his name, and saw that it was dark. He went down to the dining room but Karan was not there and had not been seen since the morning. Her room was dark; he could tell by sniffing the lamp that it had not been lit today.

Still, it wasn't that late – she was probably doing some shopping. More of her women's affairs, no doubt. Shand ate a leisurely dinner, but by the end of it, when she had still not appeared, he began to worry. The market stalls would all be closed by now. Anyway, he remembered, she had practically no money.

Retracing his steps to the place where they had separated, Shand found the shops and stalls closed and the streets empty. Evidently they were early to bed in Ashmode. One shop still showed a light, however, and after persistent knocking someone came to the door, an elderly man in a red nightshirt. He was annoyed but civil. He had not seen anyone resembling Karan.

Shand's other efforts met with a similar response, and the stars told him that it was close to midnight by the time he trudged back up the steps of the inn. Inside there was still no news of Karan. She had vanished.

Shand bought a jug of wine and sat down on the terrace in the cool. The next step was a visit to the constables, though that was one that he was reluctant to take. With that message waiting for the mayor's return, the last thing he wanted to do was draw attention to themselves.

Several hours later, the jug empty, Shand went back to his room. Karan had been very resourceful once, but she had lost that in her madness and illness. And she was not as strong as she had been. He started to feel very afraid.

After Shand left her, Karan wandered about the markets for a while. She saw many things that she would have liked to buy, including some magnificent waterskins, but all she had was a few coppers, change from purchases earlier in the day.

Strolling down the street she caught sight of a park with tall palm trees, down in a valley. She headed that way. As she passed through the arch of the park gates, someone called out hello. She turned and saw a slim young man in the uniform of an attendant, with skin that was a mass of freckles, and carrot-coloured hair. That made her like him instantly.

'Hello,' she said with a friendly smile. 'I'm just going for a walk in the park.'

He smiled back. 'There's a map on the wall around the corner. Would you like me to tell you the sights?'

'Yes, please!'

He pointed out various attractions on a coloured plan – waterfall, glade, caves.

'Caves?' said Karan, remembering Shand's lyrical description.

The youth glanced at the sun, which was rapidly descending behind the arch.

'The most beautiful caves in all the world,' he said in all earnestness. 'Though there's not enough time to see them today. Better come back in the morning.'

'I'll be gone in the morning,' she replied, discounting his hyperbole but still interested. 'What a pity. Point me in their direction and I'll just put my head in.'

'I have lanterns for hire for one copper,' he said. 'I wouldn't advise you to go in without one.'

Karan gave him a coin and he handed her a lantern. 'That way,' he said, pointing down a winding track between the trees. 'It's not far.'

Karan thanked him and set off. The path wandered in and out of the trees, dropping down steeply at times. The shoulders of the valley rose into bluffs of white limestone on either side. After five or ten minutes the track ended at a ragged opening in the bluff. 'Most beautiful caves in all the world,' she sniffed. 'But since I've come this far I might as well take a look.'

She lit the lamp and went inside, splashing through little puddles. It was a rather small cave, and drab, with a close odour of bat droppings. She turned a corner, ducked under the low ceiling into another cave, and stopped abruptly. Karan had been in caves before, most notably after she and Llian had fled from Shazmak, but those had been just grey tunnels through wet rock. Nothing had prepared her for the magnificence that now opened up in front of her.

She held up the lantern and it was like being in a palace made of cut glass. Everywhere she looked the light reflected back, the colours of the spectrum shimmering from a hundred thousand facets. The tales she'd heard of such wonders could not prepare her for the reality of this little cavern.

Outside it was beginning to grow dark. She took a step forward, then another, swinging the lantern gently to see the patterns dancing on the walls. Time passed in an exultant daze. She went a little further. The next chamber was as beautiful as the first. She stepped through into a third and saw dark cave mouths running off in three directions. Karan gazed around in wonder.

As she did so, a lanky, cloaked figure slipped through the entrance of the cave, five more following. Karan's errant talent failed to warn her – she was entranced, oblivious to everything but the play of light and colour and shadow on the countless variety of forms that the caves were made up of.

'Oh!' she said, taking a hop and a skip. She spun the lantern on its handle, twirled like a dancer, then froze.

Half a dozen figures stood across the exit, their arms folded across their chests. Hoods enclosed their faces, making puddles of darkness within which an occasional ray reflected back from their eyes. There was no way past.

Karan stepped backwards, the moving colours forgotten. She sought out with her senses but once again her talent let her down. 'What do you want?' Her voice quavered; she could not prevent it.

They did not speak but the figure on the right threw back its hood so that the light shone on grey scarred cheeks as angular as crystal, an arching nose sharp as a blade and black eyes that knew her all too well.

'Idlis!' she said, and Idlis the healer it was, the Whelm who had hunted her for months after she fled Fiz Gorgo with the Mirror last autumn.

Karan did not panic. She was not terrified; not even afraid.

She just felt an overwhelming, empty depression and help-lessness. She was so alone.

'What do you want of me now?' she asked softly.

Idlis tried to smile, a grotesque sight. 'Not to harm you,' he said hoarsely, his voice a thick bubbling that was hard to follow. 'Don't be afraid. We will take very good care of you.' He stuck out a bony hand. His skin was the grey colour of a fish; Karan was reminded of its rubbery, dead feel.

'I don't have the Mirror,' she said.

'We are Ghâshâd now,' Idlis replied. 'It's not the Mirror we want, it's you!'

Karan almost dropped the lantern. Now she *was* afraid. She took another step backwards.

'There's no way out,' said Idlis.

That's nonsense, she thought. Caves can have many exits.

Idlis sprang at her. Karan leapt out of the way. *Shand!* she cried out with her mind, or tried to, though she had no idea whether it was working. *Shand, where are you? Help!* She tried to make a sending to him but her talent was not there.

She ran, leaping puddles, ducking around stalagmites and strangely shaped knobs of rock, weaving across the cavern, following the muddy track to the next. The patterns of light shivered and danced across walls and ceilings even more entrancingly than before, but their beauty was quite lost on Karan now.

She soon found that she was not as fit as when Idlis had hunted her before. The scrambling flight through cave and cavern quickly tired her out. Karan dropped to a fast walk and looked back.

She could not see anything at all, but she knew that meant nothing. They were slower than her, and awkward rather than agile, but they would wear her down. Ghâshâd were utterly dogged. And they could see in the dark better than she could. The light from her lantern would be more than enough, but she did not dare extinguish it for fear of falling down a sinkhole.

385

Now Karan felt a faint chuckling on the edges of her mind. Some of the Ghâshâd were sensitives like her. They had tracked her by her dreams before and could use their minds to weaken her, to make her feel afraid. In the chase through the swamp forests of Orist she had deliberately suppressed her feelings and emotions, so as to stop them tracking her. It had seemed to work for a while, then her fears had broken out again and Idlis found her once more.

She remembered that night at the camp in the forest above the town of Narne, when she had *sensed* the Whelm and, powerless to resist them, had sent Llian fleeing away. What if they used *that* power again?

The Ghâshâd had a power over the Aachim, something akin to the mesmerising power that a snake has over a rabbit. That was how they had taken Shazmak so easily. And presumably, since Karan was one-quarter Aachim, why she had been so helpless that night.

Now she was plodding through a narrow tunnel whose sides could be spanned by her outstretched arms. She had lost track of distance and time, but it must have been hours; the oil in her lantern was almost gone. There was no point going any further. Stopping at a place where the cave began to broaden out, Karan put the lantern down.

I'll wait here, she thought. If they're going to take me, I'd rather I saw them coming.

That calmed her, the thought of submitting with dignity. It made her feel stronger too; she still had a little control over her fate.

The light began to splutter, to flare up and die down again. Must be water in the oil, she thought, swirling it until it resumed a steady yellow glow.

A pebble clicked back up the tunnel. They were coming! Karan held the lantern high. A shadow moved in the darkness. She fought her arm, but its trembling undermined her resolve and she had to put the light down again. Idlis, moving with that ratcheting step that was so characteristic of Whelm and

Ghâshâd, resolved out of the gloom. The others were shifting shapes behind him. Her flight had gained nothing.

Karan's knees were shaking. She had to support herself on a spine of rock, a pillar shaped like a robed and mitred priest. The diseased chuckling swelled up in her mind. She could feel Idlis's rubber fingers on her throat.

Idlis lurched towards her and at the last minute Karan's self-control broke. She snatched the lantern up, turned and ran into the dark.

Leaping through into the next cave she just had time for a momentary surprise as the light revealed a vast cavern, then suddenly there was nothing beneath her feet. She seemed to fall for a long time, sure that the fall would kill her, then plunged into an icy pool. The lamp went out, she cracked the back of her head on something, the lights came back on with a brilliant red flare and that was all she knew.

THE STIGMATA

The race continued and about three weeks after the Conclave the Aachim crashed out of the scrubby forests onto a rocky shore. Llian felt that he had been running his entire life.

'There's a fishing town called Siftah not far from here,' said Tensor. 'We'll take ship there.' He led them over the boulder-strewn headland up to the end of a long and narrow estuary, with the valley walls of pebbly puddingstone rising up steep on either side.

The people of the town knew who they were; doubtless some fast-flying message had already warned them. But it was also clear that in that remote place they cared not for foreign masters, and when Tensor asked them for a boat, took good gold from his pouch and put it on the table in front of them, they agreed readily enough. They were a dour lot, these stocky dark fisherfolk, but Tensor knew that their word was good.

A simple banquet was held that night to seal the bargain. They sat at trestle tables on the hill, feasting on baked parsnips, chunks of yellow bread dipped in pungent olive oil and sardines baked over a fire fed with rosemary branches. Llian gorged himself on the oily, herb-flavoured fish. As he was licking his fingers a wrinkled old man stood, raising a bumper of purple wine.

'Hail Tensor!' he shouted, quaffing the lot in one enormous swallow.

'Hail Siftah!' Tensor responded, downing his own beaker, and the Aachim followed his example.

For the first time in his life Llian had no interest in a drinking contest. All he wanted was a bath and sleep. He took a draught from his jar of wine for the sake of courtesy. It made his head spin.

An old fisherwoman, equally wrinkled, now stood up, holding her glass high. Llian began to think that there would be a toast for every person in the village. He groaned, took the barest sip, then laid his head down on his arms. Almost immediately someone nudged him painfully in the ribs.

'Remember your manners, chronicler,' said Shalah, twin of Xarah who had remained behind in Thurkad.

He looked up in a daze to see that his jar was full again and he was expected to drink yet another toast. Reaching for it, Llian found an inspired solution. He knocked over the jar, slumped sideways and slid gently under the table. There, to their roars of laughter, he lay down on the spiky grass and, smiling, fell asleep.

In the morning the Aachim rose dull-brained and sore-headed to find that the wind had turned, blowing so strongly from the north-east that the fleet could not get out of port. They used the time to make devices of wood and metal, light strong things of many polished pieces that slid into one, as an umbrella did, or folded down into shapes so ordinary that it was impossible to imagine the structure that lay within.

'What are they?' Llian asked.

'Trazpars,' said Asper, which was not illuminating. No one would say what the devices were for and he could only imagine that they were weapons the Aachim would use to defend themselves on the journey.

As the day passed Tensor grew anxious about the delay, though for Llian it was the first time in weeks that he was able to rest and think. He walked alone on the herb- and scrub-covered headlands, looking out across the Sea of Thurkad, or wrote notes in his journal for his *Tale of the Mirror*. The Aachim respected his need for solitude, though he was always aware that his enemy Hintis was not far away. But, though Llian still had his wallet, and enough of old Wistan's coin remained to take him back to Thurkad and beyond, if he wished it, he made no effort to get away. There was nowhere to go; no one to care about any longer.

Besides, Llian knew that he would never be allowed to escape. Tensor had some secret purpose for him, something connected to the Mirror, though it had not been mentioned since the Conclave. And the potency that Tensor had used at the Conclave: that mind-blasting spell? Why had he, Llian, been the only one unaffected?

And what of his own obligations? Llian owed Mendark a great debt, for the Magister had sponsored his study at the College of the Histories for fifteen years. Llian had often wondered what Mendark would require of him in turn. But for all he knew, Mendark could have died back at the Conclave. He had no master now.

The day after their arrival in Siftah, while walking on the hillside, Llian cut through the edge of a grove of limes. Brushing against the leaves and blossoms, a whiff of lime perfume drifted by. The image of Karan was so strong that it was like being smashed awake with a bucket of icy water.

'Karan!' he screamed to the empty sky, but it gave nothing back. He tore the end off a branch, crushing twigs and leaves and tearing his hand on thorns. The perfume went up his nose, but it could not bring her back.

Llian was torn by futile regrets. Why had he made that useless attack on Tensor at the Conclave, attracting attention to himself? But even if he could have escaped, Thurkad and all the lands around were in Yggur's hands. Even if Karan had survived, there was nothing he could do to help her now. He had no power, no will. That was held captive by Tensor too.

So, the only thing left in his life was the Histories. For years Llian had been obsessed with the idea of making his own Great Tale. A tale could only be confirmed as a Great Tale by the unanimous acclamation of the master chroniclers and that was grudgingly bestowed. Only twenty-two Great Tales had ever been so acclaimed, the last many hundreds of years ago. If he were able to make a twenty-third, he would be the greatest teller of the age.

The *Tale of the Mirror* would be his life, henceforth. As for the Mirror itself, he did not care who had it, no owner seeming fitter than any other. So he continued, watching Tensor with alternate dread and delight for what he was going to do next, making notes for his tale and bringing his journal up to date.

Tensor often went out into the night alone. He seemed to have no need of rest and little requirement for sleep. At midnight on the second night of their stay in Siftah, he returned to the camp with glowing eyes and a grim smile.

'I believe I can do it!' he exclaimed. 'But we must have a secure refuge – it could take much time.'

There was a long silence. Do what? Llian wondered.

'I say we go back east,' said Malien. 'It has long been foretold that we would abandon the west. Shazmak will never be ours again. Let us return to Stassor and make a new life there. In truth, I am not sorry; the dreams we had in Shazmak were always hopeless.'

'Yes,' said Asper the healer, striking a melancholy chord on a multi-stringed instrument. 'Our time of choice has come. We will never have the strength to pursue our ancient goals. We must remake ourselves in the present, for the future, or cease to exist.'

Blase took up the melody on a kind of flute with many stops, twisting the tune into something so sad that tears formed in Llian's eyes. He sat watching Tensor. Nothing showed on *his* face. Tensor looked around the little group, waiting to hear them all out. Finally he spoke.

'If only we could. But we are not some barbarian tribe charging out of the mountains, to be great for fifty years, then slink back to their herds and forget.' He flung out his arms in entreaty. *We are Aachim!* Think on our noble lineage. Our greatness is not power or strength, or the ability to dominate through arms. If that was all it required there would be many, even on this miserable world. Our greatness is our civilisation, our culture, our art and architecture, our music and literature and philosophy. Even under the yoke of the Charon – our works ennobled *them*! And we who came to Santhenar were their equal – Tar Gaarn! Shazmak! We cannot think to become nothing.'

'*Alcifer!*' said Malien with barely veiled sarcasm. '*Hubris! The march of folly!* We overreached ourselves and now the edifice topples. We must begin again modestly, from the foundations.'

So the debate dragged on, and always accompanied by their doleful music. The Aachim discussed things constantly, with much presentation of arguments and alternatives, and much reference to their past, their honour, civilisation and culture, things that were indivisibly bound up with them. But Llian became frustrated, for at the end they seemed no further advanced, and whenever Tensor pressed them, they always let him have his way.

'We are just a fragment of the Aachim,' Asper added. 'Just a speck flung off the wheel. Our people remain in Aachan, many more than here. Even on Santh we have greater cities: Tirthrax and Stassor. Our only chance is to merge ourselves with the Aachim of the east.'

Tensor drew himself up. 'Our folk in Aachan are born to slavery. Their culture may be no more than a whisper on the winds of time. And the Aachim of the east have taken the decadent road, merging their ways with the ways of the people around them. Only we have the strength – *the will!*'

Malien grew angry. 'Decadent! It is not my people who are prisoners of the past. We have thrived. It is to us that you always turn in your troubles.'

'But you don't care about the past. Without that, what are we?'

'We care, but we do not let it cripple us. Once we were great and that was good. Is good, to know what we were, but it does not feed us now. You must cut your lives free of the past, as we have done in the east. We do not forget. Neither do we nurture useless passions.'

'I will not be swayed,' said Tensor. 'The threat of Rulke must be expunged from the Three Worlds. Then our renascence will follow. Or, if we must fail, *let us be glorious failures*.'

That gave Llian another insight into the character of the Aachim: it's how you fail that counts! There was a shocked silence. Someone moaned, and then, as if foreboding leapt from one to another like a forest fire through the treetops, they all sprang up.

'No!' said little Shalah. 'Malien, I am afraid. The doom that fell on Shazmak is following us.'

Her outburst was a shocking thing, for the youngest must show respect for the eldest, and Tensor was much the elder of any of them. He alone had been born in Aachan. But this time the other Aachim stood behind her.

'Even the child can see the folly of this scheme,' said Asper, though to Llian's eyes Shalah was an adult woman. 'We are all bewildered by the ruin of Shazmak. Until we know the truth, nothing else has any meaning.'

The fire flickered redly on their faces. Tensor looked more grim and more fell than ever. Llian grew more afraid. Whoever won this struggle, there was no good in it for him.

'Revenge has all the meaning I require! But I am listening. If you do not follow me, where will you go?'

'Where?' Llian echoed, his voice thin against the silence. 'You are but eight. You cannot hope to take Shazmak back.'

'We must have a refuge where there is no possibility of

being trapped,' said Tensor. 'It is said that you know the Histories better than anyone living, chronicler. Where would *you* go, if you had my need?'

'The mountains of Zile?'

'Yggur could march an army there from Orist in six weeks.'

'The Great Mountains, or the distant east?'

'Too remote,' said Tensor, 'or else we must pass through lands that Yggur holds, or warlords equally tyrannical. No! We must disappear as though gone from Santhenar. There is only one way. We go north.'

'But there is nothing north of Meldorin.'

'Is there not?'

'Only the deserts of Faranda and the Dry Sea.'

'There is Katazza, and to Katazza do we go,' Tensor said. 'A delicious irony, that we should make Katazza our own and turn it against our enemies.'

'Katazza?' said Hintis and his puzzlement was echoed by several of the younger Aachim. 'What is Katazza?'

A delicious irony, thought Llian, or an impossible folly? 'Who remembers Kandor now, after the ruin of his empire? The tale is almost forgotten.'

'You do, chronicler,' he said. 'Tell my people about this place. Of all those here, probably only you and I and Malien know it.'

'I know it,' said Asper, 'but I would hear how the chronicler tells it.'

Llian looked around for a place to stand. It would be hard telling to such a hostile audience, especially here. Wherever he stood, the flame and crackle would distract them. He settled on a rock shaped like an open book and sprang up.

'The *Tale of the Rifting* is incomplete and unsatisfactory,' Llian began, 'quite the least of all the Great Tales.' He had seen an opportunity though. He would build the tale around Kandor and his mysterious death, and perhaps glean something about that puzzle from their reactions.

'Get on with it!' Tensor sneered. 'We don't want the whole

tale, just what it says about Katazza. Just the facts, and none of your teller's *voice* either.'

'Nobody tells me how to present my tales.' Llian said coldly. 'However, I will give you a condensed version that even *you* can appreciate.

'The tale begins soon after Shuthdar was hunted to Santhenar. Kandor, the least of the Charon, quickly tired of the endless hunt. Carried away with his own ambition, he saw the opportunity to pursue it unfettered, while the rest of the world was preoccupied. Kandor recognised that the key to all Lauralin was the Sea of Perion. Who controlled it could master the east, the west and the north. And the north was rich. Katazza in its centre could grow great on trade and control all the sea.

'From Katazza, Kandor wrested control of the other islands and the sea around. He made the vast wealth of Faranda his, and he was secure in his power. There came a time, some three thousand years ago, when even Rulke felt threatened by him. But not even Rulke dared oppose him openly. Kandor boasted that his empire would last as long as the Sea of Perion itself.'

'It is a great mystery why the Charon warred against one of their own,' said Malien.

'Indeed,' said Tensor, reminiscing with his eyes closed. 'They are a most clannish species, very protective of each other.'

'Eventually Kandor became so powerful that he threatened the stability of the world, and an alliance was made against him. It was even said that Yalkara joined in the alliance to break him (though others said that Yalkara, the Mistress of Deceits, set him up as a foil to Rulke). The final struggle happened at the Foshorn, the peninsula adjacent to the northern opening of the Sea of Perion, across the water from here. Even then it was an unstable place, where earth tremblers occurred daily and hot rock flowed out of the ground from long fissures.

'On this day there came an enormous earth trembler that sent waves roaring over the land up and down the coast. Even far-off Thurkad was deluged. When the waters were still again, Kandor found that the very bed of the sea had risen out of the water, closing the opening to the ocean, and is still rising to this day.'

'How could Rulke have commanded such power?' Malien asked in wonder.

'No one can,' Tensor said acidly. 'He took credit for the natural movement of the earth and the credulous believed him.'

'Within a year the sea began to fall. In ten years the level fell seven spans and every port on the sea was ruined. Then came a drought, the worst that Faranda had ever seen. But the drought went on and on, and after thirty years they began to realise that it would never end. The very climate had changed. The forests became grasslands and the grasslands desert, and the deserts so parched that nothing could live there. The millions of Faranda starved, and countless more in all the lands around the Sea.

'Kandor tried to reverse the drought. He set vast teams of slaves to digging a canal at the Foshorn. They hewed and carried, and shattered the rock with engines made specially for the purpose. More than a hundred years they slaved, all the while harried by Rulke's guerillas, so that Kandor had to raise another army to protect the diggers. And eventually they succeeded; the greatest labour ever done on Santhenar.'

'And many of our people died to make it so,' growled Tensor.

'Very many,' Asper agreed sadly. 'Two of our cities were enslaved for the purpose.'

'Kandor even thought to take a toll from all the ships that passed to pay for it. At the western end he made a great set of iron gates – two portals of rustless steel, hung on steel pins that were socketed deep into rock. They could be raised or lowered like a sluice gate, by hauling on ropes slung around two great cable wheels, and a pair of waterwheels were made to do this task. They were magnificent gates and very terrible, but they were a folly, for the Dry Sea never looked like filling again. The canal needed to be a hundred times bigger, but that was a task beyond all the people of Santhenar put together.

'The canal became the Hornrace, a violent torrent bounded by cliffs, utterly impassable. Over time it grew deeper as the race cut down through living rock, but against the Sea of Perion it was no more than a thread running down a window-pane.

'In a hundred years the level of the sea had fallen by eighty spans. In five hundred years, by four hundred and fifty spans. Islands and ridges emerged and the beautiful Sea of Perion broke up into three briny lakes: western, eastern and the greater northern one, separated by saline ridges that rose out of the sea to become desert.

'A thousand years passed. The sea was half gone. The lands were barren, the forests dead. The plains grew no crops; only nomads dwelt there. Even the fabulous mines of Faranda failed, for there was no water to work the mills.

'Kandor was still lord of the Sea of Perion, but the sea was dust and salt – he was lord of nothing. All trade had failed, for there was no entering the sea from outside. The Hornrace became a vast waterfall and the former shores formed cliffs tall as mountains.

'Kandor tried every form of mancery and sorcery at his disposal, but no one had that kind of power. Nature reigned supreme – the sea fell faster than ever. Forced to abandon his empire at last, he marched south in fury and besieged the lands held by the Aachim, beginning the Clysm. But the wealth of his empire had been consumed by the folly of the Hornrace, its strength withered by constant warring. In the end he fell, the only Charon to die on Santhenar.'

Llian turned to Malien and Asper, who sat together. 'I often wonder how Kandor died. Did the Aachim kill him?'

'We did not,' said Tensor, 'though we would have liked to. His death is a mystery that will never be solved. Continue your tale, teller!'

'Now another thousand years have gone by,' Llian concluded. 'Most of the lakes are gone. The floor of the sea is a glittering plain of salt, many spans in thickness. Few dwell in Faranda now except in the tropical north. And incomparable Katazza lies forgotten, in the middle of the Sea of Perion.'

'There is a lesson in the tale,' said Malien, 'if we will hear it.'

'I hear it loud,' Tensor replied. 'The Charon can be beaten; it is the sign I was waiting for.' He nodded to Llian, the only thanks he was going to get.

'Well, do we go to Katazza?' asked Tensor, looking around at the Aachim. No one denied him.

How things turn out, thought Llian. Katazza was my dream and now I am on my way. I wonder what I will find there.

In the end Tensor was glad of their delay in Siftah, for on the third day little yellow-haired Xarah reappeared. Her sister greeted her with glad cries and shortly more Aachim followed her, survivors of the ruin of Shazmak, a small grim band of them, with word that others were on the way. This was a reward unhoped for – Tensor looked like a man who had just inherited an unexpected fortune. Then, as the survivors told their tale of what befell Shazmak after the Ghâshâd overran it and what happened to his people there, he went so still that even the other Aachim dared not speak, though more than one of them wondered how he could have ever preferred Faelamor's word to Karan's.

'Ah, it was terrible,' said Selial, the silver-haired woman who had led the Syndics at Karan's trial in Shazmak. 'They had power over us that we could not resist. They were like a destroying swarm.'

Llian recalled Selial well, for then she had given out an air of great dignity and impartial justice. But now she was shrunken and haggard; the flesh appeared to have withered under her skin.

'How did they get in?' Tensor grated. 'Was it Karan betrayed us?'

'Karan!' Her laugh was a derisive bark. 'Of course not! The Ghâshâd knew how to disable the Sentinels and that is not something that Karan could have taught them. It was the traitor Emmant, and my fault.' Her face twisted up like a prune, but she could not weep – her tear ducts were dried out from weeping.

'How?' asked Malien from behind the throng.

'Malien, it is good to see *you*. I am to blame. I allowed Emmant to speak to Faelamor and she seduced him to it. Ah, she is an evil one! Emmant betrayed us and the Ghâshâd came, like a nightmare out of memory.'

'What of Shazmak?' cried Asper. 'Can we recover it?'

'It is forever tainted,' said another of the new arrivals, a tall man called Basitor, long and lean in the jaw, a face as red as sunburn in which were set small butter-yellow eyes. 'The Tower of Trakst fell and burned. There was much other damage, though not, I think, irrecoverable. But who would go back to a place so stained with our blood?'

That gave Llian another insight into the character of the Aachim. Another species would have fought to regain their city and built it stronger and greater than ever.

'How many were lost?' asked Asper.

'Hundreds,' said Selial, shaking her head. 'Many hundreds! But more survived than you might think.'

'Then where are they when I need them?' Tensor cried.

'Gone east,' she said in a voice lowered almost to a whisper. 'They cursed you and swore that they would never follow you again.'

Tensor looked as though he had been struck in the face, but he recovered quickly. 'Cursed I am, and thrice cursed,' he roared, 'but I am more determined than ever that mine is the right course. Come with me,' he said to the two leaders of the Shazmak band. 'We must talk further.'

Basitor and Selial walked away with him into the night and did not return for many hours. What they said was never related, nor whether they blamed him for what had happened, but at length Selial returned alone. She closeted herself with Malien and Asper, who acted as counsellors within the group.

Later Basitor returned and, even later, Tensor. He looked to have aged thirty years of old humankind, so that instead of a strong and vigorous man of later middle age he appeared old and tired and desiccated. He stumbled back into the camp, eyes staring.

'Out of my way, treacherous Zain,' he said in a voice as parched as the bed of the Dry Sea. He swung his boot at Llian, who scurried backwards, almost falling into the fire.

Tensor's eyes met the Aachim, one by one, and not one of them could withstand his gaze. 'We are ruined!' he said. 'We will never rise again. Nothing remains but revenge, and *I will have it!*' Pinning Llian to the spot with his stare, he caught him by the hair and held him high in one hand.

'I swear by the blood and brains of this accursed Zain that I will not rest until every Ghâshâd is dead – every man, every woman, every child and every babe-in-womb.'

Llian was caught between terror and horror. He struggled fruitlessly, then Tensor twisted his fingers in Llian's hair, took his shins with the other hand and began to pull in opposite directions. Llian's scalp began to burn under the strain.

'Put the Zain down, Tensor,' said Malien softly.

Tensor shook with fury. 'Scalping is not fatal. Even were I to pull his face up over his head and cut it off, enough of him would remain to serve me at the end.'

Selial and Asper stepped up beside Malien, and then one by one the other Aachim did too, all save Basitor and Hintis.

'Release him,' Malien said. 'Where is your honour?'

'Dead in the bloody ruins of Shazmak,' Tensor raged. 'I will have my revenge. I will grind the Ghâshâd to glue; tear

Rulke limb from limb and organ from organ.' He went on in a litany of violence and cruelty so horrific that all but two of the Aachim drew away from him. Suddenly Tensor broke in self-disgust.

'Aah! Get away from me, revolting Zain,' he wailed, weeping tears like blood in the leaping firelight. Shuddering, he flung Llian at the fire, sending brands and coals scattering everywhere.

Llian lay on his back, feeling the coals burning him but unable to move, as if prisoner of Tensor's will once more. All the Aachim stared at him, then Asper realised what was the matter. He sprang and hauled Llian to safety, beating out a lick of flame at the tail of his shirt.

The Aachim were already dividing into two camps: a group led by Selial and Malien who saw that they had brought this ruin on themselves, and that pursuing Tensor's folly, whatever it was, could only result in the annihilation of the Aachim; and a smaller group led by Tensor, Basitor and Hintis who were so full of hate and fear and, in Tensor's case, a suicidal self-loathing, that nothing would cause them to deviate from their course.

Llian often found Tensor's eyes on him after that, seemingly measuring him, but Tensor never spoke to him. Hintis and Basitor watched him constantly, full of cold vacant rage. Llian made sure that he was never alone with either of them, knowing that they would cut him down for the least offence. Had he not known that Malien watched over him, and Asper, Llian would have died of terror.

Next day they woke to squally weather to find that the wind had swung around to the west. By mid-morning the tide was ebbing, racing down the estuary, leaving little swirls on the surface where the seabirds congregated. They crammed into their squat fishing boat, went out with the tide and set sail for the southernmost tip of Faranda. Tensor left one of the newcomers behind to tell the secret destination to any other

Aachim who might appear. The wind drove them along at a sail-cracking pace, so that in a day and a night they had crossed the water and were landed on the shore without incident.

The Foshorn it was called, a plate of land some fifty leagues north to south and thirty east to west, shaped like the bowl of a spoon. Its handle was an isthmus so rugged as to be impassable, running north-west and blending into the northward-broadening bulk of Faranda.

The western side of the Foshorn was just a ramp of sand standing against the great rolling swells coming up the sea from the western ocean. From the boat they could see that the land was barren – mostly salt marsh or saltbush, the few streams dammed near the sea by strings of sand to form shallow, sour lakes – though the crew told them that fish were plentiful.

They unloaded into a dinghy half a league offshore, for the bottom shoaled so gradually that the fishing boat could come no closer. Shortly the dinghy ran aground on a sandbank, forcing them to wade the last few hundred paces. Llian slipped getting over the side, plunged head first into the water and might have drowned, held down by the weight of his pack, had not Tensor hauled him upright.

'You don't escape me that easily, chronicler,' he said with a hideous travesty of a smile.

They landed on the tip of the Foshorn and struck out into the sandhills at such a pace that before the dinghy had returned to the fishing boat for the last time (for they were now twenty-two) the leaders had crested the first hill heading east. Inland the hills gave way to a flat land of shallow, stony soils – arid country with scattered scrubby trees and tangles of thorn bushes.

The mountains were rugged the way they wanted to go, forcing them to divert south-east along the coastal plain. One whole day they marched through a dead forest, the silver trunks standing up like poles. Beyond that, on the morning of the third day, they saw one of the greatest sights on Santhenar.

The southern tip of the Foshorn was separated from the the north-eastern peninsula of Lauralin by the impassable chasm of the Hornrace. Down this narrow, cliff-bounded abyss, not a league across but five hundred spans to the water, the waters of the Sea of Thurkad and the Sea of Qwale roared. At its eastern end the Hornrace plunged over a precipice, another thousand spans and more, thundering endlessly down to the bottom of the Dry Sea, the greatest torrent and the most magnificent waterfall in all the Three Worlds. At the bottom the flood made a long lake that grew more saline the further east it went, eventually failing into crusts and bergs of salt.

They heard the Hornrace long before they arrived, a dull rumble that grew to a roar, then a smashing rage that shook the native rock underfoot. Closer still, the noise was a wild, animal thing so loud that even shouted conversation was impossible.

The black rock was drenched, every surface dank and dripping, coated with mosses that cushioned their timorous steps. Underneath them the rock shook like the cage of a great beast. The mist made ground and sky the same. They stepped up to the very brink, reaching it suddenly, and Llian's head spun. He swayed dangerously on the edge until Tensor dragged him back.

'I won't let you do it,' he screamed in Llian's ear. 'Look after him well, Basitor.'

Basitor squeezed Llian's elbow painfully while he looked down. Llian could feel the Aachim's arm shaking, barely resisting the urge to hurl him over. Being Zain, he was used to prejudice and discrimination, but this violent hatred was impossible to come to terms with.

They passed the easternmost of the Iron Gates, long broken, only the hinge pins, great cylinders of corroded steel three or four spans in diameter, now remaining. They continued on, walking beside the race for several hours, never speaking since nothing could be heard over the roar of the water. Eventually the Aachim stopped by two gigantic black pillars that stood guard over the Hornrace. They were carved with Aachim designs but badly fretted by weather and time. Mist swirled up from the falls and the sun shone through it, making the faintest rainbow that seemed to link Faranda and the continent of Lauralin. When the mist cleared momentarily they saw two more pillars, tiny as upright pencils, on the other side.

'The Rainbow Bridge once stood here,' said Selial to Llian, who was nearby. 'The greatest engineers and artists of our race laboured for a hundred years to make it. It was more beautiful than any rainbow you see today.'

'There must be a tale to its making,' said Llian, fascinated. How parochial the Histories that he had learned in Chanthed now seemed. How much more there was to learn out in the real world, and how much more to tell.

'There is a tale,' said Selial, 'and perhaps I will tell it one day. The *Tale of the Rainbow Bridge* ought to be one of the Great Tales of this world. The bridge was the most perfect structure we ever built, though perhaps my bias shows. My great-grandmother was the engineer who designed it.'

'Already I burn to hear it,' said Llian.

'Certainly our greatest achievement on Santhenar,' said Malien, 'but it is long gone, crushed into the abyss.'

'What happened to it?'

'The Friend of the Zain, your very own Rulke who gave the Gift, forced the earth into motion here so as to cast it down,' growled Tensor, walking past.

'Do not forget that he betrayed us Zain as well,' cried Llian, 'and we have suffered for it as much as the Aachim ever did.'

Tensor opened and closed his extraordinarily long fingers as if he had a throat in mind. 'Let us away,' he said. 'The Rainbow Bridge was once our greatest inspiration, but now it only reminds me of what we have lost.'

They pressed on, though with many a backward glance, until after dark. There had been no evidence of pursuit since well before they had reached Siftah, but Tensor relaxed not at all. They kept watches every night and all but Llian took part in them, though he generally stood through the watch with one or other of the Aachim who were friendly to him. He was afraid of the dark now.

They went by the falls of the Hornrace, a torrent so prodigious that not even Llian's teller's skills could find words to describe it. On the eastern side of the range they emerged into lands that were in the rain shadow and barren – nothing grew there but spiny grey scrub in the gullies. They crossed a narrow plain, only a few leagues in width, cut at the edge by steep gullies that amalgamated into mighty canyons. Then suddenly in the mid-afternoon they stood on the edge of a cliff that dropped away sharply, in a series of steps, all the way to the bottom of the Dry Sea. Tensor was on the edge of the vast chasm, staring.

'This is a sight that not even in my present mood can I pass by unmoved,' he said. 'We will camp here, if we can find water, and watch the sun rise in the morning over the Sea of Perion. I have not seen it since the sea dried up.' His eyes were moist. 'Once it was the most beautiful place in all Santhenar. Look at it now.'

Llian gazed down with awe and unease. The Sea of Perion came into many tales but none had prepared him for the reality of it – its vastness, aridity and desolation. He was afraid to go down onto the salt plains, even in the cool of winter. His family still lived in Jepperand, beyond the other side of the Dry Sea. He remembered well the struggles of the Zain to wrest a living from that barren land, against the withering salt-laden winds howling ceaselessly up from the sea floor. That anyone would be so foolish as to try and cross it, to take refuge in the very centre of it, was beyond his understanding. He said so to Tensor, for Tensor's rage had retreated in the past few days. The Aachim's mood was so changeable that Llian never knew what to expect from him.

Tensor inspected him in equal incomprehension. 'But we are desperate, chronicler. We must have a safe refuge where we can work without fear. A place that will stand for a month, a year, even a hundred years if it takes that long. We do not have the numbers to defend, so nature must defend for us. The crossing will be hard, no doubt of it, and the coming back harder still – if there is a coming back! But *we must, therefore we will*.'

They stood long there. The still air was very clear, though the far distance was obscured by haze. The floor of the sea looked featureless, except to the north-east, where a blocky ridge made a brown smear against the salt whiteness. One of the Aachim pointed to it and Tensor nodded.

'It was marked on the charts we kept in Shazmak, but it is many years since I studied them. I recollect that it runs north for forty leagues or so. There will be seeps. Somewhere there we'll find water.'

'And what then?' Llian asked. 'How much further?'

'I cannot say. Certainly more than a hundred leagues. Perhaps as much as a hundred and fifty, and we'll need water twice more on the way.'

There was none here, but half a league away a creek ran into a gully that plunged steeply down, becoming one of the innumerable chasms gouged into the edge of the plateau, and it was still trickling. They moved camp to it and made preparations for the journey. Food they had in plenty, bought from the fishing village, dried or smoked and neatly packed. They filled their huge waterskins and tied them to their packs, so heavy that Llian could not even lift one (his was much smaller). All was ready. It was still light. They were at leisure for the first time since Siftah.

Llian sat on a boulder near the cliff edge, though not so close that it would arouse his fear of heights and precipices, writing in his journal while the light was still good. To his surprise, for she had appeared to be avoiding him for more than a week, Malien sat down beside him.

'What do you think about this venture, chronicler?'

'If I had some idea of what Tensor intends at the end of it I might be better pleased.'

'I doubt that you would. If you knew, I think you would walk to the cliff edge and hurl yourself over it.'

'That's not one of my temptations.'

'Nor mine at this stage of my life, but when Tensor stood there earlier I fleetingly considered ending us both. He will bring ruin to your people as well as mine. Alas, I could not do it.'

As she leaned back, the setting sun flamed in her red hair. Llian almost choked with anguish.

'What is the matter, chronicler?'

'The sun in your hair – you could have been Karan, for a moment.'

She sat forward again and it was gone. 'Here,' she said, wiping his eyes with a piece of blue linen. 'Hold, what is this?' She took his face in her hands and swivelled it round. 'Open your eyes!'

Llian blinked into the sun. 'Ahh!' She released her breath in a sigh. 'It *is* as I thought when you mentioned the dream.'

'What?' he cried in alarm.

'The brown of your eyes grows speckled with white, and white freckles are coming on your hands, here and here and here. You *do* have the Gift of Rulke – the stigmata are developing.'

He blanched. 'We Zain call it the Curse of Rulke, so many of us having died because of it.'

'And you will be one of them if those who came out of the ruin of Shazmak find out. That would be cruel and unjust, but who could blame them?'

'That treachery by the Zain, if indeed it was treachery and not just an ill-judged alliance, was long ago. Are we to be persecuted until the end of time?'

'I would say yes, chronicler! We forgave the Zain, but you

and Karan came to Shazmak with the Mirror, and Shazmak fell.'

'That was not my doing.'

'But you are bound up with it! And now you display the stigmata of Rulke, our ancient enemy. The Ghâshâd were also the servants of Rulke in ancient times. How can we not think that their reappearance, and your marks, forecast his return? How can we not worry what Tensor plans to use you for?'

'Better that you put your time into ensuring that the Nightland is secure than harassing me! I was tested carefully before I left Jepperand,' said Llian. 'We all are!'

'You said that when Tensor broke the Conclave you felt pain and blindness, but it suddenly disappeared. The Gift must have been latent in you and the potency has released it. Now you are in the greatest peril of your life.'

The journal slid off his lap onto the dirt. The pages turned idly in the breeze. Llian did not notice. He was staring at her. 'Help me! I will run away tonight. Can you . . .'

'You would be found within hours and then it would be clear why you had run. Let me think.'

She examined him again. 'The stigmata are faint. Your tale of the dream made me look for them, for that is another of the signs, dream sharing. I do not think anyone would notice your eyes unless they were very near, and then only in the daytime. Keep your hat pulled down. I will stay by you so no one else will need to come close.'

'What about Tensor?'

'Perhaps that is why he brought you. If so, he will say nothing. Be careful with him. Now, down on the salt you will need eye shields anyway, else you will go blind, and that should be enough until we reach Katazza. Once there . . . Well, that is a long way away. As for the spots, I will make a stain for them.'

Llian took her hand, pathetic in his gratitude. She eased out of his grasp. 'If anyone is watching, they will wonder,' she said. 'Do nothing to arouse curiosity.'

'Why are you helping me against your own?'

She inspected him minutely, then the smile that he had seen some time ago was back. 'Because against the odds I like you, chronicler. Because we of the line of Elienor are disposed to the championing of eccentric causes. And most of all because my kinswoman Karan put her mark on you, as surely as these other stigmata, and that obliges me to protect the defenceless.'

She walked away. Llian, astounded and confused, sat by the cliff until it grew dark, not even noticing the extraordinary hues of the fading sun behind him. Only when it was fully dark did he rouse himself, pick up his journal and stumble back to the fire for dinner.

At dawn the next day Malien came to his tent with a small jar that smelled like lanolin.

'Rub a tiny amount of this on your face and hands each morning. It has a stain in it that will conceal the spots, and preserve your youthful complexion too, if that is of concern to you. Keep your hat down; do nothing to arouse attention.' She tossed the jar at him and was gone.

28

STALACTITE

Idlis skidded to a stop. 'Light,' he rasped urgently.

The woman behind him unshuttered her lantern and pressed forward to the edge of the drop, a waterfall in ancient, wetter times. They were oblivious to the revealed magnificence of the cavern, a natural cathedral. It was quite a way down.

'I heard a splash,' said Idlis. 'Karan may still be alive. Rope, quickly!'

The Ghâshâd clustered on the narrow ledge, shining their lamps down. Reflections danced in a large pool immediately below. Someone tossed a rope over. Idlis threw off his cloak, wrapped rags around his hands and slid down the rope. He went right off the end, bobbed up again then began to swim around in circles, looking down through the water.

'More light!' he shouted. 'Come down!' and several others splashed into the pool.

'I have her,' Jark-un cried, breaking the surface with Karan's limp body in his arms.

They carried her out of the water onto a smooth mound like a curved table, laid her on her side and worked her arms and legs to expel the water. Karan's chest rose; a dribble of pink water ran out of her mouth.

Idlis felt her head. The back of her skull was swollen;

there was a small cut in her hair, though scarcely bleeding. He ran his healer's fingers along her bones, each in turn; he felt her belly; he listened to her chest; he put the lantern to her eyes.

'She lives!' Idlis said. 'She is not badly harmed. The shock must have stopped the breathing, for there is no water in her.' He opened her mouth to look inside. 'Bit her tongue – not serious! Dry her, wrap her up and put water on to boil.'

All this was done with mechanical efficiency. Soon Karan was wrapped in a cloak while the Ghâshâd stood around, staring down at her, waiting for her to come back to consciousness.

Karan gave a little moan and opened her eyes. Then she slammed them shut again, fighting back the panic. She was lying on a slab like a sacrificial altar, with at least six Ghâshâd towering over her. She tensed, thinking to leap up and run, which made her head ache.

'There is no escaping us, Karan of Bannador,' said a voice that she did not recognise, a dry rustling like a snake sliding through a bucket of beetles. 'Submit willingly and you will not be harmed. Indeed, the master will reward you. But listen to this warning: *we will force you if we must!*'

'What do you want?' she croaked. Her throat hurt too.

'What do you think?' Idlis replied.

Karan closed her eyes again. What could they possibly want her for? Why come all this way after her?

'I suppose you want to use my talent,' she whispered.

'As before, so again.'

'Before?'

'It was your link that our perfect master caught and used to wake us to our true identity,' replied a gaunt woman.

Suddenly the long-suppressed memories exploded back, of that awful night near the town of Narne; the night she had sent Llian away just before the Whelm had come for her. She remembered the link to Maigraith and, inexplicably, it being

411

snatched off into dimensions that she could not even imagine.

'You want to use me to contact *Rulke*!' Struck cold with horror, she remembered that night perfectly, *now*. That was why she had closed off her talent on the way to Sith, suppressing the horrible memories at the same time.

What had come from that night was worse than anything she had suffered. Rulke had used her link to wake the Whelm, to remind them of the memory that had been stripped from them thirty generations ago: that they were Ghâshâd, his ancient servants indentured after the fall of the Zain.

So the fall of Shazmak, and the death of all those who had dwelt there, her Aachim friends had come about because of her! *My fault! My fault!* rang through her head like mortuary bells, each toll the death of someone she had known and cared for. How much more was to come?

Never again! she thought. I will *never* help you again, *willing or unwilling*. She opened her eyes momentarily, looking up at the high ceiling. A huge mounded mass of stalactites, like a cow's udder the size of a cottage, hung there. The Ghâshâd were still staring down at her. Karan shuddered. She must do everything in her power to prevent it.

There was a rubbery touch on her throat. Her eyes shot open. An old woman was bending over her, a beanpole even leaner than Idlis, though she looked to have kind eyes. 'Let us begin,' she said. 'You will make the link that you made before.'

'I can't! Maigraith, if she lives, must be far away. My link only works when I am close.'

The Ghâshâd went into a huddle, but Karan could hear snatches of their speech. 'Perhaps she is lying,' said the soft-eyed woman.

'Perhaps, Quissan,' Idlis said, 'though it is the same with our own mind-speech. If it works at all, it is only at close distances.'

'And the woman Maigraith was very special,' said scrawny Thassel. 'It was no ordinary link.'

They came back. 'Link to the old man,' said Idlis.

412

'I cannot – Shand is not sensitive. Anyway, I closed off my talent after Narne and it no longer comes when I want it to.'

This prompted another discussion, then the woman called out. 'Rebban, come forward.'

A young man, utterly blanched of skin and hair, and with pink eyes, stepped into Karan's line of sight. 'Rebban is our most powerful sensitive,' said Quissan. 'He will help you to find your talent again.'

Karan looked into the eyes of the albino. The thought of linking with him was horrible. She struggled but they held her down, wrists and ankles, and bound her to the rock. Rebban placed his colourless hands on Karan's forehead and closed his eyes. She tossed her head from side to side, trying to rid herself of the hands, but they held her head too.

She began to feel a subtle pressure on the inside of her skull, a build-up of warmth in her ears and her sinuses. She concentrated on nothing, doing everything she could to avoid the sequence that had led to the birth of the link. She took comfort from the thought that linking hardly ever worked anyway. Then Karan felt something insinuate itself into her mind, a tiny thought, the progenitor of a link. But it was alien, not something that she could ever have had herself. Panicking, she clamped right down, the thought disappeared and the hands withdrew as well.

Karan opened her eyes. The albino had gone even paler; sweat was dripping off his face. 'She is strong,' he said. 'We will have to use the *square*.'

The six of them stood around her. Idlis took some objects out of a bag, weighed them in his hand, trimmed small pieces off two that were larger than the others and handed them around, one piece to each. They chewed, swallowed, then all linked hands.

Karan knew that this was the only opportunity she would get. She tried to roll over but found that she was bound fast. The sick chuckling she had felt earlier began again, itching like an inflammation of the lining of her brain.

413

'Get away!' she screamed. 'Get out of my head!' but they kept on.

Now she felt a horrible rasping prickle, like a wire brush being drawn up and down her backbone. It began to hurt, just little pinpricks of pain at first, but they grew sharper every minute. She tried to close down all her senses, to make herself a dull log of flesh as she had been after the Conclave, but the pain and the irritation constantly reminded her of who she was.

'The link!' Quissan whispered.

'No!' Karan screamed, spitting at her face.

The link! Make the link! came a whisper in her mind. *See, we are speaking into your mind. Speak back to us; make the link.*

'No!' Karan screeched, writhing on the slab. 'I never will.'

But even as she spoke those link-thoughts were there again, and images of the master too, his majesty and his purpose, his pain and torment from a thousand years in the Nightland. *Make the link! Set the master free!*

Karan could feel her resolve bending, her mind weakening under the strain of six opposing minds as a beam bends under a load. *Free, free, free!* The pressure was intolerable.

What could she do to stop it? She would even have plunged herself back into madness if she could have, but that refuge was beyond her. She would have struck back with her mind as Maigraith had done when she was so harassed, but Karan had no ability to use the Secret Art.

Make the link! Make the link! Make the link! Make the link!

Karan gasped; the beginnings of the link grew stronger. She was being forced in spite of all her efforts. *I won't!* she thought. I won't! How can I use this power against them? What can I do? At least they can't know what I'm thinking. No one can read minds.

She writhed, she groaned, she flung her head from side to side; she struggled frantically against the bonds on wrists and ankles, trying to give the impression of utter panic before finally giving in. As she did so the Ghâshâd pressed harder, forcing the link on her till her mind crawled with it. All of a sudden Karan went still; she gave a great shudder, turned her head to one side and let her tongue flop out of her mouth, a gob of saliva run down her cheek.

The pressure eased, then Karan hurled it all back at them, sending their compulsion back into their own minds, using the strange talent that she had developed to send the dream to Llian the night before her trial in Shazmak.

Jark-un cried out. Idlis threw up his hands in shock. Rebban the albino reeled and staggered off, cross-legged, to crash into the water. Two others ran down and fished him out. The pressure vanished, then Karan exerted all of her remaining strength in a sending to Shand. Linking only worked with a very special kind of person, but she could make a sending to almost anyone if the need was dire enough.

Shand, help me! she cried, opened her eyes and sent everything she saw to him, just one instantaneous image – the cavern with its udder of hanging stalactites, the stunned Ghâshâd and the thousand glittering reflections. Then she closed it off again and lay there panting.

She must have shocked her opponents more than she had realised, for they went into the square again, trying to bring Rebban out of his brainstorm. Karan felt groggy: aftersickness from what she had done. After Rebban was restored to them and laid out on the floor to recover, they prepared food and drink, and fed her too, then some slept while the others kept guard. Karan had no idea what time it was, but surely many hours had passed since her capture. It could not be long till daylight. Eventually she dozed, woke to see that the guards had changed, and dozed again.

Later she was woken and fed once more, gruel and tea with a leafy taste. All the Ghâshâd were up now, even Rebban, talking in a circle, but she could no longer hear what they were talking about. Then someone raised their voice, perhaps deliberately.

'I say we use the hrux on her,' said Quissan. 'Force her!'

'No,' said Idlis. 'Hrux can be deadly to humans, especially blendings. There is so little of her that it would be hard to calculate the dose.'

'What does it matter if she lives or dies? I would willingly give up *my* life if it would help free the master.'

'Ah!' said stocky Jark-un, 'but dead she is no use to us at all. Alive, she may serve the master for another fifty years. This talent of hers is a precious one.'

'But first we must free him!' said the woman. 'Unless he is freed we will all go to our graves with our duty undone. It is worth the risk.'

'That is so,' said Idlis. 'We must not lose sight of our greater purpose. Loose her bonds.'

Karan's arms and legs were untied and Idlis picked her up in his arms, weighing her. He frowned, stripped her naked and, to Karan's mortification, pinched the flesh of her thighs, her belly, her breasts, her arms.

'What are you doing?' she cried, for he had the look of a butcher weighing how much meat he would get off a carcass.

Idlis ran his fingers up her forearm, squeezing in to the bone. He did the same for her legs, then flipped her over, squeezing her buttocks and probing her back from top to bottom, though quite as clinically as a butcher.

'I am gauging the fat, the flesh and the bones,' he said, taking her wrist again. 'Such slender bones you have! How do they hold you up?'

'Well enough!' she snapped.

Idlis turned away to his healer's satchel, then turned back. 'You are not pregnant by any chance?'

Karan snorted. 'Does it harm babies?'

'The contrary,' Idlis said ambiguously. 'Dress her and tie her,' he spoke over his shoulder. 'I am going to give you a small portion of hrux,' he said to Karan, 'which we use in the square to link mind to mind, to strengthen our will. I hope that it will not kill you. Its effects on your kind can be . . . unpredictable.'

'I was mad only a month ago,' Karan said, hoping to put him off. 'Likely it will send me back to that state.'

'Perhaps, though that will not prevent us from using you. Indeed, it may make the link stronger.'

'Oh!' said Karan.

'You could also develop a craving for it. That is a sad thing, hrux addiction. Indeed, that too could be a useful thing for us. Of course you never need go without it *so long as you serve us faithfully*.'

Karan said nothing at all. She felt quite lost and hopeless. 'Open your mouth,' Idlis said.

'No!'

He tried to force her but she bit his fingers. Idlis yelped. 'Hold her!' he said, then one of the Ghâshâd seized her head and held it. 'Open her mouth.'

'*No!*' Karan screamed, but there was nothing she could do to resist.

Shand, dozing in his chair, had been jerked awake by Karan's earlier cry, *Shand, help me!* and a vivid image of a cavern illuminated by lanterns. He leapt up and put his head out the door, expecting to see a dozen people running after that desperate call, but the hall was empty and the inn quiet.

It was just getting light. Already the streets were crowded, but the people had the unhurried look of those going about their daily routine. Only then did he realise that the cry and the image had been a sending to him. Shand tried to recapture the image, already fading. He saw the cave, the light reflected from thousands of facets, a mound of multi-coloured stalactites and spires and what looked like an out-of-focus group of people staring down. Then it vanished.

Someone had captured Karan, but who? If it was a response to that message from Yggur, it had been a remarkably swift one. Too quick, even if the mayor had returned.

Shand went downstairs, where the proprietor was already in the kitchen, chalking the day's menu on a board.

'Caves?' the man said, rubbing the scar on his jawbone. 'There are caves everywhere around here. I could name a dozen.'

'Which is the nearest?' Shand asked casually.

The answer was an oblique one. 'The best is a little step from here, near the bottom of the first cliff and along a league or two. The kitchen will pack you a hamper if you want to go in there. Dangerous caves though – we've lost quite a few picnic baskets that way. I'll have to charge you a deposit, in case you never come out again.'

For an instant Shand thought that he was joking, but the proprietor did not look a humorous man. 'I had in mind something a little closer,' Shand said. 'Are there any nearer – say in the area between here and the markets?'

'No, though down in the park at the back there are. It's said they are pretty enough. Myself, I've never been to look.'

'Any others close?'

'Not within an hour or two, but –'

'They'll do,' said Shand. 'Can you put me up a satchel of food and a lantern? Don't worry about the basket,' he added as the man's mouth opened.

'I was going to say you can hire a lantern there,' said the innkeeper. 'How soon would you like your lunch?'

'Ten minutes,' said Shand, heading back up the stairs, two at a time. He stopped at the markets on the way to purchase a few other items including rope and a hammer with a long handle and a heavy head, the sort used for breaking rocks, in case he had to smash his way in.

At the park he knocked on the door of the little hut inside the gate. The youth came out, rubbing his eyes.

'This way to the caves?' Shand asked, easing the pack on his back. The hammer was extremely heavy.

'That is correct, sir,' the young man said. 'Would you like to hire a lantern?'

'Two,' said Shand, 'and an extra skin of oil. Do you get many visitors?'

'Not at this time of year, though the caves are very popular in the summer. There was a young woman in yesterday, quite late. Stole my lantern,' he said sadly. 'I have to account for the loss. And she seemed such a nice person, too.'

'She the only one?'

'Another party came soon after, six of them, but they didn't hire any lanterns.' He described them.

Whelm! thought Shand. What are they doing here?

He handed over the deposit, took his lanterns and headed down the valley. At the cave mouth he checked the ground carefully but there were too many prints in the soft soil to be sure of anything. He went inside, picking his way along with the shutter of his lantern almost completely closed, knowing that he would see their lights a long way away and, equally, they would notice instantly if his tunnel was suddenly lit up.

Being obliged to make such cautious progress, hours went by without him getting very far. Several times he took wrong turnings and had to go back, for there were many places where there were no tracks at all and he had to guess which turning they had taken. At one place a great mass of the roof had fallen in and on the rock beside it were carved the names of three people, two women and a child, who must have been crushed in the rockfall. There were rude carvings of flowers and a pathetic few lines of verse. Shand bowed his head and passed by.

Eventually his caution was rewarded by a faint gleam ahead of him, a lighted oval. Shand shuttered his lamp and crept forward, finding himself on a ledge where the tunnel opened into a cavern. Below was a big pool. On the other side he saw six figures standing around a curved outcrop of limestone.

Karan lay on the slab. From here he could not see if she was alive or dead. He scanned the cavern. It was a glorious sight, had he had the time to appreciate it, the lights glittering off millions of tiny facets. The floor surrounding the pool

419

was littered with shattered rock fallen from the roof. Beyond he saw another cave where presumably the overflow from the pool went. Looking up, the roof was clustered with stalactites including a huge downward-hanging mound with the form of a cow's udder. He remembered seeing that in Karan's sending.

Shand turned his gaze back to the scene below. One of the cloaked figures went down to the water. Shand felt a chill run down his back. The jerky gait was characteristic – Whelm or Ghâshâd. No way to tell the difference.

Surely they could have come so far for only one reason – Karan! How could he combat them? Two would be his match; maybe even one, he thought ruefully. Once that had not been the case, a long time ago, however he could not remember when he had last used a weapon in practice.

Shand settled down with his back to the wall and his head in the shadow. There was not much to see – the six went into a huddle, then four settled down to sleep on the floor while the other two stood guard. They were very vigilant guards. To his relief Karan moved once or twice.

Shand ran through his options. They weren't many. He could take them on by himself, which had an inevitable ending, or he could fetch the constables. However, Shand's intuition told him that they were already looking for Karan; that the message from Yggur had been about her.

He scanned the ceiling again and eventually the udder formation caught his attention. He knew that stalactites were easily broken off. On this side he saw a fissure in the rock, extending part-way around the base of the formation. Pity he couldn't prise off a chunk. That would give them a shock and maybe make an opportunity for him.

Why not? Shand gauged the climb. Part of the cave above his ledge was in shadow; it was worth the attempt. He took off boots and socks, tied one end of his rope to a nearby stalagmite, made sure that the hammer was secure in his pack and began.

It was not a hard climb, for a recent fall had left crevices aplenty and there was an abundance of spiny protrusions to hang on to. But with his awkward load Shand made hard work of it, and he was afraid of moving where he could be seen by the unwearying sentries. Afraid, too, of breaking the tip off one of his handholds.

At the top Shand looked down to see that the cloaked figures were gathered round Karan once more. What did they want her for? He had a most unpleasant suspicion.

Shand inspected the fissure between the hanging mass and the roof. It was narrow, just wide enough to get the handle of his hammer in. Further on it ran round the mound and disappeared. Back the other way, it ended just in front of him.

Shand tied his rope, hooked the pack over a stalagmite and took out the hammer. Climbing up, he wedged himself in between two stalactites, inserted the handle in the crack and heaved.

Nothing happened – he might as well have pushed the side of a hill. He pushed harder. Still no result. He moved the handle along, progressively moving and jerking until blisters began to form on his palms and his shoulder muscles burned with the strain. It was no use.

Shand slid the handle back out and hung on a pinnacle of rock, panting. When he got his breath back he looked down. Five of the figures were still standing around Karan, while the sixth was rummaging in a satchel further down near the water.

He climbed higher, perched precariously on a ledge, and saw that the fissure began again on the other side of the knob. If he struck just there he might be able to crack off a large piece, enough to frighten them. Just then he heard Karan say 'No!'

Someone was holding her head, someone else approached her. Karan screamed, loud and terrified. Shand squinted down, cursing his old eyes. He had to do something to distract them. He put his foot on a slender stalagmite and pushed.

It broke with a snap like a carrot and plunged into the water.

They whirled, staring at the spot and the widening ripples. Lanterns were held high, angular faces searched the cavern, but they could not see him high up among the spires of stone. A hasty conference was held on the water's edge.

Whatever chance he had, this was it. Shand took up the heavy hammer, made a few practice swings, then swung it with all his might at the place where the fissure ended. The impact jarred his arm right up to the shoulder. It made a shockingly loud noise and a few chips fell, but that was all. The sound echoed back and forth around the cavern.

The Ghâshâd stood to attention. They knew that someone was up there, but they could not see him. The echoes died away, then Shand heard a series of little tap-tapping cracks. The fissure seemed a little wider than before.

As he watched, the fissure propagated around the knob of rock, the knob fell out like a plug, the stalactites moved and with an incredibly loud noise the whole great udder-shaped mass of rock fell.

Shand watched in horror as it plunged down into the pool with a smack that almost burst his eardrums. Water exploded out in all directions, a vast wave that washed over the staring Whelm and the stone on which Karan lay. A furious wind buffeted Shand. The surge rushed halfway up the walls, stinging drops struck his face, then the last of the lanterns went out and he was left, perched high among the stalactites, in utter darkness.

29

OBSESSIONS

M aigraith woke in Yggur's bed, reaching out to her lover,
the first man who had ever held her in his arms. The
bed was empty. Yggur had fled.

She was disappointed, though not surprised, knowing how
obsessed he was by his work and the prospect of catching
Mendark. After bathing and eating breakfast from the tray
that Dolodha provided, she went down to check on Faelamor.

Faelamor was as weak as ever, though still capable of
spite. 'Why do you not wear your glasses?' she said. 'Do you
want everyone to see your shameful eyes?'

'I'm proud of my eyes,' Maigraith said with a smile and a
toss of her head. Nothing could dash her good humour today.

'What are you up to?' cried Faelamor in helpless rage.

'I have taken a *lover*!' Maigraith felt a frisson of joy as she
said the words, that only a day ago would have been too
embarrassing to speak.

Faelamor seemed to sink right into the bed. 'Yg-Yg –' she
choked.

'Yes, Yggur!' Maigraith exclaimed gaily, taking pleasure in
defiance. 'My lover, my lover, my lover!' She danced out of
the room without a backward glance.

Behind her, Faelamor thrashed weakly. Her legs twitched,
the muscles of her neck corded, she foamed at the mouth

like a crushed snail. She clenched her fists so hard that her nails broke the skin of her palms.

'No ... you're ... not!' she ground out, sticky bubbles oozing out her mouth to hang off her chin like a goatee. Slowly, agonisingly, Faelamor forced herself to a sitting position. 'You're mine! When ... I'm finished –' she hung on the side of the bed, gasping, 'he'll never ... dare look at you ... again.'

Maigraith was a vital part of the great plan that she had been working toward for centuries – to smash the Forbidding and take the Faellem home to Tallallame. Their world needed them and nothing could stand in her way, certainly not this upstart, Yggur. She steadied herself, taking deep, panting breaths, calming herself while she sought those powers lost at the Conclave. Not lost, she thought despairingly, just mislaid – hidden from me. Where are they? I must have them back. Tallallame weeps for us. I am the Faellem. I must! *I will!* Even if I tear open my bowels in trying.

She forced; the pain was such that she might well have burst all her organs, but she did not care. Faelamor drew strength out of some forgotten reserve and ever so slowly an image of Maigraith began to form in her mind. She concentrated on it, making it so perfect that no one could have told the difference between image and reality. Then she brought forth the image, painting it on the air of the room.

The illusion rotated slowly while she adjusted a detail here and there – the curve of an ear, the gloss of the hair, the slope of a shoulder. Before it was nearly done she began to feel faint – the first stirrings of aftersickness, on top of all her other ills. Faelamor forced it away and completed her work.

Now she made certain small changes to the Maigraith likeness. She broadened the nose a trifle, deepened the eyes and made them glow like living fires. The skin she darkened a shade or two. As she retouched the hair from chestnut brown to glossy blue-black, more Charon-like, the aftersickness began to return, far stronger than before. Faelamor knew that she lacked the strength to resist it much longer.

Where was Maigraith now? Scrying her out with her failing powers, she found her, climbing the steps up to the battlements of the fortress.

'Go!' she gasped to the altered Maigraith illusion. 'Do your work and do it well – there will never be another chance.'

The illusion vanished. Faelamor directed it with her mind, along the corridors and up the stairs, a labour as great as carrying Maigraith on her shoulders all that way. Only when she was sure the illusion was in place did she let go. Falling to the floor, she lay unmoving for the whole of the day.

Maigraith went to Yggur's war room, but he was not there. No one knew where he was and she spent hours searching the fortress without success. Perhaps he was up on the battlements. As she climbed the stairs looking for him, Maigraith felt a shroud of unease settle over her, a queer feeling that blurred her eye and left her dizzy for a moment. A feeling that what they had made together last night could not last. Shrugging it away, she continued, though with a heavier step than before.

She found Yggur on the wall that encircled the old fortress. Maigraith stood watching his agitated pacing – the jerky motion of his limbs, the bad leg dragging, the downcast gaze. He turned at the far end and headed back.

Not until he was a few steps away did he look up. Seeing her outline in the guardhouse, he froze in mid-step. His face choked up.

'Oh Maigraith!' he began. 'I am a fool. Last night I thought –'

She sprang out of the shadows into the bright sunlight, holding out her arms. Faelamor's illusion shifted uneasily, then welded itself tight. Her eyes flared like blazing beacons.

Yggur stopped dead. For an instant Maigraith looked like a smaller, fairer, womanly version of Rulke himself. No less terrible because she was a woman; more terrifying because

Yggur had spent the night lying defenceless beside her. He imagined that she came to torment him, to possess his mind just as Rulke had.

'Aah! Get away!' he cried, shielding his face with his arms.

Maigraith froze. Her vision felt clouded, as if she was peering through a heat haze. Then, as Faelamor collapsed in her room below, the illusion whispered away like a silken nightgown falling from her shoulders.

'Yggur, what is the matter?' she whispered.

Maigraith looked herself again, though her carmine eyes seemed to taunt him. Yggur dropped his arms; his face went blank. He nodded curtly, as one would to an acquaintance that one owed money to, and limped past.

Maigraith could not imagine what had happened – could only think that she had done something last night to offend him mortally. She could feel her insides dissolving with the pain and the rejection.

Gathering her courage in both hands, she followed Yggur down to the war room, which was in total chaos. She entered not far behind, in time to hear his bellow of fury.

'What?' he screamed. '*He's got away*?'

'H-he must have been in the wharf city the whole time!' stuttered the unfortunate Chaike.

'I'll crush them! I'll raze the wharf city to the water,' Yggur roared, storming out.

Maigraith did not run after him. She knew that Mendark was not the real problem. There was something about her, but he would never say. She also knew why things were going wrong for him. Yggur was too inflexible. The skills that equipped him for war were ill-suited to managing anarchic Thurkad and rebellious Bannador. And she had undermined him – because of her he had given way to his deepest fears. What was it about her that affected everyone she met? Only Faelamor could tell her, but Faelamor never would, especially after Maigraith's earlier defiance.

For three days Yggur stalked the fortress like a madman. None of his advisers or generals could get near him, save for Vartila. He would not meet Maigraith's eye in his war room, would not go walking with her, and most certainly would not come anywhere near his bed while she was in it. Every day he looked more desperate, more haggard.

Maigraith questioned everyone who knew him, even Vartila, but no one had seen him like this before. She went searching for Yggur, eventually finding him up on the wall again. He looked nearly as bad as Faelamor had, and when he saw her coming tried to duck down the other stair.

Maigraith ran and caught him by the shoulder. 'I must talk to you. This is tearing me apart.'

'Then go,' he replied. 'I cannot hold you, nor want to.'

'Not until I know what the matter is. Did I unwittingly offend you? Or am I so dismal a lover that you cannot abide to come near me? I am willing to learn. I beg you – teach me what pleases you.'

'It is not that,' said Yggur, turning away from the torment of her eyes.

'What? I must know!'

'I'm afraid,' he muttered.

'Of what. Of *me*?'

'No,' he lied, and she knew it.

'What then? Speak to me!'

'Mendark's escape,' he said desperately. Any refuge was better than this. 'And why half of my Whelm deserted me and became Ghâshâd. What are they up to? Why Shazmak, of all places? Whatever their plan is, I am not ready for it, and they know all my secrets. *It wasn't meant to be like this!*'

Don't whine about it, she thought. Get up and do something.

Avoiding her, Yggur broke away to limp down the wall.

Clearly he wasn't going to tell her what the real problem was. How could she find out? Maigraith would even have interrogated Faelamor, but she had lain in a comatose state for the past three days. *Three days!* Ever since Yggur's strange affliction began. An ugly suspicion arose. Faelamor's symptoms were like aftersickness, but how could that be, for she had lost her powers completely? Or had she?

Fleetingly Maigraith recalled that image of Yggur looking into her eyes just as she went to sleep. He had looked afraid. The pieces fell into place: the strange sensations she had felt on the way to meet Yggur, like looking through a veil; Yggur's reaction, as if he had seen someone else, someone who terrified him. Of course – she reminded him of his enemy Rulke!

Now that she knew what the matter was, Maigraith felt strong, able to take on Yggur and even Faelamor. Yggur was not the man she'd made him out to be, but she was not going to allow Faelamor to control her life any longer. She ran after him, barring his path with her arms.

'I know what troubles you,' she said softly, 'but it is not what you think.'

Yggur trembled, looking anywhere but in her eyes.

'My eyes don't make me your enemy,' she said. Still he made no answer. 'Can you not see what Faelamor did? Did you not recognise her illusion for what it was?'

'Illusion?' he said in bewilderment.

'Come down; you will see.' She explained it on the way, making him stand behind the door once they got there.

Faelamor lay still. Maigraith put her hands on her liege's shoulders and shook her. She did not stir. Maigraith slapped her, hard enough that fingermarks blushed the colourless cheek. She slapped harder, left and right and left, and finally Faelamor's eyes fluttered open.

'What did you do to me?' Maigraith screamed.

Faelamor managed a smile of triumph. 'The fool calls himself a mancer – he didn't even suspect!' she croaked. 'You are mine and always will be.' Then she slid back into unconsciousness.

Yggur looked like a man who'd had the bones withdrawn from his legs. 'She fooled me with illusion!' he said, slumping to the floor. '*Me!*' He sat there, shaking his head with disbelief.

Maigraith's respect for him was further undermined. But she was not going to give him up that easily. She helped him upstairs, not caring whether Faelamor lived or died.

Winter passed in Thurkad, with its rain and sleet and bitter winds; and spring came at last. Yggur was continually on edge, as if he expected a greater enemy to appear and take his empire from him. Did the Ghâshâd come to prepare the way for their master? That memory of being possessed by Rulke, the haunting fear of the scorpion coming again, was very strong in Yggur now.

When Maigraith had first appeared, his disabilities had scarcely been apparent, but since Faelamor's trickery his leg began to pain him, so that sometimes he seemed to move like an old man. At such times his speech grew halting and the paralysis of his face acute.

After some weeks of mortified solitude, Yggur began to seek out Maigraith's company once again. They resumed their late-night and early-morning walks on the walls of the fortress. They were almost friends, as long as she did not press him too far; as long as she kept her glasses on. But not such friends that he ever came to her bed.

Maigraith was uneasy now – deadly insecure, though as she had always lived with the dread of having snatched away that which she most yearned for, she did not show it. She took what came, planned and worked as she had always done, yet expected nothing from the morrow.

Yggur was busy ordering and ruling the lands that he had conquered. Most of his empire was subdued already, but Thurkad was the most unruly of all the conquered provinces and must be forever watched. And across the sea at Nilkerrand, Thyllan and his deputy, Berenet, were building a great army for invasion.

'Yggur,' said Maigraith one day.

'Mnnn,' he replied, bent over a chart of Nilkerrand.

'Remember when you held me prisoner in Fiz Gorgo last autumn?'

'I could hardly forget it.'

She hesitated. Maigraith had wanted to ask the question every day for a month, but had kept putting it off. 'One day you said that if I told you where Faelamor was and why she wanted the Mirror, you would tell me who my parents were, what happened to them and why it brought such shame upon the Faellem.'

He stiffened, but kept his head bent to his work. 'You refused to tell me,' he said in a chilly voice, flicking his glance sideways at her and then away again before her eyes could meet his.

'I could not betray my liege – surely you understood that? Now things have changed and I am asking you again.' She looked quite childlike in her expectation.

'This is important to you?'

'You know it is. I am nothing without it – I have no parents, no family, no ancestors. *I must know!*'

'You have served Faelamor all your life. Why have you never asked her?'

'I soon learned not to raise such questions. The issue of my parents was a shameful one. Not one of the Faellem would ever speak about it. Yggur, you *must* tell me! I am consumed by the need to know.'

'I'm sorry,' he replied. 'I cannot. At that time I thought I knew; it was one of the things I'd learned, spying with the Mirror.'

'*Thought*? What do you mean?'

'It is not called the Twisted Mirror for nothing,' he said, still not looking at her. 'Since then I have learned just what a deceitful thing it is. Nothing that the Mirror shows can be trusted. Remember that, if ever you hold it in your hands again. It is a lying thing!' Laying down his ruler, Yggur abruptly went out.

How can that be? Maigraith thought. You used to spy

on your enemies for years – that is how you grew so powerful. That could not have come about if everything the Mirror told was a lie.

She did not want to believe him, for that would undermine the little dream she had nurtured ever since she picked up the Mirror in Fiz Gorgo and it came to life in her hands. It had called to her, offering a whole new world, a different life where she was not in the thrall of Faelamor or anyone. A life where she had value for herself. She kept thinking about what she had seen there.

Yet Maigraith could not bring herself to think he was lying either. She was slow to trust and, in spite of their unsatisfactory relationship, slow to give up trust once she had bestowed it. She said no more about the matter, but was more determined than ever to find out who she really was.

'So you haven't heard any more about Karan?' she asked when they met for dinner.

There had been tidings of Karan, a sighting in Ganport and, later, at the town of Granewys on the other side of the Sea of Thurkad, not to mention the suspicious illness of Zareth the Hlune. Yggur's efficient spies had tracked Mendark to Zile, though that was not a place over which he had any influence. But still there was no news of Tensor or the Mirror, save of their going north. The Aachim had been followed for a time, almost taken, but they had shaken their pursuers off to disappear in wild weather somewhere on the north coast. From there they might have gone anywhere.

'Not since Granewys, though I know she went north, then east. There may be news when my skeets come back. I have one or two spies in that area. She is a remarkable woman, this Karan of yours.'

'More remarkable than you realise,' Maigraith said absently.

Yggur started, then laid down his bowl of lasee and took her by the shoulders, drawing her close to him. He even dared to look into her eyes, though he did not take her glasses off to do it.

'There is something about her that you have not told me,' he said alertly. 'What is it?'

'Nothing,' she replied, shocked to find that she had aroused his curiosity. What a formidable man he was.

Yggur was not to be put off. He gripped her hands in his.

'What is it about Karan that I do not know?' he demanded. 'Are we not . . . friends? I would not keep such a secret from you.'

Would you not? she thought. She was not naive. Perhaps you do already. Yet for all her ambivalence toward him, Yggur occupied a unique place in her life and she wanted to please him, and help him too. That was what friends did for one another.

'I cannot tell you. Karan's secrets are not mine to give away.'

'But Maigraith, *do you not trust me*?'

She looked into his steady gaze and knew that she could. Why else would she be here? But she had already betrayed one of Karan's secrets. Under torture by the Whelm, she had revealed that Karan was a blending. Karan had suffered terribly for it. Nothing could induce her to betray Karan again.

'I can say nothing more. If you truly cared for me you would not press me to betray a friend.'

'If you really trusted me you would not keep a vital secret from me,' he snapped.

Denying him was hard, but she could not do otherwise. 'You just want to use her,' she said, hurt and disillusioned. 'People are just things to you – when you wear them out you throw them away.' Turning away she went up to her room, wondering if, all along, Yggur had been hunting Karan just to use her talent.

Maigraith questioned Yggur about Rulke constantly. She could not learn enough about the Charon. In the beginning Yggur had been only too happy to talk about his enemy, but as her interest grew, so did his unease.

Why did she want to know? Was she reverting to that Charon blood in her?

I've got to find out more about Karan, and Maigraith too, he thought. He had been lying before, in that distant time when he had offered to tell Maigraith who her parents were. Now he wished that he had not been. If only he had the Mirror. How he would force his will on it now and make it scry out the truth about Maigraith and Karan for him!

Lacking that, what could he do? The Faellem were all far away in Mirrilladell. It could take a year to travel there and back. But he did not even have a month. How else could he find out? Then, with a sudden thrill of horror, he saw the answer right in front of him. Faelamor! And she was already in his power.

Yggur now knew that she was greater than he. He could never have hoped to force the truth from her had she been well, for her illusions were so powerful that she could drive anyone mad. But Faelamor had scarcely moved from her bed in a month. He gathered that she had lost her powers and did not look like recovering them.

Yggur knew that the bonds of duty and obligation between Maigraith and Faelamor were still strong, for all that they seemed to hate each other. Maigraith would react violently to any threat to her liege. She could not do otherwise.

Next day, when Maigraith was down in the city and would be away for some time, Yggur slipped into Faelamor's room. She lay on the bed as in a coma, a sad, dull dishrag of an old woman who looked ready to die. Her pale hair flopped on the pillow like wet fur. The blood crawled like sluggish worms beneath her translucent skin.

He bent down over her, wondering how to go about his business.

'What do you want with me, *gah*?' she said in a shivery whisper. The old, golden eyes that were like bottomless wells flew open.

Yggur had not expected her to wake, much less confront him so powerfully. He could think of nothing to say but the truth. 'Who *is* Maigraith?'

'Leave it!' she hissed. 'She is nothing to do with you!'

'I must know. I can be a good friend in return for this small favour.'

'I prefer you as an enemy,' she said coldly.

'So be it. Then be warned, you are in my power and I will force you if I have to.' He bent over to grip her by the shoulders. '*Who is she?*'

Faelamor smiled, showing small teeth and a lot of pink gum. It was not a pleasant smile. Her hand, which was as little and thin as a claw, shot up and grabbed him by the throat. The most powerful warlord on Santhenar tried to step backwards but the colourless nails dug into his windpipe.

Yggur bowed down, trying to relieve the choking pressure. He could not understand it. He might have picked Faelamor up and broken her over his knee, but he could not imagine how to rid himself of the nails in his throat.

It's an illusion, he thought. That's all the power she has. Tensing, he straightened his legs, shooting himself upright.

Faelamor did not let go. The most brutal pain he had ever felt tore at his throat, for he had heaved her right out of bed and she hung vertically from her clawed fingers. Yggur could feel her nails tearing through his throat, ripping apart skin, flesh, arteries and windpipe. He saw blood spray out of his neck, heard his hopeless attempts to drag air into his chest, then Faelamor fell down beside the bed like a sodden rag.

Yggur reeled backwards, fell over a chair and put his fingers to his neck. That part *had* been illusion, for though there were bloody gouges down each side, he was otherwise whole.

He tried to speak but not even a croak came forth. Perhaps she had crushed his voice-box. Yggur stared down at her, this little, frail, old-looking woman who lay as limp as death. He tried to think of another way to get at her. 'Maigraith and I are lovers,' he whispered, continuing the dialogue he had begun before her fingers had cut it off.

'*No!*' she spat. 'You may love her, though I doubt it – you are too much in love with yourself and your own suffering. But to Maigraith you are no more than a way station on the road. She will never love you.'

'Who is she?' he repeated, a husk of a voice that burned when he spoke.

'Not for you to know, mancer,' she said. 'I will never tell you and she cannot. Now leave me.'

'I will not rest until I know,' he said, though he knew that Faelamor had defeated him.

'As you wish.'

'Then at least answer me this. What is Karan's secret that Maigraith will not tell me?'

Faelamor weighed him up, then smiled maliciously. 'Karan is *triune*,' she said softly.

Yggur's knee gave way; he almost fell. 'What? How can that be?'

'She has a distant Faellem ancestor. The name is in the register at Gothryme, though it has been kept very quiet.'

'Triune!' Yggur repeated. 'So she carries the blood of the Three Worlds. That *is* a rare thing, indeed.' He looked at Faelamor rather calculatingly. 'She could have a great talent; I thought so the very first time I met her. It needs to be trained. And she is in some danger, if anyone else learns of it.'

'Indeed! I want Karan dead. Now go!'

Yggur slunk out, so injured and demoralised that he could not bear to face Maigraith. But on the other hand he had learned something that could well prove vital to his campaigns. *So!* he thought. *I must do everything in my* power to bring Karan here. I will send out my remaining skeets at once.

Faelamor had lain in her room for weeks, scarcely moving, eating the food that Maigraith sent to her, taking the medicines, but seldom rising from her bed. The loss of her powers had been a devastating blow to her. She barely had any will to live and took interest in nothing.

Then Maigraith visited her the day after her confrontation and found her up and dressed, bright of eye, the rose colour back in her skin, pacing the room. The conflict with Yggur had roused her, though Maigraith did not know that.

'Time to be doing,' Faelamor said. 'My powers have begun to return. See!'

She snapped her fingers and disappeared. Maigraith was astonished. Though she knew it was just an illusion and even how it was done, she had to concentrate until her brain smouldered to find Faelamor in the room, sitting in the chair by the fire. Then all at once she was back. There was a silvery sheen on her brow.

'I have never seen such an illusion,' Maigraith said.

'Ah, that was hard work and a lot of pride and will. I am not strong, but I will be.'

Faelamor worked like a demon, exercising and practising her other powers in her room, and occasionally outside it. Once she walked right into a meet between Yggur and the puppet Assembly, and not even Yggur knew she was there, though the whole room felt uneasy and the meeting broke up early in discomfort. She laughed when she told Maigraith later, and her delight was a thing that Maigraith, who had spent many years with her, had seldom seen.

As her confidence grew, Maigraith's spirits sank, knowing that soon she would have to face Faelamor's demands once more. Then, to her surprise, Faelamor came late one night to where Maigraith sat with Yggur and announced that she was going away.

'I have a great deal to catch up on,' she said, speaking as though Yggur was not there. 'I may be gone some time. Be on your guard against this lover of yours; he is using you in every way.'

Beside her, Yggur choked and ground his teeth together, and as soon as Faelamor was gone he left Thurkad suddenly, saying only that he must inspect his troops, and did not return for weeks.

30

DELUGE

W hat have I done? Shand thought, feeling around for the rope. Unfastening it, he followed it down to the ledge where he had left his gear. The floor was running with water. One of the lamps had broken, while the other had been swept back up the tunnel and lay on its side, still burning, giving out a faint chink of light where the shutter had come open. Shand opened it all the way and shone it down into the cavern. He could hear rushing water but could not see anything, for the air was full of mist.

He used his rope to go down, hand over hand, faster than he had ever gone down a rope before. By the time he reached the bottom the air had begun to clear and Shand saw that the pool was empty, while the rock-mass lay in the middle of the depression, cracked into pieces. The whole cavern was dripping, streams of water pouring off every surface. Most of the torrent seemed to have gone down the other tunnel. There was no sign of the Ghâshâd or of Karan.

Shand raced across, leaping from rock to rock, splashing through rivulets. He saw a small foot sticking up in the air behind the table-shaped rock where Karan had been laid out. Springing up, he found her hanging down the back, held by her ropes.

'Karan!' he cried, afraid that she had been drowned or

battered to death by the torrent. He cut her wrist ropes and laid her out on the rock. Karan shuddered, spat out a mouthful of water and opened bloodshot eyes.

'Shand,' she whispered. 'Did you do that?'

'I did,' he said, sawing through the rope around her ankles.

'What happened to the Ghâshâd?'

'Washed down the tunnel, I expect. If you had not been tied you'd be with them.' He wiped her wet cheek. Her face was bruised in a few places. 'Did they do this?' His voice echoed harshly.

She touched her cheek. 'They did not harm me. Lucky I saw the roof fall; I don't think I've ever held my breath so long. How did you do that?'

'Arrant stupidity,' he said, coiling up the rope. 'We'd better get going. I wouldn't think that they're all dead, though likely they've broken bones.'

'I'm not arguing.' Karan stood up and took a few limping steps. 'Oh, I ache all over.' She pulled up her trousers, to discover that her legs were bruised all the way up.

They got away from there as quickly as they could and in a couple of hours were back outside. By then Shand was hobbling too, his boots lost in the flood. It was dark, though not late. He had not yet mentioned the skeet, but before they went into the inn he said in a low voice, 'I think we'd better go tonight. I'll settle our account.'

Karan followed Shand listlessly, afraid in a numb, helpless way. The Ghâshâd having come all this way for her, what was the point running any further?

They found a market stall that was still open, bought boots to replace the lost ones, and went searching for the shop that sold waterskins. It was closed up; no one answered their knocking.

'We've got to go,' Shand said anxiously. 'There'll be a place further down, surely.'

They collected their packs from the inn and before midnight set off on the path to the cliffs. There they bedded

439

down in a patch of scrub for what remained of the night.

At the first light of dawn, with much looking behind them they headed down the cliff path. It began as broad steps cut in the marble and, even at that hour, was busy with traffic going both up and down.

It was a beautiful day, though already a little too warm for walking under such a burden. The packs were heavier than they were used to, and the shock of each step soon made their knees wobbly. At the bottom of the first set of cliffs they turned aside into a broad path that led across the slope to a vineyard just coming into leaf. Beyond was a small orchard of dark-green lime trees covered in small bitter limes.

'Let's rest awhile,' said Karan, sitting down on the bank on the uphill side of the path and leaning back against her pack. 'I've rather a headache.'

Shand grunted. 'Not surprising.' He looked over his shoulder up the hill.

'Look, the vines are getting their leaves already. Spring doesn't come in Gothryme for weeks yet.'

'They can grow almost anything along here,' Shand replied. 'Plenty of water, no frost on the slope, shelter from the cold winds, sun all day.'

'Why isn't there a bigger city then?'

'Don't know! The further down you go the saltier the soil, and it's a hard climb back up.'

A team of carriers went by, staggering under huge loads. Karan was glad that wasn't her lot. 'I wonder you didn't retire here, instead of Tullin.'

'*Retire!*' He threw a waterskin at her in outrage. 'I work twelve hours a day in Tullin. No, I'll not retire. I like Tullin, in spite of the cold. Plenty of gellon in Tullin.'

'Gellon? Is that all?'

'I love gellon in all its forms. It is the noblest of all fruits and every way of eating it is perfect – green, ripe, dried, fermented, pickled, made into jam or chutney. Grated for its juice. Even salted gellon is good and better than ginger for the seasickness. Do you get aftersickness when you use your talent? Gellon is good for that too.'

'I could do with some now if you've got any – I feel a bit woozy.'

'Afraid not. And if I ever tired of those, there are my gellon liqueurs. I distil them myself and they are the finest in Meldorin – perhaps the finest anywhere.' He grew lyrical. 'What better reason is there to live in Tullin, since the finest fruit in Meldorin comes from there? I love my gellon trees too, for they are a large part of my life, great gnarly twisted things with their roots deep in rock, and it was I who planted them. More than a hundred years old they are. They love the cold and I love them. Yes, Tullin is all I want.'

Karan had been listening to this tirade with a fond smile, but all at once she looked taken aback. 'Is it? Is Tullin all you want, old friend? Who are you really, Shand? Are you some kind of wizard, like Mendark, to have lived so long, or do you have blood of the other human kinds in you?'

Shand turned to her, though his eyes still seemed to be looking into the distance. 'My gellon trees have given me away,' he said. 'Yes, I am an old, old man. I have lived beyond my time, though it was neither sorcery nor heritage that punished me with the ordeal of this life. I am old human, no more. Yet you are right – Tullin is my refuge, my hiding hole, and I am hiding from myself. Don't ask. That is my price for helping you, if you like. Don't ask.'

Shand looked so sad that she could not bear to look at him. Karan was immediately sorry. 'Let's go then.'

She jumped to her feet. Before them was another set of steps, but not as long or as steep as the first, and she headed down at a fast pace.

At the bottom they came out into irrigated terraces where rice and vegetables were grown, though the rice fields were at this time of the year just mud and stubble. A number of villages were scattered across the slope and, after they had been walking for three hours or so, they saw ahead a small pavilion beside the path, which turned out to be a tea house. For a copper, they drank tea and ate sweet cakes made of rice flour and dried grapes.

Nothing more was said of Shand's affairs and shortly they continued. Before dusk they stopped at a village where a tiny inn looked inviting. Again they sat on the veranda, eating their dinner and sipping green wine as the sun set, casting long shadows along the cliffs. A full moon rose, the second of their journey together. She tried to remember where they'd been the last full moon, but couldn't. Shand kept staring back up the path. Karan had often noticed him looking over his shoulder on the way down and she was worried too. But that was all she could do. The ordeal with the Ghâshâd had left her feeling lethargic; she lacked the emotional energy to be afraid any more.

Today was the thirty-third day of the month of Talmard, old-year day, the last day of winter and of the year. They were both looking forward to its closure, and a new beginning. Finally they were beyond sight of the last village. It was already hot and not a cloud to be seen. Here and there the soil was crusted with salt. A streak of green not far away indicated a seep: enough, after some excavation with their hands, to wet their headgear and fill their bags with cool water.

'How is it that the water here is fresh while further up it was too salty to drink?' Karan wondered as she filled the first bag.

Shand shrugged. 'Underground, the water goes where it wills. You can tell the fresh water seeps though, for the plants are bright green, while around the salt seeps they are brown or blue or even purple.'

They had not been able to buy waterbags to replace the foul ones. 'We haven't started yet and already I've a bad feeling about this journey,' said Shand. 'All our gear needs to be perfect, yet here we are, setting out with half our skins foul.'

'Nothing we can do about it now,' she said, sharing his unease.

When all was ready Karan looked at the pile with dismay. Enough food for thirty-five days made a formidable heap, even though it was mostly dried stuff, tightly packed. But they had carried it down. Water was the greater problem. Even travelling by night and sleeping by day they each needed four waterbags for eight days, and each bag held the equivalent of a small bucket of water.

'We need it all,' said Shand, also staring at the huge load. He had been much younger the last time he crossed, and it had been a cool year.

They donned their desert robes, loose white garments with long hoods and dangling sleeves that covered even their hands against the sun. Shand put on his slitted eye covers; Karan shivered, reminded of the Whelm. She tied on her face cloths, pulled her hood up and her floppy-brimmed hat down over it.

The food, spare clothing and cooking gear completely filled her pack. On top was tied her light sleeping pouch. She slung the four huge waterskins across her shoulders; two on the left, two on the right. Already she felt impossibly burdened; the skins wobbled against her sides with every step. She reached down for her pack, but could not lift it.

Shand threw it onto her shoulders. Shrugging her arms through the straps, she buckled them while Shand took the weight. When he released it she seemed to shrink, only her legs visible. She staggered, fumbled with the straps and flung the pack onto the ground.

Taking off her eye covers, Karan wiped away tears of frustration. 'It's too heavy!'

Shand could not but agree. What she was carrying weighed more than she did. She emptied everything onto the ground, sorting through the piles restlessly. 'There's more food than we need. You said the journey would take thirty days, yet we have food enough for thirty-five.'

'About thirty days; it may take longer.' And what if you hurt yourself, or I do? Twist an ankle, say, or get a poisoned stomach from the water. And after we get there, what if it takes days to find food? You're not carrying any reserves.'

Karan knew it to be true. Though she had, by prodigious feats of eating, regained some of the weight previously lost, her former soft roundness of face and figure had not returned. Her face was drawn and her hip bones pressed against the skin. She felt that she inhabited someone else's slim, ugly body.

'Then we've too much water,' she said crossly. 'You said the first stage is only five days – we're carrying enough for eight.'

Karan emptied one of the foul skins onto the ground. They both watched as it soaked into the sandy soil. She glared at Shand, and even he, with all his years upon him, felt subdued and poured out his last bottle, though only half. Karan seemed satisfied that he was cooperating and turned back to her work, disposing of the cooking pans, her heavy coat and other unwanted items.

'It's barely spring. Deserts can be bitterly cold at night,' Shand cautioned.

'I can't carry it!' she shouted, angry with him and her own weakness.

'Then we shouldn't be going at all,' he said, moderating his temper. 'But if we are, you will need to keep the sun off and the salt dust out.'

'I still have my cloak and hood and hat – surely not all of these clothes are required?'

Shand peered at the small pile. 'I would take it all,' he advised. 'There will be no chance for washing before Katazza. Your clothes will be so crusted with salt that they'll wear sores that cannot heal.'

'There's still too much.' She found some other oddments to throw away. 'I will eat less,' she said fiercely, swinging her hand at the pile of food parcels, sending the top four flying. Then she carefully repacked everything, took up her hat, a broad-brimmed, crumpled thing made of leather, dyed olive-green, pulled it down at the front so that it shaded her face and heaved the pack on her back unaided. It was still very heavy, but she could manage it now.

Shand looked down at the discarded parcels, weighed his own pack in his hands, then thrust them inside. Karan studied him for a moment, somehow irritated by his action. 'You are an old fool,' she said, though she knew he was right. Fatal to go at all, without the best of everything.

They set off slowly down the long slope toward the floor of the sea. Here and there were blocks of grey limestone large as houses, rolled down from the cliffs far above. In the mid-morning a thin line of green caught their attention away to their left. It was a canyon, its rocky sides falling away sheer to a floor choked with sand. The rock faces glistened with salt, but there were trees growing out of the sand. On they slogged, following the rim of the canyon, and the air was so thick that it stifled them. Already it was almost as hot as summer in Gothryme, her mountain home.

'It's not even midday,' Karan said despairingly. She had never been able to tolerate great heat. 'What's it going to be like in another month?'

'What's it going to be like on the way back?'

At the end of the first day's march they began to crunch through salt-encrusted sand. The land was barren here, except around the occasional seeps.

'I think we've lost your Ghâshâd friends,' said Shand that evening.

'We'll never lose them,' she responded gloomily.

Time to ask the question that he had been putting off. 'What did they want you for, Karan?'

Shand was shocked when she told him. 'I wish you'd let me know before. I'd not have come out here at all.'

'I'm sorry. When I . . . I closed off my talent so that it could never happen again, I must have suppressed the memories too. I didn't remember it until they began to work on me in the cavern.' She looked across the leaping flames into Shand's eyes. 'I'll never be safe from them, will I?'

'I . . . no, you won't, not until it's resolved one way or the other. The way you make a link must be unique. I never heard of anyone seizing control of one before.'

Karan didn't want to discuss it. 'Come on – we've got to get ahead of them.'

The next day was the first day of Thays, of spring and of the new year. It did not feel any better than the old one. They found a way into the canyon and for two days followed it down, taking advantage of the shade, with much looking behind them from every vantage point. Mostly the going was good, though here and there they came to a low cliff, perhaps an undersea waterfall in the days of the Sea of Perion. Late in the afternoon of their second day in the canyon, and seeming like a mirage or a miracle in that barren land, they found a long deep pool in the rock, fresh enough to drink, in a place where the gully turned east-west. At this time of year the pool, sheltered by the steep walls of the canyon, did not see the sun. Karan swam and dived in the deeper water while Shand fished at the other end with a piece of meat on a thread. He caught no fish, but a kind of yabby were to be had in abundance, so unafraid that he could catch them with his hands.

'A pity you threw away the pans,' he observed, as Karan wandered back, towelling her curls with a shirt.

'Fire would do just as well,' she smiled, turning back towards the trees.

She returned with an armload of wood and soon had a bright fire blazing there. After that, Karan drew up a flat rock and sat on it, her toes out toward the warmth, though it was not cold, then found a comb in her small bag of personal things and began to disentangle her fiery hair. Occasionally she regretted her outbursts to Shand about her hair.

446

Shand had scooped a pool in the sand at the edge of the water to keep his catch in, but the yabbies kept escaping, climbing over one another with their stalky eyes moving this way and that, their claws clashing. He built a wall of stones around the pool but even this would not contain the creatures and he had to run from one side to the other, putting them back in. A muffled snort escaped; Karan was laughing at him.

'If you'd help I wouldn't have this problem,' he said gruffly.

'Surely one silly old man is the match of a dozen *clatchers*,' she said, still laughing. 'You should have despatched them at once. The fire is ready.'

Shand saw the funny side of it. Inwardly he was delighted to see her laugh.

'*Clatchers!* Where did you get that name from?'

'That's what they're called, aren't they? We don't have them in Bannador, but I remember them from travelling with my father.'

'It's a bit like calling a baby sheep a baa-lamb. The proper name is linney.'

'Oh, *linney*.'

'But you can call them whatever you want.'

He killed the clatchers with his knife, washed the sand off and laid them on his pack. Shand attended to the chores of the campfire, watching her as he worked. The smile remained on her face for a long time as she absently combed her hair, though the tangles were long gone, staring into the fire. Once only a shadow passed over her face. Karan pulled her cloak around her shoulders and sat down again.

It was getting dark. Shand raked the coals around a flat stone, put the vegetables on it in a nest of green leaves, and raked the fire back again. When they were nearly ready he flung the first pair of crayfish onto the coals. A few minutes only to cook and they feasted, burning their fingers on the crisp shells. The clatchers made as delicious a meal as they had ever tasted.

When the last empty shells were cast back into the flames, fingers licked clean again, and they sat once more with their copper mugs steaming with fresh-brewed tea, Shand looked across the fire to her.

'You're finally recovered!' he said. 'I'm glad.'

Karan's gaze met his own, but she said nothing for a long time, thinking back on all that had happened since he found her and the other lifetime before that.

'Yes,' she said at last. 'I'm stronger, I think, than ever I was before. I'm not afraid of madness anymore. My poor mother – all these years I hated her for leaving me all alone. I understand her better now. And I owe everything to you. Whatever I have is yours – you have but to name it.'

She went gracefully to her knees in front of him, bowing until her forehead touched the sand. Shand was deeply touched. Had he ever been so honoured? But he was irritated too, knowing that he had done less for her than he should have.

'Get up, child,' he said sternly, so that she went still, thinking her gesture rejected. He hugged her and ran a hand through her curls. She inclined her head then went back to her stone. Shand had not shaved since leaving Tullin and his beard was long and thick, grey with black strands.

'Indeed you owe your life to me. Three times I had to breathe it back into you that first day. But you lived, and the rest was your own affair. I had no part in that save by accident – putting you in the custody of the Hlune. Maybe that was what brought you back. There was no room in your head for all those other struggles.'

Karan smiled at the memories. Then her thoughts came back to the topic that was never far from her mind and slowly the smile disappeared.

'Do you truly think that Llian went willingly?' she asked in a small voice, thinking back on previous conversations.

'I don't know what to think. Why would Tensor take him? What could he possibly want him for? Still, Llian is Zain and they are untrustworthy wretches all!'

Karan grimaced. 'Don't say that – the Zain are just like you and me. He never wanted the Mirror for himself; Llian cares nothing for such things. It's the Histories that he's obsessed with.'

Then she thought she had said enough, even to Shand. Karan knew that Llian burned for the tale. Perhaps he thought that Tensor would help him fulfil that ambition and so clung to him as he fled. He was weak in that way.

'Would he abandon you in Thurkad after all you suffered together?'

'I wouldn't have thought so.' Her voice was barely audible.

'Perhaps he saw you fall and fled in terror and grief, thinking you dead. Or maybe . . . he and you did Tensor much harm. Maybe Tensor . . .'

'Don't say it. I don't know what to think.' She went silent then, aching for him.

'Enough of that,' said Shand. 'I have a gift for you.' He felt in the bottom of his pack. 'I was going to give it that day in Ashmode, until you treated me so disrespectfully.' He gave her a frightful glare.

Karan did not know what to say. He looked so fierce that she felt ashamed and embarrassed.

'I'm joking,' he said. He unwrapped a small cedar box and held it out.

She opened it. Inside was a parcel carefully wrapped in felt, a small bottle of precious crystal with an ebony and ivory stopper. It was beautifully cut, very heavy in her hand.

'Oh, you can't give me this,' she said. 'It's such a beautiful, precious thing.'

'Open it.'

She took out the stopper and there came forth the most beautiful aroma of oil of lime blossom, her favourite scent and her mother's. Tears flooded her cheeks. She put the stopper back, the fragrance lingered in the air a minute, then it was gone. She sat back on her haunches, not troubling to wipe the tears away.

'Thank you. But I have nothing to give in return.'

'What you have given me back is far greater than this small gift,' he said. 'You have given me back my self-respect.'

Karan asked no questions. She knew that he would not answer them. 'Where did you get it?'

'The bottle? I've had it for a long, long time. It's very old, but fitting that it comes to you, for I think it was made in Bannador originally. I had it filled in Ashmode. The best perfume limes in the world grow there, on the slopes above the sea.'

She opened the flask again, touched a tiny amount of perfume behind her ears and in her hair, smiled at some secret thought and packed the treasure away.

Something croaked down the other end of the pool and another answered it. 'Thirty more days, at least,' she whispered. 'The waiting is unbearable. But what if Llian went willingly?'

Shand took her in his arms. 'If you are unsure it is generally wise to think the better of someone, rather than the worst. Tensor must have a use for Llian; surely he took him against his will.'

She straightened up. 'Is that what you truly believe?'

'Yes,' he said, feeling only a little bit guilty.

She thought for a moment. 'To Llian I owe my life as well – it is a much-owed life, mine. I will think the best of him, and rescue him from whatever foolish trouble he is in. Then I will take him home with me. He can write his wretched Histories in the library at Gothryme. I'm tired of mirrors and mancers and stupid war games.'

Disentangling herself, she walked away toward the pool, staring at the reflected stars. The surface of the water was as still as glass.

If only it were that easy, thought Shand, I would happily join you there. But you can no more escape from this business before it ends than I can. No one has tried harder to avoid this responsibility than I have.

31

THE TOWERS OF KATAZZA

Llian used Malien's stain on his face and hands, but it could not cover up the terror he felt every time one of the Aachim so much as glanced at him. He was always expecting to have his secret uncovered.

The next two days involved a dangerous scramble down gullies and canyons where the shattered rock slipped and slid with the least movement, and several times the Aachim started landslides that became avalanches pouring down the canyon like a river of rock, with a storm of dust and a roar louder than any noise Llian had ever heard. Often they had to find their way down cliffs or, more frequently, around them, a torment all the more acute for Llian because he dared not show his fear of heights. He dared do nothing that would bring anyone but Malien to him.

Late in the afternoon of the first day of their descent, he was standing near the edge of one of the lower cliffs, fretting, when a shadow fell across his feet. Another shadow framed him on the other side. He looked over his shoulder. A frozen-faced Basitor stood there, with Hintis beside him.

'What do you want?' Llian quavered. Once Hintis's tormenting had been fairly good-humoured but since Siftah it had become malicious.

'I want you dead,' Hintis said, baring his teeth. 'Like the Aachim you betrayed in Shazmak!'

Basitor moved toward Llian with his arms spread wide.

Llian's back was to the edge. Just knowing it was there made his skin crawl. Hintis caught him by the wrist, Basitor took the other one and they turned him around as smoothly as if they had choreographed the scene beforehand. Pulling his arms behind his back, they bent him forward so that he was leaning over the cliff.

'What say that rock down there?' Hintis said. He pointed towards a ragged red spike crusted with white droppings.

Llian imagined impaling himself on it. Bitter bile heaved up into the back of his throat.

'I prefer the round one,' said Basitor, jerking his arms hard. Llian's feet skidded in the gravel on the edge. He shrieked, sure that he was going over.

'Hoy!' shouted Asper. 'What are you doing with the Zain?'

'He is not harmed,' said Basitor, drawing Llian back from the cliff edge.

'Let him go!'

They released Llian, smiling unpleasantly, and wandered away to join the rest of the Aachim. The descent continued. Llian's knees were wobbly before he even began it.

At last, with the waxing moon showing more of the dark side every night, they reached the boulder-littered slopes that ran down for leagues to the white floor. There they searched for water and found it with a little digging at a green seep. Bottles filled, eye covers donned, as soon as the day began to cool in the afternoon they shrugged huge packs on their backs and set out toward a flat-topped mountain range in the north-east distance.

That night set the pattern for every other. It soon became apparent that Llian could not keep up the pace, so they redistributed his pack and his goods among themselves. All he carried was a small bag with his journal, personal items and a single water bottle. They walked, with three brief rests mainly for Llian's sake, all afternoon and night and well on into the following day. Then they set up camp, ate and slept. Around midday Llian was woken by an argument between Tensor and Selial, all the more furious because it was entirely whispered.

'*No more*, until we know where you lead us.'

'I lead you to refuge,' Tensor said softly.

'Don't play with words,' Selial hissed. 'Satisfy me now or go your way without us.'

Tensor became slightly more conciliatory. 'Selial, I need you – all of you. The survival of our species is the only thing I care about. But we must get back our pride. Too long have we hidden in our glorious past. We must grow again or become insignificant.'

'Then let us recover our pride by great works, not by plotting futile revenge.'

'I do plot a great work,' Tensor rumbled. 'The greatest! But look how our past wonders have been brought to ruin by Rulke. What is the point of building anew, just for him to tear all down again?'

'Bah! Still starting at phantoms, Tensor!'

'Selial, there is a secret hidden in the Mirror; *I know there is!*' His voice glowed like molten gold. 'A secret that will uplift us again.'

'What about the Zain?'

'The Zain . . . is vital.' His words were as slippery as butter. 'I don't know why, *not yet*, but I will.'

'Then call off your dogs, Tensor. Leave him alone.'

'They will not harm him,' said Tensor. 'Let them have their fun.'

In the mid-afternoon they crossed a saltscape where the ground was broken into thick slabs like icing on a cake, sometimes standing up against each other, leaving a tent-like space inside. At a brief stop Llian sat down inside one, grateful for the shade.

'Careful that doesn't fall,' Tensor said with a grim smile as he went past.

At that moment Llian began to feel a buzzing in his head like an alarm. He shook his head, blew his nose, but could not get rid of it. Then he felt someone call his name, *Llian!* It was a cry into his mind; no voice to recognise, but it made him jump. He tried hard to get it back but it vanished.

Hintis's voice came distinctly from the other side. 'How I *hate* this chronicler, Basitor! When I think that we took him in and made him Aachimning, and all the time he was laughing at us and planning our betrayal. What say you, now he's inside, we slam the lid down on his coffin?' He struck one slab a blow with his fist that made it quiver.

'I would do it right now,' said Basitor, 'had Tensor not forbidden it. It seems he has a fate in store for the Zain that will make up for all the pain he has given us.' He chuckled.

Llian's nerve almost broke then. He wanted to scream, 'What's he going to do with me?' Shivering, he slipped out the other side, and after that watched his back more carefully than ever.

When he calmed down, Llian began to wonder about that cry of warning. Karan had a sensitive talent that sometimes warned her of danger. Was he developing one too, another aspect of the Curse of Rulke?

At this time of year it was not hot even in the middle of the day, but the air was thick and hard to breathe, and the salt that crept into everything made Llian feel nauseous most of the time. Travelling over smooth salt, walking hard sixteen hours a day, they made up to fifteen leagues each day, though Llian always fell behind in the night and pairs of Aachim took turns to carry him on a stretcher.

Skirting along the base of the mountain ridge they were twice able to replenish their water bottles. The second time the water was brackish and though the Aachim did not seem to be affected, Llian could not drink it. Fortunately there was still enough fresh water left.

After that they passed beyond the ridge and struck out across empty salt desert, travelling on Tensor's memory of a map seen long ago. Five days they walked, making good time in the brooding red and yellow moonlight, and saw no hill in all that time, but on the morning of the sixth, as the sun rose, ahead and to the left of their track a mountain appeared, tall and black. There, after much searching, high up on the flank they found a soak which yielded water after hours of digging, though it was so salty that not even the Aachim could drink it.

'How much do we have left?' asked Tensor. It was new year's day.

'Three days,' said Selial, 'but only one for him.' She jerked her elbow at the shapeless lump that was Llian, hunched down under huge hat and white-streaked coat in a tiny patch of shade.

'Set up the trazpars. We might search for a week and not find better than this.'

They unfolded the devices that Llian had thought were weapons. These turned out to be cunningly made apparatuses like inverted umbrellas of black metal. Salt water was poured into an outer chamber below, it evaporated with the heat of the sun and pure water condensed in an inner chamber. By the end of the second day they had drunk their fill and had sufficient for the next leg.

'Enough,' said Tensor, scraping crystallised salt out of the last trazpar. 'At most it can be seventy leagues to Katazza.' On they marched.

They saw Katazza days before they reached it, first as a grey smudge in the distance, later a slowly growing mountain, salt-white at the base grading darker up its long steep flanks, with an icing of snow at the top. Each morning it appeared, perceptibly larger, but as the day wore on a haze came up from the salt and when the winds intensified in the afternoon it disappeared from sight.

Llian was glad when it had – he was afraid of Katazza

now. The trip had become a horrible torment. Hintis and Basitor taunted him mercilessly. He was constantly finding lumps of salt in his dinner, spiky climbing irons in his sleeping pouch, or cooking slops in his hat when he put it on in the morning. The two groups of Aachim bickered among themselves, while Selial constantly made threats against Tensor that were never enforced. To make life even more uncomfortable, Tensor's mood changes were extreme. Llian never knew what to expect from him: a grim smile or a cuff over the ear.

In five days Katazza had become a vast black mountain, its triple peaks covered in snow, but they had not reached it. The salt had given way to incredibly rugged country, broken lava in piles and billows, upthrust cliffs and knife-edged ridges, difficult and dangerous to walk on in the now dark nights, and full of steaming vents and fumaroles crusted with sulphur or coloured salts. Soon their boots were rent and scored; Llian had to bind his with wire to prevent them from falling apart. The scorpion nebula gave a dim red light, one that Llian found particularly treacherous. He fell many times, once gashing his leg from calf to knee, another time tearing open the palms of both hands, though when Asper came to assist he waved him away, too afraid, and stood with the blood dripping from his hands onto the salt-crusted basalt until Malien appeared to repair him once again.

'Chronicler,' she laughed. 'I wish you'd learn to stand on your own feet.'

Llian gave not a squeak, even when she had to put a dozen stitches in his palm. 'Will I be able to write again?' he whispered, suffering silently.

She gave him a hug that left bloodstains on her white robe. 'You'll heal!'

Finally, when all the fresh water was gone and they were down to the dregs of the brackish, driving Llian's stomach into a torment, they crossed off the black rock country onto a slope littered with boulders. Here they found a brine pool, from which they made enough water with their stills to fill a couple of skins. That sufficed to bring them to the foot of Katazza where there were seeps aplenty, beautiful cool fresh water, enough to wash in, though Llian had to be careful that he did not wash off the stain.

Tensor would not rest, even now. After they had drunk, eaten, bathed and put on their salt-crusted clothes, they turned at once to the mountain, and Tensor pressed them harder than ever, as if it was a race they were in danger of losing. It was a cruel climb after so many days on the flat, and a long one. Though they had been labouring up the ramp from the bottom of the sea for days, it was still more than a thousand spans from the base of the first set of cliffs to the flat plain that once formed the shore of the island. There all was dry and scrubby too, a desert of gritty ash that squeaked underfoot. The land was covered in saltbush and thorn thickets, littered with pumice boulders and small volcanic cinder cones, some not much taller than Llian. The earth often shook here.

In the evening they spied tall trees in the distance and at dusk reached a modest river foaming with snowmelt. Tensor stripped off his robes to wade into the chilly water. The others followed his example, though Llian found the water too cold for his liking. They swam, washed their clothes and camped by running water that night for the first time in weeks. After the oppression of the sea bed the cool, thin and salt-free air of Katazza was like a bath in a crystal-clear waterfall. Llian, however, lay on the pebbles, utterly fatigued. After weeks breathing the soupy air of the Dry Sea, this mountain air felt too thin for his lungs.

The next day they had another climb, leaving the river to scrabble up scrub-covered slopes into the mountains, where in the early afternoon they struck the remnants of a well-made road, five spans wide, that led through a ruined city toward a cone-shaped mountain. Parts of the road were torn away by deluge or landslide and the stone slabs were cracked or angled up in many places, nonetheless it was the easiest walking they'd had in a long time. They pressed on until midnight, stopping halfway up for a few hours' rest. Llian had to be carried most of the way; he was now so tired that he could barely walk.

'What's the matter with you?' Malien asked, walking beside the stretcher.

'I nearly died of mountain sickness on the way to Shazmak,' he replied. 'This feels just the same.'

'Katazza is not as high as Shazmak, though you have climbed higher, from the bottom of the Dry Sea.' She inspected him carefully. 'I think you'll get used to it after a week or two. Don't exert yourself too much.'

Before dawn they set out again, following the road which wound around the mountain. The land was barren on three sides but a series of folds and terraces contained patches of forest and bog. Toward the top they passed by a half-ruined temple, its columns sagging among the trees, and an overgrown bathing pool carved out of rock.

'We're going to be late!' shouted Tensor, abruptly turning off the road to head straight up the steep slope, almost at running pace.

'What's the hurry?' panted Llian to Asper as the other Aachim streamed after.

'He wants to be there for dawn!' Asper gave the struggling Llian his shoulder, and shortly they emerged onto a small plateau at the back of a massive building.

The sun burst up over the mountains in orange glory and lit up the tip of the tallest tower of Katazza fortress like a match being touched to a candle. They had reached their destination at last, and it was not much more than eight weeks since the breaking of the Conclave.

Llian was so taken in by the magnificence and the wonder of Katazza that he could not speak. No chronicler in the past millennium had seen it. His fears were for the moment quite forgotten.

The living rock of the mountain top had been carved flat, and near the edge they'd climbed was a paved oblong, stepped up to an enormous building. At either end the steps were divided into two by a broad ramp ten spans wide that swept up from the plateau and back down to it. Above the steps was a flat area paved in obsidian, though now the stones were cracked and the roots of huge old figs and ebony trees thrust them up into spiky mounds. Inside the paving was the massive rectangle of Katazza fortress itself, that looked between triple peaks to the south, the north, the east and the west. Snow lay in the shadows from a recent fall, for spring was only a fortnight old.

From the centre of that monstrous structure there soared multi-coloured domes and spires, at least a dozen, with minarets at their quarters. Nine lofty towers grew between the mushrooming domes, each made of spiralling cables of stone plaited together and faced with tiles so white that the sun on them dazzled the eye.

As they moved onto the plateau they saw that the tenth tower dwarfed all the others, soaring at least a hundred and fifty spans into the sky. The sunlight crept down revealing that it too was made of woven cables of laid stone, each cable as wide as a cottage – a complex spiral interwoven with all the other spirals in a pattern that was everywhere different. Halfway up and at the top the weave was circled with bands of lapis lazuli, each three or four spans wide, bordered with gold. The dome that surmounted the tower was topped with beaten platinum, shining silvery white, decorated with crimson.

Turning a corner of the fortress they realised that the tenth tower stood by itself in the centre of the plateau, but joined to Katazza fortress by a pair of metal bridges. An enormous rift ran across the plateau, lifting the stones on one side the height of a tall step, and thence beneath the tower through a pointed archway. The rift was closed up tight, though near the surrounding paved area the tower water dribbled out to stain the ground yellow and blue, and an occasional wisp of steam drifted up.

'How did the tower survive the earth trembler that did this?' Malien asked in wonder.

'It was built to survive it,' said Tensor, leading them towards the archway: The rift was already there. See how the foundations are in separate parts, cunningly made to move independently of each other.'

The Aachim passed in between two of the stone cables, exclaiming at the engineering genius that could create such a structure. Llian had no interest in that, but he could not help wonder why Kandor had gone to such trouble to build over the rift. What was it about this place that had been so important to him?

Shortly they were brought up by a curving wall, much stained by fumes. They walked all the way round, back to their starting point.

'I imagine the entrance is via the bridge from the fortress,' called Asper.

'No doubt,' said Tensor.

He marched across to the fortress. Standing on the broad step before the western door there was a look of grim satisfaction on his face.

'Though Kandor was the least of our enemies, I cannot but smile to stand here on his threshold. We have fallen, may never rise again, yet we have outlasted this enemy. And now his fortress, impregnable to all save time, will shelter us from our foes.'

He pushed the door, but it did not budge. Though it had never been secured during Kandor's two-thousand-year tenancy, nor after his servants fled, time had welded its hinges. The Aachim had to push together to free it, but the aged metal broke, leaving the door sagging. They went inside, thick dust muffling the echo of their feet and rising in little puffs at toe and heel.

Llian did not follow them – the walk had exhausted him.

'Well, here I am,' he said to himself. 'Back in Thurkad I dreamed of coming here to find Kandor's papers about the Forbidding, though I never thought that I would. Now what do I do? What exactly had Kandor said?'

Waiting until they had all gone inside, he sat down behind a tree and read once more the letter that he had stolen from the citadel just before the disastrous Conclave.

17 Mard, 4201

My dear Rulke,

I am so weary of war, and this world, that I would do anything to end it. The loss of Perion has eaten the heart out of me. Once more I beg you – share what you know with me. Say the word and everything I have is yours. I will even bend the knee to you. You know how much that takes, but I am beaten.

Something happened at the time of the Forbidding. I have spent a fortune trying to find out what it was. Was it you? Let us come together on this – we are both Charon. I think you forget that sometimes. I beg you, by the one thing that you cannot refuse, that tops all other considerations: the survival of our species.

I have written to Yalkara as well. I will gladly bring what I have to Alcifer, if you will it. I wait upon your reply.

Kandor

Llian thought back on the strange tale that had started the whole business, his new version of the *Tale of the Forbidding*. His heart went out to the crippled girl, dancing away those few hours of happiness that Shuthdar had given her, miraculously protected from the maelstrom of the Forbidding, only to be stabbed in the back soon after. What secret had she been killed to protect?

I have spent a fortune trying to find out. Well, let's see what can be learned here. Where did Kandor die? How did he die? Did he meet Rulke first? Did he leave his records here or take them on that fateful journey? I must be very careful, Llian thought. Not even Malien can I trust with this secret.

Putting the letter away, he followed the Aachim into the magnificence of Katazza. Tensor was already setting out his plan for the ordering of the fortress. The little band of Aachim hurried to do his will.

While that was going on, Llian gazed around him with the greatest satisfaction. He was recalling to his mind the many tales about the empire, set down in *The Book of Perion*. What student of the Histories would ever have thought to come to Katazza and find that the towers still stood, unchanged from the days of their glory? But he was uneasy as well, for surely now Tensor must reveal what use he planned for Llian. That came about sooner than he had expected.

Tensor turned and once again his eyes pinned Llian. 'Come with me!' he said.

They stepped together through Katazza, though every room they went into Tensor rejected with a shake of the head.

'What are you looking for?' asked Llian, anxiously.

Tensor was in good humour today, almost friendly. 'A chamber that is large enough; one that can be made secure against any attack. But more than that, one that has the right feel. To mould and direct the Secret Art as I intend, the place must be perfect.'

'Where did Kandor work?' Llian wondered, trying to understand Katazza for his *Tale of the Mirror*.

Tensor whirled. 'Good thinking, chronicler. I don't know, but maybe you do – you've read the tales of this place.'

Llian sorted through memories. *The Book of Perion* was in fact five books; thousands of pages of tales. 'Ah!' he said, after a pause. 'There is a line in *The Manceriom* that goes: *he looked down from his workbench into the fires of the rift*.'

'So where he worked must have been somewhere above the rift,' said Tensor. 'A place of great power, surely, somewhere in the Great Tower. You may yet earn your keep, chronicler. We'll try the western bridge.'

It led from the fortress into the Great Tower by a cunningly concealed entrance between the stone cables. The rock was stained and corroded by fumes. Climbing a stair that spiralled between the cables and the curving inner wall, they looked out through glass windows that were flawless, though extremely thick, down on the domes and spires of Katazza.

On the fifth level the stair terminated at a landing. They entered an open doorway so wide that all of the Aachim could have passed through it together, into a room that occupied the whole floor of the tower. It could be sealed off with a massive door of steel, but on the other side the stair was open, now sweeping up inside the inner wall to the higher levels. The floor was uncannily warm and the room had a faint brimstone reek.

'This is it,' Tensor sighed. 'I can *sense* it. A fitting place for my work as it once was for Kandor's.'

Llian was in ecstasy as he wandered the room, immersing himself in Kandor's environment. The room had the shape of a nine-leaved clover, while the ceiling was a vault made of stone arches growing out of the walls, so high that Llian counted sixty steps before the stair curved away out of sight. Dusty fireplaces of carved stone, large enough to roast an ox in, stood in each bay. All around were small tubular windows of coloured glass that passed right through the inner walls and the outer braided stone cables as well. The setting sun came in one window bathing the room in a golden light, a light peculiar to Katazza. Llian climbed the stair, finding another chamber on the next level, though not nearly as grand, and the stair continuing up.

'Hoy, chronicler! Time to get to work!' Tensor's voice came echoing around the corner.

Dust danced in the last shafts of sunlight. They began clearing away the dirt and dust, the crumbling papers and fabrics. When the sun went down they had to stop, for though there were globes on the walls no one had yet worked out how to get any light out of them, and the oil vessels contained only a waxy sludge on the bottom. The Aachim made makeshift lamps by soaking twists of rotten fabric in the sludge, and later a kind of candle from the wax, then continued their labours.

That night Malien appeared at Llian's door with a pair of spectacles made of wire and glass. The glass was so old that it had gone a purply brown. She fitted the spectacles to Llian's face without a word, examining the result with her lamp.

'That will do. Wear them in the daytime. You can say that the bright sun up here hurts your eyes, if anyone asks. And at night – well, no one has noticed so far.'

In fact no one had taken any notice of Llian all day, so absorbed were the Aachim in the wonder that Tensor had led them to. Even Basitor and Hintis spoke to him without evident malice. There was still plenty of food, so fast had been the crossing, and they supplemented it with nuts, roots and fruit that had dried in the desiccating air outside, though that was bad as well as wormy. But it sufficed until scouts returned from the north of the island four days later, with supplies bartered from the shy, forest-dwelling native people.

Now the days became like each other, with the Aachim working ceaselessly to bring their refuge into order. This was a major task, for Katazza was vast and parts were in ruinous condition. A month went by as they repaired the doors, walls and other defences, ensured that cisterns and storerooms were full and secret entrances blocked, and fixed water pumps and boilers, sewers and lights. One night Llian came in from outside and found all the lightglasses glowing, lighting up the wonder of Katazza.

In all this work he was unable to assist, except in the most menial way, for he was clumsy with his hands. Not even competent to cook the food of the Aachim to the standard that they required, he felt himself to be particularly useless. The only aid he could provide was fetching and carrying.

When that work was done they dismissed him and he was

left to his own devices. Llian was delighted. Here was Katazza to be examined and described, used to flesh out the Histories and be brought to life in the Great Tales. That was work for a lifetime.

Llian fluctuated between euphoria and despair. No chronicler had ever had such opportunities as were being offered here. Surely the *Tale of the Mirror* was already a Great Tale, though more than likely he would not live to tell it, if Malien's warnings, or Hintis's and Basitor's threats, came true.

Llian tried not to think about Karan; that was too painful and fruitless. He spent more and more time with Tensor, who for some time had been struggling to master the Mirror. At first Llian stood in the doorway, watching silently, and when this brought no response he was sufficiently emboldened to sit at the end of the bench. He felt like a schoolboy watching his teacher perform some incomprehensible rite. He felt insignificant, while the least thing that Tensor did was fascinating.

'This Mirror is changed from the one I knew,' said Tensor, staring at the glyphs flowing about its perimeter. 'It is Yalkara's work. And this –' he touched the shimmering symbol, 'it fogs my mind. But I will find a way to overcome it.'

Llian stared just as eagerly. The glyphs were a puzzle – a script that he could not read at all. How he wanted to. If Yalkara had put them there, to what purpose?

Tensor sat gazing at the Mirror, which was propped up on the bench before him. He could have been asleep – his eyes were closed – but his body was as tense as a bow.

Was he conducting some long-delayed rite of thanksgiving at the recovery of the Mirror, that oldest of the heirlooms of the Aachim. Or was he trying to find a path through the snares and deceits within it, to tune his mind to it and bring it under his control?

A day passed. Tiring of watching Tensor, who still had not moved, Llian began to wrestle with another puzzle. '*He looked down from his workbench into the fires of the rift . . .*' The rift ran right beneath the tower. Llian had scoured the floor on hands and knees for secret passages or trapdoors, but found none. The floors below this room were sealed off. What could the quote mean? Maybe this was not the right room after all.

Llian gave up and went for a walk, following a track down to a patch of forest below the southern rim of the plateau. There he found some red fruit like persimmons that had hung on the bare branches all winter and were so ripe that they almost fell to pieces in his hands. Beyond Llian saw a small lichen-encrusted dome between the trees. It was a pavilion held up with eight columns, set on an eminence of basalt beside a lookout that overviewed the forested terraces and the stony mountains beyond, and out the other side, the Sea of Perion. The pavilion was shaded by a vast fig whose cascade of ropy roots enclosed one side, pushing the columns askew, and the columns, the benches and the table inside were carved from solid serpentine.

He hesitated between the two columns that formed the entrance, stroking the silky yellow-green stone with his fingertip.

'Come in,' said Malien.

Llian started, dropping one of his fruits, which made a red splatter on his boot. As his eyes adjusted she appeared out of the background, sitting with her back against the roots of the fig tree.

'I don't want to disturb . . .'

'No matter. I was thinking about you, as it happened. How are your hands?'

He looked confused. 'Oh, they are better.'

'Come, sit down, eat your fruit.'

Llian sat beside her and offered what he had. 'I am not hungry,' she said, laughing, and he gained the impression that she thought him rather a yokel, with his hands full of dripping fruit and stains down his shirt and trousers. 'What is Tensor doing?'

'Staring at the Mirror for hours on end.'

'When you go back, watch him carefully. I want to know everything he does.'

Llian said nothing.

'Llian!'

'I'm not a very good spy. I can't . . .'

Her hand flashed out, gripping his wrist painfully hard. One of the fruits squirted its fermenting pulp and a clot oozed down his shirt, to his further chagrin.

'This is not a game that you play at tellers' school.' Malien's voice was low and savage. Llian tried to get away but she hauled him back effortlessly. Her strength was frightening, but the blaze in her eyes was worse. 'I know that to *you* the only thing that matters is the tale, but you don't understand what is at risk here. Well, let me make it absolutely clear. If he is doing what I think he is, then I will die, and you, and all of us Aachim, and Karan, if she still lives, and countless thousands of your people and all the peoples of Santhenar. And for what? The revenge of a madman – nothing more. Believe me, if there were any way to stop him I would have done so already, but he is too wary and too strong. You are in my debt and now I call upon you to repay it. *Show me your quality!'*

'Why do you not stop him?' Llian quavered. 'You and Selial could – '

'My hands are bound, chronicler. Tensor and I were partners once, and though that is long ago, I cannot strike him down. I cannot end him, and that is the only way that he can be stopped.'

'Selial is strong – I saw her stare him down at Karan's trial in Shazmak. He did as she ordered.'

'That was before Shazmak fell,' she said, so softly that he had to crane his neck to catch the words. 'Tensor is more resolute than ever. But Selial – it has burned all life and hope out of her.'

'You said it before, back at the hill where the ghosts were,' Malien continued after a pause. 'We do not have the courage.'

She let go his wrist. Llian massaged the hand until the numbness went away. 'You do not know our history, Llian.'

'I'd like to,' he interrupted, curiosity overcoming his fears for the moment.

'So often have we been undone by fighting among ourselves – not least when the Charon took our world – that now we shrink from any such conflict. We have taken folly to the other extreme. It would be going against two thousand years of history for us to restrain Tensor by force. Besides, he is incredibly powerful, the equal of all of us, even without his followers. If we force him, he will use the potency against us. Yes, he has fallen so far that he would even slay us, were we to get between him and his folly. When you are weak, chronicler, you must be cunning. So I use you. What is your choice?'

'I will do it,' he said shaken. It had been easy to avoid thinking about the results of collaboration.

'Good,' she said, and gave him a genuine smile. 'I must go.'

'What would you have done if I had refused?' he wondered aloud. He always wanted to know the alternatives – and their consequences.

Malien paused on the threshold.

'I think that Karan would understand the sacrifice, even if she could never forgive it,' she said softly. 'I would have betrayed you to Basitor.'

PART THREE

32

FARANDA BOUND

'Now I will hear your story,' said Nadiril, when the bowls were taken away and fresh ones brought. 'Tell me all of it, leaving nothing out, and I will add what I know. Then, Mendark, if it is still needful, you may ask me your questions.'

Mendark and Tallia told their stories. Lilis hunched up in her chair, listening intently but saying nothing. Her face was so alive with possibilities that it quite transformed her from the thin-faced, pointed-chin little urchin of a few weeks ago. She could not keep still; could not keep the beaming smile off her face, but every so often it would cloud over, her jaw muscles clench. Some evil memory from her time on the streets, Tallia supposed.

With the dark it became cold. The servant returned with a cloak for Nadiril and another for each of them, though Mendark had no need of his and it hung over the back of his chair.

'This is a bad business,' said Nadiril. 'Just you and me and old Wistan holding to the purpose, and I'm a useless old thing.'

'Indeed!' said Mendark.

Nadiril ignored that. 'Will you try to renew the Council?'

'Orstand is irreplaceable. Even Hennia – treacherous Zain that she is!'

'You have Tallia,' said Nadiril.

Tallia stirred, as though she was going to protest.

'Too young!'

Lilis looked as if her friend had just been insulted.

'You were as young when you first joined the Council,' responded Nadiril. His rheumy eyes met Tallia's for a moment, and it seemed that they held a question. Tallia raised her eyebrow slightly but Nadiril turned back to Mendark.

I don't want it, Tallia thought. When this business is over I am going home, and I don't think I'll ever return. She exhaled a gusty sigh.

'Times were different then,' said Mendark.

'You know best, of course,' said Nadiril, smiling innocently.

'Enough of your sarcasm and your sly little games,' Mendark said testily. 'Where have you been when I needed you these last few years?'

'Right here,' Nadiril said frostily, 'waiting for your call.'

'You haven't been to a Council meeting in ten years.'

'The Council hasn't done anything but talk. The Library needed me here, so I could answer your questions when you finally condescended to ask them. I should travel two months for you to lecture me on my responsibilities? For all his follies, Thyllan was right! The rise of Yggur, and the fall of Thurkad, does lie at your feet.'

'I was Magister, not Governor!' Mendark spat.

'Bah!' said Nadiril. 'She was your puppet, Mendark – the whole Assembly were! Face it: you're a greedy, selfish, wicked old man and you no longer have the courage for the job.'

Mendark positively shook with fury. He stood up, waving his fist in the air. 'You bloody old fool, just look at yourself, twitching in your decrepitude. I've a good mind –'

Lilis, who had been looking more anxious with every word, burst into tears. 'Stop it. Stop it!' she wailed, squeezing her eyes shut to contain the tears.

'Yes, stop it at once,' Tallia said softly. 'Look at you! What a pair of fools you are.'

'I'm sorry, Lilis,' said Nadiril. 'Do not be alarmed, child: we are old foes. What would you ask of me, Mendark?'

Mendark calmed himself, though it took an effort. 'What you know about the Mirror of Aachan. What powers does it have? What secrets does it hold and, most urgently of all, what does Tensor want it for?'

Nadiril took time to compose his words. The light of the lamp illuminated only part of his face, and not his eyes, making his head more skull-like than ever.

'Since this matter arose,' he said at last, 'I've spent some little time searching out the records. Thus far I have only three references dealing with the Mirror, all of which are second-hand. There may be others, but it will take time and the cost will be great. Still, you never went short of the Magister's gold.'

'I brought enough to pay your outrageous fees. Tell me what you have,' said Mendark in surly tones.

'There is another thing that bothers me almost as much as Tensor does,' Nadiril said obliquely. 'These Ghâshâd! Why did they take Shazmak and what are they up to now? We must come back to that. But to your question: the Mirror is scarcely mentioned in the main body of the Histories, for it seemed such a minor thing at first. The scribes had far greater devices to marvel at. Later, after Yalkara changed it, it was kept secret. Even so, it is remarkable that so little is written about it. Very remarkable.

'The first reference is in an ancient book of the Aachim, called the *Nazhak tel Mardux*. It was said to be written by Pitlis before he died, though I believe it was made after his death. The book tells of the early history of the Aachim, during the time that they held the Mirror, but it is long lost. I have never set eyes on it.'

'Llian read that book in Shazmak!' cried Mendark. 'But the idiot left it there.'

'Then certainly he must come here when he is found. The *Nazhak* may have been destroyed in the fall of Shazmak,

473

and all the more vital that what Llian remembers is written down. The second reference is to the *Codex of Yalkara*, what you might call *her* Histories. The *Codex*, if it exists at all, would doubtless be the most valuable of the sources, as Yalkara was the greatest of the users of the Mirror, and the most subtle. She was an ambiguous figure; quite the most puzzling of ancient times.'

Mendark said nothing. He was deep in thought.

'The third reference is no less obscure: a document called *The Secrets of the Recorder*. All that is known of the Recorder,' Nadiril explained, turning to Lilis, 'is that he set down the story of the struggles of Yalkara and Faelamor before Yalkara fled from Santhenar. I have only a corrupted and incomplete version. You may see it, Mendark. But of the other matters of which it is reputed to speak – Yalkara's parting injunction, the disposal of the Mirror after her departure – nothing! We do not even know who the Recorder was, except that his name was Gyllias. But that was a common name in past times; there are several mentioned in the Histories.'

Mendark was still silent.

'I fear that I've not been much assistance,' said Nadiril. 'There may be more in the Library, but none can recall it. Yet there are scrolls here that have not been read in a thousand years; books that no one can decipher. If all my scribes read for a hundred years they would not have seen a tithe of what is here. However, my feeling is that there is nothing more to be found.'

'Let me see this corrupted fragment that you have,' said Mendark. 'Llian will tell me what the *Nazhak tel Mardux* says, if we find him.'

'If he read it, he can write it down. When you find him, tell him to do so at once. I look forward very much to seeing it.'

'I venture you will have passed on by then,' said Mendark. Tallia flinched.

Nadiril fixed Mendark with a very clear cold stare. 'Not even a seer can see their own end and I certainly cannot. But my imminent death has been predicted for so long that I venture I will be at my work when you are no more than ashes.'

Mendark shuddered as though a toad had crawled up his back. Tallia diverted the discussion into safer waters. 'What of Yalkara's *Codex*? Where might that be found? Is anything known of it?'

'The Histories speak of the *Codex* only as rumour. No one has sighted it; indeed, it is not known whether it is a single book or a library of volumes. Further, and this may discourage you from looking too hard, in what language is it written? And what script? If you plan to look for it, go to the *Wahn Barre*, where her ancient fastness, Havissard, lies abandoned but inviolate. No one has ever found a way in. Now Lilis, would you excuse us for a while? Mendark and I have private business to discuss.'

Tallia walked away with Lilis to the wall that enclosed the rooftop, pointing to the lights of the city and the stars.

'I suppose you'll be leaving soon,' said Lilis with a sniffle.

'I expect so.'

'I'll miss you, Tallia.'

'And I you,' said Tallia, putting her arm around the child. 'But I'll be back.'

'What else do you want from me?' asked Nadiril. 'That's not all you came for.'

'The other is . . .' Mendark tugged his beard fretfully, '. . . I don't know if there's anything in it or not.'

'This matter about what really happened at the time of the Forbidding?'

'How did you know that?'

'My dear Mendark – the Histories are my business. I'd heard within a week of Llian giving his tale.'

'And could there be anything in it? That someone got into the tower secretly?'

Nadiril scratched his blotchy scalp. 'I have often wondered

about that over the years. I haven't seen any convincing evidence. It would be good to read the proofs for Llian's tale, but old Wistan has locked them away and they can't be obtained until his death.'

'Silly old bugger!' said Mendark vehemently. 'I've a mind to hasten that a little.' Nadiril turned a cold eye on him. 'But I won't,' Mendark added.

'So, what are *your* plans, Mendark?'

'To hunt down Tensor and the Mirror.'

'And then? Are you strong enough for the resolution?'

'I don't know. I'm old; I'm failing.'

'And if you fall, who will carry on?'

'I had hoped that Tallia would. She is capable . . .'

'But not greedy enough?'

'No. She doesn't want everything, as I did, and Rula before me. Rula! She was the greatest Magister of us all, and look what good it did her! Tallia is not hard enough. She cares too much about people. Two fatal flaws in a Magister, to my mind.'

'Not to mine,' said Nadiril, 'but then, what do I know of the burdens of your office?'

Weeks went by. Mendark spent all his time in the bowels of the Library, searching out ancient maps and documents. He was bad company, frustrated at his inability to find what he was looking for.

Finding his constant ill-humour irritating, Tallia wandered Zile, talking to shopkeepers and people in the inns. They were all happy to gossip. The war was a long way away and Zile had been conquered many times in its history. Its people were resilient, accepting. Such things happened, but after a while life would resume, not much changed from what it had been before.

She had taken to walking in the early morning. In the first days Lilis had come too, but she soon became so consumed by her work and her lessons that she could find time for nothing else.

Today Tallia walked for an hour or so, enjoying the quiet, with sometimes a solitary other walker coming silently out of the mist, nodding and disappearing again. As the sun rose she sat on a bench in an outdoor café, her favourite one. Shortly the owner came out. Her hair was white, though she was not old; a slender woman with high cheekbones and a broad beautiful face wasted on her solitary customer.

'You are early this morning, Mahl,' she said respectfully, using the courtesy title for a foreign scholar. She wiped the dew off the table with a cloth that Tallia had never seen her without. 'What can I get you?'

Tallia gave her order. 'It's cool this morning!'

'Cool!' the woman agreed. 'We'll soon warm you up – it's a pleasure! Customers are so few these days; I had none yesterday. Just wait a few minutes until I get the stove roaring. Easier to think with a bowl in your hand, I reckon.'

She left Tallia to her ruminations. White smoke gushed from the kitchen chimney. Tallia watched the smoke, musing. There had been several messages from Mendark's factors lately, reporting sightings of a small company of Aachim hurrying north by seldom-trodden ways. But the sightings all dated from the first few days after the Conclave. Since that time there had been nothing at all.

Her breakfast came, thick pancakes flavoured with nutmeg and allspice, a small jug of black sugar-cane syrup and a large bowl of hot vanilla with shreds of mace floating on the skin.

'This will get your blood flowing,' said the woman, as Tallia pushed the skin to one side and sipped the scalding drink. The flavour of vanilla and mace was overpowering. She poured the contents of the jug over the pancakes and began to eat.

'No customers yesterday? What's happening to Zile?'

The woman shrugged. 'The war, far away and all as it is. And the drought – it has lasted for thirty years now. The irrigation ditches are thick with salt and nothing grows anymore. But the west has been declining for a thousand years in favour of Thurkad and other wretched places. One day the sand will cover ancient Zile. Even the Great Library will fail.'

'That will be a sad day.'

'It's all that remains of our ancient glory.'

'The Great Library is still the glory of all Santhenar,' said Tallia.

'Perhaps, but Santhenar does not care to support it. No, Zile is finished, as surely as the Dry Sea is dry. *Not until the Sea of Perion once more thunders against the jewelled shores of Katazza Mountain will Zile rise again.* So the prediction goes, and I am sure it is a true one.'

'Katazza! Was that not a great island in the middle of the sea?'

'It was, and is still, I suppose, though all is desert now.'

A thought struck Tallia. She stopped eating, her fork in the air. Black syrup ran down onto her fingers. She licked it off absently, then suddenly put down the fork, drained her bowl and fingered coin out of her purse.

'Are the pancakes not to your taste?' the woman asked anxiously. 'I can . . .'

'They're delicious, but I just thought of something urgent. I must run, thank you.'

In the Library she found Nadiril deep in the vaults, already perched on his stool, with Lilis beside him copying from a book onto a slate. He checked her work, frowning. Lilis promptly erased the slate and started again. There were dark shadows under her eyes but she looked intensely happy.

Nadiril seemed to read Tallia's thoughts. 'Never have I had such a student,' he said. 'She will not even stop to sleep. Lilis, come read your slate to Tallia. Show her your progress.'

It was an arid account of a minor Council held some hundreds of years ago. Lilis, beaming, read the page in a monotonous voice, though with barely a stumble.

'There,' said Nadiril, as proud as if she was his own

daughter. 'One day the pupil will excel the master.' He looked twenty years younger. 'Now, back to your writing lesson. Progress is not *so* good there.' Lilis soberly bent to her slate again.

'I'm sure when next we meet you will be a master scribe,' said Tallia. The beaming smile was back again, then the import sank in.

'You are going away?' The young student reverted to the squeaky child.

'I think so, but never fear, we will be back. And if I find that Nadiril has not fulfilled the terms of the contract, *he will have me to answer to*.' She scowled fiercely at the librarian.

'What would you ask of me?' said Nadiril with a dry chuckle.

'Anything you know about Katazza.'

'Then or now? Now I suppose. Very little, really. People still try to cross the Dry Sea occasionally, though there is nothing out there valuable enough to be worth the risk. Most die. Some live to write about it. I have several accounts made in the past few hundred years. As I recall, two of them mention Katazza, though only one actually climbed the mountain. Let's go to the catalogues. Come, Lilis, here is an important new thing for you to learn.'

Just then Mendark stuck his head in through the door. 'Ah, Mendark, Tallia thinks that Katazza might be the place.'

After much searching in the dusty archives they found three reports on crossings of the Dry Sea. One was just a worn and torn map with notes on it in a tiny hand, next to scratchings which apparently indicated campsites. Katazza was marked, and other mountains, but the route had not approached it. The second was a battered notebook of some twenty loose pages, evidently having been torn from a larger one, and a beautifully drawn map. The third was a short scroll written on poorly cured leather. Most of the writing was illegible.

'There,' said Nadiril, pointing with a finger. 'The scroll

mentions Katazza by name as well as the location of a soak at the foot of the mountain where they found water. They saw snow on the peaks.'

Mendark scanned the scroll. 'But that's all!' He cast it onto the table, whereupon it coiled itself up and rolled onto the floor. Lilis scurried to pick it up, giving him a reproachful glare.

'This is the best of them,' said Nadiril, handing him the notebook, 'as you might have expected.'

'The writing tugs at my memory,' said Mendark, puzzled. 'No, I cannot say.'

'An old *friend* of yours,' said Nadiril, scarcely able to conceal his delight.

Mendark stared at him.

'Shand!' said Nadiril. 'He gave the Library many boxes of papers when he retired to Tullin.'

'*Shand!* Well, let's see what he has to say.'

'Quite a lot. There are notes on each day's travel and each camp, the map, and several pages on Katazza itself.'

'Katazza!' said Mendark. 'Who would have thought it?' He read from the first page of the notebook. *The Histories tell that there was a stronghold of the Charon on Katazza. Kandor's towers soared from the pinnacles of Katazza over the azure sea of Perion*. He has a very flowery style.'

'But the information is there. Read on!'

Mendark read the rest of it to himself, a description of the drying up of the sea, detailed notes on the journey, weather conditions, hazards and waterholes, a digression on the myths and legends of Katazza. 'Is there any record of Tensor having seen this?'

'No,' said Nadiril, 'but he came to the Library many times over the years and wandered where he would. I cannot say that he has not. Doubtless there are accounts in other libraries. He may have even been to Katazza himself.'

'I can see why he might want to hide there,' said Mendark. 'It would make an incomparable refuge for one who sought only solitude and time to order his affairs. But I must have some sign to embark on such a journey.'

The following day the sign came, a skeet from one of Mendark's factors. Among other despatches was the following: a band of big folk, led by Tensor, had stayed three days in Siftah before taking ship north in all haste to Faranda. And with them was a young man of middle height that could have been Llian.

'Faranda!' said Mendark, his mood suddenly lightened. 'Though this message was written weeks ago. Tallia, go at once to Framan, find Pender and get us passage to Tikkadel, on the Foshorn. We'll seek news of them there, then head north to Flude. I'll copy these documents and follow tomorrow. Nadiril, send word to me in Flude, if you have any news.' He gave the name of a contact.

'This is wonderful!' Nadiril beamed, not trying to hide his pleasure at Mendark's imminent departure.

Lilis, however, looked distraught. 'I did not think you would go so soon,' she said, a forlorn child again.

Tallia embraced her. 'Nor I,' she replied, 'but the sooner we depart, the sooner we will meet again.'

'Good,' said Nadiril. 'Now, Lilis, Tallia is going to look for your friend Llian. Come, tell us about your father and we will see what we can do to find him too.'

Lilis described her father as best she could, though no better than Tallia had heard before.

'What about the people who took him?' asked Nadiril. 'What do you remember about them?'

'They were foul and ugly and mean!' Lilis cried.

'That describes half the people I've ever met,' Mendark said sourly.

'Including yourself! Lilis,' said Nadiril, 'you must try to remember more, else how can we know where to look?'

'What about the boat?' Tallia asked. 'You told me they dragged him off to a boat and sailed away.'

Lilis screwed her eyes shut. 'It looked a bit like *The*

Waif – a fast boat. I remember it had red sails.'

'Did you see the name?'

She started. 'I couldn't read it. But,' she said excitedly, 'I heard people say the name afterwards. It was a cruel name, like *Stabber* or *Cutter* or *Dagger*.'

'Try harder,' said Mendark irritably. 'Tallia, you must get going.'

'She was only five at the time, Mendark.'

'If you can think of the name,' said Nadiril, 'it can be traced through the Customs records, though it will cost much in bribes.'

'I have some money,' said Lilis, getting out her purse.

'Put it away, child,' said Tallia. 'Before I go, I have something for you. Each of the people that you rescued from the Conclave paid a ransom and here it is. This will help you with your quest.' She offered Lilis a small heavy leather bag.

Lilis did not take it. She looked bemused. 'Ransom?'

Tallia pressed it into her hands. 'Perhaps that's not the right word. Suffice it to say that they paid what their lives were worth, quite a bit in most cases, and it is yours. Farewell now. I will ask at every port on the way.' They embraced again, Tallia clasped Nadiril's hand and hurried out.

Back at Framan, the downriver port of Zile, Mendark and Tallia had a wait of a few days because Pender had taken *The Waif* off on another commission. When he returned they found the boat freshly painted, every rail glistening and the deck stoned back to smooth cream wood. Another two days passed before the boat was fully supplied, which Mendark spent pacing and issuing veiled threats against moonlighting captains. But Pender was mournful for days when he learned that Lilis was not coming.

Once on board they had good tail-winds and crossed the hundred and twenty leagues to Faranda in a matter of a few days. They learned nothing at Tikkadel, except that a large party had crossed that way, a long time ago now.

They debated what to do. Mendark knew the geography of the northern lands better than most, for he'd sailed around them many times.

'I know a place where a cape of Faranda, a horn-shaped range, juts out into the Dry Sea in the direction of Katazza,' he said. 'By going that way our journey across the salt will be much shorter.'

They sailed north for days, then dropped anchor in a rocky bay, shaped rather like an egg, at the furthest, roundest part of which was a significant town, called Flude. The land north and south of Flude was barren but the town itself lay on the floodplain of a river fed from snowmelt.

'What now, eh?' said Pender.

'It would be better if he knew,' said Tallia.

'Come into the cabin. Osseion, stand guard outside and see that we are not overheard.' The door banged shut.

'We are going across the Dry Sea to Katazza, boatman,' said Mendark.

'Katazza! Then it would be well that you sign *The Waif* over to me now, since surely you will never come back.' Pender was only half-joking.

'We will return by the end of summer,' said Mendark, not smiling, 'if we return at all. Then we will have need of a boat. Where will you be at that time?'

'Right here, if you pay my hire for the next five and a half months.'

Mendark gave a derisive bark.

'Otherwise,' Pender reflected, 'I will take what passengers and cargoes I can along the coast of Faranda, and maybe even as far east as Crandor.'

'I should be sorry if you went to Crandor without me,' said Tallia wistfully.

'Well, I daren't go back to Meldorin.'

'If we rode all the way to Katazza and then marched straight back again,' said Mendark thinking aloud, 'we could hardly be back here in less than three and a half months.

So, do what you will until the month of Guffins, Pender, but be here at that time. I will pay you to wait for two months.'

They shook hands on it and next day went to the Harbour Master's office, where Pender paid Mendark for *The Waif*, the spare sails and all the ship's gear Tallia had purchased in Ganport. By hard bargaining he secured a heavy discount for wear and tear, as well as a generous price for the loss of *The Dancing Goose*. Even so, it took every tell of the vast hire that Mendark had paid him and all his other earnings too. The ship's papers were changed to Pender's name, the price counted out, and a host of documents signed, stamped, sealed and registered.

'You cannot imagine how happy I am,' Pender said to Tallia as they headed back to the boat. 'My life's dream is fulfilled. But . . .'

'But you have spent every grint you had and have no capital to run your ship, nor any reserve for emergencies.'

'How did you know?'

'I can count,' said Tallia.

'And there is the crew to pay,' he replied glumly. 'Oh farsh! I will have to put myself in the hands of the graspers, though I swore I never would again. The cost of their money is three tells back for every one borrowed each year.'

'I have an alternative proposal,' offered Tallia. 'Perhaps you would like to consider it. I have a little capital and it will weigh down my pocket sorely if I have to carry it to Katazza and back. What if I were to become your partner?'

'Even were you not to be in the middle of a hundred leagues of salt it would be a good arrangement,' Pender whooped, beamed and bussed her on each cheek.

They turned their steps to a notary, where a contract was drawn up, terms specified, next of kin listed, and then back to the Harbour Master's, where the ownership was amended once more. They shook hands and Tallia, for a payment of two hundred tells, became a one-fifth partner in *The Waif*.

They all stayed on board one more day while Mendark completed arrangements for their trip, then without ceremony they shook hands with Pender and the crew and departed with a guide and mounts.

In little more than six weeks they had ridden across the mountains and plateaus of Faranda, sent back the mounts with their guide and were camped at the bottom of the Dry Sea. The way Mendark had chosen to cross the sea was blessed by the largest stream to run from central Faranda. Swelled by melted snow, it flowed in a sinuous channel across the salt flats for many leagues before debouching into a series of oval lakes. The water was fresh, for the river had built up its bed and banks of silt over the salt, allowing trees and shrubs to grow there.

The lakes were shallow, abundant with fish and fowl. They made camp by the water, caught fish, filled their water bottles and prepared for the night's march. The distance to Katazza was sixty leagues and more, but they were fit, rested and well-fed.

The march had been no hardship for Tallia – she had travelled longer and harder, this last year. However, it had been years since Mendark had taken such an arduous road and the past weeks had worn him down.

'What will we find at Katazza, I wonder?'

'Doubtless not what we're expecting,' said Mendark. 'Let us hope that Tensor is there, else we have come a long, hard road for nothing. And a longer and more weary way back, whatever the result.'

'And if he is, what then? Equally we might hope that he is not.' You were not the equal of Tensor before, went her unspoken thought. Why should this time be different?

Mendark had often thought about this question on their long journey, but no answer had come to him either. 'I cannot even guess,' he said. 'It's too far away. How many does he have with him? What's his state of mind, what does he propose? All unknown. I must be there, before he uses the Mirror.'

After ten wearing but uneventful marches, most spent in the brutal lava country that had so troubled Llian, they reached the precipitous flanks of Katazza. A patch of green had caught their eye hours earlier and they made their way to it, scrub nourished by a spring of sweet water issuing from the base of the cliff. After filling their water bottles, which still contained a few days' worth, they trudged north along the base of the cliffs, looking for a way up.

For a day and a half they marched. They came by several more springs – some fresh, others already salty – and in the afternoon of the second day chanced upon a set of tracks leading toward a cleft that could have been the way shown on the map.

'What's this?' said Mendark, looking around anxiously. 'Are these Aachim?'

Tallia laughed. 'Hardly, old friend,' she said. 'Look at the size of them.'

'And there are only two,' said Osseion. 'These are the marks of a man about your weight, but footsore and weary; see how they drag. The other are much smaller: a child, perhaps?'

Mendark examined them. It was evident that they were old, for the afternoon wind carried salt dust into everything and there was a powder of salt in the bottom.

'There may still be wild people living on Katazza,' said Tallia. 'It's large enough and the snow lasts into the spring; there must be water all year round. Such people might come down for purposes we know nothing about. There may be pools with fish or plants they like to eat.'

'Perhaps, but let's be cautious. Small need not mean harmless.'

They trudged on up the slope, following the prints, still wondering how they would get up the lowest set of cliffs.

The tracks went into the cleft. There they hesitated, for the sun was low.

'Shand's map was not exactly clear about the way up,' said Mendark, sitting down to consult his copy yet again.

'I'd say his track was further north,' Tallia said, looking over his shoulder. 'I vote for continuing,' she went on, seeing Mendark's doubtful frown. 'The sooner we're off the salt the happier I'll be.' She rubbed her neck where the crusted collar had chafed it. 'Let's try it; the first cliff is not that high.'

The cleft, a shear through the basalt, ran all the way up, though save for two places where it was choked with fallen rubble the passage was no more difficult than climbing a staircase. Still, by the time they reached the top they were all panting and it was almost dark. They found themselves on a rind of gently sloping land, a narrow terrace littered with huge round boulders and terminated by another set of cliffs: black, salt-encrusted extrusions like giant pillows piled one upon another.

The terrace was difficult to walk on, for it was very irregular, full of pits and hollows and collapsed caverns filled with soil and rubble. They picked their way through it. Across their path lay a cluster of boulders. Umbrella-shaped trees shaded them.

'I'm worn out,' Mendark said, flopping down.

'I can smell water,' said Osseion.

He helped Mendark back up. They clambered into the cool gloom under the canopy, making their way between the boulders. Now Tallia could also smell the odour, so heightened were her senses. Osseion parted the foliage to reveal water trickling from fissures in a head-high shelf of rock. Mendark splashed it on his face then drank from his hand.

'Fresh,' he said to himself, 'though it has an iron taste.'

None of them could think of anything but a cool drink and rest. Even Osseion had forgotten the tracks below. As Mendark stooped to the trickle again, someone sprang from a boulder and crashed without warning onto his back, flattening him against the ground. A hand jerked his head back by the hair and a blade was at his throat. A sharp object pressed into Tallia's back. Osseion's hand flashed for his own knife, then halted in mid-air.

A salt-roughened voice croaked. 'Don't even twitch or I'll cut his throat.'

33

A WARRANT

The morning after their dinner of roast clatchers, Karan and Shand set out early. She had not slept well, for Shand's worries about the Ghâshâd had woken in her a nagging fear, and she was afraid to dream lest it lead them to her again.

By midday the walls of the ravine began to shrink until they were no higher than the banks of a river, offering scant shelter from the sun, so at that point they put up the tent and rested for the remainder of the day. At sunset they dug a hole in the middle of the ravine. Finding good water, they filled all their water bottles, gathered twigs and leaves for cooking from a stranding in the channel and set off.

They travelled quickly in the starlight, soon reaching the salt plains. At first the salt was rough beneath their feet, like freshly ploughed ground, but later it became smooth as a table, with a surface crust crunching beneath each step. Further out it was as hard as rock and in places had been heaved up in a jumble of sharp-edged plates. They marched all night, then, as soon as the sun rose and the heat of the day could be felt, put up the tent again.

Karan's fears, which had retreated on the march, built up again like an approaching storm. She hardly dared to sleep. Whenever she closed her eyes she imagined them creeping up on her.

That evening, after they had eaten a frugal meal of stale flatbread with the last of the fresh meat barely singed with a few handfuls of their fuel, Karan asked Shand about their route.

'Let me show you,' he replied, and, squatting down, began to draw with the point of his knife in the salt. 'Here is Ashmode behind us, and here the cliffs that mark the northern edge of Lauralin. Get your finger out of the way until I'm finished! This is the coastline of the Sea of Perion.' The knife carved a shape somewhat like a sideways-squashed oval with a couple of indentations on the left-hand side. 'Out here in the middle, opposite the high plateau of Faranda, lies Katazza.'

A lozenge oriented in a north-westerly direction appeared in the middle of the sea, almost due north of their present position. 'Between Katazza and here there was once a scatter of islands. Now they are mountain peaks. We will be able to see them from a long way off, unless the salt haze is very bad. Which it often is, I recall. But there are also peaks that weren't tall enough to be islands before the sea dried up, and it is unlikely that we will find water at those.'

'How can we tell?' she asked. 'We might spend days searching around the base of a mountain for water and there be none.'

'We might. This is the most hazardous enterprise you have ever embarked upon. Four waterbags – *eight days*! We might very well die, you know. More people have died trying to cross the sea than have survived it. But then, I am not just anyone. You could have picked no better guide, if you only knew it. I think we will get there.'

'Boastful man,' she murmured.

'Actually, it's quite easy to pick the difference. The smallest mountains are steep and pointed, those a little higher have flat tops while the highest of all have a terrace or a plain halfway up, where the shore used to be before the sea went dry. Above that there are smaller hills or mountains, the part of the island that was once above water. Those are the ones we'll try for. And on the highest peaks of all there should still be snow visible. We are assured of water there, though it may be a long climb to get it. Others may appear barren but still have seeps, and these we should be able to tell by green growth. But I think the taller mountains are further to the north, so perhaps our challenge will come quite soon.'

'Is there anything else I should know? I thought it would just be smooth salt all the way.'

'It is in many places but not down the centre of the sea, the direction we take. Some places have no salt at all, only bare black rock freshly oozed out of the earth, sometimes too hot to touch. That land is difficult to walk in and dangerous too. Away from the centre the salt is thick and hard and relatively smooth. Most of the taller mountains are there, but for Katazza herself. And that is the way we must go.'

'We must cross this black rock country to get to Katazza?'

'We must, and it is bad country, as rough as anything you have ever been on. But then, the whole of the sea is deadly.' He stood up. 'Shall we go?'

They tramped across the salt, heading north. It was the easiest walking of their whole journey, on that flat and featureless plain where there were no landmarks. They set their course by the Southern Diamond, whose longer axis pointed behind them to the pole. At midnight, under a bright yellow moon, they stopped for a drink and a mouthful of flatbread, now so stale that it crumbled in their mouths.

'How far have we come?' asked Karan, weary despite the easy walking. The thick air was exhausting to breathe. 'How far to go?'

'Of my paces, we have come about sixteen thousand since we ate. That would be three leagues, or a little more. But to Katazza, maybe another hundred and fifty leagues.'

'Seven leagues for the night, if we keep up this pace,' Karan calculated gloomily. It was an impossibly long way.

'Twenty days and more were it all like this.'

'Which it is not, as you will see. And the nights will get shorter and the days hotter as we go along.'

'We've got to go faster,' Karan said. 'I'm worried about Llian.'

As soon as the sun rose it became very hot, so they pitched the tent, hammered the pegs into crumbly salt and crawled inside to swelter and doze away the day.

It was their second night on the salt. Already they should have sighted the first mountain, where they planned to replenish their bottles, but nothing interrupted the progress of the plains. In the early hours they reached a place where the salt was thrust up in vast broken plates as tall as buildings, very difficult to negotiate in the dark, though they would provide glorious shade in the daytime. Karan plodded along, head down, scarcely looking where she put her feet. Today the brooding feeling that they were being followed had not gone away.

Suddenly Shand shouted 'Stop!' and at the same instant Karan's feet went from under her.

She had stepped on a steeply sloping slab of salt, a ramp that ran down into darkness. Karan fell desperately twisting around to save herself, and cracked her nose. A long way down, a few bright stars were reflected in a brine pool. Another step and she would have gone all the way to the bottom.

She grasped Shand's hand and pulled herself back up, her nose dripping blood.

'I'm sorry,' he said, mopping blood off lip and chin with the baggy sleeve of his robe. 'I wasn't quite quick enough. Fall into that hole and I'd never get you out. This place is too dangerous in the dark. We'll have to camp.'

All around them the slabs of salt stuck up like miniature peaks, making triangular caves that provided better shelter than any tent, warm in the night-time but cool by day.

'Would there be any fish in these pools?' Karan wondered, when the rosy dawn had woken them.

'No idea, but I have a line if you want to try.'

She looked down into the brine pool, a jagged sinkhole with water five or six spans further down. The fall would have broken bones. The water was an oily green, and still. She had thought to have a swim but the look of it made her shudder and she would not even put the fishing line in.

Karan went exploring a salt cave instead. The caverns seemed to go on forever, splitting and rejoining, opening out into triangular spaces much taller than her head, then just as abruptly closing into conduits where the salt was crushed together, leaving cracks that only a snake could have squeezed through. Everything was white, confusing the mind like walking in a snowstorm, and away from the entrance it was difficult to tell wall from floor or ceiling, except by feel. She found a place where it was deliciously cool and slept the day away, for once a rest completely free of dreams.

'Karan, get up! We're being followed!'

Karan pushed his hand away sleepily, the words taking a long time to sink in. '*What?*'

'I saw them from up top. They'll be here in half an hour. See if you can *sense* what they're after.'

Her stomach tried to tie itself in knots. Not the Ghâshâd again; she could not take it. 'Where? Who? Ghâshâd?' Karan felt so panicky that she could only think in single words.

'I don't think so. Can you *sense* anything?'

She strained with her mind, but nothing happened. Her talent did not like to be forced. 'No!' she said.

'There's something else. A message skeet came in the day before your adventure in the caves.'

'What!' Karan glared at him, hands on hips. She was livid with anger. 'Why didn't you tell me! I've been worrying for days that we were being followed.'

'After what happened, I didn't want to alarm you unnecessarily,' he said. 'But I did find out who sent it – it was Yggur!'

'Yggur!' He would never give up either. 'That's as bad as the other. Don't hide things from me! I'm not going back. I'll die first.'

'Nonsense,' said Shand placidly. 'What about Llian? Who will get him out of trouble if you give up now?'

'Llian! How easily you manipulate me.'

'I merely encourage. Let's see what we can do. I think that there are only two of them.'

'Two! Well, we are practically unarmed, unless old Shand has some powers that he has been keeping to himself.'

'Not anymore,' said Shand. 'There's no point trying to hide from them, so do as I tell you. Conceal your gear in one of the caves, then come back and brush away your tracks very carefully.'

'I'm not sneaking away like a coward.'

'Do what you're told! They don't want me, do they?'

'What are you going to tell them?'

'I'll think of something. Perhaps I'll say that you fell in the sinkhole and drowned.'

Karan looked down at the green water, shivering.

'If I am taken or killed,' Shand went on cheerfully, 'you must turn back to Ashmode. Don't dare go on to Katazza on your own.'

'If you are killed it will only prove the worthlessness of your advice,' Karan retorted. 'Of course I will go on. Give me that map you've been scratching at.'

'I'm not dead yet,' laughed Shand, pushing her away. He climbed back to his observation post. 'They'll be here in half an hour,' he called down. 'Precious lot of good your talent is! Get rid of your tracks.'

Karan did as she was bade, hid her pack way down in the white-out, then wriggled back through small crevices until she found a place high above the camp. She blocked the way

494

behind her with salt rubble and waited. She could not see very well, but she should be able to hear what was said.

There were two of them, a man and a woman, both tall, lean and weatherbeaten. Their robes were ragged but they were fit and alert, and they stood well apart.

'I am Gwossel Snu, a serjeant of Ashmode,' said the woman. 'Praide here is my constable.' She nodded toward the man. 'I have a warrant for the red-haired woman who left town with you.' She held out a piece of paper, unrolling it so that Shand could read the description. There was a sketch as well, a passable likeness of Karan. 'See, the warrant comes all the way from Thurkad, with the Seal of Yggur himself. And look, here it has been countersigned by the mayor of Ashmode.' She seemed concerned to prove the legality of her commission. They were like that in Ashmode. 'Where is Karan Fyrn of Gothryme?'

'Dead,' said Shand sonorously.

To Karan, the rest of the talk had come indistinctly, though she got the gist of it. But the word 'dead' rang in her ears. She shivered and scrunched herself up in her crack.

'Dead!' exclaimed the serjeant. 'How so?'

'Alas, we were walking in the cool of the dark, last night, when she fell into a brine pool and drowned,' said Shand sadly.

'And what is your name?

'My name is Shand and I come from the village of Tullin, near Chanthed on the island of Meldorin.'

'Drowned, you say. Then we must see the body,' said the man.

'It sank to the bottom,' said Shand. Then realising his mistake, he added, 'It wasn't this pool, but one of the others.'

There was a long silence. 'No body would sink in this water,' said the woman slowly. 'It is too salty.' She stared at Shand, very suspiciously. 'Show us the pool that you say she fell into.'

There were only two other brine pools nearby, but no tracks led to either of them.

'Twice you are proven a liar,' said Gwossel Snu coldly. 'And look,' she called to her fellow, 'there is blood on his sleeve!'

'My nose,' said Shand weakly, but already the man was behind him, binding his hands.

The serjeant inspected the sleeve, sniffed it. 'Shand of Tullin, I charge you with the murder of Karan Fyrn of Gothryme at this place. Be warned, we are sworn officers of Ashmode, and whatever you say will be retold at your trial. Be also warned that attempting to escape is proof of guilt and legally you may be slain.'

They lashed Shand to a pillar of salt, then searched the whole campsite carefully, even climbing down to the pool to probe the green water with a staff. On the way back up the man found the place where Karan's nose had bled.

'Look, here is where he did the deed. Vile murderer!' he cried and when he reached the top gave Shand a vigorous blow in the belly, doubling him over against his ropes.

'Enough!' said the woman sternly. 'Come, we must search the place thoroughly. The evidence seems clear but this fellow is obviously a great scoundrel. It may all be a trick.'

They searched the caves, and all around the brine pool, but Karan had done her job well. Already night was falling.

'So,' said Gwossel Snu. 'You dragged her all this way and then you killed her, poor child. What did she have that was worth the killing, I wonder? Will you confess? No? No matter. You stabbed her, did you, weighed down her body and flung it in the water? We will drag it in the morning, but these pools can be bottomless. I doubt we will ever find her. Pity. Alive she is worth five tells, but dead without proof, only one. We will sleep until the early hours, Praide, and then head back.'

Karan, wedged up in her tiny crack, was in a quandary. Her death was perfect, but what was she going to do about

Shand? Even if she could free him, how to stop them from following?

With the night it quickly grew cool. Karan took a sip from her water bottle, peering down at the camp. She was starving but her pack was a long way away. The camp disappeared in the darkness, then the stars came out and later the scorpion nebula, casting a faint red light over the saltscape. The upthrust plates looked like ancient standing stones, places of power and witchery. The shadows moved, making her think of the Ghâshâd again. Karan had to force herself to ignore that dread, to concentrate on the job at hand.

The officers fed themselves and Shand, then the woman slept while the man kept watch, and after a few hours they changed. Karan crawled down into the main tunnel, moving carefully, making no sound.

Gwossel Snu sighed, rested her head on her coat against a block of salt, and did not move. Karan slithered out towards Shand's pillar, but before she got there the woman yawned audibly and stood up. Karan cursed. Her plan depended on freeing Shand – she could not possibly handle two.

She went rock-still, trying to look like a salt boulder. A poor disguise, just here where the ground was smooth. The woman strode across to Shand, checked his bonds, then scanned the camp. Her gaze passed over Karan's shadow without noticing her, and the woman headed back to her post. She stared around her, uneasy. Karan dared not move.

Finally Gwossel Snu yawned again, turning to look the other way, towards Shand. What am I going to do? Karan thought. I'll have to take her now. She drew her knife, knowing that it wasn't in her to kill the woman in cold blood. Creeping forward, her heart hammering wildly, she reached up. The woman was a good head taller.

Her hand went over the serjeant's mouth and nose from behind; she pressed the knife against her throat. 'Don't move,' Karan hissed, hoping that her bluff would not be called. 'Down, on your belly!'

'Praide!' the woman screeched, then lashed backwards with her boot, smashing it into Karan's ankle.

It was like being kicked by a horse. Karan went over sideways, the impact jarring the knife out of her hand. She scrabbled after it, desperate now, snatching it just as the woman kicked again. The boot struck her in the hip, then Karan scuttled off.

Gwossel Snu was big and tough, a trained fighter, too much for her to handle. Behind her Karan saw Praide rising to his feet.

'Shand!' she screamed, hobbling toward him, closely pursued.

She tripped over something, one of the packs. Karan swung it hard at the woman's knee, collapsing her, then hacked at Shand's bonds until they parted.

'Take the man,' she whispered, rolling into the shadows as the woman limped after her. From there Karan sprinted around a knob of salt, climbed up the rough side and crept over the top. As the serjeant ran by, Karan dropped onto her back and brought her down.

'Don't!' she grated, pricking the knife hard into the back of the serjeant's neck. The woman tensed. Karan pressed harder onto the knife. 'I mean it,' she panted, and suddenly her opponent went slack.

Afraid of a sudden attack, Karan put a knee in her back to hold her there, pulled out the long sleeves of the woman's desert robe and tied them behind her back, a straitjacket that should hold her for a little while. There was a scuffle in the darkness, grunting and thrashing and swearing. A robed shape loomed over her and Karan rolled out of the way, feeling for her knife.

'It's me,' panted Shand.

Karan collected the enemy's boots. They could bind their feet with rags, sufficient to get home, but without proper boots they would never dare follow across the salt. Shand flung their weapons in the pool.

'I trust the murder charge is dismissed,' he said to the serjeant as he shouldered his pack.

Her eyes glittered. 'There are severe penalties for obstructing justice.'

'You took your time,' Shand remarked as they walked away.

'It takes time to come back from the dead,' Karan laughed. 'I knew you weren't worried.'

'I was, but I shouldn't have been.' He tousled her already tangled hair. 'What a partner you are.'

Preoccupied with the dangerous country, it wasn't until they stopped at dawn that Karan realised Shand had been hurt. One eye was completely black and so swollen that he could barely see out of it.

'What happened . . .?'

'He got me with his knee, the wretch. My hands were numb. He almost had me.'

Karan took a swig from her bottle. 'Yuk!' she said. 'Why didn't we take their water bottles and give them our foul ones?

'Too bloody stupid,' Shand said wearily.

That night the land began to ramp upwards. They began to encounter lumps and domes and pinnacles of rock protruding from the salt, some of them with a salty icing, others just black rock with a crust of crystals in the crevices. Karan spent the greater part of the night trying to recover her talent, but she could hardly remember how it had worked. It was not there at all.

Far from their escape heartening her, she felt greatly discouraged, harassed. Desperate to get to Katazza, she was constantly hurrying now, pressing Shand hard, taking risks with her own safety.

Late in the night, when they were both silent and worn out, Karan looked up from her trudging to see a black barrier ahead.

'What's that? It looks like a cliff.'

'It is.' He did not even raise his head.

The cliff was further away than it had seemed in the starlight and it was almost dawn when they reached it, an escarpment of black basalt some three or four spans high. It stretched beyond sight, south-east and north-west.

'Let's camp,' said Shand. 'This place will give us shade all day if we pick the spot.'

'We haven't gone far enough,' she replied, dog-tired, but driven to keep going.

'Far enough! I'm depressed.'

'What's the matter?' Karan asked as she picked her way through fallen slabs of basalt to a smooth patch of salt. Here it was like sand, loose granules that would not support the tent pegs. She had to stake the tent out with lumps of rock.

'I'm worried,' said Shand. 'We should have seen the first mountain before yesterday. I hadn't thought to get into this kind of country for days.'

'Maybe the map you remember was wrong.'

'Could have been. But this country can change too. Earth tremblers can thrust rock up through the salt and let it fall again.'

'But not mountains, surely! Let's worry about that after breakfast. What are we having today?'

'Mouldy onion rice, same as yesterday.' He unwrapped what was left from their last cooked meal and broke the congealed lump in two. Karan nibbled on her piece.

'This cliff won't stop us.'

'No, though they become higher toward the centre. There are some mighty ones near Katazza.'

He washed down the last of the rice with a swig of warm water, slightly foul, and stood up. 'Let's go up; the air's always clearest in the first light. I want to make sure that we're heading the right way.'

At the top Shand hauled himself onto a spire that stood above the cliff. As he had said, the cliff grew higher to the west, but there were no mountains in that direction, nor to the north. Nor, as far as they could make out, to the north-east.

Karan looked at Shand. 'I have water for four or five days.'

'The map was wrong,' Shand said, overcome by weariness.

'I won't go back.'

He climbed down, making for a higher pinnacle a few hundred paces away. From the top he scanned the horizons. Just then the rock quivered.

'What was that?' Karan was alarmed to feel the solid earth move beneath her.

'Earth trembler!'

'Can you see anything?' Her anxious voice carried clearly from the top of another spire.

'Nothing but the Grey Cliffs behind us.'

'How many days to water?'

He came to the base of her perch. 'That depends on our path. If we go east, four or five days. North-east, maybe a week.'

'East it is, and we must go hard so that we can be there in four.'

'Harder, and we use more water,' said Shand. 'Still, I think we can make it.' He mopped his forehead. 'Let's get out of this sun.'

They repaired to the tent, cool in the shade of the cliff, to sleep a better sleep than they had for days. Karan woke in the mid-afternoon, covered in sweat. The tent was still in shade, but a few steps away the sun sucked the sweat off instantly and the salt glare was a blinding, burning pain at the back of her eyes. She pulled the hood down over her face and felt in a pocket for the eye covers, realising just what Idlis had suffered on that day near Sundor last autumn.

The eye slits made it possible to see again, but there was little to see, just white salt and black rock, whirling salt devils here and there, and the afternoon haze. It was too hot. Deadly hot! She slunk back to the shade and the tent to lie staring up, to toss and scratch, for she itched all over, but there was no more sleep.

In the late afternoon they headed east and before dark were out of the rocky country, back onto the plains of salt. They made a hard night of it, boots crunching in the soundless dark while the stars wheeled, walking so fast that they sweated, though there was a cold breeze blowing. In the early hours Karan had to stop several times with leg cramps.

Dawn blushed the featureless salt to rose but wind-borne dust blocked any sight of the cliffs to the east. Karan swayed on her feet and had to catch hold of Shand's shoulder to keep herself upright. Her lips were so dry that the skin was flaking off. 'How far have we gone tonight?'

'I lost count. Ten leagues at least. A good march, even in such easy conditions.'

Suddenly all the blood drained out of Karan's face. 'I don't seem to have any strength left. And I itch all over. This heat is drying me up. I feel that I could just blow away in the wind.'

'Help me with the tent, then get inside.'

When it was up Karan crawled in and lay on the ground, too tired to eat or drink. 'I'm all dizzy,' she croaked. When Shand came in a few minutes later with a bowl of dried meat shavings mixed with chopped onion and a few pieces of lime, she lay on her face as though unconscious.

'Karan!' he cried. 'What's the matter?'

She did not move. He heaved her onto her back. Her eyes rolled up into her head. Shand lifted her up. Her skin was as dry as crackling. Her eyes fluttered and she seemed to see him, even lifted her hand to him, before it fell back to the ground.

34

THE STING OF THE SCORPION

S hand prised Karan's teeth open and felt her tongue. It was as dry as paper. 'Bloody fool!' he said, jerking the stopper out of a skin and dribbling water into her mouth. He held her head back until the water had gone down, then gave her another dose. After a minute or two some water went down the wrong way. She choked; her eyes flew open.

'My head hurts,' Karan said sluggishly. 'My blood feels thick.'

'When did you last drink?' He held the skin to her cracked lips. She swallowed, gasped.

'I can't recall. A . . . long time ago.'

'Did you drink anything on the march last night? You didn't, you stupid, stupid child!'

Her hands came up, fastening onto the waterskin. It shook, spilling a few drops on her lip. Shand steadied it while she took a larger swig.

'I was being careful, saving the water. After a while I didn't feel thirsty anymore.'

He inclined the flask; she gulped the fluid. Her eyelids fluttered, those striking green eyes looking straight up at him. 'I'm sorry. I suppose I've been a little foolish.'

'A little,' he said grumpily, 'though I doubt that any harm has come of it. Now will you listen to me! I know why you're pressing so hard, but you can't keep doing it. You're risking your life, and mine too.'

'I'm sorry,' she said.

'I will give you a lesson in surviving in the desert. *The* lesson. You can't save water by not drinking it.'

She looked blank.

'You need so much a day, no less, for every drop you lose must be made up. Travelling at night and sheltering by day, you have to drink half a bag each day. If we walked in the sun a whole waterbag would not be enough. Once you have lost two bags full and not replaced it, you die. For me a little more, since I am bigger. The only way to save water is not to lose it in the first place. Never go into the sun. Move as little as possible in the day. Where there is shade, *use it*! And don't go so fast at night that you sweat. I should have made that clear before we set off.'

'I feel better now.' She sat up and swigged another mouthful. 'Oh, this water is awful.'

'And will no doubt get worse.'

Karan recovered quickly, though her head throbbed and she felt thirsty all day. It was hot, for there was nothing to shade the tent. That night they took it more slowly, but still made nearly eight leagues, and in the clear dawn light saw the cliffs in the distance.

'How far now?' she mused.

They had reached a place where the salt stood in angular plates again, taller than Shand, and erected the tent beneath an overhang that would provide shade for most of the day.

Shand consulted his map and made a few more marks on it, the day's progress. 'It's maybe fifteen leagues to the cliffs, but we should find water well before that. I have three parts of a skin left, a foul one. How much you?'

'A full one and a dribble, both foul.'

'Let me see you drink some then.'

She pretended to look sulky but drained the second skin, a large mugful. After midnight, a dark night, for there was high cloud before the stars, they crossed out of the salt plains onto gently up-sloping land and by dawn found that the cliffs were much nearer, barely a day's march away. The air was completely still, so thick that it stifled, despite the sun being a finger's breadth above the horizon. They scanned the country but could not see the least tinge that might suggest water.

'We won't be able to see it in the dark,' she said, it being the time of the new moon. 'I vote we continue north-east for an hour or two while it's still relatively cool, and maybe again late in the afternoon. Then even if we don't find anything, we'll still be able to turn north and reach the cliffs during the night.'

Shand nodded and thus they continued. They found no water before it became too hot to move, but in the afternoon trudged over an imperceptible rise and saw an oasis before them, a gully with a ribbon of green along it.

'Stay calm,' said Shand, putting his hand on Karan's shoulder. 'Let's be sure that we can drink it first.'

'It'd have to be better than this,' Karan said, gagging as she sipped from her bottle.

'And beware, the most venomous creatures on Santh inhabit places such as these. Even the ants can bite so hard that you will not be able to walk for a week.'

'I will brave the ants. Oh, to soak my aching feet.'

The oasis was just that, a place where the land changed within a single step from salt-crusted, sterile wilderness to grey saltbush and then to a brilliant green herbfield, with a band of tall, strap-leaved trees running up the gully for a few hundred paces. Above and below that was nothing but sand. Karan walked the length of the oasis and back down again, enjoying the humid shade, but found no standing water.

When she returned, very crestfallen, Shand was excavating a hole with his knife in the centre of the gully, labouring through fibrous roots, digging out moist black sand and rotting leaves. 'If you want to soak your feet you'll have to dig your own,' he said. 'This is for drinking.' A small amount of dark water began to accumulate.

'I *will* dig my own,' she replied, tossing her head, and, taking her knife, went upstream to a place where the banner of forest was broader and the ground was soft.

Shaping a piece of wood into the form of a trowel, she began to dig. She smelled woodsmoke but continued her excavation, lost in a sensual daydream about Llian. Finally Shand came looking for her. Karan was working in a crater almost the size of a bath, the wet soil sailing through the air and plopping on the heap behind her. Her boots lay to one side, covered in mud. There was water up to her ankles. She beamed at him, rinsing the mud off her hands.

'If we were staying for a week I would make a swimming hole.'

'Very good,' he said. 'I'm glad to see you're not in such a hurry anymore. It's dinnertime.'

She fell in beside him, still distracted by her daydream. 'What feast have you prepared tonight?'

'Well, I dug out a couple of your clatchers for starters, but they're only little. And there is a tree in fruit. Here, try one.' He pulled from his pocket something that resembled a grey nut shaped like a small banana.

'How do you eat it?'

Shand squatted down by the fire. 'Stick the point of the knife in thus, twist, and the halves of the shell come apart. Oops!' He picked up a lump of white fluffy stuff that looked like kapok, brushed the dirt off and handed it to her.

'You eat this? What's it called?'

'No idea. I call it dumpling fruit. Try it.'

She picked off a piece of the sticky fluff and put it in her mouth rather tentatively. 'Oh, it's sweet!' She finished it off. 'It does rather stick to your teeth though.'

'Yes, it's better cooked. And there's more.' He showed a hatful of brown seeds or berries. 'Desert peas. They make very good soup though they take a lot of cooking.'

They ate a handsome dinner of spicy pea soup and a roasted clatcher apiece, washed down with steaming tea sweetened with dumpling fruit. It was beginning to get dark. Karan went back to the pool for her forgotten boots. Shand was just rinsing the dinner mugs when he heard her scream.

He sprinted up the gully. Karan lay on the ground, trying to tear her boot off. 'Something bit me,' she cried.

Shand lifted off the boot, shaking it out on the sand. A small red and black scorpion fell out, trying to scuttle away on crushed legs. He brought his boot heel down hard on it.

'It's all right,' said Karan with a weak smile. 'It doesn't hurt anymore.'

'Not a good sign,' Shand grunted, winding the cloth belt of his robe tightly around her leg from knee to ankle. He tore off her sock, slashed open the bloody mark on the ball of her foot, kneading it so that the blood flowed freely, and sucked out the wound, spitting blood on the ground. His tongue began to go numb.

Perspiration literally burst out of Karan's forehead, then her head lolled on her shoulders and her eyes rolled back. Shand lifted her across his shoulder and ran back to the fire. Reefing out a burning stick, he thrust the red-hot end against the wound, holding Karan's ankle with fingers of steel while she thrashed and screamed. Finally he tossed the stick back into the fire, pressed a wet cloth to the bloody mess, salved and bound it and put her sock back on to keep it in place. He splinted her leg from ankle to hip so that she could not move it.

Karan subsided into moans and shudders and, without warning, threw up her dinner. She became very cold; her lips went blue. All her garments could not warm her, and she slipped into a coma-like sleep. Shand shook her awake, feeding her with tea sweetened with his dumpling fruit. The pain was terrible, almost unbearable. Folding cloth into a pad Shand forced it between her teeth. She bit down hard, her hand gripping his so strongly that it hurt.

She slept again for an hour or two, then woke with Shand's eyes on her. 'What a brute you are,' she said weakly. 'Did you have to burn a hole right through me? I don't think I've ever hurt so much.'

'That was a deadly scorpion you put your foot on. Lucky it stung you on the hard skin underneath. On the toe or the ankle, I probably couldn't have saved you. That's why I burned the wound: sometimes heat makes the poison harmless. But now look what you've done. I told you to beware. Katazza is out of the question – you won't be able to walk for a week.'

Karan said nothing, just turned her face from him, suffering the night away, and cursing her carelessness. In her agony she kept having flashes of premonition about Llian, who was always in peril. Once or twice in the night she caught sight of the scorpion nebula. It seemed brighter than ever; she felt that it mocked her.

They were laid up for two more days before Karan could even put foot to ground, but after that she was restless to go. Though limping like an amputee she would not even think of turning back, so Shand whittled a crutch for her out of a sapling.

'We can't go straight back out,' he said. 'I don't dare until your foot is healed. Anyway, the food's running low. However, thirty or forty leagues north and east of here the Truno River, the largest in Lauralin, empties into the Dry Sea. It's a land of lakes and marshes, a place to get lost in, but there are fish and game in abundance. We'll head that way and see how your foot goes. Now promise me that you'll be careful; if we are to go on to Katazza, we can think of nothing but how to get there safely.'

It was an agonisingly slow hobble to the lake country, for Karan's foot would not heal while she walked on it. They spent a fortnight there, drying fish fillets in the sun. Shand filled their foul waterskins with salt, hoping to cure them. Eventually Karan's foot was sufficiently better for them to strike out across the salt, heading north-east, following the oases.

The journey took another thirty days and more, but there was little to tell about it. Each day was the same as the previous but hotter. The sun rose, crept across the cloudless sky and reluctantly set again. If they were lucky there would be a salt cave; if slightly lucky, an upthrust slab of salt; if unlucky there would be no shelter at all and they would have to sleep in their tent on the hot salt.

Karan had all the time in the world to brood about her life and try to make plans for the future. She was twenty-four. Most of her adulthood, she now realised, had been wasted in travel. She felt trapped in this journey that had no end. More urgently, she had a growing urge to make up for lost time, to provide Gothryme with an heir.

The last part of the journey took much longer than expected because they had passed off smooth salt onto broken basalt with edges sharp as knives, deadly to slip on, full of cracks and cavities, some that gave off steam or a blast of heat. This country was too dangerous to traverse in the dark, so they had to restrict travel to morning and evening. There were thrust-up cliffs and terraces everywhere, each a difficult and hazardous climb. In the awful heat, they used much more water.

About sixteen weeks after the Conclave they reached a small barren peak, a horn of rock that thrust up more than a thousand spans from its grey skirts of broken rock and salt. Finding no water there, they tightened their belts, pulled their cloaks about them and set out for the next mountain, a peak that they had seen briefly the previous day, before the mirages shredded it and the haze came up from the salt. They could not tell if it was high or low.

'How far to go?' asked Karan. 'I've not much water left, nor food.'

'Too far,' said Shand irritably, clutching his stomach.

'There must be water somewhere.'

'There's no must out here. Some of these islands were barren even before the Sea of Perion dried up.'

'But even on barren islands you can generally dig a well and find water. The rain must come out below.'

Shand snapped at her. 'No must, I said.'

Karan was too cranky to think straight – they both were, and irrational too. 'You said that you'd made this journey twice before. How could you forget where the water lies?'

Shand's face darkened. 'I've not been *this way* before, as I've told you several times.'

They trudged on through the night, making their way by the stars, bickering until they no longer had the strength to do even that. The following day was very hot, very hazy, and they sweltered in the tent all day and caught nary a glimpse of the mountain. On they marched that night. Sometime after dark they felt the gentlest slope beginning to rise beneath their feet and, to their joy, in the light of the pre-dawn, saw the triple peaks, Katazza surely, to the east of the path they had been following.

It was already scorching, though the sun was barely a hand's breadth above the horizon. Shand looked wracked. Karan pulled the brim of her hat even lower.

'We went too far west in the haze,' said Shand. 'Right past the southern end – we're looking back at the western side now.'

Karan would have wept but her eyes were too dry for tears. 'You mean we could have been there days ago?' She rubbed crusted eyelids.

Shand abruptly doubled over and staggered off behind a yellow-stained knob of rock. She heard him vomiting for ages.

'What's the matter?' she asked, when he reappeared.

'The gripe! My water tastes like a rat died in it.' Putting his hand over his mouth, he dashed back behind the rock.

As they approached Katazza, fuming rifts appeared in the ground, crusted with crystals of coloured salts and sulphur, and vents that oozed a red-hot paste of rock. The ground shook constantly, sometimes so violently that they were thrown off their feet. Cooling rock around them cracked like toffee. Smaller mountains clung to the skirts of Katazza on this side, their craters spewing smoke and ash. Once the tallest of them ejaculated a spurt of red lava that took hours to flow down the mountainside.

They wove their way through a cluster of boiling brine springs and fountains gushing steam. The levees all around were coated with a fur of needle-like crystals. The air stank of sulphur, making their eyes water and their noses run, and each breath burned their throats. A raft of purple scum had drifted up one end of the last brine pool.

'We can eat that,' said Shand, bending down to scoop some up in a pot.

'What is it?' she asked dubiously.

'No idea – it grows in boiling water and it's good to eat – that's all I know about it.'

He squeezed the water out and they spooned the scum from the pot. It was like grainy foam, with hardly any taste, but it filled their bellies. It stained their lips purple too.

'What a horrible country,' said Karan, almost as ill-at-ease as she had been in the wharf city. 'Is Katazza like this at the top?'

'Not at all. Something to look forward to.'

The gripe got worse. By the time they reached the base of the mountain, clawing through desolate country between the little cones and the southern flank of the island, Shand was in agony. His water was gone but for half the contents of the last Granewys bag, now so foul that it almost made him vomit. He would not share it with Karan.

'It can hardly make me worse,' Shand said. 'Drink your own – if you get the gripe as well, we're finished.'

By the next morning his water was gone and Karan had little more than half of her last. Even on it, Shand's stomach complaint got worse, crippling him and wasting precious water in vomiting and diarrhoea.

He lacked the strength to climb the long slope to the base of the cliffs, so they lay in the tent all day in scorching, sweltering heat, for though they were in shade the ground was as hot as the air. That evening, before setting out again, they ate the last of the food and drank Karan's water, every drop. There was no point in keeping a few mouthfuls for later. Shand hurled his up again before they had gone twenty paces.

'Sorry!' he said, wiping his mouth on the hem of his ragged, salt-saturated robes.

Karan gave him her shoulder. After an hour they came upon a seep that bled into a large clear pool part of the way up the slope, but it was saline and so bitter that it was undrinkable. In their desperation they tried a little but it gave them stomach cramps. Afterwards they were thirstier than ever. Shand lay down by the pool, clutching his belly. He could barely walk. Karan was terrified that he was going to die.

After a long rest in the shade he felt better, though nearly dead from dehydration. Karan went fishing in the pool and came back with several small flat fish. They ate the juicy flesh raw, which seemed to make the thirst diminish, but Karan knew that without water Shand would die in a day, and she would not last much longer. All that night they staggered on, and before dawn found by smell a tiny seep of water at the base of the cliffs, not enough to fill their bags even if they stayed there all day, but enough to save their lives and give them a little to carry with them.

In the evening they pressed on again and eventually found a way up the lowest cliff of Katazza onto a narrow platform. Another scrambling hour or two and they reached a south-facing ravine where the sun never reached. Here at last they found signs of moisture, grey leathery plants in the base of the gully, and further up, a trace of green. The cliffs seemed to go up forever. Shand was too weak to climb any higher.

'Tomorrow will be better,' he said, skinning a tuber that Karan had dug up.

Karan said nothing. She was so hungry that she could have eaten a raw rat. All she'd had today was a clump of ant eggs dug out of a nest with a stick, and it had cost her more than it was worth in bites. Her legs and arms were spotted with little red swellings.

The terrace had patches of scrub in deep gullies and seeps of iron-stained water. Better water was found once they dug in moist places. They found grubs and lizards to eat, and more tuberous roots that were probably not poisonous, so they would not starve; at least, not immediately.

'Tomorrow we'll try,' Shand repeated the next day, but he was so ravaged by the gripe that Karan knew he would never be able to.

Tomorrow came, but Shand was unable to get up, and when Karan returned from the hunt with a large lizard – food for several days – he showed scant interest in eating it.

'Go up!' he said, raising a limp hand. 'Get help.'

'I'm not going to leave you,' she said, though she was torn between her care for him and her yearning to find Llian. There were times when she could almost sense Llian, and what she sensed frightened her.

'You'll have to or we'll both die. Take the food and go.'

'You'll die if I leave you!'

'I've all the water I need,' said Shand, giving her a weak smile. 'And a little bit of food. It takes weeks to starve to death – you'll be back long before then.'

Karan hesitated. She really longed to go; it was a burning flame inside her. But she couldn't leave him.

35

A TREMENDOUS INSULT

Whave hen Llian returned, shaken from his interview with Malien, he found Tensor still sitting on his ebony chair, his forearms flat on the broad workbench that ran the length of the wall. The bench was ebony too, thick planks polished by wear to a silky smoothness. The bench reflected the Mirror, and the Mirror reflected Tensor's face: the glossy dark hair, brushed back in waves from his broad brow, the long straight nose with its thick bridge, and the dense curling beard that concealed the lower part of his face.

As Llian watched, Tensor slowly arched his back and gripped the frame of the Mirror with each hand. It shook, steadied and an image appeared; precisely the image that Llian had seen in Thurkad last winter.

He saw a desolate landscape, gloomy with pitch-dark shadows. A plain was dotted with steely-grey masses, structures like clusters of bubbles. The plain was gashed by a deep rift crusted with grey frost; an iron tower leaned over it as if frozen in the act of falling. In the background, mountains stabbed the sky like shards of pottery. A small red sun attempted to break through wild storm clouds, but it was doomed to fail.

It was Aachan, or perhaps Tensor's memory of that worldscape, already thousands of years old. Did it still exist?

Was it unchanged from that distant, innocent time before the flute?

Yet this image was different from Mendark's. It was alive – the sun and the moon moved in the heavens, the clouds drifted, the light waxed.

But that one scene was all Tensor could extract from the Mirror and, as the days passed, his stern confidence began to fall away. He tore his hair, shouted angrily at Llian and even raged at his fellow Aachim. Malien was pleased when Llian reported this to her.

Tensor smashed his great fist down on the bench so hard that the Mirror jumped into the air and toppled over. 'Why will it not open? Why? *Why?*'

'*Yalkara locked it, and there is only one key. I have that key,*' said Llian, thinking aloud without thinking.

Tensor's wild-maned head jerked around and Llian was shocked to realise that he had begun to collaborate, that he wanted Tensor to succeed with the Mirror, in spite of Malien's dire forecasts. That like a sot with his ale he *had* to follow this tale to the bitter end, no matter how much he might regret it later. No! he thought. I must record the tale, but I don't have to aid him. Let him do it himself, or not at all.

'What?' cried Tensor.

'Nothing,' said Llian, sidling away. 'I was wrong.'

Suddenly he found himself caught about the throat and lifted high in the air. '*What did you say?*' Tensor roared, shaking Llian like a rat. Llian choked. Tensor dropped him to the floor and put a foot on his throat.

'Faelamor . . . said it, at the Conclave,' gasped Llian as his face went purple. Blood trickled from a graze on his chin. His arm had gone numb from landing on his elbow.

At once Tensor turned away, seeming to have forgotten that Llian was there.

'So she did! What can she have meant?' he said thoughtfully. 'How locked? *How locked?*' He paced the room. 'Faelamor never held the Mirror, except briefly in her struggles with Yalkara, and not at the end. So, if it *is* locked, it was not she who locked it. Only Yalkara can have done that, and she is long gone. But to what purpose? Often have I wondered about Yalkara. It was said that only one man ever saw into her mind.'

'And what is the key?' Llian wondered. 'Faelamor said she had the key.'

'Who can tell? Perhaps she forced the secret out of Yalkara?' Tensor went out, muttering to himself.

When he came back, Llian said, 'I've heard that the Aachim laid aside the Mirror in ancient times because it was so perilous to use.' He was hoping Tensor would fill in some of the gaps in its history.

'Perilous indeed, and it was I who did so – even though it was my most precious thing. I smuggled it here to Santhenar in the first place. That was a dangerous business! It was forbidden to carry objects between the worlds.'

'Why?' asked Llian.

'Because they are liable to transform in dangerous ways, as the flute did. And the Mirror too! Had I been caught, it would have been the end of me. Then Kwinlis (who led us before the traitor Pitlis, chronicler, since I can see you are about to ask) used the Mirror. He saved us at the cost of his own life . . .' Tensor sat silently, staring back across the ages.

'After that, no one could use it. Whatever Kwinlis had done to the Mirror was beyond our understanding. It lay neglected, unguarded in our archives, and at the fall of Tar Gaarn Yalkara stole it. But now I *must* work with it, whatever the cost, and I will. Why would she lock it? How can it be locked?'

Tensor picked up the Mirror, that small, apparently insignificant thing, and brought it close to his face. His face was further aged, further diminished. Despite the brave words he was losing confidence. It all seemed to have been for nothing. Shazmak had been destroyed because of his blind pursuit of the Mirror and now he found that he could not even use it.

While this was going on, the Aachim had been working unceasingly on their own projects, to make sure that Katazza was secure. As the days rushed by even Malien began to relax when it became clear how Tensor was struggling and failing. Eventually Llian became bored with the lack of progress and spent more of his time exploring the myriad rooms of Katazza and its towers.

One day he found a pleasant room at the top of the Great Tower, just below the platinum dome, where he could look out over the sea. When he leaned out as far as he dared he could see the top of the gold and lapis band that encircled the tower below his room. It was warm in the daytime, with the sun slanting in, but the nights were bitter, for the large embrasures were open to the mountain air. There he sat day after day, for there were weeks to record in his journal.

When that was brought up to date Llian began his casual, circumspect search of Katazza for Kandor's records. And since Tensor did not call him, or seem to have any need for his services after all, he spent less and less time in the workrooms, until Malien pointed out that his usefulness as a spy would disappear if he was never there to watch.

Llian had searched everywhere but had found not the least scrap of paper, and finally decided that he must have help.

'Why do you want to see Kandor's papers?' Malien asked coolly.

'The Histories of the Charon are poorly known,' he said, feeling safe in the half-truth. 'The *Tale of the Rifting* is the weakest of all the Great Tales. Anything I can learn here must improve it.'

She stared into his eyes and eventually he had to look

away. 'There is more, chronicler. Give me the real reason and maybe I will help you.'

'That *is* the real reason,' Llian protested, but she was not satisfied.

'I know you, chronicler. There is more than you are saying.' Her grey-green eyes stripped him naked.

He went through the mysterious ending to the Forbidding and what Tensor had told him in Shazmak, showing her the stolen letter from Kandor to Rulke.

Malien listened carefully, sniffed the paper, even tasted it with her tongue. 'It looks to be genuine. How did Mendark allow you to keep such a vital document?'

'Er . . .' Llian was ashamed to admit his larceny. 'When I returned he was so angry that I didn't get a chance to tell him about the letter. He would not see me before the Conclave, and afterwards . . . There was no afterwards.'

'So! No one knows about this but you and me?'

Llian had an uncomfortable feeling about where this was headed. 'That's right.'

'Then I'll keep it.'

'But it's –'

'*It's mine*, you were going to say. I don't think so, chronicler. You've done more than enough harm already, collaborating with Tensor. I know what you've been up to. If there *is* anything behind this letter, do you think that we would allow you to bargain it away to Tensor in return for some other secret? Would you give a baby a razor to play with?'

'Then what about –?'

'Kandor's archives? I'm glad you haven't found them. Henceforth they shall be forbidden to you. And if you try to get in to them . . .'

'You will betray me to Basitor,' finished Llian.

Malien smiled. 'I'm glad you understand me so well. He suspects you, you know. Were it not for Tensor, and for me, the skeet would have dined on your brains long ago. So, we are friends again?'

Llian was not that resilient. He put his head in his hands. Malien touched him lightly on the shoulder and disappeared.

The next time Llian walked along a seemingly innocent corridor of the fortress, a certain door was bolted and sealed with a lock as big as his head. He was back to where he started. Worse, since what he wanted was so close and he was barred from it.

Time passed but still Tensor gleaned nothing from the Mirror. Winter was long gone and spring had melted the snow from all but the tallest south-facing peaks. His science had proven unequal to opening the Mirror but perhaps his long-suppressed inner senses might open the way.

One night in late spring, as he sat brooding before the Mirror, staring at the changing yet unchanging scene of Aachan, the self-control that he had maintained for so long drained out of him and he allowed his memories free rein of the distant past, a time when he was a young man in Aachan, an apprentice artificer in the service of Rulke. That was even before the time of the flute, an impossible age ago. He recalled the lessons, the trials with clay and stone, metals and timbers, and the master shaper, Aoife, who had taught him. She had made the Mirror and given it to Tensor for his outgift – a simple seeing device, not uncommon on Aachan.

He drifted back to that time, to that first moment when he took the Mirror in his hands, tuned his mind to it and *saw*. It had only been a little way, not even across the city, but he'd felt the whole of Aachan open to him. Later Tensor had learned to direct the Mirror to other seeing devices and, once or twice, something that had never been done before, to see practically anywhere he wanted to.

He let the memories drift back and saw himself as he had been long ago – the delight in life; the youthful strength and exultation. The euphoria became so strong that he could do anything and, as he picked up the Mirror, he was once more back in that evening long ago, and without a thought the Mirror opened to him!

All day he played and dreamed, but when he emerged from his dreams Tensor realised that the Mirror had opened at a primitive level, below the deceits, snares and delusions of later ages. He knew that the distant past could not aid him. And the younger part that held Yalkara's secrets was still locked to him.

Tensor spent two days and a night before the Mirror, neither eating, drinking nor sleeping. He seemed to be in a trance, save that his eyes followed the images flickering across the luminous surface, more quickly than Llian could follow. After a minute Llian's eyes were so strained that he became dizzy and had to go outside.

Llian could not work out the nature of the information that Tensor was seeking or sorting through, for it varied through words and drawings, scenes urban and rustic and of wilderness, manuscripts and plans, faces and meetings, music and voices speaking, and almost every aspect of life on Santhenar (and Aachan) that it was possible to imagine. Once he even saw the image of Tensor himself, a young and achingly handsome man.

One time Tensor groaned so loudly that Llian, who was up on the next level, came running down to see what was the matter. Whatever had so stirred Tensor – joy or despair – the image was gone. He sat rigid, trance-like, the scenes flickering on his face as before.

In the middle of the night Llian was wakened by a metallic crash and ran in to find Tensor banging his head on the ebony bench. His scalp was bleeding, a torn-out lock of black hair clutched in one fist. Llian put his hand between Tensor's bruised forehead and the bench and after a couple of bangs Tensor laid his head down and his fists relaxed, though his eyes were still open.

Llian found the Mirror against the far wall. There was a

tiny indentation in one edge but it was otherwise undamaged and the images continued to race across it. He squatted down, entranced, and once thought he saw his own face there, but it was gone in an instant. Time stood still. He had no idea how long he spent in that position, then the Mirror was plucked from his fingers and Tensor propelled him out of the room with a foot in the middle of his back.

Llian lay on his pallet for hours in the darkness, unable to sleep, strange scenes replaying themselves on the inside of his eyelids. He felt a profound longing to hold the Mirror again, though as the night passed the images faded to a blur, and the longing too, and he slept.

He was woken by a furious roar and once more found himself high in the air with Tensor's hands about his throat, being shaken like a dog.

'What has she done to it?' he screamed.

Llian squeaked something incomprehensible and again Tensor dropped him from on high, this time onto the relative softness of his pallet. The aged wood smashed under him.

'What has she done to the Mirror?' Tensor cursed Karan and her father, and all her ancestors, in strange oaths that Llian had never heard before.

Llian was overcome by an anger so furious that he lost all sense. He grabbed one of the splintered side bars of the pallet and, as Tensor lunged forward, struck him violently in the groin. Tensor froze, clutching himself. Llian quickly rolled out of the way and stood up, stick in hand.

'Never say that again,' Llian said in fury, 'or I swear I . . .'

Tensor shuddered and slowly drew himself to his full height. His fists hung in the air like melons. Llian held out the weapon before him, then Tensor's arm swung lazily and sent it flying.

'How could she have changed it?' Llian said, desperately running backwards. 'Remember Faelamor's words at the Conclave.'

'Do not remind me of my shame, you *worm*!'

That set Llian to wondering about the Conclave and Maigraith. Her appearance had been carefully stage-managed by Faelamor, clearly designed to shock. But whom had she been aimed at – Tensor or Mendark?

'Karan did nothing,' he yelped. 'Whatever was done to the Mirror, it was one far greater than Karan who did it.'

Tensor glared down at the paltry human who opposed him, raising his fist to smite him. Llian leapt backwards out of the way.

'She didn't even know enough about the Mirror to draw an image out of it,' Llian panted. 'You know that she has no power of that sort.'

Tensor sat down suddenly, with a grimace and a whooshed-out breath. He did not speak for a long time, in evident pain.

'Yes,' he said eventually. 'I made sure of that long ago.'

Llian went very still. 'What did you say?' he asked in an icy voice.

Tensor's mouth closed like a trap and wrath exploded from him once more. 'By the powers, chronicler, I begin to regret that I did not splatter your brains across the wall. Say one more word and I will.'

He advanced on the cowering Llian, whose mouth hung so wide he could have put his fist in it. 'You think to fool me with your glasses and your pastes?' Tensor roared. 'I have always known what you were, just as I know that you spy for Malien. Keep well this in mind – the minute you are of no use to me, not Malien or a hundred of her kind can save you from my fury. *Now get out!*' Picking Llian up by the scruff of the neck and the seat of the pants, he flung him out the door and slammed it behind.

Llian wobbled his way out of the tower and went in search of Malien. Once again he found her in the serpentine pavilion under the fig tree. She was sitting with her knees up under her chin, staring dreamily out across the sea.

'What now, chronicler? He has mastered it?'

'No! But he knows everything. The stigmata, my spying for you, all.'

'He is a clever and cunning foe! I did not think it could be kept from him.'

'Malien, I haven't come to you as a spy today,' Llian said cautiously.

She raised a ginger eyebrow.

'He accused Karan of having done something to the Mirror; insulted her gravely. I became angry and struck him in his manhood with a piece of wood. I fear I hurt him badly.'

Malien was awestruck. 'Chronicler, I am astounded! You have done him a tremendous insult, though that part of him is a little ... desiccated. You are bolder than I thought, a *veritable tiger*!' She laughed. 'This counts as not attracting attention, does it? How is it that you remain alive?'

'I wonder myself, though I merely repaid his own insult. He was going to smash me, then I told him that Karan had no skill at the Secret Art, and he stopped and said to himself, *Yes, I made sure of that long ago*. I demanded to know what he meant. Tensor became angry again, told me that he knew what I was up to, and flung me out of the room.'

'After the stroke, you still questioned him? I conclude that you are not a tiger after all, but a lemming.'

Llian ignored the jest. 'What did he mean?'

She sighed. 'I don't know. No, wait! I was there when Karan first came to Shazmak as a girl, for though I dwelt in Stassor I went to the west a few times to visit Rael and my friends there. It was evident when Karan appeared that she had a great talent. That is not surprising in a blending. Years later I learned that little had come of it. Again not surprising, as a brilliant boy singer may lose the power of song when a man. From what you say, Tensor did something to prevent Karan's talents flowering. That is a crime and a great wickedness, though it has been done before. What danger could she possibly have presented? I'll try to find out.'

Llian kept well away from the workroom for the rest of

the day but when he sneaked through late that night to get to his sleeping quarters, he found that Tensor had regained his composure, though he still grimaced when he sat down. It was as if the event had never happened.

'Look, chronicler,' he said amiably, tapping his finger on the Mirror, 'Faelamor was right. *The Mirror has no power, none at all. What it has, if you can read it, is knowledge, and many, many secrets.* That's what she said and for once Faelamor was telling the truth. It has no power that I can find or, knowing how it was made, can even imagine. I was looking for some force within it . . . as though it was a ring or some other device of magic. There is none, or at least, none in the part that I have been able to unlock.'

'Then what use is it to you?' Llian asked.

'The Mirror has knowledge, libraries of it. Perhaps, hidden within it, are the secrets I need, for I know such things existed in ancient times. They all failed after the Forbidding, yet only three hundred years ago Yalkara made a gate and fled back to Aachan through a flaw in the Forbidding. What I have to do is find that secret and put it to work.'

Llian did not know what to think about this obscure discussion. 'What secret?' he cried in an agony of frustration, but Tensor said no more.

Tensor spent more long days and nights before the Mirror, using it differently now. He dug into the secrets of the past: past lives, past deeds, past treacheries and betrayals. He was driven, scarcely able to tell the difference between what he saw in the Mirror and what happened in the world around him. And he was by turns good-humoured, indifferent, morose, vengeful – and malign.

Then one day, as Llian watched, Tensor seemed to see something that Llian could not. He sprang up.

'What is it? What have you found?' Llian asked, captive of the excitement. 'Have you cracked the code?'

'No, *but my way is clear*! More I will not say.'

36

THE ARCHITECT
AT THE GATE

After he made this discovery, Tensor worked unceasingly. All day and all night he sat at his table before the Mirror, sometimes staring for hours at a single image. At times he seemed mesmerised by the past. Entranced he would sit there, his stern face alive with joy or wet with tears. Sometimes the images were like life, and Llian, peering over his shoulder, could see people walking back and forth, or peering out of the windows of tall towers, or fleeing in terror before the march of armies. Yet on other occasions the scenes appeared to be symbolic – most commonly a triplet of still, black lakes with the huge Aachan moon hanging above, but not reflected.

Once Tensor worked without a break for three days – eyes staring, writing furiously on a bark scroll, seemingly oblivious to hunger or weariness. Then he flung himself on a pallet on the floor and slept for a few hours, at the end of this time awakening so suddenly that his head literally jerked up off the pillow. He scrambled up in haste, ran back to the table and, touching the Mirror to life again, resumed his frantic writing.

Llian brought all this to Malien, though after the first day his duties as a spy became less onerous, for Malien herself or another of the Aachim stood there watching and though

Tensor knew they were there he took no account of them. The Aachim, even those who had fled Shazmak and supported his every mood and plan, grew afraid. Finally they could take no more. Their fear of what he was going to do overcame all other terrors.

'We are dreadfully afraid, Tensor,' said white-haired Selial, looking more withered each day. 'In the past you never sought for anything but the well-being of the Aachim, always subordinating your own desires to that greater end. But in Shazmak we gave way to you, in recognition of all that you did for us. We cautioned you to beware your own folly. You did not and Shazmak fell! Still we followed you. But no more, no more! Not into the disaster that you are planning now!' She gasped, a twisted cry of pain.

'Aye,' said Tensor. 'My folly it was that led us to this end. But not mine alone! Each of us chose to hide away from the world, to live in the past, to avoid our enemies rather than to confront them. We lost those skills that we needed for our survival. Grave treachery brought our enemy into Shazmak and our safeguards failed: we submitted!'

'Treachery indeed,' said Selial, 'and as always, it came from among us. I am to blame. I should have seen it.'

'Whatever! I will not be swayed,' said Tensor softly. 'The Ghâshâd came to Shazmak and we lacked the will to oppose them. We fell like millet under the scythe.'

'We own that,' said Malien.

'But the folly was chiefly mine,' Tensor went on in a low voice. 'The old way, the way of the Syndics, will serve us no more. We must learn anew a more primitive way. Committees will serve us no longer. Who will take command?' He said this softly, in his deep voice, using no rhetoric to sway them. 'You are right to upbraid me – but who will you choose in my place?'

The Aachim looked at each other, but found no leader there; none with vision enough. Malien said, 'We cannot find a leader. We will not abandon the old ways without one. The Syndic shall lead us.'

Tensor seemed not to have heard her. 'You're right,' he said. 'I have violated your trust. Why should you follow me? Choose yourselves a leader,' he repeated more loudly. 'I will follow. I am too weary to carry this burden any longer.'

He sat down on the floor, so that they had to look down at him, but even so it was they who were discomforted. They tried to urge Selial forward but she bowed her head.

'We cannot find a leader,' Malien said again, 'and so we have none. The Syndic must lead.'

'I will not be led by a committee,' Tensor repeated. 'After Tar Gaarn we gave authority to the Syndics. Look what came of it!'

Malien shook her fist at him. 'You stole it back!' she spat. 'That's what became of it.'

'Choose or I go my own bitter way.' Tensor bowed his head, quivering with suppressed tension.

The Aachim conferred among themselves. Eventually Selial came back with their answer. 'The Syndic stands.'

Tensor let out his breath in a whoosh. 'Then I must hew my own path,' he said in anguish.

'No,' said Selial, a muscle spasming in her cheek. 'We will never follow you again. Obey us or become outlaw. We depart tomorrow for the eastern cities. The preparations will begin immediately. You will surrender the Mirror to us.'

Tensor looked ghastly. He stood up painfully, moving up the corridor with shuffling steps. Passing Llian, he gripped his arm. 'Come,' he muttered. 'There is much to do before the morrow.'

Having made their decision, the Aachim would go at once in the cool of the morning. They hurried back and forth, checking their equipment and packing food into small parcels. Every day's delay would add to the hardship of the journey, for it was late spring now and the Dry Sea was baking under a sun that would not be hidden by clouds for another two hundred days. The way to the east could be the most difficult of all.

Llian was devastated. Katazza had promised so much, but all he had gained were a few more chapters to a tale that had no ending. Now it would never be finished.

He hung around, feeling useless, then Tensor had a sudden change of mood. 'Go away!' he roared, 'and with something of a sense of relief Llian joined the other Aachim in the fortress, glad for once that there was some task at which his hands were useful. He was bemused by the change in them, and in Tensor. Why had they rebelled? Why had Tensor given in? Truly he knew nothing about their kind.

After the hardships of the trip here, he could scarcely bear to think of the return journey. He had also reached a certain rapport with Tensor. Though it was evident that Tensor did not trust him, he seemed comfortable with his wit and quick understanding. Tensor had taught him something of the Aachim script that few outsiders knew, and to a chronicler that knowledge was a treasure beyond contemplation. Why Tensor had done this he did not know – to give away a secret that had been guarded for so long showed how desperate he had become and how little hope he really had.

They finished their preparations; they slept, though Tensor did not. They rose again in the dark, took up their packs and their gear, crossed the bridge to the Great Tower and waited on the landing. Finally Tensor appeared at the top of the steps.

'Have you made your preparations?' asked the Speaker, for Tensor carried nothing but the Mirror case in one hand.

'Indeed I have,' he replied grimly.

'Then give me the Mirror – I will take custody of it in the name of the Syndic.' Selial smiled and held out her hand. Tensor did not smile. Llian noticed that his knuckles were white. A shiver went up his back.

'Alas,' he said, 'I renounce my species and my world. I am no longer Aachim. I will never give up the Mirror. You may go, but I remain in Katazza.'

Perhaps the Aachim had expected something of the sort

for they all surged up the steps. As they reached his landing Tensor put up his hand. They stopped at once.

'Do not move against me.'

There was a long, tortured moment when it seemed violence might be done, Aachim against Aachim, yet none wanted it. Tensor backed slowly away and the Aachim did not pursue him. At the next flight he called 'Llian!'

Llian resisted but once more found himself in Tensor's thrall. He felt his legs move though he willed them be still. Malien grabbed his arm. Tensor put out his own hand towards her.

'Would you force me to raise my fist against *you*?' Tensor rasped. 'I will.'

'Stay here, if you so choose,' she said. 'You know that I cannot do you harm, but Llian goes with us, and the Mirror too.' She cast a glance over her shoulder. 'Does the Syndic support me in this?'

Selial stepped forward, and one by one they all did, even Basitor and Hintis.

The veins on Tensor's neck bulged. 'I *will* use it,' he warned. 'Think what you do!'

'No!' she cried. 'No more shall we give way to your fancies and follies; you are insane!'

He reeled. 'Then insane I be. And I say this – *look* at him! Tear off the glasses, wipe away the stain. What do you see? A Zain who bears the stigmata of Rulke! A collaborator among us! A treacherous, vile Zain of the line that betrayed us in aeons past, never to be trusted again. Will *you* have him, Basitor? Will *you*, Hintis? Will *any* of you, except she who has protected his secret ever since we left Thurkad?'

Llian was almost beside himself with terror. Basitor strode forward, plucked off the glasses and ground them under his heel. He tilted up Llian's chin. 'Look at his eyes,' he said.

Hintis tore open Llian's shirt. 'See the white spots on his breast.'

Selial inspected the evidence. 'He carries the Gift of Rulke –

the stigmata are plain. But he cannot be punished for the crimes of ancestors long dead. He has committed no crime.'

Basitor spat on the floor. 'The Gift is crime enough for me, after what happened to Shazmak. Comes he with us, I will twist his head off his neck at the first chance.' He held up a pair of hands the size of garden forks.

'And I'll hold him while you do it,' said Hintis. 'Too long have we suffered our enemies when we should have smitten them.'

Malien met Llian's eyes. 'I'm beaten, chronicler. Our ghosts will walk the pages of the Histories. Karan, forgive me!' She opened her hand, letting Llian's wrist slip out.

Finding the pull of Tensor's will irresistible now, Llian crept towards him. Tensor gripped his wrist as he had at the Conclave.

'What now?' asked Tensor. 'Do you enforce your edict on me or not?'

Selial agonised but could not bring herself to raise her hand. The moment was balanced, then Tensor flung Llian through the door, slammed it closed and barred it. The Aachim rushed the door and beat their fists against it, bold now that his presence was gone.

'That won't hold them,' said Tensor, his great chest heaving.

Llian was dragged up to Tensor's work chamber, which was designed to survive anything but the complete destruction of the tower. Tensor crashed its metal door, locked bars thicker than Llian's body, made active other defences that Llian did not understand, then looked back with grim satisfaction. Now that the decision had been made, he seemed to revel in the conflict.

Llian was desperately afraid, though relieved that he did not have to face the Dry Sea just yet. And he saw that Tensor had not been idle – he had a great store of food and a tank of water in one corner.

Tensor noted the direction of his gaze. 'Hope that there

is enough,' he said, 'for until I've learned the making of a gate into the Nightland and brought *him* forth for my revenge, we do not leave this place.'

As if nothing had happened he sat down at the bench and resumed the work that had been interrupted the previous day. Not long after there came a fierce banging on the door. A low-pitched whine followed it, rising to a furious grinding and grating sound. Later they must have used a kind of blasting powder, for there was a dull boom and the whole tower trembled. The silence that followed hung heavily, testing Llian's nerves. Yet the door was unbreached.

'They'll never break it,' said Tensor, without looking up. 'Kandor himself made it to be impregnable.'

Some time later the Aachim returned with other devices and a high-pitched wailing began, rising and falling, finally breaking into a screech that set Llian on edge. Evidently they employed some kind of machine against the door but though the noise went on for hours they made no progress.

The sun set. Tensor continued his work in silence. The barring of the stair had left all the upper floors of the tower at his command, for there was no other way up. Without the wholesale demolition of the Great Tower they were safe.

When Llian stirred in the morning Tensor was still working with such furious energy and concentration that he did not even look up when food and drink was put before him. Nor did he react when the noises at the door resumed. Again there came a hollow *boom* and the whole room shook. A stack of food packages tumbled to the floor; the Mirror fell face-down on the table. Only then did Tensor give a weary sigh and turn toward the door.

The clamour let up for a moment, long enough for Llian to hear the end of his sentence: '. . . I have done it!'

Staggering to his pallet, Tensor flopped onto his face and plummeted into sleep. Even the attack outside, violently renewed, did not disturb him.

This chamber was built for Kandor himself, thought Llian, luxuriating in that thought. It was made with all the skill of the Aachim and the cunning of the Charon at the height of their power and ingenuity.

The attack did not even dent the door. While Tensor slept, Llian picked up the scroll. It was a long document, closely written in the Aachan script in a tiny neat hand. He had not yet been taught enough to decipher it, but recognised an occasional word. There were drawings too, though they formed no pictures that his mind could accommodate, except for small ones along one side of the scroll, doodles perhaps. Great arches were depicted there and other ornately framed apertures of various dimensions and shapes. And several times a word appeared that he recognised or a symbol that he took to mean 'gate'.

So Tensor had found the secret of gates – portals that linked one place to another – or thought he had. A way of escape! Perhaps (Llian felt a secret hope), a way back to Meldorin without suffering the torment of the Dry Sea.

Suddenly he was shocked into immobility by a presence behind him. He whirled to find Tensor standing there. Tensor smiled at the furtiveness, though he did not appear to be bothered by the deed.

'Yes, it is a gate,' he said, 'and why should you be surprised; there has been much talk of them. The principle is simple but can I make it? And will it work?'

He was interrupted by a disembodied voice issuing from a solitary high slit in the wall. A quavery voice.

'Tensor! Tensor! We are pursued.'

Tensor smiled at this. 'Pursued?' he said, pretending astonishment. 'Who pursues?'

'We cannot say. They are coming from the south.'

'See how we have fallen!' Tensor said to Llian. 'A few solitary individuals approach, doubtless starving and half-dead, and we tremble. Before the Ghâshâd came, a legion would not have daunted us here.'

'Seek not my advice,' he shouted through the wall. 'I have renounced leadership.' After that, only silence came from outside.

Tensor turned to the making of his gate device, while Llian looked on in wonder. The Aachim proceeded with utmost confidence, though what he made did not remotely resemble the earlier drawings. He did not need to measure, but judged lengths by eye and weights by heft. He took his materials from nearby, from the higher chambers, adapting the design according to what lay to hand.

Tensor mined the rooms for metal and stone, removing stone from the inner walls, using tools that he made himself, shaping it easily and locking it together with metal pins. And he shaped metal with the same apparent ease, with similar simple tools. His skill and his feeling for his materials were awesome, and he appeared to take great pleasure in the shaping.

The gate that he made was a simple, beautiful thing, in the form of a pavilion, just a stepped pad of stone and seven slender stone columns supporting a metal dome. It was beautiful yet lacking in symmetry; characteristically Aachim. Yet simple though it was, it still took many days of tireless labour.

Llian could not sit idly by while Tensor laboured, and now that he had been abandoned by the Aachim and lost the protection of Malien, he no longer felt any constraints. At first he just sat, watching and listening, but he became so fascinated by what Tensor was doing that he began to question him and offer suggestions. Soon Llian was completely captivated by Tensor's ideas and the knowledge that he was gaining, what no other chronicler could have known. As time went on Tensor needed to compel him less and less. Llian was close to working as a partner with him. A collaborator he was named, a collaborator he would be.

He questioned Tensor constantly, about the languages and scripts of Aachan and the Histories of the Aachim, and Tensor answered him freely. Llian soon knew enough to read most of what Tensor had written on the scrolls, though it consisted of thoughts about the theory, philosophy and construction of gates, and was not of any lasting interest to him.

Llian's questioning had a greater purpose. He still planned to translate *Tales of the Aachim*, the book of Aachim Histories that he had committed to memory in Shazmak. He made a start on that task too. For Llian was a master chronicler, and as the Histories were his art, their languages were his science, the meat to his bread. He learned quickly, driven by his own consuming need to know as well as the knowledge that this opportunity would never come again. That was what drove him most of all – today, tomorrow, it could all be snatched away, and he would not have learned enough to continue by himself. I am nearly as corrupt as Tensor, Llian thought. What would Karan have thought of me? That sobered him for quite some time. He dreamed bitter, lonely dreams of her that night, but in the morning woke to reality. Karan was lost, and Tensor was right here.

One day his work, his life and these dreams were shattered. Tensor suddenly stood up, dusted his hands, stepped back and looked at the pavilion gate.

'It's done,' he said. 'It's good. It's ready and so am I.' He turned to Llian. 'And soon I will put *you* to the use for which I brought you all this way. We shall see then who is the greater.'

37

AN UNEXPECTED MEETING

T he man emitted a throttled squawk of terror. He could not
speak, for the weight on his back had driven the breath
from his lungs and his mouth was pressed into the dirt.

Then a woman spoke and there was a chuckle in her
voice. 'Get off him, Karan. We're on the same side now.'

Karan started. The voice was familiar though she could not
remember whom it belonged to. She twisted her victim's head
around roughly, trying to make out his features in the gloom.
Once identified as Mendark, she put the knife away and
climbed off his back, even put out her hand and helped him
to his feet, though with evident dislike, and made a play of
wiping her hand on her trousers afterward. Old memories
surged back from the terrible time before the Conclave.

'*You fool, Osseion!*' raged Mendark, spitting out dirt. 'Did
you lose your eyes and your brains along with your finger?'

Each party was so astonished to see the other that, for a
long minute, nothing was said. Finally Tallia took Shand's
hand.

'Well met,' she said, 'though you look absolutely shocking.'

Shand put his own knife away and lurched forward. He
was gaunt; his tanned skin had a yellow cast. 'I've been ill,'
he croaked. Abruptly he dropped the knife and crumpled to
the ground.

'Shand!' Karan cried, falling to her knees beside him. Tallia bent down over him too.

'It's all right,' he said weakly, barely able to raise his head off the grass. 'I've had the gripe for weeks. I thought I was going to die here.'

'I've a medicine will fix that,' Tallia said, flinging things out of her pack. 'By morning you'll be ready to climb mountains.' She shook various powders into a mug, filled it with water, stirred the mixture and held it to his mouth.

It went down his throat in one huge swallow. 'That's nearly as foul as my water was!' he choked.

'It needs to be. But it'll block you up so tight that you'll need a corkscrew next time you go to the jakes.' She laughed merrily. 'So, Shand, this is what you were up to that night in Tullin when you introduced me to Pender. I wondered.'

'I didn't imagine that I would ever end up here,' Shand replied. 'I didn't know it until we reached the very edge of the Grey Cliffs, Karan and I. It's a long way from Tullin to Katazza, and I at least am glad to see you. We can tell our tales and discuss our objectives later: doubtless they are not too different. For now, good food is what we need, and plenty of it.'

Tallia went to where Karan stood alone, looking uncomfortable. Karan eventually held out her hand. Tallia took it, then embraced her, to Karan's surprise.

'I left you behind at the Conclave,' said Tallia. 'There were too many people to take care of and I couldn't carry you. When I came back you were gone. I've never stopped feeling guilty about it.'

'Your job was to bring the living to safety and you couldn't even manage that. I don't see why you feel guilty about the dying,' said Mendark, still angry.

'Nevertheless,' said Tallia to Karan, flicking a dismissing hand at Mendark, 'I am shamed.'

'I do not blame you,' said Karan. 'It was the best outcome for me, as it happens. Though I'm absolutely starving.'

'We have food,' said Mendark, still looking at Shand in amazement and Karan with outright hostility, if not malice.

'Then get it out of your pack, lard-belly,' she cried. 'We've been eating lizard for the last two days.'

'And here is my friend, Osseion,' said Tallia.

Osseion gave Karan a huge grin. 'I have heard your tale more than once, Karan. I am very pleased.'

She extended a hand gingerly. It disappeared into his four-fingered paw but to her surprise his grip was gentle.

'I am the captain of Mendark's guard,' said Osseion. 'I protect him from people hiding behind rocks with knives. Today I lose my job.' A low, rumbling chuckle welled out from deep in his chest. 'You were very quick. I think we will be friends, you and I.'

Karan thought so too, deciding that she liked him best of all. They followed Shand through the darkness to the trees where their camp was established. There, sheltered from the evening wind, she rekindled the coals in a stone fireplace as Tallia unpacked a food bag. She and Tallia chopped food into a pot while Osseion filled two smaller ones with water from a red-stained spring.

Mendark was still smouldering from Karan's assault. With her knife pressing his windpipe he had known fear such as he had not felt in centuries. Worse, he had given way to that fear and everyone knew it. He could not let that rest.

'Easy to tell she's from Gothryme,' he said loudly as Karan speared a bit of raw onion and ate it off her knife. 'She has the manners of a manure-bagger.'

There was dead silence. Karan's eyes locked with his over the fire. The back of his neck crawled, then in a single blinding movement she flung the pot, contents and all, at his face. Had he not ducked it would have knocked his teeth out. With a choked gasp, Karan stumbled away into the night. Rather too late Mendark recalled their first meeting, when he had tried to take the Mirror from her. Karan had *sensed* what he was going to do before he knew it himself, and reacted more quickly than his eye could follow.

Tallia picked up a brand from the fire and, with its light, gathered the scattered food. She was so angry that the torch shook in her hand.

Shand gripped Mendark's arm, tight as a wrench. 'You fool! You left Karan behind, though you wanted her badly enough when she had the Mirror. Since then she has walked all the way from Thurkad and crossed the Dry Sea by the longest way, three times your well-fed jaunt, cushioned by the Magister's gold that drags your purse down so.' Shand went pale; his free hand clutched at his belly, but he mastered himself. 'She is the most courageous person I know, and the most loyal, and I value her above a hundred of you. I swear I'll fling you down that cliff before I see her harmed, Mendark! Now get out of my way!'

Shand sought Karan out in the darkness. She had not gone far for there was nowhere to go but along the narrow terrace between the lower cliffs and the upper. She was sitting at the edge with her feet hanging over, crying silently. Shand sat down beside her carefully, because though he had no great fear of heights, he had a healthy respect for the edges of cliffs. He put his arm around her slender shoulders, holding her wordlessly.

'Mendark!' she spat. 'How I hate him. He pretended friendship once, the stinking, greedy hypocrite.'

'You mistake his motives, Karan. It is not greed that drives Mendark, not in the ordinary sense. Duty perhaps; the Magister must put all other things below that.'

'He failed as Magister and his wallet is still the size of a pumpkin! He's a greedy, evil, malicious man.'

'The duty cannot be put aside so easily, nor the office. A Magister is not a mayor to be elected and cast down at whim. It is a lifetime position. While Mendark breathes he must put the duty above all things. He has been faithful to his responsibilities and no more corrupted by his long office than any other might be. He has many weaknesses, as have

I, and even you, Karan. He likes his position too well and the power that goes with it. A proud man does not like to have his nose pressed into the dirt.'

'I have never been blind to my own faults,' she said in a small voice.

'Nonetheless, we need him,' Shand said, taking her hand. 'He has a part to play in this story of the Mirror before it is done.'

'And you, whom I love and respect, take his side. I am lost.'

'I do not take his side. I present both sides. I will protect you, if it comes to it. But how can we go to Katazza and do our business like this, eh?'

'I can hardly bear to speak to him,' Karan whispered. 'But I have sworn an oath to you. If you require it, I will endure him.'

'I *ask* it,' said Shand. 'Now let us go back; my belly still hurts.'

He stood up. Sniffling, Karan followed him back to the camp. There they found the food recovered and the pot simmering merrily. Karan was so hungry that she could barely restrain herself from spooning it from the pot, but Mendark's previous remark made her draw right back into herself, to sit quietly out of the firelight. Then she saw Shand's eyes on her and remembered her duty.

She went across to Mendark. He took a half-step towards her, then stopped uncertainly. Karan went the rest of the way and forced out her hand. Mendark took it, held it for a moment, then bowed his head to her and each turned away. The tension went out of the gathering; they took up their plates and ate.

By the morning Shand's gripe was gone but he was still weak, so they stayed there for another day. Now it was time to go. They were on the moist south-western side, sheltered from the sun, and as they set out the morning light began to flood across the plains, touching the white with pink, highlighting the mounded sea floor and casting crescent-shaped shadows behind the salt dunes. The sea looked cool, beautiful, peaceful. In the west the mountains behind the high plateau of Faranda stood out huge and clear, seeming only a few leagues away.

Above them the cliffs were rounded masses of black basalt, threaded with fissures, chimneys and passages. Karan climbed the first hundred spans easily, though the footholds were a long way apart and more suited to the tall folk, Osseion and Tallia. Karan was uncannily sure-footed, leaping from one hold to another like a mountain goat, though her boots were falling to pieces. The sole of one was held on with rope.

She climbed for an hour, drawing steadily ahead of Shand and Mendark. Tallia came up around an outward-jutting mass of basalt and found her sitting on the ledge above, binding a gash on her foot with a piece of rag. The cut was a deep one and the blood flowed freely. She dabbed casually at the wound, then sat staring out across the sea. Tallia sat down beside her. The others were toiling along far below.

'Your boots!' she said.

'I have another pair,' Karan answered absently. 'I'm saving them for the way back.' She looked very contented, oblivious to her injury. The scrap of bloody rag fell through her fingers unnoticed to flutter away down the cliff.

'How much you've changed since we first met,' said Tallia. 'You seem happy today.'

'I am happy. This journey has been good for me. When I think back to what I had become before the Conclave, how I drove myself, how I matched my will against the wills of others much stronger than me until it drove me mad, it's as though it happened to someone else. What a strange, obsessive time that was for me! How remote it seems now; how meaningless! There was nothing driving me but a promise to someone who had taken advantage of my good nature – Maigraith. What right did I have to choose, to decide that

Faelamor should have the Mirror, more than any other? What do I know of the future, or the dangers we face, or how to overcome them?'

'What does anyone know? The Histories are littered with failures and follies and disastrous decisions made by the wise and the powerful; those whose destiny it was to rule. Look at Tensor! The more schooled to power, the greater the disaster when they blunder. Why should not your own judgment, made in good faith rather than pride or self-interest, not serve as well?'

'Pride drives me too.'

'Pooh,' said Tallia, unimpressed.

'I owe Shand everything,' Karan said softly. 'I can hardly tell you what he's done for me.'

'He is a good man.'

'I am stronger than I was before all this began. Happier too, though I can't say why. Even if Tensor fails, eventually we must go back, and the journey will be cruel in the summer.'

'If *he* comes,' Tallia thought aloud, 'there will be no going back.'

Karan was not listening. There was just one thing on her mind. 'Llian is up there – I *know* he is.'

Just then Shand and Mendark came toiling up, their faces flushed. Osseion followed easily, in spite of his monstrous pack. Karan was silent, looking briefly at Mendark and then away again, but when Shand appeared, panting and his lips grey, she jumped up at once. Tallia was on her feet too, her face a picture of concern.

'Are you all right, Shand?' she asked gravely.

'Don't worry, I'm not dying. I'll rest here with Karan a while. My legs have forgotten all about climbing and my belly still hurts.'

Mendark, Tallia and Osseion moved on up the slope.

'Shand, you look terrible.'

'I've felt better. Tallia was right about the corkscrew! But enough of my sad tale. We will soon be in Katazza.'

'Yes, and Llian is there,' she repeated.

'Maybe,' he cautioned. 'Don't get ahead of yourself! A lot could have happened in the past months. Now listen to me.'

He stopped abruptly, staring upwards, but nothing happened except that there was a rattle of falling pebbles to one side. The others were still moving steadily up, almost to the base of the next set of cliffs.

'I've often wondered about your part in this, Karan. You are special in some way, more special than your poorly developed talents indicate, and you're here for a purpose. There will be a climax at Katazza and whatever happens you will be at risk. Be careful.'

Karan could think of nothing that would trouble her once they got there. 'Yes, of course,' she said absently.

She jumped up, grimacing as the weight went on the cut that she had still not bandaged. She bound it swiftly with another bit of rag, turned it around her slender ankle, tied it and strapped her broken boot back together.

Shand went silent. She can think of nothing but the arms of her lover, he thought. Ah well, I remember that too. I hope she gets what she desires. Who could possibly deserve it more? Llian had better appreciate her.

The day passed, and another, before they climbed the last cliff, the steepest, stood on the ancient seashore and saw the mountains of Katazza towering above them. But there was a surprise awaiting them.

Directly in their path, unmoving, were six Aachim. Tallia and Osseion, who were leading, stopped abruptly.

'Well, Mendark,' she said. 'The moment that you put off planning for has come.'

'They don't look hostile,' said Karan. 'Let me go first.'

'Stay where you are,' Mendark replied. 'Hold up your hands.'

They did so, and shortly the Aachim raised their hands to show good faith.

'We will go forward cautiously,' Mendark said.

When they were close, Karan saw two that she knew: Selial, from her trial in Shazmak, and Malien, Rael's mother, whom she had not met for many years. She ran forward.

'Malien,' she wept. 'Oh, Malien, I am so sorry. It was all my fault.' She threw herself at Malien's feet.

'Karan,' said Malien, lifting and embracing her, weeping shining tears onto her curls. 'Ah, my Rael. I had such hopes. But he was a true son of Elienor.' They clung together while the others approached.

'I am Selial,' said the white-haired woman, 'and I speak for the Syndic and the Aachim. Well met, Karan.' She named the Aachim – Xarah, Shalah, Iennis and Basitor. Karan introduced her group.

'Without asking your business here,' said Selial, 'or your businesses (for we watched your separate approaches with our spy glasses), I give you ours. I will be offensively blunt. We have a grim tale to tell. Tensor has taken the Mirror and locked himself away in the Great Tower, defying the Syndic. He has cast off his heritage – repudiated the Aachim. We believe that he has found the secret of making gates and is constructing one at this moment. He is unhinged, but cunning. We cannot stay him nor even gain entry to his chamber. I am afraid that our doom is very close. If you can aid us, Mendark, it may sway the balance.'

'Our interests coincide,' said Mendark. 'I will do what I can.'

Karan was almost bursting with impatience, but now that the politenesses and the urgent business were done, she could not restrain herself.

Selial held up her hand. 'Before anything, there is an uncompleted matter regarding Karan. A residue from her trial in Shazmak. Karan, come to me.'

Karan looked alarmed but she obeyed.

Selial looked stern, judicial. 'I must inform you that, in your absence, three days ago this Syndic reopened your trial. We found that you were indeed guilty of one of the charges, namely, bearing the Mirror into Shazmak and failing to render it up to us. As you know, the penalty is death. Furthermore, we found that you had, by unknown means, deceived the Syndic.'

Karan fell to her knees. Of all the things that might have happened in Katazza, this was the least expected. Selial signed her to rise.

'However, on the first crime we absolved you, in the light of further events concerning the Mirror, for it has become clear that you acted in our interests better than we knew ourselves.

'On the second crime, though you are also guilty, no penalty is set because such a thing has never before occurred. We require only that for our Histories you tell how the deception was done.'

Karan bowed her head.

Selial smiled. 'Now you may ask the question that concerns you so greatly.'

'Where is Llian,' she cried. 'Is he here?'

'I'm sorry,' said Malien. Karan's face blanched.

'Nay, not that,' Malien amended, touching Karan's cheek. 'He is in Katazza, and in health, though I had to repair him many times on the journey. I am afraid Tensor has him and they are locked away together. But, dear me!'

'What?' cried Karan, alarmed again.

Malien was smiling broadly. 'He has a kind of charm, this Llian of yours. But Karan, dear me, he *is* a fool!'

It was still a march long and hard to Katazza, for the land rose steeply and very broken, barren and littered with round black rocks. Only in the deeper valleys was there vegetation, here a scrub of olive trees writhen with the years, dried-up black fruit still scattered on the ground, there a patch of ghost gums, their bleached trunks leaning out over a dry watercourse.

As the path wound higher and the valley became deeper, they passed through patches of forest where the shade was cool. It was not possible to reach Katazza that day, for though in leagues it was not far, it was an exhausting climb and their lungs had forgotten how to get what they needed from the thin air.

For Karan the trip passed in a daze. The strange landscapes – the plains coated with ash and volcanic bombs, the fumaroles and geysers, the cinder cones and deserts of ropy lava, the deep valleys filled with the strangest trees she had ever seen – might have been her back garden at Gothryme, for all the note she took of them. She could think only of one thing and even when, at dusk, they reached the top of the mountain, and stood before the extraordinary braided towers, an architecture that existed nowhere else on Santhenar, she gave them not a second look.

'Where is he?' she cried at the western door of the fortress.

Malien smiled and pointed. 'There in the Great Tower. Go through this door, up to the third floor, across the bridge to the tower, then follow the stair to the fifth level. You will see the marks on the door. But you cannot get in.'

Karan was already gone, racing through the halls past Aachim who stared at her in astonishment. She ran with her boot flapping, up the stairs and over the bridge, stopping only to cast off the broken boots. She darted between the woven columns of stone, across the landing and up the coiled stairs, not feeling the ache in her side. Her heart was pounding as if it would explode out of her chest. Sucking at the unaccustomed thin air, she reached the fifth level and skidded across the landing to the massive door that sealed off the chamber, the stair and all the great height of the tower above.

The door was solid steel, scratched and scarred from the Aachim's earlier attempts, but neither damaged nor even dented. She pounded it with her fists but she might as well have beaten against the side of a mountain, for her blows did not make a sound. The door closed into the stone on all sides. It was impossible to get in or even speak through it.

Wait! High above, beside the door, there were slits in the stone. They were too small for the smallest child to get through, but perhaps she could call to him and reassure herself.

Karan ran down a floor, where she had seen a bench and some planks. Hauling them up, she swung one of the heavy planks violently at the door. The crash tore it out of her hands, embedding a splinter deep in her palm. The shock went up her arm to the shoulder. Chastened, she bashed the end against the door over and over, to be sure that she had their attention. She stacked the bench and the planks, climbed up on top, precariously balanced, and standing on tiptoes was able to put her face to the slit.

'Llian, Llian, are you there?'

38

THE TWISTED
MIRROR

Once again there was a pounding and a crashing at the door, a tremendous vibration.

'Fools,' said Tensor, but as the racket went on he became irritated. 'I am Aachim no longer!' he shouted. 'You have no hold on me.'

A shiver wavered its way up Llian's spine. This was different. 'Shut up, you fool,' he whispered, cupping his ear.

Behind him Tensor clenched his mighty fist, then he lowered it again.

Pressing against the door, Llian caught the faintest whiff of perfume – lime blossom – and he *knew*! Another shiver passed up his back and made the hair stand up on his head. Tears started from his eyes. Tensor was staring at him, staring at the slit high on the wall as well, and his own eyes were ablaze.

Suddenly a voice came through the slit. A pure young voice that Llian had given up as lost months ago in Thurkad; mad, brave, going quietly to her death. Waves of goosebumps passed over his skin. The lump in his throat was so big that it choked him.

'Llian, Llian, are you there?'

'*Karan!*' Llian croaked. He leapt in the air, screaming her name. 'Karan, can it really be you?'

'Llian,' came her voice. 'They said you were here. Come out!'

'I cannot,' wept Llian. 'Tensor will never allow it.'

Karan cursed vividly, fluently, imperiously. '*Tensor!* Let him free. He has no part in this.'

Tensor had been staring up at the slit, his eyes shining, though with what emotion Llian could not be sure. It was almost as if Tensor wanted to believe in her. But her imperious manner came up against his pride and his will, and though perhaps he still loved her, he could not forgive her for the fall of Shazmak, her fault or not. He could not humble himself.

'Betrayer, go away.' Turning back to the pavilion, he renewed work on his gate.

'Fool!' Karan roared through the slit. 'This is your doing, not mine. Look! Here are your people locked outside, striving to save you from your folly. Llian, Llian, have you not told him?'

'Yes,' whispered Llian, ashamed of his collaboration with Tensor. 'But he will not listen.'

There was a long silence. What was Karan thinking? Llian knew that there was *nothing* she could do. He stood at the base of the wall, looking up at the slit. Pushing a bench across, he put a stool on top and clambered up. Peering through the slit, all he could see was a lighted rectangle at the further end.

'Karan,' he called softly.

At once a shadow appeared at the other end; a froth of red hair.

'Karan. Let me see your face.'

She moved her head back so that the light caught the tangled mass of hair, that unique, magnificent red, and her familiar lovely face. Her nose was burned from salty wind. Her round cheeks were hollow. She was the most beautiful sight he had ever seen.

'Karan,' he said, not bothering to wipe the tears away. 'I

548

thought you were dead. I scarcely dared to hope that you might be alive. How did you get here?'

'I walked! Shand carried me out of the Conclave and brought me back to life. We fled Thurkad, wandering, and when we came to the shore of the Dry Sea I knew that you were out here somewhere. I've come to take you home.'

Her self-assurance brought up deep memories and made him smile. Reality snatched it away again. This prison was beyond her skill to breach.

'Give me your hand,' he said. She put her slim arm through the slit and their hands clasped somewhere in the middle of the wall. Her hand was small and warm and he stroked it with his fingertips, running them up the back of her wrist, feeling the bump where the broken bones had not knitted perfectly.

'Karan, you are a miracle.'

On that first night Karan spent an hour with Llian, just gazing at his untidy face, talking to him through the slit and holding his hand. But she was too impatient to be long satisfied with that, and next day came only briefly to the wall, in the morning and the evening and at other odd times. Llian wondered what she did with the rest of her day, for he could have spent hours there. So in her absence he went back to his study of the Aachim script that Tensor had begun to teach him and his translation of Tensor's scrolls. After a while the enthusiasm came back, though not as fiercely as before.

He thought constantly about Karan and asleep he dreamed about her, though that was no more satisfying than the waking. All he saw in his dreams was a slice of her face framed in a dark rectangle.

Now that his life had a new hope, Llian began to worry about what Tensor wanted from him. What aspect of the Gift of Rulke did he need from Llian, and how would he turn it back on Rulke, if that was what Tensor intended to do?

Now Tensor too took pause. The gate was made but his assurance fell suddenly from him. Was it that he knew not how to use it, or that the coming of Karan had brought out all his self-doubts, his guilt, his follies and his fears? A part of him longed to beg her forgiveness but his pride would not allow it. Another part wept for the desolation that was Shazmak, blaming her for being the mover of it. If she had never gone to Shazmak none of this would have happened. He doubted Llian even more. What if Karan turned this weapon against him too? And he had cut himself off from his people – living death for an Aachim. Every part of his life and being was brought to nothing.

Tensor felt pitifully alone and fearful. Despite what he showed to the world, he was afraid. He had no friends, no brothers, no people. What he did was for himself alone or for the hate that had been there longer than anything; but that was not enough. His dreams had failed; the Aachim would never recover. There was nothing more he could lose.

Nothing remained: he was an outcast with no bonds, no strictures. Nothing was left other than hatred and revenge. Nothing could take that from him save death and that he would gladly embrace when this was done.

Buoyed up by these thoughts he went back to his experiments with the gate. How was it to be activated, opened, directed across space to its destination, and brought back here again?

Llian watched, appalled, enthralled as Tensor fitted the Mirror to a plate set on one of the columns of the pavilion. It slipped into place. Tensor touched it to life. He spoke a word. A succession of images – alien places – drifted across the face of the Mirror. The images moved faster, blended, disappeared.

Tensor was rigid with tension, staring at the Mirror, his other hand clenched tightly about the black metal case. Then he lifted his hand. The flow stopped suddenly, settled on one image, a gloomy room, a dim-lit chamber, though it was

550

the soaring audience chamber of a palace. A sombre figure was seated in the shadows.

Tensor cried out, thrusting Llian behind him with a single sweep of his arm so that he fell, half in and half out of the pavilion. Tensor's other arm was held high and for a moment he remained motionless. Llian saw the other figure start and look around, then Tensor swung down his upraised arm with a great cry.

The floor of the pavilion rocked beneath them. A torrent roared in Llian's ears. The breath was snatched from his lungs. All light fled from the room. His head was pulled in one direction, his feet in another. His empty stomach heaved up acid, burning his throat and sinuses. He tasted blood in his mouth; he had bitten his tongue. Then he began to hallucinate. The skies pulsed with light and colour; cables of flame and darkness writhed around him; there was a noise like thunder. He felt a shocking blow in the back and fell senseless.

Llian realised that he was lying on the floor beside the pavilion. The lamps still glowed in their brackets. The experience seemed no more real than a nightmare after waking. The pavilion stood in the same place as before; nothing had changed, except there was a crack in its stone floor. Nothing had happened after all.

Something ran from his nose, wetting his lips and chin; something thick, sticky, salty. He pushed himself to his feet and staggered across to the Mirror. It showed nothing but his face, and that was a mess. His mouth and beard were red with blood and his nose was bleeding. He had bitten his lip as well as his tongue. His eyes were starred with red veins; his hair was wild.

Karan's voice came hollowly through the wall, close to panic.

'Llian, Llian, is everything all right? What are you doing?'

Llian realised that Tensor was nowhere to be seen. 'It's Tensor,' he shouted, scrambling up onto the perch. 'He's made a gate and gone through it, and not returned.'

Karan swore. 'Don't go with him. Keep away from him; never aid him. Swear that you will not.'

'He has a power over me – like Emmant had, only much stronger. That's how I came to be here.'

She thumped her fist against the wall, then there was silence. Evidently she was thinking. 'Pathetic, weak-willed fool!' she cried, though without venom. 'That's not good enough. Give me your hand.'

He extended his hand through the wall.

'Your hand is so cold. Oh, look at your face! He is mad! Now, swear that you will not aid him.' Llian was just about to do so when the tower shook. 'Go,' she screamed, 'hide before he returns. Wait for me.' She pulled her warm hand out of his and her face disappeared.

Llian sat on the step of the pavilion. What was Karan thinking? There was nothing she could do. The Aachim had already tried every way.

What if Tensor never came back? What if he had been consumed, or opened the way for his enemy? Already Llian had spent more than a week barricaded in with Tensor. He could starve here.

There was a *crack!* behind him and Llian was tossed off the step. He turned to see Tensor appear in the gate, in fact in a duplicate gate slightly out of alignment from the original. The two blurred into one again. Tensor lurched, falling to hands and knees. His garments were in tatters and there were claw marks down his right cheek and shoulder. Blood dripped from his fingers onto the floor. He swayed there for a moment, looking straight at Llian but not seeing him, then his eyes unglazed and focussed once more. 'How the gate hurts!' he said.

Karan had evidently not gone far, for she was back at the hole almost immediately.

'Llian?' she called.

'Rulke?' said Llian to Tensor at the same time.

'Not Rulke,' Tensor said hoarsely. His eyes stared right through Llian. 'Nothing like. It was a horror, a nightmare. *The Mirror lied!*' He turned away and sat down heavily at his bench, already suffering aftersickness. 'The old tales name it the Twisted Mirror, the Glass of Delusions. But I chose to think that I had mastered it. Fool that I am! Delusion within the Mirror, and delusion without.'

'Then why do you toy with it still? It is a rare fool that commits the same folly twice.'

Tensor bridled and Llian leaned away instinctively. 'My whole long life has been lived for this moment,' Tensor said. 'Could you, all else torn away and destroyed, abandon the Histories, the prop of your life?'

'No, but . . .'

'Llian? Llian?' came Karan's panicky voice.

Tensor smote one of the columns of the pavilion with his great fist so that the dome shook and chips of stone fell in his hair. 'If you have nothing useful to offer, then say nothing,' he roared. Then he jumped up to the hole in the wall and bellowed at Karan. 'Stop your damned puling, 'less you want me to use him in my next experiment.' He seemed struck by the idea. 'There's something to think about. The gate must be tested, and who better to test it with.'

There was silence from the other side of the wall, then Karan screamed, 'Llian, run and hide. I will come for you. If you harm him, Tensor, I will curse you and your descendants for a hundred generations.'

'Do what you will,' he said indifferently. 'I am already cursed. Llian, come here. I see that you have an idea in mind. It had better be a sound one, for you will be the first to try the gate.'

There was a crash outside, as if Karan had fallen off her perch.

Llian backed away. He *had* realised something, but wasn't sure whether he would be worse off by telling Tensor or by keeping silent. He was terrified of the gate now. *The Mirror lied!* Of course it had and he knew why. Where would it send him in its malice?

'Tell me!' roared Tensor, shaking him, using his power over Llian, and in Llian's mind the urge to speak became irresistible.

'When first you began to use the Mirror,' Llian squeaked, 'it seemed that you needed from it only the secret of making the gate.'

'Making the gate and using it. That is so.'

'But you have put the Mirror *into the gate.*'

'I must be able to see the destination.'

'If you put the Twisted Mirror into the gate, how can you know if it shows true? How can you expect it to?'

Tensor struck Llian a fierce blow on the shoulder, knocking him to the ground, but he picked him again at once and dusted him off. 'By the orange moon of Aachan, chronicler,' he boomed, 'were you not a wretched, treacherous Zain, a scoundrel and a fool, I could almost admire you.'

He disappeared up the stairs, searching the other parts of the tower for metal suitable for the making of another mirror.

Llian had now completely lost his fascination with the Mirror and with the gate. Karan did not answer his calls so he went back to his eyrie at the top of the tower, trying to make a pattern of all he knew about the Charon, about Rulke and about the Mirror. All the mysterious incidents, like his first meeting with Shand, an old man who had seemed to know more, to be more than he should. Now Shand was here too. Llian recalled Karan's dreams after they fled from Sith; he had even shared one of them. It had been a nightmare about Rulke, held prisoner in the Nightland. A prison made to weaken him, drain him. So Tensor had said, and Thyllan too, at the Conclave. *But had it?*

He remembered his earlier forebodings, going back almost to his first meeting with Karan. Even the ordinary people on the road seemed to have sensed some coming cataclysm:

that something moved with slow patience towards a hideous consummation.

But Llian had no answers and, in the end, thirst drove him back down again. Once on the way the tower shook. Llian wondered if that was the Aachim trying to get in or just another earth trembler. The pavilion stood in the middle of the room as before, though the mirror frame had been remade. At the bench Tensor was working on his new mirror, giving it the final polish. It was larger than the Mirror of Aachan, with a slight coppery shimmer, and he had found time to chase a pattern of swirls on the margins. As Llian watched he gave it a final rub, snapped it into the frame and stood back, checking it, his head to one side.

Tensor turned to Llian, smiling enigmatically. 'What was that business between you and Malien?'

Llian wasn't sure what he was talking about. 'Business?'

'A letter you brought here,' said Tensor impatiently.

'Oh!' Llian wasn't sure that he should speak about it. *Would you give a baby a razor to play with*? Malien had warned him. But then, Tensor *had* told Llian to look for Kandor's records in the first place. 'I stole a letter from the citadel archives in Thurkad,' Llian said. 'It was from Kandor to Rulke, and it raised questions about the time of the Forbidding. But Malien took the letter and locked the door of Kandor's chamber of records so that I couldn't get in.'

'I doubt that you would find anything there anyway,' said Tensor. 'However, you have a way about you. You have done me some service and I would repay you. Get in the pavilion.'

'No,' cried Llian in a panic. 'I no longer want to.'

'That's not what you said on Tisane Mountain, when you went out among the ghosts. You said you would do anything for the tale. In you go.' He picked Llian up by collar and belt and threw him sprawling into the pavilion.

Llian tried to scramble out but was hurled effortlessly back.

'Take this,' said Tensor, skidding a lamp across the floor at him, 'and hold on.'

Images whirled across the new mirror and, with a whack, Tensor sent Llian flying back out into a dusty, journal-laden room. The air made a sucking sound behind him then he was alone. The gate was gone.

39

THE GREAT TOWER

Karan ran outside and stood beside the rift, staring up at the tower where Llian was held. No way in! She walked the outside of the great building twice but no solution came to her. Eventually her wanderings took her to the little patch of forest and the pavilion of serpentine, where she sat in the cool and the quiet, trying to think. She had been there for several hours when Malien came in silently, reacting (Karan sensed) as if sorry her refuge had been invaded.

'Are things not well between you and Llian?' Malien asked.

'As well as the wall permits.'

'Something's the matter – what is it?'

'Tensor has used the gate!'

Malien was shocked rigid. 'I hoped that he would fail, as all others have.'

'I'm dreadfully afraid. He plans to use Llian to test it. What if he never comes back?' Karan covered her face with her hands. 'How I can get to him?'

'You can't, unless you can fly, or climb like a spider. They are secure as long as the food and water last – at least a month.'

Karan was silent for a long time. 'Climb!' she said thoughtfully.

'I wasn't speaking seriously. We've investigated every way.

The towers are faced with glazed tiles, made so that no one could cling to them even if they were a brilliant climber.'

'I am a brilliant climber,' said Karan immodestly. 'I was taught by the best in Shazmak.'

'But have you looked closely? You haven't, for you've been mooning through the wall for days. Come up on the roof. There's a better view of the Great Tower from there. I'll show you why it cannot be climbed.'

They clambered up onto the steep roofs of the fortress which were covered in flaking tiles of slate and schist shipped from far across the sea. Karan picked her way along box gutters of solid copper filled with a sediment of shining mica, between gorgeous enamelled domes and jewelled spires, across to where the braided towers thrust up for heaven. They circumnavigated the bases of the clustered towers, finding the glazed tiles to be as smooth as the day they had been put there. As they came around the south side of one tower into the shade Malien said, 'See, Katazza was designed to be unclimbable.'

'Unclimbable when defended. Tensor can't defend it alone. I could smash pegs through the tiles into the stone from top to bottom.'

'By yourself?' said Malien. 'Wait, look here!'

The tiles had once been bonded at the edges to make a slick surface, but the freeze and thaw of aeons had cracked the bonds. Where the sun never reached, the joins were threaded with mosses and lichens. Here and there a clump of ferns had established itself in a crack.

'If the Great Tower's the same . . .' cried Karan. 'Come on!' She clambered down, raced across the bridge and at the other end climbed up on the rail. Reaching up, she put her fingers in a crack and lifted herself up, broken boots scrabbling at the joins. She jumped lightly down, took off her boots and tried again. Soon she was well above Malien's head, moving steadily sideways and up. She called down.

'Well, it may have been impossible two thousand years ago, but I'm sure I can do it now. I'd come up here, cross above that smooth patch, and then up in the valleys. For look,' she was becoming excited, 'there are a few places, up there and there, where you can see plants growing. The gaps must go up quite a long way.'

Malien moved back along the bridge to get a better view. The tower grew out of the ground, a braid of nine stone cables each many spans across, formed into a complex, interwoven spiral. About six floors up, three above the height of the bridges, the braid passed beneath a pair of stone doughnuts with a downward-hanging metal skirt, a defence that would be difficult to cross. Halfway up, at least eighty spans, was a vertical band of polished lapis lazuli, brilliantly blue in the golden afternoon light, with narrow gold bands at bottom and top. That section would be particularly hard to climb. Above that the cables spiralled up for another sixty spans or more, then a second vertical pitch of gold and lapis, and beyond that a relatively easy climb up and through the tall embrasures below the platinum dome.

'If any tile is loose, fatal to rely on it,' said Malien. 'And there may be many places where the joins are sound.'

'Most of the time it's not a vertical climb and if I had a handful of spikes and some rope, I could make my own footholds. Even if I slipped I'd slide rather than fall, and the rope would save me. It's not impossible. Admit it.'

Malien was sorry to have spoken in the first place, though she was forced to admit that it was not completely impossible. 'But dear Karan, there are three problems. Firstly, you can't go up barefoot; the edges will cut your feet to shreds. Secondly, you do not have any spikes.'

'I beg you to make some for me.'

'I will not. I refuse absolutely.'

'Then I will make them myself. I have seen it done. I think I can do it.'

'*You!*' Malien's scorn was withering. 'I never yet met one of your species who understood how to work metal.'

Karan wisely forbore to mention Shuthdar, he who had

made the golden flute and begun the troubles of the Three Worlds so long ago. 'Maybe not, but if the master refuses, the apprentice must make do with the skills she has. With or without them, I am determined to try.'

'Oh, very well.' Malien made careful measurements by eye. 'They will be ready early in the morning. But please tell no one about it.' She turned to go.

'Wait!' Karan was looking at Malien's boots. 'You have small feet.'

'No, I never lend my boots. Anyway, they are not as little as yours.'

'Please. They are perfect for climbing.'

'Ahhh! All right, anything! Anything you want. Come to my room, rifle my most precious belongings. Why not?'

'You said there was a third problem,' Karan said, laughing.

'How will you get over those projecting courses at the top. There are no tiles there, just blocks of polished lapis.'

'I will fling up a grapple iron, if that part proves un-climbable.'

Malien frowned. 'It's a long way. I doubt if you could throw an iron that high.'

'If it were light enough I could.'

'It might be better if you whispered to Llian to let down a rope from the top, securely tied.'

'Would you trust your life to a rope checked by Llian or a knot tied by him?' Karan said with good-natured scorn. 'Anyway, he is terrified of heights. More likely he would fall before I got there, or throw out the rope without tying it first. How could I climb with him fainting and dying his deaths above me?'

'So you need a grapple iron made as well, do you? There won't be much sleep for me tonight.'

'Less than you think, for I require a small hammer with a pick end as well.'

'Anything else? A portable bathtub so you can arrive refreshed for your lover?'

'That will suffice, thank you,' grinned Karan. 'Oh, and strong light rope at least . . .' She stared up at the top of the tower. 'Seven or eight spans. No, make that . . .'

Malien put her hands on her hips and stared Karan into silence. 'I judge that you will need at least ten, so I will bring twelve. Until tomorrow then, just after sunrise.'

Llian spent a hungry day and half the night in the chamber of records, for the gate did not come back and the door was still locked from the outside. His mission was not fruitful though. Few of the countless documents in the room were readable, and those that were readable were irrelevant. What had Kandor said in his letter? *I spent a fortune trying to find out what it was.*

Spent a fortune! If he had paid spies and chroniclers to dig into the past, there should be reports of their findings in tongues that he could decipher, not in this wretched Charon script that no one could read. What else had he said? *I will gladly bring what I have to Alcifer, if you will it.* To prove his case to the other Charon, Kandor would have had to bring original documents. But a cautious man, with an abiding sense of the Histories, as this vast room showed, he would have kept copies that were faithful in every detail. Llian searched until the very instant that the gate cracked into view, but found nothing.

He leapt into the gate without a backward glance. It popped him back to Tensor's work chamber suffering no more from the transit than a headache and a feeling of disorientation.

Tensor was pleased with the results of the test. 'The new mirror is much better than the original,' he said, tapping his long fingers on the edge of the table. 'Everything is as clear as if I peered through a window. So, Llian, you haven't found what you were looking for? Somehow I didn't think it would be there. Kandor was the most subtle of the Charon. He would not leave such important documents in the obvious place.'

That was no help at all. Anywhere in Katazza, or outside it for that matter, could be a subtle hiding place. Frustrated and feeling queasy from the gate, Llian collected food, drink and cloak, and headed back up to his eyrie to sleep for what remained of the night.

It was cold when Karan emerged just before dawn. A chilly breeze fluttered the fern fronds growing on the tower. Malien was already waiting, just where the bridge passed into the Great Tower, a bag in her hand. She showed Karan the contents wordlessly: six flat steel spikes each with a ring on the end, an iron grapple like a tiny anchor, a short piece of thin rope and a longer coil, a hammer and a canvas belt with loops for hammer and spikes. Karan installed these in their places, tied the end of the longer rope to the grapple and with Malien's assistance made a harness around her waist and chest using the shorter rope, leaving a length dangling to tie to her spikes.

Malien sniffed the air, which smelled of lime perfume. 'You reek!'

'The subtlest dab,' Karan said smugly. She examined the rope, which was no thicker than cord. 'It's rather thin. Are you sure . . .?'

'It won't break,' said Malien coolly. 'Nor fray, not on the sharpest edge.'

'How will I carry the grapple?' Karan wondered. Malien produced a tiny canvas backpack.

'There is a water bottle in there, too, and some dried peaches.'

'I should have asked you for a clip to attach the rope to the spikes. Too bad! I'll just have to tie it each time.'

Malien produced two small shackles, tested the spring-catches, and Karan tied one in the middle of her safety rope and the other to the free end.

'You made *these* last night?'

'Of course not – we brought such things with us! Now,

make sure to hammer the spikes in well, otherwise if you fall hard they may pull right out.'

'Of course!'

Malien offered a pair of boots, worn at the toes. They had hard soles made for climbing.

'My boots! Thank you.' Karan put them on. 'They fit well enough.'

'*My* boots, and I'll have them back as soon as this is over.' She glared at Karan ferociously.

Karan lowered her eyes but could not hide the grin. Now it was time to go. She strapped on the belt, shrugged the little pack over her shoulders, buckled it on and checked everything once more.

'Oh, it all feels rather heavy.'

'If by that you mean will I go instead, don't bother.'

Karan snorted and turned to the wall.

'You'll need your hat.'

Karan picked up the broad-brimmed, sweat-stained, faded thing and crammed it on her head.

'Hold on, tradition must be followed!' Malien made a step with her hands. Karan put her foot on it, sprang up onto the bridge rail, then levered herself up to the first crack. Another heave and she was above Malien's head. She followed the path that she had mapped out the previous day, crossing the plaited doughnuts easily. Even the metal skirt proved not to be a problem for there was a split right through it.

'No difficulty so far,' she sang out. Malien raised a hand and turned away.

Karan found the climb a relatively simple one for the first third, for there were many gaps and cracks and the way that the tower was made up of spiralling woven cables of rock meant that the cable she was climbing was well below the vertical, except where she had to cross over one of the weaves.

Once she passed over a small glass tile, and looking through it saw down a conduit into a lighted room to a bench covered in papers. It was Tensor's work chamber, she realised, but he was not within the line of sight. Neither was Llian.

She needed to use her spikes only three times in this part of the climb, each time where another cable of tile-covered stone was plaited over the valley she was climbing. The first time she pounded her spike in with her hammer, clicked the safety rope into the ring with the shackle, tested it, then stepped up. She did the same with a second spike and the second shackle, stepped up and bent down to knock out the lower spike. She struck one blow too many, it flew out and skidded away down the valley between two spirals.

'Five to go,' she thought, annoyed by her carelessness.

Karan had disappeared. Shand had known that she would not be contained for long. Going outside, he found Malien leaning on a tree trunk near the top of the eastern steps, staring up at the tower and the mountains behind. Her face was blotchy and tired, as if she had not slept all night; sweating about Tensor, no doubt. Selial stood a few steps away, the de facto leader of the Aachim now. She turned to Shand. Malien flicked a glance upward then walked away. Apparently she did not want company.

'This gate will ruin us,' Selial soliloquised. 'Tensor has led us into folly and we gave in to him like mice in front of a snake. There was a time he would have obeyed, had we directed him, but no more. We are come to the end of the Aachim of Shazmak. What a place for it, so far from everything we love.'

'There are other cities of the Aachim,' said Shand, 'greater than ever Shazmak was, before it fell.'

'But they are barely Aachim anymore, so changed are they, so reduced. They have not kept to the old ways. Santhenar has drained them of their vigour and nobility. They are become almost *human*.' The emphasis was such that she might have said *beast*, for the Aachim never used the word 'human' to describe themselves, only in relation to old humankind, who were regarded as inferior. Then, suddenly realising what she had said, Selial was mortified.

'Oh!' she said, and her lined face became purple with embarrassment and shame. 'Forgive me. My distress made me forget . . .'

Shand smiled. 'I beg your pardon,' he said, cupping his hand around his ear. 'I did not catch what you said.'

The flush slowly faded, though the shame remained, to be out-mannered by one of *them*.

'And there are Aachim in Aachan too, a multitude.'

'There may be, though we were never a fecund race, and after the Charon came . . . But many came to Santhenar. Very many. We have no knowledge of Aachan anymore. It has passed out of our lives. The Charon were iron to us.' She nodded formally and went inside.

Malien came back to lean on the tree again. Shand looked over the countryside. Nothing had changed since he was here more than a hundred years ago, except that the forest had advanced a little. He looked up at the tower spiralling far above and, as he did so, caught a flash of white, a pale face. Shand was not surprised, but when he saw her clinging there he was shocked and afraid.

He heard a tap-tap-tap, then *spang!* and something metallic came bouncing down, faster and faster, struck a spiral near the bottom and sailed though the air over their heads. Shand's heart missed a beat. He stared at the horrified face of Malien. They both looked upward. Nothing further happened. No small body came hurtling down. Shand wandered over and picked up a flat metal spike the length of his forearm.

'It's well made,' he said, holding it out to her.

'I spent all night making them.' She hefted it in her hand.

Shand looked up again. Karan was no longer in sight. If anyone could climb it, she could. He stared at the tower for ages, lost in thought.

How long had he been daydreaming? Hardly any time at all, it seemed, for the sun appeared to have stood still in the sky. But Malien was gone.

Back inside, Mendark had formed a temporary alliance with the Aachim, who were experimenting with a device that they hoped would shatter the great door. Shand watched Mendark's arrangements with secret amusement.

'Come and help us,' Mendark cried. 'You know something of such machines.'

Shand, interested despite himself in what they had made, examined everything carefully as though he were going to operate the thing himself. He walked around, saw the precautions they were taking, the protections they had assumed, and the strength of the great door. Then he shook his head, walked away to the kitchen and brewed a pot of tea. He could see that the thing would fail.

Mendark looked after him with an expression half of puzzlement, half of anger. 'Old fool,' he said to the Aachim next to him, and turned back to his work.

Llian sat in his high seat at the very top of the tower, watching the dawn. He had heard a little of Karan's tale, baldly told through the slit in the wall, but the barrier inhibited conversation and she had quickly given it away. He knew how she had got here, and with whom, but not why. Was she still after the Mirror? If so, to what end? What would Karan do now? Knowing her as he did, he knew that she would do something.

He knew that there were others outside as well, Mendark, Tallia and Shand, but Karan had said nothing about them. He was reminded of his debt to Mendark, however. No doubt as soon as this was over he would be called on to repay it.

For hours Llian sat in his eyrie as the sun crawled up the sky. Far out across the Sea of Perion the first dry storms of the season were developing, whirling salt dust high in the air, where the westerly winds caught it and carried it all the way across the Dry Sea, to fall in Jepperand, the land of the Zain, and other barren places.

The snow was almost gone from the peaks of Katazza

now; even their southern sides were mostly bare, blue-grey falls of rock. Spring was passing swiftly, racing towards the long and scorching summer. The sun glittered on the twisting, columnar flanks of the fortress and its myriad towers, towers that seemed, despite their age, as smooth and polished as glass. He looked down and out, surprising himself with his daring, to see the walls of his own tower. Llian counted nine cables of rock twisted together in a complex braid, with an encircling band of lapis and gold halfway up, and another, projecting one ending four or five spans below him. Looking closely Llian saw that moss grew in cracks and lichen crusted the surface on the south side. Curious how life flourished in the most forbidding of places.

A movement caught his eye far below, not far above the lower lapis band. Llian leaned out to see what bird or rodent had made its home in that clump of wiry fern. No *animal*, he realised, scarce able to draw breath. No animal had such a curious form, like a hand scrabbling to cling to the stems. Then it pulled itself up, and he saw a pale face outlined by red hair. Not even Karan could have done it in Kandor's time. But now up she came, creeping with fingers and toes, occasionally hammering in a spike and clipping her rope to it.

Llian felt sick just watching her but he could not tear away his gaze. She was a long way below him and the work was slow; clearly exhausting. Several times a handhold or a foothold failed and she slid as much as half a span before catching herself in some miracle of dexterity that was beyond Llian's thought. He recalled other times with her, other climbs, but still could not see how she could do this one. Once she rested her knee lightly against the stem of a tiny bush while she gave her arms a rest. The brittle stem snapped and she fell, sliding down the curve of the cable; but the spike was well home in the crack, the rope held, and she was brought up sharply by her harness. He turned away, wanting to vomit, but it was impossible not to watch.

Around midway, perhaps sixty spans above the doughnut-shaped base, the climb became much harder, for the spiral changed pitch to run almost vertical, and above that was the sheer band of lapis and gold. At the same time the handholds became fewer, the mortar here being sound.

Karan passed over a vent through which a vaguely sulphurous warmth issued – a chimney, she supposed. She realised that she was tiring rapidly, was much more tired than she should be from what had been, so far, a relatively simple climb. A year ago she would have gone three times this height, and much faster, before being as weary as this. Shortly after, the whole tower trembled, and had she not been clipped on, she would have fallen.

The steep pitch was only ten spans or so but it took more than an hour, and in that time she twice thought she was going to fall. That would be perilous even if her spikes held, weak as she was. Now, as she neared the top of the vertical pitch, Karan had to rest after each spike, each step. Once a huge chunk of lapis lazuli, worth a fortune back in Thurkad, flaked off under her spike and whizzed past her face.

Finally she banged in the last spike, reached the top and stood on a narrow ledge, like an annulus around the midpoint of the tower, where she could actually sit in safety. Nonetheless she hammered in a spike, clipped her harness to it and sat down dangling her feet over the edge. Blessed relief! Her calves ached. She massaged them and the middle of her back as best as she could reach, sipped from the water bottle and sucked on a dried peach. It tasted sweeter than anything she had ever eaten.

Karan looked down and it was satisfying to see how far she had come. Don't look up just yet, she told herself. Rest, relax, get your strength back. She looked up. So far to go! So steep! Impossible ever to climb that far!

A germ of self-doubt crept in. She banished it, took another sip of water then stood up. Her calves began aching at once, her knees felt weak and the wrist she had twice broken throbbed. To distract herself, Karan hammered in another spike, though it was not really needed. She put her foot on the first, unsnapped the shackle, clipped it into the higher spike and stretched up. Her knee wobbled; the self-doubt was back.

I will not think! I will *not* think! she told herself, bashing the next spike in with a mighty blow. The whole tile came off, and tile and spike fell in a long curve, striking once far below.

Four! You fool, Karan. You'll need that, surely.

The breeze was cold on her damp brow, despite the clear skies and the warm sun. To distract herself, Karan thought back on other difficulties that she had overcome. She settled on her escape through the tunnels of Fiz Gorgo after stealing the Mirror. She had been in greater peril then because it had been quite out of her control.

I *can* do it and I *will*, she told herself, and as she climbed she relived that experience and found that it helped. By the time she reached the sewer door at Fiz Gorgo and was wrestling with the hinges, murky water over her head, she was more than three-quarters of the way up. It was then that she caught sight of a face staring down at her from an embrasure of the chamber below the dome. Not Tensor, surely. No, but almost as bad. Worse! *Llian!*

Oh, Llian, go away! How can I climb this last bit with you staring at me? She had never liked being watched when she was trying to do something difficult.

Now the weariness came back strongly and the distraction did not work anymore, for she saw her every action – every fingerhold, every spike, every tremble – as if she was watching herself, and in this self-absorption she began to make mistakes. She knew that she was near the end of her strength. Was there something she could throw away to reduce the burden a little? Maybe the water would feel lighter inside her. She gulped it down, ate another dried peach, tied the grapple on her back and dropped the pack. It slid away down the curve of the valley she had just laboured up. Karan climbed another step. It was no easier than before.

On she went, slower and slower. Now she was close enough to see Llian's face. From where she clung, coming up to the lapis and gold overhang, for him to be visible at all he must be leaning out dangerously. Poor Llian! It will kill him when I fall.

The realisation that she was expecting to fall shocked her. And as she approached the overhang her spirits ebbed even further, for it was much more difficult than it had looked from the ground. Even when she had been fit and strong, climbing every day, to cross the overhang and get up this vertical pitch would have tested her. Her calves were screaming – must rest! Must rest! She hammered her spikes in, two above and two below, tested them carefully, clipped her safety rope through the rings of the upper ones, stood on the lower ones and slumped.

Ah, but I have my grapple. That will make a difference. She got the iron out, a little thing not much bigger than her hand and fingers. Karan leaned out as far as she could and peered upwards, trying to see an easy way. There was no easy way; no more tiles, no more gaps. Above was a narrow band of gold, then smooth polished lapis for three spans or so, a join here, a join there, and another gold band at the top. The precious stone was pitted from time and the elements, but the pits were shallow, fatal handholds. Beyond that, the tiled woven cables ran up to a ledge below the windows.

It looked at least seven spans above her head to the windows through which she must throw her grapple. A hard throw almost straight up, grapple and rope, from this precarious roost. Could she even throw it that high? It would be difficult, for she had to lean right out to clear the overhang and aim at what was, from this angle, a very narrow slot. But at least Llian was there to fasten it; that would make it easier. Below each window was a long pole that once must

570

have held pennants or flags. Momentarily she thought of throwing for the pole, an easier target, and getting Llian to secure the rope from there, but she dismissed that idea at once. Far too dangerous for him.

She prepared herself, making knots in the rope to aid her climb, checked again that the safety rope was secure; inspected her two shackles and her spikes. The long loops of the rope hung loosely from her left hand. She ran the end of the rope twice around her hand in case she missed, steadied herself on her pegs, gripped the upper spike in her left hand, hefted the grapple and flung it, instantly grabbing the spike with her right hand and letting go her left so the rope could fly.

Too short! The distance must be further than she'd thought. She clung to her spike and braced herself as the grapple fell back. It struck the ledge above her, shot past her head and fell at frightening speed. Reaching its fullest extent, it jerked tight around her hand as though it was going to tear the flesh from the bones. The shock went right up her arm, wrenching her shoulder badly.

'Ahhh!' Karan cried.

'Are . . . you all right?'

'Yes,' she snapped, gritting her teeth until the pain and the shock subsided. She pulled the grapple back up and examined her hand. It was already bruised blue in a band from front to back, two huge blood blisters growing even as she watched. She steadied herself for the second throw, though this time she wound the end of the rope twice around a spike, tied it and let the loop hang down.

She threw the iron again, as hard and high as she could, an anxious bad throw. Too hard; too high! It soared above the window, curved back down and the rope wound itself around the end of the pennant pole. Llian and she stared at each other.

'I could crawl out and free it,' he said in a tiny voice.

'Might as well jump straight away,' she said under her breath, and as she had that thought her capricious talent set off such a clanging in her chest that she cried out, '*No! It won't support your weight.*' Her talent seemed to want to protect Llian more than it did her.

So saying she gave the rope a mighty jerk, hoping that it would slip off the end. Rotten metal groaned, the pole snapped off and speared down at her. Karan flattened herself frantically against the stone, gripping her spikes. The pole clanged off the overhang, whistled past her head and fell, trailing the rope.

Snap! The rope twanged tight, ripping the spike out of the crack, shackle, safety rope and all. Karan's feet were wrenched off the lower spikes and she was dragged down by the weight of the pole. She screamed. The harness knots slipped, the ropes tightening around her chest like twin nooses. She stopped in mid-air with a jerk that shook her like a doll. The other spike and shackle had held!

Far below, the pole bounced at the end of the rope. Karan was stretched between the weight of the pole and the spike that still held. She would have shrieked but the harness had pulled so tight that she could barely take a breath. The pressure was slowly squeezing the life out of her. The knots felt like bolts being pushed through her flesh.

She felt for the knife at her belt, then realised that if she cut the torn-out spike free she would fall. She tried to get the ring of the spike out of the shackle but the clip was jammed under the weight of the pole. She reached below the spike, sawing at the rope attached to the grapple. As Malien had said, it was very tough. It kept springing away from the knife. Then inspiration came. If she could force the point of the spike down, the weight should pull the rope right off, and pole and grapple would fall.

Karan put the heel of her hand on the ring of the spike and forced. It hardly moved, such was the tension on it. The knots of her harness slipped again, tighter yet, making her cry out, a small breathless squeak. She put her knife away and sucked in a tiny breath which the harness squeezed straight out again.

Fireworks danced in her eyes. She thrust the spike down with both hands. One of the blood blisters burst but she did not feel it. Slowly the spike moved from vertical to horizontal. Now it pointed slightly down, though the ring was slipping on blood. How it hurt! She couldn't hold it!

She let go with one hand to wipe the blood away and the spike immediately sprang back to the vertical. Llian was shouting but the words made no sense to her. Something about coming down.

Coming down! 'No!' she screeched.

Sucking a cupful of air through her teeth, Karan pushed the spike down. Not daring to relax, she shook it furiously, lubricating it with her blood. Suddenly the coils slipped away. She was free, swinging on the end of her safety rope. She felt around with her toes, found the two lower spikes and settled herself on them, every muscle trembling.

The pole fell, clanging and banging, bounced clear of the tower and turned end over end, the grapple swinging wildly on the end of its rope. She watched it smash into the middle of one bridge. The sound seemed to take a long time to come back up, an enormous bang. Soon a group of people appeared outside, pointing and shouting.

Llian was screaming at her. 'Karan, are you all right? Karan, speak to me!'

She could not care. Drenched in sweat, all she wanted to do was lie down, curl into a ball and pull the covers over her head, as she had done in the miseries of her childhood.

Minutes passed. Llian was still shouting above. She felt very cold.

'Yes, I'm all right!' she screamed, just to shut him up.

But she wasn't. The whole of her chest throbbed, her head ached and there was a bruise on her temple though she had no memory of hitting her head. She pushed herself up on the spikes, leaning out so she could see him.

'It was corroded right through,' he said. 'Lucky thing you stopped me –'

'Shut up!' she snapped.

'How are you going to get up the last bit?'

'I don't know. Leave me alone!'

Karan leaned out again. At the top of the vertical pitch there seemed to be a bit of a shelf, a few spans above which were the window embrasures. If she could just get onto the shelf she would be safe. Examining the lapis band, the panicky feeling began to come back. It was much smoother than the lower one. She had made such climbs in the past, but not when she was at the end of her strength.

She knocked out one of the lower spikes, installing it higher, just below the overhang. Karan fastened on, tapped out the next spike and tried to haul herself up. It hurt shockingly. I can do it, she told herself, stopping for a rest, but her confidence was gone. She unclipped the spike that had pulled out earlier, reached to the edge of the overhang and tried to bang it in the gap between gold band and lapis slab. She mis-hit, cracking her thumb a terrible blow and sending the spike singing through the air. She swore but it didn't make the pain any less, didn't bring the spike back.

It took half an hour before she crossed the half-span of overhang and hung on the lower edge on her three remaining spikes. Her bad wrist burned, strengthless. The weight of her belt and hammer seemed to be urging her down. She sagged on the rope, resting her cheek on the ultramarine stone, looking up at Llian. Poor Llian!

For once he seemed to understand her state of mind. 'Wait!' cried Llian. He disappeared from the opening.

She looked around, thought about hammering a spike in that gap just up there, then decided not to. Yes, I'll wait, as long as you like. I'll just hang here for a while, she thought. It's quite peaceful now. She closed her eyes.

40

A CONTEST OF INJURIES

Llian had climbed right out the embrasure and down onto the ledge outside, the only way he could see Karan. It was hard to concentrate there, for the height made him dizzy and he was afraid his sweaty hands would slip on the stone. Karan had only a few spans to go but she was not going to make it. She had nothing left to give. He could tell that she knew it too.

Finally she stirred, but moved only from one spike to the next before stopping. Even from here Llian could see her arms trembling. Her muscles would no longer obey her will. She closed her eyes as if she wanted to sleep. That really alarmed him.

'Wait!' he cried uselessly.

He jumped back in through the embrasure, looking around wildly for something to use as a rope, knowing that a rope would hardly last a hundred years without losing strength, much less a thousand. But he saw nothing. He could not recall any rope below, either. It would have to be his cloak.

He thrust his knife into the heavy cloth, forcing it through the tough Aachim weave, which was like light canvas but made of a thread impossible to tear and difficult to cut. He hacked it into thick strips, alternately climbing out to check on Karan and going back to his job. Finally he had enough roughly cut material for about eight spans of rope. He knotted the lengths together, made a loop in one end, tied the other around the stone-framed embrasure and tested it with furious jerks.

Satisfied that it would hold, Llian flung it over the rail. After knotting and tying, it reached only four spans below the window. Not far enough, by two or three spans.

Throwing off his boots, and without even thinking of his terror of heights or what he could possibly do when he got to the end, Llian put his leg over the sill and climbed out onto the window ledge. Taking hold of his rope he continued down onto the tiled cable section, but even this close he could not see any handholds. It was easy going down, bracing his feet on the wall and moving from one knot to the next. Suddenly he was at the end of the rope, hanging with both hands from the loop, his toes scrabbling at the stone. He looked down, realising just how far it was to the bottom. One slip and he would fall all the way. The spiralling columns of white seemed to draw his eyes down. His head spun, his stomach heaved.

'Ahhh!' he cried.

Karan's eyes snapped open and her white face stared up at him. She was only three spans below his feet.

'Go back!' she hissed.

He reached down with his toes for a foothold, feeling the strain on shoulders and forearms. The rope wobbled. Llian's gaze, moving aimlessly through the air, crossed Karan's face. Their eyes locked.

'Go up,' she screamed.

He saw a sudden blind terror in her eyes and knew that it was for him. His sweating fingers slipped on the rope, then his toes found a hold, the narrow shelf above the lapis band. He slid down onto it.

'No!' cried Karan. 'Don't let go of the rope.'

Too late. The loop slid from his fingers and he crouched down against the rock, terrified, unable to believe what he'd got himself into. The rope swung gently back and forth above him. He was trapped on the ledge with neither courage to go down nor skill to get back up. Llian was even afraid to stand up, sure that his knees would press against the wall to push him off. The platform – if a sloping terrace of rock narrower than a bookshelf could be called such – seemed to be growing slick beneath his feet. He curled his toes into a crack.

'I can't go up,' he cried. 'I'll fall.'

'You're too close to the wall,' she screamed. 'Lean out.'

But he couldn't; she could see that. She knew it anyway, remembering the cliff path at the ruins near Tullin and the climb down beside the great falls of Shazmak. Llian was terrified of heights. Karan's heart was thumping so hard that she thought it would split open. He was going to die because of her. In her mind's eye she saw him fall, a plunge that seemed to take hours, then break himself on the hard paving stones far below. It was this that roused her, the knowledge that he could do nothing to save himself.

Suddenly the way opened up in front of Karan and she found a trickle of strength that she didn't know she had. She unclipped her rope, tapped out the lowest spike and forced herself up onto the highest. Reaching up, she banged the spike into a tiny gap between the slabs of lapis. Chips of blue gemstone showered down on her hair. She tried to attach her rope but the clip would not go through the eye of the spike, no matter how she tried. The eye was squashed flat.

Karan fastened onto the spike she was standing on and tried to hammer out the lowest one. One blow and it snapped off, a flaw in the metal. She unclipped, climbed onto the top spike then realised she was in trouble. She could no longer reach the lower one to knock it out. She'd have to go up the last bit, the hardest and most dangerous of all, free-climbing. *I can't do it*, she thought, but one look at Llian swaying on the platform and she knew she must.

Up she went again, crabbed sideways to take advantage

577

of another crack, then stretched sideways again to a crevice she could press her toe into, if she could get it there. Something numbed her screaming arms, her trembling fingers for just long enough and she did it. She got a toe to the cleft, her fingers onto the sloping ledge, and forced herself up until her face was level with Llian's feet. Her sweaty fingers slipped on the edge.

Karan jammed the point of her hammer in, then tried to pull herself up. Her muscles refused to budge. Llian gave a muffled groan. Trying again, with a convulsive movement she was beside him on the ledge, gripping his shirt tightly. She reached up but the rope was beyond her fingertips.

'Get the rope!' she said urgently.

Llian was swaying dangerously, not game to open his eyes. Karan felt a burning pain in her chest. She pushed him back against the wall, slammed her pick into a beautiful crack and looped her rope around it, not that it would hold if they fell. Her knees almost folded with relief. No, you can't relax yet! Quickly, before your strength fails. Holding Llian with one hand, she struck him in the face with the back of the other.

'*Open your eyes, you bloody idiot!*' she screamed. '*Get the blasted rope!*'

Llian snatched at the loop and clung to it like a lifeline.

'Now hold it tightly and don't let go for any reason. Stand firm while I climb you. Are you ready?'

'Yes,' he whispered.

Karan weighed him up but was not satisfied. She sawed a length off her safety rope and tied it tightly around his chest. The other end she took in her teeth. Slipping beside Llian into a crack, somehow using handholds that he could not even see, she climbed above him, reaching out with one foot, resting it on his shoulder, holding the makeshift rope in one hand, just a moment, even those few seconds of relaxation a marvellous relief, but knowing that she dare rest no longer. The other end of Llian's rope she clipped to the loop, the fabric of her trousers caressed his face then her weight went off his shoulders and she went up the cloth rope like a sailor, onto the glorious window ledge, up the smooth walls below the window then in to safety.

'Come on!' she cried.

Llian tried, but climbing ropes was not one of his skills. He half-climbed, was half-hauled up and over the wall, and dumped unceremoniously onto the floor. Llian stood up unsteadily to lean against the wall, panting. Karan lay flat on the floor, gasping, and for a long time she could not move at all. Her muscles were locked in cramp.

Finally she rolled over, pushed herself to her knees and crawled unsteadily over to Llian. Her face was white and she was trembling all over, but the miracle had happened. She was alive and he was, and they were together at last. She stood on her knees and opened her arms to Llian.

'That was the stupidest thing that you have ever done,' she said. 'And the bravest.'

Llian said nothing. He had no words and needed none.

Eventually Karan stirred. Her legs were as limp as lettuce.

'Go down and get me something to eat, Llian. I'm weak as a baby –' She grinned suddenly, her old self, 'or a master chronicler! And try to be discreet; I don't imagine that Tensor will be glad to see me.'

He crept down the long flights of stairs, all the way to the chamber where Tensor laboured still. Having not been there for half a day, it was only natural that he should go to the stack of food packages against the wall, to the cistern and fill his water bottle. But Tensor looked up at him as he passed and his eyes glinted.

'So she's come for you, has she? Take care that she treats you better than she does her own. An astounding climb – I praise her courage and her skill. But there's no way down save through this door, not for you or for her. No need to sneak any longer; take anything you want. Only be sure that

I will come for you in my need.' He turned back to his work.

Llian scuttled away with his packages, the water and a big blanket. 'He knows you're here,' he gasped when he reached the high room again, breathless and dizzy from the climb. 'He says there's no way down.'

Karan was stretched out on the rags of Llian's cloak.

'Close the door,' she said, and Llian forced the stone slab against time-frozen hinges. He could find no means to lock it, but wedged it shut with some pieces of broken stone. She held up her good hand to him. Llian pulled her to a sitting position.

She caught sight of the jade amulet hanging about his neck and recoiled as if she had been stung. 'What's that?' she said sharply.

'The charm my mother gave me.'

'Oh, take it off quickly. I can't bear to see it.'

Llian put it in his pouch. Emmant the half-Aachim had used it to trap Karan before trying to throttle her. 'I'm sorry,' he said. 'If it wasn't so precious to me I would have thrown it away. But Malien has taken the enchantment off it.'

'I don't mind you having it,' she said. 'Just don't wear it when I'm around. Please.'

She opened one of the wrapped packages, keeping her left hand closed so that he would not see the huge blisters and bruises. There was dried fruit in one package, hard dark bread in another and goat cheese in a third, that the Aachim had bartered from the shy people of the forests. Llian had also brought a kind of cake bursting with fruits and nuts. She cut small pieces off each. Llian passed her the water bottle.

'Aren't you afraid that he'll come up?' he wondered after they had finished.

It was early afternoon. The sun cast rectangular shadows across the floor. Llian stretched out on the blanket in the shade. Karan lay on the rags with her head on his chest. She opened an eye, looking up at the inside of the platinum dome.

'I'm not afraid of Tensor now. I did what was right and he knows it.'

Llian was not so sure, but he wrapped the packages and put them away without replying. He caught her eye; they both looked away. It had been so long since they were together, carefree, that they did not know how to begin again.

'Look at you,' Llian said, staring at her. 'You are positively *thin!*'

'There's no need to be rude! Get me back to Gothryme and I will soon be round as an egg.'

Karan tried to stand but her muscles had grown stiff. She flopped down hard on her bottom.

'It hurts too much,' she said to Llian's frown. 'This is the worst I have ever felt.'

'What hurts?'

'Everything. My feet, my legs, my back, my arms, my head.'

He caught her hand, the bruised one this time, and tried to lift her up.

'Ow! Ahh! Let go!' She jerked her hand free and thrust it into her armpit, squeezing it against her side.

'I'm sorry! What's the matter? Give me a look at your hand.'

'It's all right,' she said stubbornly. 'Leave me alone.'

She did not want him to see how badly she was hurt. Llian felt kept at bay, and wanted to retreat, but he steeled himself.

'No, I won't. You forced yourself back into my life and now you have to put up with me. Show me your hand.' He knelt down beside her.

Their eyes met. I push but he doesn't back away, she thought. This is a new phase. Well, not before time. She held out her hand. It was blue and black, bruised round and round, with a blood blister the size of her little finger between thumb and finger, and a larger one that had burst on the other edge of her hand.

'Karan!' he exclaimed. Taking her wrist, he inspected the black and bloody hand, front and back, then drew it to his lips.

How gentle he was. The touch stirred the hairs on the back of her neck.

'That is just *one* of the wounds I took for you,' she said with a trace of a smile, 'while you were on your walking holiday. And each one a debt that you must repay. How you will slave for me.' She grinned in anticipation.

'Walking holiday!' he said in indignation. 'I have more scars than I can count. Do you call abduction, beatings about the head, strangulations, death threats and hurlings over cliffs a holiday?'

'Loudly the teller boasts, but who can tell fact from tale? I would see the evidence. See, here is another of mine and you have shown nothing.'

Karan brushed her hair back off her forehead. Llian put his lips to the lacerated lump. She tried not to flinch.

'I have a kiss for each one. That is how I will pay these debts you so harp on.'

'A kiss! Then you can start at the bottom,' she said laughing. 'My feet have at least a hundred . . .'

Llian promptly sat up and tugged at her boot. 'No! Don't! I was joking. They're filthy.'

The boot slipped off, revealing a very threadbare and faded green sock. The sock came off, and the other. Her feet were marked with a dozen scars and bruises. She wiggled her toes, revelling in the freedom and the coolness. Taking her foot in his hand Llian drew it to his lips, and the tiny hairs on her legs stood up. He ran his lips down the side of her foot, across her toes, back over her instep and in a circle around her ankle. Karan shivered.

'I see a few little scars, most healed long ago!' He gave her a sly sideways glance, his cheek resting on her shin. 'Scant evidence, for all *your* boasting.'

Karan withdrew her foot. 'There are others. I haven't seen

582

the worst myself yet. I feel bruised all over. Look where the scorpion got me.'

Llian inspected the hard, scarred hollow. 'It's an awfully big scar for such a small animal,' he said, caressing it with his lips.

Karan described Shand's brutal remedy with the firestick.

'Still, I have bigger and better ones.' He showed his palms, which were scarred across from his falls in the basalt country, and the long mark from calf to knee.

'Falling over doesn't count,' said Karan, though she nuzzled his hands anyway. 'Scars must be earned ones.'

'Even if earned by carelessness?' He laughed, touching the scorpion wound again. 'Haven't you anything better?'

Karan showed a myriad other scars. Llian kissed each one while pretending scorn.

'Is that the best you can do? While I am taking spears in the side, you stub your toe?'

Her smile disappeared. 'Spears in the side? Surely you're making it up?'

Llian pulled up his shirt. The wound was long healed, just a purple-brown pucker against the pale skin, though a full handspan long, and it had a thicker lump in the middle. 'That is Malien's stitchery. A breath to the left and I were dead.'

Karan could almost feel the spear entering her own ribs. She touched the scar with a finger that shook. 'I did not know. I did not even *sense* it.' That felt like a personal failure. She laid her cheek against his side, squeezing the tears back. Llian's heart thumped reassuringly, though very fast.

'It was only a few hours after the Conclave. I don't even know what you were doing then.'

'I was unconscious. It was two days before I knew anything, Shand tells me.'

'You lay there for *two* days!'

'No, Shand found me in the night. I don't want to talk about that just now. I want to know what happened to you.

Your *Tale of the Mirror* must be a long one already,' she murmured with eyes closed, curving her slender fingers around his side, along the scar. Her moving hand slipped under his shirt, across his chest.

'How came this about?'

'Long enough the tale is and the teller even has a small part in it, though I will cut that out later. To be in your own tale is not seemly. I opened the door of Tensor's villa, trying to get back to the Great Hall, and a spear came at me. Where would we be if I had escaped, I wonder? Anyway, that's all there is to tell. I'm no hero.'

'I have another,' she said, showing a tiny mark just above the hairline of her temple.

He inspected it with casual disdain. 'She's growing desperate now,' he mocked. 'I've done worse damage combing my hair.'

'I find that hard to believe,' she replied, running her fingers though his tangles. 'But there is a real tale here.' She told the story of the Ghâshâd and the caves. He pulled her face against his chest so that the end of the tale was muffled, meanwhile picking chips of lapis out of her hair and arranging them in a good-luck spiral on the floor.

'Not bad,' he said at the end, 'but I haven't finished with my scar yet.'

'Two tales from the one scar,' she sniffed. 'And you call me desperate.'

'See this lumpy bit? That is where the stitches burst open when Tensor flung me over a cliff.'

Once more Karan felt the tears stinging her eyes. 'A cliff! You weren't joking?'

So Llian told her about that adventure as well, and his various other ones, while her eyes grew wide. 'You are not the person that I met at Tullin,' she said, putting her lips to the scar.

Nor was she, but the game was not ended yet. 'Now, back to your chapter of woes. I still don't see you topping mine.'

'I can, though I am a little shy to do so.' She hesitated. Then slowly she unfastened her shirt, slipped it off her shoulders and let it fall on the rags of his cloak. Her white skin was shockingly bruised and burned by the rope harness in a band above her waist, and another above her breasts, and these bands were joined by lines of bruises running from waist to shoulders and down to her waist again at the back, the knots leaving larger welts above and below her breasts that were bruised black.

Shocked, Llian knelt and laid his cheek against her belly. She ran her fingers through his knotted hair.

'Is it agony? I dare not even kiss you.'

'It is painful enough,' she replied. 'My ribs feel like they've been squashed flat. Nonetheless, I must demand what you promised.'

Llian lifted his head and looked her in the eyes. 'How I love you,' he said.

'I love you too,' she said. 'My fee, if you will.'

He examined her with exaggerated slowness, teasing her for her impatience. The slender curve of her neck, feathered by a few red tendrils, the shapely ear peeping out of the wild hair, the silkiness of her skin, the translucency of her breasts. The terrible welts.

'It would take an infinity of kisses.'

Karan leaned back, stretching out her arms behind her. From the top of her head to the base of her spine, all was a-shiver. 'There is the night,' she said.

They were gifted with the remains of the day and the night. Though after dark it quickly grew cold in the open mountain air, neither wanted anything but to be alone with the other. Perhaps Tensor respected that wish for he did not come near. Or perhaps he was busy with other things. They made a fire from crumbly bits of wood, rotten old furniture, enough to boil water for tea and to warm and cheer them. Llian used a small-leaved grey herb that the foraging Aachim had brought back. It made a sweet, overly fragrant brew, not what either was used to, but it was hot and it served.

Llian lifted his mug to his lips. It was too hot. Something else must be said. 'There is a precaution . . .' Llian began.

'Late as usual. I thought of that weeks ago,' she said.

'How could you know that I was even alive? You schemer!'

'Hush! Come here! I'm cold and I'm tired. Stop hogging that blanket. Come and help me make the bed.'

Karan looked at the remnants of Llian's coat with disgust. They re-spread the rags on the floor, wrapped themselves in the blanket and clung together the whole night. Not sleeping much but not wanting to either; just taking pleasure in each other, dozing and waking, watching the strange northern stars wheel, and feeling at peace. And dozing once more.

Though when she was awake Karan wondered more than once about her talent. It had come back so strongly when Llian had been in danger that she felt bruised inside from it.

In the early morning they limped below, hand in hand, wondering what Tensor would do. Creeping around the corner of the great stair that looked down into his work chamber, they found the room empty. Karan stood there at a loss, having prepared for a confrontation that had not eventuated.

'Why did you aid him, Llian?' she asked carefully, so it came as a question rather than a criticism. She was feeling full and content. What was to be would be.

Llian was silent. How he regretted his collaboration over the past months. He had been caught up in the project: the irresistible urge to find out what would happen next. 'Aid him?'

'I heard you talking about the Twisted Mirror.'

'Oh, that! He was going to test the gate with me. I couldn't bear to think where I would end up if he directed it with the Mirror of Aachan, so I pointed out that he should make a new mirror if he wanted to see true.'

Knowing Llian, Karan wasn't quite satisfied that this was

all there was to it, but she did not question him further.

Suddenly there was a boom, a rush of agitated air and Tensor appeared in the middle of the pavilion. His hair was wild and his eyes glowed. He started forward then checked, unbalanced as if the floor was lower than expected. Karan gripped Llian's hand tightly. But their fears were groundless – Tensor was quite consumed by what he had come from.

'*I've seen him!*' he said.

That normally stern figure could scarcely contain himself and they caught a glimpse of what he had been like before the unyielding regimen of the Aachim had stripped him of his boyish enthusiasm. He had to tell someone what he had done.

Tensor's natural caution had not deserted him. 'When I tested the new mirror and found it to work, I did not attack the Nightland. Instead I built a secret spy-hole, a tiny gate, bypassing the Watch. A spy-gate bounded about with protections and safeguards. I've had my nose to the flaw in the Nightland all day.

'Rulke was in a great chamber,' he continued, 'on a chair grand as a throne. Parts of a *construct* lay all about – a pitiful device, one of those complex things that the Charon so love, full of wheels and levers and unknown parts and strange energies. So intricate a thing to do such a little task. He looked old and weary. Though I had a hand in its making, I would never have believed that the Nightland could have so drained him.'

'Don't be fooled,' said Karan. 'I have dreamed him many times. He is potent beyond your strength.'

Tensor laughed. 'Dreams show only what *he* wants you to see,' he scoffed. 'I have *seen* him; my eyes do not lie. He sits there still, fooling with his constructs, believing that he can make his own way to freedom. Fool! There is no escape from the Nightland, only release. I will set him free *forever*.'

He laughed and they saw that he was completely captivated by his own dreams.

'You are the fool,' cried Llian. 'You are Rulke's dupe. He shows you what you want to see.'

Tensor's eyes narrowed. 'He is stronger than I hoped, but weaker than I expected. He is cunning, but so am I. And I have a weapon.'

'Tensor,' said Karan, 'I beg you in the name of our kinship.'

'It was you who devalued that currency,' said Tensor, turning away. 'I will not be swayed.'

Tensor returned to his experiments, his tuning of the gate. Several times more he played with it, disappearing with a whip-crack and a sucking of air, later reappearing with a boom and a rush of air. Sometimes he was gone for hours, at other times only a minute or two, as he explored the intangible boundaries of the world and the Nightland. He was away much longer the last time and came back white and sweating. Without saying anything, he ran up the stairs.

Llian dozed on the floor while Karan prowled restlessly, turning the one question over and over in her mind. What was this secret weapon? What weapon had there ever been against Rulke?

She paced. She sat. She walked around and around the pavilion, looking at it from all sides. Why had he brought Llian all this way? Why would he want a chronicler?

'Llian,' she called out. '*Llian!*' She shook him by the shoulder.

He drifted awake and, seeing her face, smiled up at her.

'Llian, wake up.' Still she shook him. He put his hand over hers.

'I'm awake, Karan,' he said calmly. 'What is it?'

'What happened at the Conclave? At the end?'

'When Tensor took the Mirror?'

'Yes. Tell me what happened then.'

It was perfectly clear to Llian even now. 'He looked up at Maigraith, and something in her face shocked or frightened him terribly. He raised his arm at her, but put it down again as if he did not have the courage. Someone called out, "*No!*"

I think it was you. Your hair was standing on end, your hands beating the air. Someone else cried out too – Maigraith perhaps. Tensor put out his arm, there was a flash and Nelissa was dead, thrown against the wall. You were on the floor – at first I thought you were dead as well. Everyone was knocked senseless, even Faelamor, and then Tensor took the Mirror.'

'But you were not down?'

'I was but only for a few seconds, and wondered why I was spared. It was like a gate closing in my mind and another opening. I saw you lying there and a rage took me. I picked up Nelissa's stick and struck Tensor over the head with it. It didn't harm him, though, and he said something like: *I have need of you*. He caught my arm and I couldn't resist him; I still can't. His power over me is like the power that Emmant had, but much greater, though only when he wills it.'

'But what does he need: the chronicler or the Zain? Is that exactly what he said?'

Llian thought. 'Not exactly.' This was a part of his training that he had not had occasion to use for a long time. 'What he said, and these are his precise words and exactly how he said them, was: *You alone are unaffected. I have need of one such as you. Come to your reckoning, chronicler*.' Llian spoke in a very deep voice, not quite as deep as Tensor's but a close imitation. 'Then he took me by the hand and led me away. I managed to free myself and ran back to where you lay, but he exerted his will and I could not resist him.'

She said slowly, 'There was ever only one weapon against Rulke that the Aachim spoke of – a potency developed ages ago. It was to find a defence against this that the Zain were corrupted in the first place. You told me that yourself. You must carry the Gift of Rulke after all.'

'I do,' said Llian. 'It seems that it was latent and the potency released it.'

'But what he did at the Conclave was not planned, so he can't have known about you then.'

'*You alone are unaffected,*' Llian repeated.

'Of course! That's what gave you away.' This was worse than she had imagined. Rulke set free, and foolish, defenceless Llian to be Tensor's shield. He must plan to use the Gift against Rulke, but how?

Just then Tensor came running back down the stairs and his eyes were blazing. He sprang into the pavilion, roared out a new instruction and the mirror answered. Its light was like a bronze searchlight on his face. He spun around on his heel and cried, 'Llian. Llian of Chanthed! Come, this is the time.'

Llian began to walk toward the pavilion. His reluctance showed in his face, his stiff-legged gait, but he came. Karan clung to his arm but could not hold him. She had to let him go.

Llian reached the pavilion, took the steps like a robot, and stood by Tensor. Tensor caught Llian by the arm, the image on the new mirror drifted, steadied.

Karan choked.

Tensor opened the gate.

41

THE PROSCRIBED
EXPERIMENTS

It was the middle of Bunce now, the last month of spring, but in Thurkad a blazing day, as hot as summer. Maigraith sat in Yggur's work chamber, as she had long ago in Fiz Gorgo, watching him at his art. He was working at a brazier, casting powders and metal filings into the fire, then passing various devices – an amulet, rings of several sizes and colours and designs, a glass sphere – through the multi-coloured flames. Maigraith shuddered. Magical devices were forbidden the Faellem and though Maigraith was not one of that species, the prohibition was burned into her too.

What was he working at? She neither knew nor cared, only that, whatever it was, it did not work the way it should. There was something about the place that blocked him – or maybe something lacking in him. What power there was here acted against him. He needed a better place to work, but there was no better place in Thurkad.

Though her liaison with Yggur had never regained the intimacy of the first week, they had found in each other something that, however weakly, still held them together. The relationship was a prickly, repressed, mute thing though: neither could talk about it.

'How I hate this place!' Yggur said vehemently. 'Thurkad swelters half the year, freezes the rest, and stinks all year round. I can never tame such a city, not if I take it apart stone by stone and put it back again.'

Maigraith wondered why he tried to – surely the wickedness and corruption of Thurkad was written in the blood and sinews of its people, and whilever they lived, so would the city have their character.

He flung his tools down, paced across the chamber and back, and immediately took them up again. The room was dark and so humid that the walls sweated. Yggur preferred such places for his workings, seeming to draw power not from the stars but from the dampness and the earth.

'I cannot come to grips with the way you use the Secret Art,' Maigraith said. 'That my security should reside in some object, some thing beyond my understanding or control – that would frighten me.'

She was sitting on a low couch on the other side of the room beside another charcoal-filled brazier, warming a dish of jasmine-scented oil. She wore a long cream skirt and a plum-coloured silk blouse, high at the front but undone to the third button. As she leaned on a slender arm, her shining mahogany hair, cut straight across, brushed her shoulders. Her skin was as smooth as cream; the sad curve of mouth, once her signature, was almost erased and once she even gave a faint smile as she looked up at Yggur.

'Yet all your life you have allowed yourself to be controlled by another – one no greater than yourself. You have endured that domination, fighting against it then submitting again, allowing it to tear you apart. If Faelamor were to come back today and demand a trial of you, would you not go? In her eyes you have no value but to serve her.'

'My whole life has been duty to Faelamor,' said Maigraith. 'I don't know anything else. How can anything else fulfil me?'

'Look at this ring.' He slipped it off his finger, a thick annulus made of two silver rings and a gold one between them, beaten into one. 'It gives me power and it can you too, if you will learn to accept it. But not Faelamor. How could she teach you what is forbidden her? Maigraith, you are different – *you are not Faellem*! You can have my kind of power too, if you allow yourself. I tell you, rather would I hold my security in my own hand, knowing that it will last as long as I have strength and will to maintain it, than leave it to the uncertain favour of another.'

Maigraith lowered her eyes. Such talk confused and frightened her: rebellion against duty, striking out into the unknown, tampering with what was forbidden. Once before she had rebelled against Faelamor but she had soon returned, for she knew nothing else.

In fact she *had* gained some small measure of self-confidence during Faelamor's long absence. In spite of her reservations about Yggur and his evident unease with her, it was good to care for someone and be cared for. That was something that she had not previously allowed herself to experience in a life that was already much longer than her youthful features indicated.

Yet there were aspects of Yggur that disturbed her greatly – his harshness, his casual cruelty, the contempt that he showed for his faithful Whelm servants. Moreover Yggur did not complete her. She was always wanting more from him and knowing not only that he was unable to provide it but that he did not even know how to. He had not come to her bed since that very first time. There must be something wrong with her. Even so, she hungered for his body.

Abruptly the door was kicked open and a Whelm stalked in. It was Vartila, her bony knees clacking as she walked. Maigraith drew back into the shadows. She had never got over Vartila's dominance of her in Fiz Gorgo.

Yggur's face grew red. 'What is it,' he said testily, 'that you disturb me at my work?'

Vartila smiled, showing grey teeth filed to points. The Whelm smiled so seldom that the sight was a matter for disquiet. Maigraith recalled other contests between Vartila and Yggur, struggles in which more than once she had got the upper hand.

Vartila skidded a leather wallet of despatches across the bench at him, insolence bordering on insubordination. Yggur did not challenge her. The months since Faelamor's disappearance had gone so badly that he dared not alienate her.

'I'll read them later,' he said, trying to recover face in front of Maigraith.

'Read them now,' rasped Vartila, 'or there may be no later.'

'Tell me what they say,' he growled.

'As you wish. One,' she held up a witch's forefinger, bony and long-nailed. 'Another shipment of supplies vanished between the wharf and the wharf city yesterday. That's three this month!'

Yggur sat down suddenly. His mouth moved but no sound came out. 'S-Send General Fwandi down immediately. Order half the Fourth Army in, if necessary.'

'You only *have* half a Fourth Army,' said Vartila, 'what with casualties, desertions and the pox. If they go in there, they won't come out as an army – if they come out at all.'

'What's the matter with this place?' he raged. 'I've cleaned up this cesspit, brought them law and order, and the whole city curses me.'

'Thurkad lives by corruption – it's rotten from top to bottom.'

'Why can't they see that they're better off?'

'Ha!' Vartila snorted mirthlessly, holding up another finger. 'Thyllan has raised a mighty army, thirty thousand at least, and is massing across the sea. He'll soon have enough ships to invade.'

'I have five armies – a hundred thousand seasoned troops!' Yggur spat.

'Spread over two hundred leagues! You'd be hard pressed to put twenty thousand in the field without risking the lands you've already conquered. And morale is bad and getting worse.' Vartila looked him in the eye. Maigraith could see his unease. A third finger went up. 'Another matter – the Ghâshâd are coming out of Shazmak. Already they try to seduce your Second Army in Bannador.'

Yggur felt a prick of fear. He knew if he didn't get rid of her he would scream. 'I've heard enough,' he said curtly.

'There are other problems,' Vartila began.

'Then deal with them!'

Maigraith was shocked. Before the conflict with Faelamor he would have dealt with them himself to the smallest detail.

Vartila bowed low and went out. Yggur caught Maigraith's critical eye on him. She began to take her glasses off, then stopped at the look on his face. Another problem, just as insoluble. He still could not control his fear when he saw the colour of her eyes, so she wore the glasses all the time now.

'I'm sick of this!' Yggur shouted, smashing bowls and crucibles off the table. He no longer wanted his empire but could not relinquish it. Power was just a means to an end, and the end was his long-nurtured revenge against Mendark and Rulke. But lately he had begun to doubt that he had the capacity for it.

Maigraith caught his shifting glance. He turned away, tearing at his hair. 'It doesn't work!' he cried, looking so tormented that despite herself she felt pity for him.

'What doesn't?'

'My Art – it's all going wrong. I can't see my way any longer.'

'You're trying too hard,' she said. 'Come here.'

'Aah!' he groaned. 'I can't face it.'

Face what? Her? 'Come to me!' she said in a commanding voice.

He came across, limping worse than ever, and took her warm hand. His fingers were cold. Maigraith shivered at the touch, but put her arm around him and drew him down. He shuddered, resisting her. She felt a sudden, overpowering anger. *Am I so pathetic that I must beg?* she thought, furious with herself for having put up with this for so long. *Damned if I will! If someone must come to heel it will be him, not me.*

She channelled all her fury into the powers that had lain dormant in her for many months – hardly used since Fiz Gorgo, in fact. Maigraith made a sending, changed it into a compulsion and flung it into his mind.

Do my will, for once! Embrace me, take comfort from me and give me comfort – now and tonight!

Yggur shook like a tree in a gale. Maigraith strained to overcome his resistance until needles of pain began to grow behind her temples. Suddenly his eyes rolled back in his head and he fell down, his cheek coming to rest on her breast. Maigraith was amazed. *He submitted to me; he did my will after all!*

His wiry beard scratched her, not unpleasantly. She put her arm around him, pulling him against her. Eventually, realising that he was watching her with a look of wonder, she stroked her hand down across his brow, brushing his eyes closed. She left her fingers resting on his eyelids, sending a delicious warmth through him, a calming contact. The perfume of her skin rose through the thin fabric and brought harmony, peace, contentment. Maigraith looked serene, queenly.

There they lay for an hour or more, and the rising and falling of her breast with every breath was like the swelling of a wave against him, washing over him, cleansing him and dissolving his cares until he fell into a gentle sleep. She did not sleep but was lulled into a dreamlike contentment, a peace that felt no duty, no burden of obligation, no fear of ill-worth or failure. She, too, closed her eyes and drifted into a oneness of spirit that seemed to suspend time and place.

Night fell. The brazier died down to a few points of orange that winked out, one by one. The two dreamed on, though now it felt cold: oddly cold for the season in steamy Thurkad, and the cold and the dark began to intrude into their dreams, becoming a twisting and a tormenting thing that conjured visions of dark palaces glazed with ice, towers leaning oddly from red-illuminated hilltops, and a swirling mist that was blacker than the darkness. The mist folded around them, then parted briefly. A noble, impossibly handsome, cruel face was revealed, and indigo eyes in which a living fire glowed.

The dream brought Maigraith awake, troubled: afraid of the strength of the seeing, yet drawn to that face. She opened her eyes. The yellow moon, three-quarters full, shone through a high window. All at once Yggur's heavy head quivered in her lap, then he jerked himself upright, staring straight through her.

'Did you feel that?' he asked hoarsely.

'I saw a vision. A dream of the Aachim, I took it to be, mixed up with fragments of Aachan, and at the end a face that haunts me.'

'Rulke!' he said. His eyes were staring, his breathing heavy. He fought to maintain control, not to lose face.

'But you've often dreamed of Rulke – you told me so.'

'Never like that! Never did he appear so aware, so waiting, so confident in his strength. And there was something else – a shivering of time and space as if someone was trying to shrink the distance between there and here.'

'Tensor!'

'I'm afraid that he has used the Mirror, but how? And to what use?' His face became still as he spoke, and his words correspondingly more compressed, until the right side of his face was as rigid as stone.

'What can be done to stop him?'

'Nothing. Tensor went to Faranda and walked into the sand. I cannot find him. Cannot stop him. Here I am, the most potent warlord in all Santhenar, but powerless.'

He pushed himself up and limped back and forth. At the

narrow window he stared out at the moonlit roofs of Thurkad below and the silvery harbour, busy even at this hour with his boats.

Maigraith remained where she was. Until she came here nearly four months ago, her life had gone at breakneck speed, always rushing toward a purpose of someone else's choosing. Then the Conclave broke all that. That was one of the reasons why she had remained with Yggur in spite of her ambivalence toward him – a rebellion against Faelamor. It had given her the space to take control of her own destiny. But the stronger she became, the weaker he seemed.

Later that night the door opened silently. Faelamor stood there, returned from wherever she had been these past months. Faelamor's voice was as cold as her eyes. She caught Maigraith's eye and Maigraith felt her strength dissolve, her rebellion a foolish indulgence that Faelamor had allowed her to get away with. But no longer.

Faelamor spoke directly to Yggur. 'Tensor threatens us all, attempting the Nightland in this way.'

Yggur was shocked to hear her say what he had not dared to think about. 'How can you know?'

'It is one of the things I *know*, that is how I know it. What are you going to do about it?'

'I know not where he is or what power he uses. What can I do? No more than arm myself against Rulke as I do now, in case Tensor fails.'

'In *case* he fails?' Faelamor was scornful. 'Tensor is in his dotage. He will bring the Clysm back upon us and you do *nothing*!'

Yggur grew wrathful. 'Your lineage is greater than my own. Look to your own abilities.'

'I do, though power must be matched with power, and we Faellem do not have that kind of power. If we did, be sure that I would not lack the courage to use it. *Can you not see*, you who are famed for daring the Proscribed Experiments?

Or has that youthful courage failed you? Use that ability again and find him, else we are done.' She disappeared through the door without further word.

Yggur sank his head in his hands. Maigraith sprang up. 'Could you? *Could* that way be used to find him?'

'Perhaps, though my mind shrinks instinctively from the Proscribed Experiments. Every cell and nerve is saturated with the memory of that last attempt. It feels as if Rulke left a poisoned spike in my brain and, whenever he thinks of me, it throbs.

'My life has been spent in cautious striving, Maigraith, in never undertaking a thing until I know all possible consequences and have prepared myself for any of them. The youthful genius that I was before Rulke was imprisoned is gone forever. *He* might have done it, but the man – methodical, unimaginative – that replaced him? I do not think *he* could. In these things confidence is paramount, and since coming to Thurkad I have lost mine.'

He went back to his work, but shortly slammed his instruments down again.

'I can't concentrate. *The Proscribed Experiments!*' He pondered. 'There is one that might succeed. If Tensor has indeed put a gate against the Nightland, it might be used to trace him; even take him. If only I knew more about the gate.'

'Do not allow the taunts of Faelamor to drive you to a folly,' Maigraith said. 'Long have I endured them and I know better than any how they bite. But know also that she never taunts in anger or without a purpose.'

'I understand that,' he replied, his voice indistinct.

'Anyway, it's too late to think about that now. Come up. The morning is a better time for such thoughts.'

To her surprise, Yggur did come to her bed and they embraced each other with a passion and an urgency that neither had ever felt before. Afterwards Yggur went quickly to sleep. Maigraith lay awake staring at the painted ceiling in the dim light, trying to puzzle out Tensor's purpose, and

Faelamor's, and what might be in the mind of Rulke too. Perhaps that was why the lovemaking was unsatisfying; she now felt a different yearning.

For a moment in her earlier dream she'd felt her spirit meld with Rulke's. His face had seemed to become wistful as he looked at her. And she had felt his burning urge to be free – free of the Nightland and the centuries of imprisonment. Maigraith suddenly felt that torment in herself, at her own long subjection. Rulke's knowing indigo eyes woke a hunger in her, like the hunger she'd first felt when she looked on the Mirror in Fiz Gorgo. That she was here for a purpose.

Maigraith drifted back to sleep and dreamed that Rulke was her lover; a dream so wild and passionate that her moans woke Yggur. Later, in her sleep, she felt the lack of his warmth beside her and was sure that he had cast her to the awful Whelm. Sleep became a nightmare from which she could not seem to wake.

The night had crystallised Yggur's inchoate thoughts into a plan. When next he sensed Tensor trying his gate he would attempt one particular Experiment – but only the summoning part of it – to draw the gate away from the Nightland toward him. He would use another power to capture the gate and go through into Tensor's refuge. He shied away from the next step – he had no idea what to do once he got there.

He formed the sequence in his mind, working through it over and over so that when the time came he could stitch the Experiment together seamlessly. Maigraith whimpered beside him and turned over, clutching at his arm. He touched her shoulder; she murmured and lay still again, and he too slipped back into sleep.

As the sun rose, there suddenly came into his dreams that curious sense of warping that he had dreamed earlier, only stronger now and more purposeful. Maigraith began to toss wildly beside him, moaning with a passion that she had never demonstrated with him. Abruptly she sat up, her dreadful eyes open though she was still asleep. Yggur stared at her in horror. His enemy was everywhere. He had to do something now! He sprang out of bed, threw on a robe and, still half in his dream, ran down to his workroom. In the manner of the Experiment that he had tried so long ago, he reached out and twisted the fabric of reality. Peering through the curtain of time and distance Yggur realised that it was Tensor, and that he had succeeded with his gate. Here was the chance, if he could dare it, but it had to be now.

Yggur saw clearly his destination – and the improbability of his return. He snatched up the instruments that he needed; his hands shook. The warping grew strongly, urgently, bending the light in the room, breaking up the shapes so that not even the door was recognisable. Yggur reached out and caught that questing, insubstantial thread that Tensor sought to attach to the barrier of the Nightland. How that hurt! It was almost as bad as the time of the Experiment, slicing through his brain like razors. He drew the thread gently to him, anchored it and the gate followed.

With a *bang* the gate smashed open, sucking the air out of the room in a whirling cloud of white, the papers on his desk, pulling everything down a black tunnel to nowhere. The vortex tried to drag him in. His bare feet slipped on the damp floor and he clutched desperately at the brazier, knocking it down in a flurry of ash and charcoal.

'No!' he cried. He was not ready, could never be ready. Yggur felt like a man who had jumped into the ocean, thinking that he could swim, then suddenly understood that his skills were nothing before the power of the sea. If he went through that gate he would drown in it, be engulfed by the torment that Rulke had done to him long ago. Already he could feel the scorpion arching its sting to strike him.

Someone appeared in the distorted doorway, a tall woman, lean and hard, with grey hair and filed teeth. It was Vartila the Whelm! She knocked Yggur out of the way and raced past.

'Fool!' she spat, throwing herself into the gate.

But as she passed through, the illusion slipped for a moment, and Yggur saw a much smaller woman there. It was not Vartila at all, but Faelamor. The gate brightened as she passed through, then faded to nothing.

His papers rained down like confetti. Yggur picked them up absently, arranged them on his desk and stumbled back to bed, ironically the one place where he did not feel like an utter failure.

42

'COME FORTH, COME FORTH'

As soon as the gate opened Karan realised that something had gone terribly wrong. It opened with a roar, with a whirling and twisting of the air in the room and a giddy wrenching inside her mind. Then came a blast of warm moist wind that lifted her bodily to drop her hard on her bottom. Banners of mist formed, tumbled and disappeared in the dry air of Katazza.

Tensor stood before the opening, great legs spread wide, cloak flapping, one hand a manacle around Llian's wrist. Frost grew on Tensor's beard and his hair, ageing him in front of Karan's eyes. His other hand was held out before him, reaching into the gate, the emptiness. The earth trembled; the whole tower shook. The floor seemed hotter than before.

The gate had been drawn astray and only Karan knew it. It was the smell that gave it away. Her senses were acutely linked to her memories of places and things, and the air that came through the gate had a close, damp odour that she recognised instantly. Thurkad! She had been to no other place that had that smell, compounded of spice and damp, rotting rubbish and the filth of countless people living on top of each other, so different to the sterile cold salty air of Katazza.

Tensor did not know and that astonished her. *He did not know!* For he was reaching out, standing on the tips of his toes, almost choking with the anticipation.

'Come forth! Come forth!' he cried, and the frost began to melt away from his beard.

Nothing happened for a long moment; then, without warning, the rush of air diminished and Vartila the Whelm appeared in the gate, running, stumbling, her eyes staring out of her bony face, her pallid, long-toed feet flapping in loose sandals. Tensor seemed shocked out of his wits, for he took a long time to react, to realise that the gate had been snatched out of his control.

The sight of Vartila aroused memories that Karan would rather have let lie. Long hours she had spent in Narne last winter, bound to an iron bed, watching that hatchet face above her, the bony hands doing their passionless violence on her. Llian knew her too from the night he had burned the old house down and set Karan free.

Vartila dodged by Tensor's outstretched hand, springing past him out of the pavilion. Tensor's face flooded with hate and rage.

'Ghâshâd!' he cried mistakenly and flung out his arm to obliterate her.

She let fly an illusion already prepared. The room spun with impossibilities so powerful that Karan's guts tried to heave themselves out her mouth. She covered her eyes and clung to the bench to stop herself going insane. Tensor squeezed his head between his hands, attempting to clear it.

Vartila skidded to a stop in front of Karan, staring at her in consternation. 'How did you . . .?' she cried.

Tensor spun around, then back to the gate, unable to tell what was real and what was illusion. The gate was already fading; the rush of air ceased. Vartila raised her hand to Karan, then her features seemed to shift. Karan was on her knees, weakly holding up one arm. She could not understand why Vartila would want to kill her.

For a moment they stood frozen, then the tall woman shrank and Faelamor stood there. Tensor rocked on his feet, his confidence undermined by her appearance, the one who had brought doom upon Shazmak.

Faelamor flicked her wrist and what Karan saw was too much for her brain to hold. Her eyes revolved in sickening circles, casting her down into a whirlpool. Faelamor drew a knife. Llian tore his wrist free and ran at her, sending her flying across the floor.

Tensor raised his hand to let fly the potency. Then he hesitated and Llian knew why. Once used, he would be weakened by aftersickness. What if his worst enemy appeared while he was helpless? He dared not risk it.

At his motion Faelamor jerked like a puppet, the potency eating into her brain before he even released it. This time it would kill her. She screamed, '*Keiollellioullallillime!*' and every object in the room broke into twenty images. It was impossible to tell what was real and what was merest illusion.

Twenty Tensors went into slow-motion, hands going up and out, freezing then falling back. Nothing was real. Llian's head was whirling. He closed his eyes and kept crawling to where he knew Karan lay. They cracked heads, then twenty Llians picked up as many Karans in their arms.

Evidently the conflict could be heard outside the chamber, for the attacks on the door were resumed violently. Llian retreated up the broad stair, feeling for each step with his foot. As they turned the corner the illusions began to fade.

'I'm all right now,' Karan whispered. 'Put me down.'

He stood her on her feet but her knees wobbled and she grabbed his arm. They heard feet on the steps below.

'Quick, upstairs,' she said, feeling her way along the wall.

'Are you sure you're all right?'

'Just a little dizzy – it's getting better though. Don't let her see you,' Karan whispered, putting her head between her knees. 'Oh, I feel quite faint.'

It was a long haul up the stairs to the topmost chamber.

She had to rest several times on the way but they did not hear the footsteps again. Once inside, Karan wedged the door shut and stood with her back hard against it.

'What happened?' Llian asked, trembling.

'The gate came from Thurkad. How could Tensor send it so far astray?'

'Maybe Faelamor drew it there. Why does she hate you so?'

'I don't know! Is there anything left to eat? I'm starving!'

There were two packets of sweetcake, very rich with fruits and nuts. She broke one in two, offering Llian half.

'How can you eat!' he exclaimed.

'When I'm frightened, I eat,' she said, gobbling it down. 'Did you see her face back there? What have I ever done to her?'

Just then the door shook, moved fractionally open with a scrape of stone, then stuck. It shook again, as if a shoulder had been put to it.

'It's her!' Karan whispered. 'What are we going to do?'

Llian banged it closed again, but Faelamor's voice could not be stopped. It came clear and high into the room, and there was magic in it, one that Karan was peculiarly susceptible to. Even as Llian watched, she drooped in the dust like a dying swan, only her eyelids flickering to show that she was still conscious.

Faelamor's words impacted heavily on Llian's brain too. Slowly came the realisation that she was spinning a tale to mesmerise them, weaving it with all her mastery of illusion and enchantment. How bold she was, to use his own telling skills against him – truly she must have great powers and great confidence in them. He was struck with admiration.

Perhaps because the charm of his teller's *voice* was so powerful, Llian was able to resist the desperate urge to submit. But now she called directly to him, and despite everything he grew afraid. No, this was one duel that she could not be permitted to win.

To distract himself he began to speak a tale of his own.

It was a long and tragic story, chanted in an ancient and formal rhythm that was overpoweringly hypnotic. He embellished and embroidered it as few others could have done; using all of his strength and his teller's *voice* and once Faelamor's voice faltered, though only on a single word.

Then her voice came back stronger than before. Llian did not raise his, though he worked his hopes and fears and dreams of Karan into his tale. Faelamor faltered, cracked again, then only silence came from the other side of the door.

Still Llian told, until he was driven into oblivious ecstasy by his creation, as if the room in which he stood was a block of marble and each word he sang a tap of his sculptor's chisel, carving the stone away, bringing forth the exquisite form beneath.

Karan sat up, all dusty and dishevelled, looking up at Llian. She had never heard such desperate inspiration.

Other times when Karan had heard him tell, it had been for the pure joy that comes from mastery of the art. Now he told for their lives and love. But his tale was not of the traditional teller's love, that which strikes in an instant like a bolt of fire. Rather it was the maturing passion that swells until it is strong enough to move the earth. He told also of the reverse side – the terror of knowing that it can all be torn apart by some chance thing: the indifferent brutality of fate.

Llian's telling was not a defiance but an entreaty. Defiance would not have touched Faelamor's fierce and ruthless heart, but Llian's entreaty did. Karan could sense the tears falling on the other side of the door, the rain in the heart of her enemy. For Faelamor had not always been as she was now. She had been young when she came to Santhenar, in love with life as only the Faellem can be.

At last the tale ended, one of the most beautiful that had ever been told. Llian, wrung dry, slumped against the wall.

He could do no more, even if Faelamor were to force the door at that moment.

Karan put her arms around him, overcome by tenderness. The long silence seemed to stretch out forever. The sun slanted lower, pierced in through the western embrasures to touch Karan's hair to a blaze of copper and lit the tiny hairs of her forearm where it lay on Llian's shoulder.

Faelamor tried another enchantment to make him sleep. Llian had no power over this one. He was already half there. The charm tipped him over the edge of a well, he slid to the bottom, landed on a cloud of down and slept. Karan grew drowsy again but she could not sleep, *must* not sleep.

The silence seemed to stretch out to infinity. Then Karan's talent showed her the other side of the door, her enemy rising slowly to her feet. She sensed Faelamor rising, the distant dreaming, the memories of another life on Tallallame and of a greater love fading; just a bittersweet nostalgia remaining.

Karan sensed Faelamor at the door, thrusting the door wide, stepping into their refuge. Fleetingly there came a vision seen through Faelamor's eyes: a large room, bright windows open to the sky, two people small against a wall. A man dreaming with his eyes open; a woman, her arms about him protectively; terribly afraid.

Karan looked up at her enemy – Faelamor down at hers. The silence stretched out. Karan hugged Llian one last time, then shook him and stood up. She was of the size of her enemy. Llian rubbed his eyes drowsily.

'Go,' said Karan softly to him. 'This is my battle. I don't know why it is or what I have done, only that if it must be, I would have it now.'

'Stay, Llian of Chanthed,' said Faelamor. 'You have shown your worth as a teller. Now I need the master chronicler to tell me something.'

'In that case there is a price and you know what it is,' Llian whispered.

The moment was drawn out like a thread of spider's silk. Llian rose, still holding Karan's hand.

'My price,' he said again, staring into Faelamor's eyes.

'Ahhh! You cannot know what you ask.'

'Why do you hate Karan so? What harm has she done you?'

'She is brave and I honour her, *but I hate and fear what she is*. Believe me when I say that I would not lift a finger against her for myself. What do I care about my life – I have lived long beyond what I ever wanted. But Tallallame cries out for us and we do not come. It has been foretold; she is the one!'

'*The one?*'

'I say no more.'

'Nonetheless, she is the price.'

Faelamor took a shuddering inward breath. A wave of goosepimples passed up her bare arm, seeming to press out the translucent skin from beneath. She let out a tiny sigh. 'I was a proud fool, thinking to use that weapon against you. My charm is revealed as mere illusion, but your tale was *real*.' She put her hands over her face, then her fingers parted and cold ancient eyes stared at him. 'I cannot refuse you.'

Llian watched her silently, noting her distinct Faellem characteristics: the lustrous skin, the deep feline eyes, the way she spoke and moved. All this he needed for his tale. He had now met two of the three off-world human species: Aachim and Faellem. No other chronicler had had that opportunity in a very long time. But Llian was not sure that he wanted to meet the last species – Charon!

'Watch her well,' Faelamor said coldly, 'for I tell you now: there will be no other lives given.'

She slipped through the door and they heard a bar thud down. They did not even go over and try it.

Night fell. The stars came out one by one, brighter in this lonely sky than they had ever seen them. They drank the last of the water, divided the final food packet between them and licked up the crumbs, wishing they'd brought more; they clung together against the night cold and later the pre-dawn wind that came in the open windows to swirl around the room. They spoke together in hushed tones though there was none to hear. Later that night the scorpion nebula climbed high in the sky, burning brighter and blacker and fiercer than ever before, and its arching sting might have struck anywhere within the Dry Sea or any of the lands of Santhenar beyond.

No noise penetrated the length of stairway, the thickness of door that lay between them. They speculated on what might have happened below. Perhaps Faelamor had used the gate. Maybe Tensor was off on his explorations again. There was no way of telling. Karan paced back and forth, unable to bear the silence and the inaction.

She sat down beside Llian, taking his hand. 'I'm afraid,' she said. 'I've a bad feeling about how this is going to end.' She examined his broad, strong hand, remembering his caresses, wanting them now. She had what she wanted – all she had to do now was get them safely home. But in her mind's eye all she could see was foreboding: a whirlwind of darkness, herself hurled out of it one way, Llian cast off the other.

Llian gave her a wan smile. 'Gates are trouble; such things were never meant to be.' And he could not stop thinking how, without his collaboration, Tensor might never have had succeeded at all.

Ever since Tensor had barricaded himself inside, the Aachim had been working furiously to break in. Yet every method they tried: from above, from below, from outside – all had been anticipated by Kandor long ago. Nonetheless, what one engineer could construct another could take apart, and since the first report of Tensor using the gate, the Aachim had redoubled their efforts, working day and night.

Shand was in the stone-vaulted cooking room making yet another pot of chard. There was an outcry up the stairs, so loud and prolonged that he was able to distinguish individual voices. He already knew what the trouble was. They had been arguing for days, the same tedious counsel of caution, appeasement and despair from Selial and her band, while a smaller group, mostly those that had survived the ruin of Shazmak, proposed ever more violent and outlandish solutions. Mendark and Malien tried to rouse the conservatives and soothe the hawks, though to little effect.

Mendark was closeted now with three or four of Selial's group, working on a new scheme that involved a kind of blasting powder made from crystals gathered in the dung pits of the old stables, sulphur collected from the fumaroles further down the mountain, and other secret substances. Tallia had spent all day with the twins Xarah and Shalah, grinding each material with exquisite care and blending them in different combinations. Then she tested each formula outside, making terrific bangs and clouds of black smoke. Sausages of the chosen powder were being sealed into a number of key places, to be set off in the correct sequence.

'Make the calculations again, just to be sure,' said Mendark, and the Aachim ran to do what he required. Mendark was not afraid to command but they could see that he weighed the risks carefully. They were glad to follow him for the time being.

Shand went back to the kitchen. Before he was finished, Mendark stuck his head through the door.

'Shand, come out here! Tell me what you think!'

Taking his bowl of chard, Shand went upstairs to inspect the new scheme. He walked around, noting the size and placement of the charges. Tallia staggered in carrying another crate of blasting sausages. She looked very cheerful, though her eyes were red and she was covered in black soot.

'Well?' said Mendark impatiently as Shand took a deliberate slurp from the bowl. 'I swear you are as bad as Nadiril.'

'Thank you for the compliment. It might work, though

611

this charge will blow the plug back out at you.' He prodded at it with a weatherbeaten finger. 'And this one – likely you'll bring down the whole tower. Still, you're the engineers and I'm the chard-boy.'

Mendark and the Aachim conferred, worked on a new set of calculations and made changes along the lines that Shand had proposed. As Shand turned back to his cooking, Osseion took him by the sleeve.

'There's going to be trouble as soon as that door comes down,' Osseion whispered, rubbing his jowl with a four-fingered hand. 'We'd better be prepared for it.'

'What trouble?'

'Well, since we arrived I've had nothing to do but keep watch over old Magis. Gives me plenty of time to see what's going on. Five or six of these Aachim folk, you probably know the ones, have worked themselves into a state. Basitor and Hintis are the worst. I've seen it happen before – berserker! The worst enemy of all in battle because nothing but death will stop them.'

'I hadn't realised it had gone so far.'

'It hadn't until today. But they've made a great store of fermented fruit juice, poor man's wine, and they've been drowning in it all day. Sometimes that stuff is enough to make you crazy. You'd better watch out. Those two in there will be the first to go once the door is opened.'

'Karan and Llian? I hadn't thought of that. Where's Tallia?'

'Gone back outside. I'll fetch her.'

While he was waiting, Shand took Malien and Selial to one side.

'I was afraid of that,' Malien said after he had explained. She pushed her fingers through thick red hair. 'Now is the time, Selial. We must make our stand or perish.'

'Llian is the key,' said Selial, who looked absolutely ghastly – white-faced, shrunken, her eyes staring.

'Yes! As soon as the door opens we must carry him away. There are fifteen of us but only seven loyal to Tensor. At least, I hope that's all. He would not dare act without Llian.'

'What is the plan?' Selial whispered, clinging to the door.

Shand did not like the look of her at all. She was breaking and could not be relied upon. But he could hardly warn Malien in front of her.

'I will go for Llian,' said Malien. 'You must support me and bar their way afterwards while I get him away.'

Not long after there came a series of cracking explosions, so close together that they blurred into one, followed by a vast *BOOOOMMMM*. Dust whirled in the air. Rubble crashed down on metal.

'That's it,' whispered Malien. 'Our time has come, Selial my friend. Aachim against Aachim. What a terrible day. Don't fail us now.'

43

HIDEOUS STRENGTH

'What do you want from me?' asked Llian as Faelamor came back.

'It has to do with the Forbidding,' said Faelamor, 'that imprisons us on Santhenar as surely as Rulke is himself imprisoned; that will allow nothing to pass between the worlds. Nothing, *save my enemy Yalkara*! You think *you* are mine enemy, ha! Llian, I would have you tell me what happened after the death of Shuthdar. And be quick about it.'

Llian jumped. Did she know that he had been searching for that secret for the past year?

'There is not much to tell,' said Llian. He told her the ending of the *Tale of the Forbidding*, but said nothing about his own researches since leaving Chanthed nor the strange business about the murder of the crippled girl that had aroused his curiosity in the first place.

'There must be more than that,' said Faelamor.

'There are details in plenty,' said Llian, 'of the movement of armies, the number and disposition of troops, the fighting, the casualties. I can even tell you the colour of their banners, if that is what you wish to know.'

Faelamor dismissed armies and banners with a slash of her hand.

'I can tell you how they found Shuthdar, who was there, of the storming of the tower, what it was like inside when it was over.'

'Who was there at the end?' Faelamor asked, unable to disguise her eagerness.

'There were whole armies, led by the greatest leaders of that age. So many kings and queens, autarchs and dictators and generals were there that you could have filled a game board with them. Rulke, of course; Kandor too; Kwinlis, the first Magister of the Council; several other Aachim –'

'Tensor?' she interrupted.

'He was there at the beginning but, after the flute was destroyed, the Aachim saw into the void and fled in terror. There were countless others, though the lists of the minor people are contradictory. The destruction of the flute left a halo of death for half a league around the tower, yet strangely not inside. During that time the Forbidding sealed off the Way between the Worlds.'

'Go on!'

'Hours went by before anyone dared cross that field of corpses and go inside. I think that the first to enter the ruins were Rulke, Vance (a minor noble), Baggus, Yalkara –'

'Yalkara! *Yalkara!*' She almost choked on the name. 'I have not heard that before. Tell all.'

'It is not widely reported. The records of each of the major armies show that their general was first, but another report, written by the Princess Nangaiya, gave this list. She was a reliable recorder. Even though the outer stones of the tower glowed and ran like slag in a foundry, they went in. No one else dared, so altered was the reality of that place, so nightmarish. Yalkara was badly burnt but they found nothing. No one did, though afterwards they took the tower apart, stone by stone. The golden flute must have been destroyed for no trace of it was found.'

'Yalkara was searched?'

'Everyone who entered was stripped naked in front of the

rest. Even Rulke submitted but, of course, nothing was found. There was nothing to be found.'

Faelamor's face was expressionless. Had she learned anything of value? Llian could not tell; the mask was back on her face. Abruptly she left, blocking the door behind her again.

'I can't bear this,' said Karan, almost screaming with frustration. 'What's going on down there?

Llian had no answer. They stood side by side at the southeastern embrasure, looking out across the sea. It was a bright morning, so clear that a mountain peak could be seen in the distance, sharp as a tooth, as the rising sun touched the horizon behind it. Once or twice the tower shook, but that was not surprising – the earth often quaked here. Looking down to the sea, where the night still lay in obsidian pools, they saw that one of the little cones at the foot of Katazza was erupting fire again, lighting up the steam and ash that billowed halfway up Katazza Mountain.

'So,' said Karan, 'it keeps coming back to your *Tale of the Forbidding*. It was the beginning and maybe it is the end of it all, too. What have you learned since you tried to rescue me from the citadel?'

Llian had almost forgotten that abortive flight through the corridors of the citadel and its gruesome ending. He told Karan about Kandor's letter.

'The tale keeps coming up, but I find only dead ends. I'm beginning to think that it is all wishful thinking.'

'I don't,' said Karan. 'I have a *feeling*, just as I did when I first heard your telling. What a night that was for me!'

'I . . .' Llian began.

Just at that moment Karan saw Faelamor in the doorway.

'Hush,' Karan said, and putting her arms around Llian, stood up on her toes and stopped his mouth with her own.

Faelamor wedged the door closed, sat down on the floor and pulled out from its tube a coil that slowly unrolled and hardened into a plane. She held it up in shaking hand. Tensor had left it carelessly on the bench and was off on another of his explorations. She had the Mirror at last.

'I thought you were forbidden to use magical devices,' Llian said, hoping to learn more about the Faellem.

'More than prohibited – it is our oldest taboo.'

'Then . . .'

The strain was evident on her face now. 'I have broken the taboo,' Faelamor snapped, 'and will pay dearly. Now leave me!'

'What's this!' Faelamor exclaimed, shivering. 'This script was not here when I last fought Yalkara.'

Llian peered over her shoulder, fascinated. The Mirror was blank but for the fiery moon symbol and the silvery glyphs around the border. She counted the glyphs with a fingertip.

'There are ninety-nine,' Llian said, 'But only thirty-three different ones. Some are repeated many times, others not so.'

'So it's not a decoration,' she said. 'It means something.'

'I've not seen that script anywhere else,' Llian said.

'I –' her voice went hoarse. 'I don't like it – I dread that it is a trap.' Faelamor was as tense as wire, the blue blood beneath her skin moving in jerky pulses, the muscles contracting in spasms as she forced herself to overcome her dread.

'Can you use the Mirror?' asked Llian, the teller in him watching her as eagerly as he had Tensor before her.

'It is locked and the key is back in Thurkad.' She did not look up. 'Yet I saw Yalkara employ it in times past.'

Nothing happened for ages. Karan went back to the embrasure and her study of the eruptions down below. An explosion sent splatters of solidifying rock wheeling through the air almost as high as Katazza.

Just then the Mirror opened with a burst of white light that highlighted Faelamor's face from below. Words and scenes flashed across it with dizzying speed. He tried to see but she swung her little fist at him.

'My eyes only, chronicler,' she grated.

Llian rejoined Karan by the window. They looked out till their bellies felt empty again.

'Where are you, mine enemy?' shouted Faelamor, rising to her feet and holding out the Mirror before her. 'Where are you, Yalkara?' But that image, the one which the Mirror must have reflected more than any other, it would not reveal.

Faelamor's whole arm went into spasms, the Mirror shaking like a leaf in a gale. 'Come forth, enemy mine. Show yourself to me. Even from the Mirror will I have your secret!'

They wondered what she wanted from it. What ancient power had she honed like a sickle in the countless years of waiting? What force could she hope to direct against an enemy that was but a shadow on the glass?

'Where are you?' she repeated, raging at the thought that once again Yalkara had frustrated her. The mask of Faelamor's remarkable face cracked. Holding the Mirror close, her hand trembled. Then, a perversity of the Mirror, it became an ordinary mirror again, showing her deranged and hate-filled face.

For an instant Faelamor stared at what she had become, then flung the Mirror away. It skidded across the floor, momentarily a smiling face appeared, then it was a mirror again, reflecting the ceiling.

'Laugh!' Faelamor said softly. 'I know what you left behind. I found it and broke it, and all your plans and hopes with it. But from it I have forged a greater implement and it will free us. You will not defy me!'

Suddenly remembering her prisoners, Faelamor whirled. Llian's mouth hung open but Karan was deadly quick. Her hand was upraised, her forearm bent back over her head, the little knife shining there.

'I *know* you now,' said Karan. 'Your image is fixed in the back of my mind with all my other enemies and each time you even think of me it burns me. Move the smallest muscle and this knife will go into your eye so hard that it will come out the back of your head. And then the Faellem will truly have something to weep about, for they will *never* return to Tallallame.'

Faelamor went still. Her eyes flicked sideways at Llian and Karan's fingers quivered.

'Do not,' Karan hissed. Suddenly the danger was over, Faelamor whirled and went down the stair again, leaving the door open.

'That was a deadly moment,' Karan said, looking into his eyes. 'She gave away something that she may regret, I think.'

Llian gave a muffled curse.

'What?'

'I've been puzzling for ages over those glyphs around the border of the Mirror.'

'What about them?' Karan felt an icicle run down her back.

'I bet Faelamor does know the language. I should have bargained.'

'*Llian* . . .' said Karan in a dangerous tone of voice. 'You just can't help yourself, can you?'

He quickly changed the subject. 'The world could be ending down there and we wouldn't know it.'

'I'd know it,' said Karan. 'All right, I can't bear it either. Let's go down, carefully.'

They crept down the interminable windings of the stair. It was very quiet.

'Hang on,' said Karan, halfway down. She was limping badly. Llian sat on the stair while she prodded her calves with her fingers, wincing.

'Are you all right?'

'My muscles are still sore. I'll have to take it slowly. Rub my legs.' She pulled her trousers up to her knees, lay back on the cold step and closed her eyes, luxuriating in his touch. The step vibrated beneath her.

'That's funny,' she said dreamily.

'What?'

'It felt like the step shook. See, there it is again.'

The whole staircase quivered. She sat up.

'An earth trembler?'

The stair shook violently. To Karan it seemed that a wave passed along and up the solid stone. It shook again, then there was a great *boom!* and a metallic clang followed by the rumble of falling masonry. A dusty, smoky wind rushed up the stairs. Karan gripped Llian's hand.

'They've broken the door to Tensor's chamber,' he said.

'At last! Not even Tensor can stand against all of them and Mendark too. Soon it will be over. Let's go down.'

They continued, hand in hand, but a couple of spirals from the bottom heard the sound of running feet and two Aachim hurtled up the curve of the stair: Hintis and Basitor. Llian moaned, slipped over, then tried to scramble back up on hands and knees.

'What's the matter?' Karan cried.

'They want me dead –'

The Aachim's faces were so grim that even she, who knew them both, quailed.

'No, leave him be,' she cried, but Hintis caught both wrists in one giant hand and she was helpless.

Basitor twisted Llian's arms behind his back, bound him and dragged him down the stairs. They were gone from sight very quickly. Hintis thrust Karan down on the step.

'Stay!' he said. 'Do not interfere.' He loped off, taking five steps at a stride.

Blinking tears out of her eyes, Karan followed. The air here was smoky; it was hard to see. She rounded the last curve of the stair, looking down over Tensor's chamber. The door had fallen outwards, leaving a hole twice as wide and high, piled with rubble. There was a zig-zag arch at the top where part of the inner wall had collapsed. The dusty air still whirled and something burned among the masonry. A wavering trail of white smoke curved around the ceiling before dissipating up the stair.

Karan eased her head around the corner. The destruction had been confined to the doorway. The rest of the room was undamaged, though it was littered with chips of stone and plaster, and the papers from Tensor's bench were scattered. Tensor stood within the pavilion, thick legs spread, one arm upraised. Just outside, a guard of six Aachim faced the doorway. Evidently they had joined the rebellion.

As she watched, Hintis finished binding Llian to one of the columns and Basitor leapt out the other side of the pavilion to his appointed place. Karan limped to the bottom of the stairs. There she saw Malien circle round to the other side of the pavilion, creeping among the overturned benches and tables. The rest of the Aachim, with Selial to the fore, had fanned out between the pavilion and the broken door, but they hesitated, unwilling to make war on their own.

Malien looked back as if waiting for the Aachim to do their part, but they remained frozen. She was very tense. Suddenly a knife flashed in her hand and she sprang onto the platform. Tensor scrabbled backwards as she leaned forward with the knife, then Hintis kicked out with both feet, striking her brutally on chest and shoulder. Something snapped audibly, she gave a tiny muffled cry and tumbled out of the pavilion like a rag doll.

Tensor went as white and still as marble, shrieking as though the injury had been done to himself. For all that, he did not go to her aid. Hintis stalked across to join the other guards. Selial started towards Malien but the renegade Aachim raised their weapons and once more her courage failed her.

Karan raced across, pierced through the heart. Malien was breathing but there was blood coming from her hair, her ear and her shoulder. Her shirt was drenched, bone protruding through the skin. Karan felt faint. She tried to lift Malien but found her surprisingly heavy and the movement shivered her face in agony.

Karan cut off a sleeve and pressed a pad over the wound to stop the bleeding. She had no idea what to do about such injuries. Surely Malien was going to die. Then the folds of dusty air parted and, like a miracle, Shand appeared beside her. Karan wept in relief – Shand always knew what to do.

As he bent down, Hintis and Basitor whirled and came at him, wearing identical expressions of berserker rage. Hintis hacked wildly with a curved sword longer than Karan. The air might have been a corpse that he was trying to dismember.

Shand pushed himself to his feet, hands hanging loosely by his side. The Aachim were head and shoulders above him. Hintis leapt, the sword swinging in a violent arc that would cut Shand in two. Karan's hand flashed to her knife but she was far too late.

Shand looked up at his attacker. 'Don't,' he said softly, but the tone of his voice made her flesh crawl, so icy with menace was it. He moved one hand in the air.

Hintis's long hair stood up vertically; his pupils dilated until his eyes became black holes looking forever inward. His feet tangled and cast him on the floor. The sword clattered away. Basitor's jaw dropped so far that Karan could have stoked his mouth with a shovel.

'Go away,' said Shand more softly yet.

Hintis was so desperate to escape that he scuttled off on hands and knees, abandoning his sword. Basitor loped away, head down and long arms swinging like a running ape. Shand turned back to Malien, looking just like old Shand again, but for the glacier that slowly melted from his eyes. He said nothing and Karan said nothing, but he got up very slowly and painfully and they carried Malien out over the rubble, past a death-like, hang-dog Selial, and laid her down beside a stretcher on which lay Tallia, with her eyes closed and a rude bandage around her head.

'Oh, what's happened to Tallia?' cried Karan.

Shand's face had gone a greenish-yellow and his eyes were glassy. 'Hit by a piece of rubble when the door came down,' he whispered. 'I think she'll be all right.'

'Are *you* okay, Shand?'

'I overstretched myself,' he said hoarsely, 'and I'm going to suffer for it.'

He tried to peel the shirt away from Malien's shoulder but his hand was shaking so much that he could not grip the cloth. Karan did it for him, revealing the ugliness of the wound. She looked toward the door, torn between her duty to Malien and her need to look after Llian.

'Go,' said Shand. 'He has only you now.'

'Ahhh!' wailed Karan. 'Malien . . .'

He touched her arm. 'Ask yourself what she would want you to do, then run. I've cleaned up on a dozen battlefields. This is not as bad as it seems.'

Malien groaned and opened her eyes. Karan wept. 'Karan,' Malien whispered. 'You must stop him or we are all finished.'

'What does he want Llian for?'

'The Gift . . .'

'Yes, but what?'

'Tensor plans to use the Gift to amplify his . . . spell,' she tried to raise her head but could not. 'So that not even Rulke can resist it. To use him like a living lens.'

'Llian . . .'

'It will break the lens. Quickly, Karan.'

Karan kissed Malien on the brow, spotting it with her tears, then ran. From the top of the rubble she saw Selial pleading with Tensor, but Tensor had gone mad too. Having condoned such crimes, there was no going back. He flashed a black staff in her face. Hintis, his curved sword and his boldness recovered, hacked the smoky air into chunks right in front of Selial, forcing her back to the gaggle of Aachim. In the pavilion Llian was slumped against his bonds, convinced that his doom was only minutes away.

623

In Thurkad Yggur had spent the day locked in his workroom, rigid with fear. He was mortified by his failure at the gate, but the thought of leaping into that whirlpool as Faelamor had done and baring his throat to the void was a terror that he dared not face. He tried to distract himself with work, slaving with his sorcerous tools – stones and rings and other things in which his power resided (he hoped it still did) – until his hands shook, but no distraction was proof against this. Finally he took down the most hazardous devices in his armoury: an uncut emerald – a six-sided prism as long as his hand – and a perfect ruby the size of a grapefruit. These were objects that he had never dared try to command before, but it was time for desperate measures.

What was that racket outside? He realised that it had been going on for ages. Mastering his fear, Yggur wrenched the doors open, but it was just Maigraith, bearing food and a cooling draught. Anyone else would have shrunk back before him but she merely looked up at him from under her lashes and smiled in that funny way of hers, as though it was a new thing she was trying to learn.

She was not wearing her glasses. The light touched the colour in her eyes and Yggur shivered. Her smile faded away.

'Come in,' he said roughly, grabbing the platter out of her hands.

He told her what had happened in the night. 'Faelamor went through the gate and I was too afraid to follow.'

Maigraith drew away. 'Faelamor went because she had no choice, and she goes not to fight your battles but her own. You can rely on her for nothing.'

He could tell that Maigraith was disappointed in him. It stung. The tables had truly turned.

'Perhaps if you did not wallow in your terrors quite so much,' she said with just a hint of acid, 'you might be able to overcome them.'

He buried his head in his hands.

'Tell me what to do,' said Maigraith, thinking that it would help him. 'Bring the gate here and I will go through it.'

'It would be the end of you.'

'Perhaps. I have no fear of that.'

'I have,' he groaned.

'We'll do it later,' she said. 'Come up!' Once more he followed her.

Eventually the fear of what would happen if he did not act began to overwhelm Yggur's other terrors, and in the black hour just before dawn he reached the point where he had to rid himself of his nightmare, one way or the other. Either he conquered it or it must overcome him. He could never go back to that time of torment when Rulke had possessed him; had crouched within his brain like a giant scorpion, stinging him again and again.

There it was again! That warping of the shadows of the night, a twisting of reality so that dreaming and waking could hardly be distinguished. Yggur woke with a cry, face set rigid, drenched in sweat. The emerald on the bedside table glowed like luminous mist. Maigraith was sitting bolt upright beside him, staring into the night. She put her hand on his wet forehead. Yggur buried his face against her shoulder with a moan. She held him tightly.

The sun crept up. No, he thought, *I must face it!* He reached blindly for the emerald and sought for the gate again. This time it was much harder than before. Soon the warping grew so intense that the very air twisted the images of things on the other side of the room. The walls shivered, broke up like a picture in a distorting mirror. The air became as cold as winter. Mist condensed in flat layers which began to drift in spirals, whirling into the centre of the room.

Now! It must be now! Yggur wriggled free of Maigraith to fling on a gown, cape and boots. The ruby was in one pocket of his cloak, the emerald in his hand. The leaden air had to be consciously swallowed but it clotted like cold porridge in his lungs. He forced himself to breathe, to concentrate, to pick the gate out of the ether and bring it to his hand. For a moment he was prey to the scorpion again, and the non-image he held in his mind began to slide, but he squeezed the emerald and wrenched the vision tight.

Suddenly the displaced air cracked as a gate appeared before him. It was bigger than previously: a pavilion, a dome supported on slender columns, and the mist spiralled in and roared through the gate to nowhere. His long hair flapped, stinging his cheeks. Yggur thrust the emerald inside a pocket and stepped forward, his bad leg burning like fire. His cloak billowed out, trying to rush past him into the gate.

Again he hesitated, the air pulling him in but his feet dragging. He had brought the gate here but was afraid of trying to control it – afraid that it would overpower him. In a panic, trying too hard, he tore the emerald out through the side of his pocket. Thrusting it out toward the gate he shouted a command. Green light streamed out between his fingers. He sensed a door opening and a wild surge of power leapt into the emerald. For an instant Yggur felt that he could do anything, overcome anyone, then it faded. The gate roared back and opened its maw, sucking the sheets and blankets off the bed, pulling everything loose in the room to itself.

A wail came from behind him. It was Maigraith, naked from the bed, her chestnut hair wild, her hands up around her mouth, crying, 'No, Yggur. Don't use that!'

He could barely hear her above the rushing of the wind. Her image wavered, the background breaking into streamers, Maigraith distorted to face and skull and staring eyes. A silken gown tore off its peg and struck him in the face, writhing and smothering. Yggur tossed his head. The gown caressed his cheek and fell into the gate.

'*Maigraith!*' he cried, terrified, and reached back to her for help.

She stretched out her beautiful arm to him. For a moment Yggur teetered, unable to choose between two fates, then the scorpion stung him again. That could not be borne for another instant, even if it was to kill him. One side of his face was all warped up, but the other had gone rigid as stone. Yggur turned, gasped a breath that might be his last and threw himself into the gate. His parting words came too softly to survive the roar of the wind. He faded away to nothing.

Maigraith took a step toward the gate. It drifted sideways. Another step. Again it dipped away from her. She sprang at it but the gate began to move, glided across the room, slowly revolving, and bounced off the far wall with a shower of plaster. Wallpaper was torn off in strips and sucked inside.

She ran at the gate, a furious burst of speed, and almost touched it, then it jerked itself away, repelled by her, snapped shut and disappeared with a bang that brought down half the ceiling. The rushing misty air was suddenly stilled. Eventually the dust settled and the room grew bright with morning light.

'Do not go,' she said softly, but it was far too late. She was left alone, just she and the Whelm. Maigraith turned back, dressed herself without knowing what she put on, then lay down in the bed. It was white with broken plaster. She pulled the covers up, waiting with quiet desperation, sure that her taunts had driven him to this folly.

He did not return.

As Karan stood in the doorway, staring at Llian so hard that it was surprising he did not look up, Mendark crept up the stairs with bowed back and hunched shoulders. He glanced at her vacantly and she was shocked to see how old and worn he looked, until she recalled that it was one of his abilities. At the same time, sensed but not seen, Faelamor ghosted by in the other direction. Each of them was searching for the best, safest vantage for the coming struggle, as she should be.

Suddenly Tensor leapt up for his mirror, shouting to Basitor. Something was amiss: the gate was working of its own accord. The smoke glowed, the dust in the air sparkled, hot moist air belched outward. Again Karan smelt the humid stench of Thurkad. Yggur this time, she knew without knowing how. *Yggur!* Shades of their encounter in Fiz Gorgo stirred her hackles.

The mist continued to belch from the gate, mixing with the smoke and dust until the Aachim were but shadows in the fog. The floor grew damp. Karan blinked beads of moisture from her lashes and crept on. She tried to reason with herself, to reassure herself that she was no longer of any interest to Yggur.

As she edged around the room, the earth trembled again. At first she thought it was another explosion, but there was no noise at all, just a shuddering of the floor. Then as she slipped past one of the fireplaces, the tower lurched and she heard the most hideous screeching, like all the banshees of the world howling in agony. The floor tilted slightly, then back the other way; the tower jerked upwards, halted, jerked again. The screeching stopped, the shifting foundations locked together once more. Then the floor dropped and rolled under her feet, stone grating on stone.

Karan looked around frantically. A circle of stone a few paces across had dropped about the height of a step and was sliding beneath the floor. A lighted crescent appeared, growing wider like a swiftly waning moon until it was entirely open – a circular hole where the hearth had been. Sulphurous heat drifted up. She sprang backwards onto solid floor and peered gingerly over the edge. The hole passed down through all the levels of the tower, for she could see each floor, circle after circle. She counted quite a few. They were only on the fifth level, so the shaft must run deep underground. At the bottom it glowed orange – the rift? Well, whatever was down there, Llian was more important.

Without warning the gate boomed open behind her, the sound echoing round the room. Scraps of parchment and clothing whirled in the air, shredded by the gate. It was indeed Yggur. How tall he was! His cape writhed against his back and shoulders as if the gate had given it life.

Tensor froze, midway through his potency. It was no use against *this* enemy. They drifted together, two big dark-haired broad-shouldered men, then exploded apart. Yggur skidded out of the pavilion across the gritty floor. There he came face to face with Mendark, standing four steps up the stair.

Mendark could not have been more shocked, more dismayed. This he had never expected, could not have prepared himself for. Yggur, equally surprised, recovered quickly and burst out laughing. He moved sideways so that his back was to the wall, so that he could see Mendark and Tensor at the same time. When Yggur raised his hand, Mendark could not stop himself from flinching.

Yggur felt that surge of power again. His self-confidence was back. Thurkad was Mendark's; it – and, he suddenly realised, Maigraith – had sucked all the life out of him. But here he knew he was more than Mendark's equal.

He scanned the room, assessing the dangers – Mendark, Tensor and, somewhere in the fog, Faelamor. Better find out where. Then he noticed a curious glow over by one fireplace. He caught his breath. Could it be? he thought with growing excitement. Can this be *the place*?

And as he crept closer he was sure. Yes, it was the *rift*, the very place where Kandor had worked for so long – one of the most powerful sites in all Santhenar. It must have opened when he'd commanded the gate. Dare he go down? His fingers slid across the emerald in his pocket. It felt dead again, but down there he could charge it with such forces as not even Rulke could resist. That thought sobered him for a second. If Rulke came, a weapon of surpassing power would be required to overcome him. And this was it. Yggur knew he could do it now.

He looked around. None of his enemies was visible in the fog. Squeezing the emerald in his fist, he put his leg over the side of the pit and began to climb down.

The pavilion was empty but for Llian, and Karan could barely see him through the clouds of gushing saturated air. Now the fog cut him off. She went onto her belly and slithered up the steps. There were small puddles of condensed moisture on the floor.

'Are you all right?' she whispered, looking up at Llian from the floor. Water dripped from his chin onto her cheek.

'So far. What a tale I am going to tell!' He smiled his familiar lopsided grin, though it only lasted for a second. Poor Llian. Despite the bravado, she knew he was terrified. She wanted to take him in her arms.

Karan sawed at the tough ropes around his feet. Her knife was blunt; it seemed to take a long time. She stood up, sliding her small body up the length of him, keeping him and the column between her and Tensor. The contact was a comfort. She hacked at his wrist bonds. One came apart but the other resisted the knife.

Lightning flashed near the staircase. The visibility improved a little, the Aachim appearing out of the fog like a row of pillars. Thunder whip-cracked and small pieces of stone showered down from the ceiling. A fragment rang on the dome of the pavilion. For a moment Karan felt dizzy; then her vision cleared and through a gap in the mist she saw Yggur looming over Mendark. The vapours closed again, and with a massed shout Selial and her Aachim rushed the pavilion guard.'

The renegade Aachim stood firm, weapons clashed, somewhere Tensor roared, *'Hold them!'* and leapt out of the fog right into the pavilion with the black staff in his hand. Catching sight of Karan he thrust it at her like a spear. She weaved out of the way, the staff passing between her and Llian, and Tensor tossed her down the steps as if he was pitching hay. Llian struggled furiously but could not break the last bond.

Tensor clouted him over the ear with his free hand, dropping the staff to shout, 'Hold them, whatever it costs!'

He touched his new mirror back to life, trying to wrench the gate back to his will.

Abruptly the rushing wind, the belching mist was cut off. The inside of the pavilion went dark, an inky blue-black shadow. Swords clashed in the background, then fell silent as a note near the upper register of hearing skirled out from the space where the gate had been. Karan, still lying on the floor, put her hands over her ears. The note wailed up the register, making one ear ache, then went beyond her hearing. The whole pavilion rocked and disappeared. Everyone stared at the vacant space. Two seconds later the pavilion was there again, but rotated, for now Llian faced Karan from across it. It blinked out again, the music moaned and sobbed, the pavilion reappeared rocking on its foundations and a zephyr puffed from it. The gate was open once more.

But this breeze was not born in Thurkad. The air was bitterly cold and had a hard, metallic smell. The darkness blew away in the centre. Karan looked down a corridor so long there seemed no end to it. The light in the corridor was icy blue, like the cracks of a glacier.

The wind intensified until it howled out of the portal; icicles started to grow downward from the top of the pavilion. Karan's fingers ached from the cold. Tiny flakes of snow whirled around the ceiling of the chamber.

An ominous shadow began to crystallise in the ice-blue distance. Tensor whooped, lunged and lifted Llian bodily by the shirtfront. The half-sawn rope snapped. Holding him high, Tensor roared out his defiance.

'Come forth. Come to me! Pitlis, rise and see how I avenge you!'

He slowly raised his right fist. A golden halo sprang into life around it. Karan felt the hair stir on the back of her head. Faelamor wailed and suddenly became visible in mid-flight, racing for the protection of the broken wall.

Shand, appearing in the doorway, screamed, 'Get to shelter!' and disappeared again.

'Yes, get well clear,' Tensor said gently. 'What I did at the Conclave is nothing to what I will do here.'

The Aachim slowly backed away. Hintis was stretched up on the tips of his toes; his eyes seemed to have been sucked back into the middle of his head.

'No, Tensor,' he shouted. 'You swore!'

'*Ha!*' cried Tensor madly, the radiance rising like wisps of steam from his fist.

The whole room could feel the potency building. Llian clutched his temples; his head felt about to explode.

Tensor raised Llian even higher, mouthing some unheard formula. The shadow within the gate advanced till it was only a couple of spans away but it seemed to hesitate, afraid. Tensor's fist flared, Llian screamed, the shadow wavered. He screamed again, thrashing his arms and legs, biting his tongue till bloody foam dripped from his mouth.

Karan felt the feathery touch of the bewilderment that she had suffered at the Conclave. Tensor was toying with Rulke, but there were only seconds to act. She knew that this time the potency, once he let it fly at full power, focussed and amplified by the Gift within Llian, would kill her and everyone in the room. Before that, Llian would be jelly on the floor. His immunity could not save him from such power as this.

'Help!' Karan cried, levering herself to her feet, and Osseion, who had hitherto stood by Mendark, broke free and ran toward her, roaring and clubbing the paralysed Aachim out of the way with great swings of his fists. The diversion was just enough. Karan grabbed a broken lump of marble the size of a brick, bounded up the steps and, with both hands, hurled it full in Tensor's face.

There was a grotesque SNAP! Tensor reeled and dropped Llian. His arms windmilled the air; blood fountained from his nose. The shadow roared. A blast of frigid air blew out the glowing fist. Tensor slipped on the bloody floor and went to one knee, holding his arms up before him as the shadow grew in the gate. Karan tried to roll a stunned Llian out of the way but waves were bursting in her brain, blinding her. Then Osseion, blood dripping from a cut eyebrow, swept Llian up in one arm, Karan in the other, and leapt out of the pavilion.

Halfway across the room he dropped them both on their feet and screamed, 'Run!' They fled toward the dubious shelter of the stair.

Tensor forced up a feebly glowing fist and let fly the disintegrated fragments of his potency. A shockwave fled outwards, buffeting the snowflakes, knocking the Aachim over like pins. The room went dark.

A ruddy glow seeped from the hearth. The shadow swelled and shrank in the lesser darkness. Tensor choked; the potency failed. Suddenly the gloom inside the pavilion was rent by a jagged flash, like lightning, and there came a triple boom like the laughter of a giant. Tensor staggered backwards and fell down the steps. The pavilion, undamaged through all the previous conflict, went momentarily translucent, faded completely before becoming solid again.

The air in the chamber grew ever colder, swirling out and up, searing them with each breath. The gate was empty. Then with a thunder of rushing wind a dark figure appeared in the centre, black hair flowing, black beard bristling, carmine eyes glowing. He was more than massive – a giant of a man whose head pressed up the domed ceiling of the pavilion. There were fetters about his chest and legs, heavy chains, but now trailing out behind him like scarves in the wind. He stepped forward, bursting the irons, flinging them away. The stone burst into flames where they fell.

Rulke came, more powerful than ever, and no one could control him. A second flash split the pavilion down the middle. The front part fell into rubble around him, just three columns and the metal dome remaining, framing him from behind.

Tensor looked around wildly, his beard smoking with

blood, noble nose flattened against his face. The potency had failed; Llian was gone and now the aftersickness began its excruciation. His courage could not withstand all that. Tensor broke, clawing his way across the room, desperate to get away.

Rulke advanced toward them, force irresistible. He was dressed in black on black; a scarlet cloak flared from his shoulders; ebony boots sheathed him to the knees. He looked around the room, seeking out his enemies.

Karan heard a low whistle, like a kettle steaming, that grew and swelled to a roar that shook the floor. Abruptly the glow at the hearth was blacked out as a dark figure shot out of the hole, soaring through the air as if the streaming cape was a wing. Yggur landed on his feet, bounced, then thrust his fist up to the heavens. Shards of light burst out of the emerald, splinters of pain in their eyes.

'Meet your doom, Rulke!' he cried, his face almost splitting open in his glee, and hurled the stone at his enemy.

Rulke stood frozen as the crystal tumbled toward him, end over end. Then at the last moment he snatched the emerald out of the air. The light grew so bright that it shone right through his fingers, muddy green. Rulke enclosed it in mighty fists, writhing as if the emerald was white-hot. He squeezed it ever tighter, doubling over and pressing his hands into his stomach.

'*Thar ng Caxit!*' Yggur roared, in a forgotten tongue. 'Burn him! Burn my enemy to char!'

The emerald flared so brightly that the bones of Rulke's skeleton could be seen. He shrieked, he wept, almost torn apart by the power of the emerald, but he did not let go.

Yggur stood like a frozen runner, one arm forward, one foot in the air. He reached blindly into his belt for a knife to deliver the *coup de grâce*. Then Rulke's whisper grew as he found the words of the counterspell. His face was shockingly twisted; smoke rose from his hands. The glee began to fade from Yggur's face.

There was a brittle smash. Rulke opened his hands. Emerald sand rustled to the floor. He stood up on his toes, yelling out his pain and his exultation.

Yggur dropped the knife and began to back away. 'It didn't work,' he said uncomprehendingly. 'Why didn't it work?'

'This is a Charon place,' Rulke said impatiently. 'Kandor found the rift, built the Great Tower on it and tapped its power for two thousand years. How arrogant you are, *old human*, to think you can just walk in and use it! How ignorant!'

He clenched his smoking fist. Yggur gave a vast bubbling cry of agony and convulsed on the floor, trying to tie himself in a knot. He arched his back, tore at his hair as though attempting to rid himself of something that clung to his skull, but it tightened its multi-clawed grip on him, overarched the sting and struck him in the throat.

44

THE BIRTHRIGHT

Karan's head hurt. Everyone in the room was stricken by aftersickness from the power that had been used there. No one had the courage to oppose Rulke: not Mendark, not Yggur, not Faelamor, not Tensor. Across the room the Aachim stood in a tight knot, holding each other up against the after-effects of Tensor's potency, weak though it had been. They were leaning forward together as if trying to stand against a gale. Desperately afraid, they had no answer to Rulke, just waited for his blow to strike them. How many times had the Charon mastered them before?

Yggur was writhing on the floor. Karen recalled the first time she had met him. It had been in Fiz Gorgo half a year ago, when she had stolen the Mirror. Yggur had shown no mercy then and his strength had been terrible. Never had she feared anyone so much. In a flash of insight she saw Maigraith weeping. They were lovers. Surely there must be some good in him.

She leapt up on the stair rail and cried out in a ringing voice, 'Together! We must attack him together. He cannot resist us all.'

Rulke whirled to see whence came this new nuisance. As he did so, Faelamor stood up. That seemed to shock him.

He had not known that *she* was there, did not want to risk himself against *her*. He hesitated.

'Together!' Faelamor echoed.

She ran down the steps, calling out in the melodious, lilting language that was the speech of the Faellem. Rulke stopped, looking this way and that, unsure which adversary would strike first. She crossed directly before him and Karan held her breath, thinking that Faelamor was going to overpower him without effort. Could it all be this easy?

It was not. Faelamor ran with quick short steps straight past Rulke, the Mirror in one hand. She gained the ruined pavilion and it instantly shimmered with ghost fire. The gate remained open! Everyone stared at her, unable to believe that she would abandon them. Tensor shook his head, levering himself to his knees.

'The Mirror is mine!' he cried thickly. 'You shall not have it.' He reached out to her with his long fingers and the Mirror clattered to the floor.

Faelamor leapt after it but it slipped further away and, no matter how she strained, she could not reach it. She shrieked, such was her desperation to get the Mirror back, but though she stretched until it seemed her shoulder would come out of its socket, it kept sliding away, then Rulke put his boot on it. Shaking with aftersickness, she began to speak the syllables of another illusion. Tensor put his hand up and it flared a bilious green.

'No!' he cried, spitting blood. 'I will reduce you to an atom. No Faellem can stand against this.'

Faelamor was beaten – Karan could see that. He could strike her before her miserable illusion was complete and this time Faelamor would die. She backed away into the pavilion. Rulke watched her with narrowed eyes. Her foot skidded on a piece of stone, a fragment of the gate. Snatching it, Faelamor peered into the new mirror on the bracket, wrenched the gate to her destination and with a soft little pop she was gone.

Rulke had been watching the disarray of his enemies with a pained smile. 'Three down!' he said softly. Pink fluid dripped from his burned fingers.

He flung out his arm, the dome of the pavilion glowed red and blue, sailed off and clattered across the floor, spinning like a top. One of the remaining columns toppled, leaving two standing. He turned, making his outstretched right hand into a fist, grimacing at the pain. Yggur, who had lain silent all this time, screamed. Rulke directed his other hand out towards Tensor, who fell to his knees, his mouth gaping though he was incapable of sound. He reached forth in supplication.

No one dared to move. Yggur's helpless cry struck right through Karan. How contemptible were the Aachim, who did not even have the courage to defend each other? If no one else dares, I must, she said to herself, feeling at her belt. In a blinding movement she hurled her knife at Rulke.

Rulke whirled at the sudden movement and threw up his hand, but he had been too long in the Nightland. His reflexes were dull. The knife went straight though the palm of his hand and wedged between the bones. His face became incredibly cold, though whether from pain that he could hardly have felt in a thousand years, or from humiliation, it was impossible to tell.

He shivered, dropping the bloody hand to his side, clutching as if the knife had gone in there. He stared through Karan, looking back over forty centuries.

'Two cuts, Elienor! Any but you.' He was lost, then his eyes slowly focussed. *'Who are you?'* he whispered. 'You are not Elienor at all. You are not even Aachim.'

'I am Karan Elienor Melluselde Fyrn and I come from Gothryme,' she replied. 'Not Aachim, yet I am of her line.'

'Karan,' he smiled, though not pleasantly. 'That is good. *Elienor* was ever safe from me. So, *this* is your semblance! When I followed you before, I thought you tall and dark with a beak for a nose and feet like paddles. I knew you from the inside, but never did I guess that you would have *her* likeness. Had I realised, I would not have used you. But done is done. I have a greater use for you yet. Come here!'

He flicked his wrist, the knife clattered to the floor and a spray of red spattered the room. Everywhere a drop fell on flesh, it seared. Shouting a word, the stone steps on which Karan and Llian stood crumbled to powder, flinging them down. He took a step towards them. Karan was defenceless. Had he wished it he could have embedded her in the wall.

His foot kicked the Mirror that Faelamor had abandoned. Rulke bent swiftly to pick it up. He looked at it long and hard, while Karan held her breath, wondering what he saw there. It was clear that he did see, for the reflections flickered on his face. Then he cast it aside.

'A toy – a trinket of the Aachim!' he said contemptuously. 'What need have I of such clumsy devices – I have a better. Ah, but it is good that I came – *you* are just what I need for my project.' He stared at Karan and Llian, and each feared for the other.

'How fortunate that I did not slay you just then, little Karan. Come to me. I can use *you*.' Rulke's eyes seemed to glow the way Karan remembered from her dreams of long ago.

He stepped toward her and Karan backed away, looking around frantically for Llian. He was supporting himself against a block of stone behind her, holding a knee gashed from the fall. She took his hand and they back-pedalled through the rubble around the room. Silence, but for the shuffle of their feet against the gritty floor. Rulke advanced, head and shoulders and chest above her, twice her width, three times her bulk. His hands were huge; with the fingers spread they could have enveloped her skull. He moved noiselessly, though the sound of his breathing carried through the room.

Karan was terribly afraid. Just then her boot skidded on something and, looking down, she saw that she'd trodden on her blade, lying where Rulke had flung it. She dived for the knife.

She almost got it. The bloody handle burned her fingertips, but an unseen force skidded it out of reach. Llian pulled her to her feet and they continued their backward dance.

'Stay!' Rulke said. 'What use this game? You are mine.'

She did not stop. She could see a faint halo between the two columns that were all that remained of the pavilion, and the glimmering of a plan came to her. If there was no other escape she would flee to Thurkad as Faelamor had done.

'*Stay!*' he thundered, and Karan was frozen to the spot. What could she do? She realised that Tensor was just to her left. Was there anything left of him?

'Tensor!' she cried. 'Remember that day, twelve years ago, when all the Sentinels in Shazmak rang at once? You came to the gate of Shazmak and found on your doorstep a shabby proud girl. She said to you then, "I have come home" and you picked her up and held her in your arms. I am that girl, Tensor, and I love you still. Do you not care for me?' She reached out her arms to him.

Rulke was looking on with amusement and now he laughed. 'Better you asked that question before smashing his nose in,' he roared.

Her plea struck through the aftersickness, waking Tensor to his folly and his shame. Suddenly he broke and jumped between Karan and Rulke, swinging his arm like a wheel. But the aftersickness betrayed him; he was slow as senility, slow as death.

Rulke struck him aside with contemptuous savagery. Tensor fell to his knees, broken by the blow, his big frame misshapen. He tried to rise again and even caught Rulke by the leg, but was hurled away like an attacking dog. Karan wept, began to run to Tensor's aid, then stopped. Rulke blocked her way. She was trapped! Tensor lay still. His eyes looked up at her but he could not move. 'Leave me,' he whispered. 'Save yourself!'

She looked around desperately. Everyone stood paralysed, coming neither to Tensor's aid nor her own. 'Please, someone!'

No one dared to move after Tensor's brutal fate. Karan clutched Llian's hand, dragging him backwards, her eye darting this way and that. Nowhere to go. She saw Shand in the doorway. Old Shand, who consistently denied that he had power, but always seemed to be able to do something in an emergency.

Shand looked beaten now, though. He was sagging against the door, spent from his previous defence of her. How could she ask him to do more? But someone had to.

'Shand,' she pleaded. 'Help me!'

Shand pushed himself away from the wall. Rulke turned, drew back his shoulders, spread his legs and smiled scornfully.

'Help her, old man, if you dare. *Blast me to ruin!*'

Shand's face nearly cracked in half with the effort, the agony. Finally he achieved something with his hands. The floor vibrated but nothing further happened.

'Try again, you old fool,' shouted Rulke, laughing himself to scorn. He turned back to Karan.

He might have reached out and touched her, but he seemed to be enjoying the chase, taking pleasure in baiting her, in driving her just where he wanted her. She stepped up onto the platform and came up against that halo that still clung to the rubble. At once a bright light flared between the columns.

Why not? Karan thought. There's nowhere else to go.

'Karan, don't!' cried Shand from across the room.

He spoke too late. Rulke lunged at Karan and she jumped backwards into the waiting gate, dragging Llian with her. It flared brightly, two brief pulses, and boomed them away before fading to nothing.

For a moment no one moved. Rulke began to laugh again, a deep rich sound.

'Did they know where the gate has taken them, they might have been less willing to enter it,' he said, wiping his eyes.

'Truce, Mendark!' whispered Yggur at the same time. 'You can atone for your ancient crime. Help me!'

Mendark had been trying to look weak and insignificant, biding his time, waiting for the opportunity when Rulke was off guard. Now he saw it. Mendark knew how to free Yggur of Rulke's hold; in fact he had always known, and that was at the root of the hatred between the two. But neither hated each other as much as they feared Rulke.

Slipping up behind Yggur, Mendark put his fingers to the sides of his head. His fingers appeared to slide right through the skull. Yggur's face went blank and he slumped down, groaning nonsense.

Mendark drew upon knowledge long forgotten, powers that had not been used since the time of the Experiments. He reached deep into Yggur's mind and did what he should have done back then – he tore out the poisoned spike, severing the mind-forged manacles that had shackled Yggur ever since.

'Yggur!' Mendark whispered. 'Now's our chance.'

Yggur shook his head, dazed, weak. He was free at last, free as he had never been since that distant time. But he did not move. Nothing could hold him back now but his own fears, and hold him back they did – the nightmare could not be overcome that easily. He trembled in Mendark's arms.

Mendark, realising that the opportunity was nearly lost, let Yggur fall and sprang to his feet. He was terrified but he did not show it. Rulke was many times his equal, if he was ready for the conflict. But maybe he wasn't.

He stepped over Yggur to face his enemy, the bravest thing he would ever do. Taking a deep breath, struggling for control, he raised his hand and cried out in a harsh voice, 'Rulke! Come, test your courage on me. You hesitate? Then feel *this*!'

Rulke was jerked right around. He stumbled, off-balance, and Mendark let fly a blast that sent him reeling backwards. Rulke recovered quickly, spoke a word and Mendark's arms and legs began to twitch convulsively. His feet danced wildly, faster and faster until they were no more than a blur.

He screamed then with a wrench took back command of his limbs. He issued a counterspell which made sweat break out on Rulke's forehead. Rulke tried to break back, an effort that made him clutch at his heart.

Mendark went white under the strain, staggered and slipped to one knee. 'Come on!' he screeched to the rest of the company as he hauled himself up again. He took another step toward Rulke, looking as commanding as he must have done in his prime.

At this the others, sensing that the tide had turned, began to draw in around him. Crippled Tensor was on his knees, but he too raised his arm. Yggur, still dazed, forced himself to his feet. Mendark lifted him while Osseion stood on his other side, almost as big as Rulke. Even the terrified Aachim seemed to have gained some courage. Shand supported himself in the doorway, watching and waiting.

Rulke hesitated. The balance was tipping against him. He could not allow himself to be caught unprepared, surrounded by *all* his enemies. He began to back away, perhaps understanding that they had no plan. Maybe they were not ready for the great confrontation either and he could escape as long as they did not realise their advantage. The Nightland was broken. *He was free!* That was all that mattered. The battle would take place another time, another place. Rulke leapt backwards towards the ruined gate.

'He's weak!' Shand shouted. 'Attack him, all together.'

Mendark was fastest. He sent the new mirror spinning from its bracket, flying across the room so hard that it crumpled when it struck the wall. The gate was useless without it.

Rulke ducked between the two standing columns, sending them toppling backwards at his pursuers, leapt over the rubble pile and fled up the stairs. Once again Mendark took control. 'After him!' he shouted, barely avoiding a falling column, and sprinted like a young man. The others followed – Yggur and Osseion, a swarm of Aachim and then Shand. Two Aachim came more slowly, carrying Tensor on an improvised litter.

Halfway up Rulke began to falter – the Nightland had sapped him. On the twelfth level they almost had him, but he crumbled part of the wall down at them and raced upwards.

Osseion clambered over the rubble. 'Hold it!' shouted Mendark, gasping for breath. 'You're not his match. We must stay together.'

A thousand steps later they reached the top – a lurching, staggering band. The door was wedged shut. 'Smash it!' Mendark gasped. Eight shoulders struck it such a blow that it was flung open. Rulke was at an embrasure on the other side, looking out, his great chest rising and falling like a bellows.

'There's no way down,' shouted Mendark. 'You're trapped! Give yourself up!'

Rulke laughed in despair, spitting furies that curdled the rock of the walls. The platinum dome began to sag like latex.

They held back until Tensor's panting bearers appeared at the door. 'All as one,' Mendark cried. 'Now!'

This time their courage did not fail them. Finding strength in their hatred and rage, they exerted their combined power in a great blast of light that focussed right on Rulke's chest and flung him, arms and legs beating the air, straight through the embrasure.

They gave a ragged cheer, dumbfounded at their sudden success. 'It was easy when we stood together,' said Yggur.

'He can't survive,' said Mendark, his face lit up in exultation. The victory was his and it was very sweet. Let them call him a failure now! 'The fall will kill him, though he be Charon.'

'Too easy,' said Shand, limping across the room.

They hobbled to the embrasure to watch the fall and witness the death, but found that it was not the end of him after all. Rulke was clinging one-handed to one of the great

644

pennant poles. His face was bright with the agony of his burned hands and there were knots in his arms and legs, but he looked them in the eye, one after another.

'Hear the foretelling retold,' he said so softly that they had to strain their ears to hear him over the whistling wind.

When the dark moon is full on mid-winter's day, I will be back. I will crack the Forbidding and open the Way between the Worlds. No one has the power to stay me. The Three Worlds will be Charon evermore.

They all looked out, but the moon had already set. It was only a few days off being full, but presently none of the dark side was showing. Shand said in reply:

Break down the golden horn,
Wish the glass unmade,
Fear the thrice born,
But beware the thrice betrayed.

Rulke's face was unreadable. Mendark stretched out his arm, so weak that he had to support his elbow with his other hand. Pointing to the base of the pole that held Rulke above the abyss, Mendark groaned an oath. The pole cracked and failed, just as the other one had only days ago.

Rulke let go to hang in the middle air, seeming to defy gravity for a moment. The pole dropped away from him. Then he fell, faster and faster, and every eye watched his progress toward the hard metal rail of the bridge far below. But before he reached it he threw up his arms, his clenched fists met above his head, making an 'O', the same blue-black darkness that had heralded his arrival burst out in all directions and Rulke vanished.

Mendark was peering over the side. 'What happened?' he asked. 'I lost sight of him.'

'He's gone,' said Tallia, whose eyesight was keen.

'The Nightland has drawn him back,' croaked the crippled Tensor.

'Then nothing has been achieved from your folly,' Selial said bitterly.

'Less than nothing. He is stronger; we are ruined. I take the name til-Pitlis. I name myself the worst traitor and the biggest fool of all time.'

The company stared at each other, then every one of them looked to Shand, wondering about Rulke's prophecy and his reply. The dark face of the moon, blotched black and purple and red, was an ill-omen. Only rarely was it turned completely towards Santhenar on mid-winter's day, hythe. But a *full dark* moon in hythe – no one could recall when that had last happened. No one knew what Rulke's words signified, or Shand's reply, and Shand said no more.

'Let us go,' cried Mendark. 'Katazza is finished.'

They turned away down the interminable stairs, suffering cruelly the pangs of aftersickness. At the bottom, as they passed by the ruins of his gate, Tensor groaned and stirred on his litter. 'Bring the Mirror to my hand. Do not leave *it* here. I must have it.'

'You fool,' cried Selial, shaking with rage. 'Will you not die? I will throttle you myself before I let you put your finger to it.'

Old Shand went across and took up the Mirror, which still lay where Rulke had cast it. 'I will take charge of this,' he said, 'in memory of the one whose birthright it was.'

He put it in his pocket, and though everyone wondered at his words, none disputed him.

THE END
OF VOLUME TWO

VOLUME THREE
DARK IS THE MOON

continues the novel

GLOSSARY

of Characters, Names and Places

Aachan: One of the Three Worlds, the world of the Aachim and, after its conquest, the Charon.

Aachim: The human species native to Aachan, who were conquered by the Charon. The Aachim are a clever people, great artisans and engineers, but melancholy and prone to hubris. After they were brought to Santhenar the Aachim flourished, but were betrayed and ruined in the Clysm, and withdrew from the world to their vast mountain fortress cities.

Aachimning: A friend of the Aachim.

Aftersickness: Sickness that people suffer after using the Secret Art, or being close when someone else uses such power, or even after using a native talent. Sensitives are very prone to it.

Alcifer: The last and greatest of Rulke's cities, designed by Pitlis the Aachim.

Almadin: A dry land across the sea from Thurkad.

Aoife: The master shaper who made the Mirror. She gave it to the young Tensor for his outgift, or graduation prize.

Ashmode: An ancient town looking over the Dry Sea.

Asper the healer: An Aachim, one of Tensor's company.

Asrail: Daughter of Ulice, a tavern-keeper in Thurkad who is an old friend of Shand.

Assembly: The puppet government of Thurkad, dominated

by the Magister on the one hand and the Governor of the city on the other.

Bannador: A long, narrow and hilly land on the western side of Iagador. Karan's homeland.

Basitor: A bitter Aachim who survived the sacking of Shazmak.

Berenet: The second of Mendark's chief lieutenants, a dandy.

Blase: One of Tensor's Aachim band.

Blending: A child of the union between two of the four different human species. Blendings are rare, and often deranged, but can have remarkable talents.

Blustard: A drunkard who knows everything going on in Thurkad.

Booreah Ngurle: The burning mountain, or fiery mountain, a volcanic peak in the forests east of Almadin. The Charon once had a stronghold there.

Calendar: Santhenar's year is roughly 395.7 days and contains twelve months, each of thirty-three days.

Chaike: One of Yggur's officers, a thin nervous man.

Chain of the Tychid: A ribbon of seven very bright stars and many fainter ones, visible in the winter sky at southern latitudes.

Chanthed: A town in northern Meldorin, in the foothills of the mountains. The College of the Histories is there.

Chard: A kind of tea.

Charon: One of the four human species, the master people of the world of Aachan. They fled out of the void to take Aachan from the Aachim, and took their name from a frigid moonlet at the furthest extremity of the void. They have strange eyes, indigo or carmine, or sometimes both together, depending on the light.

Chert: One of Pender's crew on *The Dancing Goose*.

Chronicler: A historian. A graduate in the art and science of recording and maintaining the Histories.

Citadel: The Magister's palace in Thurkad, an enormous fortified building.

Cloak, **cloaked**: To disguise oneself by means of illusion.

Clysm: A series of wars between the Charon and the Aachim beginning around 1500 years ago, resulting in the almost total devastation of Santhenar.

College of the Histories: The oldest of the colleges for the instruction of those who would be chroniclers or tellers of the Histories, or even lowly bards or king's singers. It was set up at Chanthed soon after the time of the Forbidding.

Compulsion: A form of the Secret Art; a way of forcing someone to do something against their will.

Conclave: A forum held in Thurkad to resolve some crisis. It is arbitrated by the Just, a selected group of judges or high officials. The last Conclave was held to resolve the ownership of the Mirror, but Tensor used his potency and stole it.

Construct: A machine partly powered by the Secret Art.

Council; also **Council of Iagador**, **Council of Santhenar**, **Great Council**, **High Council**: An alliance of the powerful. With the Aachim it made the Nightland and cast Rulke into it. After that it had two purposes – to continue the great project and to maintain the watch upon Rulke.

Dancing Goose, The: Pender's second boat.

Darsh: An untranslatable Aachim epithet (very offensive).

Dirhan: Customs officer in Sith and friend to Pender and his estranged wife Hassien.

Dolodha: A messenger girl; one of Yggur's servants.

Elienor: A great heroine of the Aachim from the time when the Charon invaded Aachan.

Elludore: A large forested land, north of Thurkad.

Emmant: A half-Aachim, librarian at Shazmak, who conceived a violent lust for Karan and attacked her. She killed him in Thurkad.

Faelamor: Leader of the Faellem species who came to Santhenar soon after Rulke, to keep watch on the Charon and maintain the balance between the worlds. Maigraith's liege.

Faellem: The human species who inhabit the world of Tallallame. They are a small, dour people who are forbidden to use machines and particularly magical devices, but are masters of disguise and illusion. Faelamor's band were trapped on Santh by the Forbidding, and constantly search for a way home.

Farsh: A mild obscenity.

Festival of Chanthed: An annual festival held in Chanthed in the autumn, at which the Histories are told by the masters and students of the College.

Fiz Gorgo: A fortress city in Orist, flooded in ancient times, now restored; the stronghold of Yggur.

Flute; also **golden flute**: A device made in Aachan at the behest of Rulke by the genius smith Shuthdar. It was subsequently stolen by him and taken back to Santhenar. When used by one who is sensitive, it could be used to open the Way between the Worlds. It was destroyed by Shuthdar at the time of the Forbidding.

Forbidding: See *Tale of the Forbidding*.

Fyrn: The family name of Karan of Bannador, from her mother's side.

Gah: An insulting term for one of the old human species, who are generally considered to be inferiors.

Galardil: A forested land, east of Orist.

Galliad: Karan's father, who was half-Aachim. He was killed when Karan was a child.

Gannel: A river beginning near Chanthed and flowing through the mountains to the sea at Ganport.

Garr, **Garrflood**: The largest river in Meldorin. It arises west of Shazmak and runs to the Sea of Thurkad east of Sith.

Gate: A structure, controlled by the Secret Art, which permits people to move instantly from one place to another.

Gellon: A fruit tasting something between a mango and a peach.

Ghâshâd: The ancient, mortal enemies of the Aachim. They were corrupted and swore allegiance to Rulke after the Zain rebelled two thousand years ago, but when Rulke was put in the Nightland a thousand years later they forgot their destiny and took a new name, Whelm. They sacked Shazmak just before the Conclave.

Gift of Rulke; also **Curse of Rulke**: Knowledge given by Rulke to the Zain, enhancing their resistance to the mind-breaking potencies of the Aachim. It left stigmata that identified them as Zain.

Glass: Colloquial term for the Mirror of Aachan.

Gothryme: Karan's impoverished manor near Tolryme in Bannador.

Granewys: A miserable coastal town north of Thurkad.

Graspers: Moneylenders.

Great Betrayer: Rulke.

Great Library: Founded at Zile by the Zain in the time of the Empire of Zur. The library was sacked several times, but subsequently re-established.

Great Mountains: The largest and highest belt of mountains on Santhenar, enclosing the south-eastern part of the continent of Lauralin.

Great Project: A way sought by the Council to banish the Charon from Santh forever.

Great Tales: The greatest stories from the Histories of Santhenar; traditionally told at the Festival of Chanthed, and on important ceremonial occasions throughout Santhenar. A tale can become a Great Tale only by the unanimous decision of the master chroniclers. In four thousand years only twenty-two Great Tales have ever been made.

Grint: A copper coin of small value.

Gyllias: The Recorder.

Hakasha-ka-najisska: A forbidden potency (mind-blasting spell) developed by the Aachim against the Charon. Zain carrying the Gift of Rulke are immune to it.

Hassien: Pender's wife, who left him in Sith.

Hennia: A Zain. She is a member of the Council of Iagador.

Hintis: An extremely tall Aachim with woolly hair.

Histories, The: The vast collection of records which tell more than four thousand years of recorded history on Santhenar. The Histories consist of historical documents written or held by the chroniclers, as well as the tales, songs, legends and lore of the peoples of Santhenar and the invading peoples from the other worlds, told by the tellers. The culture of Santhenar is interwoven with and inseparable from the Histories and the most vital longing anyone can have is to be mentioned in them.

Hlune: The lanky people who rule the wharf city of Thurkad and control all ship-borne commerce there.

Huling's Tower: The place where the golden flute was destroyed.

Human species: There are four distinct human species: the Aachim of Aachan, the Faellem of Tallallame, the old humans of Santhenar and the Charon who came out of the void. All but old humans can be very long-lived. Matings between the different species rarely produce children (see **blending**).

Hythe: Mid-winter's day, the fourth day of endre, mid-winter week. Hythe is a day of particular ill-omen.

Iagador: The land that lies between the mountains and the Sea of Thurkad.

Idlis: The least of the Whelm, a healer and longtime hunter of Karan and the Mirror. He became Ghâshâd and went to Shazmak.

Iennis: One of Tensor's Aachim.

Jark-un: The leader of a band of the Whelm, once rival to Vartila, but now a Ghâshâd.

Jepperand: A province on the western side of the mountains of Crandor. Home to the Zain; Llian's birthplace.

Jevi (**Jevander**): Lilis's father, taken by a press-gang seven years ago.

Kandor: One of the three Charon who came to Santhenar. He was killed sometime after the end of the Clysm, the only Charon to die on Santh.

Karama Malama: The Sea of Mists, south of the Sea of Thurkad.

Karan: A woman of the house of Fyrn, but with blood of the Aachim from her father, Galliad, and old human and Faellem blood from her mother. This makes her triune, though she does not know it. She is also a sensitive and lives at Gothryme.

Lake Neid: A lake in the swamp forest near Fiz Gorgo, where the half-submerged ruins of the town of Neid are found.

Lar: An honorific used in Thurkad.

Lasee: A pale-yellow brewed drink, mildly intoxicating, and ubiquitous in Orist; fermented from the sweet sap of the sard tree.

Lauralin: The continent east of the Sea of Thurkad.

League: About 5000 paces, three miles or five kilometres.

Librarian: Nadiril the Sage. He is also a member of the Council of Iagador.

Library of the Histories: The famous library at the College of the Histories in Chanthed.

Lightglass: A device made of crystal and metal that emits light after being touched.

Lilis: A street urchin and guide in Thurkad, whose father Jevi was press-ganged.

Link, **Linking**; also **Talent of Linking**: A joining of minds, by which thoughts and feelings can be shared, and support given. Sometimes used for domination.

Llian: A Zain from Jepperand. He is a master chronicler and a teller. A great student of the Histories.

Magister: A mancer and chief of the Council. Mendark has been Magister for a thousand years, save for a brief period when illegally overthrown by Thyllan.

Maigraith: An orphan brought up and trained by Faelamor for some unknown purpose. She is a master of the Secret Art.

Malien: An Aachim, Rael's mother; once consort of Tensor.

Malkin: Temporary leader of the Assembly of Thurkad, a flabby coward.

Mancer: A wizard or sorcerer; someone who is a master of the Secret Art.

Mantille: An Aachim; Karan's paternal grandmother.

Master chronicler: One who has mastered the study of the Histories and graduated with highest honour from the College.

Master of Chanthed: Currently Wistan; the Master of the College of the Histories is also nominal leader of Chanthed.

Meldorin: The large island that lies to the immediate west of the Sea of Thurkad and the continent of Lauralin.

Mendark: Magister of the Council of Iagador, until thrown down by Thyllan. A mancer of strength and subtlety, though lately insecure due to the rise of his longtime enemy, Yggur.

Mirror of Aachan: A device made by the Aachim in Aachan for seeing things at a distance. In Santhenar it changed and twisted reality and so the Aachim hid it away. It also developed a memory, retaining the imprints of things it had seen. Stolen by Yalkara, the Mirror was used by her to find a warp in the Forbidding and escape back to Aachan.

Moon: The moon revolves around Santhenar about every thirty days. However one side (the dark face) is blotched red and black by volcanic activity, and because the moon rotates on its axis much more slowly, the dark face is fully turned towards Santh only every couple of months. This rarely coincides with a full moon but when it does, it is a time of ill-omen.

Nadiril: The head of the Great Library and a member of the Council.

Narne: A town and port at the navigable extremity of the Garr.

Nazhak tel Mardux: A book of Aachim tales which Llian committed to memory in Shazmak.

Nelissa: A member of the Council and Prime Just of the Great Conclave; she was killed by Tensor's potency.

Nightland: A place, distant from the world of reality, wherein Rulke is kept prisoner. Rulke attempted to use the power of the city-construct Alcifer to break the Forbidding, but it failed. The Council used the Proscribed Experiments to force Rulke into a bubble formed out of the wall of the Forbidding, which subsequently became the Nightland.

Nilkerrand: A fortified city across the sea from Thurkad. Thyllan's refuge.

Old human: The original human species on Santhenar and by far the most numerous.

Orist: A land of swamps and forests on the south-west side of Meldorin; Yggur's fortress city of Fiz Gorgo is there.

Orstand: A justice and member of the Council. Mendark's oldest friend.

Osseion: The captain of Mendark's guard, a huge dark man.

Pender: A masterly sailor who carried Karan and Llian from Narne downriver to Sith, then on to Thurkad.

Perion, Empire of: Kandor's empire, which collapsed after the Sea of Perion dried up.

Pidgon: An estuarine jellyfish, only edible if you are desperate.

Pitlis: A great Aachim of the distant past, whose folly betrayed the great city of Tar Gaarn to Rulke and broke the power of the Aachim. The architect who designed Tar Gaarn and Alcifer, he was slain by Rulke.

Port Cardasson: The port of Thurkad.

Portal: See **gate**.

Potency: An all-powerful, mind-breaking spell developed by the Aachim as a weapon against the Charon, but effective against all but those Zain who bear the Gift of Rulke.

Proscribed Experiments: Sorcerous procedures designed to find a flaw in the Forbidding which could be used to banish Rulke forever. Hazardous because of the risk of Rulke taking control of the experimenter.

Rael: An Aachim, half-cousin to Karan, son of Malien and Tensor. He was drowned helping Karan to escape from Shazmak.

Read: Truth-reading. A way of forcing someone to tell the whole truth.

Recorder: The person who set down the tales of the four great battles of Faelamor and Yalkara, among many other tales. He is thought to have taken the Mirror (after Yalkara finally defeated Faelamor and fled Santh) and hidden it against some future need. His name was Gyllias.

Rula: The Magister before Mendark. She was regarded as the greatest of all.

Rulke: A Charon of Aachan. He enticed Shuthdar to Aachan to make the golden flute, and so began all the troubles. After the Clysm he was imprisoned in the Nightland until a way could be found to banish him back to Aachan.

Runck: A sewer swab.

Rustible: One of Pender's crew on *The Waif*.

Santhenar, **Santh**: The least of the Three Worlds, original home of the old human peoples.

Sard tree: A tall tree that dominates the swamp forests of

Orist. Its papery bark is used for writing scrolls and its sweet sap for brewing lasee.

S'Courcy: A villain who controls the labyrinthine back streets and underworld of Thurkad. A sickly, bloated spider of a man.

Sea of Thurkad: The long sea that divides Meldorin from the continent of Lauralin.

Secret Art: The use of magical or sorcerous powers (mancing). An art that very few can use and then only after considerable training. Notable mancers include Mendark, Yggur, Maigraith, Rulke, Tensor and Faelamor, though each has quite different strengths and weaknesses. Tallia has much skill but as yet insufficient training.

Selial: An Aachim woman, leader of the Syndics in Shazmak, who escaped after the city's fall.

Sending: A message, thoughts or feelings sent from one mind to another.

Sentinels: Devices that keep watch and sound an alarm.

Shalah: A young Aachim woman, twin to Xarah.

Shand: An old man who works at the inn at Tullin and is more than he seems.

Shazmak: The forgotten city of the Aachim, in the mountains west of Bannador. It was captured by the Ghâshâd, after they were woken from their long years as Whelm.

Shuthdar: An old human of Santhenar, the maker of the golden flute. After he destroyed the flute and himself, the Forbidding came down, closing the Way between the Worlds.

Siftah: A fishing town on the north-eastern coast of Meldorin.

Sith: A free city and trading nation built on an island in the River Garr, in southern Iagador.

Skeet: A carrier bird, grey or blue-grey. Large, ugly and ill-tempered.

Slukk: A Whelm epithet (very offensive).

Span: The distance spanned by the stretched arms of a tall man. About six feet, or slightly less than two metres.

Stassor: A city of the Aachim, in eastern Lauralin.

Sunias: An Aachim woman from Shazmak.

Syndics: A ruling Council of the Aachim, sometimes a panel of judges. None can lie to them in formal trial.

Tale of the Forbidding: Greatest of the Great Tales, it tells of the final destruction of the flute by Shuthdar more than 3000 years ago, and how the Forbidding sealed Santhenar off from the other two worlds.

Talent: A native skill or gift, usually honed by extensive training.

Tales of the Aachim: An ancient summary history of the Aachim, the *Nazhak tel Mardux*, was prepared soon after the founding of Shazmak. Llian read and memorised it in Shazmak so he could translate it later.

Tallallame: One of the Three Worlds, the world of the Faellem. A beautiful, mountainous world covered in forest.

Tallia bel Soon: One of Mendark's two chief lieutenants. She is a mancer and a master of combat with and without weapons. Tallia comes from Crandor.

Tar: A silver coin widely used in Meldorin. Enough to keep a family for several weeks.

Tar Gaarn: Principal city of the Aachim in the time of the Clysm; it was sacked by Rulke.

Tell: A gold coin to the value of twenty silver tars.

Teller: One who has mastered the ritual telling of the tales that form part of the Histories of Santhenar.

Telt: A small, timid people who live in the wharf city of Thurkad and are indentured for life to the Hlune.

Tensor: The leader of the Aachim. He sees it as his destiny to restore the Aachim and finally take their revenge on Rulke, who betrayed and ruined them. He is proud to the point of folly.

Terror-guard: Yggur's Whelm.

Tess, **Tessariel**: A fishing captain working out of Ganport.

Thel: One of Tensor's Aachim.

Three Worlds: Santhenar, Aachan and Tallallame.

Thurkad: An ancient, populous city on the River Saboth and the Sea of Thurkad, known for its wealth and corruption. Seat of the Council and the Magister.

Thyllan: Warlord of Iagador and member of the Council. He intrigued against Mendark and briefly overthrew him as Magister.

Tirthrax: The principal city of the Aachim, in the Great Mountains.

Tisane Mountain: A ghost-ridden place.

Tolryme: A small town in northern Bannador, close to Karan's family seat, Gothryme.

Torgsted: One of Mendark's guard. A cheerful, reliable fellow.

Triune: A double blending – one with the blood of three different human species. Triunes are extremely rare and almost always sterile. They may have remarkable abilities. Karan is one.

Troix: A river north of Thurkad.

Trule: An Aachim man of Tensor's band.

Tullin: A tiny village in the mountains south of Chanthed. Shand lives there.

Twisted Mirror: The Mirror of Aachan, made in Aachan in ancient times and given to Tensor, who smuggled it with him to Santhenar. Like all objects taken between the worlds, it changed and became treacherous. So called because it does not always show true.

Ulice: Proprietor of a cellar bar in Thurkad. She can procure anything, for a price.

Vartila: The leader of a band of the Whelm. She remained Whelm and served Yggur after most of her people reverted to Ghâshâd.

Voice: The ability of great tellers to move their audience to any emotion they choose by the sheer power of their words.

Void, the: The spaces between and beyond the Three Worlds. A Darwinian place where life is more brutal and fleeting than anywhere. The void teems with the most exotic life imaginable, for nothing survives there without remaking itself constantly.

Vuula Fyrn: Karan's mother, a lyrist. She committed suicide soon after Karan's father, Galliad, was killed.

Wahn Barre: The Crow Mountains. Yalkara, the Mistress of Deceits, had a stronghold there, Havissard. A place of ill-omen.

Waif, The: Pender's third boat, formerly a blacklisted smuggler's vessel, *Black Opal*.

Way between the Worlds: The secret, forever-changing and ethereal paths that permit the difficult passage between the Three Worlds. They were closed off by the Forbidding.

Whelm: Servants of Yggur, his terror-guard. See also **Ghâshâd**.

Wistan: The seventy-fourth Master of the College of the Histories and of Chanthed.

Xarah: A young Aachim woman, twin to Shalah.

Yalkara: The Demon Queen, the Mistress of Deceits. The last of the three Charon who came to Santhenar to find the flute and return it to Aachan. She took the Mirror and used it to find a warp in the Forbidding, then fled Santh, leaving the Mirror behind.

Yetchah: A young Whelm woman who hunted Llian from Chanthed to Tullin.

Yggur: A great and powerful Mancer. Formerly a member of the Council, he now lives in Fiz Gorgo. His armies have overrun most of southern Meldorin.

Zain: A scholarly race who once dwelt in Zile. They founded the Great Library about 3000 years ago. They made a pact with Rulke and after his fall most were slaughtered and the remnant exiled. They now dwell in Jepperand and make no alliances.

Zareth the Hlune: One of Yggur's lieutenants.

Zile: A city in the north-west of the island of Meldorin. Once capital of the Empire of Zur, now chiefly famous for the Great Library.

Zurean Empire: An ancient empire in the north of Meldorin. Its capital was Zile.

GUIDE TO PRONUNCIATION

There are many languages and dialects used on Santhenar by the four human species. While it is impossible to be definitive in such a brief note, the following generalisations normally apply.

There are no silent letters, and double consonants are generally pronounced as two separate letters; for example, *Yggur* is pronounced *Ig-ger*, and *Faellem* as *Fael-lem*. The letter *c* is usually pronounced as *k*, except in *mancer* and *Alcifer*, where it is pronounced as *s*, as in *manser*, *Alsifer*. The combination *ch* is generally pronounced as in *church*, except in *Aachim* and *Charon*, where it is pronounced as *k*.

Aachim Ar'-kim	**Chanthed** Chan-thed'
Charon Kar'-on	**Faelamor** Fay-el'-amor
Fyrn Firn	**Ghâshâd** G-harsh'-ard
Iagador Eye-aga'-dor	**Karan** Ka-ran'
Lasee Lar'-say	**Llian** Lee'-an
Maigraith May'-gray-ith	**Neid** Nee'-id
Rael Ray'-il	**Shuthdar** Shoo'-th-dar'
Whelm H'-welm	**Yggur** Ig'-ger
Xarah Zhá-rah	

**LOOK OUT FOR FURTHER VOLUMES
IN THIS SPELLBINDING SERIES:**

A SHADOW ON THE GLASS
Volume One of The View From The Mirror

DARK IS THE MOON
Volume Three of The View From The Mirror

THE WAY BETWEEN
THE WORLDS
Volume Four of The View From The Mirror

by Ian Irvine

Orbit titles available by post:

☐ A Shadow on the Glass	Ian Irvine	£6.99
☐ A Cavern of Black Ice	J.V. Jones	£7.99
☐ King's Dragon	Kate Elliott	£6.99
☐ Aurian	Maggie Furey	£5.99
☐ Colours in the Steel	K.J. Parker	£6.99
☐ The Thief's Gamble	Juliet E. McKenna	£5.99
☐ The Empire Stone	Chris Bunch	£10.99

The prices shown above are correct at time of going to press. However, the publishers reserve the right to increase prices on covers from those previously advertised, without further notice.

orbit

ORBIT BOOKS
Cash Sales Department, P.O. Box 11, Falmouth, Cornwall, TR10 9EN
Tel: +44 (0) 1326 569777, Fax: +44 (0) 1326 569555
Email: books@barni.avel.co.uk

POST AND PACKING:
Payments can be made as follows: cheque, postal order (payable to Orbit Books) or by credit cards. Do not send cash or currency.

U.K. Orders under £10	£1.50
U.K. Orders over £10	**FREE OF CHARGE**
E.C. & Overseas	25% of order value

Name (Block letters) ....

Address ....

....

Post/zip code: ....

☐ Please keep me in touch with future Orbit publications

☐ I enclose my remittance £ .

☐ I wish to pay by Visa/Access/Mastercard/Eurocard

Card Expiry Date